THE LOVE SONGS OF W. E. B. Du BOIS

HONORÉE FANONNE JEFFERS

4th ESTATE • London

4th Estate
An imprint of HarperCollins*Publishers*
1 London Bridge Street
London SE1 9GF

www.4thestate.co.uk

HarperCollins*Publishers*
1st Floor, Watermarque Building, Ringsend Road
Dublin 4, Ireland

First published in Great Britain in 2022 by 4th Estate
First published in the United States by Harper in 2021

1

Designed by Leah Carson-Stanisic

A catalogue record for this book is
available from the British Library

ISBN 978-0-00-851645-1 (hardback)
ISBN 978-0-00-851648-2 (trade paperback)

Set in Dante MT
Printed and bound in the UK using 100%
renewable electricity at CPI Group (UK) Ltd

MIX
Paper from
responsible sources
FSC™ C007454

For James William Richardson Jr.
and Sidonie Colette Jeffers:
brother and sister,
heart and heart

And for my mother,
Dr. Trellie Lee James Jeffers,
who gave me our land
and our people

FAMILY TREE

MICCO CORNELL'S FAMILY

Unknown married Nila Wind (1747–1797)

- Micco (Jonathan) Cornell (1764–1840)

Micco (Jonathan) Cornell married Mahala Norman (1766–1838)

- Bear Norman Cornell (1785–1845) and Jonathan Norman Cornell (1785–1846) (twins)
- Arthur Norman Cornell (1787–1847)
- Eliza Rose "Lady" Cornell (1802–1870)

AHGAYUH'S FAMILY

Ahgayuh "Aggie" Pinchard (1800–1865) married Midas Pinchard (1798–unknown)

- Tess Pinchard (1821–1865)

Tess Pinchard married Nick Pinchard (1817–unknown)

- Eliza Two Pinchard (1840–1934) and Rabbit Pinchard (1840–1869) (twins)

Eliza Two Pinchard (later Freeman) married Red Benjamin (later Freeman) (1845–1875)

- Sheba Liza-May Freeman (1861–1882)

Sheba Liza-May Freeman

- Clyde Nick Freeman (1877–1941) and Benji Nick Freeman (1877–1944) (twins, unknown father)
- Charles Nick Freeman (1878–1939) (unknown father)
- Adam Nick Freeman (1880–1956) and Abel Nick Freeman (1880–1956) (twins, unknown father)
- Maybelline "Lil' May" Victorina Freeman (1882–1918) (unknown father)

Maybelline "Lil' May" Victorina Freeman, unmarried liaison with Thomas "Big Thom" John Pinchard Sr. (1860–1924)

- Pearl Thomasina "Dear" Freeman (1900–1987)
- Jason Thomas "Root" Freeman (b. 1907)

Pearl Thomasina "Dear" Freeman married Henry John Collins Sr. (1905–1959)

- Miss Rose Collins (b. 1920) and Henry John "Huck" Collins Jr. (b. 1920) (twins)
- Annie Mae Collins (b. 1927)

Annie Mae Collins

- Pauline Ann Collins (b. 1944) (unknown father)

Miss Rose Collins married Hosea Leroy Driskell (1910–1974)

- Roscoe Nick Driskell (1938–1966)
- Jethro Leroy Driskell and Joseph John Driskell (1939–1939) (twins, died in infancy)
- Norman Hosea Driskell (b. 1941)
- Maybelle Lee "Belle" Driskell (b. 1943)

Maybelle Lee "Belle" Driskell, married

Geoffrey "Geoff" Louis Garfield (b. 1943)

- Lydia Claire Garfield (b. 1966)
- Carol Rose Garfield (b. 1969)
- Ailey Pearl Garfield (b. 1973)

SAMUEL PINCHARD'S FAMILY

Samuel Thomas Pinchard (1785–1868) married Eliza Rose "Lady" Cornell (1802–1870)

- Victor Thomas Pinchard (1826–1891) and Gloria Eugenia Pinchard (1826–1859) (twins)

Samuel Thomas Pinchard, unmarried liaison with Mamie Pinchard (unknown–1817)

- Nick Pinchard (1817–unknown)

Victor Thomas Pinchard married unknown

- Thomas John Pinchard Sr. (1860–1924) and Petunia May Pinchard (1860–1915) (twins)

Thomas "Big Thom" John Pinchard Sr. married Sarah Marcia Dawson (1868–1888)

- Thomas John Pinchard Jr. (1888–1957)

Thomas "Big Thom" John Pinchard Sr., unmarried liaison with Maybelline "Lil' May" Victorina Freeman (1882–1918)

- Pearl Thomasina "Dear" Freeman (1900–1987)
- Jason Thomas "Root" Freeman (b. 1907)

Thomas John Pinchard Jr. married Lucille Anne Sweet (1885–1954)

- Cordelia Sarah Pinchard (b. 1925)

Cordelia Sarah Pinchard married Horace Rice (1925–1982)

ZACHARY GARFIELD'S FAMILY

Zachary Pierre Garfield (1919–1979) married Claire Mignonette Prejean (b. 1920)

- Geoffrey "Geoff" Louis Garfield (b. 1943)
- Lawrence Garfield (b. 1945)

They that walked in darkness sang songs in the olden days—Sorrow Songs—for they were weary at heart. And so before each thought that I have written in this book I have set a phrase, a haunting echo of these weird old songs in which the soul of the black slave spoke to men. Ever since I was a child these songs have stirred me strangely. They came out of the South unknown to me, one by one, and yet at once I knew them as of me and of mine.

—W. E. B. Du Bois, "Of the Sorrow Songs"

CONTENTS

❖

◆

SONG

◆

We are the earth, the land. The tongue that speaks and trips on the names of the dead as it dares to tell these stories of a woman's line. Her people and her dirt, her trees, her water.

We knew this woman before she became a woman. We knew her before she was born: we sang to her in her mother's womb. We sang then and we sing now.

We called this woman back through the years to our early place, to our bright shoots rising with the seasons. We know her mingled people. How they started off as sacred, hummed verses. And now, we go back through the centuries to the beginning of her line, to a village called The-Place-in-the-Middle-of-the-Tall-Trees. And we start with a boy, the child who will change everything on our land.

Wait.

We know you have questions, such as, if we tell the story of a woman's line, why would we begin with a boy? And to your wonder we counter we could have begun with a bird's call or with a stalk of corn. With a cone from a tree or a tendril of green. All these things lead back to this woman's line, whether we mention them or not. Yet since our story does not follow a straight path—we travel to places here and across the water—we must keep to the guidance of time. To the one who first walked past a tall, grass-covered mound in a particular place in the woods—and we have questions as well, for, despite our authority, we cannot know everything.

And so we ask if a child cannot remember his mother's face, does he still taste her milk? Does he remember the waters inside her? Can you answer those questions? No, and neither can we. Yet, we remind you that many children commence within women, and thus, this is why it is completely fine that we begin with a boy.

And so we proceed.

The Boy Named Micco

The boy lived on our land. Here, in a Creek village that was between the wider lands straddling the rivers of the Okmulgee and Ogeechee, near the Oconee River, which crawled through the middle. Though Micco had playmates among the children of his village, he was an unhappy little boy, for he felt the tugging of three sets of hands. Whenever this tugging began, he felt confused and miserable.

There were the hands of his father, a Scottish deer skin trader named Dylan Cornell. There were the hands of his mother, Nila, a Creek woman who belonged to a clan of the highest status in their village, the Wind clan. The little boy's parents were yet alive, but the hands that pulled at him the strongest were of a man who probably was dead, though no one knew for sure. They were the hands of his mother's father, a man who appeared one day in the village.

This was in the years after 1733 and the arrival of James Oglethorpe and his ship of petty English criminals, what he called his "worthy poor." They were those who had been sentenced to death or hard labor for the stealing of an apple or a loaf of bread or some other trifling thing.

When Oglethorpe came to our land, he thought he found a comrade in Tomochichi, the leader of the Yamacraw people, another tribe of our land.

Yet Oglethorpe had not made a friend. Tomochichi had not made a friend, either. He'd only encountered a pragmatic white man determined to set anchor and build a colony for his English king. Tomochichi had seen white men before, so he was interested in trade, which was a long-standing commerce. There had been Englishmen moving along the paths, going north and south and east and west, for more than a hundred years. Though Tomochichi was a wise leader and probably smelled greed on Oglethorpe, he had no idea of what would follow: sin.

For the original transgression of this land was not slavery. It was greed, and it could not be contained. More white men would come and begin to covet. And they would drag along the Africans they had enslaved. The white men would sow their misery among those who shook their chains. These white men would whip and work and demean these Africans. They would sell their children and split up families. And these white men brought by Oglethorpe, these men who had been oppressed in their own land by their own king, forgot the misery that they had left behind, the poverty, the uncertainty. And they resurrected this misery and passed it on to the Africans.

And now we reach back even further.

The Grandfather of the Boy

The young man who would become the grandfather of Micco was perhaps eighteen or nineteen when he appeared next to the tall mound that marked the entrance of The-Place-in-the-Middle-of-the-Tall-Trees.

The young man was barefoot, and his soles were thickened and rough. His gray-colored shirt and pants were wrinkled, and even to those who were standing far away his garments gave off the smell of mildew—which made sense, because when someone asked him in English how he had arrived at their village he only told them that he had been walking when he'd arrived at a river. Then he'd found that he was hungry, so he had tried to seize a catfish at the edge of the water but had fallen into the river. He talked with his hands, making wide gestures and animated facial expressions—even more so when he described falling into the river—and the villagers laughed. Yet he did not want to offend. He laughed along with them.

"Where do you come from?" an elder of the village asked.

"Over there." The young man pointed vaguely. He smiled some more, and when the elder asked another question—where was he headed—the young man said he meant to go south.

"Truly?" The elder looked back wisely at the rest of his cohort, and the other men held this elder's gaze.

Then there was more talking and more asking. But when the young man told them a very small man the size of a child had pulled him from the river and led him through the woods to the mound at the edge of the village, then the small man suddenly had disappeared, the elder gave his cohort a new, surprised look. Now this? This was a different matter altogether. And so the elder and his cohort clustered, whispering in their own language while the young man smiled and nodded as if he understood the snatches of words that he was hearing. He did not understand at all. The elders were whispering about what the young man meant when he had said that he was headed "south."

They did this because the young man who had found his way to the village was a Negro.

Thus, the elders assumed he was headed to the lands that the Spanish called "Florida," and that the young man was looking for certain Seminoles. The people who lived in The-Place-in-the-Middle-of-the-Tall-Trees knew much about the Seminoles, because the Seminoles had once been a part of the Creek people before they had broken off to form their own nation. And the Seminoles gave sanctuary to Negroes, taking them into their villages. They mated with Negroes, too.

And so if this young man with mildew-smelling clothes was seeking the Seminoles, that meant that he was not free.

Though slavery wasn't legal yet in the territory Oglethorpe had settled—that would come years later—there were ways that the English or Scottish got around the law. And one of those finagling men owned this young Negro, which meant that somebody might come looking for him and that somebody might try to cause some trouble. Ordinarily that would mean the people in The-Place-in-the-Middle-of-the-Tall-Trees should take hold of the young man, carry him back east, over the Oconee River, and collect a reward from the English or Scottish person who owned him. Yet the young man had mentioned that a very small man had pulled him out of the river. Could this mean the young man had encountered one of the "little people"? These were supernatural beings and when they chose to show themselves it was a serious matter indeed. The small man would not be happy if this chosen young man was betrayed.

While the male elders talked, they tried to ignore the nudging and giggling from the women of the village. The women were looking the young man over: Though he was not tall, he was inordinately handsome. His forehead was high, and later, the people would discover that was a natural characteristic—he did not pluck around his hairline, as some men in the village did. The young man's kinky hair stood at some length. His dark-dark skin was smooth. His muscles were well formed. His teeth were white as sweet corn, and when he smiled, there was a warmth to his entire face.

As the older women watched the young man, they reminisced about the days when they still visited the moon house during their bleeding times, when their breasts were high and their bellies did not carry pouches of fat. And the younger women who still saw the moon fantasized about rolling on top of the young man and riding him fast, like a warrior chasing battle.

The male elders came out of their huddle, and their leader asked the young man what was his name?

"My name be Coromantee," he said.

Yet we can tell you, the young man was lying; this was not his real name.

And we can tell you that, though he had been born here on our land, his mother had been born across the water. She had been pushed out of her mother in a place in Africa called "Gold Coast" by the English, who had been traders in slaves and riches and goods for many years. The white men had invented an aberration and called the African people of the Gold Coast "Coromantee." In the future, no one would know where this term had come from, or why the white men had invented it, only that, as white men are fond of doing, they decided that whatever moniker they gave those that they encountered was right. And so when the white men traded with the residents of the Gold Coast: Coromantee. When the white men took the Gold Coast women for temporary wives: Coromantee. When they herded these people into the dungeons of the slave castles along that coast: Coromantee.

We can tell you the origin story of this young man's grandparents,

and the origins of their parents, until we reached the very beginning of what you know as time. We can tell you the lives of gods—
but truly, don't you want to return to this charming young man
with the beautiful, dark-dark skin?

He stayed more than mere days in the village, for each time the
young man declared his intention to go south the elders urged him
to stay. They did not want him to leave. When Scottish deer traders
came through the area, their arrival was never a surprise, and by
the time these traders rode their horses into the village, the villagers
had hidden the young man they had begun to cherish. Eventually,
he was so loved and admired that he was adopted by a Creek family
who was of the Panther clan.

Thus, the young man's name became "Coromantee-Panther."

From an uncle in his adopted family, he learned manhood skills,
as is the Creek way. He learned how to use poison on the water or a
net to catch smaller fish and how to catch the bigger ones by grabbing into their mouths. He should ignore the pain of their bites. And
Coromantee-Panther told his new uncle he was grateful for these
skills, for he had not been allowed to learn how to feed himself in
the place from which he had escaped. That is all he would say, and
because Coromantee-Panther seemed sadly pensive whenever he
mentioned the time before he came to the village, the uncle did not
ask him to elaborate.

Coromantee-Panther showed himself to be courageous. Once
while hunting a bear attacked his uncle, who would later say a red-
colored spirit—a spirit the color of war—entered his nephew,
giving him strength. Right when the bear jumped on the uncle,
Coromantee-Panther leapt on the animal's back, slit its throat, and
pushed the bear off the uncle before he suffocated from the weight.

"That was risky, eh?" The uncle spat out red phlegm and laughed
along with his adopted nephew. When they brought the dead bear
to the village, the family feasted on its roasted ribs as the uncle told
of the courage of Coromantee-Panther. The tale would be repeated
for many years among the people. Coromantee-Panther did not
have a chance to prove himself in battle, however, for the village in

which he lived was called a "white" town because it was committed to peace. There were other villages throughout the Creek confederation who believed in war, and they were called "red" villages. The young men of these villages would shed blood without thought. Yet Coromantee-Panther was a hunter who brought more than enough meat to his adopted family regularly, proving himself capable of supporting a wife. There were many young women who wanted to marry him, too, though they knew he'd probably been a slave and he continually repeated his intention to leave the village and go south.

In times to come there would be other Negroes who made their reputations, men who contained warriors' spirits. Who would marry Creek women who birthed strong children and some of those children would prove themselves, men like Ninnywageechee and Black Factor, men with dark-dark skin and bushy hair, who rode hard without fear and spilled much blood in honorable ways.

The eventual wife of Coromantee-Panther was a young woman of the highest rank, from the Wind clan. She had strong ankles, lean calves, and a beguiling space between her top front teeth. Perhaps she was beautiful, though all young women are beautiful in their ways, and this is not that kind of story. Like all offspring she had a name, given by her mother, but we shall call her "Woman-of-the-Wind."

She caught the eye of Coromantee-Panther by indirection, because she did not place herself in front of him to win notice. Rather, her absence reckoned with his interest and he began to look for her. To watch her cutting meat into strips for drying. Other young women came to Woman-of-the-Wind to tell her that Coromantee-Panther had asked for her. She would look up from pounding dried corn to see him smiling at her. She was self-conscious about the space between her two front teeth; also, she considered too much humor to be a sign of foolishness, but she couldn't help but smile back at him.

Though the young Negro wasn't as high of status as Woman-of-the-Wind, she was taken aback by her feelings when he offered her the skin of the bear that he had killed.

"I have much affection for you," Coromantee-Panther said. His Creek language skills were rudimentary, but he had practiced that phrase with his adopted uncle. When he touched his chest and gestured to Woman-of-the-Wind, she put aside the corn. She took his hand and walked with him deep into the woods to a spot where they lay on the bearskin. He was not an experienced lover, but his sincerity made up for what he did not know. He pleased her greatly that night and many nights to come.

Soon, Woman-of-the-Wind and Coromantee-Panther were married with the blessing of her clan, and he moved his belongings into her family's hut, as a married Creek man did. At least, that is what happened during those times, before everything began to change.

The Daughter of a Powerful Union

The young woman's devotion to Coromantee-Panther was strong, but she did not want to hinder him on his journey south. Thus, on the day that he finally left the village—twenty-three moons after he had arrived—when the elders gave him a horse and supplies, and had taught him to read the marks on the sides of the trees to find villages that would be friendly to him, Woman-of-the-Wind did not inform Coromantee-Panther that her womb was heavy with his seed. She only dearly loved the twin babies that she gave birth to, a boy and a girl. The girl's name was Nila. The boy's name was Bushy Hair. Both children would have their father's courageous, red heart, though each would take their own path to claim that mettle.

In time, the twins grew, and Woman-of-the-Wind was courted by men of other clans in the village. Not only was she desired because of her high status, but also, she had been the only mate of Coromantee-Panther, who had loved her dearly. On the day that her husband left, he had clung to Woman-of-the-Wind and wept before she pushed him away, telling him go to the south. Go to his freedom, and she would remember him always, and Coromantee-

Panther had slid onto the bare back of the horse the elders had given him for his journey. Woman-of-the-Wind would never marry or mate again.

Surely, such a woman was extraordinary, and when the daughter of Woman-of-the-Wind came of age, Nila had many suitors as well. She was a rarity in her village, beautiful in a very odd way. Nila had her father's dark-brown skin, his kinky hair, and his warmth. She had her mother's entrancing space between her top teeth and her high status. Frequently, young men from her village and other surrounding villages came to present Nila with meat and softened deer skins to win her favor, but Nila did not want an ordinary man for her husband. She was arrogant, and her weakness was her vanity. She had been told too frequently how wonderful she was, that, as the child of Coromantee-Panther and Woman-of-the-Wind, there was no one as special as she was. Thus, when a handsome, blond Scotsman named Dylan Cornell began to travel to the village for trade, Nila accepted his proposal of marriage.

Woman-of-the-Wind tried to intervene; she told her daughter that she'd had a bad dream about Dylan Cornell, but Nila would not listen. It was only after she married the white man that the wisdom of her mother's dream rang. Dylan told her that he would not be moving to Nila's village, as Creek men did, and that he would only visit every three moons. Also, he revealed that he had another wife, a white woman who lived far on the other side of the Oconee River, in a town where other white people lived. When Nila told Dylan that she would travel with him, that she did not mind sharing his dwelling with another wife so long as they could all live peacefully, he laughed at her. He told Nila she looked like a Negro. The only way he could carry her to the east of the Oconee was as his slave, for when Nila had been a very little girl, the law had changed in the territory where Oglethorpe had landed: Negro slavery was now legal.

Nila could not believe her husband had dared to compare her to a slave. Her heart filled with red anger—the inheritance of Coromantee-Panther—and air whistled though the space in her front teeth. Nila poked her finger in Dylan's chest and told him the obscurities of her mind, and then her husband struck her.

She touched her cheek in shock, but her heart was still red. "I would sleep very lightly, if I were you, Dylan Cornell. For I am going to burn your manhood with coals. And I would be careful about eating as well. I will treat you like a sturgeon and poison you."

Yet Nila did not keep her word. She did not burn or kill or poison her husband, for he sidled next to her and begged her forgiveness. He stroked her kinky hair and told her he did not know what had come over him, and Nila's red anger paled, and she consented to lie with him. It would be like this every time Dylan struck her on his visits to the west. He would fool Nila into believing that his nature had changed and she would believe him until the moment he struck her again and called her names that began with "black." Dylan told her she was a "black wench" or she was a "black devil." He told her she looked like a slave.

Yet in those early days Nila still held out hope, and when she became pregnant Dylan was tender with her. Their child was born in an interval between Dylan's visits. When he returned, Nila allowed Dylan to rename the baby "Jonathan," though she had called the boy "Micco." Moons after the baby's birth there were two more visits where no striking occurred and Nila reasoned that time had changed her husband. However, on the subsequent visit once the baby was walking, Dylan began to strike Nila again and it was worse than before.

Nila did not dare tell anyone about how she suffered with her Scottish husband, especially Bushy Hair, who was protective of his twin sister as he had been the baby to emerge first on the day that they were born. Her arrogance kept her from admitting that she had been foolish not to listen to her mother's dream. She kept her shame inside, for she didn't want her family to be ridiculed in the village, for the people to marvel that the extraordinary daughter of Coromantee-Panther and Woman-of-the-Wind had thrown herself away on a white man who beat her.

Nila learned to raise her arms to catch the blows so that her bruises would not show on her face. She learned to hope that Dylan's visits every three moons would end, but he continued to visit. Sometimes she was lucky and sitting in the moon house when his visits occurred, for Dylan did not know how to count the days to avoid her womanly seclusions. Yet other times, she was not fortunate, and she tolerated his embraces, for Dylan would force himself on her. Nila drank a tisane made from wild carrot seeds to keep from being with his child. On the rare times that didn't work, Nila would brew another tisane of wild ginger root, drinking this to expel the contents of her womb, or, as a last resort, boil the berries of the pokeweed.

The Incident of the Cracker

Nila's only son would grow to be tall, but Micco looked neither Negro nor Creek nor Scottish. His hair was dark, but it was not kinky; it crisped into tight waves. After his fourth year, his skin darkened to a brown that was the color of pecans. He had picked up selfishness from Dylan Cornell, whose visits had slowed to every six moons. The Creek had not learned yet about locks or being selfish with food and goods—that would come much later—but Dylan inculcated a love of property to his son. Whenever other children picked up something belonging to Micco in his hut, he would snatch it back.

"Mine! Mine!" the boy would scream.

Micco soon became a very lonely child, for other children began to avoid him, and, because he was a boy, when he reached the age of four or five it was frowned upon for him to hover around his mother and the women of the village. Though he ardently looked forward to his white father's visits, Micco didn't receive much attention from his father, either, except when his father insisted that he learn how to read so he could know the most important words to the white men besides their laws: the book that Dylan called the Bible. These lessons were so important to the lonely little boy that when his father hit his mother Micco turned his head and tried to ignore his mother's weeping. He would lie at the foot of the spot where his parents slept and pretend not to hear Dylan forcing himself on Nila, her sad begging for Dylan to please stop, because Micco lived for the mornings when his father would roughly nudge him with a foot and say, "Good morning, boy." This wasn't much, but Micco grabbed at these bits of affection, as children crave the love of their parents.

His only friend was his uncle, Bushy Hair, who spent time with the boy when he was little and took over his manhood training when he grew older. This training was Bushy Hair's responsibility, as was the way of the people. Like his sister, Bushy Hair had his father's courage as well as his sweet charm and kindness. He talked to the boy, listening as if he were a grown man. Bushy Hair did not laugh at Micco, either, when his arrows did not fly straight at low-flying birds or slow deer, and his voice was not harsh when Micco ran from the water of the creek when a fish bit his hand. Bushy Hair was patient. When Micco eventually shot an arrow straight and killed a fat bird, and when he withstood the gnaws of the fish on his hand and threw it on the banks of the creek, Bushy Hair smiled and told the boy, well done, nephew. You are a great hunter, and Micco felt much love inside.

This peace that Micco felt would be broken, because in his fifteenth year there was trouble between the people of the village and a white man who had settled on the other side of the Oconee River. The people called him a "cracker," for the sound of his whip when driving his five head of cattle right up to the boundaries of the village. The cracker was a stringy man in both hair and body, and ornery, too. He didn't try to keep his cattle from running through the village cornfield, laughing when women had frantically waved to warn him. He had made obscene gestures at the women as well. Several times, men of the village had ridden out to the cracker's farm, a shoddy place with a tiny cabin he had erected without the permission of the people. The men had talked to the cracker, warning him about his animals. He would nod his head in agreement but then kept driving his cattle onto the village grounds.

One morning a village woman was not quick enough to grab her toddling child from the path of the cracker's cattle and her child was trampled to death. Though the village was a "white" place of peace, this insult could not remain unanswered. A group of younger men rode out to the place where the cracker had set up his pathetic farm, but the cracker was ready for a fight. He pulled out his long gun and trained it on the four men who stood in front of him. However, the cracker had not considered that his back was unprotected. There was a fifth man behind him: Bushy Hair, who made quick work of the cracker and left him dead.

The cracker's wife had been standing at the window of her cabin watching the scene play out. She had screamed when she saw Bushy Hair hit her husband with his ax. He had been so quick she hadn't been able to warn the cracker. She screamed more, a sound of hopelessness, and one of the men wanted to go inside the cabin and kill the wife. This was understandable as this man was the father of the dead toddler.

Yet the three other men did not want to harm the cracker's wife; they still wanted to adhere to peaceful ways as much as possible. Bushy Hair listened to both sides, then asked the toddler's father to leave the cracker's wife unharmed. They had solved the problem of blood revenge, according to Creek ways. In times past, if someone in one village was killed in anger by someone in another village, the two places would get together, consult, and the culprit would be handed over to whichever village had been wronged. The white woman's man was dead, Bushy Hair reasoned. She wouldn't remain, especially since they were taking her husband's cattle back to the village.

Perhaps Bushy Hair's kindness had been his mistake, for the cracker's wife found her way east of the Oconee and reported the killing of her husband to a headman in a town populated by white people. Bushy Hair found this out when his brother-in-law came for a visit only a moon after the killing.

Upon his arrival, Dylan Cornell marched straight to the elders of The-Place-in-the-Middle-of-the-Tall-Trees. Standing in the ceremonial grounds—turning his body so that the sun highlighted his yellow hair—Dylan declared that whoever had killed the cracker had broken the law and must be surrendered to the leaders of the white men.

The head elder scratched his chin, unconcerned by Dylan's passion.

"Whose law?" he asked.

Dylan swept his arm. "The law of the government of this land!"

"Whose government? Whose land?"

The debate went on in this circular fashion. The other elders asked questions, such as, would the white man's government come to the village? No, Dylan said. The cracker only had been one man. No one was coming this far out to avenge him, but the murder was a matter of honor. The elders tried to explain to Dylan that indeed the cracker had violated honor according to the Creek ways, but Dylan did not listen.

Someone else asked permission to speak: it was Bushy Hair.

"You're shaming our family, my brother." He told the truth. Nila was not at the meeting of only men, but the male members of the Wind clan sat in the gathering, and they were mortified.

Dylan Cornell left the next day, and Nila was happy to see him go. Yet within only one moon he returned. He professed that he missed his son dearly and that he wanted to take Micco on a trading trip across the Oconee. Nila didn't want Micco to go. She'd had a dream that Dylan would try to take her son from her, but she knew if she tried to stop her husband, she would have to tell the people in the village what she had been enduring at his hands. She was frightened of revealing her shame, and she was frightened of losing her son. It was a prison made by the violent hands of her husband, but she had one option left to her. She asked her brother to accompany Dylan and Micco on the trading trip, and she was relieved that Dylan agreed. Not only that, he promised Bushy Hair much bounty.

It was dark in the early morning when the two men and the boy left. Only Dylan rode a horse with a saddle. The other two rode their horses bareback. There was much friendly talk from Dylan because Dylan did not know that his brother-in-law despised him.

Though Bushy Hair had no idea that the white man had physically abused Nila over the years—he did not have the gift of dreaming, like his mother and sister—he was repulsed by the white man on general principle, for over the years Dylan had earned other marks of contempt.

The white man did not partake in the sacred green corn celebration.

No one in the village ever wanted to hunt with him, either, for Dylan could not use a bow and arrow, only his long gun. And he stomped through the forest like a full-grown bear, too, which scared away the game.

Further, while it was true that Dylan was expert in the language of the Creek people, he'd used his expertise to whine fluently about the killing of the cracker, yet hadn't uttered one sentence of sympathy for the toddler who had been trampled.

Micco had no idea the enmity that his uncle held toward his father. He was happy to be in the company of his two favorite men and didn't question why his usually sweet uncle only grunted in response to Dylan's chatter. Yet halfway on the journey to the Oconee River, Micco was awakened by the sounds of struggle between his uncle and father. They were fiercely fighting, and unlike most men who bully women, his father was not backing down from the fight. He was heavier and taller than Bushy Hair and this gave him an advantage. The two men rolled on the ground in battle, and when Bushy Hair finally got the best of Micco's father, the white man called out for help, using his child's English name.

"Jonathan, Jonathan, help your father! Help me, my son!"

This was a choice no child should be forced to make. Micco didn't know what to do as he watched the struggle. He didn't want to choose, but he remembered how Bushy Hair had always made him feel good inside with his loving words. And he remembered how Dylan had hurt his mother, leaving bruises that she'd had to cover with long sleeves, even in the heat of summer. So the boy made a choice: He trotted to the site of the struggle and kneeled at the head of his father. The boy took out his knife, grabbed hold of his father's chin, and slit his throat. Then Micco sat there on the ground and wailed, rocking back and forth with blood covering his hands.

His uncle let his nephew cry for a long time before touching the boy's shoulder. Bushy Hair told him, gently, that they had to bury his father according to white men's ways. They could not leave him for the wild animals. That would not be right. After the body was put into the grave hole, Bushy Hair told Micco that he had not wanted things to go this way, but Dylan had jumped him in his sleep. Micco looked at his uncle for a long time before asking, was this the truth? And Bushy Hair told him he would never lie to him. Yes, it was true, and he did not know why Dylan had attacked him.

Uncle and nephew spent a moon hunting and sleeping late. Bushy Hair told stories of the wily rabbit that constantly found himself in trouble with the wolf, but who always found a way to get loose, because the rabbit was a very smart creature who could not be caught. During that moon, there was a peace that Micco had never known, and he was happy, though he awoke sometimes with his face wet: his father now came to him in dreams.

When Micco and Bushy Hair returned to their village, it was Micco who decided to tell his mother that his father had died from eating tainted fowl, prepared by a white man at a trading destination. Micco said it was too difficult to bring his body back. He did not need to pretend sadness at the death of his father, for he did grieve. Yet his mourning ran alongside relief that his father never would hurt his mother again.

Nila was no fool. She had shared a womb with Bushy Hair and had carried Micco inside her body and fed him from her breasts. She saw the glances her brother and son gave one another, and she knew that one or the other had killed Dylan. Yet her own grief wasn't over her husband. She only mourned the guilt of her son. Nila made a long face and cried and beat her chest over Dylan, but inside she was leaping. Though no longer young, Nila still visited the moon house for her bleeding times and reckoned she had two or three summers before her woman's change. She was of high status, and there were younger men in the village already giving her nice looks, even at her age. The elders of the village told her her husband had been a white man and not of the people. Therefore, Nila didn't have to mourn Dylan for four years, as Creek women were required to do when they became widows. She could shorten her grief time to four moons, as Creek men did. After her mourning period, Nila intended to choose a Creek man as her second husband, for a Creek man understood the responsibilities of the people and knew about the requirements of loyalty to the family of his wife.

Nila warned Micco that no matter who his father had been or how friendly white men might seem, they would never truly love or respect the Creek people. That was her first gift to her son. The second was the cow that her brother had given to her from the five head of cattle that had been split up among him and the others, after the killing of the cracker. Nila wanted no part of that bounty. She wanted to be free of the possessions of white men.

The Scourge of Mr. Whitney

And so the sin was intrusion, as when a neighbor calls at the entryway and when there is no answer walks inside anyway. Or when there is an answer, he kills his neighbor and pretends the dwelling was empty. When the Englishmen and Scotsmen came to the land of the people, cattle took over. It was no paradise before, but there were rules followed by the Creek, the descendants of beings who built Rock Eagle and hunted the deer and gave thanks before they dressed the meat. Who ate the corn and kept its season sacred.

And then the treaties, the agreements between these intruders and the people, all of which would be broken, and the land that would be taken—and taken again.

There was the Treaty of Savannah in 1733.

The Treaty of Coweta in 1739.

The Treaty of Augusta in 1763. Ten years later, a second treaty in that same place.

The Treaty of New York in 1790, and the realization that our land would be fertile for short-staple cotton, and after this, there came an

invention by a man named Eli Whitney. Think of him, a man stew-
ing in the juice of mediocrity, the blankness of his legacy breathing
down his neck, tinkering with his rude invention. Or did a slave
invent the gin, as some have said? Workers tend to have more genius than the boss, to reduce the strain of labor. Whoever its inventor, before the gin, one daily pound of cotton. After, fifty pounds,
more slaves, very few deer, many cattle and pigs, and running talk
of planting, for the gin was a way to separate good from evil. More
specifically, cotton bolls from seeds.

The intruders on the land weren't Englishmen or Scotsmen anymore, because a revolution had been fought. Now they were "Americans," "white" men, and though to the Creek the color white
meant peace, that word meant something else to the intruders.

And now those called Coromantee or Igbo or Wolof or Fula were
"Negroes" or "slaves."

And now the Creek were "Indians."

And there was the Treaty of Colerain in 1796.

The Treaty of Fort Wilkinson in 1802.

The Treaty of Washington in 1805, and our land was no longer
what the people called it.

Now the white men called us "Georgia."

The Tracing of the Line

When we follow the centuries to come, a family will remain in our
same place. Here on our land. The-Place-in-the-Middle-of-the-Tall-
Trees will be called another name: Chicasetta.

The family won't know the original name of our land, nor the
name of that first, taken African of their line, the one whose mother
had traveled over water. Nor will this family know about the Creek
woman who was already here. They won't know the names of
Coromantee-Panther, of Woman-of-the-Wind. Those will be lost to
everyone but us.

There will be generations that lie between the people of The-
Place-in-the-Middle-of-the-Tall-Trees and their descendants: a woman

who will be named Eliza Two Pinchard Freeman, also called Meema. She will marry a man named Red Benjamin, and he will take her last name.

And Meema will bear a daughter named Sheba, who will grow up to be free with her love.

And Sheba will bear Clyde, a son. His father's name will not be known by her family.

And Sheba will bear Benji and Charlie, twin boys, for a different, unknown man.

And Red Freeman will pass away, his death making Meema a widow woman and Sheba a half orphan.

And Meema's daughter, Sheba, will continue to be free with her love: for another unknown man, she will bear Adam and Abel, also twins. And for a last man, Sheba will bear a girl named Maybelline, called Lil' May. Hours after this baby is born, Sheba will die in a lake of blood.

And Lil' May will give birth to Pearl. And ten years after Lil' May bore her daughter, she will bear a second child. A boy, Jason, though his family will call him "Root."

And Pearl will marry Henry Collins. She will bear the twins Miss Rose and Henry Jr., called Huck. After many childless years, she will bear Annie Mae.

And Annie Mae will bear a daughter, Pauline, for an unknown man, and then she will leave this child behind in Chicasetta.

And Miss Rose will marry Hosea Driskell, and she will bear Roscoe, a troublemaking handsome boy. And Miss Rose will bear Jethro and Joseph, the twins who will die in their cribs.

She will bear Norman, another son.

And finally, Miss Rose will bear a daughter, and she will rejoice. This girl will be named Maybelle Lee, though she will insist that her family call her "Belle."

And Belle will bear three girls: Lydia, Carol, and finally, a last daughter: Ailey, who will learn to honor a line reaching back to people whose names she never will know. To praise the blood that calls out in dreams, long after memory has surrendered.

I

If a man die shall he live again? We do not know. But this we do know, that our children's children live forever and grow and develop toward perfection as they are trained. All human problems, then, center in the Immortal Child and his education is the problem of problems. And first for illustration of what I would say may I not take for example, out of many millions, the life of one dark child.

—W. E. B. Du Bois, *Darkwater: Voices from Within the Veil*

DREAM AND FRACTURE

◈

I'm three going on four, and there's a voice. Like that song my mama
sings sometimes.

Hush, hush

Somebody's calling my name

But it's not my mama calling me. It's Lydia, my big sister. She's
the one calling and I love her very much.

"Ailey, baby, it's time to get up. Come on now. We're going to
Chicasetta today. Don't you remember?"

Her voice pulls on me, but somebody else holds on. Somebody's
calling my name. It's the long-haired lady. I love her very much, but
I don't know what she's saying. She's rocking me in another place.
She's singing to me, but I don't know the words, and the long-haired
lady tells me pee-pee. *Go 'head, right now. Let it go.*

But I don't want to. I don't want to pee-pee 'cause it's gone be a
yellow wet spot in my bed and Lydia's gone feel sorry for me. She's
gone say, "Oh, it's all right, baby sister. I'm not mad." But I don't
want nobody to feel sorry for me. I want to be a big girl, but I can't
hold it and the wet spot's here and I'm awake and the long-haired
lady's gone.

———

I'm four going on five, and I'm riding in the brown station wagon.
Mama's got her hands on the round thing, and we're going and going. I'm screaming for Daddy. Where is he? Lydia's touching my
head, rubbing.

"Don't cry, baby," she says. "We had to leave him home. He has
to work at the hospital to make money for us. Remember what I
told you?"

But I don't remember.

Coco's in the back with all her books. She's nine already. Lydia's
eleven going on twelve, but Coco's in the same grade. She's smarter

than everybody, but Mama says she loves all her girls the same. And we are going and going, and I'm screaming, and Coco's pulling at my braid.

Mama turns that round thing and we're on the side of the road. We ain't going no more and the cars go by and make the station wagon shake.

She says, "Coco, give me that paper sack." She pulls out a chicken leg and I'm hungry. I reach for the chicken and Mama pulls back. "Are you going to be a good little girl?"

And I say yes, and she gives me the chicken and I eat it, and I love her very much, even though she yells sometimes. Then we are going and going for a long, long time. There's a long dirt road and there's a house and a bunch of people on a porch. A bunch of grown-ups and everybody stands and waves except for an old, white lady sitting in her chair, and I say, "Why's that white lady there? Is that Aunt Diane's mama?"

And Lydia tells me, "No, baby. We left Auntie at home. That's Dear Pearl, she's our great-grandmother, and she's only light skinned. Please don't hurt her feelings."

Mama's getting out the car and everybody here knows everybody, but I don't know nobody and I'm real, real mad. Then a man with white hair comes down into the driveway, and he looks white, too, but I remember what Lydia told me. I don't want to hurt his feelings.

I say, "Are you a Black man?"

Mama says, "You should remember him, Ailey, you're a big girl now."

The man says, "All right, now, give the child some time."

I say, "My name's Ailey Pearl Garfield. My mother's Mrs. Maybelle Lee Garfield and my father's Dr. Geoffrey Louis Garfield."

The man says, "My goodness! That's a lot of information."

He has eyes with all kinds of colors. Real strange eyes, but I think I remember him.

I say, "Is your name Uncle Root?"

He says, "What a brilliant child!"

He picks me up, and he holds me, and I feel safe, and I love him very much.

———

I'm six going on seven in the big kitchen in Chicasetta. I know everybody now. I know my granny's Miss Rose and she lives in one house. Her sister's Aunt Pauline and she lives in another house. Their brother's Uncle Huck, but he only comes out of his house once a week. He has a boyfriend that he kisses on the mouth, but I'm not supposed to know that. I know their mama is Dear Pearl and her brother is Uncle Root. I know my mama's brother is Uncle Norman. All the grown folks can tell me what to do, even if I don't want to listen.

It must be a Saturday or maybe a Sunday, because Baybay and Boukie ain't here. *Aren't*. They come during the week and play with me. Baybay's mama drops them off and we run and we play, but they don't talk proper. And my mama says I have to talk better, but sometimes I forget. In the kitchen my granny is putting biscuits and grits and sausage on a plate, and Mama tells her that's too much food. I'm already chubby.

Miss Rose says, "You leave this baby alone and let her eat in peace." She pours coffee for Mama, but my sisters and me can't have no coffee. *Any* coffee. We have hot chocolate.

Coco says, "Actually, there are stimulants in chocolate as well, similar to caffeine in the coffee."

Mama says, "Stop talking back to grown folks. Just be grateful for the plentiful food on this table and the hands that have prepared it."

It's time for the grocery store, 'cause Mama ain't gone eat folks out of house and home. *Isn't*. But Coco don't want to go to town. *Doesn't*. She wants to stay with Miss Rose to help make preserves. She promises she will be well behaved and try not to be rude.

Then, we are in the station wagon, I'm sitting between Lydia and Mama. I'm full of breakfast, and my mama and sister smell real good, like grown ladies do. I'm happy listening to the radio, but then that white lady sees us at the Pig Pen. She don't know that Lydia is with us. *Doesn't*.

Lydia don't look like none of us. *Doesn't.* Daddy's got brown eyes, but he looks like a white man. Mama's dark like chocolate and little and pretty. She makes her hair straight with a hot comb and blue grease. I'm dark, too, but not like Mama. I got red in my skin underneath the brown like my granny. Coco's eyes and skin match, like caramel candy. Her nose is wide like Mama's, and she's real short, too. Her hair's like Mama's, and it grows real long. Lydia's hair is long, too, but won't hold a curl. But in the back of her head, she's got a kitchen. It grows in curls like mine. That's how you can tell that she's a Black girl. She's got a gap in her teeth like Mama's too. Her skin is light but not like Daddy's. She looks like she went out in the sun and stayed a long time and got a tan. But Mama says Black folks don't get tans. We already got some color. And Mama don't care if folks are ignorant about her children. *Doesn't.* She carried all of us in her belly and we belong to her and we should love her very much.

It's cold in the store. When Mama pushes the cart up the aisle, the white lady waves at us. Mama waves back and says good morning, and the lady and her cart come our way. She's old like my granny and has a pink shirt and a jean skirt. Her brown shoes are ugly. I don't like those shoes.

The white lady says, "You are so good with children."

Mama says, "Thank you, ma'am. I try my best with these two. There's another one at home."

"How long have you been in service?"

"Ma'am?"

The lady touches Lydia's shoulder. "This one won't need a nanny soon, and my daughter has a little boy who'd just love you. Let me give you her number. She'll pay well." The white lady puts her hand in her purse and pulls out a pencil. She puts her hand in again and has a smooshed piece of paper, and Mama frowns, but then she smiles. She says Lydia is her daughter. They have the same teeth, but Lydia is getting braces next year.

"Gal, you're funning me!" The white lady shakes her finger close to my mother's face, and I say, "Ooh," 'cause you ain't never supposed to put your hand in somebody's face. *Aren't.*

Mama steps back. She's still smiling.

"I promise I'm telling the truth. This is my daughter, and I ought to know. I was there for the labor, all seventeen hours of it."

The lady points her finger at my sister. "Are you telling me this here is a colored child?"

Then Lydia starts singing our favorite song about how she's Black and proud. I start dancing, shaking my booty. Mama tries to grab my hand, but I run behind Lydia. The white lady turns pink. Then she pushes her cart away.

Lydia says, "I'm Black."

Mama says, "Don't you think I know that? And who're you talking to? You know better than to cause a scene in public!"

Mama walks away, and Lydia pushes the cart and puts our groceries back on the shelves. The bacon and the cereal and the mushy, light bread. At the checkout, she buys me a candy bar and says she'll hide it for me so Mama can't see, but in the parking lot the station wagon is gone.

Lydia holds my hand and we wait for Mama. We wait and wait, and then Lydia says we're going for a walk. My legs start hurting, and Lydia kneels and tells me climb on her back. She starts walking again. There is a house, and I think I remember this place. The red flowers. The bird in the tree: *coo-coo, coo-coo*. I climb off Lydia's back, but before we knock Uncle Root opens the door.

"Young lady, before you start, my name is Bennett, and I'm not in this mess. This is supposed to be my summer vacation, so I'm not getting in the middle of this. And I told your mama the same when she called and woke me from my very enjoyable nap. Come on."

We follow him through the living room and into the kitchen. Lydia sits in a chair and pulls me onto her lap. She puts her chin on top of my head, but her lap is too skinny. Her bones hurt my booty.

Uncle Root picks up the phone on the wall. "Hello? Miss Rose, I have your grandbabies." He waits and there's squawking.

"Say she's still mad, huh? This one over here is 'bout a wet hen, too. Well, what did Maybelle Lee expect? Children don't have any sense. Did she think they'd just wait at the store while she drove around? She should know better. If this was Atlanta, no telling who'd have these girls."

More squawking, and he makes a silly face. "All right, Miss Rose. Okay. All right. That's fine." He hangs up and tells us our granny says we should spend the night in his guest room.

Lydia says, "That sounds fine."

I say, "Yeah, that sounds fine."

"But first, young ladies, let's ride over to the Cluck-Cluck Hut. Get us some chicken and biscuits and French fries. Matter of fact, let's stop back by the Pig Pen for some ice cream. I got a pie in the freezer and we're about to have us a party. Power to the people!"

He raises his fist.

I say, "Ooh wee!"

Before it's time for bed, Lydia asks Uncle Root for another sheet to put underneath me. I'm scared she'll tell him what I told her about the long-haired lady, but Lydia don't say nothing. *Doesn't.* That night, the long-haired lady comes to my dream, but she only sits with me. In the morning there's no yellow stain. Lydia tells me that's what she's talking 'bout. Two nights in a row with no wetting the bed. Who's a big girl?

And I say, "I am!"

"Give me some skin, big girl!" I hit her hand hard and she turns her palm down: "Now, on the Black hand side!"

For breakfast, Uncle Root makes us cheese and eggs and pancakes topped with butter and syrup. He says he knows how to feed some hungry children. Don't play him cheap.

Then we are going and going in his long car back to the country. At the driveway, we all climb out of the car, but Uncle Root tells me to stay with him. Let my sister go first. The screen door opens, and Mama comes out to the porch and down the steps. My sister runs to her. She's crying, and Mama hugs her and rocks her side to side.

Lydia says, "I'm sorry."

Mama says, "It's all right, darling. It's okay."

———

I'm nine already, because my birthday was a week ago. I'm looking for Lydia to walk to the creek with me. It's Friday afternoon. Bay-bay James's mama came and got him and Boukie Crawford, and I'm bored. If my big sister comes with me to the creek, she'll break off pieces of the sugarcane and give that to me to suck until the juice runs out. But when I call her name, Lydia doesn't answer.

I run to Coco on the front steps. "Come on! Let's go to the creek! Let's go!"

"You sure are full of energy. You need to settle down."

Coco fusses like an old lady and looks like one, too. Her hair's braided and wrapped into two buns. She climbs up from the steps and calls through the screen door, asking can we walk to the creek?

A voice comes back. "You taking the baby?"

"Yes, Mama, I got her."

"All right, then. Y'all be careful."

Coco takes a long stick from the pile by the side of the house. There're blackberry bushes on the way to the creek, and the stick'll protect us from snakes. Then she decides which way. We can walk north, but then we'd hit the soybeans that Uncle Norman's planted. After that, there's a forest with trees and shadows, like in a fairy tale. That scares me, so we take the longer way, walking east through the peach trees until we come to the dirt road.

Now we have to choose again. If we take one direction we'll walk out to the highway, but that's not allowed. If we walk the other di-rection, we'll go past the burned-down plantation house and the old general store. That road will end at our family church, Red Mound. So we have to turn west again: that's the way to the creek. There, we see a light-green pickup truck parked on the grass, and Lydia on a blanket on the ground. Her long hair's out of her plaits. Her shirt and bra are off, and I see her breasts. There's a man standing over her. A grown man. Tony Crawford, Boukie's cousin. Tony goes to our church, and he is naked, and he's stroking his long, long penis.

Coco slaps her hand over my mouth and drags me by my hand

back to the main road. She starts running, as I try to keep up. Slow down, I beg her. My legs are tired. She doesn't stop until the plantation house. I breathe fast, my hands on my knees.

"Coco, why was Lydia naked? And that man Tony, too?"

She sighs and stays quiet for a while.

"Okay, like, she was hot, Ailey. It's really hot today—and—and—that's why she had her shirt off. And—and—the man—he was trying to compete with Lydia. It was a game, okay? Just a game to see who could pee the farthest. And—and—boys urinate standing up instead of sitting down. With their penis. That's what that thing was."

"I know that. I've seen a penis before, lots of times. I saw Gandee's in the bathtub. He made me touch it, and it stood up like Tony's."

She socks my shoulder.

"Ow, stop, Coco! You're heavy-handed!"

"Don't you ever say that again about Gandee. Do you hear me? Ever, to anybody. It would hurt Mama's feelings real, real bad. She would cry all the time and wouldn't stop. And you don't want that, do you? Pinky swear?"

I think about that awhile. I like to think now. I don't like people pushing me around.

"What about Lydia? Would her feelings be hurt, too?"

"Definitely." Coco sticks out a short finger and I hook mine to hers and I swear I never will say a thing. On the walk back to the house, she starts talking to herself. She's like an old lady again, only she curses under her breath. She says she's glad that Gandee's dead. She damned sure is. That low-down motherfucker. That nasty asshole.

Lydia's gone at dinnertime, and Mama walks through the house, out the door, and into the field that Miss Rose says is her front yard. Mama calls my sister's name. She asks Coco and me, do we know where our sister has gone? No, ma'am, we say, but then it's dark. There are no streetlamps out in the country, only june bugs. She starts calling people on the phone, and Uncle Root and Uncle Norman and Aunt Pauline come to the house. Aunt Pauline sits with my mama on the plastic-covered sofa and reads out loud from her

Bible about the Lord is her shepherd, and she shall not want, but my mama's still upset.

Then she calls my name and kneels down in front of me. She asks again, had I seen Lydia?

"Tell me, baby," Mama says. "It'll be all right. I won't be mad at you."

When she begins to cry, I tell her about what I saw at the creek, but I don't tell about Gandee, so maybe my pinky swear wasn't broken. Coco's mad at me. I can tell. She stares at me hard.

Mama tells me what a good girl I am, then she calls the sheriff's office, though my granny begs her not to. No telling what the law would do to a colored man, once they get hold of him, but Mama doesn't care. She calls anyway, but the sheriff says she needs to call back the next day. He couldn't do anything until Lydia's been missing for twenty-four hours.

Uncle Root starts calling Black folks in town, asking them about my sister. He tells them she's very light-skinned with long hair in two braids to her waist. She's tall, too, but she hasn't yet filled out, so she looks her age, which is fifteen going on sixteen. And have they seen her with Tony Crawford?

I'm not hungry at breakfast, and neither is Coco. We sit on the front steps of the porch and that's how we see Lydia in the passenger side of Tony's truck. Lydia opens the door, but Tony must have said something, because she stops before she kisses him on the mouth. That's what Mama sees when she comes out of the house, before Tony drives away. She yells down from the porch to Lydia. She tells her she better not move. My big sister stands, shaking, and Mama runs out to the field, through the peach trees. She comes back with a switch, and Lydia starts screaming.

The screen door slams, and my granny walks onto the porch.

"Wait a minute now, Belle. Let the child explain."

"What explanation? That nigger kissed her!"

The screen door slams again. This time, it's Uncle Root.

"Maybelle Lee. Don't do this, beloved. Please don't. This isn't like you."

But Mama starts stripping the leaves off the switch, and my big sister is screaming even louder.

"Cry all you want! Go ahead! But you're going to get this whipping. And let me tell you why. You're getting whipped because you scared the shit out of me. I was wondering where you were and whether you were alive or dead! My fifteen-year-old child . . ." Mama shakes the branch in my sister's direction. Tears leak from her eyes, but she doesn't wipe them away. ". . . and your granny didn't even want me to call the police! Said if I did, Tony Crawford might end up killed, because that's the way they do Black men in this town. But when I called the sheriff anyway, he told me fast girls run away all the time. That's what he called you! A fast girl! He didn't even care about you, because you were somebody's Black daughter. So I started to pray. That's all I could do, Lydia. Pray that nigger wouldn't kill my child. That she would come back home."

I'm standing in front of the porch and crying, and Coco's on the step behind me. She hugs me around the shoulders. Mama drops the peach branch and falls to the ground. She starts to holler like at church. To wave her hands like when the Spirit comes around, only Mama doesn't sound happy. She doesn't sound blessed by God, and Uncle Root runs down the steps and pulls her into his arms. He tells her not to cry. Please don't cry, beloved, but Lydia doesn't move from her place in the yard. And my sister's still screaming.

At church on Sunday, I sit between Coco and my granny. On the other side, there's Uncle Norman. Nobody else from our family is there. Nobody's been talking much since my sister came home. I feel bad this morning, so I wore a dress that Lydia made for me. I twirled in my dress to make her smile, but she didn't say anything and I hope she's not mad at me for tattling.

Before the sermon, Mr. J.W. leads us in a song. He's the head deacon, and he gives one line and then we give it back. But Mr. J.W. has a very bad voice, and even though I'm sad about my sister, I want to laugh. I cover my mouth, because I don't want to get in trouble.

Elder Beasley stands up from his chair. He goes to the lectern and flips through his Bible.

"The text that I take this morning comes from Genesis, chapter four, verses one through thirteen. Y'all got that?"

I have my own Bible. It's white leatherette. My granny gave it to me for my birthday, and I find the pages because I read really well. I'm proud of myself and I put my Bible on my lap and pretend I'm a grown lady. I wave at the air with the cardboard fan that has the picture of the blond Jesus and the lambs.

Elder Beasley reads to us about the story of Cain and Abel. How Adam knew his wife and then she conceived, and when Cain and Abel grew up, Cain killed his brother.

"Cain is a murderer, ain't he? There ain't no doubt about that. He is a low-down, nefarious criminal! He killed his own brother because he was jealous. He didn't have faith enough to say, all right, now, God has not seen fit to praise him. That's done made him mad, but he didn't say that, maybe, he needed to pray and ask, 'Lord, what do you want from me? Forget about my brother. What is it I can do? How can I get that favor you bestowed upon Abel? Am I doing something wrong? Help me, Lord. Give me just a little sign.' But, y'all, Cain didn't do none of that. No, he had to act a fool and take and kill his brother, and then he received his punishment.

"Some of y'all sitting up in here, you done had hard times. You struggling. You got bills to pay and no money. Some of y'all's children, they done fell in love with the world and they have disappointed their people. Some of y'all are raising grandkids that those children done left you with. I ain't calling no names. We don't need to do all that. I'm just telling you I know what you going through. That's what a pastor is for, but I'm not only your pastor. I'm your brother in Christ—"

The door to the church creaks open. Tony Crawford and his mama walk up the center aisle. When they pass me, I see his face swollen red and purple. One eye is closed, and Tony walks like he's real tired. Everybody in the church starts whispering, but Elder Beasley tells us, Amen, let us pray.

———

I'm thirteen going on fourteen, and it's a June morning. Mama and I have been up in the dark, preparing for the journey to Chicasetta. By the time she makes breakfast, the sun is flirting with the sky. My father arrives, home from working the night shift in the emergency room. But my sisters aren't there in the kitchen, as Mama fixes plates for Daddy and me. Grits, eggs, and sausage biscuits. No coffee for me; I'm still too young.

She gives Daddy instructions. Don't forget, there's Tupperware in the deep freezer with directions on the lids. He has to defrost and then put everything in a pan before he puts it in the stove, otherwise the plastic will burn and smell bad, too.

He pats his thighs. When she settles on his lap, he kisses her cheek.

"Woman, you do know I'm grown."

"I don't want you to go hungry."

"I need to lose weight anyway. I'm pretty sure I can miss a few meals."

"But don't be eating out every day. That's not healthy. There's plenty greens in that Tupperware."

"I'll be fine. I'll just miss you, woman."

"How much? Tell me."

They banter back and forth, but I want them to notice me. "Are you going to miss me, too?"

"What kind of question is that?" Daddy asks. "You are my precious baby girl! Of course I'll miss you. Who'll beat me in chess while you're gone?"

"Anybody can beat you. You don't know how to play."

Mama laughs, and he tells her this is certainly her daughter, because I sure can cut a brother off at the knees. She hits his shoulder lightly, and he kisses her, only this time on the mouth. They start ignoring me again, talking in their low, "just us" tone.

This summer's different: When we start our journey south, only Mama and me in the car. Lydia's down south already. She's going to be a junior at Routledge College, studying social work, and I've been so lonely in the City without her. Lydia's the one who used to wake me up in the morning, kissing my face with loud smacks. Who congratulated me that my twin bed was dry, the year after the long-haired lady had stopped coming to my dreams. Lydia, who debated with me about which clothes I should choose. Who told me that I wore jeans too much and, when I protested that our cousin Malcolm wore jeans every day, the one who told me this was true but that Malcolm wasn't as pretty as me. She's my best friend, but she's gone all the time now, except for summer.

Coco's gone from the City, too. She's headed to her third year at Yale. She was accepted early, and now she's on the premed track. She called last week and told Mama she was taking the bus down to Chicasetta. Yes, it's a three-day ride, but she wanted to see more of the country. And don't worry about her ticket. She'd already saved up from her emergency fund.

It's a strange ride in the station wagon. I don't squeeze between Lydia and my mother. There's no slapping at Coco's hands as she reaches over the back seat and tugs my braids, and when we pull into the driveway at the farm, Dear Pearl's not there on the porch. She's gotten older. She doesn't like to be out in the heat. Still, it's a surprise not to see her waving her church fan, to see, instead, my sisters waiting for Mama and me up on the porch. That's when Uncle Root rises from his chair, his gait spry; he doesn't hop down the steps, as in past years. He takes his time, and when he kisses my cheek I notice I'm the same height as he is.

My playmates don't come around anymore, either. Last summer I started my period, and Mama told me I was getting to be a young lady. I couldn't be running around with musty roughnecks smelling themselves. Mama said Baybay James and Boukie Crawford are a year older than me and boys that age want to get into mischief, but they weren't doing that with her daughter.

Come day, go day, as the old folks say, and the hours are so quiet. I wear a beat-up hat while we pick weeds in the garden. My sisters are quiet. Coco is fascinated by the dirt, rubbing it between her fingers, and Lydia can't focus on her weeds. She straightens and puts her hand to her forehead, shading her eyes. Like she's looking for something in the distance.

My mother's so happy, though. Happier than I've ever seen her, and every day, she climbs in the station wagon and goes visiting. The news she brings back isn't that exciting. Somebody had a baby. Someone else is putting in a den in their garage. Or maybe, flowers have been planted in the front yard around those cement blocks propping up another family's trailer. One evening, her eyes shine as if she'd been on an adventure. Like she's been sipping a glass full of magic.

I'm sitting on the porch with useless hands: I don't know how to sew quilt pieces. My stitches are too large, my granny says, so I should sit a spell. Enjoy the company, but I'm pouting. My sisters have gone to the American Legion, and I'm forbidden to go. I'm too young, they said. I wouldn't even be let inside the Legion, let alone able to buy a drink.

Mama's an expert sewer, but she only keeps the pieces of cloth in her lap. She rocks in her chair, smiling, and Miss Rose asks, what's gotten into her? Had somebody took and gave her some money?

"No, ma'am, I'm just happy! I got three daughters and all of them doing well! I've done my worrying over them. They gave me a few gray hairs, but it looks like things will be all right. Only four more years and my baby will be done with high school." She pats my leg, as if I need reminding that I'm her last child.

"Don't shout till you get happy," Aunt Pauline says. "Remember, the Devil always working." She's the pastor of her own church.

"That's fine," my mother says. "But I'm the one who raised these girls. Not Satan."

My granny tells them, don't fight. It ain't nice to do that, and Aunt Pauline says she was just saying. She reaches and squeezes my granny's hand. She says she's sorry, but days later my great-grandmother passes away.

Dear Pearl dies way before her time. She had been eighty-seven, but that's a very young age in our family. She should have had ten more years, though it was true that Dear Pearl had let herself go after she became a widow. She got fat, stopped wearing her bottom partials, and her daughters had to harass her to get in the bathtub twice a week. She didn't have the sugar diabetes, though, even though she loved cola and peppermint candy. Her doctor had told her it was a miracle she was reasonably healthy.

Nobody knew when it had happened. Dear Pearl went to bed early, skipping supper and saying she was gone lie down. Her cane tapped slowly as she walked back to her bedroom. The next morning, we heard Miss Rose calling her mother. When Dear Pearl didn't rise, my granny said she was getting in more sleep, which Dear Pearl surely deserved. Hadn't she worked hard all her life? Let her settle under that chenille spread. My sisters and I sat in the kitchen, while Miss Rose puttered around, cutting slices of streak-o-lean. Cracking eggs and pouring in heavy cream she'd bought from the farm down the road. My granny doesn't believe in store-bought anything. During the summers, she cooks two sets of breakfasts: one for herself, my mother, and Dear Pearl, and another for my sisters and me. After breakfast, Miss Rose put the cooked meat and the biscuits in the oven but threw out the scrambled eggs. She went out to the garden with my sisters and me and plucked some weeds. When she came back it was lunchtime, but my great-grandmother hadn't yet risen. When Miss Rose went into the room, it only took a moment for her to know something was wrong, and her cries climbed into full-blown screams.

My granny's a cheerful, smiling woman who offers perky words whenever you need them, but after she finds Dear Pearl, her tears are steady. I worry that she might not have any more water to give. I offer her full glasses, along with shoulder pats.

"Thank you, baby," she says, but she keeps right on crying.

In a few hours after Dear Pearl is found, Mr. Cruddup, the Black mortician in town, pulls his funeral hearse up to the house. He solemnly greets my family and whispers his condolences. Only after he leaves with Dear Pearl in the hearse does Uncle Root arrive. He told my mother he didn't want to see his sister carried out with her face covered. Uncle Root's in his baby-blue seersucker suit, his red-and-blue-striped bow tie neatly centered, but he seems very sad. He sits in one of the plastic-covered chairs in the living room, his chin on his fist, and stares at the wall. Every hour, Mama sends me over with a full plate. Doesn't he want to eat something? It might make him feel better. But the old man only shakes his head.

The day before the funeral, I ask my mother if we have time to go to Macon to buy me a dress. I don't have anything appropriate, only jeans and sundresses, but Mama goes to her room. She comes back out with a navy-blue dress with lace at the collar. There are low, dark heels, pantyhose, and a slip, all in my size.

"I had a dream about Dear passing, so I packed this for you. But I put it out my mind. You know, sometimes I dream about something and it never even comes true. I was hoping it would be like that this time."

Ever since I was little, my mother would say that in Chicasetta it wasn't a rare Black funeral that went badly, it was a rare one that didn't. And there aren't any cremations, either. Black folks in Chicasetta don't believe in that: it's not natural. That's what they have the insurance man for. You pay him every month (or every two weeks, depending on the schedule), and no matter how poor you are, you have enough for a suitable burial. If you're too poor for the burial insurance, Mr. Cruddup solicits donations for the homegoing. He's closemouthed about your business, too. Mama says you can control the casket, the flowers, what part of the Black cemetery in town you're laid to rest in, but you can't control the guest list. It looks bad keeping somebody from paying their respects. What's more complicated is when someone in your family misbehaves.

Before the funeral, Mama tells me a secret, one I should never mention: Aunt Pauline isn't Dear Pearl's biological child. She raised the baby girl as her own after Annie Mae, the child's mother, abandoned her. Annie Mae's my granny's blood sister, but she's been gone so long that if her child hadn't been given a photo of her, Aunt Pauline wouldn't have even known the woman if she passed her on the street. The photo and a few stories are all that's left of Annie

Mae: Her favorite color. (Blue.) That she played the trumpet like an angel of God. That she never could stand wearing a dress.

My granny never had made a sign that Aunt Pauline was adopted, and the two of them were so thick. So it didn't make sense when my granny cut a jig at Mr. Cruddup's funeral home, screaming that she wanted a white coffin, instead of the maroon one Aunt Pauline had picked out, Mama says—she was there at the funeral home when it happened. But then again, Aunt Pauline wanted to control the scriptures, to read Psalm twenty-three, instead of Ephesians, chapter two, verse eight. Aunt Pauline pulled out their mother's Bible to show which scripture she'd loved the best, but Miss Rose told her that didn't count for nothing. Everybody knew their mother never had learned to read. Mr. Cruddup whispered he would leave them to make the choice, but even after that Miss Rose and Aunt Pauline argued about what food to serve at the repast. One wanted pork chops, pound cake, and rolls. The other wanted fried chicken, sweet potato pie, and biscuits. At least they could agree upon the greens.

It takes Uncle Root to bridge the feud. When he shows, Mama tells me to go back to my room with my sisters. Grown folks are talking, but she doesn't fuss at me when I hang in the doorway of the living room. I hear the old man tell my granny and Aunt Pauline they ought to be ashamed of themselves. What kind of daughters behave this way, when their mother has only recently been called to Glory? It's a scandal, and if the two don't start acting right, he'll make the decisions for the homegoing and the repast himself. He's paying for most of it, after all. Because that fifteen-hundred-dollar burial policy his sister had taken out didn't begin to cover the cost.

Thursday afternoon, we walk into the funeral as the organist plays an instrumental of "Precious Lord," lingering on every third note. Our family moves behind the white casket carried in by white-gloved men. We can't hold all the mourners for Dear Pearl at our family church, so the venue's been moved to the gymnasium of the new high school. Men carry in flowers and announce the last name of a family as they hold up each arrangement. So many flowers, as if a garden's bloomed under the gym's basketball net. All the older ladies wear hats. When Elder Beasley steps behind the podium, there's a flurry of white, as those same women pull out handkerchiefs. He begins with Psalm twenty-three, before moving to Ephesians.

Later, at the repast in the high school's cafeteria, my mother says, what a beautiful homegoing. The adults at our table nod in agreement as they nibble at their plates of fried chicken, pork chops, greens, and candied yams. Those store-bought, faintly sweet, white rolls that everyone in the south seems to like, and biscuits that have chilled. There are many different flavors of cake. No one at our table mentions how the always dignified Uncle Root wept loudly behind the podium during his eulogy until my mother had gone up and hugged him, before walking him back to his seat. Or that Uncle Huck had been too broken up to attend his mother's funeral, so he'd sent his boyfriend in his stead. The mourners only remark that it's so nice that Miss Rose and Aunt Pauline have made up. At the grave site out on the family farm, they'd watched as the casket was lowered into the ground and the two sisters held each other.

"Mama, don't leave," they'd screamed. "Mama, please don't go!"

THE DEFINITIONS OF SIDDITY

◈

A week after the funeral of my great-grandmother, Mama and I packed the station wagon again and left my sisters behind in Chicasetta. Coco insisted on taking the bus back up to New Haven, and Lydia drove her little car the twenty-five miles over Highway 441 to her own college campus. I should have been excited: Finally, I was starting at Toomer High, but I didn't have anybody to help me get ready. To make sure I looked like I was in high school.

When I was little, Lydia would unravel my four braids, oiling my edges with the blue grease from the medicine cabinet. She'd put ribbons in my hair, and tell me I was beautiful with my brown face and my brown eyes. It didn't matter what Nana Claire said. She was just jealous of me, because she was pale as a corpse and you could see her creepy blue veins. And brown skin was the most beautiful, so I could sit in the sun as much as I wanted. Nana was mean, Lydia insisted. I shouldn't pay any attention to her.

I wanted a teenaged hairstyle, instead of braids, for the first day of ninth grade. Lydia would have helped me to wash my hair and roll it, so I could sit under the dryer. But Lydia wasn't there, and Mama told me nothing was wrong with my hair the way it was. She'd been saying that since middle school.

The morning of the first day of school, I gave myself a pep talk while looking in the bathroom mirror: *You're absolutely fine! It's going to be okay! It's a new school this year, and you'll be really popular there!*

A knock on the door. A rattling of the doorknob, but I was locked inside.

"Are you in there talking to yourself?" Mama asked.

"That's my business," I called. "But it's an intelligent conversation."

"Don't you get smart with me, little girl."

I looked at myself and then took down my braids. I pulled my hair back in a long ponytail, sprinkled some water on my edges, and brushed them down. There. That might do. And in my room, I dressed in my best jeans and name-brand, button-down oxford shirt. I put shiny pennies in my loafers and repeated my inner pep talk. But the kitchen felt bigger with only me at the table, as my mother clicked around in her schoolteacher's outfit, her high heels and green dress. She forgot to tell me how pretty I was without Lydia there to remind her. There was a loud greeting at the front door as Aunt Diane let herself in with her key, followed by my cousins Malcolm and Veronica. Malcolm went to Toomer High, too, so we'd be riding together.

When the station wagon pulled up to the front of school, my mother stopped the car and unclicked her seat belt. I begged her, for the love of God, to please just drop off Malcolm and me. We already had our homeroom assignments and our class schedules. Please don't embarrass me. Mama's face was hurt as she fastened her seat belt again.

In the front hallway of the school, Malcolm hovered.

"You okay? I can walk you to your homeroom. That was mine, three years ago."

"I'm fine, okay? This isn't the first day of kindergarten. I'm not Veronica."

He tapped my shoulder lightly. "All right, then, killer. Hold it down."

By lunchtime, I was feeling hopeful. A girl in my English class had told me she liked my shirt and my penny loafers. She was adorable. Brown with deep dimples and curvy by fourteen-year-old standards. Her relaxed hair fell below her shoulders, there were gold hoops in her ears, and her brand-name oxford shirt was identical to mine, except it was pink while mine was lavender.

"You look dope, girl," she said.

"Thanks!" I said. "You, too."

Her name was Cecily Rester, and in the cafeteria she waved me over to the table, where she sat with four other stylishly dressed girls. I'd been walking beside Malcolm, but when she waved I put more distance between my cousin and me.

"Is it okay if I sit with those girls?" I asked.

"Do your thing, killer."

He headed over to a table of guys, and I set my tray down at Cecily's table.

"Is that your man?" she asked.

"Definitely not! He's my cousin."

"Ooh, girl! That's good, because that dude's a nerd."

Everyone at the table laughed. If I laughed, I'd be disloyal to Malcolm, but I did anyway. I told her I couldn't help who I was related to. They laughed again, and I looked over at my cousin.

One of the other girls said that he might be nerdy, but he was fine as hell, with those waves. He looked like El Debarge.

"Whatever," Cecily said. "Ain't nobody tryna get with Malcolm Garfield. Ain't his mama a white lady?"

The next day, when I entered the cafeteria, she waved me over to her table, and the next days after that, too. She and her friends were popular. I could see that from the way the other freshmen in the cafeteria looked in their direction, but Cecily and her friends never looked back, unless it was to point someone out for ridicule. She began joining me on the steps after school as I waited for Aunt Diane to pick up my cousin and me. I was glad Mama was on bus duty at the school where she taught, so that it was my aunt's glossy Volvo instead of my mother's old brown station wagon that pulled up daily.

My cousin sat with Cecily and me on the steps, but in the car after, I told him my friend and I had things to talk about. I lowered my voice: beside me, my baby cousin Veronica was napping in her car seat.

"Like, girl things," I said. "Like really private things we'd be embarrassed to talk about in front of boys."

"Are you talking about menstruation?" my aunt asked. "There's no need to be shy about that. It's a natural part of any young girl's life, and he already knows—"

"Naw, naw, I get it." Malcolm's face was pink, as he fumbled with the seat belt. "It's cool, killer. I'll wait somewhere else. Do your thing."

———

I'd never had a girlfriend before, except for Lydia, and a sister had to love you. That was the blood contract, and I supposed that's why I had my father's mother as a friend, too. Nana Claire wasn't very nice, but she was family.

I was her favorite; or rather, I was the only grandchild she tolerated. My sisters weren't to Nana's liking, and the feeling was mutual: they made fun of her behind her back. Nor did she want to spend time with Malcolm. Boys were savages, she told me. She'd only tolerated her own sons as a mother's cross to bear. And Veronica was going on five and thus too taxing on the nerves.

Nana was unlike any woman in my mother's family. She wore coral lipstick to match her nail polish and powdered her nose and cheeks daily, even if she never left the house. Nana did not cook like my Chicasetta granny. The only recipe she knew by heart was for her Creole cookies, which she only baked on holidays. She employed a maid because she didn't do housework. A lady had to worry about her hands, and Nana wore white cotton gloves to bed every night, slathering her hands with petroleum jelly before the gloves went on. She never went outside without a hat, and she warned me that if I wasn't careful to protect my skin, I'd have the complexion of an old fishwife when I turned thirty. Nana never seemed to sweat, either. No matter how high the temperature, her brow remained fresh, and she was lovely smelling. Her aroma took you to a better place in the world, where there was no hunger or war or southern relatives who ate repasts of pig offal and covered their living room furniture in plastic.

Nana and I would take our Saturday field trips. I'd spend the night, and the next morning, we would dress in church clothes and take a taxi to Worthie's, the department store downtown. I would sit outside the dressing room waiting for her. When she emerged wearing one of the conservative yet expensive outfits she'd tried on, I'd clap for her, as if she were a fashion model.

When we returned from shopping, we would sit in the anteroom outside her bedroom's inner chamber. Nana in her wing chair, while I sat on the floor. She'd turn the pages of one of her photo albums. She had hundreds of pictures, some in albums, others in special binders. There were pictures covering the red-painted walls of the anteroom, too, in silver frames, and more in the bedroom. Pictures of my grandfather Zachary, whom his grandchildren had called "Gandee." My father and Uncle Lawrence as small children dressed up for Easter. My sisters and me in matching, fancy dresses. My cousin Malcolm standing behind Aunt Diane, a hand on her shoulder as she held a bald baby Veronica.

She pointed to an older photo in the album. Tucked into four corner holders.

"This was taken at the Vineyard. 1938, I believe. Or '39. It was before the war, though."

"World War Two, Nana?"

"Yes, Ailey. How old do you think I am? That was almost fifty years ago, so I suppose I am close to my dotage. But don't tell anybody that."

Nana handed me another photo. "This is Mrs. Richardson and me when we were young girls."

"I think I remember that lady. She died, didn't she?"

"Yes. Poor thing. Breast cancer. Can you believe I was ever that young? That's me, on the right. I'm the blonde."

Two very pale girls wore bathing suits. The brunette wore a modest, almost dowdy suit. It wasn't a color photo: the blond girl's hair looked white in its pageboy style. The halter of her suit's bosom was shirred, and the bottom exposed lots of thigh.

"Mother complained so much about that suit, but I told her, 'It's the new style, and I'm going to live until I get married. Really live!' I'm glad I did. The war cut into our fun, and I went gray so early, right after Lawrence was born. You can't wear gray hair past your chin. It looks unkempt. Don't you think so?"

"Yes, ma'am."

"Ailey, how many times have I told you that 'ma'am' is servant talk and we are not servants? At least we are not on my side of the family."

"I'm sorry."

"I wish your mother wouldn't take you down to that backwoods metropolis every summer. It's ruining you. Here's the cottage on Oak Bluffs. It's getting difficult to travel now, but do you know why I still go, Ailey?

"No, ma—no, Nana."

"I go because there are Negroes like me there, people with whom I feel comfortable. We are accomplished, we are quiet, and we never make trouble. If you adhere to those rules, you will have peace with others."

Then, Miss Delores would knock and bring in a tray, balanced on her right arm. This was the woman my mother forbade me ever to call a "maid." I wasn't allowed to address her by her first name without a handle attached. It didn't matter that she cleaned Nana's kitchen and bathrooms. That she cooked the roasted chicken that she then cooled and placed on the tray, alongside water crackers, crudités, and thinly sliced cheeses, and walked the tray up the stairs to serve my grandmother and me. Miss Delores had babysat me as a toddler, my mother told me. I needed to give her some respect.

When Nana and I finished eating, I wouldn't press the servants' button that had been installed in the corner of the anteroom long before I was born. I'd take the tray down while Nana changed into her silk pajamas. When I returned, she would turn on the television and smoke a cigarette fitted into a jade holder. I wasn't allowed to tell anyone she smoked, especially my parents. I would sit on the love seat at the foot of her bed, but it was hard to concentrate on the movie. When my grandmother talked, she expected me to turn and look at her.

On the television screen, *Stormy Weather.* Lena Horne sang next to a greasy-headed man playing the piano, an outrageous, feathered cap on her head. Now there was dancing, and Miss Horne shimmied in the middle of adoring men. Her voice was mediocre, but her presence carried the scene.

"Isn't Lena Horne beautiful? There was a girl I went to school with who was even prettier than that. But it wasn't Toomer when I went. It was the City Preparatory School for Negroes. Goodness, I can't even remember that girl's name. What was her name?" My grandmother took a puff of her cigarette and blew it out. "But I remember her face like it was yesterday. I was so jealous of that girl."

"You, Nana?"

"Every woman has her insecurities, Ailey, especially if she doesn't know a man's heart." She pulled on her cigarette. "God, I despise Bill Robinson! For the life of me, I don't know why they cast him in this movie! He looks like an ugly monkey." Puff. Puff. "Ailey, do you want to hear a secret?"

"Sure, Nana."

"I first saw *Stormy Weather* over at the theater on Sixth Street, but I didn't sit in the balcony. What do you think about that?"

"Um . . . okay."

"Ailey, it was against the law back then. The theater on Twenty-First Street was for Negroes, so we could sit wherever we wanted. But the one on Sixth Street was segregated. Only whites could sit on the first level. If you were Negro, you had to sit up in the balcony. I could have been arrested."

"Weren't you scared, Nana?"

"Of what? Nobody knew. I'd leave your father at home with the housekeeper and pass for white all the time. I had plenty fun in those days, and your grandfather never knew a thing about it." She winked. "Oh, here's the best part! Watch."

On TV, Lena performed her legendary song, and my grandmother sang along.

———

To me, Cecily Rester was as beautiful as Lena Horne, and when she began to pay me attention at school, I knew this was my chance. Not only for non-kin female companionship, but to be popular. I felt the euphoria of power, but also fear. In just a few weeks I'd seen Cecily turn ugly on one of the lunchtime crew. I didn't want to be the flower withering beneath her gorgeous sun.

Usually everyone was safe, however, because the daily target of Cecily's derision was most often Antoinette Jones, a girl who was in my second-period English class. Antoinette wasn't popular in school. Word was her mother was a crack addict. She didn't even talk to anyone except Demetrius Woods, a boy with whom she rode the bus to and from school. Her brother by a different father, some said. A cousin, others insisted, but everybody agreed that Demetrius and Antoinette looked in need of several pork-heavy meals, along with many biscuits and side dishes.

"That girl is so damned weird," Cecily said. "Look at her. She makes my skin crawl."

She pointed at Antoinette standing in line for the bus. The girl's book bag was torn, and she was trying to keep the top closed with both hands. She climbed on the bus awkwardly, still holding on to the book bag.

"And what's up with that damned hair? It's not even two inches long. Antoinette's, like, chronically baldheaded or some shit. I went to Wells-Barnett Elementary *and* Fauset Middle with that chick, and, like, in five years, her hair didn't grow."

"Maybe she got a bad perm. That's kinda sad, don't you think?" My mother had warned me about picking on people, even behind their backs. Did I want to be like Nana, thinking my farts were special? But I couldn't tell my new friend that we were being mean. I wanted to sleep over at her house like the other girls who sat in the cafeteria with us.

"No, it's not sad," Cecily said. "It's stupid. Why'd she keep going back to the same beautician who burned her hair out? Stupid, baldheaded heifer."

She stretched out a shapely leg, picking a mote from her tights. Antoinette's bus drove away, revealing a billboard illustrated with our First Lady's solution to drug addiction: JUST SAY NO! Beside those words, someone had spray-painted rhyming lines: NANCY REAGAN IS A CRACK HOE!

I didn't worry much about Antoinette, at the cruelty pointed her way. Not just by the students, either. The teacher of our English class constantly embarrassed her. Like the day Mrs. Youngley diagrammed sentences and asked Antoinette about the identity of a word on the board. Antoinette whispered her confusion, but our teacher kept prodding, "Don't you remember? I told the class only yesterday!"

"No, ma'am."

"Didn't you even take notes?"

Antoinette shrugged.

"All right. That's fine. I'll give you a hint. It's one of the eight parts of speech."

She paused, eyebrows raised haughtily, but Antoinette only looked down at her desk. When our teacher called on others, they had adolescent loyalty. They didn't know, either, but I raised my hand. I waved it enthusiastically and shouted that the word was a verb. I beamed when our teacher praised my intelligence, throwing a smug glance at Antoinette. Saving the memory of her stupidity to share with Cecily and the rest of the crew at lunch. But I didn't have time to tell my story, because an hour later, Antoinette completely altered the trajectory of my short-lived social life and entire high school education.

When she appeared at my locker, it was like a scene out of a horror movie: I closed the locker door and there she was, shocking me into a low scream.

"You getting on my last nerve, bitch," she said. "The way you think you so cute."

"What did you say?"

I don't know which shocked me the most: that Antoinette finally was speaking to somebody besides Demetrius Woods, or that I outweighed her by about fifty pounds and was inches taller, but she didn't seem intimidated. A group of girls crowded around us and there was Cecily. She cautioned me in a loud voice to kick that heifer's ass.

Antoinette repeated herself, pointing her index finger in my face. Before that I'd quickly planned to offer peaceful rhetoric, as our principal had counseled at assemblies, but now everyone was watching. Seeking peace would be a punk move.

"Uh-uh," I said. "I don't think I'm cute, neither."

"Yes, you do, bitch," Antoinette said.

"No, I don't! And—and—don't you keep calling me no bitch! And—and—you better get your finger out my face!"

"I'ma call you whatever I feel like, you siddity bitch. And you think you better than everybody 'cause you light-skinned and got that good hair. Bitch."

My mother had told me that all hair was wonderful, no matter the texture, and that it was ignorant to separate hair into categories of "bad" and "good." Furthermore, anybody could see I wasn't even close to light-skinned. Even in the wintertime I approached mahogany—but it was too late to explain, because then Antoinette slapped me across my face.

The crowd roared: "Oooooooooooo!" She kept striking me until I fell, then she straddled my stomach, yanking my hair, until Malcolm broke through the crowd. He pulled Antoinette off me, and she kicked at the air, but he told her nobody was going to hurt her. Stop kicking. He set her on her feet, standing between us. Soon, a teacher arrived on the scene and marched Antoinette and me down the hall and to the first floor to the principal's office.

I was surprised when my father showed up. He told me that my mother couldn't take off from her job. So he'd told his receptionist to reschedule his patients' appointments. In Principal Perry's office, my father and I were informed that I was suspended. It was Wednesday, I couldn't come back until Monday, and further, this was going on my permanent academic record.

"But Mr. Perry, that's not fair!" I said. "Everybody saw that girl jump me!"

"Ailey. Please." My father put out his hand, his signature, calming gesture. "Mr. Perry, I'd ask that you reconsider your decision. Look at those scratches on my child's face. Clearly, this was not her fault or a fair fight."

"I'm sorry, Mr. Garfield."

"It's doctor."

"Pardon me?"

"I'm not a mister. It's Dr. Garfield."

"My apologies. I have a doctorate, too, but the kids call me 'mister.'"

"That's lovely, but I'm a board-certified physician. General practice, though I am trained in surgery, in case someone gets seriously hurt. And you never know when that's going to happen."

"Oh, I see. How nice."

"I think so."

Mr. Perry cleared his throat. "Anyway, my decision is final. I think I'm being very fair. The other girl is suspended as well. We have a zero-tolerance policy for violence here. I'm sure you can understand."

My father asked me to go outside to the reception area. He would come get me soon, he told me, but he stayed inside the office for another thirty-five minutes. When he emerged, he took my hand like when I was little. In the car, he turned the ignition, before turning it back off.

"Ailey, you know I'm always on your side, right?" His baritone was low, unhurried.

"Yes, Daddy."

"And you know you can tell me anything, and I'll treat you fairly?"

"Yes."

"So give it to me straight: Did you do something to that girl to provoke her?"

"You mean Antoinette?"

"Yes, her. Your principal told me, that girl comes from a very disadvantaged background and some particularly cruel kids pick on her about her clothes and the way she looks. I know that sometimes, kids can get in groups—"

"Uh-uh, Daddy! I didn't say nothing to that girl! We don't even speak!"

"So you're saying she jumped on you for absolutely no reason?"

"Yeah. She just, like, snapped. I don't even know why. Maybe she's got mental problems. Something."

Daddy patted my arm. "I didn't mean to hurt your feelings, darling. I was just checking, but I already knew the answer. Your heart is too big to ever be mean."

At home, he told me I was not suspended, but the principal had decided that I could stay home to calm down. When I returned on Monday, I wouldn't have detention, either, and he thought that was a very reasonable decision on Mr. Perry's part.

"Your mama will be here soon. Maybe she'll make fried chicken. You can have both the breasts, if you want."

"I'm not hungry. I just want to lie down."

"Aw, darling. All right, then. There're vitamin E capsules in the medicine cabinet. Go wash your face and start rubbing that oil on those scratches. Three times a day, okay? Don't forget. You don't want those marks to get permanent."

If I hadn't gotten my ass beat, the next two days would have been fantastic. My father stayed home with me, and we watched a talk show and three soap operas. He ordered pepperoni pizza with extra cheese and didn't even hide the box in the trash. This was a special occasion, he said. We needed unhealthy food to make things better. Besides, my mother had given him permission.

That Monday, my cousin tried to hold my hand when we climbed out of my mother's station wagon. If I hadn't been too embarrassed— I was fourteen damned years old, after all—I would have let him. Instead I let go and walked behind him, my eyes on the ground as we entered the school. I could hear the whispers of *There she go* and *Did you see Antoinette beat that ass?* as I somehow made it through the hall and up the steps to my homeroom.

In English class, Antoinette wasn't there. She'd been suspended, but the other students twisted their mouths my way. They felt self-righteous now: I was the villain. If anything was worse than getting beat down in public, it was snitching to the principal.

When Mrs. Youngley called on me, I told her I hadn't read the assignment.

"That's not like you, Ailey."

"I know. I'm sorry, ma'am."

I wasn't hungry at lunchtime, but I filled up my tray. I wanted something to hold in front of me, a barrier between me and my shame and ridicule. I walked past tables and more whispers until I saw Cecily and the crew. I smiled in relief: here was my oasis. When I set my tray down, Cecily was holding court, telling a story. The other girls giggled, and I joined in.

I waited for Cecily on the steps, after school. I'd already brushed off her spot, because she didn't like sitting in dirty places. She was careful with her clothes. She was late showing, but when she sat down in the clean place I'd made for her she greeted me warmly. Asked how I'd been doing since the fight. She moved into her usual derision of Antoinette: her lack of hair, her stupidity, and this time, I eagerly laughed. I didn't feel sorry for Antoinette anymore. She deserved everything Cecily threw her way.

It was a safe, beautiful half hour, and then I saw the Volvo nudge forward in the line of cars. My aunt beeped the horn.

Cecily touched my arm. "Look. I really like you."

"Thanks. I like you, too."

"You're super cute and you dress really nice. And that's important, because I can't hang with anybody tacky. But it's like this. Even though that heifer jumped you, you snitched. And I can't have snitches around me. I got a reputation to protect."

My smile dropped. Blood thudded in my ears.

"No, Cecily! I didn't snitch, neither!" I didn't care about lying. There had been only two witnesses in the principal's office. She couldn't check out my story.

"Yeah, you did. Otherwise, how come you're here and Antoinette got suspended? Not that that heifer didn't deserve it."

"I don't know! I just, like, wasn't suspended."

She gave me a pitying look. "Uh-huh. Sure."

"Cecily, please."

"I'm sorry. But me and my girls voted. For what it's worth, I took your side, but you lost. You can't sit with us no more."

Behind me, my cousin called my name, and my voice trembled with urgency when I told him, just a minute, okay? One minute, and he walked down the school steps. My breath came heavy as I tried to figure out something to say that would save me.

My aunt beeped the horn, longer this time.

"Your ride is waiting on you, girl," Cecily said.

She picked up her book bag, unzipped it, and began looking inside for something. She didn't look up when I spoke to her, and when my aunt laid on the horn, I picked up my own bag and headed toward the Volvo. In the back seat, Veronica was napping in her car seat. On purpose, I bumped into her with my arm. Her eyes opened momentarily before her head rolled to the other side.

———

For two months, I'd called Lydia's dorm phone every Sunday evening, to talk about how I'd finally made a friend. When I lost the companionship of Cecily, I called to tell my big sister I was lonely again. However, I hadn't been able to catch her. My mother told me not to worry—Lydia was a junior in college. She had her own life now, but I kept calling. Trying. The young women who answered the phone would shout down the hall.

"Lydia Garfield, telephone! Lydia Garfield!" A long pause. "Sorry, she's not in."

One evening in early November, my big sister rang the house after dinner.

"Lydia, I'm mad at you," I said. "I tried to call last week for your birthday."

"Aw, baby, I'm sorry. Will you forgive me if I tell you a secret?" She gave a squeal and I forgot my irritation.

"What?!"

"Baby sister, I'm in love!"

"Oh my God! Tell me everything!"

"His name is Dante Anderson, he's from Atlanta, he goes to Morehouse, and he's super cute!"

"Dante? Like the *Inferno*? What kind of name is that?"

"It's a great name. The best name there is. And you be nice, because I'm bringing him home. I'm asking Mama for permission."

My sister and her beau appeared the day before Thanksgiving. They made a striking couple. Dante was much darker than she was and flagrantly handsome. He was polite, too, giving a submissive "yes, ma'am," when my mother banished him to the basement let-out sofa. She told him this was an old-fashioned household.

The next afternoon, the rest of the family gathered. Of the younger generation, Malcolm was our only boy. He sat on the floor with Veronica, pretending to drink from her tea set. Coco was quiet, answering questions about college in monosyllables, but Lydia was our butterfly, keeping everyone laughing with her stories, like how somebody in her college dormitory had accidentally set a small fire with a hot plate, and Lydia's dorm mother had run outside in a fancy silk negligee—but had forgotten to put her wig on. On my boom box, she played a mixtape with her favorite holiday song on a loop, "This Christmas," by Donny Hathaway. It was Thanksgiving, she said. The season had started.

Right after dessert, she disclosed truths in segments. She was going to transfer to Spelman in January. The paperwork had gone through, and Dante was graduating from Morehouse that next year. Then she hit us with the rest.

"We eloped, y'all! We're married! Me and Dante got an apartment in Atlanta!" She pointed a finger at Mama. "And before you ask, I'm not pregnant. I'm still on the Pill."

My grandmother gasped, and my mother asked, didn't Lydia have any shame, talking about her inside business? People were eating. Children were in the room.

"I'm not a kid anymore," I said.

Beside me, Mama swiveled. She pointed her finger at me, close to my face. "Ailey Pearl Garfield, is anybody talking to you? You need to learn to be quiet when grown folks are speaking. Or you gone learn to deal with my teaching you, and you don't want that."

Mama turned back to my sister. Across the table, Lydia had put her arm around Dante.

"How could you do this? Have you lost your mind? You just turned twenty-one two weeks ago!"

Lydia didn't seem upset. She smiled, as if my mother wasn't shouting. "You were around that age when you and Daddy got married. And then you had me. Y'all did all right."

"Girl, you think I wanted that? I was supposed to be going to graduate school, but I got pregnant! That's why I got married, Lydia! That's why I had a damned baby at twenty-three years old!"

Mama put her hand to her mouth. Except for my mother and sister talking, everyone else had been quiet, but now I couldn't even hear breathing. Then Mama rose, picked up a serving bowl, and walked back to the kitchen.

At the head of the table, my father pushed back his chair. He held out his hand to my sister's husband, and Dante stood. They shook hands, but when Dante tried to let go, my father held on. He cleared his throat a few times.

"Brother, you better take care of my baby. I'm not playing with you."

"I will, Dr. Garfield. I promise. I won't let you down, sir."

My father and Dante stood there, and then my father pulled at him again, and they embraced. Daddy pounded the younger man on the back. When they parted, my father's face was wet. The younger man sat down, and my sister kissed his cheek. She rubbed her lipstick off his skin.

But still, nobody else said anything. We just sat there, I don't know how long, until Nana announced it was time for my father to call her a taxi, but he said no, he'd drive her. It was a holiday, after all. After that, Aunt Diane began collecting plates. My sisters and I tried to help her, but she told us that was all right. She had it. When Aunt Diane's arms were full, she went into the kitchen, but she didn't return, either.

The next morning, the newlyweds were gone, and Coco packed for New Haven. She asked my father to take her to the bus station. The dorms were closed, but she was going to stay with a friend.

Within days, my mother called the new number Lydia had written down for her, along with her new address. But there was a message whenever Mama called: she had reached a number that was no longer in service or had been disconnected. My mother called Uncle Root, telling him she needed him to go to Atlanta and see about her daughter. She gave the old man the address, but when he drove to the neighborhood, there was only an empty lot. Then he called someone he knew in Spelman College's admissions office, but he was given the news that they had no record for my sister's transfer.

◆

SONG

◆

The Village Becomes a Farm

Twenty years had passed, and a new century had begun. Since Nila had given Micco his first cow, much had changed in the village and in the people's land near the Oconee River. More white men along with their wives and children had pushed further west, bringing their ways of collecting days on paper, instead of recording moons. There were many small battles between the Creek people and these whites, for they had brought cattle and pigs with them, which trampled the land, and they killed too many deer.

Bushy Hair had inherited the tendencies of Coromantee-Panther and, though he had stiffened in age, when young men from the village began to fight the white men—the children and grandchildren of Englishmen and Scotsmen—Bushy Hair was filled with red courage and rode into battle. He died in one of these fights and his name was sung with grief and gratitude.

Yet battle was different when it occurred on paper and in assaults on the mind. The white men—the Americans—wanted everything and did not respect the ways of the people. Even those who represented themselves as friends encouraged domestication among Creek men, that they should farm the land, instead of letting women do it. The most annoying were the Christian missionaries who intruded at odd times to advocate baptism and the romantic practice of the man on top instead of on the bottom or from behind. They insisted that anyone civilized knew the latter two were unholy and, moreover, encouraged the rheumatism.

After his uncle died, Micco felt more confusion, especially when the elders of The-Place-in-the-Middle-of-the-Tall-Trees decided to combine their village with another. Nila begged her son to move with her, but his desire for property, a hankering he had inherited from his father, became stronger. He wanted to make his own way and it pleased him that after the villagers left, he could walk the land and know that he owned it all. As he had in his childhood, he whispered to himself, "Mine! Mine!" This was land Micco could give to his children after his death. A legacy, for he had married as a young man.

Micco and his wife, Mahala, had twin sons and a third son. Each had American names, as Mahala had insisted. Then, when Micco thought that Mahala had gone through the change, for she had stopped her intervals in the moon house—the only Creek way she followed—Mahala had become pregnant and gave birth to a little girl. Her mother named her Eliza, but her father would call her "Lady."

Mahala was a mestizo, the daughter and granddaughter of mixed-blood children of white men who had mated with Creeks. Mahala's skin was very pale, her hair light brown, and her eyes blue instead of brown. She had met Micco at the trading post near her family's home by the Oconee River. Mahala's father had impressed upon her his own ways—that women should obey their husbands—and after Micco and Mahala married in a tiny Christian church near the trading post, she had moved her belongings to his village and his house, instead of Micco following his wife, as a proper Creek man did. In fact, Mahala did not even speak the language of the people. Her parents had forbidden it in their home, and when Micco spoke to their children in his dialect—for he had taught them—and they responded in kind, Mahala grew petulant. She accused her husband and children of making fun of her, an insecurity made more potent when they laughed at her in reply.

Mahala was ambitious for her husband, and at their biannual journeys to the trading post, she urged him to buy another cow, as well as a couple of pigs. These trips allowed her not only to visit with her parents, but to covet the lifestyles of the whites. In addition to livestock, Mahala began to bother Micco to purchase slaves, whom traders brought to the post. Initially, Micco was resistant: though his wife was unaware of his Negro blood, he was sensitive about the idea. He had seen slaves before, naturally, though they had been Creek. The village had kept people in bondage, because of a revenge trade in the aftermath of a murder, or when captives were taken in war. Yet buying a person who had not committed any wrong, or whose clan or village had not transgressed, did not sit well with Micco. Still, his wife pushed him, and one summer, when a slave trader found his way up the path to Micco's farm, he paused to speak to the man.

The trader rode a horse and carried a long gun. He was accompanied by a stoic-looking mulatto boy. The boy held on to a chain that was connected to four shackled Negroes: three men, and a woman who was young with large eyes and a mane of thick, kinky hair. Micco knew he did not want to purchase this woman. She stirred a man's desire in him, and she would be a temptation. Yet a slave could not say yes to him in the dark, and rape was not in Micco's nature. He almost sent the trader away until Mahala came to the opening of their hut and berated him, saying that she needed a slave. Hadn't he promised her one long ago, along with a cabin like her father's? Micco ended up buying the oldest slave in the bunch for a pittance, only fifty dollars. Though the man walked upright and, when his mouth was forced open, every one of his shining, white teeth was in place, the trader told him he had to be honest. This slave had been taken from Africa thirty years before, and thus, was well past his prime, but the trader assured Micco that he was getting a good bargain. The trader had put the slave through his paces on the coffle journey, and he was a hard worker who could labor for many hours at a time. The slave's name was Pop George, and he was patient with Mahala as she sent him on many errands and spoke to him in a sharp, superior voice.

It was a simple life for Micco's family. Time passed without incident, with the wife cultivating vegetables and fruit, and the husband hunting in the woods with his sons. When they left the territory of what had once been the village—which Micco now called a "farm"—there would be rare occurrences in which they encountered white men, but these white men were never hostile. Perhaps they didn't even know they were seeing Indians, for Micco and his family no longer dressed in the old ways, and when he and his sons gave greetings, the white men waved back. Then there was a sad time for Micco, when his sons came of age and decided to leave the farm and find their Creek relatives, but he understood. The three of them needed wives, and they wanted to find their mates among the women of their people.

Without his sons, Micco began to fish more. Gradually, the fish had come back to the creek now that the villagers had gone, and Micco liked to let his thoughts overtake him as he placed his hands into the water to grab the fishes' mouths. Fishing was patient work, and he had memories of Bushy Hair, how his uncle had been so kind to him. There were moments when Micco shed tears of nostalgia over his uncle, but these were happy memories. Yet when his thoughts turned to Dylan Cornell, he pushed that ugliness aside. It was too painful: the moment when Micco had grabbed the chin of his father and pressed a knife against the throat until blood gurgled.

Whenever patricide particularly tormented him, a small man would appear to him at the creek. He said his name was Joe, and he was the height of a child. He had the dark-dark skin and the tightly kinked hair of a full-blood Negro, and he informed Micco that he had known his grandfather, Coromantee-Panther, many years before. That it had been Joe who had guided his grandfather past the mound into the village proper. Though the small man seemed young, Micco did not challenge his word, for Nila had told him the story of Coromantee-Panther's appearance. Her own mother had told her the same and that "one of the little" was not to be challenged. Yet Joe was friendly and gave Micco ease. At the creek, he would settle upon the bank.

The Arrival of the White Man with Strange Eyes

Owning so much land made Micco largely content, and Mahala was happy, too, once he finally built her a cabin that looked like her father's, instead of a Creek-style hut. Micco had been lonely. He was glad that Joe had decided to make his acquaintance. A few months later, Micco made another friend as well when a young white man appeared on the farm. He didn't appear to be looking for any trouble. He only rode up to the cabin, got off his horse, and tied the reins to the post.

The stranger was young enough to be Micco's son, and he looked somewhat like Micco's father: he was blond, and his hair shone in the sun. His eyes were strange-colored, changing every moment. Now blue, now green, with hints of orange and gray, too. His sympathetic manner seemed a benediction to Micco.

In the times to come, some would say Lady answered the door, that this white stranger had a conversation with her and fell in love. And that he immediately asked Micco for her hand in marriage. This story about Lady is untrue, however, for she was a toddler when the white man arrived. Yet she'd answered the door, of a manner, since Mahala had been carrying her in her arms.

The Negro named Pop George would say that the moment he stopped praying for making do and started praying for mercy occurred not when the white man entered the cabin for the first time, but when the white man took his first bite of peach. It was summer and he was offered dinner, a savory stew of cured venison, garlic, onions, and turnip roots. For dessert, there were large peaches, grown on the farm. Despite its juiciness, the stone was firmly tucked inside, so the white man used his tongue to slowly coax it from the flesh. He made an injudicious sound.

These are the incongruities of memory. It is hard to hold on to the entirety of something, but pieces may be held up to light.

Micco's young visitor was named Samuel Pinchard, and the two men became fast friends. Micco offered the old-style Creek hospitality to the young man and let him sleep inside the cabin on one of his sons' vacant beds. In the dark early mornings, Mahala made corn porridge for both men and poured rich milk into Samuel's coffee cup, adding spoonfuls of sugar. When Samuel complimented the sweetness of the milk, she was pleased. She was the only one of her family who drank milk from cows. Her husband and daughter—and her sons before they left—could not tolerate it. After breakfast, Micco and Samuel went to work, milking the cows and turning them out to feed. They slopped the pigs that Mahala had insisted Micco purchase. Then they turned to chopping at trees. Micco had told his friend he should stay awhile; he would help Samuel build his own cabin on the farm, along with the assistance of Pop George. The second cabin was built, and once Samuel moved in, he helped Micco and Pop George cultivate more acres. Micco was open to advice and agreed that it was a good idea to plant cotton. During this time, the terrible dreams that he had been having about the murder of his father ended: he took that as a good sign.

The Suggestion of a Comrade

When happiness is upon us time does not slow down. As Micco's grandfather Coromantee-Panther had done in days past, Samuel Pinchard would make noises about moving on from Micco's farm. This frightened Micco, as he was afraid of loneliness. Whenever Samuel threatened to leave, Micco would cringe at the prospect of the dreams of his murdered father returning. He would beg Samuel to stay, and the young white man would sigh and say all right, just a bit longer.

One spring evening in Samuel's fifth year of living on the farm, Micco confided some fears to Samuel over dinner. On paper, Micco had always passed for white, using the last name of his father, Cornell. Yet as more Americans pushed west, and as the land between the Ogeechee and Oconee rivers—and now, even close to the Okmulgee—was ceded by Creeks who had betrayed the people, Micco was afraid. He had a wife and children and owned slaves like a white man, but Americans didn't even use the guise of friendship anymore. They had taken to killing Creek people on sight. If his secret was revealed, he was a dead man and his family would be homeless and destitute.

So Samuel kindly offered a suggestion to Micco: the land should be registered in a white man's name, and Samuel was willing to be that man. Micco was unsure, but his wife made encouraging movements with her fingers, motioning that Micco should listen to his friend. Then she prepared a second helping of supper for the two men. As Samuel ate Mahala's food and made hearty sounds, Micco offered a suggestion to his friend. He would sign a piece of paper giving the farm to his friend, if Samuel would agree to marry his daughter in two years. She would be only ten years old, but that was the age of consent for white people to marry in Georgia. However, Micco stipulated that Samuel would have to wait to consummate the marriage until Lady reached the blood of womanhood or the age of sixteen, whichever came first. Samuel readily agreed.

After dinner, Micco went down to the creek. He didn't usually fish in the dark, but he knew the water well. When he placed his hands in the water, he could sense that which he could not see. Joe was there, sitting on the bank, and as Micco fished he talked to Joe of his plans to give his only daughter in marriage to Samuel. The man was white, but then again any male who married into a woman's clan was bound as kin, so it would ensure that his land stayed with their family. It seemed like a good plan to him.

Joe said no words, but he grunted, which Micco took as agreement. He caught no fish that day.

The next morning, Samuel climbed upon his horse. He told Micco he was riding to the town called Milledgeville to fill out the paperwork for the farm. He smiled as he told Micco he'd even decided on a name for the establishment. It would now be called "Wood Place."

Samuel stayed gone for two weeks, and Micco was very afraid. On the day that his friend rode up to the cabin, Micco was filled with happiness. Yet Samuel seemed a changed man. He was no longer obsequious, and his voice seemed deeper. In three more days, the slave trader appeared with his mulatto helper, who was now a young man who tugged a chained coffle of five slaves. Money was exchanged between Samuel and the trader, and Samuel informed

Micco that these were the new slaves who would build another cabin where Micco, Mahala, and their little girl would live. This structure would be located on the extreme south side of the farm, and Samuel would continue his outrages: he'd take over the cabin on the north side, the place Micco and his family had built and called their home.

A Series of Changes

As another five years passed, Samuel took over more of the running of the farm, especially after a minister married Samuel and ten-year-old Lady. She continued to live with her parents, but Samuel took walks with her, chaperoned by Mahala. Upon his return from these walks, he was even more authoritarian. When Micco tried to offer advice to Samuel about the farm he still considered his own, his new son-in-law took it as an opportunity to remind Micco of the papers that were registered in Samuel's name with the white men in the town of Milledgeville. And Samuel continued to purchase more slaves.

Micco was upset, but he'd never been a warrior. He was a farmer, and in the years since Samuel had arrived at Micco's farm more white men had settled in the area. There was even a white man named Aidan Franklin who had moved his family on top of the mound that rose on the edge of what used to be the village of the people.

Yet even with his small, daily aggressions, Micco wanted to believe that Samuel and he remained friends. Samuel often smiled with sincerity in their encounters, which confused Micco. Surely such a nice man could not be an enemy. He must be perceiving things incorrectly. And Micco would receive the white man with hospitality in his little cabin, which was now surrounded by slave houses, until the next day, when Samuel would commit another tiny outrage, and then another. Mahala, however, refused to blame him for their reduced circumstances and still treated him kindly. It was her husband toward whom she directed her wrath, during the nights, when their daughter was asleep.

One Sunday, Samuel came to visit. Mahala rushed to serve Samuel some of her precious tea in one of the china cups painted with pink flowers. She had harangued Micco for these cups and their saucers, the matching plates and bowls, and the silver place settings that he had to save for each year, one setting at a time. After drinking tea and smiling charmingly at Mahala, Samuel asked Micco outside to talk. He had a matter to discuss. In the dirt yard in front of the cabin, Samuel causally broached the matter of Micco's African blood.

He knew Micco's heritage: In the first year after Samuel had come to the farm, the Creek man had confided about his grandfather Coromantee-Panther. It was information Micco never had intended to share, but he'd been so happy for a friend, he'd become giddy with affection and camaraderie. Yet he'd been wise enough to ask Samuel never to tell anyone else. Micco wasn't entirely foolish; he knew he was giving out dangerous information. Even Mahala didn't know; Micco had never told her, because he knew that she worshipped white people and despised Negroes. With each child that Mahala had given birth to, Micco had prayed to his wife's Christian god that none would betray his African line, but the prayer had been answered slant. His twin sons were white-skinned but had wide noses and full lips. His third son had been born with blue eyes, but his skin had turned brown in his fourth year, so that Mahala continually had bathed him in buttermilk and screamed at him to stay out of the sun, though this boy had only laughed at her as he ran outside to play or hunt. With Micco's daughter, that god kept laughing, for though Lady's skin remained very pale, her eyes hazel, and most of her brown hair straight, there were tight kinks that grew at her nape. Mahala sometimes wondered if someone had cursed her with the old medicine she'd ridiculed in the past. Why else would her children have these strange features?

As Samuel observed the copse of trees on the horizon, he remarked that it would be such a shame if Micco's heritage were revealed. He could become a slave. Even Micco's sons, who had gone to live in Creek villages, could be tracked down and put in chains. But Lady would be the worst, because men in the Louisiana territory would love to use her for their base desires: a Negro girl who looked completely white would be in great demand. However, Samuel always would keep Lady's secret now that the little girl was his wife. There was no reason to be afraid. He'd only wanted to remind Micco of the trust that lay between them. And remembering the past nectar of friendship, Micco held out hope.

The day that Micco finally understood he'd been deceived by Samuel Pinchard began with a minuscule event. Micco had gone fishing and told his Negro, Pop George, to have four buckets of water waiting when he returned to keep his fish fresh. But upon his return the buckets were still empty. Micco sent for Pop George, who told him Samuel had ordered him to accomplish other tasks. Only then, Samuel had said, could he turn to filling Micco's buckets, and the white man had slapped Pop George several times to induce obedience. Every time the Negro had finished one task, Samuel had given him another thing to do. Pop George had not had time to fill the buckets. While telling this story, he referred to Samuel as "Master." When Micco asked why, the Negro told him he had been ordered to do so by the white man.

The grandson of Coromantee-Panther became angry, an emotion he'd never truly felt before. His heart shaded with red, and he raised his hand to strike Pop George, who did not crouch or beg, but simply stood there. The Negro's face was not impassive, however. Though he was a slave, he looked at Micco with pity. That was when Micco recalled the words of Nila many years before, when she'd told him that white men were not to be trusted. And Pop George—the man Micco had purchased for fifty dollars years before—felt sorry for him, for Micco actually had believed a white man could be an Indian's friend.

That evening, Micco went to the creek, seeking out his only remaining comrade. Micco needed counsel, but the small man Joe could not be found. And he was not there the next day or in the days to come. Though Joe would return to the farm that had once been a village, he would never show himself to Micco again.

And Micco still hadn't solved the riddle: which sets of hands he should lean toward.

II

Self-realization is thus coming slowly but surely to another of the world's great races, and they are to-day girding themselves to fight in the van of progress, not simply for their own rights as men, but for the ideals of the greater world in which they live; the emancipation of women, universal peace, democratic government, the socialization of wealth, and human brotherhood.

—W. E. B. Du Bois, "Evolution of the Negro"

WHAT IS BEST

❖

It was the Friday before winter break at Toomer High. Mama knocked on my door, telling me we were going to take a girls' day. I didn't have to go to school, and she'd arranged for a substitute to cover her class. We were going to have some fun.

"For real? Can we have pizza?"

"We'll see. But let's go out."

"Where're we going, Mama?"

"It's a surprise, baby. Wear something nice, though. Not jeans."

I wore a plaid kilt and a pink sweater but slipped on my penny loafers. Mama was in heels and a blue wool dress with a matching self-belt. The pearl earrings my father had bought her for their anniversary hung from her lobes. We buckled in and she drove to the toniest part of town, where the streets were cobblestone, and pulled up to a new, L-shaped building. There were four floors and wooden shingles on top.

"Mama, why are we at Coco's old school?"

"Don't get upset." This was what she usually said right before she was about to upset me. "We're going to talk to the admissions counselor here."

"No, Mama! Uh-uh!"

"Just keep an open mind, baby. If you don't want to transfer, you don't have to. But please be polite, okay? Don't embarrass me in front of that white man."

Inside, the school counselor told us to call him by his first name, because at Braithwaite Friends School everyone was on a first-name basis from the students on up to headmaster. Which meant I couldn't call the counselor anything, because I'd been taught that children shouldn't address adults by first names. I couldn't tell him that, though, because that would be correcting an adult, which I was also forbidden to do. This was a no-win situation.

The counselor informed us that I had placed in the ninety-ninth percentile with my reading and writing scores on the state's secondary school standardized tests. He didn't say how he'd received my test scores, only that my language skills were quite surprising since I'd lagged over a year behind in science and math. He didn't want to give me those percentiles, however. That would only discourage me.

"I know that Ailey can catch up," Mama said. "She's a very hard worker."

This charade had gone way too far. I turned to my mother and she looked back at me. Her eyes narrowed, and her lips pursed for a quick moment, before her face was brushed free of emotion again. That's when I knew: my mother had sat me in the fool's chair.

The counselor picked up a small stack of folders and straightened them by knocking them on top of the desk. "All right, but we can't take her for this spring semester. That's too soon, I hope you understand."

"I understand," Mama said.

"But I'll have a place for her next fall," he said. "And I have high hopes for your sophomore year, Ailey. Your sister Carol was a superlative student here and fully integrated into school culture."

The counselor had been smiling in an encouraging way, but when he said "integrated" he paused and blushed. He looked down at his files, as if he'd said something naughty. At the end of the interview, he began filling out the paperwork needed for my enrollment at Braithwaite Friends School.

————

My mother wasn't much into art. She tended to use books as decoration instead: one wall of our living room was taken up by custom shelves. The former owners had installed them, and when the real estate agent had walked my mother through the house and she saw those shelves, she'd instantly put down a bid. And then there was a child's quilt that had been passed down in my mother's family that hung on my parents' bedroom wall. Its edges were tattered, and its scattered stars had faded to an anonymous gray, so my mother had framed it and sealed it in glass.

Aunt Diane had given Mama her only official piece of art, a reproduction of a Norman Rockwell painting. A poster, really—though Mama had that framed as well—that depicted a little Black girl named Ruby Bridges on her first day in a segregated school, back in 1960. In the painting, she wore church clothes: A dress with petticoats underneath. Ankle socks and Mary Janes. The faces of the federal marshals escorting her were hidden, but anyone looking at the painting understood why they were bookending her. There was implicit, hushed violence in the brightly colored scene: tomatoes had been thrown at the child, their brutal juice clinging to the bricks. Ruby was in kindergarten, so she couldn't read the word "nigger" scrawled on the brick wall behind her.

Sometimes, when a bad event was reported on the news, something that a white man had done to a Black person, or when President Reagan used one of his inside terms meant to low-rate Black folks, like "welfare queen" and such, my mother would get to talking about Ruby Bridges. How, even at six years old, she'd been so brave. To hear my mother, the way she wrapped her words in intimacy, you'd think she and Ruby had been best friends.

That afternoon, as my mother and I drove away from Braithwaite Friends School, I fumed in the car, afraid to snap, to tell her what I really thought of her betrayal. Not only that, but the deception involved. My mother didn't drive straight home. She wheeled around the City to out-of-the-way places and began to talk of Ruby Bridges, the patron saint of integration.

"I know Braithwaite doesn't have a lot of Black kids. But look how brave Ruby must have been. This'll be a walk in the park compared to what she went through. It's 1987. And you don't transfer until next fall."

I said nothing.

"And these white kids at Braithwaite? They all come from good families. Wealthy families. They're nothing like those crackers that used to stand outside Ruby's school. Coco went to Braithwaite, and see how great that worked out? She's at Yale!"

I took in a deep breath, as my aunt did when she was trying not to yell at my cousin Veronica, whom we called "demon child" behind my aunt's back.

"I don't want to go to school with all those honkies. I don't care how rich their families are."

"That's not nice, Ailey. Your aunt's a white lady. What would she think if she heard you talk like that?"

"I think Aunt Diane would agree with me. She married Uncle Lawrence, didn't she? And have you ever seen any of her white friends? Like that lady she loves so much at her counseling job. The one she talks about all the time. Have you ever met a white lady named LaTavia?"

"That's beside the point, Ailey. The point is, you're being prejudiced—"

"Oh, my God! I know you did not just say that! Besides Aunt Diane, you can't stand white people—"

"That's not true! What about Miss Cordelia from down home? She's white, and there's Father Dan at church here—"

"I can't believe you're trying to play this off!"

"Ailey Pearl Garfield, are you calling me a liar?"

Oh, damn.

I took another deep breath.

"No, Mama. I'd never. But aren't you always telling me that besides Aunt Diane, white folks aren't to be trusted? That all white men do is go after us? And now you want to send me to school with them? Like, what about what happened to Uncle Roscoe—"

"Don't you dare bring that up!"

For twenty minutes, she said nothing, but when we pulled up to our street, her mouth was trembling. She told me she didn't know how I could take her dead brother's name in vain, just because I wanted to win an argument. That was so mean, especially when she only wanted the best for me, the way any mother would.

Inside, I stomped up to my room, though when the smell of

chicken hit the hallway, I came down to dinner. The meal was a quiet, tense affair, even with my extra chicken breast and sweet potato pie for dessert. After I finished eating, I left the table without excusing myself and made a production of walking out of the room, my hand to my forehead, like the white girls on television. Then my father knocked on my bedroom door. Come on down. I could bring my book if I wanted, but in his office, he'd set up the board.

I lay on the beat-up leather couch.

"I don't feel like chess, Daddy. I'm in a very unfortunate mood."

"I see. Well, we can just sit here. I don't mind. I enjoy your company." He put his pipe in his mouth. He liked to suck it after dinner. It had been years since he'd filled it with cherry tobacco, but he liked the taste of the stem. My mother called it his sugar tit.

I kicked the back of the couch. "How can you be so calm when my life is being ruined?! I don't want to transfer schools!"

He took the pipe out, setting it on his desk. "Darling, come on now. It's okay."

"But I want to stay at Toomer! I can't be at that other school with all those honkies!"

"All right, now. Don't be upset. Let's look at this logically." He closed both his hands into fists, and I sat up on the couch. "Let's weigh the pros and cons. Let's say you go to Braithwaite Friends. You can call up Coco. Get her notes and rap about the social situation."

Daddy offered his thumb to mark the "pro," and because I wanted him on my side, I withheld vital information, such as nobody said "rap" anymore for "talking." It was 1987, not 1967.

"Next, ninety-nine percent of Braithwaite's students attend college. And eighty-seven percent of those students go on to the Ivy League—"

"And one hundred percent of everybody there are pasty-faced honkies. And anyway, Daddy, I don't know if I want to go to the Ivy League."

He extended a thumb on the other hand.

"I hear you. The presence of honkies is a big con. But another pro is that you have a fresh start at Braithwaite Friends without worrying about getting beat up. So we've got one con and four pros. Let's turn to Toomer High."

He put his hands back into fists.

"There are no honkies," I said. "That should be, like, two fingers."

"I'll give you those, then. And you feel very comfortable among other Black students. Let's give that credit for two more pros."

Four fingers. My chest felt light. It was going to be okay.

He held out the other fist.

"Now let's list the cons for Toomer. Your cousin Malcolm is graduating in June and probably headed to Howard, so he can't look out for you. Con. Last fall, the City public schoolteachers went on strike and have threatened to go on strike again. Con. There's a crack house three blocks down the street. Con. You got jumped by some unstable lunatic who tried to rip all your hair out of your head. Con. She scratched your beautiful face, too. Con. You got sent to the principal's office. Con. If I hadn't pulled out the business card of our family attorney and threatened to sue the school system, you'd have a suspension on your permanent academic record. Con.

"Thus, which school do you think I want my precious child to attend, Braithwaite Friends or Toomer High?"

I looked at his hands and the weight returned to my chest. He'd run out of fingers on the "con" hand.

"This is a complete setup."

"Ailey, please don't be mad at your daddy."

"Too late. And don't you expect me to play chess anymore. You're a horrible opponent anyway. Worse than me, and I didn't think that was possible."

"You wound me deeply with those statements. And here I thought I was coming up on Bobby Fischer." He put the empty pipe in his mouth and then took it back out. "Girl, you are just like your mama!"

"I'm ignoring you, Daddy. I might never speak to you again."

I lay back down, flipping through the book that Nana had given me. It wasn't a proper romance novel. Nobody ever got busy on a yacht in Greece, but it was good. This was the second time I'd read it, but it had aged well.

"This novel is by a Negro friend of my mother," Nana had told me. "Miss Jessie Fauset would take tea at our house, whenever she visited the City. She was the assistant to the great W. E. B. Du Bois. Don't you find that interesting?"

In my head, I gave the characters British accents, like on *Masterpiece Theatre*. They weren't like the characters in the book Uncle Root had mailed to me. Back in the late 1930s, he had run into the book's author at a party in the City, and Miss Zora Neale Hurston had been quite stylish, with a feather in her fedora, and fur trimming her blue duster. Uncle Root and she got to drinking the bug juice she'd brought along, and after a few sips of that, they talked about the best way to fry a catfish—head on or head off—but he had to cut the night short. Aunt Olivia had been shooting Miss Hurston and him dirty looks.

As I read, I forgot I was supposed to be angry, and when my father took his break from making his notes on his patient files, I told him the story. My father told me that Uncle Root had been wise to back away from that situation. No man could sleep soundly lying next to a jealous woman. It just wasn't possible.

At Sunday dinner, Nana was smug. Private school was what she'd wanted for me all along. Ever since my big sister had attended Toomer High, she'd warned my parents it was not an appropriate place for children from the best families. It had been a lovely institution back when it was the City Preparatory School for Negroes, but those days were long over. She talked past me at the dinner table as if there were an empty seat beside her and told my parents thank goodness they had come to their senses. She pointed a slightly gnarled, coral-painted finger in my direction.

"Belle, you really should be training a more careful eye on her. Her oldest sister already has set a bad example. Lydia couldn't even get into a good college with those mediocre grades of hers. And then she brought home some ruffian that she married?"

I looked down at the table; no one was supposed to tell my grand-mother that my big sister had disappeared.

Mama gathered the empty plates, scraping them into a bowl, a girlhood habit she retained from helping her father slop the hogs. She headed to the kitchen as my father announced he hated to break up a great evening, but he had patient files to read; he would call Nana a taxi.

When Nana lifted her face for a farewell kiss, Daddy ignored her. He walked toward the kitchen and met my mother, who was com-ing back out with pie. When he kissed her cheek, she closed her eyes and smiled, but later that night she let him have it.

"Miss Claire raised boys," she said. "What the hell does she know about my parenting skills?"

I couldn't see from my hiding space in the hall, but I expected my mother was rolling her hair, that my father was sitting at the bedside taking off his wing tips. No slip-ons for him, because one never knew when a crack fiend would hit him over the head at that clinic where he volunteered. They could try to steal his shoes, but the double knot would trick them.

"Baby, ignore her. You see she doesn't upset me. You know why? Because I don't even pay attention. You have to learn to flip the 'I can't hear Claire' switch on."

He cursed—he was fighting with a knot.

"That's easy for you to say," Mama said. "She doesn't blame you for anything that goes wrong. No, this whole Lydia mess is my fault. It's bad enough your mother has been turning my baby girl against me since she was a toddler. Thank the Lord I still have Coco."

"Belle."

"Oh, so now I'm crazy." Her voice turned loud and drawled. "So when Miss Claire tells Ailey to wear a hat outside, she don't mean, *Don't get as dark as your own damned mama.* Tell me I'm lying. Go 'head and say it."

"Woman, did I call you a crazy liar? Don't you put that on me." He would be holding his hand palm down, his placating gesture.

"We both know Claire Prejean Garfield is mean as a stomped-on rattlesnake. That's why I married me a sweet girl."

"Don't you try to jolly me along, Geoff! I'm so tired of your damned mother! I did the best I could to raise Lydia, and she was a good girl until she met that nigger. I tried to tell you about that boy, but no, you couldn't take my side."

"I only said Dante seemed nice enough. I mean, he had bad table manners, but was that really the end of the world?"

"I told you, I had a dream about him! And my dreams are never wrong. Remember when I used to have those dreams about you, back in the day?"

"Woman, please don't throw that up in my face. That was nearly twenty years ago."

"I'm just reminding you, don't make fun of my dreams."

"I'm not. You're not the only one who's worried. Lydia's my daughter, too."

"But you didn't carry her in your body. I did."

———

It was past midnight, well past the hour when phone calls were allowed in a southern Black woman's house, but there was repeated ringing. Silence and the phone rang again. It was March, but the nights were still cold and I hopped across the freezing wood floor to answer the phone.

"Garfield residence."

"Baby sister? Is that you?"

"Lydia?! Where are you—"

The phone was snatched from my hand. Before my mother spoke into the receiver, she pointed to my room. *Go back to bed.* I left my door open, and she closed it firmly. But I put my ear to the door and heard her murmuring on the hall phone. I couldn't make out the words, but I could tell when she'd hung up. Minutes later, I tiptoed back down the hallway until I reached my parents' open doorway. My mother's suitcase was open on the bed.

"I thought I told you to go back to bed," she said.

"What did Lydia say?" I asked.

"I'll tell you later."

"I can't sleep."

"Do you want me to tuck you in?"

"No, I'm too big." But I let her follow me into my room. She spread the comforter back over me up to my chin. Was that better? I nodded, and she told me, no matter how big I got, I'd always be her baby girl.

In the morning, Mama was absent from the kitchen, as was my breakfast. I walked to the refrigerator and opened it, pulling out a package of cheddar cheese and an apple. I told myself this was good. I didn't have to go to school, and I could eat whatever I wanted, but then my aunt walked into the kitchen, leading Veronica by the hand. She'd already dropped off Malcolm and had come back to get me. This was Aunt Diane's late morning working at the counseling center.

Her voice was perky as she exclaimed she'd brought me a blueberry muffin and a sandwich. I followed her out to the car and watched her wrangle Veronica into the car seat and tell her yes, she still had to sit there. "Please be nice for Mommy. Don't be naughty." Before she turned on the ignition, Aunt Diane told me my mother had flown to Georgia.

"But don't worry, we'll be staying with you. Won't that be nice? Just like a big slumber party!"

"When is Mama coming back?"

"I don't know, darling." She smiled and handed me the paper lunch sack. "Have a great day! I'll see you this afternoon."

My aunt stayed in Coco's room with Veronica, while Malcolm slept on the living room couch. My father spent more time at the hospital, only coming home to sleep or change clothes. He'd leave with paper sacks filled with Aunt Diane's blueberry muffins or banana bread.

Every evening, my uncle came by for dinner, which meant some kind of soup and a big green salad, because my aunt didn't believe in stuffing the body at night. Uncle Lawrence would sit with Aunt

Diane on the couch, though when he tried to get her to go down to the basement with him—because he had something very important he wanted to talk about with her—she pushed his shoulder impatiently. She asked him couldn't he control himself for a few days? Did everything have to be about him and his needs?

I didn't sleep well while Mama was away, waking in the dark. The long-haired lady from my dreams was back. She took my hand and led me to a small clearing surrounded by trees, where she pointed to a grassy spot. I sat beside her. Unlike years past, I couldn't see her face, though, and she no longer urged me to make water. We only sat together on the grass.

Every night at nine, Mama called to tell me she and Lydia were fine, though she couldn't put my sister on the phone. After a minute or two, she would tell me she didn't want to run up the bill, so she wouldn't hold me, but she loved me and please be good for my aunt. Don't cause any trouble. When Mama hung up the phone, I'd call Coco's dorm room at Yale, uncaring of long-distance charges.

"So what the fuck is going on?" Coco asked. "She still hasn't told you? Daddy neither?"

"Uh-uh," I said. "I barely see him, and every time she calls, she just says she's all right, Lydia's all right. That's it."

"This is some certified bullshit. Did you ask Auntie what's going on?"

"Like she'd ever tell me, if Mama won't. All she does is give me pancakes or muffins."

"At least you get a good breakfast. I know you hungry from all that soup and salad."

"Well, Auntie is a white lady, so she can't make collard greens."

"You better not let Auntie hear she's white. She thinks she's an honorary sister."

We laughed, and then Coco turned serious again. "Shit. I knew that dude was some fucking trouble when I saw him."

"How'd you know?"

"I had a dream about him."

"You sound like Mama."

"It is what it is. Okay, let me go. I gotta test tomorrow."

It was an early Sunday afternoon in May when my mother returned. Outside, the chill in the morning air finally was gone and the rosebushes in our tiny front yard were no longer sullen and bare but budding into promise. My aunt and I sat on the couch in the living room, watching *Meet the Press*. Malcolm sat in the armchair, holding his sleeping sister on his lap. She was napping too late, which meant she'd be up all night looking to play and acting ugly when her mother insisted it was bedtime.

The key jiggled in the front door, and my mother stepped inside. Seconds later, Lydia followed. Mama's greeting was casual, as if she hadn't been gone for two months, but everyone else in the room cried their surprise. The noise woke Veronica, who began to clap her hands and laugh. I rushed to the foyer, hugging my big sister. When I put my arms around her, she was so skinny her bones dug into me.

I craned my neck, looking into the foyer.

"Where's Dante? Did he not come with y'all?"

Neither of them answered, and when I asked my question again, Mama told me act civilized and let folks get in the door. Don't be bum-rushing. They'd just come off the road and she had to call our people. They needed to know my sister and she had arrived safely, and then she had to call my father.

She squeezed my aunt around the waist.

"Diane, you can call your man first, though."

A half hour later, my uncle arrived. His clothes were rumpled, his curly, salt-and-pepper hair grown over his eyes. He shook his keys dramatically. Come on, he said to my aunt. She could leave her car and pick it up tomorrow. Just come on, and no, he didn't want to stay and eat. This had gone on long enough. But my aunt overruled him. It was Sunday, and my mother was cooking an early dinner. Wouldn't it be lovely to sit down as a family, all of us together? My uncle called his wife's name, but she kept sitting on the couch.

"You can leave if you want," Aunt Diane said. "But I'm hungry, and so are my children." She gestured to my cousin, who was standing, holding his sister. She told Malcolm sit down. They weren't going anywhere, not yet.

An hour later, my father came home and called out from the foyer. One of his colleagues was covering for him at the emergency room, but he had to be back by midnight. When he saw my sister sitting on the steps, he opened his arms. Hug his neck, he ordered. She stood up slowly. Walked hesitantly into my father's arms. He hugged her close, then pushed her away.

"Don't you scare your daddy anymore. Don't you scare him like that again."

"I promise."

"All right, now. You know us middle-aged Black men got bad nerves."

Lydia giggled, and he pulled her back in. Kissed the top of her head, until my mother came from the kitchen. Then he trotted to my mother, his round stomach bouncing. He picked her up, and her feet dangled for seconds.

"I feel a poem coming on!" Daddy shouted.

"Oh Lord. Somebody come get this Negro." But Mama couldn't stop smiling. She laid her head against his chest and raised a hand to rub his belly.

There was plenty heavy food for dinner. My mother's meat loaf, macaroni and cheese, sweet potatoes, corn bread, and the mandatory collard greens. My sister hunched her thin shoulders, concentrating on her plate. She'd been so quiet since her arrival. I'd followed her up to our room, pushing my dirty laundry off the twin bed that used to be hers. Wait just a few minutes, I'd told her. I'd get some fresh sheets and change the bed, while she'd murmured that was all right. Don't make any trouble.

I didn't worry about her silence at dinner. I was just happy to see the faces of my mother and sister, and to eat real, seasoned food. At the table, I smacked my lips gratefully at the taste of garlic and onions and paprika, as Mama urged my sister to eat. She reached over with a knife and fork, cutting the meat loaf into pieces.

My sister ate a very small bite. "Mmm, this is good."

"I know it's your favorite, darling. There's banana pudding for later."

Lydia ate another small bite, then put her fork down. She apologized for her lack of appetite, but Mama told her it was just exhaustion from that long drive.

After another half hour, my uncle began making loud hints that it was time to take his family home. Mama told him stay awhile. There wasn't any hurry, and plenty of food and sweet tea. When he insisted it was time, she made him sit down for a couple more minutes. Let her pack up some plates before they left. She'd made an extra pan of corn bread. She knew how he loved some corn bread.

After the rest had left, my sister excused herself. I followed her, leaving our parents cuddled up on the couch. Their whispers broken only by soft laughter. The sound of their many kisses. Up in our room, I tried to talk to my sister, but she was still quiet as she hung up clothes from her suitcases and slipped into flowered pajamas. When I asked her where had she gone, and what about Dante? She slipped beneath the covers of her bed.

"I'm tired, Ailey. I don't feel like chatting."

She turned her face to the wall. Her breath deepened into sleep, but I lay in my own bed, unable to rest. The air conditioner came on roaring. When I slipped into the fog of a dream, the long-haired lady was there.

———

That June was strange. No farewell sleepover at Nana's the night before she and Miss Delores traveled to Nana's cottage on Martha's Vineyard for the summer. And no rising with my mother to pack the station wagon for our own trip to Chicasetta. No sticking my head out the window to watch as we drove away from our house with my mother scolding I better put that head back in the window before I had an accident. Mama informed me there would be no summer in Chicasetta. She'd been gone from her husband too long after spending so long down south with Lydia, and she didn't want to leave my father again, not so soon. Besides, I needed to get back to a routine anyway.

"What about Miss Rose? What about Uncle Root?" I asked. "They'll miss us!"

"You can call them every Saturday. And this is a perfect time to catch up on your reading."

Nothing made me grind my teeth more than spending an entire summer in the City. I missed the chance to walk outside, to see sky and earth and trees. Lydia must have felt even worse, because there was no vacation for her at all. She had to enroll in summer school at Mecca University to retake two of the classes that she'd failed the previous year. She was diligent, rising at dawn. She would wake me and pad down the stairs, while I followed, wrapped in a blanket. In the kitchen, I begged for a cup of coffee, and she poured in cream and the brown sugar from the box saved for baking. She laid out bacon on a cookie sheet and mixed up biscuits, pressing them into a smaller pan. Soon, Mama would join us, scrambling eggs, pouring in the same heavy cream, sprinkling dried things and cheese into the mixture, and stirring up a large pot of grits.

Another hour, and Daddy would sit down to the hearty meal, still sleepy from a night working the emergency room. My mother would eat her bland breakfast, grits with a banana, and they'd read their identical morning papers, because neither liked to share. Before heading out to his practice, he would pause at the door of the kitchen, sniffing deeply. Bacon smelled so good, like the memory of young love.

"Your father thinks he's a poet," Mama would say.

"I was in another life," he'd reply.

During the days, I surprised Mama by helping with housework before going off on my own to read. In the evenings, Lydia would sit on the living room couch and I'd settle between her knees on a floor pillow, and Lydia would scratch and oil my scalp.

"I'ma cut off all this hair, Ailey. I need me a curly wig."

"Give me that comb so I can burn those strands. Don't you put no roots on me."

"You sound like Miss Rose! She's always thinking somebody's trying to root her!"

"Don't she, though?"

We watched tapes of television shows that I'd recorded on the VCR. I had two years of *Dynasty* on tape, and I kept a running stream of commentary to catch Lydia up. Alexis Carrington was our girl. She knew how to fling insults and hands like she had some Black in her.

If we didn't watch television, we went to our room, lay on opposites sides of Lydia's bed, and took turns reading out loud to each other. Lydia had all of Alice Walker's books, but *The Color Purple* was the one she'd read eight times. It was like visiting Chicasetta every time she read it. When it was Lydia's turn, she had different voices for each character, and it was like when we'd gone to see the movie. I'd only been twelve, but that winter break Lydia had lied that she was taking me to see *Out of Africa*. Mama had quizzed us when we returned. What was the plot? It was about Africa, we said. Yeah, yeah, and a white lady and a white man. A love story, and it had a really nice ending. Happily ever after. We repeated the story at dinner, but when Mama went to the kitchen with the dishes, Coco had whispered she was onto us. She'd read *Out of Africa*, and unless the movie had seriously changed the story, it should have been depressing as hell. The protagonist had syphilis.

Nana returned from her vacation on Martha's Vineyard in late August, a week before I began classes at my new school. The public schools already had started, and so had Lydia's regular fall classes at Mecca. Nana called nearly every day, extending an invitation to me, but I didn't want to give up my time with my sister. I finally had Lydia back, and if Mama didn't exactly treat us as adults, she didn't intrude on our time together. At Sunday dinners, Nana made her displeasure known. She gave monosyllabic answers when Aunt Diane or Malcolm tried to engage her in conversation and pushed away little Veronica when she tried to sit on her lap. And she made snide remarks about Lydia needing summer school. As for me, Nana monitored the amount of food on my plate. It wasn't ladylike to take second portions, and my being tall couldn't hide the fact that I should drop twenty pounds.

She waited until Mama served dessert before announcing she wanted to go home. Yes, now. No, she didn't want to drink a cup of tea, and Daddy would sigh and push back his chair.

"All right, Mother. I'll take you home."

One evening in our room, I told Lydia I felt sorry for our grandmother. She didn't have any old-lady friends to hang with, except Miss Delores.

"That's because Nana's a bitch."

"Lydia!"

My sister put a hand to her mouth. She raised her eyebrows.

"Oops. Did I say that out loud?"

"You shouldn't talk that way. It's not nice."

"No, it's not. See how guilty I look?" Lydia crossed her eyes, and I tried not to giggle.

"Baby, you know Nana doesn't count Miss Delores. Claire Prejean Garfield would rather be stranded on a desert island than be friends with her dark-skinned maid. And that's why nobody likes her."

"Lydia, don't say that. She's not perfect—"

"That's an understatement—"

"—but Nana still needs love."

"Baby, your heart is too big. You have to learn to be a little colder."

———

Lydia didn't point out the change in my mother's schedule, that Mama not only picked up Lydia and me from our different schools, she dropped us off in the mornings, too. That Mama didn't dress up in her stylish, feminine clothes on early weekday mornings, tapping around in the kitchen in the heels that made her inches taller. There was no big leather purse filled with folders or student papers. It took me an entire week to notice that she was wearing tracksuits in shades of blue or pink and designer tennis shoes that kept her feet close to the ground instead. When I asked why was she dressed so casually—was she teaching physical education now?—she told me she had decided she was tired of teaching those little badass kids at Wells-Barnett. They had worked her nerves for years, and it's not like she needed the money. Between Daddy's practice and his moonlighting at the hospital, there was more than enough, and besides, she had a family to see about.

I didn't challenge my mother's change of heart. It made sense to me that she'd want to stay home in more comfortable clothes and read the books she wanted, ones that weren't written for third graders. Maybe she'd lost the excitement for the smell of chalk and the sound of high, needy voices. I could understand, because I'd lost my desire for school, too, ever since that day Cecily had sat beside me on the steps and told me she couldn't be my friend anymore. After that, I'd brought a sack lunch to school and eaten it while locked in a bathroom stall. That way, I wouldn't have to look at Cecily and her crew.

I didn't regain any enthusiasm when I enrolled at Braithwaite Friends. There were only twelve other Black students in the entire upper school—what they called the sophomore, junior, and senior grades. If I hadn't had Lydia back, I don't know what I would have done, because it was lonely at Braithwaite Friends. Really lonely. At Toomer, I'd been popular for all of two months, but at least everybody there was like me. The only white person at Toomer had been the art instructor. In her office she'd hung prints by Romare Bearden and Elizabeth Catlett. Braithwaite Friends was not just in another part of the City. It seemed to occupy a minuscule country all its own, one where there were no combinations on the lockers or padlocks because it was assumed that the students didn't steal. The cafeteria was called the "dining room," and the options were varied and delicious, not like the single, processed meal at Toomer that you either had to eat or go hungry. There were three kinds of soups. A salad bar with raw, bright vegetables and both creamy and vinaigrette dressings. Hot entrees were made to order, and if you were vegetarian someone in the kitchen came up with a creative concoction and put parsley on the side of the plate.

It was hard to figure out the financial or social pecking order at Braithwaite Friends. Nobody seemed to be an outcast, and nobody had bad teeth, either. There were straight teeth or braces in these kids' mouths. On their bodies, neat, clean clothes, but nothing too stylish or ostentatious. Someone who looked like a nerd might have lots of friends and you'd find out that his father had given him a Mercedes for his sixteenth birthday. Mama had told me to seek out the Black kids. Undoubtedly, they would be lonely, too, but the twelve others in my tribe looked at me blankly whenever I offered my special, colored-person smile, which communicated that we were in this integration thing together. In the dining room if I put my tray down next to someone Black, they would rise and relocate at another table, sitting down in a sea of whiteness. The Black girls were the worst: none of them knew how to fix their hair. Besides me, every single girl relaxed, but didn't grease at all. Their dry edges looked so broken and defeated.

After a month at Braithwaite Friends, only my teachers had made the place bearable. I'd never known teachers who asked for kids' opinions and discussed ideas with them instead of telling us what we should think.

Ms. Rogers was my literature teacher. She was about thirty, with a short brown bob. Like the other teachers, she was usually casual, dressing in khakis and button-down shirts. On the rare days that she wore a dress with her flat shoes, students would ask why was she so fancy? Did she have a date that night? And she would smile and tuck a strand of hair behind an ear. Though she kept insisting I call her by her first name, I refused, and when I compromised and called her "Miss Angela," she'd tease me and look behind her, as if I was talking to someone else. Her class was my favorite, though.

"What about these sonnets?" Ms. Rogers asked. "Let me know what's up!"

In the front row, Sunshine Coleman raised her hand.

"In the Dark Lady poems, I've noticed Shakespeare draws a correlation between light as good and dark as evil."

"So great! Really profound! Anyone else? Anyone?" Ms. Rogers gave me the encouraging teacher eyeball, and I scooted down in my chair. "So we've talked about theme and subject. But what about the way Shakespeare writes a poem? What about his rhythm and meter?"

Lizbet Welch raised her hand. Only twelve, she was the tenth-grade genius freak. She didn't even have boobs yet. "The iambic pentameter is obvious. But when one scans the poem"—she looked around defensively—"um, the stresses tend to occur with his most vivid imagery."

"Yes!" our teacher exclaimed. "That's exactly right! Astounding!"

In the row in front of me, Amber Tuttlefield raised her hand. She and I were in another class together, American History, along with Chris Tate. He was the Black guy who acted like her boyfriend. Whenever he looked Amber's way, his face was adoring as Amber raked her fingers through her blond hair. It fell to her tailbone, and sometimes she'd fling the hair back and it would land on my desk.

"I think this whole discussion is really mean and it makes me sad."

"'Mean' how?" Ms. Rogers asked. "Expound, please."

"Like, why does everything have to be about Black and white or whatever, when true love sees no color?"

"Amber, that is certainly some insightful food for thought. Thank you for sharing your profound feelings." Ms. Rogers held her hand to her chest in the approximate location of her heart.

At the end of class, I stayed in my desk watching Chris whispering in Amber's ear.

She laughed, pushing his arm. "You're such a fucker!"

Ms. Rogers looked up from her desk, frowning. A few beats passed, and then she returned to the papers on her desk. The teachers at my new school were serious pushovers. They let these rich white kids call them by their first names and when a student cursed they didn't even glance over their shoulder in case an adult overheard. At Toomer, if a teacher heard you cursing, it was an automatic suspension.

Amber rose. When she walked in front of Chris, he stepped in reverse a few paces. Between his fingers there was a piece of paper. He dropped it on my desk then ran after Amber.

There were no buses after school. Everybody waited for their rides home. Chris and a group of white boys kicked a cloth ball among them, bumping into the other kids waiting for their rides. A few of the kids looked annoyed, but most laughed. It was finally Friday. Being an asshole was for the beginning of the week. Chris almost fell backward, but Amber rushed over and grabbed hold of his upper arm. She shouted, "Up!" as she pushed. He located his balance, smiling into her eyes, and her cheeks turned dark pink. Watching them, a stitch formed in my side, but I arranged my face into a pleasant façade. Mama had told me to exhibit my best behavior at this school. Don't drop my guard and don't lose my temper, because if anything bad happened those white kids would stick together, so I pretended joy at witnessing Chris and Amber opening their eyes wide, apparently shocked at the miracle of Friday afternoon.

Mama inched the station wagon forward in the queue of cars, honking the horn. Lydia opened the car door.

"Hey, baby," she said. "Did you have a good day?"

On the grass, Chris and Amber were talking. A wind blew, and she flicked her blond hair out of her face. The other boys restarted the game without him.

———

I took a week, studying the paper Chris had slipped me. There was no name, but there was a phone number, and a handwritten message: *You're so _fine_ and I want to _get_ with you!*

I looked for ciphers in those nine words. Was this simply an overture of friendship? And why, when Chris had behaved like the rest of the unfriendly Black kids in this school to my face? Monday morning, I took my time finding an outfit and decided on the one that I'd worn the previous fall, when Mama and I had visited the counselor. My kilt and special sweater with my penny loafers. When I walked into Ms. Rogers's classroom, Chris's expression didn't register that I looked amazing, which was disappointing. But at the end of the lesson he gave me a quick wink and I decided that I would take a chance.

Still, I waited to call him, until an evening after dinner when everyone would be occupied. My father was at the hospital, moon-lighting. My mother and my aunt were sitting in the kitchen, talking. Aunt Diane had left Veronica at home with her husband to let him know that it was a new day. Men should be responsible for childcare, too. My sister was in the office studying, and I tiptoed upstairs like a sneak thief. I dragged the hall phone by its long cord into my bedroom and shut the door. From underneath my pillow, I pulled out note cards with conversation starters, and placed them on my comforter: *I enjoy listening to public radio* and *Zora Neale Hurston is my favorite author* and *Unless it's summer, my mother doesn't let me eat processed foods.*

The lady on the other line was quiet-voiced. "Tate residence."

"Hello, this is Miss Ailey Garfield. I'm calling for Mr. Christopher Tate. May I speak to him, please?"

"One moment."

A series of clicks, and then another quiet-voiced lady.

"This is Camille Tate."

"Hello, this is Miss Ailey Garfield. May I speak to Mr. Christopher Tate, please?"

"Oh, hello, Ailey! This is Mrs. Tate."

"Um . . . hello, Mrs. Tate, ma'am. How are you?"

"I'm well, Ailey. And yourself?"

"I'm fine, ma'am. Did you have a good day?"

"I had a very good day, dear, and thank you for asking! Chris said you had impeccable manners. I see he was right, and what a lovely surprise. So many young people these days are so rude."

I talked with Mrs. Tate, running through my polite arsenal, but it was exhausting. There were no openings to broach the starters I'd laid out on the bed. By the time Chris came to the phone, I didn't know if I had any more to give.

"Hey, girl. Why'd you take so long to call me? Damn."

"Well, you know."

"Well, you know," he repeated, in a high, girlish voice.

"You're so crazy."

We made plans to meet behind the lower school building—the

younger kids left thirty minutes earlier—at two thirty on Tuesday, one of the days Amber left early for her three-hour-long piano lessons, Chris said.

If he wanted to make a change, he shouldn't be talking about his current girlfriend, but I put that out of my mind. I had other problems, such as inventing a plausible lie to fool my mother.

The afternoon of our rendezvous it was chilly out. I wore two extra T-shirts under my sweater, but then I was overheated. I took off my down coat, laid it on the ground, and sat with my book bag beside me. I'd told my mother there was a study group for biology that met after classes. I felt no shame. Technically, I was telling the truth, since I'd used my half hour after school let out to study.

After a few minutes, Chris showed. "What'cha doing sitting on the ground?"

"Waiting on you. Take a load off."

"You talk so funny, Ailey."

His skin was smooth: so far, he'd escaped acne. His hair cut low and neatly brushed. He rested his head against the bricks of the building, regaling me with tales of that stupid cloth ball game. He'd wanted to attend a public school with a real soccer team, but his parents had vetoed that.

"But at least now I have a reason to like it here," Chris said.

"What's that?" I asked.

"You, silly."

Walking through the halls and holding hands, so that people witnessed our love. Stopping every now and then to kiss. That's how I pictured us.

"Girl, when I saw you in class, I was like, who is that? She's so fine. And you don't even care what the white kids say about you."

I wondered what they said about me, but I wanted to keep up my cool impression.

"Not really."

He swiveled his head, looking for eavesdroppers. "But you know, fuck these honkies, right?"

"Sure, I guess."

He gave me a quick peck on the lips. I touched his face, but he quickly grabbed my hand. We went back to talking about that stupid cloth ball game, but I caught something about his father.

". . . I never see him," Chris said. "He's always at the hospital."

"Is he a doctor?"

"Yeah, a surgeon."

"My daddy's a doctor, too. He's in general practice, but he works emergency. I only see him at dinnertime about three times a week."

"We don't even see mine then."

I gave his hand a sympathetic squeeze. He squeezed back.

———

"Hey, Mama? I'm going out tonight, okay?" Lydia scraped at a soggy vanilla wafer in her dish of banana pudding.

"Going where?"

"To the preseason game with one of my sorors. I can give you her number so you can talk to her."

There were the three of us that night. Two sisters and a mother at the table, lingering. We used our spoons to pick at the remains of our dessert. We were full, but sugar beckoned.

"No, I don't think so. Coco's not here to chaperone." Mama rose from the table and when she returned from the kitchen, she carried foil. She covered the pudding dish, pressing around the edges.

"So no, just like that?"

"You need to be studying."

"I can go out on a Saturday night if I want to. I'm almost twenty-two years old, Mama."

My mother turned to me. "Ailey, if you don't stop looking in grown folks' mouths when they're talking. Go do your homework."

"I did it yesterday. I'm finished."

"Ailey Pearl Garfield, did you hear what I said? I'm not playing with you!"

Upstairs, I lay on my big sister's bed, reading. On the transistor radio, the preseason game was on: Mecca was losing to Albany State: *"And it's GOOD!"*

I was dozing, when I felt Lydia lie down beside me. We moved into our old position, my head resting against her feet.

"Lydia, where's Dante?"

"You can't tell anybody I told you. It has to be our secret. Do you promise, Ailey?"

She nudged at me until I sat up. I promised her and she told me she'd gotten in trouble last year. She'd been hanging out with a bad crew and, well, she'd started using drugs.

"For real?" I looked down at her comforter, focusing on the seashells and waves. I didn't want her to see my face. The shock there and the disappointment. I didn't want her to be ashamed.

"That's why Mama came south to see about me. She put me in a rehab center so I could get better. So I could get off the drugs."

"But what about Dante? You still didn't tell me what happened with y'all."

"We broke up. We're not together anymore."

"But, like, maybe y'all can get back together. If you had a fight, you could say you're sorry and he could say he's sorry—"

"No, baby. That's over."

"Oh. Okay. Are you sad?"

"Yeah, baby, I am. I'm real, real sad. That's why I don't want to talk about Dante. It just makes me want to cry."

Lydia had told me a serious secret; it was only right that I offered one in return. For seconds, I considered telling her about Gandee, what he had done to me in the bathtub when I was little. How he'd threatened to kill my sisters and mother, and then me, if I ever told anybody. And even though Lydia was my best friend, she was like a second mother to me. I didn't want Lydia to think less of me, to decide that Gandee had made me something other than the good girl she thought I was.

Instead, I confessed to Lydia about Chris. That I'd been meeting him behind the upper school on the days I told Mama that I was studying late. He already had a girlfriend, and I knew I should feel guilty that he was two-timing, but I didn't. Because Amber was that white girl in my class that I'd told Lydia about, the one who flipped her hair on my desk.

"You don't have anything to feel sorry for," Lydia said. "I mean, no, it's not the best situation, but be honest. He probably was with that white girl because there weren't any Black girls. At least not any who don't have jacked-up perms. Remember how Coco used to complain about that school? There weren't but six Black kids there."

"It's thirteen of us now."

"Whoa-dee-whoa, look at all them Negroes! Thirteen is a race riot!"

I laughed and touched her hand. "You so silly, Lydia!"

"Baby, think about it. That Chris guy just wants a girlfriend who looks like him, and then here you come, all beautiful and brown and super cool. And you know how to fix your hair. How could he resist all this?"

Lydia waved her hands at me, like I had a superpower. She made me sound so interesting, like one of the characters in her favorite book. I laid my head back down on her feet and listened to the game. Mecca had scored a touchdown. Our side was starting to win.

PERMISSION TO BE EXCUSED

◆

Coco looked like she had cancer. That's what Mama said when my sister let herself in, dragging her suitcase behind her. It was a Friday in mid-October, the first weekend of fall break. Our mother ran and hugged her, then chastised Coco for taking a taxicab from the train station.

"All you had to do was call. You know I would have driven down to . . ." Mama stopped and gave a low cry. "Lord have mercy! What did you do? You look like a cancer patient!"

Coco touched her head, stroking the inch of red-brown waves. There was a part in the left side of her cut. "You don't like it? I love it! All I have to do is slap on some Murray's and sleep in a stocking cap. And did you know the barbershop only costs ten dollars? Ten dollars! That's all the brothers have to pay. Can you believe that?"

"But why would you cut it all off?" Mama's voice wavered. "I took such good care of my little girls' hair."

"Aw, Mama, you sure did. And I appreciate you. I appreciate you so much, but I can't afford to get my hair done every week. It's, like, forty dollars and three hours every time I go—"

"I would have sent you the money! You know that—"

"I know, but then I had to get those relaxer touch-ups every two months, and that's, like, thirty extra dollars? And who knows how dangerous all that sh—" She caught herself. ". . . that mess is in those relaxers? Those carcinogens going into my blood? No, ma'am. I had to give it up."

Mama kept saying there had to be a better compromise than a woman looking like she had one foot in the grave and another on a slick of bacon grease. Maybe Coco could have let her relaxer grow out and just press and curl or do a wet set? And how did she expect to get a boyfriend with a bald head when she already dressed like a field hand?

I sat on the bottom step of the staircase, watching them. Two small women, identical except for their skin and hair colors. Both delicate-boned with feet that my father marveled at, for how could any person walk on feet that tiny, especially two women as tough as them?

A tap on my shoulder, and Lydia settled beside me. "You gone say 'hey'?"

"I'm just waiting for your mother to wind down. That's gone take a while." We laughed, and the sound made our sister turn to us. Her greeting was brusque as usual, but there was gladness on her face. Her eyes crinkled when she asked what did we know good?

Mama walked behind her, hugging her around the waist.

"Look at this! All my girls together! God is so good, ain't he?"

Her daughters answered in a chorus: "All the time."

She called the hospital and left a message for Daddy, but he couldn't take off from the emergency room. It was Friday night and weekends were the worst time in the City. People getting shot or going crazy from drugs, but that next morning, we heard his voice calling from the living room. His heavy step as he walked into the kitchen. The top of his green scrubs stretched over his belly.

Mama called from the stove, where she was stirring a pot. "Grits?"

"You know it. Sausage and toast, too. No coffee, though. I'm going to try to lay this body down and sleep. I got the late shift again tonight."

He walked around the table to Coco and kissed the top of her head. "I like this cut, girl! Very elegant!"

"For real, Daddy? So I don't look like a cancer patient?"

"What fool said that?" he asked.

Coco snorted, and I looked at my mother spooning grits onto a plate. She added three patties of sausage and two pieces of toast, then carried the plate and a mason jar of preserves to the table. She placed the food in front of my father.

"Thank you, woman," he said.

"You're welcome." She went back to the stove and fixed her own plate. Grits and toast, but no sausage. When she sat down, Daddy asked, was anybody going to tell him what fool had told Coco that? What kind of person would be so heartless?

"Your child is signifying." Mama gestured with her fork. "I'm the fool who said it. Me, and I'll say it again. She doesn't look healthy with that haircut and I don't know why a Black woman with all that long, pretty hair would chop it off."

"Oh, I see." Daddy dug into his own plate, even when Coco scolded him for the sausage. Surely, that couldn't be healthy for a man of his age and weight. Not only that, he was a Black man, and thus at a higher risk for hypertension, heart disease, and stroke.

He licked a finger. "So what you're saying is, if I give up my sausage, more for you? I see your strategy, girl. This is how you Ivy League Negroes trick people."

He put his fork down and laid his hand against Coco's cheek, patting. She rolled her eyes but didn't move away when he said, look at this. All his ladies together at the kitchen table, eating grits and ridiculing him. It didn't get any better than this.

"I was just saying that!" Mama hit the table lightly.

My mother was capable of surprises every now and then, and she proved it that night at dinner. She asked Lydia, were there any parties that weekend? Maybe she'd been invited to something?

Lydia sat up straight. "For real? My soror Niecy is back for fall break."

"Is she a good girl?" Mama asked. "Not any trouble, right?"

"No, ma'am. She's real nice."

"Okay, you can go, but you gotta take your sister along, so she can chaperone."

"What?" Coco asked. "I don't want to go. I don't even know those people."

"Getting out will do you good," Mama said.

"I am out," Coco said. "I'm here. Why I gotta go someplace else?"

"Because you're almost twenty and you don't need to be stuck in the house. Just look out for your sister, please."

That evening, I followed Lydia around as she prepared for the party. I'd only seen her dolled up for church in Chicasetta, and even then the outfit she wore was modest. Miss Rose didn't go in for flesh on the Lord's day. The orange dress that Lydia chose for the party stopped well above her knees and clung to her narrow waist, wide hips, and plump backside. Mama liked to say Lydia might have gotten her skin color and hair from the white folks, but anybody with sense could look at that ass and know there was a Negro in the woodpile.

Lydia put a socked foot into a long, black boot and zipped it up her leg.

"I want to go. I could wear something real cute, too."

"You wouldn't have to dress up. You're gorgeous all by yourself." She zipped up the other boot and held out her arms. "Come here."

"No. I'm very mad at you."

"It's not my fault, baby. You know Mama isn't letting you go to a college party. Now stop being mean and come here."

She wiggled her fingers and I moved into her arms. She smelled nice but foreign. Not a soapy girl anymore, but a woman. She walked to the hall, and I followed. Coco was waiting for her at the foot of the stairs, wearing the same jeans and Yale sweatshirt she'd been wearing that morning. I suspected the gold hoop earrings and red lipstick were a concession to Mama.

I went back to the bedroom and pulled out *The Color Purple* from the bookshelf. It was my turn to read that evening, and I'd been practicing the character's voices. Celie's tone would be high and trembling, but after she found her strength and purpose, her voice would deepen. And Mister would be a nasty bass, like the low-down scoundrel he was. I sat on the couch, reading *The Color Purple* until they returned. Neither one seemed to notice me, though, and at breakfast time, Lydia didn't rise early as she usually did. When I came down for breakfast, Coco's bag was sitting at the bottom of the stairs. In the kitchen, Mama tried to get her to take a later bus, but Coco told her she needed some rest before classes in eight days. Her manner was brusque when Mama asked her, how was the party? Did they have a good time? In a few minutes, her taxi honked outside. A quick squeeze around Mama's waist and a kiss on the cheek, and Coco was gone.

———

"What did I do?" I asked.

"Nothing, baby. I just need my space."

Lydia was in our closet, her voice muffled. She hugged an armful of hanging clothes, lifted them, and freed the tops of the hangers from the closet pole. She huffed under their weight and walked down the hall into our sister's room.

I followed behind her.

"But you didn't need it before. And Coco needs her room for when she comes back."

"She's not coming back. She's going to medical school next year. She'll probably get an apartment."

"But what about the holidays?"

"I'll sleep in your room, like always. Don't you want your privacy?"

I didn't answer, and she walked back into the bedroom that we'd shared only the night before. The one that wasn't our room anymore. It was only mine. She pulled more clothes from the closet until her side was empty.

"Okay, I think that's it. I'm tuckered out. I think I'll sleep through dinner."

"It's Wednesday. *Dynasty*'s on tonight."

"I'm sorry, baby, I can't. I have to study. Tape it for me? We'll watch another time."

She nudged me out the door of Coco's room, and then closed the door in my face. I heard the click of the doorknob locking.

I sat on the couch alone that night, watching *Dynasty*. On my lap, a notebook. I took notes on the plot, so that I could be sure to catch up Lydia. I didn't have her memory, how Lydia could not only remember the plot, but facial expressions and body language, too. My mother came and sat with me, but she asked too many questions, like why did that brunette lady keep trying to fight the blond lady when it was clear the blond lady could take her? And why would any man in his right mind have his first wife and his new wife living on the same property? It didn't make any sense.

"It's complicated, Mama. I don't have time to explain."

I went upstairs in the middle of the episode and knocked on Lydia's door, but she didn't answer. At breakfast, Lydia laughed when I told her that I was mad at her. That she was kicking me to the curb now that she was in college. Don't start an argument this early in the day, my mother said. Lydia was older, and grown people needed their privacy.

After days of knocking on my sister's locked bedroom door with no answer, I called Nana's house. When Miss Delores put her on the phone, I asked if I could visit that weekend. That is, if she wasn't busy. When I came over that Saturday, she told me she wanted to discuss important matters. I was a young lady now, and it was time that she imparted serious information to me. For example, why a woman must choose her mate wisely.

It was a theme she returned to later that evening, during the commercial break of our movie. That night, it was *All About Eve*.

"You need to be very careful with the male company you keep. For example, look at the young man that Lydia brought home. It was obvious from the very beginning he was unsuitable."

The break ended, but I didn't look at the television.

"Why do you say that, Nana? I thought Dante was really nice."

"Didn't you see that boy? He was so dark! And that hair!" She shuddered dramatically. "And his table manners. What on earth did Lydia see in him? Women push the family forward, Ailey, not backward. You are very, very brown, so you must find someone much fairer than yourself. You must think of your children. Why, when I met your grandfather . . ."

I tried to listen politely as she insisted on strolling through her history with Gandee. Their courtship, when he'd seen her on the campus of Mecca University in her pink-and-green sorority jacket. She'd been leaving the Humanities building, her books clutched to her chest, and he'd called out, "Hello, beautiful!" He'd convinced her to come with him that evening to meet his parents, who hadn't been prepared for company, but had made do. Zachary Sr. didn't say much, but Lila McCants Garfield had graciously excused herself and taken her son into the kitchen. She'd whispered it was bad enough that he'd pushed a visitor on her at the last minute, but now this. They were liberal Negroes, but not so much so that Zachary could bring a young white lady home. No, Mother, he'd explained. Claire was Creole, just like them, and when they'd returned to the dining room, my great-grandmother had been euphoric. She'd embraced the young, blond girl, shouting, "Welcome to the family!"

I looked at the bedroom wall intently, until I almost couldn't hear Nana's voice talking about Gandee. What a great catch he'd been. How kind he'd been, at least, in their early years. He'd promised her that she could go on to medical school after they married. She'd taken the required classes in college and had earned the best grades. Then she'd gotten pregnant with my father, and that had put an end to that. As she kept on with her grievances, how the direction of her life had been hijacked, it seemed that my head was wrapped in cotton. I scanned the silver-framed photographs hung on the wall. So many, but not one picture of Mama anywhere. Why had I never noticed that? I'd never noticed, in all the years I'd been coming to this house. Never—

My grandmother called me back. "Are you listening to me?"

"Yes, Nana."

"Then what did I just say?"

"Um . . ."

"I knew it! You weren't listening. How rude!"

"Yes, I was, Nana. You said, women push the family forward."

"I said far more than that."

"I'm just summarizing, Nana. I heard everything you said. I understand. I get it."

"Good girl. Remember, willful ignorance is not an appealing trait in a young woman."

I shifted my gaze to Bette Davis, tossing her hair and flaring her nostrils. I didn't feel like watching this movie anymore. And I didn't want to be in this room, either; I didn't care how lonely I was.

"Nana, it's been a very long day and I've got homework to finish tomorrow. I should tuck in."

"Are you asking my permission to be excused?"

I waited a few seconds.

"Uh-huh. Sure, Nana."

"Yes, Ailey. You may be excused."

That next morning, I rose early and called myself a taxi without even leaving a note to explain why I wasn't attending Mass with her. I paid the taxi driver with my emergency ten dollars and felt grown when I told him to keep the change.

At home, my mother was sitting on the couch, almost like she knew that I'd be returning early. She patted the spot beside her, saying that she needed to talk to me.

"Your sister's gone away again for a few days. Actually . . . well . . . it's going to be more like a month."

"Where'd she go, Mama?"

She told me, I was a big girl now, so she would tell me the truth. My sister had been in trouble with drugs. I tried to fix my face, to mirror one of the actresses in a movie that Nana loved. Mama wasn't fooled, though. She touched my hand, saying she should have known I'd work things out. I'd always been such a smart child.

That evening, I consoled my mother at dinner; it was just the two of us. It was early November, I pointed out. Lydia would miss her birthday and Thanksgiving, but she'd be home for Christmas. And Coco would take the train down from New Haven and she and I would roll our eyes at our big sister playing that Donny Hathaway holiday song that she loved so much. It would be all right.

———

Two weeks later, my mother told me Lydia had disappeared again. She'd run away from the rehab center. My father had looked for her, but she couldn't be found. Mama said she'd wanted to keep Lydia's problems a secret from the rest of the family, but now that my sister had disappeared, she'd have to let everyone know. We were a family. It was our right to worry.

I was in the kitchen when Mama told me. She put a breakfast plate in front of me, but I pushed it away. I put my head down on the table and cried.

JINGLE BELLS, DAMNIT

I didn't know how much I actually didn't know until I enrolled at Braithwaite Friends. How I had treaded water at Toomer High, never having to work too hard to get the highest marks. I was frightened by the possibility that I wasn't as smart as my teachers and my parents—and even Uncle Root—had told me I was. What if I couldn't keep up? Not only would I disappoint everyone in my family, I'd be humiliated in front of all the white kids at my school, so I rose earlier than anyone, in the pitch dark. I sneaked downstairs and made coffee and made sure that I washed out the carafe and dumped the grounds before Mama came down to make breakfast. I stopped eating in the school dining room at lunchtime and ate my homemade sandwich in the picnic area while I studied.

I started written assignments weeks ahead of time, because my teachers required papers that were much lengthier than the one-hundred-and-fifty-word paragraphs that had been assigned at Toomer. Now I had to write at least three papers during the term. I called up Coco to complain, but she told me my new school was like college on purpose. Those rich, white folks expected their children to get into Harvard or Yale, or at the very least Brown or Dartmouth. Teaching somebody to write a short paragraph was not going to get it, but the good news was that when I went to college I'd be so prepared that I wouldn't be pressed.

In my history class, we had begun a Civil War unit. Mr. Yang and I conferenced ahead of time about my final, longer assignment on the role of Blacks in that conflict. He said he expected that I would maintain a high level of engagement, because my Lewis and Clark essay had been very thoughtful.

"You weren't, like, mad, Mr. Yang?"

"About what? You earned a ninety-four. Does that sound like a mad grade?"

"I just thought, like, you know, what I said about how white people ruin everything might have hurt your feelings."

He leaned forward, whispering. "In case you hadn't noticed, Ailey, I'm not white. But please don't tell anybody. I've kept that secret for so long."

When he laughed, I thought, *I could look at Mr. Yang all day.* His skin was flawless, like in a beauty commercial. You couldn't even tell he had pores. And his shoulder-length, dark hair was so sexy.

"The way you compared the Lewis and Clark expedition to the aftermath of Christopher Columbus's landing in America was pretty brilliant. Your language was a little strident, and I would like for you to lean more into fact-based argument—this is, after all, a history class—but I like your honesty. It's refreshing that you aren't afraid to speak your mind. Ms. Rogers tells me you're an excellent student in her class, too, and you have a real flair for language."

"Ms. Rogers said that about me?"

"She sure did. But we'd both like you to speak up more in class. You tend to be so quiet, and I don't know why. You're so full of great ideas in your essays."

"At my last school they didn't like us to talk so much."

"Well, let's try to work on that here, all right? This is a different environment. A chance to make a fresh start."

"Yes, sir, Mr. Yang. I won't let you down."

He smiled. "Your manners really are impressive, Ailey. Please give my compliments to your parents."

During history class, I kept Mr. Yang's words close. I remembered my home training as Amber softly sighed and raked her fingers through her blond tresses. I decided to ignore her and focus on Chris. On the back of his neatly trimmed head. He'd wanted a super-high-top fade, but his mother had told him absolutely not. He could get creative in college if he wanted to, but so long as he was under her roof, her son wasn't going to look like some rapper. As I silently willed him to turn around, Amber's hair struck my cheek; she had flipped her hair back.

I looked at the bright strands on my desk, wishing for scissors so I could cut off that shit and hand it back to her. Instead, I took the tip of my pen and gently pushed her hair off my desk. I ripped a piece of paper out of my notebook and began writing. I folded the paper. I didn't wait until after class to rise, as I usually did. I tapped Amber on her shoulder.

"Hey, this is for you." I handed the folded paper to her.

Chris looked back at us, his eyes widening.

"What's this?" Amber asked.

"Oh, just a little poem I wrote for you. I think you'll really love it."

"Really? Gee, thanks!"

"You are so welcome."

The rest of the day, I thought about Amber reading my note. It made me so happy, but when school let out Chris was waiting for me in our spot, holding the piece of paper I'd given Amber, as if it was a bloody knife.

"Ailey, you made her cry! How could you tell her that you were concerned about her hair touching you, in case she had head lice?"

"Because I am. How do I know where that white girl's hair's been?"

"Ailey, why are you so mean?"

"It's not my fault that heifer doesn't have any manners," I said. "Why's she always throwing her hair back on my desk anyway? Do I look like her damned beautician?"

"She told her friends about the note, Ailey. And now everybody's talking about you. Don't you even care?"

"No, Chris, I really don't."

He was very insecure. I'd learned that in three months of secret dating. He was popular, but he put up with a lot of shit from the white boys he hung around with. They wanted to sing the "nigger" part in the rap songs they listened to when Chris visited their homes, and he laughed and pretended it was okay. I'd asked, why didn't he just tell them that it hurt his feelings? But he'd told me he didn't want them to think he wasn't a good sport.

"I'm supposed to be your girlfriend, Chris. Not Amber. Or do I just not count because I'm a Black girl?"

"Ailey, don't say that! Yeah, you count! But everybody's not tough like you. You don't need anybody. You're, like, a soccer team all by yourself."

"Are you trying to call me fat?"

"No, girl! I just mean, it's like when you walk through the hallway, you don't look left or right. You just keep gliding."

He was supposed to be my boyfriend, but he didn't understand me. I didn't look at anybody in the hallways because I was afraid people were laughing at me. Or I was hoping they didn't catch me pulling my shirt down, because I didn't want anybody looking at my big booty. I wanted friends so badly, sometimes my stomach hurt, but it was so hard for me to make friends who weren't blood relatives— I didn't know why. And did kin even count as actual friends?

"You know what they say, Chris. It's better to be feared than to be loved."

"Who says that, Ailey?"

"I can't remember. I read it in a book somewhere."

"You talk so funny sometimes."

He began to kiss me, pushing his tongue into my mouth, as I leaned back on the wall. He begged me, unzip his pants, please, touch it, oh, please, but I refused. When he pressed against me and started grinding, I closed my eyes. His movements didn't feel good to me, but I felt powerful, that I could make him tremble and pant. I was in control, and that was important, because I was tired of people either telling me what to do or lying to me. I wasn't going to take it anymore.

"Ailey, oh God," he whispered.

There was screaming, but it wasn't him. It was Amber: she had found us, but he didn't tell her I was his real girlfriend. He pulled away from me and tried to do up his zipper as he started after her, yelling her name.

I walked away.

When Mama brought me the phone that evening, she told me it was that boy again, asking for homework. Her voice was strained, lower than usual. She'd sounded like that ever since Lydia had run away from the rehab center. Mama had started walking the halls at night again.

I waited until she closed the door. "I'm busy, Chris. What do you want?"

"Um, it's like this: Amber and me broke up. You want to be my girlfriend now?"

I put down the receiver and considered what my life had become. Only fifteen, but already, I was a pre-slut. I'd let a boy use me for sex—or something close to sex, at least—without getting anything in return. Two boys, if I counted Gandee, but he was a relative and dead.

"Hello? Hello? Ailey, are you there?"

"Yeah, I'm here. I'm just listening to how pathetic and, like, insane you are." The storm came over me quickly. I was so tired of people lying to me, tired of being treated like a fool. "In fact, I hate you! I wish you were dead!"

"Damn, Ailey. For real? It's like that?"

His voice was small, and my heart slowed some, as he begged me not to kick him to the curb. He was sorry. He wouldn't do me wrong again. Just give him another chance.

"Fine. I'll think about it until after Christmas break, and then I'll let you know."

"But that's forever."

"Christopher Allen Tate, don't push your luck. I said I'd talk to you in January. In the meantime, I suggest that you reflect on your asshole behavior." I used a terse, businesslike tone so that he would understand that he wouldn't be getting to third base with me for a long time to come. "You made a fool out of me in front of that white girl. And I am not a woman to be trifled with."

"Ailey—"

"But please remember to give Mrs. Tate my best. Please tell her I wish her happy holidays and a very prosperous New Year. Now goodbye."

The next afternoon, I was washing my hands in the bathroom when Amber appeared with Sunshine and Lizbet. She was weep-

ing, which made me angry. Why was she singing her betrayal like a
Metropolitan Opera soprano? She should have more pride.

"How could you do this to me?" she asked.

Lizbet hugged Amber's waist, and Sunshine stepped to me, pointing her finger close to my face.

"You're a man-stealing hussy, Ailey Garfield. Don't you have any
female solidarity? Didn't you know that Amber and Chris were in
love?"

This wasn't the best time to mention he had come after me, or
that his mother had encouraged our courtship. One false word, and
it would be a repeat of the Antoinette Jones debacle, but these white
girls might kill me, or worse, yank out even more of my hair. I'd be
permanently baldheaded, a victim of violent alopecia.

Sunshine twisted her mouth. "You walk around this school with
your nose in the air like you're better than us, and then you think
it's completely okay to kidnap somebody's boyfriend. That's you,
Ailey. Miss Selfish Superior Bitch."

She turned to the others, and they nodded.

I stepped closer, until Sunshine's finger almost poked me in the eye.

"No, actually, I'm Miss Selfish Superior *Black* Bitch. And I transferred here from Toomer, so I'd be careful, if I were you. But if
you're feeling froggy, go 'head and try me. I'd love to whip your ass
and get expelled. Because I don't want to be at this fucking school,
anyway."

I counted in my head until Sunshine dropped her finger. Then I
balled my fists and flexed at her. When she jumped away, Amber
and Lizbet moved with her. I pulled a paper towel from the dis-
penser, dried my hands, and walked out, clutching the towel. I know
I should have been careful about turning my back, but by that time,
I felt safe.

———

I'd always known that Nana thought light-skinned and white people
were superior, but I'd willfully overlooked that. Even when she'd
remark that my sisters were prettier than me, it didn't chafe—wasn't
I my grandmother's favorite? When Nana boldly insulted Dante's

color, however, that struck close to blood. My mother was even darker than Lydia's ex-husband, and now Mama's hurt complaints throughout the years came back to me, with new meaning: That all Nana's friends were fair enough to pass for white. That Nana insisted I wear a hat when sitting in the sun so I'd get no darker. That Nana never had approved of my mother as a daughter-in-law, but had adored Aunt Diane from first sight.

At Toomer High, whenever somebody talked badly about somebody's mother—or even hinted at a maternal insult—there had to be a fight. That was a point of honor. But how could you fight your elderly grandmother? And so I stayed away from Nana. On Thursday afternoons, I'd leave messages with Miss Delores, telling her that I couldn't spend the weekend with Nana because I had homework. My other excuse was cramps—I didn't reveal that Daddy gave me two codeines a month after I'd told him the agony in my midsection made me ponder whether I wanted to face the next thirty-five to forty years of menstruation.

But then Nana called my house. When I picked up, she asked to speak to my mother. Minutes later, Mama knocked on my door.

"That was your grandmother."

"I know. I answered the phone, remember?"

"Ailey, she's so upset. What's happened? Y'all used to be so tight."

"Nothing. I'm just busy, trying to keep my grades up."

"So you're going to kick Miss Claire to the curb? You can't study over there?"

"Mama, please don't try to be cool. It's kind of really sad."

"All right, I will set my coolness aside. But, baby, she's an old lady. I know she can be cantankerous, but she depends on you. You're her only friend."

"Are you actually feeling sorry for Nana?"

"Folks get crotchety when they get old. I expect I will, too. You remember how mean Dear Pearl was?"

"She wasn't so bad. She was all right."

"That's 'cause you didn't grow up with her. I remember this one time we were in church, and Mr. J.W. James, he got up and said he

needed to testify about how good the Lord had been. He wanted
to sing Him a song. The elder said all right—this was the one before Elder Beasley. Now the whole congregation knew Mr. J.W., he
never could sing a lick, and we just didn't say anything to keep from
hurting his feelings, don't you know. But Dear Pearl? She did not
care one bit! She stopped Mr. J.W. right in the middle of 'Amazing
Grace.' Told him if he was trying to praise the Devil, he shole was
doing a good job. But if he wanted to praise Jesus, he needed to shut
up and sit his ass down."

My mother laughed so hard, she plopped down on my bed. I
didn't want to laugh along, but I couldn't help myself.

"Child, in church! In front of God and everybody! Ailey, I laughed
so hard, I thought I was gone pee-pee! But Mr. J.W. never did care
how mean Dear Pearl was. When she died, he was so broken up at
her funeral."

"I remember. He couldn't stop crying."

My mother touched my hand. "Ailey, please go see your grandmother. It's the holiday season. Nobody should be alone during the
holidays, especially an old lady. I know she's hard to take, but we
don't know the troubles she's seen. And we never will, either, because Miss Claire's a prideful soul."

When Mama collected me from school on Friday, I told her I
needed to pack for that weekend. I'd call Nana at home and see if
she was free. At the red light, my mother put her foot on the brake.
She pulled my face to hers, kissing my cheek.

"You are such a good girl. I'm so proud of you."

But when I called my grandmother, she didn't seem grateful. She
acted inconvenienced, letting me know she'd have to change her
plans for the weekend. Exactly what those plans had been, she didn't
say, but at tea the next afternoon, she pulled out my midsemester
reports. My mother had turned them over to her. It was Nana's right
to see them; she was helping to pay for my school tuition.

"Ailey, I'm amazed by your biology grade, and not in a good way.
This B minus is unacceptable. You don't seem to understand what
your responsibilities are in this family. I'm very disappointed in you."

As she continued to berate me in ladylike whispers, I closed my eyes. Unlike others, who raised their voices, when my grandmother was angry or wanted to emphasize something she lowered hers, forcing me to ask her to repeat herself. This resulted in her raising her voice and speaking slowly and loudly, but at least I didn't have to be a dog to hear her.

"Ailey, are you going to be a physician or not? Because with this biology grade, there's no way you'll be accepted into a college that will prepare you for medical school."

I blew on my Earl Grey. When I looked up, she regarded me with disdain.

"Nana, I don't think I want to be a doctor."

"But we talked about this a long time ago."

No. You talked about it. I just went along.

"I know, Nana."

"Is that all you have to say for yourself? Do I need to remind you that there are five generations of physicians in the Garfield family, going back to the nineteenth century?"

"No, ma'am."

"Ailey, how many times must I remind you about that servant talk? My God!"

When I didn't respond, she stretched out a coral-painted thumb and forefinger. I prepared myself; my grandmother didn't hit, but on rare occasions she could be an expert pincher. I was saved when Miss Delores knocked on the open door of the antechamber. Her large, rectangular glasses sat near the tip of her nose.

"Mrs. Garfield, there's somebody downstairs asking for you."

"Could you perhaps be more specific? Somebody such as whom?"

"I really can't say." Miss Delores tilted her head to the side. Her lips were clamped together.

My grandmother placed her cup on the saucer. She placed her hands on both arms of her wing chair, braced herself, and stood. As she left, she closed the anteroom door behind her. I waited a few seconds, then stood, walked to the door, and opened it in careful inches, listening to the voices downstairs. Nana was upset, her voice wavering, and there was another voice at shouting volume. It was my sister Lydia.

Letting go of the doorknob, I took off my shoes and stepped into the hallway in my socks. My sister's voice was even louder now, as she told my grandmother how Gandee had been a monster. A dirty old man who gave her nasty magazines to look at while he played in her panties. That he put his thing in her mouth and made her suck on it. How he'd told her if she said anything to anybody he'd kill everyone she loved, including her younger sisters.

"And you're worse than he is!" Lydia shouted. "Leaving me with him, and I was nothing but a child! You and your goddamned shopping trips! You ought to be ashamed of yourself!"

"Oh, Lydia, I swear, I didn't know! Oh God! Oh, please forgive me!"

"You owe me! Now I want to see my baby sister! I know she's here!"

As Lydia screamed my name, I crept further down the hall, but my collar was pulled from behind. When I jerked out of Miss Delores's grasp, my hand hit her shoulder.

"So you're going to beat me up now, Ailey?"

"I'm sorry, Miss Delores, but you can't grab on me! You're not my mama."

"You're right, but I do have your mama's phone number."

"I don't care. Call her all you want."

"All right, then. And when I do, I'll tell her your sister showed up high as a kite and telling lies on a dead man. And then her baby girl hit me. The one I used to change diapers for."

Tears leaked from my eyes, but Miss Delores was relentless.

"You're standing there crying, but what about your mama? Don't you think she's been through enough with Lydia? How many more tears does she have to shed?"

I watched her walk down the hallway toward the stairs, before I turned and went back inside the anteroom, leaving the door open. Downstairs, my grandmother sobbed loudly, but her cries couldn't cover Lydia's rage. She called Nana a color-struck, mean old bitch. She called her a pimp for little girls, and then there was another raised voice: Miss Delores, who told my sister she needed to leave right now. Leave this house, and if Lydia didn't, she could wait and shout at the police all she wanted.

The noise stopped.

For an hour, I waited for my grandmother, but when a shadow appeared in the anteroom's door, it was Miss Delores again. She told me my grandmother had gone out shopping. I should get my things; she would drop me off at home.

For days after that, I called Nana's house. Maybe she knew where my sister was. Several times a day, I left messages with Miss Delores, but my grandmother never returned my calls. I didn't sleep well, thinking about what my sister had screamed that day. What it meant: Gandee had lied to us both. He'd hurt Lydia, and then he'd hurt me. We both had kept Gandee's secret, kept our pain inside to protect everyone else in the family. And now I couldn't even tell Lydia how sorry I was about what had happened to her. I didn't even know how to make myself feel better.

———

On Christmas morning, Nana arrived at our house by taxi looking fresh and blameless, wearing the Chanel suit she'd bought in Paris on a family trip overseas, back when my father and uncle were teenagers. She handed me her purse and a platter of Creole cookies, then plucked at the tips of her gloves, like an actress in an old movie, and criticized my outfit.

"Ailey, in my day, we used to dress for a holiday dinner. I was not aware that dungarees were proper attire for receiving company."

My parents emerged from the kitchen. All morning, my mother had been padding around in slippers, but she'd put her heels back on now. She wore her pearl earrings.

"Hey, Miss Claire! My, don't you look pretty? I've always loved your Chanel!"

When my grandmother turned to me, asking, what on earth was that awful-smelling mess, and were we supposed to eat that, my father began shouting. Was she going to spoil every goddamned holiday? Jesus H. Christ, how long could this go on?

I made an alarmed sound: I was surprised by my father's anger. He was the calmest among us, the one to settle our female disputes. No matter how grumpy my mother was, I couldn't remember when he'd ever raised his voice to her, or to Nana, either. But lately, ever since that day Lydia had headed back to rehab, my father had been snappish. He'd put on weight, too: his belly had gotten even rounder.

Mama had her own surprise that evening. Instead of ignoring my grandmother, she put up a hand, telling my father she was tired of this situation and she was going to finally handle it. As she moved closer to Nana, her tone was a tranquil purr.

"Miss Claire, you know perfectly well those are collard greens you're smelling. And when it's turnip greens season, we're going to eat those, too. You've been coming here for Sunday dinner, Christmas, Thanksgiving, Easter, and your birthday ever since Dr. Zach died, and I always serve greens at my table. Now, I was reared to respect old folks, and that's why I have tolerated your utter lack of manners throughout the years, how you sit at my table acting as if I'm trying to poison you, and criticize me behind my back to my own children. I've put up with you because I know you are a lonely, bitter woman without a true purpose driving your life. However, we have reached the end of the line. Do you understand me, Miss Claire? If you persist with your rudeness, I'm going to prepare you a lovely holiday plate, call a second taxi for you, and throw you out of the house that I helped buy with my teacher's salary. If that is your wish, you let me know."

Under the sheen of powder, my grandmother's face colored.

Mama put her hand on Daddy's shoulder, balancing as she took off her heels and left them on the floor. She advised my grandmother, be careful not to trip over those shoes. She'd hate for Nana to break any bones. Then Mama walked in her stockinged feet back to the kitchen, with my father and me following.

In the kitchen, my mother picked up her wooden spoon and went to the stove. My father perched on the table's edge.

"Ailey, do you know that your beautiful mama is the best wife a brother could ever ask for? I love her, and I love me some greens, in almost equal proportions. And I sincerely hope there's an extra ham hock in those greens, because I love me some pig meat, too."

My mother lifted the lid of a pot; when the steam rose, she leaned back. She tried to keep her lips pressed together, but laughter escaped. Daddy hopped from the table and dance-stepped up to the stove, offering his hand to her.

"Come on, woman. Let's take us a turn."

"Geoff, if you don't stop acting silly, you better. And you know it's not a ham hock in that pot. I used smoked turkey wings, like your doctor told me to."

"Who cares what he says? The more pig for me, the better! Oink, oink!"

She swatted at his shoulder with the spoon, but he caught her by the waist. He kissed her on the forehead, and she closed her eyes.

"Ailey, put those cookies on the table and take some cheese and crackers out there." Her eyes still were closed. "That should tide over you-know-who until we sit down."

Throughout dinner, my grandmother's signature bon mots were absent. She was quiet, in between offering meek conversation starters, which I ignored. I loaded attention on my cousin Veronica, who twirled to show me the petticoats under her dress. Malcolm had grown a scraggly goatee and was trying to get a spades game going.

"I know how to play now," Malcolm said. "The brothers in my dorm taught me."

"Spades is for suckers," Aunt Diane said. "The trump doesn't even change! Bid whist is what real adults play."

"Aw, you talking trash!" Malcolm said.

She laughed. "And I can back it up, my dear boy."

"Sure can," my mother said. "I taught Diane how to play bid whist back in 1968. Now get those cards from the kitchen. Let me show you how to run a Boston on somebody."

Coco waited until we'd finished dinner to call. After everyone had their turn talking, I picked up the extension in the upstairs hallway and pulled it into my room. She hadn't returned home since her fall break. When I asked why, she told me studying for the MCAT was a lot of work.

"Carol Rose, you missed some holiday fireworks."

"Uh-oh, girl, what happened?"

"Your grandmother showed out, as per usual. She talked about the greens again, but this time Mama got her told."

"Aw, shit! Are you serious?"

"Mm-hmm, girl. It was real good. You should've been here."

"Damn, I hate I missed that! But I don't get it, though. Doesn't Nana know greens keep you regular?"

We laughed over the familiar, revolting rhyme of my mother: *A banana in the morning and greens at night / Will keep your bowels moving just right!*

There was no talk of our sister, my worries about whether Lydia had a holiday meal or whether she was safe. I hadn't told Coco or anyone else what had happened at my grandmother's house. I'd become a gourd filled with secrets: my own and Lydia's. That we both had been hurt as little girls by a man who was now dead. I'd been filled for so long, I didn't even know what it felt like to be happy and empty.

Soon, our silences extended, and finally, my sister and I said our farewells. An hour later, a taxi arrived for my grandmother. When I heard the horn, I walked downstairs to the foyer, where everyone stood. Merry Christmas, Nana, they called. We love you very much.

At midnight, my father left for his shift at the hospital, and the house emptied. I offered to help my mother clean the kitchen, but she told me the work would do her good. Go on to bed. But upstairs, I couldn't rest. Around two in the morning, I heard my mother walking the halls. I went down and heard the low sounds of a record on the turntable. It was Aretha, singing to her man. Asking, why wouldn't he let her love him? Mama was on the couch. She pointed to the banana pudding dish on her lap: Did I want some? She only had one spoon, and she gave it to me. As we listened to Aretha's soprano pain, I ate my fill, scraping the sides of the dish. I don't remember dozing off, but in the morning, I was covered with a blanket.

◈

SONG

◈

⊙ ⊙ ⊙

The Loss of Africa

We know of those taken from the place called Africa, captured by men who had transgressed against flesh for a long time. The Africans who stole others and kept those folks for themselves. The Africans who stole others and sold those to the Europeans who would take them over the water and humiliate and sometimes torture them for life. We know about the dark-dark folks who never would see home again.

We know dates. We know hours. We know disbelief. We know mourning.

We know about the years even before 1619, and the years that would come after. We know about those Africans who arrived in a place that the English called Jamestown, Virginia.

We know which villages these Africans lived in before they were stolen, their collection of conical, huddled homes. Domestic birds running on the ground of a courtyard, feathers of black and red. A goat tied to the side of a hut and, every morning, a mother rising from her pallet, tossing grains in a pestle. And we try not to weep over what was lost to these folks.

We know about an enemy from a neighboring village. We know of strangers who saw wealth in meat rocking bone. The names of the captives are lost to everyone but us. Their tribes. Their children, if they had them. Their beloveds they'd hoped to marry in ceremonies of laughter and wine. The rivers passing through their nations. Their words for a rooster cock-crowing. For a delectable fruit, skin the color of red intruding yellow. For their warbles and ticks of joy.

On that English ship that would land in Jamestown the enslaved probably weren't locked in irons. That time would come later, after the sailors saw the Africans look at water and sing. Leap overboard and the sharks swim to meet them. These "twenty and odd" folks would begin as bloody vectors, spilling lines across continents. More Africans enslaved by the English would arrive on ships.

You already know that we know laws as well.

We know 1662 and the words set down in the Virginia colony: partus sequitur ventrem, Latin for "that which is brought forth from the belly." And so African—now Negro—women's children would no longer follow the status of their fathers, as had been English common law for centuries. With dark children, their mothers would decide their fate. If a woman was enslaved, her children would be enslaved. If a woman was free, her children would be free. And if enslaved, somehow, a mother would try to hold on to her child, to keep her child from being sold. And if separated, her child would forever grieve. This is what happened to a girl named Kiné, a girl from across the water. A girl whose line would become tangled with our people who lived here, on the western side of that ocean.

The Stories of the Mother

Kiné had been born in Africa. Of this time there was one story she would repeat as she braided the hair of her cherished daughter, the product of the surprising love she found with Paul McCain. The story she would tell when she and her child dug in the garden beside Paul's mother, Helen, or when Kiné brought water to Baron McCain, a man who was stiff with Kiné but who turned tender at the sight of his granddaughter.

The present that reminded her of the past: The way Beauty held her head. Or the sound of Beauty singing. It would bring up a memory of across the water, in the compound of Kiné's father. And children, who had been her siblings, the offspring of the four wives and three concubines of Kiné's father.

Kiné's father had not been a very wealthy man. However, as her mother had liked to say, he had been very blessed and able to raise the pillar of charity high, as Allah commanded. Kiné's father had five slaves, male and female. The three females were concubines, low-status yet beautiful women seized as captives during war. Though the concubines warmed his sleeping mat, the father also had four wives, of which Kiné's mother, Assatou, was the first. Being first wife meant Assatou was in charge of the compound. She was a fertile woman and had given her husband several children; all but Kiné were sons.

The day had been pleasant, starting in the dark morning with first prayers. Kiné had been playing by herself while her youngest brothers had practiced writing their Arabic letters in the dust before heading off for lessons with their teachers. The oldest sons were out of the compound, occupied by business that Kiné only thought of as manly, since it was a mystery to her. During the midday, there was a soup with dried fish for lunch. In preparation for dinner, Assatou killed a chicken, wringing its neck in a drama of squawking, before dropping it into a pot of boiling water and plucking the feathers. That would be her contribution to the largest meal. As first wife and the daughter of the district's marabout, a holy man with great power, Assatou didn't worry about jumping around to please a man. She'd given her husband sons before giving him a daughter, and she never caused trouble. Her place in the household was secure; the proof was in the heavy gold in her ears and around her neck.

The mother and daughter beat the garlic and peppers in the pestle. *Bum-bum. Bum-bum.* The child was tiny for her size and struggled to lift her mortar. *Bum-bum. Bum-bum.* Assatou adjusted her long head scarf, to keep her hair covered. She admonished Kiné to do the same. The child was bored, so to keep her occupied, the mother told stories. She began with the terrible monster of the river folks, the Ninki Nanka, who had the body of a crocodile and the head of a giraffe. Also, long scales covering his tough skin, which was white underneath its belly, like the toubab, the white strangers in their midst. This monster breathed fire to paralyze its victims before eating them. This is why good little girls should stay close to their mothers and not wander about.

Then the mother began a story about the hare and Boukie—the filthy hyena—and how the hare always was tricking the latter. Assatou had arrived at the point in her tale where the hyena had the smaller animal in his grips, when the group of men walked into the courtyard. They had the muscled strides of purpose.

"Salaamalaikum," Assatou said, sweeping her hand to include all the men. Peace be with you.

"Malaikum salaam." Only the tallest man returned the greeting. His voice was loud, as the six other men looked at their sandals.

Assatou continued in Wolof, "Na nga def?" And how are you?

A rushed greeting indicated bad manners, but the tall man didn't care; he waved his hand impatiently. He didn't want to go through the polite rituals. He asked her, where was her husband? Even at Assatou's polite response—sir, her husband was at her father's compound—the tall man kept talking loudly and she leaned back, meeting his eyes. Assatou was the cherished daughter of a marabout, and she took no disrespect, not even from her husband. She spoke sharply to the tall man, reminding him to respect her house, but the tall man pulled back his hand, and then slapped her. Kiné cried out, and the other women and girls in the courtyard did, too. But this was only the beginning of the agony.

Then there were hours and days that roared as Assatou, Kiné, the other wives, her father's concubines, and their female children were walked along the road. Kiné never would see her brothers and father again. The women and girls were tied together with rope as if they were captives of war, and the younger boys were marched in another direction.

The tall man ended their walk at the wooden front door of a one-story house; instead of mud, this house was built of plaster. When the door was opened, an older light-skinned woman answered. Though she wore a heavy, English-style dress, her hair was wrapped in the traditional way, in cloth that was green and patterned. She had the gold earrings and bracelets of a woman who had received her bride price from a wealthy man, but she was a Christian: she wore a golden necklace with a cross pendant.

The light-skinned woman was a signare, a woman of English and African blood who'd been given by her family as a wife to an Englishman for as long as he stayed in Africa. In this small district, this woman was the only one of her kind, but closer to the coast, there was an entire community of signares and their families. In-between women who were neither true wives nor concubines. They spoke two languages, Wolof and English, or sometimes, Mandinka and English, but were infidels who had left aside Allah and clung to the skinny Jesus that hung on a cross. Like their white fathers and husbands, the signares traded in slaves.

The signare spoke flawless Wolof to the tall man who pushed the women and girls inside the house, through the courtyard, into a large, bare room with no furniture. There were mats woven from river reeds scattered about the floor and two buckets in the corner for relief. For the next few days there was only millet for meals and no meat. There was no water for ablutions before prayer, but Kiné's mother kept her composure. She told the women and girls that Allah would forgive them for praying with dirty feet, hands, and bodies. For now, give thanks that they were alive and surely all would be sorted out.

Yet in the time that followed, a younger woman came and whispered news, looking over her shoulder. Her head was wrapped in the traditional way, too, with lengths of patterned red cloth, though the cloth was frayed. The woman was a slave in the household. The slave woman told Assatou, may Allah bless her and her father, the marabout. Assatou's father had once promised the slave woman that he would pray for the slave woman's family, who had been captured in battle to the east, sold, and gone to an unknown land. She had cried many salt tears and when the marabout gave charms to the slave woman, magic that would bring her spirit peace, he had asked for no payment. And in a matter of days, the slave woman had found that peace. She had become reconciled to her lifelong role in the signare's house, and the signare had become nicer and less sharp in her words. The slave woman was sure this was because of the marabout's charm.

When she told Assatou that her husband had been accused of heresy against the faith, Assatou's shoulders dropped in relief. There was no servant of Islam more devout than her husband. Yet then the slave woman reported what happened when Assatou's husband was brought before the district's imam. The imam had been at odds with Assatou's father for years, and by extension, her husband. The imam had brought witnesses to lie about Assatou's husband, and indeed, his entire family. They claimed her husband had been spied lying on his mat in the mornings instead of rising and completing ablutions for the dawn prayers. That he had been seen stumbling in the road, drunk with spirits. The men swore that her husband kept a pig in his courtyard and had butchered this meat and passed it around to his family to eat. And the witnesses said that Assatou's husband and other mature family members ate heartily and drank many daytime cups of water during the month of Ramadan. Thus, none of this man's family were true Muslims, and this is why they had been given over to the imam as slaves. The imam had decided to keep Assatou and the grown women as his concubines, but to sell the rest of the family, including Kiné.

Assatou slumped, weeping, and the slave woman begged, please, do not blame her. Forgive her, please. Balma, the slave woman was sorry, and Assatou replied she did not blame the woman. And she would bless the woman's name when she was able to make proper ablutions. Her voice had none of the haughtiness from the time when she had ordered house slaves and concubines to bring her this and bring her that. Assatou pulled Kiné close to her, digging in her nails.

Come to your mother, child, she said. Come to your mother. Every few seconds, Assatou whispered this. It became a continuous chant as she rocked back and forth on the floor of the room. It became a scream the next day when the men came to the house of the signare to take Assatou back to the imam. The tall man shouted at Assatou that his master was a kind man. He had allowed her to stay with her daughter for this time, in order to make her goodbyes. Then the tall man picked up her like a sack of millet or a newly killed animal as she kicked and bit and reached out her hands to her little girl. That was the last time Kiné saw her mother.

And then there were many, many days of walking until they came to the edge of the river. Across the river was James Island, named so by the English who had taken over that spot, fighting other white men from other countries for control.

The men put Kiné and others in a canoe and they rowed to the island, where white men waited. There, their clothes were taken from them and Kiné and the other women and girls were put in a stone-walled room with no windows. There was no bucket for relief, only a corner, and a terrible smell. At times, a white man or two would come to the room to pull out an older girl or woman, and there were new screams. And Kiné put her hands over her ears and rocked back and forth. In the stone-walled room Kiné could not be sure how many days passed—perhaps ten—before she and the other women and girls were taken from the room. Not to satisfy the white men's desires, but to be loaded into the bottom of a ship that had sailed up to James Island.

Next came a journey she could not track, because she could not see the moon or the sun from the dark hold of the ship. At times, she was pulled up onto the deck into light. Other times, sailors with appetites visited the female side of the hold, turning women and girls into profane vessels. Kiné was spared this physically, but she bore witness. One of her comrades—if she could call her that—was tossed overboard after she died, succumbing to her bowels. The sailors threw her into the sea without the sheets used as shrouds for the two white men who had perished on board. The sharks tore at Kiné's comrade, the water filling with her meat. It was the nature of those sea-swimming things: brutality seeks what is nearest.

After three months of lying in her own mess on wood, Kiné arrived in western land, on this side of the big water. She arrived in Savannah, Georgia, where she was doused with buckets of water to clean her off, and given a rough cotton dress. Then she was put on another ship, a much smaller one, and sailed up the river to Augusta.

"And then what happen?"

Kiné's daughter would ask this over the years until she was old enough to understand her mother's anguish. Kiné would only look away to the side as the people in her homeland did whenever something sorrowed or shamed or frightened them. She was still an African, no matter how many years had passed.

Kiné had been purchased that day in Augusta by Baron McCain. He had brought his young son Paul with him, and Kiné was put on a horse with Paul, who held her safe by the waist. They rode a long time through wilderness to a farm that was across a river, a few miles from the new federal road.

Before Kiné, Paul had been the only child on the farm, and Paul and Kiné played together like any other children. Kiné also helped Paul's mother, Helen, take care of the three-room house and the chickens and the one pig and the cow and the large vegetable garden and the corn patch. Helen McCain was a mixed-blood Creek woman, as Baron's own mother had been, and she was lonely out in the wilderness without her family. She had lost several babies, some in the womb, and some after birth, which had brought her much grief. Baron cherished his wife, and so he'd saved for three years to buy her a slave to help keep her company. Kiné was a child who would have time to grow up, a girl who could be devoted to Helen all her life. While Kiné helped Helen with the labors around the small farm, the woman told her stories of the wily rabbit who always tricked the other, larger creatures who wanted to bring him down. The stories reminded Kiné of the tales her mother had told her in their courtyard.

Neither Baron nor Helen could have dreamed of Paul and Kiné falling in love when they came of age, that the two children who played together after their chores would become inseparable. However, these were the early years of the place that would become Georgia, and after some alarm when Paul informed them Kiné was expecting a baby, the McCains gave in to logic. They were mixed-blood themselves. These things happened and—though there was no marriage in a church, as during that time, Christian ministers would not marry an African and an Indian—the two young people pledged themselves to each other. Then Kiné moved into Paul's room in the back of the one-story house. When their child was born, she was named "Beauty" by her grandmother, and there was con-

tentment for Kiné working in the garden with her child and her beloved's mother, as she learned the earth and the uses of plants from
Helen. As the older woman told Beauty stories of rabbits on this
side of the ocean, so Kiné shared her own tales of creatures, while
keeping her pain to herself. And no one ever stopped her from per-
forming her prayers five times a day.

"And then what happen?" Beauty would ask again.

"Nothin' else, baby," Kiné would tell her daughter. "I'se here now,
and so is your daddy. And we both loves you. That's all you need to
know." And she would take her daughter into her arms.

A Terrible Journey

There were years of happiness for Kiné and then tragedy: Baron
and Helen died of a sickness that struck the territory, and Kiné died
soon after. Undone by his losses, Paul began to take to drink, to go
off into the wilderness for two or three days. While he was gone, his
daughter, Beauty, tended to the farm, keeping a gun and a long staff
by her side to scare off animals.

One morning after an extended, drunken absence, Paul returned
with a woman, riding in front on his horse. Paul didn't say where
the woman had come from, but she was neither a Creek woman
nor a mestizo. She was white and, based on her rough manner and
reddened hands, she was not from a family of means. Paul seemed
bewildered by his new wife's presence even as she moved into the
larger room where his parents had slept. When Beauty went to her
father, complaining that her grandmother had told her this bed
would go to Beauty after Helen's passing, Paul told her she was being selfish. He had been very lonely. Yet the white woman didn't
stop Paul's drinking and in months he sickened and died.

After the burial of her husband, Beauty's stepmother pretended
not to know that the small farm now belonged to Paul's daughter. One morning she told Beauty she had a great surprise for her.
Beauty was relieved; perhaps she and her stepmother would finally
be friends. They rode the horse together until they came to the

federal road that had been cut through the lands of the Cherokee and the Creek. There, a white man and a young mulatto stood by a wagon. The mulatto grabbed Beauty. As she struggled, she saw the white man hand her stepmother money, and she understood: Beauty had been sold as a slave to a trader.

It was a weeklong journey in the wagon as the slave trader stopped other places and acquired more slaves. During the day, there were only two corn cakes apiece for each slave. At night, cooked streak-o-lean to chew on. Throughout the day, blessed sips of water. It snowed in stingy specks or they were plagued with freezing rain. The two little girls were lucky; they were allowed to sit in the back of the wagon. Beauty and the other woman walked behind without fetters. There were purchased men, too, chained together behind the horse of the trader. Beauty was also lucky; she'd been wearing shoes when she was sold. The others in and beside the wagon were barefoot, and the other woman caught frostbite. The mulatto boy held the woman down while the trader did the ax work. When the screaming started, Beauty made a bare spot in her mind. She crawled into it.

Now the woman with no feet sat in the wagon. She cradled the little girls and gave them their water. Beauty slowed her walking and held hands with the woman. During the times of rest, Beauty braided the hair of the little girls in rows like corn, as her mother had worn her hair. When the wagon stopped for the next to last time, a white man came out from a large cabin and picked up the woman with no feet. The rags wrapped around her stumps fell away, exposing raw meat to the cold. The woman dropped into a faint. Beauty fainted, too, and when she awoke she was in the wagon and the woman with no feet was gone. The little girls were gone, too.

Beauty crawled back into her bare space, and when she was sensible again, she saw that she stood in the middle of a field. Woven between the twigs of the plants was whiteness, though not as pure as snow or as beautiful as the tail of a deer. She shielded her eyes. There was a voice behind her, speaking English.

"All this be cotton." She turned to see a very small man: he was the height of a child and his short legs were bowed, like twigs bent before breaking. "All that over there be cotton, too. Ain't no way to get away from it. It'a follow you into your dreams and it'a be sleeping beside you on your cooling board."

Beauty was wary. This man was the size of a child, but as such, he might be "one of the little." She had to be careful. Helen McCain had spoken of these little people—powerful supernatural beings who would walk through ordinary people's lives, but who could not be trusted. If disrespected, they could cause terrible events.

Then the small man surprised her: he spoke in the language of Kiné, who had taught her child the simplest of greetings in the Wolof of her African home.

"Salamalaikum," he said.

"Malaikum salaam," Beauty said haltingly.

"Na nga def?" he asked.

She could not pretend she didn't hear him. It would be bad manners to do so. "Ma ngi fi. Na nga def?" Beauty replied that she was fine, though she lied. And how was he?

"Jamm rek, alhamdulillah." The small man told her he only had peace, praise God. He continued to talk in English—about this and that—before he told her his name was Joe.

"My name be Beauty."

"Naw, baby. That ain't your name no more. You be called 'Ahgayuh' now."

"My name be Beauty!"

She stamped her foot. She didn't know much Cherokee—they were not the people of her grandparents—but she did know that "Ahgayuh" meant "woman." If her grandmother Helen were alive, she would have been outraged at the insult.

Joe bowed in defeat. "A'ight, then. But let's go now, 'cause a storm be coming soon. Hear that thunder roll?" He grabbed her hand, but she snatched it away. Shook loose her mind, trotting. She ran to the fields. There was no place to go. She ran one way and there was a

white man blocking her. She ran the other way and a white boy
came toward her. She turned and there were red lights in her eyes
and then she wasn't in the field anymore. Beauty was in a ship somewhere, wood upon water. So much water. So many folks and they
were naked and they were shaking chains and there were sharks
following the wood upon water and the folks were holding out their
hands to her but she couldn't help them and they were lost from
their home and she was lost from her home and everyone she loved
was dead and someone was whispering *leave this place* and *there
will be too much sorrow here* but there was no way she could leave
and the red lights lifted from her eyes and Beauty saw the field and
that's all she would remember.

The Changing of Beauty's Name

Beauty was not allowed to recover from her losses. Her grandparents, her mother, her father. To grieve the day that she had been sold
for the first time. Or grieve the day in the wagon when the women
and the girls had been taken. Or grieve the day she was sold to Samuel Pinchard, the owner of the plantation called Wood Place.

Slaves were not allowed to lie on a quilt-covered dirt floor and
weep. Neither women nor men nor children. They weren't allowed
to sleep for days on end, so that blankness would cover the soul or at
least take away a memory briefly. Tears and sleep were not luxuries
cast to slaves. There was only work. When the cock crowed for
work. When the sun rose for work. When the sun fell until the stars
cut the dark. Beauty hadn't learned this in her grandparents' house,
but her senses knew it now. And when she heard the work bell ringing the morning after she was sold, she washed her hands and feet
as her mother would have bidden her. She whispered a prayer to
the God who had ninety-nine names according to the teachings of
her mother's people. And she followed the folks from her cabin as
they drifted outside.

When Beauty approached the Negroes who lived in the three
Quarters cabins, asking them the whereabouts of the small man

who called himself Joe, she was told no such person lived on the farm. They were sure, and Beauty suspected that the small man had been a vision, as the ship had been. Such as her mother would see when Kiné had stared into the distance for minutes at a time. Sometimes, when Kiné had roused, she'd shaken with the authority of her knowledge.

Beauty's daily work on the farm was tedious, but her grief was alleviated by a man who lived in her cabin. He was gentle and spoke with the wisdom of the elderly, but he appeared as young as Beauty's father had been before he died. The folks in the Quarters called this man Pop George and said he was much, much older than he looked. Yet, incredibly, all his teeth were in place. It was a wonderful thing when Pop George smiled, and when he laughed, even more so.

In the evening, Pop George told stories to the children, whose parents sat a distance away. They pretended that they were watching their little ones, when really they were listening to the stories, too. The Quarters-folks insisted that Pop George was nearly one hundred years old. When Beauty told him this, though, he laughed his entrancing sound and said folks in the Quarters were funning her. None of these peoples knew how to count, and he didn't neither. He would chuckle as someone protested, uh-uh, Pop George. They won't lying. He knowed they was telling the truth.

Pop George told Beauty that, indeed, he had been born over the water in that place known as Africa. And he had been purchased by the father of their mistress, the girl the Quarters-folks called "Miss Lady." This had happened before Lady had married their current master, Samuel Pinchard.

Since her arrival, Beauty had seen Lady a few times. She appeared as a white girl, but one day, Beauty had seen the girl with her father, Micco. Instantly, Beauty had recognized this man as a mulatto, for his features were a combination like her own. When she imparted this information to Pop George, however, he put a finger to his lips.

"Don't be saying nothing like that again, chile, 'less you want to feel the whip."

And Beauty felt her skin chew over with anger that Lady, a girl who appeared no older than fifteen—a girl with Negro blood—was allowed to live as a white woman. That Lady lived free and high above others and lived in a house with a wood floor, instead of dirt. That here this girl was called Lady, while Beauty had been given a new label, "Ahgayuh," which wasn't even Creek!

In time, Beauty's new name was shortened to "Aggie," and she decided that she would answer to this, to keep pure the name her parents had given her. For she had been made by two people who had loved each other, and each night under the tattered quilt that she had been given she would take out her memories and wrap herself tightly in them. She was owned, but her memories were not.

III

Out of the North the train thundered, and we woke to see the crimson soil of Georgia stretching away bare and monotonous right and left. Here and there lay straggling, unlovely villages, and lean men loafed leisurely at the depots; then again came the stretch of pines and clay. Yet we did not nod, nor weary of the scene; for this is historic ground.

—W. E. B. Du Bois, "The Black Belt," *The Souls of Black Folk*

DEEP COUNTRY

◈

When I was little, I had expectations of the seasons. Summer was for joy: the ride with my mother and sisters down the interstate to Chicasetta and seeing the Peach Butt in Gaffney, South Carolina. The tall structure that was supposed to look like a piece of ripe fruit but instead looked like somebody's ass. Picking weeds with my granny, my sisters, and sometimes Aunt Pauline, and sitting on the porch after supper. Running through the peach, pecan, cedar, pine, and oak trees. Nothing barred my way, within reason. So long as I was with one of my sisters or, if alone, within earshot of my mother's voice, I went wherever I wanted. I was free.

Autumn, winter, and spring contained my trials. There was contentment during the week at home with my sisters and parents. But on the weekends there were the hours spent at the house of my father's parents. Those terrible Saturday intervals when Miss Delores took her half day and Nana went shopping. When those women abandoned me to the baths that Gandee would draw for us. When he threatened me that, if I ever told anyone about what he did to me, he would kill everyone I loved. I believed him, so I kept his secrets.

I had trusted the adults around me: my parents, the elders down in Chicasetta, Nana, even Gandee. Because I was a child, I'd believed what they told me, no matter how kind or cruelly they behaved. I lived surrounded by a fence made up of trust, one I'd assumed couldn't be knocked down. But the day I heard Lydia yelling in my grandmother's foyer, I walked up to that fence. The barest of touches and it fell so easily. This was the barrier separating my childhood from some other place. I wasn't yet an adult, but my childhood was gone forever.

Before I'd heard my sister's revelations, it hadn't occurred to me that Nana might have left me on purpose all those Saturdays up until the year I was seven and Gandee died. I wasn't sure that Nana had known what he was doing to me, but then, I wasn't sure she hadn't. And when I considered Nana's behavior over the years—her casual rudeness toward my mother, her inability to consider anyone's feelings but her own—I couldn't come up with enough evidence to defend her.

I didn't confront Nana, though, because there was something that I needed from her. That June, I didn't want to be in Chicasetta by myself, thinking about my sisters. Lydia had disappeared. In a way, so had Coco, who'd phoned me to say a vacation wasn't possible for her. She had graduated from Yale, and her medical school classes at Harvard University had started that summer. She had too much work to do. In Chicasetta, there would be no place I could go without thinking of the two of them. So I had a new plan: I was headed to Martha's Vineyard, where I would stay with Nana. Up on the Vineyard, I could come and go as I pleased. And I could see Chris because his parents had a cottage on the Vineyard, too. Nana didn't know that, of course, and neither did my mother. Only Lydia had known.

When I told Nana my summer plans had changed, she told me she'd be so happy to have me spend the summer with her. She took my hand and squeezed it, and I waited before I slipped away. Even her touch made me sick to my stomach. I could only play my game so much. But though I knew I was letting Lydia down, I kept on visiting Nana every weekend to get what I needed. I never mentioned the things that my sister had shouted that day.

———

By February, I'd told Chris I'd forgiven him, after his longing looks in school, and several contrite phone calls. I consented to meet him behind the school again, and he brought me presents. A pair of sterling silver earrings in a blue box. A mixtape he'd recorded for me of his favorite R & B slow jams. Chocolate chip cookies that his mother had made. He declared that he loved me, and I let him grind against me, outside my clothes.

In March, I promised Chris that we'd go all the way after my sixteenth birthday up on the Vineyard. I made him think it was only his idea, but it wasn't. I was tired of being a virgin and trying to be everybody's good girl. I only wanted to be myself.

In April, I told Mama that New England had great libraries, perfect for an avid reader. I praised the weather. On the Vineyard, the breezes chased away heat. No need for air-conditioning.

In May, I mentioned that Miss Delores spent the summers on the Vineyard. She did all the housework and cooking. I wouldn't be a burden if I spent the summer with Nana, instead of down south in Chicasetta.

Mama and I were in the basement, sorting laundry. She liked to gear up early for our trip.

"Ailey, you do know your grandmother passes for white on the Vineyard?"

"Oak Bluffs is in the Negro section of the Vineyard."

"I thought we hadn't been Negro for some time—"

"But Uncle Root says Negro, too—"

"And Miss Delores is traveling with her now? Doing what? Miss Claire lives in that cottage all by herself. How dirty can it get? And a Black woman who can't make biscuits or scrub her own damned toilet? I have never heard of such. I don't get it. Kunta Kinte and them got snatched from Africa so they could clean somebody's house, and now your grandmother does it to somebody else?"

"Nobody's forcing Miss Delores to clean up. She's not, like, a slave. She gets a salary."

My mother put a towel to her nose, sniffed, then handed the towel to me.

"Does this smell funky to you?"

"No, it's fine."

She threw it in the dirty laundry pile. "I'll wash it anyway. Look, God knows I've tried with Miss Claire. But the fact of the matter is something's off with that lady. She doesn't even associate with anybody who can't pass. Besides us, that is."

"That's not true," I lied.

She made a farting noise with her mouth. "Miss Claire gets on my last nerve, the way she celebrates her color. It's sick and strange, that's what it is. And I'm not sending my last child up there for her to make you sick and strange, too."

"I want to go to the Vineyard. Please."

"No, baby. Something might happen."

"Like what? I might get hooked on crack? My name is Ailey, not Lydia." As her face crumpled, I smirked.

Mama began counting out loud. When she reached ten, she sighed. "Ailey, why are you being so mean? I don't deserve this. I gave up being a teacher to look after my girls—"

"I am so fucking tired of hearing this story—"

"Have you lost your goddamned mind?" She raised her voice to shriek. Took a breath, and then stepped back several paces. "Ailey Pearl, I'm the adult here, and I'm supposed to have some sense. So I'm going to ignore this tantrum, because you're upset about your big sister. I am, too. But know this. You fix your mouth to cuss at me one more time and I'ma get real crazy on you. Now take your little disrespectful ass to your room. Go on, before I forget you're my only planned child."

That evening, Mama ignored my sulks at dinner. There were the two of us, and she had fried chicken and made biscuits. She put greens on the table but didn't chide me to eat them. She'd made my favorite dessert, too, sweet potato pie, and let me drink coffee with her with no admonition that it would stunt my growth.

We sat together with no words, and after my second cup of coffee, I apologized to her, looking down at the table. I told her there was no excuse for my behavior and I hoped she would forgive me. Then she squeezed my hand and said she was sorry, too. She cut me another slice of pie but told me I needed to start packing in a week or so for Chicasetta. We were going to have a real nice summer down home.

———

On past nights before the Chicasetta journey, I'd set the alarm clock early. I liked to be in the kitchen with my mother, just the two of us, to have her to myself. That morning I woke early as usual, but in the kitchen, Aunt Diane was there, setting out her blueberry muffins. She told me that my father had a heart attack during his shift at the emergency room. Mama was with him now at the hospital.

I hadn't seen my father in several days, not since Sunday dinner. He had been quiet, like he'd been for months. Not his usual laughing self. I'd tried to get some banter going, putting my fork in a huge piece of meat loaf, and teasing that I deserved it more than he did. But he didn't catch on: he'd told me, sure, darling. Take it. He knew he needed to lose some pounds: his last two checkups, his doctor had been angry.

Aunt Diane pulled me into a hug, and I wept, my face mashed against her hair.

"What happened?" I asked when I'd calmed down enough to speak.

"I don't know, darling. But he's going to be just fine. The good news is he was finishing up his shift volunteering at the clinic. The other doctor arrived just in time to help him. Geoff's at the hospital now."

She put a blueberry muffin on my plate and told me Veronica was asleep upstairs in the guest room. They'd come in last night but hadn't wanted to wake me. I took a small bite of my muffin in between sips of the coffee she poured for me. I knew from past experience that my aunt didn't believe in overeating. I needed to make my muffin last, though she'd allow a second cup of coffee.

I breathed in the steam from my mug and thought everything would go my way finally. And no, I wasn't a bad person for thinking that! My daddy was going to be fine, and I could go to the Vineyard like I'd planned. I sipped my coffee and tried not to smile.

"Are you packed?" Aunt Diane asked. "Do you have enough toiletries? I always forget and leave something behind whenever I go back to Maine. My parents live in the tiniest town, out in the woods. It's thirty miles from the closest drugstore! Do they have a drugstore in Chicasetta? You'd think I'd know, as many years as Belle's been going. And I went there once, when you were very little, but for the life of me I don't remember."

"Um . . . I thought I'd be spending the summer with Nana. You know, up on the Vineyard, since Mama is looking after Daddy and can't come. I don't, like, want to be selfish. I know he needs her during this very difficult time." I tried to sound as convincing as I could. To be mature and understanding.

My aunt told me I was so kind and considerate, but I was going down south by myself in two days. Mama already had called a travel agent. "And it's going to be so fun for you on the plane! Your first time! I'll drive you to the airport!" Her voice the same exclamatory singsong as when she talked to Veronica.

I was too cranky to appreciate my first ride on an airplane, or the way the blond flight attendant hovered over me, making sure I was taken care of. She gave me extra packets of nuts and let me keep the whole can of soda when she passed by my seat. But she wouldn't pour me a cup of coffee, even when I reasoned that I was sleepy. It was very early in the morning.

"Coffee will stunt your growth!" she declared.

"I'm five seven and a half and one hundred and sixty-five pounds. I'm done growing."

She patted my shoulder and told me there was enough caffeine in my soda. Drink up.

At the arrival gate in Atlanta, Uncle Root walked toward me with open arms. "Welcome, sugarfoot! How's your daddy?"

I didn't return his embrace. "He's fine."

"Excellent! God is good!"

"Uh-huh." I was determined not to be friendly. Just because I'd had to go to Chicasetta didn't mean I had to be happy about it. He took my bags, and I trailed him to the parking lot and his long, black town car. He unlocked the passenger door and it groaned open.

"That door is loud," I said. "And this car is a gas guzzler."

"That's the point," he said. "Negro men like big cars. We don't believe in conserving energy. After all we've been through, we deserve to be wasteful."

Uncle Root laughed, chucking me under the chin. I wanted to laugh, too, but wouldn't give him the satisfaction. When he turned on the classical station, the radio man solemnly whispered, "It's

ninety-nine degrees in the Atlanta metropolitan area," before he introduced "The Flower Duet" from *Lakmé*.

"How was your flight, Ailey?"

"Like a ride at Six Flags. I thought I was gonna throw up and then
die when the plane crashed."

"I will take that to mean your journey was unpleasant."

I leaned against the car window, closing my eyes.

"Ailey, did I ever tell you about the time I met Dr. W. E. B. Du
Bois? You know who that is, right?"

"Can't you just let me take my nap?" I wanted to close my eyes
and dream of the Vineyard, of the beach in front of my grandmother's cottage populated with bourgie Negroes.

Uncle Root raised his voice and continued.

"I entered Routledge College in the fall of 1922. I was fifteen, and
my father sent me there. The school at Red Mound didn't go past
eighth grade back then—that wouldn't happen for a very long time.
At Routledge, I had a professor who loved himself some Du Bois.
His name was Mr. Terrence Carter Holmes, and there used to be all
these rumors he was communist. He loaned me his copy of *Darkwater* and told me to be careful with it. After that, I just kept borrowing
every book by Du Bois that Mr. Holmes owned.

"That next fall, there was a rumor on campus that Du Bois would
be visiting Atlanta University. The great scholar himself! A friend
told me. Robert Lindsay was his name, but we called him Rob-Boy.
He was very good people and came from wealthy folks. You could
always borrow a dollar if you got in a tight spot. That was some
money in those days.

"Rob-Boy and I decided to drive to Atlanta. He was from there, so
we would stay overnight with his parents. The last thing we wanted
was to be caught after dark by some crackers. We woke early that
next morning and after driving in Rob-Boy's car, with no water or
food, we were hungry. We hadn't thought to pack a sandwich or
even a bottle of Coca-Cola. But my hunger didn't dim my enthusiasm. I thought about the conversations Dr. Du Bois and Rob-Boy
and I would have. We'd let him know that we didn't agree with the

bootlicking policies of Booker T. Washington. We wanted to be intellectual, free Negro men, not somebody's farmers!

"At Atlanta University, we found out where Dr. Du Bois was staying. We ran up the stairs to his building—three flights, I'll never forget it. We knocked, and the great scholar answered, himself."

Uncle Root twisted the radio knob, lowering the volume.

I sat up. Despite myself, I was interested. "It was Dr. Du Bois? For real?"

"Indeed, it was him! He didn't have a lot of hair left." The old man ran his fingers through his thick silver curls. "And he was shorter than I was, but he had a way about him."

"Sort of like Elder Beasley at church?"

"Exactly right. He knew he was important, and everybody else did, too."

"What'd he say, Uncle Root?"

"'Yes?' he asked. I had to catch my breath. Those stairs had tired me out. 'We came to see you, Dr. Du Bois! We came to see the great scholar!' 'Well,' he said, 'now you have seen me.' And he closed the door in our faces."

"That was it?"

"That was it."

"Permission to speak freely?" Since I'd started high school, the old man had allowed me three curse words per week, if I didn't slip up in front of other elders.

"Permission granted."

"Dr. Du Bois seems like a real asshole."

The old man giggled. "Oh Lord! Please, don't ever speak of him that way in public. I beg of you."

"I won't, but doesn't he sound like an asshole to you?"

"No comment, and you only have one curse word left this week."

He pulled the car onto Highway 441.

———

No matter how many times I've navigated that stretch, there is a feeling. The odor of cow manure. County Line Road and a long, red dirt driveway. The peach trees: an entire continent when I was a little girl. Cotton planted almost two centuries ago, and then soy-beans to rest the soil.

Miss Rose sitting on a porch. Beside her, a bushel basket of ripe peaches or tomatoes. The drunkards buzzing, but easily smashed with a swat. Early mornings, she starts singing, "What a Friend We Have in Jesus," and that's your cue to rise. To eat the heavy break-fast that will keep you full all day. Once you've helped her with peel-ing those tomatoes or peaches, there are weeds to be plucked from the garden, from around the vegetables that will show up fresh on the supper table. Fish need cleaning if Uncle Norman comes through with a prize. After dinner, the piecing together of quilt tops from remnants until the light completely fades. The next morning, it starts again. A woman singing off-key praises to the Lord. The sweet fruit dripping with juice. The sound of bugs.

I thought of what Mama liked to say: to find this kind of love, you have to enter deep country.

CREATURES IN THE GARDEN

❖

Without my sisters and mother, the sameness of the country was grating. There were only two television stations, and both came in grainy. It was hot—so hot—and though there was the air conditioner unit in the living room, the plastic-covered furniture trapped the heat.

When I rang the hospital on Saturdays to check on my father, my mother wouldn't put him on the phone. He wasn't well enough, she said. Coco called down from Boston, but she was useless, talking in confusing, technical terms—she thought she was a doctor already.

"What does that mean?" I asked. "Is he going to die or not?"

"Yes," Coco said.

"Why would you say that? You're so mean!"

"I'm trying to dispel this fantasy you have. Very few Black men live to be senior citizens, especially ones who've had heart attacks."

"Coco, I'm only fifteen years old! Can't you let me have my dreams?"

"All right, then, Daddy'll be fine. He just needs to change his diet and lose seventy-five pounds. Is that what you want to hear?"

"Yes, it is."

"I'm glad you're happy. And by the way, you better be careful with boys. You know what I mean."

On the mornings when my granny's hymn-singing didn't drive me from bed, she would knock on my door.

"You ain't up yet, girl?"

"Miss Rose, I'm still sleepy."

"You too young to be tired. Come on and get this breakfast."

As we ate, she gave her regular advice: don't worry about my father. I needed to put everything in the Lord's hands, because He was in control and nobody else. If I kept busy, I wouldn't worry, so she ordered me to pluck weeds from the garden with her and Aunt Pauline, who walked over from her house across the field. We followed Miss Rose, walking between rows so as not to squash the vegetables. The dirt flew everywhere, in my two plaits, underneath my nails, as I plucked weeds, the oppressors of food. They had to be killed, violently wrenched from the earth before they put down roots: Pull. Throw in the aluminum pail. Brush the dirt from your hands. Repeat.

Miss Rose bent over, her broadness lifting the faded dress she wore. The backs of her fleshy knees were crisscrossed with stretch marks and purple, broken veins. As she plucked weeds, she offered non sequiturs: Zucchinis took over any patch. Snapping beans had given her arthritis in her left hand. A long time ago she had ground her own corn grits and meal, but now she bought them ready at the store. It was too much work and her arthritis made it hard to grind now. She paid no mind to the rabbits hopping around the edges of her garden. That's what the chicken wire was for, to keep them out. On the other side of the wire was the clover patch where my former playmates and I had searched for four-leaf specimens. But it served another purpose: the clover diverted the rabbits from human food.

"Who told you that?" I asked.

"I don't recall, baby," she said. "Just seemed something I always have knew 'bout rabbits—hand me that there bucket."

I pretended I didn't hear the broken verb. In the City, my mother and Nana ruthlessly corrected my grammar, but down south I wasn't supposed to get above myself. There'd be trouble if I insulted an elder.

"All these bunnies running around, how come Uncle Norman isn't out here with his shotgun?"

"Shotgun for what, baby?"

"He loves to hunt, I mean."

Aunt Pauline straightened, a long weed in her hand. She called over to me, chiding my foolishness. We don't eat no rabbit in this family. That was crazy talk, she and Miss Rose explained, they don't eat no rabbit, they don't eat no squirrel, and they don't eat no possum. 'Cause all them creatures is kin to rats. Aunt Pauline returned to pulling weeds, as Miss Rose said, a body needed some pride. No matter how poor she was, she didn't want to eat rats, and none of they family, neither.

"So we leave the rabbits alone," Miss Rose said. "We let 'em eat the clover and that'll keep 'em away from our garden and away from the poke salad."

"What's that?"

"Poke is sorta like spinach, but it grow wild. It's some out there, going toward the creek. Dear Pearl used to love her some poke, but I never did get the taste for it. Maybe 'cause if you don't cook it right, poke'll poison you. And you know rabbits can't cook nothing! They get on my nerves, shonuff, but rabbits is still God's creatures. And sometimes, we creatures got to look out for each other. Hold on, baby."

Miss Rose raised her hoe and swung, separating the head of a long snake from its body. I belatedly screamed, and Aunt Pauline stepped over green things toward us. She picked up the two pieces, dripping blood, then dropped them again. She told my grandmother, wait, and then walked to the house. After some minutes, she returned with a dish towel and wrapped the snake pieces in the cloth. She walked to the edge of the garden plot and dug a small, shallow grave with her hoe.

I looked at my granny, but she shook her head at me and put her finger to her lips as Aunt Pauline waved us over to the hole where she'd placed the snake's dismembered body. She bowed her head. Miss Rose followed suit, but I stood there, looking at the bloodstained dish towel until my granny put her fingers on the back of my neck and gently pushed my head down.

"Father God," Aunt Pauline said. "Father God, we want to ask your forgiveness for causing the death of this creature. He didn't mean us no harm. He wasn't nothing but a rat snake crawling in this garden. I don't know why he was here, Father God, but he gone to Glory now. We ask that You receive him into Your loving arms. We ask that You bless the soul of this poor rat snake right now. In Jesus's name, Amen."

"Amen!" my granny said. "Bless him, Lord!"

Other days, I joined the two of them in peeling peaches, which I didn't like. I never could get the skins to peel thin enough, and it was boring work, because all they did was gossip: Elder Beasley needed a new deacon. Mrs. Alconia Jones knew she couldn't afford that new double-wide. Mr. Albert Booker T. Crawford Sr. chased young girls down to the American Legion, though he'd lost his nature.

And they talked about my big sister, right in my face.

"Pauline, I want you to keep Lydia in prayer. That girl's mama don't even know where she is. She just up and disappeared."

"Um, um, um. You know the Devil don't never sleep."

"Say that! Ain't it the truth?"

I was afraid to show my anger, but I fidgeted. Instead of sitting on this porch while they low-rated my big sister I could have been up in the Vineyard. I could have been losing my virginity to Chris Tate right that minute.

"Don't mind the baby," my granny said. "I think her womanhood finally coming down and it's making her peakish."

"Miss Rose, why do you have to say stuff like that?" I asked. "Dang!"

"But you is peakish, ain't you?"

"I've already got my womanhood." I inserted nastiness into my voice. "I got it three years ago, for your information."

"Ain't no excuse for you, then. So why don't you take your mean self for a walk? Go down to the creek and keep them ghosts company. Mean as you is, they probably scared of you."

Aunt Pauline laughed. "I know that's right!"

I walked to the side of the house and picked up a long stick, in case of snakes. It didn't matter to me whether they were poisonous or not. And if I ever got up the courage to kill one, I damn sure wouldn't pray over it. At the creek, there was a half circle of citronella pots on the bank, and a patch of dirt where the grass had died. I heard a car and got ready to run, but it was only Baybay James and Boukie Crawford, driving an old Eldorado. Baybay turned off the ignition, but the radio stayed on. When he climbed out, he was inches taller than I was. Seventeen and some change, he'd grown so much since the last time we'd played together.

"What y'all doing out here?" I asked.

"We just riding," he said. "Miss Rose let us come out, long as we clean up our trash and don't get in no trouble."

"But where'd you get a car?"

"My daddy. You like it?" He ran his hand over the hood.

"It'll do." I waved at the passenger in the car, but Boukie was silent. "What's wrong with him?"

"I guess he shy."

Baybay went to the trunk and took out a blanket. He told his friend, come on out and speak, like he had some home training. Come on, now.

"A'ight, I'ma get out," Boukie said. "But you tell this girl, don't nobody like no tattletale. I still ain't forgot that whipping you made me get when you lied on me."

"No, I didn't!"

"Yes, you did!"

"Fine, Boukie. But how many times you gone keep bringing that up?"

"As many damned times as I want. How 'bout that?" He pulled out a packet of weed and papers and began to roll a joint. I sat cross-legged on the blanket as they stood, smoking. Boukie told me, no, I couldn't have none. So don't even ask.

Baybay stayed out of it, when Boukie talked smack. As a best friend, he couldn't openly dispute, even though he had been trying to court me since childhood. When we were little, he'd put his arm around me in lover's solidarity, but I was of the opinion that he showed his teeth too much, which reduced him to a simpleton. I didn't want him for my man.

I walked over to Boukie and punched him in the arm, so he'd know I was full of contempt and painful possibility.

He stuck his tongue out. "That ain't hurt."

———

I don't remember when Boukie Crawford and Baybay James had become my playmates. They were like the orchard in the field that my grandmother called her yard; it was no use trying to investigate where any of them had come from. They simply existed.

Baybay's mother worked full-time caring for the elderly and paid my granny to babysit her son. She dropped him and his best friend off five times a week. It was a two-for-one financial arrangement since the boys were inseparable.

Boukie and I constantly squabbled even then. I annoyed him because I wouldn't disobey my granny's orders. No playing in the ruins of the plantation house. No going down to the creek without my sisters, and no climbing the pecan trees, either: the last time I'd fallen, resulting in stitches at the town hospital. Boukie didn't care, though. He liked to sell wolf tickets in word and deed: he squinted his eyes and talked smack.

When Baybay came up with the idea about the peeing contest, my competitive side came out. They weren't grown men like Gandee, so they didn't scare me. I was eight and they were nine, but I was chunky where they were lean. And I'd already beaten up Boukie a few times.

Moments later, I stepped out of my shorts and day-of-the-week panties—Thursday—but the sound of the screen door paralyzed me. Piss ran down my legs while Miss Rose walked down the steps.

"Ailey, why you naked? Did you have an accident? I thought you stopped that last year."

She called my name a few more times, and I wept in fear. My mother didn't spank or hit, but down south the rules were different. She had told me my granny had a right to chastise me however she saw fit.

When I was able to unstick my tongue, I saved myself.

"Boukie the one made me take my panties off."

Miss Rose processed that information, then walked a few yards through the field, until she found a peach tree. She broke off a long switch, came back, and stripped it of its leaves, as the boys howled. Boukie got the worst of it. When my granny went back into the house, he told me that God was going to get me, "'cause you made us get a whipping."

"I ain't make you get no whipping. You and Baybay the ones started it."

"But you was in it," Boukie said. "So you supposed to get a whipping, too. We the Three Mouse-tears."

"The what?"

"The Three Mouse-tears. We supposed to stick together. Ain't that right?" Boukie turned to Baybay who nodded his head and showed his teeth, though tears dripped off the bottom of his chin. "You better tell Miss Rose you was in it. If you don't, you a lie, and that's a sin." He solemnly clasped his hands together in a convincing imitation of Elder Beasley, down to church.

"But I don't want no whipping," I said.

"A'ight, then, you better watch out for Jesus. And we ain't playing with you no more, neither."

Baybay gave me a farewell hug, a kiss on the cheek, and whispered that he loved me, but Boukie ignored me for two whole hours, until their ride drove up to collect them.

Three days later, I made a mistake and drank orange juice with my breakfast—something I tried to never do on Sundays given my fear of the wasp-infested church outhouse. I was sitting in the amen corner when that orange juice hit me, and the urge to pee came down. It was right after Elder Beasley preached and one of the church sisters caught the Spirit, the wood floor of the church shaking with the Holy Ghost, and before Baybay's mother gave him and Boukie the inevitable pinch for being mannish.

Before too long, I wiggled around on the pew.

"What's wrong?" Lydia held a church fan and, like our granny, rocked as she fanned.

"I've got to go," I said.

"Can't you hold it?" she asked.

"I'm trying." Wiggle, wiggle, oh, wiggle.

Two of the church sisters thought I'd gotten happy, and wasn't that a blessing for such a little girl? Just like Jesus when he was a little boy. They rushed over to fan me, because the Spirit could take the air from your body.

"Let it go, baby. Just give it over. He'll take care of you."

Thankfully, a lady on the other side of room hopped up with the Spirit, and she was fat; no telling what sort of damage if she fell out on somebody. They left to attend to her, allowing Lydia and me to walk to the outhouse.

She saw the wasp only after I'd worked down my lace tights. She told me to stand motionless. It worked its way over. Zigzagging. Twirling. Flip-flopping in the air. I wanted to do what Lydia ordered but I was frightened. I ran away from the wasp and fell over, but not before peeing on my tights and my patent leather shoes, and I got stung anyway, right on my booty.

At the outhouse, the boys were waiting for their turns to go, and when Boukie saw me running out with my dress up, and then falling down with my business exposed, he laughed, pointing his finger in spiritual accusation. Ever the gentleman, Baybay put his hands up to cover his eyes, but I could see he was peeking through his fingers.

The next morning, Baybay's mother dropped the boys off as usual, and Boukie went back on his promise never to play with me again, and Baybay followed suit. We still ran around, made mud pies, and fell from trees, but every so often, Boukie made sure to remind me, no longer were we the Three Mouse-Tears. And in a few years, he was right, because Mama told me I couldn't spend time with Baybay and him anymore. Young ladies had to be careful.

———

Before they drove off, Baybay had asked me to ride with them, but by the time he showed up in his Eldorado, a week had passed. There had been several phone calls to secure permission to spend time

with my former playmates. There had been a round of calls to Uncle
Root from Baybay's grandfather, Mr. J.W. Then another round of
calls from those two men to my granny. After that, Miss Rose had
placed a call to Mama. She stayed huddled on the kitchen phone
for twenty minutes before she put me on the phone.

"Ailey, I don't know about this. But your granny and Uncle Root
told me it'll be all right. So I'm going to have faith."

"It's just Baybay and Boukie. It's not like they're criminals."

"But they are boys. And boys are always up to something. I'm not
trying to have you come back here full of somebody's baby."

"Mama, that is so nasty."

"You know what else is nasty? Being a teenage mother. So I want
you to promise me that you'll be a good girl."

"I promise. I totally do, Mama. Can I go now?"

"Wait just a minute. And another thing: you watch those boys.
Any kind of ungentlemanly behavior—I mean the smallest thing—
and that's the end of your time with them. Because I don't want to
have to leave your daddy on his sickbed and come kill somebody's
knucklehead son and then hide the body. But I will. And that's my
right hand slapped by Glory."

"All right, Mama. Okay. Can I go now?"

"Yes, you may. I love you very much."

I thought that would be the end of the warnings, but when the
boys showed up at the farm that Saturday, my granny was full of
vinegar.

"Y'all listen to me good." Miss Rose looked over her glasses. "Either one of y'all try some funny business with my grandbaby, I'ma
cut off some privates, and then kill somebody."

"Miss Rose, please! You're embarrassing me!" I tugged on her
arm, but she moved forward, poking her finger into Boukie's chest.

"I'm talking more special to you, Albert Booker T. Crawford the
Third. I know how the mens in your family is."

As soon as we pulled out of the yard, he started fussing. "Why
that old lady up on me like that? That won't right!"

"Man, it's cool," Baybay said. "You know she just protective."

"But I ain't even did nothing!"

"I know." Baybay lowered his voice. "But . . . you remember . . . you know . . . that thing that your cousin Tony did to somebody's sister? She probably just remembering that."

I looked out the window. This was too much, everybody bringing up stuff about Lydia. Maybe this had been a mistake, trying to hang out with these dudes. This was a lot of drama just to go for a ride.

"Exactly, though. Tony. Not me. I don't even fuck with him."

"Come on, partner, shake it off," Baybay said. "We 'bout to drink us some wine, smoke a couple joints, and have us a very entertaining evening. Am I right?"

Baybay worked at the Cluck-Cluck Hut, and they gave him free chicken whenever he wanted. We ate a box while he drove through downtown, taking each corner slow. Through the square, past the old movie theater and the abandoned dime store. Then over the railroad tracks, where we stopped at the Six-to-Twelve Package Store, where Baybay motioned to Mr. Lonny the Wino. He was the old man who stood guard outside and cleaned up for the owner. If you gave Mr. Lonny a tip, he would buy your wine for you. But that day, a brown-and-tan car was parked on the corner when Baybay pulled up.

"Shit," Boukie said. "There go the sheriff. Keep driving."

"Naw, I'ma stop. If I drive off, it'll look bad, and I'm not trying to get arrested."

Mr. Lonny came to the car, and Baybay and he shook hands. The old man asked about the family, smiling his toothless grin. He patted Baybay on the shoulder and told him, God bless.

Then we drove back out to the farm. At the creek, we debated music.

"Can't we listen to something besides James Brown?" I asked. "Prince or somebody?"

"Prince sing like a girl," Boukie said. "And he wear high heels and ruffles and shit. Plus, a woman start messing with a Black man's music, it's all over."

"I don't believe I see a man in this car. Even though you'll probably be thirty when you graduate high school. You've been left back
three times."

"I only got left back twice, Ailey! My birthday come early!" Boukie waved his hand. "Man, forget you."

He lay back on the crushed velvet and closed his eyes. I took off
my seat belt and leaned over the seat, looking at the two boys. They
had identical haircuts, low fades with a side part. Baybay's dark skin
and white teeth were downright pretty. The other boy was too
light for me, but I couldn't deny it: Boukie was handsome. His eyelashes were criminally long.

"Um, anyway, can't we expand our horizons?" I asked.

"What you mean?" Baybay asked.

"Can't we, like, listen to some classical music or some opera?"

"Sweetheart, you got to understand something. Mad Dog Twenty-
Twenty, that's my favorite wine. And Mad Dog and opera, they don't
go together. Opera make you want to drink some white wine in a
Volvo. Some Chardonnay or something like that. But listen to this."
He turned up the eight-track and James Brown hollered. "Now,
James make you want to drink some Mad Dog in a Cadillac, don't
he? This is an Eldorado, to be more specific, but James don't sing
Chardonnay music, and this ain't no Chardonnay car."

HAPPY BIRTHDAY

❖

Every day, I looked in the mailbox, hoping for something from the City. Chris had promised he would write me three times a week, but there was nothing from him, even on my Sweet Sixteen birthday, which no one made special. Coco didn't call, much less send a card, and neither did Nana.

On the farm, my granny baked me a chocolate cake from scratch, but she didn't know she was supposed to sing the birthday song. And when Uncle Root gave me a package, I foolishly let my hopes get up, until I saw it was a hardcover book. He told me it was a first edition of *The Souls of Black Folk*. He nodded decisively, as if the matter of my happiness was settled.

I hugged the book to my chest, faking delight. "Wow. For real? Thank you so much."

I'd been looking to my father to save the day, to send down one of his usual, inappropriately expensive gifts. Daddy only mailed me a check.

"I told your mama what to buy," he said. "But she said you'd want the money."

"But you always get me something nice. And I never told her I wanted a check. Where's she getting this from?"

I didn't know that my mother was listening on the other extension. "You should be happy with that check! Some folks don't even have clothes or a roof over their heads or a decent plate of collard greens and corn bread."

"I'm sorry, Mama—"

"—your father had a heart attack! I've been taking care of him, night and day, since he was released from the hospital. But I'm so sorry I ruined your birthday. I know that's more important than anybody's health."

She hung up.

"Oh God," I said. "Now she's mad."

"Don't worry, darling," he said. "I'll smooth it over. It'll be fine. But I don't like this strict diet your mama's got me on. No bacon, no cream in my coffee, no eggs. I didn't even know your mama could make food taste bad, until she started listening to my doctor. You didn't hear me say that, though. I don't want to end up in the hospital again from a beating. Your mama beats me all the time, and yet I love her desperately."

"You're silly. She does not."

"She's capable of it. I hope you know that."

His laughing turned into a coughing fit before he caught his breath. I told him, please take care of yourself.

The next day, Baybay was at work but had loaned Boukie the car. He told me he had a birthday surprise for me: he was taking me to the mall in Milledgeville. Boukie acted like that was a big deal, and I guess it was. Chicasetta only had a dollar store that sold everything from towels to clothes, now that the old dime store had shut down.

At the mall, we encountered a group of girls coming out of the department store. I recognized one who attended Red Mound irregularly. She was cute but shaved her eyebrows off and drew them back on with black pencil. The summer before, she'd been sitting between the boys, and in the middle of the foot-washing ceremony, she'd left. I'd assumed she was visiting the outhouse, which you couldn't pay me to go near after the wasp incident. Boukie left minutes after, and then Baybay. None of them had returned until near the end of services. When the girl walked to her seat, there'd been runs up and down her stockings.

Boukie walked away a few steps, talking to the girl. Her friends looked me up and down, and I crossed my arms.

"Rhonda, it won't my fault I ain't call you," Boukie said. "My mama had forgot to pay the phone bill."

"Ooh, you lying!"

"Don't be like that."

"And anyway, you coulda walked to my cousin Pookie house and called."

"Why I'ma do that? I ain't even know he was some kin to you."

By the time he drove us to the creek, the june bugs were out, and so were the mosquitoes. He lighted the citronella pots and laid the blanket on the grass. I was nervous, because blankets went on a bed and my mother had warned to stay out of beds with boys. She'd told me that when my period came. She'd given me that advice, along with sanitary napkins, though I'd wanted tampons.

On the blanket, Boukie moved in close to me, but I leaned away.

"Is Rhonda your girlfriend?"

"Who?"

"That girl at the mall, Boukie? The one you were talking to?"

"Why you need to know all that?"

"I'm just curious."

"I see. You curious. Naw, baby, she just my friend. Like you and me is just friends."

I stood up and brushed the back of my dress. When I gave him my hand to pull him up, I didn't look in his face. Those eyelashes might have changed my mind.

When his summer schoolteachers threatened Boukie with failing, there was no more riding in the Eldorado, but the other boy still visited. My granny had no problem asking Baybay to complete chores at her house. On his days off, he pushed the mower around the big field and trimmed the hedges at the house front. When Baybay finished, he and I would sit on the plastic-covered couch in the front room, waiting to eat Miss Rose's delicious, heavy meal, our thighs slurping against the plastic.

One Saturday she told us, get out her house and go walking. We were too young to be sitting up underneath the air conditioner. It would make us sick. Baybay and I walked across the field to the burned plantation house and sat on a blackened wall. We trailed our feet in the dirt. He slid closer, and when he kissed me, it wasn't anything spectacular. Just a few smacks on the lips.

"That's enough," he said. "I don't want to be disrespectful or nothing."

The next weekend, Baybay and I took a drive into town. It felt more formal without Boukie there. He was rude and profane, but he did like to talk. Baybay didn't say much as he maneuvered the Eldorado through the narrow highway into town. At the Six-to-Twelve, he handed money for wine to Mr. Lonny, who returned with a paper sack.

Behind us, there was a flash of blue lights. The short beep of a siren.

Baybay touched my knee. He handed over the sack and told me put that under my seat. Real quick. "And don't say nothing, okay? No matter what happens, be cool."

When the sheriff walked to the car, Baybay didn't seem nervous. His hands were on the wheel at the ten and two positions. He smiled at the white man who leaned into the window.

"Hello, Sheriff Franklin, sir. How are you this afternoon, sir?"

The man smiled back. "Baybay James, right?"

"Yes, sir, but my mother named me David."

"That's a real good name."

"Thank you, Sheriff Franklin. I appreciate that, sir."

"Baybay, can I see your license and registration?"

"It's in the glove compartment, sir. Can my girlfriend get it for me?"

I looked at Baybay and raised my eyebrow.

The sheriff leaned further into the window. "Young lady, please open the glove compartment."

My hands were trembling, but Baybay was patient as he directed me, his hands still on the wheel. His license and registration were in his wallet, and that was under that *Jet* magazine. Right there. See it? When he handed the items over to the sheriff, the man didn't even glance at them. Instead, he asked Baybay, if he searched the Eldorado, would he find anything else?

"You might, sir. I got a calculus book back there."

"What you need that for?"

"I'm in advanced math at school, sir."

"I think I did hear you were going to college. What about you, young lady? You planning on college, too?"

I didn't say anything until Baybay spoke my name.

"Um, I guess so . . . sir."

"Well, isn't that nice? Both of y'all going to college. Ain't that something? I bet everybody is real proud."

"We hope so, sir," Baybay said.

When the sheriff handed over the license and registration, his smile dropped. It was like a cold wind blowing. Not enough to chill me, but enough to give me goose bumps.

"Boy, don't let me see you at this liquor store again. You hear me? Not until you turn twenty-one. I see you here again, I'm arresting you and Lonny. And I'd hate for you to have an arrest on your record, especially if you got something in this car besides a math book. Jail don't agree with college boys."

Baybay nodded his head. "I understand completely, Sheriff Franklin. Thank you, sir."

The sheriff straightened. His smile was back, his gray eyes warm and kind. He tipped his hat to me.

"Young lady."

Baybay didn't say anything on the drive back out to the country, and he didn't steer the car onto the road that led to the creek. He stopped in the driveway in front of the house and let the car idle.

"I thought we were going to hang out," I said.

"I didn't know if you still want to," he said. "I thought you might be mad."

"About what?

"You know. The sheriff and all that. I didn't want for that to happen. I'm sorry, Ailey."

"Cops stop Black dudes all the time up in the City. That wasn't your fault. He's just an asshole."

"You sure you're not mad?"

"No, but I was really scared, though. That guy was creepy."

"I was scared, too."

"You were? You seemed so calm."

"That's how you gotta be. But my heart was beating real fast. Still is." He lifted his T-shirt, then took my hand and put it on his bare skin. "See?"

His chest was so warm. I wanted to lay my head there, but then I felt weird for thinking that.

"So we gone hang out or what?" I asked, and he backed out of the driveway again.

At the creek, he laid the blanket on the grass, then told me wait a minute. He would be right back. He'd left something in the trunk. When he returned, he had a small, rectangular box in his hands. He sat down, but with distance between us.

"I was working on your birthday. But I did get you something. I didn't want to give it to you until we were alone."

In the box, there was a pen and pencil set.

"Did you buy this yourself?"

"What you mean, Ailey?"

"Like, did somebody pick this out for you? Like, a girl?"

"No, Ailey. I chose it myself. You don't like it? I can get you something else. Give it here."

He held out his hand, huffy, but I put the box on the blanket.

"I love it, Baybay. I really do. Thank you."

I scooted toward him. Tugged on his shirt, telling him, sit closer to me. This time when we kissed, there was plenty tongue. He lay back on the blanket and we kissed some more.

Soon, he asked, was it okay if he touched my breasts? I took off my shirt and he reached behind me, unfastening hooks, but I put my hands over my breasts. He touched one of my hands, tugging at it, then lowered his head to my nipple. Licked and sucked until I thought I would lose my mind.

He looked up. "Ailey, do you love me?"

"Sure, I do. You're Baybay."

"No, I mean, do you love me for real?"

I thought about it. "Yes, I do."

"Call me by my government name, then. Call me David."

It sounded peculiar, as if he'd gone down to the courthouse and changed it. When he asked, did I want to be his girlfriend? I agreed. It seemed the polite thing to do. Then he asked permission again: could he put his hand in my shorts?

I buried my head in his chest. I thought about Gandee, what he'd done to me in the bathtub. Those nasty things that made me feel dirty. But then again, Gandee had been an old man, and I hadn't had a say in the matter. And David was only a boy, and so sweet. Maybe it was all right if I did with David what I already wanted to do. Maybe I wouldn't be dirty.

"I say something wrong, sweetheart?" he asked.

I shook my head.

"You sure, Ailey? We don't have to do anything else. I promise I won't take advantage of you."

"Yes, I'm sure, David. I really want to."

He unzipped my shorts, easing a hand inside my panties, and, oh, it was so wet, he told me. I put my arm over my face, but he said, don't be embarrassed. He liked it wet like that, and did that feel okay? I nodded, lifting my hips, and he nuzzled the side of my face, finding my mouth. We kissed as he moved a finger around. He wanted me to feel good, he told me, flicking a spot. He slipped the finger inside me slowly. When he started sucking my nipples again, I reached for his fly, but he moved his hips.

"Stop, okay?"

"What's wrong, David?"

"We got to go."

"It can't be curfew yet."

He stood, jogging in place. Breathing hard. I held out my hand, but he stepped back. Turned around for a few seconds, talking to himself. When he turned back, he told me he had to fold the blanket. Come on, and I headed for the car. I tried not to cry, wondering, what had I done wrong? Did he think I was gross for letting him touch me like that?

At the house, he opened the car door for me. "You're not mad at me, are you, Ailey?"

"I guess not."

"I gotta work tomorrow, but can I see you on Sunday? After church, I mean?"

"For real? Yeah! I mean, sure."

When we kissed, he moved his hips back. "Go on inside, please. I don't want to get you in trouble. I love you, sweetheart."

"I love you, too."

When I let myself in, my granny called out from the back. In her bedroom, a window fan moved a slight breeze.

"I'm a little sleepy, Miss Rose. Can I go to bed?"

"In a minute. Come on in and sit with me, baby."

I settled beside her, but not too close. I didn't want her to smell David's aftershave.

"You know, Ailey, I didn't want your mama to leave here. My only daughter. My baby girl. I missed her so bad, even though her college was right up the road."

"Yes, ma'am."

"Then she married your daddy. I was sad, 'cause I hoped she'd marry somebody down here. But your mama never really belonged here. Some places make you feel good for a while, but you can't stay. You real smart, Ailey, so you know what I mean, don't you?"

"Yes, ma'am." I didn't have the slightest idea what she meant, and I wanted to get to bed, to remember the moment David had put his hand down my shorts.

"Tell me the truth, and whatever you say, your granny won't be mad." Miss Rose looked at me, her eyes moving back and forth. "Are you still a good girl?"

"Do you mean am I a virgin?"

"Ailey Pearl, don't you play with me."

"Yes, ma'am. I am still a good girl." I hoped I was telling the truth.

"Oh, thank you, Jesus." The words came out in a whisper. When I went into her arms, she kissed my face. "You go on to bed, baby. Me and Pauline need help with peeling tomorrow."

PECAN TREES AND VARIOUS MISCELLANEA

◆

Though Uncle Root and his late wife had visited his relatives often, they hadn't ever lived long in Chicasetta. They'd both taught at Routledge College, and resided in the faculty house until she passed away in the late '50s. Their apartment had been small, but Uncle Root told me they'd liked their lodgings. They were only twenty-five miles away from family, but far enough to maintain their privacy.

It took two decades after Aunt Olivia died for Uncle Root to buy his first house in Chicasetta. That place had been in the designated Black part of town—called "Crow's Roost"—but the street that the old man had lived on was the fanciest one in that neighborhood, where the one Black doctor, one Black lawyer, and every Black teacher had lived. In the mid-1980s, Uncle Root had bought his second house in Chicasetta, after he'd retired from teaching. He was the first African American to live in his new neighborhood, which was called the "silk stocking district" among the white families in town. He'd bought the house at a rock-bottom price when an elderly white couple passed away—the wife, and soon after, the husband—and their children had no desire to move back home. The house was imposing, with nine huge rooms, ten-foot ceilings, and a wraparound porch.

Mere hours after Uncle Root moved in, somebody left a bucket of spoiled fried chicken crawling with wormy, opaque bugs on his front porch. The next week, a case of malt liquor. Then a ripe watermelon, which he'd kept, and it had been quite delicious. It took months for the harassment to stop.

When I asked Uncle Root why he'd purchased a house in a neighborhood where he knew he wasn't wanted, he replied it had been 1985, not 1885. Further, he liked to stomp on people's last nerves, and since he'd retired and didn't have a job to keep him occupied, fighting with racist white folks gave him pleasure. Those things left on his porch were harmless, he told me. Nobody had burned a cross on his lawn or tried to hurt him. And he wasn't scared of violence anyway. If one of those crackers decided to actually come for him, well, he'd lived a good, long life. Whenever God called him, he'd be satisfied.

But Uncle Root's mother might have fainted if she'd lived to see her son owning a house in an all-white neighborhood. Even the father of her children hadn't lived in the same house as she had. There had been a racial dividing line on the farm, which was the road that edged the lawn of the old plantation house. Once you crossed that road, you were in the African American portion of the farm.

The other advantage of where the old man lived was that his very good friend lived close by. The day we visited, a younger Black lady answered the door.

"Good afternoon, Miss Sharon! You're looking stunningly beautiful as ever."

When she smiled, there was gold at the front. "Mr. Root, you a mess!"

"I take that as the highest compliment."

In the living room, a silver-haired white lady sat on the sofa. She wore a fancy paisley dress. Her earrings might have been diamonds, too, but she wore slippers over stockings.

"Jason! Come hug my neck."

He kissed both of her cheeks, European style. "Ailey, this is Mrs. Cordelia Pinchard Rice. You met her a very long time ago."

I didn't remember her, but I shook her hand. "Hello, ma'am. It's so nice to see you again."

"It sure is! It's six months of Sundays since I've seen you. You were so little. And don't you have the nicest manners? You sit with me, honey."

Miss Sharon served sweet tea in crystal glasses and slices of pound cake on china plates. She left the pitcher, and I drank two more glasses while the old man and Miss Cordelia talked. The library wanted to add another room and was begging for money. That big oak in front of City Hall was eaten through by rot.

On the return walk, he told me that the old white lady was his niece.

"Nobody else would call us relatives, least of all Cordelia. But yes, we are related. Big Thom Pinchard was her grandfather. His wife died in childbirth, but the baby boy lived. Tommy Jr., named after his father. When he grew up and married, his wife had Cordelia."

"Ladies died having babies? For real?"

"Ailey, women always risk their lives in labor. That's one reason it's so important to cherish mothers always. Isn't that right?"

"Yes, sir."

"After his first wife died, Big Thom met my mother, Lil' May, and fell in love with her. Because she was Negro, she couldn't be his legal wife, but she had my sister and me. That was a big scandal in this town, but my father didn't care. I was eleven when my mother passed away. The Spanish influenza epidemic, don't you know? I've never loved another person the way I loved her, not even Olivia. I don't think my heart ever recovered from my mother's passing."

He was sharing a secret, like a friend. I needed to respond, to let him know I understood the moment. I tried one of the phrases Mama often used talking on the phone with our relatives.

"Shonuff?" I walked closer to him, brushing against the seer-sucker jacket.

He cleared his throat a few times. "Yes, indeed, sugarfoot."

"I'm so sorry for your loss."

"I appreciate your saying that. Your mother is named for mine. Did you know that?"

"Yes, but she changed it last year. She gets cranky now when Daddy calls her Maybelle Lee. He does it to tease her."

"Sugarfoot, let me ask you, what kind of name is 'Belle Marie'? Doesn't that sound pretentious to you?"

"Well . . ."

"Look at you. So loyal. How about we go back to my house, and I'll try to teach you how to beat me in chess?"

He put his arm around my shoulders, and I put my arm around his waist. We slowed down our stride, as country folks like to do.

At the house, he pointed out the pictures on his credenza, naming everyone. Many of their subjects had passed on, now only living within the frames. He pointed out the largest image of a man, a girl, and a very little boy. The man and boy were white.

"This was taken at the 1895 Atlanta cotton exposition." Uncle Root tapped each figure in the picture. "That's my father. That's my mother. And that's my big brother."

Big Thom was a portly man dressed in a light-colored three-piece and a straw hat. He towered over Lil' May, a petite, dark girl in a striped dress; her hair was braided in a coronet, and she stood very erect and serious. Tommy Jr. stood between them, holding the hands of both, but his head leaned into Lil' May's side. The boy smiled, revealing missing front teeth. A happy blond child in his sailor suit.

"My sister and I hadn't yet been born. Mama was thirteen here, so my father must have been, oh, thirty-five or thirty-six? Something like that, and way too old for my mother. After she died, Big Thom used to tell me, he'd been a complete gentleman. He didn't start courting Mama until she turned eighteen, but I've always wondered if he said that to seem a better man than what he truly was. He built the house for her after Pearl was born. Cordelia let us live in the house after Tommy Jr. died, and that's where your granny lives now. I was supposed to move in and take it over after Pearl passed away, but I already had my own home. And even if I'd been homeless, I wouldn't have lived in that house for anything in the world. My mother was ostracized by our entire Negro community for living there. They shamed her for being my father's mistress. And then they shamed me because I carried his skin color. And if I moved into that house, it would be like I was all right with that. And I wasn't all right! So goddamn that stupid-ass house!" He caught his breath. "Goodness. Excuse my language, sugarfoot."

"You're fine, Uncle Root. But you only have one more curse left for the week!"

I nudged him, and he laughed.

———

One day, when we returned from visiting Miss Cordelia, David was waiting for us on the porch. Uncle Root and he greeted like grown men, giving each other the latest soul shake. In the house, the old man asked, did David want to play a game of chess?

"I can't play too well."

"Neither can Ailey, but I'm doing my best to teach her."

I stuck my tongue out at the old man, and then he went to get slices of pound cake and coffee. He told us he'd put plenty cream in the latter. He didn't want to stunt our growth. We sat there an hour, chatting, and he told his Du Bois story, which David never had heard. Then Uncle Root asked us, did we want to go on a trip? But all he did was drive out to the family farm. We turned off and drove on the road out to the creek, and he stopped at a boarded building, where a chubby gray cat appeared through the weeds. When we climbed out of the car, David gave me his hand to hold.

"That animal's nearly old as I am," the old man said. "I guess eating rodents keeps her spry."

"You mean like rats?" I asked.

"Don't be afraid, sugarfoot. Brother David will protect you."

I looked at my boyfriend, and he gave me a quick wink. We followed the old man through overgrown grass. He stopped and told us this was it. This was the place he wanted to show us. David made an admiring, polite sound, but I wasn't having it.

"You drove us out here to show us a patch of grass?"

"Ailey, there's a tree, too. A very special tree. This spot is where I was almost lynched!"

"Like, killed?"

"Would I lie to you, sugarfoot? It was 1934, and my wife and I decided to move back south. Olivia and I both had finished our doctorates at Mecca University. I hadn't been home for a while, and she decided we should drive on down. I wasn't too keen, but she was the boss of me, so I gave in.

"It took us a week. We made sure to travel during the daylight because a lot of roads went through the woods. We had some gallons of gas in a can, but only sandwiches to eat. Some jugs of water, too. Olivia was a brilliant scholar, but she wasn't much of a cook. Neither was I. When we arrived here on the farm, she was napping, and I didn't want to stop at the house just yet. We had all sorts of presents for my sister's children, but I wanted to bring a sack of candy.

"It was a Saturday here at the store. Lots of folks, but during those times, Negroes couldn't be waited on until all the white customers were served. That was one of the many things I didn't miss about this place. Why I didn't want to come back.

"My white half brother was the owner of the store, and when I raised my hand in greeting, Tommy Jr. waved back. I didn't want to stand in line with the other Negroes. So I decided to pass, and I got in line with the whites. When I got to the front, Tommy Jr. winked, filled my sack with candy, and wouldn't take my money. But when I left the store, Jinx Franklin recognized me.

"Now, the Franklins had always spread around that they used to own Wood Place, before the Pinchards had swindled it from them. I don't know whether that was true or not, but I do know, they didn't like how Big Thom had put certain Negroes over them, and now Tommy Jr. was doing the same. The Franklins were angry that my sister, Pearl, and her family lived in what most white people in this town thought was a big, fancy house, when the Franklins were living in run-down cabins and sharecropping on Pinchard land.

"But I was a young knucklehead! I didn't care about those Franklins. And I didn't think anything could touch me. So when Jinx called my name and put a 'nigger' behind it, I was ready to fight! I pulled out my switchblade and turned around. When I came at him, he tripped and fell backward, and that quick, I was on top of him!"

"Aw, dang! You let him have it!" David raised his free hand and the old man hit it. They laughed with deep, male sounds.

"I sure did! I straddled him good! I had my switchblade in one hand and was punching him in the face with the other. But those Franklins never did fight fair, and in a minute, two of them pulled me off and yanked the knife out of my hand. Another tossed a rope up over a branch of that there pecan tree. I was biting and kicking, and then Olivia woke up, and she started screaming, and all the Negroes who'd been in the store scattered. It was chaos!"

Uncle Root spread his arms wide. Seconds passed.

"What happened?" David asked. "Don't stop there!"

The old man sighed. "Well. As I was saying my final prayers and preparing to meet my beloved mother in the afterlife, Tommy Jr. walked down those steps." He gestured to the rotting porch of the store.

"He was a tall man, but unlike our father, he was rail thin. He called out to those Franklins, 'What-all's going on here?'

"Jinx wiped the blood off his mouth, and said, 'This nigger jumped me.'

"And Tommy Jr. said, 'Looks like he did more than jumped you. Looks like he whipped your tail.'

"Jinx and the rest started grumbling about uppity, half-white niggers, and Tommy Jr. said, 'If you let that nigger get the best of you, that's your business, but if you kill him, then you in my business, because that there nigger is my brother, and everybody here knows it. Y'all Franklins better let him go, or you can pack all your belongings on that wagon, and your women and children, too, and get off my land by sundown, which is about three hours from now.' Then he walked back up those steps. I'm telling you that you could not hear those Franklins make a sound as they climbed back in their wagon.

"I went over and calmed Olivia, and we drove up to the house to see my family. When Tommy Jr. showed on Sunday to sit with Pearl on her porch like he always did, I told him I hadn't appreciated his calling me a nigger, but he said I would have appreciated swinging from that pecan tree even less, and he wasn't about to apologize. That's how my brother was. A savior one minute, and a white racist the next. I have to admit, he protected me that day from those Franklins. But they did not forget what my brother did. That family has a long memory."

He put a hand on David's shoulder.

"And my young brother, that's why you need to be very careful up at that liquor store, when you're getting Lonny to buy your wine."

My boyfriend looked down at his feet, and I squeezed his hand.

"I'm not judging you," the old man said. "I was young once. But I told you this story for a reason, because Jinx Franklin is Sheriff Franklin's daddy. That's the kind of brutal stock that man comes from. And I don't care how many years have passed; that man is just like his father. There are all kinds of stories out there about how that sheriff treats Negro men when he arrests them. Do you understand what I'm saying? Look at me, now. I'm not angry at you, my brother."

David raised his head. "Yes, sir, Dr. Hargrace. I understand."

"Good. Because this is a tiny town. Everybody knows everybody here. And that means that the sheriff knows who you are, and equally important, he knows who Ailey is. He knows Ailey is part of my family. That her granny lives in that house Big Thom built for my mother. Even now, Sheriff Franklin is one of the few in his family who made it out of poverty. You can't tell me that doesn't scrape him wrong. So I don't want either of you in danger. The both of you have to be careful. You hear?"

We nodded, and Uncle Root told us, all right, he was done lecturing.

"But you two young folks come with me. I want to show you one more thing."

David and I walked with him over to the pecan tree.

"You see here? See these cuts? These showed up a few days after the commotion at the store. Somebody tried to chop this tree down. We never found out who did it, and it never bore fruit again."

We stood there awhile longer, with Uncle Root patting the pecan tree and sighing. Then he told us we should drive on up to the house to visit my granny. Her feelings would be very hurt if David didn't stop by and speak.

AN ALTERED STORY

◈

"Let me have some more wine," I said.

"Uh-uh," David said. "It's your first time. Sip that slow. That Mad Dog is sneaky."

"Aw, give the girl some more," Boukie said. "She can handle it."

He poured more wine in my mason jar. Mr. Lonny hadn't bought the liquor; one of Boukie's older brothers had purchased it. That night, he was at the creek with David and me, and ready to celebrate. Boukie had passed summer school and could play basketball when the season came around. He wouldn't be left back again and twenty years old by the time he finished high school. I drank my wine and tried not to resent the intrusion as I stared at David, thinking of his kisses, his unashamed affection.

When David lit the joint, he held it away from me, but when Boukie's turn came, he filled his jaws with smoke. He pressed his lips against mine. I opened and took in the smoke.

David frowned. "Y'all need to stop tripping."

My head clouded, and I went to the Eldorado, climbing into the back seat. The boys got in the car, too, though in the front.

"Stay up in front here with me," David said.

"You scared?" Boukie asked. "You want me to sing you a lullaby, too?" He gave a long laugh; he was high.

"Just don't go back there, man."

"You want to go first? That's cool. Save some for me, though."

"I ain't playing with you, Boukie. You try to go back there, I'ma have to make some trouble."

There was a long silence, and I was glad. I wanted to sleep.

"So it's like that, Baybay? You done had yours, but now, I can't have mines?"

"Man, I ain't had nothing."

"Nigger, you ain't slick. I know what y'all been doing."

"I ain't lying, Boukie. That girl's a virgin."

"She don't act like it. She act like she want to give away some pussy. And I'm ready to take it."

"She high! She don't know what she want! And I ain't gone do her like that. That's my lady, man. I love her."

"You know what, Baybay? You just rude. That's what's wrong with you. You ain't got no manners. Now, one thing you can say about me: Boukie Crawford is a polite motherfucker."

He slammed the car door when he left. I listened for him to come back, but he didn't, so I slept until David shook my shoulder. It was almost curfew.

I pulled David to me, unzipping his pants, touching him. I urged him, go get the blanket, go get it right now, and he told me we had to go, but he left and returned with the blanket. Shortly, we were out of our clothing and underwear, but he maneuvered beside me. It was safer that way, he told me. He didn't have a rubber.

I moved against his thigh in slow, wet circles. Wrapped my fingers around him, squeezing.

"Come on, David. Let's do it. Let's do it right now."

"Oh, shit. Naw, girl. We gotta stop."

"Don't you want me?"

"You know I do. All the time. I can't stop thinking 'bout it."

"Then how come?"

"You promise you won't get mad?"

I stopped moving. "You have somebody else, don't you?"

"Uh-uh, I don't have nobody but you. I love you, girl. I love you so much. But I promised my granddaddy I wouldn't."

"How would Mr. J.W. know?"

"My granddaddy, he knows 'cause . . . I kind of, like . . . got a reputation. I been with a lot of girls. You mad, Ailey?"

I thought my first time would be his, too, but I could be understanding.

"No, that's okay. But, like, who was it?"

"None of your business. Stop being so nosy."

I took my hand away.

"Why are you acting like this?" Then I remembered that day when I'd asked Boukie about Rhonda. I thought further back, to that time the three of them had gone to the outhouse at Red Mound. "Oh my God! Rhonda? You and her?"

"Listen, listen—"

"You and Boukie both screwed her? So that's why he thought—"

"Ailey, not at the same time! I promise, sweetheart! I swear to God . . ." He began explaining rapidly. He'd been with Rhonda the previous summer, but she wasn't his girlfriend. Just somebody he was messing around with, and one night on the phone, she said she'd slept with Boukie, so she didn't want David anymore. And that had been fine with him, because he didn't want her, either.

But I screamed at him. I told him he could have that stank girl, if he wanted her. When I told him I had somebody back home in the City, and I bet he wouldn't turn me down when I wanted to fuck, David started weeping. He hugged his naked arms and talked through sobs. Please. He loved me. He was so sorry, please, but I kept putting on my clothes. I reminded him it was after curfew.

When he drove me back to the house, I told him, don't ever call me again. Don't come by my granny's house, either.

————

Uncle Root had taken over the center of the chessboard. One of my castles, both my knights, and half my pawns were gone.

"Go ahead and mate me," I said. "I need to get back."

"You have plans with David James?"

I made an ugly face. "No, I'm done with him. I told Miss Rose I would help her fill the preserve jars."

He leaned down, squinting at the board. Sighed, then captured my other rook.

"What happened, Ailey? I thought you two were thick as thieves. Was he not a gentleman? Am I going to have to beat him to within an inch of his life?"

"No, he was fine, I guess."

"And what about that other one? That Crawford fellow. There haven't been any fisticuffs between him and David James over you? Because it's clear you've evolved into quite the femme fatale."

He made a silly face.

"Uncle Root, don't make fun of me! I really loved David. I thought he was a nice guy, but he broke my heart."

"I'm so sorry. What did he do?"

This old man was my friend. My only friend now, but he was an adult. There was no way I could tell him what had happened out at the creek. That I'd been naked when David and I had our falling-out. There was no way I'd tell him about what happened with Gandee, either. That all this time, I'd broken my promise to everybody. I wasn't really a good girl. I never had been. I'd just pretended to make everybody else happy, and look where that had gotten me. I had a broken heart and I was still ashamed.

I moved a lonely pawn forward. "I don't want to talk about it, Uncle Root."

"All right, I won't pry. Would you like to hear about the time I met the great W. E. B. Du Bois?"

"I know this story already. You met him, he was an asshole, and he slammed the door in your face."

He lifted a finger. "But, Ailey, you haven't heard the rest!"

"Fine. But please make this quick."

"I will try. Now, Rob-Boy and I were standing there like the presumptuous young fools we were. Then, across the hall, another door opened and Dr. Du Bois's friend and assistant, Miss Jessie Fauset, came out."

I looked up from the board. "I know her!"

"Ailey, she's been dead over twenty years. You can't possibly know her."

"I meant Nana gave me one of her books to read."

"Really? From what your mother tells me, I had no idea the lady had such good taste. Which book?"

"*Plum Bun.*"

"Ah! That's my favorite one! So back to my story. Miss Fauset invited us inside her room and a young lady was sitting there. She was a history major at Spelman College—very precocious; only sixteen—and had walked over to meet the great scholar. She didn't say whether Dr. Du Bois had rebuffed her, too, but I suspected as much.

"Miss Fauset was taking tea. She'd already poured a cup for the young lady, and she left and came back with two other chairs and invited Rob-Boy and me to stay. After some wonderful conversation and some excellent cookies, we took our leave and began walking to the side street where Rob-Boy had parked. Yet across the yard, I heard the young lady calling, 'Mr. Freeman! Mr. Freeman!' I'd left my hat in Miss Fauset's room, and the young lady was waving it high.

"The three of us walked to the car, and Robert drove her back over to Spelman's campus. It was only a couple of blocks away, but already, we both were smitten with her. She'd memorized that entire page on double consciousness from *The Souls of Black Folk*! But I was more charming than Rob-Boy, if I do say so myself. I lied and told her I was a junior at Routledge and twenty, when I was a freshman and a year younger than she was. I found the nerve to ask permission to write her, and she consented. It was a three-year, long-distance relationship with no visits. After my third letter, I confessed my age. I was so afraid, but I didn't want to lie anymore. She was very angry with me for several months, but somehow we worked it out. After graduation, we enrolled in graduate school up in the City at Mecca University. We truly were kids, but we knew what we wanted. And we married."

"The young lady was Aunt Olivia?"

"Correct. Olivia Ellen Hargrace. The best woman in the world, after my mother. And that's why I took her last name."

"Okay . . . but what does any of this have to do with David?"

"Well, Olivia forgave me, in my youthful foolishness. Do you think you could do that with David James?"

"Why are you being so nosy? Did he say something to you?"

"Ailey, I can neither confirm nor deny that."

"But you're my uncle, not his! And I thought we were best buddies!"

"Wait a minute. Don't get your pressure up. Let me explain."

"I gotta go. Take me back to the farm—"

"No, no, please listen. Give me a chance."

I sighed. Leaned back on the sofa and folded my arms. "Fine, Uncle Root."

"Thank you. Now, you are indeed correct. Despite the difference in our ages, you are my closest and dearest friend. I adore you to the moon and back, but I'm a man of honor, Ailey Pearl. And just as I would never betray your confidences, I cannot betray Brother David's. I can tell you, however, that he has never said anything negative about you. Whenever he speaks your name, it is always with sincere reverence and affection. I hope that reassures you."

"Whatever. I don't care what he has to say anyway."

"I'm sure you don't." He looked at the chessboard. "Lord, child, that's checkmate again! You have to learn to protect your queen! Let's start over and see if I can school you before I take you back to the country."

"But, Uncle Root—"

He held up a hand. "No, sugarfoot. Your granny's preserves can wait. Mastering chess cannot."

SONG

Why Women Are Strong

Back when her name had been "Beauty," Aggie's grandmother had told her men were stronger than women, save one exception: women's times of bleeding. Helen had said in the moon house women bled and watched the fire. They talked together. They sang together and told stories. To men, this place was a curse. Blood was a curse. A smelly stain on the thighs of the weak. Yet women knew the power of dark jewels. That the moon house was not for the cursed and the weak but for the strong and the blessed.

Helen explained, their power was why women had to stay away from men during their bleedings. Though Helen had been a Christian, the old Creek lore had been passed down to her and she knew a story of a great Creek warrior. This warrior had ridden his horse so fast, to regard him was like trying to catch lightning. His clan had been powerful and undefeated, and the men that they conquered in battle, they had insulted by comparing them to women.

The warrior was very careful about who cooked and served his food, too, and came within his reach. He had several wives that he insisted live far apart, so that they would not bleed together; thus, he was never in the range of a woman "on her moon." Yet one evening, a young maiden from an enemy village sneaked into this warrior's village. This maiden was in her bleeding time, and instead of sleeping and living in a moon house, she was freely walking about. Thus, when she walked around the undefeated warrior's hut, she touched the walls. At the cooking pit in front of his hut, she waited until the other women's backs were turned and stirred the pots. That night, when the warrior called for a woman to warm him, the maiden volunteered. As the maiden and warrior kissed, she whispered that she had a surprise for him. When she disrobed and he saw the blood on her thighs, he yelled and reached for his knife. The warrior easily killed the maiden, but by then, it was too late.

The next time the warrior rode into battle, his clan was defeated, and the time after that, the warrior was killed.

How Aggie Was Brought to the Moon House

One day, as Aggie was headed to the fields with her chopping hoe, Carson Franklin stopped her. He was the son of Aidan, the white man who had moved his family to the shadow of the mound many years before. Carson still lived on that same land on which his own sons still could not make cotton grow.

Carson was the overseer, in charge of the Quarters-folks working in the field. He told Aggie he needed her to walk with him to the moon house. And Aggie was afraid, as she had heard from women in the Quarters that Carson had dragged them to the moon house and attempted to ravish them, but he proved incapable. And when Carson was unable to rouse himself with these slave women, he beat them instead.

Ordinarily, the moon house was unused: it was off-limits to the Negresses on the farm. Aggie had seen them abashed as their bleeding began. They ran from the fields with red stains on their skirts. These embarrassing moments had happened to Aggie as well. This farm was not like the place where her mother and father and grandparents had lived, where bleeding women, including Aggie and Kiné, were allowed their privacy and sacred space. As a tiny girl, Aggie had stayed at this small cabin with Kiné, until she was old enough to leave her mother's breast and be cared for by Helen. When Aggie had entered the cabin because of her own blood, Kiné and she had stayed there together again. It had been a precious time, just the two of them.

The day Carson told her to follow him, Aggie walked behind him at a distance, praying that he would not try to hurt her. They walked across the fields and deeper into the woods. When they came upon the moon house, Aggie tensed, but Carson seemed nervous as he told her go on inside. Go on, now. Then he walked away.

When Aggie knocked on the door, Lady answered and, with

blushes and shy words, told Aggie she had begun her first bleeding time. She was fourteen—this was the era when girls did not bleed as early as they would in future times. Aggie had never spoken to the girl with whom she was expected to keep company. The first interval that Aggie stayed in the moon house with her, there was silence between them, as she and the girl shared the tasks of cooking simple stews from the supplies that had been left for them in the yard. Thankfully, Lady did not expect Aggie to attend to washing her soiled undergarments: she shook her head bashfully when asked. And Aggie was grateful for the break from field work. She didn't ask Lady how she had been chosen to keep her company.

By the fourth set of days together in the moon house, there was greater ease. And something else: Aggie's own cycle had synced with Lady's. That month, she followed the girl behind the cabin to the space where the two special buckets were. She waited for Lady to finish washing her women's rags, to spill the pink water to the ground, and then stick her hands in the other bucket to wash herself clean with clear water. Then Aggie held out her hands for both buckets, so that she could fill them with water for her own washing. She and Lady exchanged a smile. That evening, they told stories to each other, tales of animals that talked. Lady gave a small "Ah!" when Aggie confided that her father had been the son of two Creek mestizos. When Lady confided that her father and mother were mestizos, Aggie remembered Pop George's words: she did not want to anger this girl and feel the whip's fire. And so Aggie did not say, not only was Lady's father part Creek, he was part Negro, too.

That month, after Aggie took her final, cleansing bath and returned to the field, Carson Franklin told her she no longer would work in the cotton. Now she would work alongside Pop George, looking after the children who had not yet lost their front milk teeth. Within a year, Aggie and Pop George would share their own two-room cabin, which sat a hundred steps from the larger cabin of their master, and Aggie would treat the man as her father. Some of the Quarters-folks began to refer to Aggie as a "yard nigger," but after Pop George scolded them, they stopped. After all, Aggie tended to their children and loved them as her own—see how she gave the children hugs and kisses? Won't nothing to be mad at Aggie 'bout, Pop George said. And the Quarters-folks deferred to him, as he was their elder. They were kind to Aggie, and in time, they came to respect her greatly.

The Kitchen House

Two years had passed since Aggie had come to the farm, and as with each cotton harvest before it, changes were made at Wood Place.

Samuel Pinchard charged his overseer with finding Quarters-men to cut down remaining trees on the new portions of land he had acquired. He had bought farms bordering Wood Place from yeoman farmers, those who had cleared some of their land on their own already to plant crops, but who hadn't been able to make their land profitable. Samuel gave them pennies on the dollar for each acre.

Samuel was planning to build a grand structure with the trees the Quarters-men cut down, what he would call his "big house," even as, like other slaveholders, he would stand aside while the Quarters-men did the building. In the future, Samuel would talk about the house he had "built," as though he had labored alongside those dark men, straining his own muscles. It was slow-going work for the Quarters-men, transporting the pine trees, cutting the trees into planks, and sanding the planks smooth. Samuel wanted his big house to be perfect. That would take some time, but in the interval he had the men build a kitchen structure two dozen feet away from the future back of the big house. The kitchen needed to be close enough that his own food still would be warm when brought to him, but far enough away so that if the kitchen caught fire—as many kitchens did in those days—the flames would not spread to the big house.

Yet there was no cook except Lady, not yet, and no children for Lady, either. In the moon house, she confided to Aggie that her husband did not sleep in the double-rope bed Micco had given them as a wedding gift. Samuel either slept on a pallet in their cabin's front room, or elsewhere on one of his nighttime journeys.

The year of the building, Samuel walked around his property, smiling and waving at the Quarters-folks. They smiled back and dipped their heads submissively, though they did not like him: he was a white man and the owner of slaves. Nor did they trust him. And when his mood changed, the Quarters-folks told each other, see there? For on those days, Samuel's face would register great misery. He would straddle his horse and ride off. In a day or two, he would return in a jocular mood. He brought rock candy and passed it out to the children. He thanked the Quarters-folks for their labor, and Aggie began watching him for signs of drink. She remembered similar behavior with her father, when Paul would dive into his cups. She was afraid that Samuel might sell the plantation or gamble it away. And then the family that she had cobbled together—Pop George, the children, and all the Quarters-folks—would be lost again, and misery would descend.

And besides Aggie's own selfish interests, she worried about the others of her community. There were now thirty-two Negroes on Wood Place, and there was at least one baby born each year. The welcoming of new life should have been a joy, but the enslaved mothers were anxious. Though Aggie had not birthed her own children, she worried, too, about those children that she and Pop George tended and loved. At each new year, for January first was the time of settling debts. If Samuel Pinchard was reckless, this would be the time of selling slaves. Families would be split up. Children might be sold from their parents, as had happened when Kiné was sent over the water.

In June of Aggie's second year at Wood Place, the kitchen house was finished, and in July, a trader's wagon pulled up to the farm. He was not the same trader who had brought Aggie to Wood Place; word had traveled that this trader was now dead.

It was not January, so who was Samuel planning to sell? And why? Aggie's mind flipped through the Quarters-folks but could not locate whom Samuel might discard. Then she saw a woman hop down from the back of the wagon. Samuel appeared in the yard, counted over money to the trader, and cheerfully waved the Negress into the new kitchen house.

The next morning, Pop George told Aggie that the woman's name was Tut, and she had been purchased as the cook. Not only that, the woman required a child to work as her kitchen help. At midday, Carson Franklin was quiet. Usually he stalked the fields, calling out to those folks he didn't feel were spry enough in their labors. He carried a whip coiled by his hip but did not use it. Samuel had instructed him never to whip the Quarters-folks; Carson could slap them with an open hand, though not strike with a fist. Carson liked to yell at the folks. Don't waste no sunlight, he would shout. However, this day, he walked from the fields with Mamie, a very thin, lovely girl who had been purchased the previous new year.

Mamie was an odd child: in the evenings, after her labor had been through in the cotton fields, she would walk to a particularly large pecan tree, sit underneath the tree, and conduct conversations. However, Mamie's sweet nature and her beauty had brought her acceptance in the Quarters, even with her strange ways. Such a child needed care, not ridicule. Though she was old enough to work the field, Aggie in particular had shown the child special treatment. They both were motherless and shared a terrible kinship.

When Aggie and Pop George saw the overseer with Mamie, they sat up in their chairs. They exchanged glances, but thankfully, Carson was not walking in the direction of the woods where the moon house was located. Instead, he walked Mamie toward the kitchen house. That evening, when her young charges were back at their parents' cabins, Aggie headed to the kitchen house and peeked through the new glass windows. She saw Mamie sitting at the pine table, peeling potatoes. She returned to Pop George and reported what she had seen. This is how everyone in the Quarters found out that Mamie was the new cook's assistant.

Within a matter of days, there was a disturbance: screams tearing through the night from the kitchen house. Aggie would not hear these screams, as it was her woman's interval and Lady and she were in the moon house. Yet upon her return, Pop George reported that Mamie insisted a monster had come into the kitchen house. The monster covered her mouth in the night, trying to steal her breath. However, when Aggie consulted the new cook that Samuel had purchased—the woman named Tut—the woman was unconcerned. She insisted Mamie was only having nightmares.

Thus, Aggie forgot the child's stories of monsters, aided by the fact that she had fallen love with a man of the fields.

The Courting of Aggie

When Aggie first met Midas, she was not impressed. Though he had the pretty dark-dark color of Aggie's mother, he was short and skinny, with an abundance of hair that wasn't groomed frequently, so that it congregated in rowdy clumps.

Aggie ignored Midas when he waved at her during his midday break, when she and the children pushed the babies out to the fields in a wheelbarrow so their mothers could nurse them. In the evenings, Midas sat in the back of the group of children and listened to Pop George's stories. Midas seemed to enjoy the tales more than the children and laughed and clapped his hands. On Sundays after supper, Midas was forward: he walked to the cabin door to pay his respects to Aggie. He smiled, even when Aggie told him she didn't have no time for him. When she shut the door in his face, Pop George would chide, why ain't she let the boy have a few words? Midas won't tryna hurt nobody, but Aggie would suck her teeth and move to tend to her pot of greens. Pop George worked around her, though, for, after a few weeks of rebuffs, the next time Midas showed, Pop George called a welcome from inside the cabin. Come on in, he hailed Midas. Don't be standing in the door, like he won't raised right.

Aggie continued to frown at Midas when he stopped by the cabin, but she began to look forward to seeing him. From eavesdropping on his talks with Pop George, one Sunday evening, she learned that Midas's mother had been stolen over the water. Though Midas

had been sold away from her at the age of ten or eleven—he didn't
rightly know his age—he remembered that his mother had wanted
hot peppers with every meal, even breakfast, and Aggie hid a smile,
for Pop George could never get enough of hot and spicy meals. And
Midas knew from his mother's stories that her father had been a
man whose job it was to remember the history of a single family in
their village, going back for hundreds of years. Midas didn't know
what that kind of man was called, until Pop George chimed in, saying, over in Africa, they called that a "griot." And such a man shole
was mighty and great. As Aggie sat there, listening to Midas and
Pop George talk, she remembered that her mother's grandfather
had been called a "marabout," which Kiné had told her was somebody who had power of Spirit. More than a preacher. A man who
knew about medicines and roots and plants and things in the air
that couldn't be seen, but still existed. An important man. A man
with power, and now she knew that one of Midas's folks had been
important and powerful, too.

That was the evening that she tapped Midas on his shoulder to
alert him, do not be startled, and then, as he continued talking, Aggie began to drip almond oil from the bottle Lady had given her
as a gift. Aggie rubbed the oil into Midas's scalp, gently separating
the clumps of his hair, while he halted talking, attempting to remember his thoughts. Pop George laughed and told him, take his
time, lil' brother, and the next Sunday, Pop George said he was
an old man. He needed his rest, so he was gwan lay down. Midas
turned to leave, but Aggie called, sit on back down. She pointed to
the braided rug that covered the dirt floor. She pulled out a chair
and settled behind Midas, until his head was between her knees.
She rubbed more oil into his hair. Then, with her nails, she carefully
traced patterns and braided his hair like rows of corn.

Two more Sundays: each of those visits, Pop George said his
rheumatism was acting up. He would lie down some more, though
he walked to the next room as smoothly as before. On the third Sunday, Aggie was no longer present at the cabin, as it was her woman's
seclusion in the moon house. Yet on the fourth Sunday, Midas did

not remark on her absence, and she was glad that he knew that matters of the moon house were not to be discussed with men. Eleven
Sundays went by, and on the twelfth, Midas appeared at the cabin
with a battered hat on his neatly braided head. He pulled off the hat
and asked Aggie to marry him, and Pop George clapped his hands,
saying it was about time. He was ready for some grandbabies.

"Ain't gwan be none of that," Aggie said. "I'ont want no chirren."

Her frown was deep, though it softened when Midas told her
whatever she wanted was fine by him. She and Pop George was all
the family he needed. And he shole wanted her to braid his hair and
scratch his dander, too. He smiled, offering his hand, and when Aggie took it, Midas lifted her fingers to his lips.

Bad Dreams in the Night

Midas was a good listener to Aggie, after he moved into the two-
room cabin she shared with Pop George. Even when she did not
talk, Midas listened to her body, as they slept on the corn-shuck-
filled mattress ticking in the front room. On her sad days, when she
thought of her mother and father, Aggie's feelings would wash over
her. She would reach out to Midas to keep from heeding the call of
the knife she used to cut vegetables and salt pork, to avoid unsealing
the seams of her body. Midas seemed to know when these times
came upon her. After they jumped the broom, he tolerated her lack
of outward affection. He told her he knew how she felt inside.

Yet even Midas's goodness could not keep the truth of the plantation from showing its evil side.

It is said that someplace on this earth there is a god whose face is
made of the sun and the moon, and that this god can see everything
during the light and everything during the dark. Humans are not
like gods, all-seeing and all-understanding. They do not see what
others see. A human has a side that is blind. But the purpose of a god
is benevolence. And at times, a divine being will share knowledge
with a human, out of mercy or sheer whimsy. The night the Ninki
Nanka revealed itself to Aggie was one of these times, when the

moon was a mere slice in the sky. When a voice woke her from her sleep.

It was her mother's voice, and whenever a well-behaved child hears her mother's voice, she must answer, so Aggie did.

"Mama?"

She did not know whether she was asleep or awake when she rolled from the bed and lifted Midas's arm. She was barefoot, and she lit the lantern—another gift from Lady—and opened her cabin door. Taking a long stick from the woodpile outside, she began walking, both hands occupied. When she felt lost—for, even though she knew the farm, it was foreign in the dark—the voice that sounded like her mother would keep calling. She walked until she heard the shrill sounds of a child screaming, overridden by the howls of a beast. At first these sounds were faint, but as Aggie walked closer to the creek, they became louder.

Her mother's voice urged her on, like a grip on her arm or a push on her back. At the creek there was a horse tied to a tree. The animal was chuffing in distress. And there, on the grassy bank, the monster's body covered a screaming child. The monster's scales were gone and only its pale skin was left. Aggie put down her lantern so she could grip the long stick in her hand. She approached the back of the Ninki Nanka and began to hit its body until it wailed in pain. She kicked the monster, and it finally fell off the child, then she told the child, run, run. The child did not run, however, only crouched nearby. Yet the monster heeded Aggie's words, and as it ran past the lantern, she saw it was only a man: her master, Samuel Pinchard. He ran naked to the horse, put a foot in the stirrup, and climbed onto the saddle.

Aggie walked to the lantern and picked it up, then went back to the child, who was naked, too. Aggie lifted the lantern, and as the light cast its godly benediction, she saw the child was Mamie.

"Come here, lil' sister," Aggie called. "I ain't gwan hurt you. Come here, baby."

Mamie crawled to her and grabbed on, whimpering. Aggie took off her shawl and wrapped the child in it and they sat together on the grass. They stayed at the creek until the rooster in the barn far away made its urging crow. For several days that followed, she gave her responsibility for the Quarters-children to Pop George, in order to care for Mamie. No one saw Samuel during those days, though Pop George asked everyone about him. And Aggie pondered the stories of her mother, about the creatures that her African grandmother had told Kiné of, in a courtyard, long ago. Were there truly supernatural monsters stalking the water? Or were these monsters only white men who walked on two legs, abominations but not strangers? Only dangerous because they were familiar—in one's home, in one's temple, on the dirt of natal land?

I V

The Negro race, like all races, is going to be saved by its exceptional men. The problem of education, then, among Negroes must first of all deal with the Talented Tenth; it is the problem of developing the Best of this race that they may guide the Mass away from the contamination and death of the Worst, in their own and other races. Now the training of men is a difficult and intricate task. Its technique is a matter for educational experts, but its object is for the vision of seers.

—W. E. B. Du Bois, "The Talented Tenth"

You misjudge us because you do not know us.

—W. E. B. Du Bois, "The Talented Tenth"

BROTHER-MAN MAGIC

◈

After I returned to the City, the old man would call me every Sunday. He tried to keep his peace, but when winter came, he began throwing hints about David, that he had asked about me. Maybe I wanted to give the young man a call.

I was too embarrassed to confess that David had mailed me letters and cards for two months that fall, asking me for a second chance. And I'd been planning to forgive him—after making him suffer a sufficient amount of time—until I received David's very last letter in October. In it he confessed, he knew his cause was pointless. He still loved me, but he'd started dating another girl. Her name was Carla Jackson, she was real nice, and David hoped he and I would always be friends.

And so I reconciled with Chris Tate instead, who'd been looking pitiful in the hallways at school. He'd call my house, pretending to ask for homework, and when my mother hung up on her end, he'd beg me to get back together. He hadn't been seeing anybody else. He promised. In November, we returned to our regular spot behind the lower school.

Chris was a good kisser, but his other idea of romance was to grab my breast with one hand and pump it, as if seeking pasteurized, whole milk. He'd pull my hand and place on the front of his jeans.

"Touch it, Ailey."

"No. You don't deserve it."

"Please. I'll take you to the movies."

I nudged him away. "That's not the logical order of things. First you make me your girlfriend. Then you take me to the movies. Then I jerk you off."

"I thought you were my girlfriend. I asked you two weeks ago, and you said yes."

"But it doesn't count if no one else knows. And what about my mama? You know she's crazy."

He put my hand back to his fly, telling me, let him take care of that. If there was anything he knew how to do, it was how to handle a mother.

That evening, my mother knocked on my door. "Ailey, I just had a strange conversation. It was that boy that calls for homework all the time. Chris Tate?"

My chest clutched, but I kept my voice casual. "He called you for homework?"

"No, baby, of course not. But I think that boy has a crush on you."

"What? No. Uh-uh."

"Something's going on when he takes twenty minutes of his telling me how pretty and nice you are, but that you won't pay him any attention."

"No, I won't, because he's gross! And, like, super slow."

"Don't be mean, baby. Boys sometimes lag way behind, but they catch up. That's a natural fact."

She sat down on the bed. "Ailey, please don't be mad, but I invited him over for dinner on Sunday."

"Oh my God! Oh Jesus." I hoped my acting skills were holding up.

"Give the boy a chance. He can't be that homely, and you're old enough to keep company. Date. Go out. Whatever you young folks call it. And it's not like you've got that many options at school with nothing but white boys. Though you know I'm not prejudiced."

"Sure you're not, Mama."

On Sunday, Chris showed with a bouquet of red Gerbera daisies for my mother. He wore khakis, a white dress shirt, a blue blazer, and a red tie. He was polite, shaking my father's hand, and he listened to the stories of my aunt and mother. Chris's table manners were flawless; I saw Nana watch him with grudging approval as he took small bites and used his cutlery properly. He'd even rested his fork on his plate at meal's end.

I sat at the other end of the table and produced my most obnoxious behavior. I rolled my eyes and sighed loudly at intervals. When

I went in the kitchen to help my mother with dessert, she told me, stop being so rude. Chris was good-looking and his father was a doctor. I could do worse. And see how he'd thanked her for the wonderful meal?

"I've got a feeling if you gave him a chance, you might actually like him."

"As if," I said.

When it was time for Chris to leave, my mother produced a sweet potato pie, wrapped in aluminum foil. She told him it was for his mother, and she invited him back the next Sunday, discreetly pinching my back when I protested. The next time he called for "homework," she knocked on the door, grinning.

"It's your man."

"Ew, Mama. Please."

There were more Sunday dinners, where I made a show of warming to Chris, as my mother watched beaming. I followed her into the kitchen, carrying dirty dishes, and she urged me, go sit on the couch with the boy. Talk to him. He sure was good-looking, wasn't he?

During Christmas vacation, she suggested that Chris take me to a Saturday matinee. Wouldn't that be nice? After she called Mrs. Tate, of course. And examined Chris's insurance papers and driver's license, and the mechanic's report for his used BMW. My father was at the hospital working, but he would want to know she'd checked everything thoroughly. Chris told her he would go out to the car and get the paperwork. When he shut the front door, Mama told me, don't tell her she didn't have good taste in men.

When Chris collected me that Saturday, I told him we really had to watch the movie. My mother would be expecting a detailed description of the plot. But I'd brought an old jacket with me, and I draped it over his lap during the show and slipped my hands inside his pants.

By spring break, Mama trusted Chris enough to drive me to the City library for a study session, but instead, that morning, he and I headed to the Planned Parenthood clinic. He'd been begging for sex ever since Christmas, and I wanted it as much as he did, even as clueless as he was about the female body. I was sixteen and about to explode, but I didn't want to get pregnant. And I didn't trust Chris with taking complete responsibility for birth control.

At the clinic, I was afraid I'd be ashamed, but the receptionist treated me politely, not as if I should be worried that she would call the fake phone number I gave her and report me as a whore to whatever stranger answered. When my name was called, there were pleasant crinkles around my nurse's blue eyes. In the exam room, she asked, had I ever been sexually active?

I hesitated, thinking of Gandee. "I'm not sure. Nobody's been inside there, though."

"Let's call that a 'no,' then."

She talked me through the pelvic exam, stopping when I flinched. "You're doing great, Ailey. I know this isn't fun."

"Sure it is."

"Then you're the first woman in the history of the universe who enjoys this. I hate mine. I always have pepperoni pizza afterward."

I lifted on my elbow. "You get these, too?"

"Every woman does. Or she should."

"Geez."

"That pizza's sounding pretty good right about now, isn't it? Okay, lie back down. I'm going to do the anal exam. Here we go."

"Ouch!"

"I know, honey. Just a few more seconds. You're very, very brave."

When I limped to the lobby, brandishing my packet of birth control, Chris did a victory dance. In the car, he was all over me.

"Don't get too excited," I said. "I've got to wait awhile for these pills to kick in."

He reached into his jacket pocket and pulled out a handful of the colorful free condoms the clinic offered.

"Damn, Chris, did you leave any for the other people?"

"They had their chance. You snooze, you lose."

"Okay, but let's stop at the pharmacy. I want to get some of that jelly stuff."

"These have the spermicide on them. I checked. I'll be careful. I promise."

Chris's mother was away until that evening, so his house was empty. I wanted things to be special, suggesting a picnic, but inside, he wedged me against the kitchen counter, fumbling with the front of my jeans. When he couldn't find his way past the zipper, he gave up and grabbed at my crotch. I sighed and told him, sure. He led me upstairs, squeezing my hand. On his bed, he pulled at my jeans, repeating how much he loved me, then fumbled with the condom. When he lay on me, he grabbed at my crotch again, searching, while I told him that wasn't it. That was the wrong hole. Finally, he found the proper place, and there were thirteen seconds of incredibly painful pressure, as if I had to make a bowel movement but couldn't.

He kissed the side of my face and told me again that he loved me.

"What do you mean?" I asked. "Is it over?"

His face was hidden in my neck, but he nodded. His breath deepened and he went to sleep on me. I wanted to kick him in his exhausted balls. He didn't remember that he was supposed to hold on to the condom afterward, either. It had slipped off inside me, and I ran to the bathroom when he turned over, deep in sleep. I squatted and snagged the condom with my fingernail, wrinkling my nose at the mess.

A few days before this disgusting moment, Mama had conducted the sex talk with me. She wasn't accusing me of anything, she'd said. She only wanted to talk, because I was a young lady, and I needed to know a few things. Such as, prayer wasn't an effective form of birth control. It had seemed a silly statement, and I'd laughed at her seriousness. But it hit me what she meant when my period was four days late. During that time, I sat on the toilet at least ten times a day, waiting for blood, and asking God to spare me, this once.

After that, every time Chris and I were together, I withstood his awkwardness, telling him, don't squeeze my breasts like that, and I needed more than a few seconds of kissing to get ready. And I thought of David, how I hadn't been able to wait for him to touch me. How he'd been so gentle, and I'd been the one to pull him to me whenever we were alone. But David had a new girlfriend. She was receiving his tenderness.

Chris and I were a couple, though. My patience had won out. Instead of Mama dropping me off at school, Chris picked me up each morning, that fall of our senior year. My dream of us walking though the hallways was fulfilled, and before we headed to our respective classes, he kissed me and strutted off. We even planned to attend college together, down south. I'd convinced him to apply to Routledge College, giving him a list of distinguished alumni. There were plenty of physicians, too, in case Chris wanted to study pre-med. When Mama suggested I apply to Harvard or Yale, I told her there was no way I was spending another four years surrounded by honkies. And I didn't want to attend Mecca, either. What kind of adulthood apprenticeship would that be, living at home with my parents? She told me, all right, I was her baby, but she knew I would be safe in Georgia. I'd only be a few miles up the road from Uncle Root.

We avoided talk of my sister, how she'd attended Routledge, too. In two years, we hadn't heard from Lydia. No phone calls, no letters. I'd matured enough to know mentioning her name would only cause my mother grief. But I'd go into Coco's room, where Lydia had moved to escape me. I'd close the door and take down a box of my sister's belongings and go through her keepsakes from college: Smiling photos of her with her friends. Graded assignments that Lydia had saved with her professor's complimentary comments written in red ink. I pulled her Beta Alpha Beta orange-and-white sorority jacket off the hanger. I put it on and rubbed my hands along the sleeves. I'd decided I wanted to pledge Beta, too; it would bring me closer to Lydia, even if I didn't know where she was now.

In April of senior year, a large blue-and-gold envelope came in the mail, addressed to "Miss Ailey P. Garfield." On the front, an encircled heart. A motto curved at the top and bottom: "My Whole Heart for the Lord."

Inside the envelope, a letter stating that Routledge College was delighted to accept me to the class of 1995. On a separate sheet, a list of what the college deemed as "necessary" items: notebooks, typewriter or word processor, ballpoint pens, towels, twin sheets, twin mattress pad, twin comforter. Finally, there was a list of required clothing for female students, such as, I needed to bring "appropriately modest attire for everyday wear," a formal gown, a semiformal gown, dark heels, and at least one dress suitable for mandatory chapel, also "appropriately modest."

"What kind of sexist crap is this?" I asked.

Mama cackled. "I hope you enjoy spending four years in the late nineteenth century. Get your mind right, because if you think President Bush is conservative, you ain't seen nothing till you go to Routledge." She and I were in my father's office, sitting on the dilapidated leather couch, folding laundry. Daddy was in the roller chair, holding his empty pipe.

"Don't scare the child," he said. "Our alma mater isn't so bad. I have very fond memories, particularly of February 1966. Yes, indeed."

"Stop being naughty in front of the baby," she said. "And when we were there, it was the women they bothered. The men could do whatever they wanted. Routledge hasn't changed that 'appropriately modest' shit since we went there."

"And what's chapel?" I asked. "And why do I need a dress for it?"

"Chapel is church, baby," she said.

"But I'm an atheist. That's why I don't go to church."

"No, you're not. You're just too lazy to get up on Sunday. There are no Black atheists."

"That's not true, Mama."

"All right, then, name me one, since there're so many."

When I looked to my father, he shook his head so slightly, I almost missed it. It was a marital pact, his pretending a devout, religious belief and my mother pretending he wasn't a fraud.

"See, Ailey, you can't name even one," she said.

"I could if this wasn't a Christian Negro pop quiz."

"Watch that tone, Ailey Pearl. Remain graceful in defeat."

———

My final rendezvous with Chris occurred on the floor of his basement, the week before high school graduation. He lay on top of me,
drowsy, and told me he was going to miss me so much. I kissed
him, saying that was all right. The summer was only two months,
but after all, we'd see each other in the fall. And after our first year
of college, maybe we could get an apartment together.

That's when Chris told me he wasn't going to Routledge. He'd
been accepted to Princeton.

I shifted my hips, pushing him off. "You didn't tell me you were
applying to other schools. Did you even send an application to Routledge?"

"Ailey, I'm sorry. But my dad went to Princeton. He was expecting me to go."

"So what are we supposed to do now?"

"I don't know. Maybe . . . we should break up?"

I shifted to face him. "What?"

"I mean, I don't really know if I can do long-distance."

"You couldn't tell me this before you got laid?"

"I guess . . . I wanted us to have a good time. You know, one last
time."

"Negro, give me a break! You came in, like, seventy-seven seconds! You're the worst lay ever."

"You don't have to be so mean, Ailey."

"You're the one who fucked me and then dumped me! You lying
asshole!"

I kept my voice down so Mrs. Tate wouldn't hear me through the
vents. That way, she could pretend she didn't know that, instead of
listening to CDs on the stereo, we had sex on her basement floor.
And sometimes on top of her washing machine.

For weeks afterward, I was huffy with Mama, though I didn't
inform her of my breakup with Chris. I'd manipulated her into approving of my relationship with Chris, but somehow I was angry
at her, as if it were actually her fault that I'd been with him. I
blamed her for his bad behavior. If she'd had one of her dreams

about Chris, he wouldn't have made a fool of me. But she didn't fuss at me or tell me to mind my home training. She didn't ask about the whereabouts of Chris, only offering at dinner that being a young person was so hard. We were alone at the table, the night before our Chicasetta journey. She went to the kitchen and brought out a huge slice of pie, setting it before me. Then she poured me a full cup of coffee and topped it off with cream. I was a young woman, she told me. I'd probably done all of my growing.

The next morning, the back of the station wagon was packed to capacity, with my new comforter and pillows for my dorm room, and sacks full of granola bars and tiny boxes of raisins. Most of my books would occupy Uncle Root's downstairs library. Mama asked, had I remembered to pack my birth control pills? Because she wasn't raising any more children.

"I don't know what you're talking about. I'm not even sexually active."

She released huffs of laughter. "Child, please. I found those pills three months ago."

I was so embarrassed, I didn't speak for an hour after we began our drive. She let me listen to National Public Radio instead of her Aretha mixtape, and she didn't keep talking when I pulled out a book. But then we passed the Peach Butt in South Carolina, and the old excitement hit me. I put aside my reading, and she told unedited versions of stories I'd heard as a little girl. We gossiped about relatives in Chicasetta: that Uncle Norman never had been married twice; that fiction had been created to explain my cousin Lee Curtis, who was an "outside" child. When Aunt Barbara-Pam had learned of L.C.'s existence, she'd shown up to the mistress's house and shouted through the door, threatening to cut her throat. For a fortnight, until my uncle received his paycheck from his second job, he'd worn the clothes his wife had ruined with splatters of bleach.

At the turnoff on Highway 441, Mama turned in the direction of Madison. She pulled into the gas station, and when she finished pumping, she knocked on my window and asked, did I want to drive? It was mostly open road from there on, she said, and I had my driver's license, so unless I did something stupid, I wouldn't kill us. We weren't in the old station wagon anymore. It finally had died, back in March. My mother had cried a week over her car, then dried her tears and bought a used Volvo, identical to my aunt's.

When I drove up to the house off County Line Road, I was proud. My elders gave looks of surprise when I opened the driver's door. Uncle Root came out into the yard to hug me, and I missed the days when he had carried me in his arms.

That summer, my mother joined me in Chicasetta. She had taught my father to make his own breakfast: a bowl of oatmeal with skim milk and one patty of her homemade turkey sausage. And she had frozen his dinners. He would be fine for eight weeks.

Sitting on my granny's porch, peeling tomatoes and peaches, I bristled at the circle of elders. They asked me what ailed me, but I didn't tell them I was lonely. Even Boukie would have been welcome company. The summer before my senior year, he'd shown at my granny's house; to my surprise, Boukie had apologized for his behavior that night at the creek. He shouldn't have tried to do me wrong. And he informed me he'd started attending Mt. Calvary every Sunday.

But now Boukie was a settled man. He and Rhonda were living together and expecting a baby. As for David, he had an internship with a law firm in Atlanta and shared an apartment with two other students at Morehouse. And my granny told me he and that girl were still keeping company. David appeared at the family reunion, though, heading to the picnic table where the old man and I sat.

David was friendly with me, asking, how was I doing? And was I excited for college? I refused to answer his overtures, remembering how he'd moved on from me after pretending to be so in love. I was hoping he would leave the reunion, but he stayed. He and the old man talked and laughed, hitting the table in their mirth, while I sulked at their brother-man magic.

When Uncle Root rose, and said it was time for the three of us to visit his pecan tree, I told him I didn't feel like it. I wasn't finished with my barbecue. The two of them could go ahead without me.

WE SING YOUR PRAISES HIGH

◈

At the age of fifteen, Uncle Root had enrolled in Routledge College because he'd had no other choice for education in his town: the segregated school for Negroes at Red Mound Church only had gone to eighth grade. This was the excuse Big Thom gave him, at least, but truly his third child had confounded his white father.

First off, the boy was mean: he barely spoke to Big Thom, and when he did, it was only to ask for money. And Uncle Root had been discovered naked in the bushes with Negro girls (who also were naked). It was a good thing Uncle Root was a fast runner; otherwise, he would have caught more than one beating from an angry father. More than that, it was only dumb luck nobody had gotten pregnant. And Uncle Root was getting into fights with white boys, too, taunting them with big words. His father was constantly having to pass out cash and threats to keep his Negro son alive.

So Big Thom sent Uncle Root up the road to Routledge College, where his love of books was nurtured. There, in a history class taught by a tall, thin man, the boy read *The Souls of Black Folk* for the first time.

"Do you have any more books by that Du Bois fellow?" he asked.

"A few," his professor told him. "But be careful with them."

Though only teenagers when they met, Aunt Olivia had calmed Uncle Root down. After they graduated college, they traveled together to the City for graduate school. There, they married young. Study calmed Uncle Root further, and he was a dedicated student at Mecca University. He finished his master's and doctorate in history in record time. It had been easy, he would say, researching and writing about the freed slaves who'd migrated to the City after the Civil War. Aunt Olivia was a perfectionist—it had taken her a bit longer to finish her dissertation on the free Negro women of nineteenth-century Philadelphia. Then Uncle Root took her back south to Chicasetta.

Uncle Root and Aunt Olivia taught at Red Mound Church School in Chicasetta, and it seemed that he was a changed man. But shortly thereafter, his bad temperament reappeared when Uncle Root took his frustrations with the conditions at Red Mound Church School to the white members of the Chicasetta board of education. Uncle Root was furious that, while the board finally had allocated a tiny budget for his school, during harvest times the three rich planters in town—including Tommy Jr.—would send their foremen to the school to collect the Negro children to work in their fields. And the textbooks for Red Mound were in horrible shape. The used books were years out of date, pages always were missing, and sometimes the white students who had previously used them had scrawled "nigger" and "jungle monkey" and other epithets inside. After that contentious meeting, Tommy Jr., a member of the board, told his brother it was time for him to leave town. And that evening, Tommy Jr. sat on the porch of the rented house where his brother and his wife lived. The white man had a shotgun across his lap, in case one of the members of the board had friends among the Franklins.

After Uncle Root and Aunt Olivia left Chicasetta, they decided it was time to teach on the college level. Of course, they couldn't find employment at white universities. White colleges didn't hire Negroes in those days, and though Uncle Root could pass, his dark brown wife could not. But at each Negro college where the couple taught, Uncle Root had a habit of arguing with his department chair and then quitting his job on a dime. There had been Hampton Institute in Virginia, Lincoln University in Pennsylvania, and the Elizabeth City State Colored Normal School in North Carolina. At that rate, they were going to run out of Negro institutions.

When the joint offer came from Routledge College in 1938, Aunt Olivia was thrilled, but barely a month in, her man began grumbling. That time was different, however. The morning he told Aunt Olivia he was planning to quit his teaching job, and she warned him she wasn't going to pack up again. Her husband didn't believe her. He performed his tried-and-true maneuver of persuasion, leaning in to kiss that place on her neck—nudging her crinkly hair to the side—but she shoved him away.

"Don't you dare touch me."

In case he didn't get the hint, Aunt Olivia locked him out of their bedroom in their two-room campus apartment. This was a sobering moment for her young husband. After four days of his sleeping on the hard settee in their front room and his desperate knocking on their bedroom door in the wee hours, his wife served her husband breakfast. There was the excellent bread that the cooks in the campus refectory baked each day, and the home-cured ham and peach preserves her sister-in-law had given them on their last trip to Chicasetta.

She poured Uncle Root's coffee, and then she asked, had he heard about the materials in the college archives? But her husband sulked; he was feeling neglected and lonely.

"Such as?" he asked, finally.

"You're not acting very nice. I don't know if I should tell you what I found."

"Olivia, please don't toy with my affections."

"Just go over there and see."

She let Uncle Root back in their bedroom, but she made him do his own research. It took months of almost daily visits to Mr. Temple, the college librarian, for Uncle Root to gain access to the college archives. And it was another two weeks before he found a letter, sent in 1901, back when Dr. Du Bois had taught at Atlanta University. In those years, the great scholar's travels through the sometimes-dangerous southern countryside had landed him at the Georgia Institute for Colored Girls—the original name of Routledge College.

Dr. Du Bois had sent the principal of the school a note of thanks: *My dear Mrs. Routledge, I am so grateful for your warm hospitality during my brief visit. It was an honor to witness your important work of educating your girls. The memory is fond, for I know that you share my devotion to our people and understand the grave responsibilities of Negro women.*

You are the salvation of our Race, for without women like you, our people surely would perish. Yours very truly, W. E. B. Du Bois.

That short note was enough to keep Uncle Root in Georgia. Whenever he needed encouragement, whenever he required a reminder of why he worked for very little pay and even less appreciation at this small college out in the Georgia countryside, he would return to the archives to examine that brief collection of sentences.

———

For my birthday, my mother gave me a surprise: my own car, a red hatchback with fifty thousand miles on the odometer. She hadn't wrapped a huge bow around it. There was no fanfare when Uncle Norman drove it into the yard, but I did a hip-swiveling dance and wrapped my arm around her shoulders and told her how happy I was, while she told me, calm on down. And I wiggled some more when I saw the brand-new CD player in the dash.

"I don't know what the young people are listening to these days," she said. "You have to buy your own music or let me know."

She let me drive her to Routledge College in August, so she could settle me into the dormitory. She taped up my posters of Denzel Washington and Angela Davis and placed roach poison cartridges in the corners. A new purple comforter went on the bed with shams and a bed skirt to match, and my books overflowing my one shelf and stacked in the corner. She met my roommate, Keisha Evans, who was from Milledgeville and sat with Mama on the floor, the two of them talking like home folks until it was time for my mother to leave. Uncle Norman was coming soon to take her back to Chicasetta, but I made excuses for her to stay, suggesting that I drive us to the waffle place on the highway. Mama agreed, but as we were walking out the front door of the dorm, my uncle's truck pulled up.

"Oh, baby, I think that's my cue! Give me a hug." She clasped me briefly and climbed into the pickup. She waved, and then they drove off.

Up in my dorm room, I sat on my fluffy purple comforter and

cried, and my roommate hugged me and assured me that everything would be fine.

My initial days on campus were jarring. Routledge College occupied its own, tiny self-contained town of Thatcher, Georgia. The
campus wasn't even half the size of the farm my relatives rented,
but with nearly one thousand students crowding into that small
space. The only restaurant was the Rib Shack. The only shop, the
bookstore; along with textbooks, it sold college and Greek parapher-
nalia, laundry detergent, stationery, feminine hygiene products, and
personal toiletries, all at ridiculously high markups.

Coming from a liberal private school, I was shocked to find out
that the college motto, "My Whole Heart for the Lord," was taken
very seriously by some students. It was a rallying cry for Jesus freaks
on campus, like my roommate, Keisha. Our first Sunday together,
she rose at six thirty, turning her radio to the R & B station that
switched to gospel on Sunday.

I'd exaggerated to my mother; I wasn't an atheist, but I didn't
believe in slobbering on God, and I hadn't planned on attending
chapel services, either. We were allowed two cuts a semester in order to attend our "home church" in the area. I'd intended on taking
mine immediately and lying that I'd visited Red Mound. If closely
questioned, I was prepared: I had jotted down scripture notes from
summer services.

I lifted my face off the pillow. "Hey. Um . . . Keisha? Darling?"

"Good morning, Ailey! Praise God!" On her face was a patina of
joy. Her pressed hair was out of the curlers and lay neatly next to
her cheeks. Her unpainted complexion was a smooth cocoa brown,
her figure recognizably devastating, even under the "modest" dress
she wore.

"Look, sweetie—"

On the radio, CeCe Winans hit a celestial note, and my roommate caught the Holy Spirit. When she began jumping and clapping
her hands, I knew sleep was fruitless.

A week into the first semester, our dorm mother called a meeting in the lobby to air student concerns about the appalling conditions in our one-hundred-year-old dorm. In the evenings, the water in Routledge Hall bathrooms was fine, but in the mornings, it was rusty with unidentifiable clumps. There was no air-conditioning, and on each of the three floors, the ceilings were so high, window fans couldn't push out the heat. Many of us had spotted rodents that were either medium-size mice or small rats, but no one wanted to get close enough to make sure.

I stayed quiet, because already I had a reputation for being stuck-up, even though I hadn't told anyone that my parents were alumni. But Roslyn "Roz" Fauntleroy didn't worry about anyone thinking she suffered from superiority. She took to the floor of the lobby to carol her discontent.

"I didn't come to the sticks for this craziness," Roz said. "I'm already not getting any financial aid—my daddy makes too much money for that welfare check they pass out. He's not paying full tuition for me to dodge some rats." Turning to our dorm mother, she squinted, a direct sign of insolence.

Mrs. Stripling's auburn wig tilted wearily over her eyebrows. "It's called a Pell Grant, Roslyn. And you don't have to shame our students in need."

"I'm not shaming anybody. I'm only telling y'all, my daddy is a lawyer. And he will sue this school if I get bit by whatever's running around here."

After the meeting, Roz walked up to Keisha and me. She wanted to know, what did we think about this bullshit?

"It's a shame, shonuff."

Keisha looked down at the floor. She was in love with Jesus, and I waited for her to say that the body was God's temple, and that included her mouth, thus, cursing was a violation of temple laws, but Keisha gave Roz a pass. I sighed in a bored way, pretending I was above this whole discussion. When I'd called my parents about the dorm problems, Daddy said he was passing the phone to Mama, who told me I could have attended Mecca University and stayed at home. But since I thought I was grown and I was so anxious to leave

my parents, I shouldn't let little things like vermin and some colorful water get in the way of my higher education. And please don't
forget to say "hey" to her old roommate, Mrs. Giles-Lipscomb. She
was the college librarian now.

A day after our dorm meeting, when Roz had asked to move into
our room on the first floor, Keisha had argued our large room could
hold another twin bed easily. I'd parried that Roz seemed very bossy
and I'd left my mother at home, but Keisha had countered with an
appeal to my guilt.

"Ailey, that girl lives on the third floor, and there's no air-
conditioning! You know it's too hot up there. It's the Christian thing
to do."

"Okay, but when you get tired of Roz's mouth, don't you come
running to me. You tell it to Jesus. Ask Him to fix it."

Yet in our room, Roz would sometimes speak in whispers—
one never knew who was listening at the door—and it was during
those times that Keisha and I grasped that she wasn't as tough as
she seemed. In those moments she would draw us closer, tell us the
secrets required for any true female friendship: Since Roz's parents
had divorced, her mother and she were struggling financially. They
shared a one-bedroom apartment in southwest Atlanta. Whenever
Roz visited, she slept on the let-out in the living room. And while
it was true that her father was an attorney and that he made too
much money for Roz to receive financial aid, that was only on paper. He paid for her tuition and her books but complained that his
new family—with the woman he'd left Roz's mother for—required
too much money for him to cover the rest. So during the summers,
Roz worked as a secretary. Her father's grandmother had bought
her a used car, but the rest was on Roz.

Though Keisha's early morning habits were annoying, she looked
after Roz and me. She woke us early every morning before breakfast so we could study together. She was a social work major on
scholarship. Roz was an English major who planned to be a lawyer.
I was majoring in premed. I took my classes with the other premed
freshmen, and only saw my roommates in our room, at meals, and

on Fridays, when we returned to the chapel's congregational space for the requisite Freshman Orientation.

When Dr. Charlemagne Walters, the dean of students, lectured the freshmen in the college chapel, he told us what he thought to be the most salient facts about Routledge College. We were required to memorize everything. Dean Walters started his first lecture by giving us the background on the two founders of the institution, Mrs. Adeline Ruth Hutchinson Routledge, and her spinster sister, Judith Naomi Hutchinson. The latter was a deeply religious woman who had died four years after the Civil War, in 1869. Dean Walters told us that Adeline's desire to start our college originally had begun with her sister's idea for a school for Negro girls. That's why even though Judith had passed away four years before the official founding of the college, her name was listed along with Adeline's as a founder.

When Dean Walters talked about the founders, he would pull out his handkerchief and dab his eyes.

"Our people, our people! What a mighty race!"

He told us the original mission of our college was to lead students to seek knowledge in a way that adhered to Christian values. The school motto was chiseled in the marble floor of the library, surrounded by a lapis lazuli Valentine's Day heart, which represented that same muscle of Judith Hutchinson. We were never—ever—supposed to step on the heart. Yet what our Freshman Orientation professor could not explain, despite his copious knowledge of our college's history, was why, in one hundred eighteen years, the board of trustees had never appointed a second female president of our college. The only woman who'd occupied that role had been Mrs. Routledge herself, but even then, she had called herself the "principal."

When I asked about the gendered redundancy of our college administration, Dean Walters paused and tilted his head to the side. He was a diminutive man, only a couple of inches taller than my mother, and he overenunciated every word.

"Tell me this, Miss Garfield. Do you question why there has never been a female president of our great nation?"

"Actually, I do, very much."

The students in the chapel gasped and looked back at me.

"I see," he said. "Miss Garfield, I don't know why the board of trustees in their infinite wisdom selected these esteemed men to lead us. I just think it's a coincidence they are all men."

Neither could Dean Walters answer why the institution had gone coed in 1922, eighteen months after Mrs. Routledge had died, and a year after her daughter had married Mr. Thierry De Saussure and then appointed him as the second leader of the school. He was the one who had begun calling himself "president," and who had decided that the school would be called "Routledge College," instead of "Georgia Institute for Colored Girls." According to the official origin story, Mr. De Saussure thought that allowing male students to matriculate would increase enrollment, since the college was located in a remote part of Georgia.

I raised my hand again.

"Miss Garfield, I'm trying to get through this material by the end of class. What is your question?"

"I went to the library and looked up old yearbooks."

Dean Walters perched on his toes. "Did you, now? Wonderful!"

"Yes, sir, I did. When you gave us the handout to read, I thought I might do some more research."

"Well, that is simply fantastic!"

"Thank you. And I counted the numbers of female and male students from 1922 to 1990, and what those numbers show is that Mr. De Saussure's coed strategy has been a complete failure."

The students whispered.

Roz poked me.

Dean Walters came down on his heels. "That is simply not true."

"I'm sorry, but it is," I said. "While the number of students rose from three hundred or so students in 1922 to almost a thousand in 1990, the percentage of male students has remained around nine and a half percent. So why didn't one of the other presidents decide to have Routledge go back to an all-female school?"

"Because we already have Spelman College in Atlanta and Bennett

College in North Carolina, and those are colleges for African American women. Now let's move on—"

When I raised my hand again, he cut me off.

"No, Miss Garfield. We have finished. We are through. I know
you come from the City, so let me explain that down south, when an
elder says, let's move on, that means, *Stop talking, young lady, because
you aren't offering anything important to the discussion.* Do you understand, Miss Garfield?"

"Yes, sir."

Though I was the daughter of college alumni, I hadn't yet told
anyone. I didn't want to sit in the "bourgie section" of Freshman
Orientation, the first rows of chapel pews, where alumni's kids clustered. They were referred to as "grandchildren," since their parents
had been formed in our college's pulsing Negro womb. The bourgie section gave enthusiastic cosigning to Dean Walters, smiling
with no irony when he referred to Routledge as "the Harvard of the
South." They already knew the words to the college hymn, "Dear
Routledge, We Sing Your Praises High"; unlike me, they didn't have
to constantly look down at the cheat sheet throughout the song.

Some other freshmen tried to buck Dean Walters's indoctrina-
tion, such as Abdul Wilson, who walked around in red, black, and
green outfits with matching knitted caps. He chewed on a long twig
and insisting on calling out, "Hotep," when he saw my roommates
and me on campus. He got under Keisha's skin—she'd reply that
she blessed him in the name of Jesus, and switch right on past him.

The day Dean Walters led us on the tour of Freedom Library,
Abdul committed a horrible faux pas: he stepped on Judith Hutchinson's lapis lazuli heart. We had started our tour in the basement,
where there were twenty new computers that had been donated by
an alumnus. We stood and admired the screens, and then we filed
up the back steps into the dark and frightening stacks, where the
books were kept, and where there were study carrels. Dean Walters
told us there were three levels of books in the stacks, and more in
the reading rooms. When we came out on the first floor, Abdul was
at the end of the line, with my roommates and me. He deliberately

walked into the middle of the lobby floor and stepped on the heart. Then he smiled.

Mrs. Marie Giles-Lipscomb walked from behind the counter and began yelling. "What are you doing? Get off the heart! This is a sacred symbol! You might as well be stomping Jesus on the cross!" She gestured at the floor with both hands, but Abdul deliberately lifted a foot and put it right back on the heart.

Our professor turned, saw the scene, and started yelling, too. Abdul stepped back several paces from the heart, but Dean Walters quickly followed, making sure that he stepped around the heart on his path. He stood very close to Abdul. Though he perched on his toes, he was too short to get into the younger man's face. But his menacing words carried.

"Boy, I see you smirking," Dean Walters said. "But let me tell you, this is not a joke. That's the last time you step on the heart. Do you hear me? You put any part of your body on that heart and I will expel you by the end of that day. I don't care if you have a stroke near that heart, pass out, and accidentally fall on top of it. I will expel you. Now, you walk back over there to our librarian and you apologize for your ungentlemanly, rude behavior."

Abdul hurried over to Mrs. Giles-Lipscomb, who folded her arms at his approach. Whatever he said, he whispered it, because I couldn't hear him. The librarian's frown only softened by a few degrees, and as he kept whispering apologies, she gave a short nod. She turned and walked behind the counter. Abdul walked back to our class group.

We continued on our tour, walking into the main reading room, where a velvet cord blocked off a large, framed sepia-toned photograph of Mrs. Routledge and Miss Hutchinson, our two founders. Though the women were sisters and dressed identically in long, dark dresses with full skirts, they looked nothing alike. One woman was very fair, the other very dark, but both women looked grim, as if somebody had told them something that ruined their day, moments before the picture was taken.

As we filed from the reading room back through the lobby of the library, the librarian gave Abdul a nasty look. On the mezzanine, there was an exhibit of graduation class portraits. The class photos didn't begin until the 1920s, Dean Walters explained. That was when Violet Routledge De Saussure, the founders' daughter and niece, came up with the idea to document the college's legacy. In the earliest pictures, most of the faculty, administrators, and students were so pale, they were racially indeterminate, though I thought I recognized a very young, cocky-looking Uncle Root in the class of 1926.

Keisha tugged on my shirt hem and leaned close. "These supposed to be Black people?"

"I think so."

"They sure don't look it."

Roz walked behind us, whispering, be quiet and look at the pictures. She could trace her Routledge legacy back four generations through her mother; one of the racially indeterminate students in the class pictures was her ancestor, though the bloodline had thickened through the generations. Roz was my mother's chocolate color, with a heart-shaped face, thick-lashed eyes, and full lips with a small mole at the right corner. She wore her relaxed hair in a braided bun that other students whispered was a cheap wig. Yet besides Keisha and me, no one seemed to notice her beauty. The guys on campus chased after the palest women, the lighter the better.

But then came the Friday afternoon when the air conditioner in the chapel stopped working. It was one of those early September southern days. The temperature had risen to a freakish place in the nineties, and everyone in the chapel was sweating. Dean Walters went to find maintenance, warning us, do not leave. He would be checking roll when he returned.

Beside me, Roz fanned herself, sighing; she was about to pass out. She reached to her neck and pulled out her bobby pins. Her braid fell to her waist.

"Ooh, girl." Keisha unraveled Roz's braid, and whispers began in the chapel. Wait, that wasn't a wig, after all? That was her real hair?

The next morning, when our roommate pinned up her braid, Keisha walked behind and yanked out the bobby pins.

"No, uh-uh, Roz. You look like an old lady with that bun."

"You got your nerve. Where you get that ugly dress? Your grandma?"

Keisha didn't even acknowledge the insult. She pulled Roz's hair into a loose ponytail, asking me to get a rubber band from her purse. I searched past the packets of disposable handkerchiefs and loose peppermint candy until I found the band, and after Keisha was done, we both clapped our hands. We remarked how beautiful Roz was, as she told us to stop ribbing her up. She didn't have any money to give us.

That was the morning that six guys stopped us on the way to breakfast. They all directed their conversation to our roommate. The next morning in mandatory Sunday chapel, Keisha had to elbow two brothers out of the way when they tried to sit on either side of Roz. Shame on them, Keisha said. Trying to flirt on the Lord's day, but she was grinning.

———

At the next Freshman Orientation, Dean Walters focused on the change to the curriculum of the college.

When Mrs. Adeline Routledge had been alive, the college had aligned itself with the principles of Du Bois and featured a liberal arts curriculum. In theory, the students of Routledge College were supposed to provide a buffer between the folks living in the Georgia countryside and the white citizens of the state; graduates were charged to go out into the world and present an example of what glories the race could accomplish when its members put their minds to it. However, in practice, the college had been viewed as rabble-rousers by whites in the community, and interracial relations were violent. In 1916, two Black male faculty members were murdered on their way back from a visit to Atlanta, and in 1919, another disappeared and was never heard from again after he tried and failed to protect his wife from gang rape at the hands of five white men.

Tensions settled greatly in 1924, however, when Mr. Thierry De

Saussure, Violet's husband, added a vocational track to the schedule of courses, similar to the academic track of Tuskegee Institute in Alabama, led by Booker T. Washington. Though the move was applauded as timely and practical by Routledge's all-white board of trustees, in late September of that same year, there were protests from the faculty—Black and white members alike—who encouraged the students to join them; three-quarters of the student body refused to attend classes, and the other students sat looking silly in empty rooms. Mr. De Saussure responded to the protests by firing half the faculty and giving those truant students the weekend to decide whether they would attend classes again on Monday morning or be expelled. Without their faculty leaders, the students' courage folded and they refilled the classes, including the new agricultural science courses for the young men, and the domestic courses for their female counterparts; those classes would be eliminated in 1985, but Mr. De Saussure's proclamation was well recorded in college history:

"Miss Adeline founded this institution on nothing except love for our people and never-ending prayer. If need be, I will rebuild Routledge College on those two humble foundations."

Abdul raised his hand. "Why'd that De Saussure dude add that vocational track like at Tuskegee? I don't get that. Everybody knows Booker T. Washington was an Uncle Tom."

"Really? Who is this everybody?" our professor asked.

"Like, everybody in Philly."

"Tell me, do any of your friends carry guns in Philadelphia?"

"Yeah, we got them jawns." Abdul looked around severely, like he planned to shoot up the entire bourgie section.

"Down south, civilized Black men don't carry weapons on our persons. We carry our intellects. Down here, African Americans must learn how to improvise. That's what Mr. Booker T. Washington did at Tuskegee, and what Mr. De Saussure did here as well. He knew that certain southern whites did not want African Americans going to college, so he tricked those whites by requiring the vocational track. That way, they wouldn't know he also was teaching us science, math, literature, and foreign languages. And I am grateful for that improvisation, because this school was still standing when I enrolled in the fall of 1954, instead of being burned to ash by the Ku Klux Klan. Aren't you happy about that?"

The bourgie section nodded and turned to look at Abdul, but he stayed quiet, fingering his twig like a talisman.

Dean Walters moved on to the timeline of the buildings on campus. The plantation house had been built by Matthew Parson in 1856. The barn, no longer standing, had been built in the same year. The schoolhouse predated the college's official founding year, built in either late 1871 or early 1872.

Keisha raised her hand. "Can I ask you something? I thought this was 'sposed to be a Black school."

"Indeed, Miss Evans, this is an institution of higher learning for African Americans, though we have been an equal opportunity college since our founding. All are welcome here."

"But if this is a Black school, how come most of those folks in the library pictures look like that?"

"Like what?"

"Like they white people."

The bourgie section gasped.

"Well, they are not white people, Miss Evans. You can be assured that those students are African American."

"Well, they way too light for me."

"That is a very rude thing to say. Now let me get back—"

I raised my hand. Roz poked me, but I leaned away from her.

"Why's it rude? She's only being honest."

Dean Walters put the chalk in the board's tray. "Your mother and father are both alumni, Miss Garfield. I believe that they were in the class of 1966. That is correct, is it not?"

From around the chapel, there were whispers.

I shifted in my chair. "Yes, sir."

"And both of your parents are African American. Correct?"

"Yes, sir."

"And each of your four grandparents are African American. Correct?"

"Yes, sir."

"And I would bet that the members of your family come in many different shades. Correct?" He perched so high on the toes of his wing tips I expected a plié. "Miss Garfield, I have met your father, and I was taught by Dr. Freeman Hargrace, your great-great-uncle. Would you want someone saying either of them was too light when God made him this way? No, you would not. Further, this kind of discussion creates discord within our African American ranks. And we don't want that, do we?"

Dean Walters picked up the chalk and returned to the timeline of campus buildings.

Keisha placed her hand on my arm. She gave me a tender squeeze.

By the following afternoon, the campus gossips had anointed my roommates and me with a new nickname. They called us "The Too-Light Crew."

LIBERTÉ, ÉGALITÉ, FRATERNITÉ, GODDAMNIT

From the time I was born, my parents had put aside money for my college, the same as they'd saved for my sisters. But my regular eavesdropping had informed me they hadn't counted on Coco being a genius and requiring expensive private school, and then equally expensive Ivy League college and medical school. Nana had helped them with my tuition at Braithwaite Friends, but the cost that had hit them the hardest was Lydia's rehab. They had been too proud to ask Nana for help. My parents hadn't counted on spending so much money for my sister to recover in a safe environment.

In my last year of high school, I'd no idea what I'd study in college—now that Coco was in school to be a doctor, I thought I'd be off the hook for carrying on that particular family legacy. I'd been mostly concerned with earning high grades so I wouldn't let those white kids I went to school with think they were smarter than me. I did know that whatever I finally chose as my profession, I wanted to spend time with books. Many, many books, but during a rare Saturday at Nana's house, after my mother plied me with guilt to visit the woman, my grandmother hinted about my parents' financial worries. What a shame. Truly, so sad, and these days, college wasn't enough. Postgraduate studies were necessary in this new economy, but why borrow thousands in student loans when she would be happy to help? However, there was one caveat: I was required to attend medical school to secure her financial support. She wouldn't be paying for my studies in any other field. And we needed to spend more time together, too, so that we could talk about my future plans in the medical profession.

Nana had taken a sip of Earl Grey and shifted the subject: There was a new Van Gogh exhibit at the City High Museum. She'd been wanting to see it for a week. She would call a taxi for us. Even though I didn't want to be anywhere around her, I made a choice: I needed

Nana's money to pay for my education, or at least some of it. I couldn't let my parents try to bear that burden alone.

I was exhausted my first semester at Routledge taking classes on the premed track. Physics, biology, biochemistry, calculus. Showing up for those everyday labs that somehow only earned me one hour of credit. I attacked my studies with vigor, but whenever Nana wrote me, congratulating me on my chosen profession, I didn't write back. I'd open her letter, pull out the twenty-five-dollar check she'd included, and drop the letter in a shoe box under my bed. Whenever the box filled, I'd throw the letters in the trash can on my dorm floor.

Five days a week, Keisha, Roz, and I rose in the dark morning. One of us would heat water for tea on our forbidden hot plate. Then we'd throw on robes and go downstairs to the dorm lobby, where there would be other young women studying as well. Two hours of that, then breakfast in the refectory, where I drank several cups of cola before going to classes. At noon, I downed a caffeine pill with lunch.

Throughout the day, I'd silently repeat the facts of the body, but I was less interested in cells, systems, and connective tissues, and more in the backstories, as when my elderly anatomy professor entertained his students with tangents. A retired physician from Alabama, Dr. Turner told us about the Tuskegee experiment of the 1920s and '30s, when the government refused to cure a group of Black men with syphilis, just to watch the disease's horrible progression. Another tangent was about Dr. Turner's white professor in medical school. He had reminded his students that it was a well-known, scientific fact that the colored race didn't have the same filial affections as other races. They didn't feel physical pain much, either, the white professor had said. You could cut into their flesh with a scalpel and they wouldn't even flinch.

"Can you believe the nerve of that white man?" Dr. Turner asked. "Making up science like that?"

After classes were over, I ate dinner with my roommates and walked to the library alone—Keisha didn't believe in late hours. I'd stay at the library until it closed at ten, then walk to my dorm and sit in the lobby with earphones on and study some more. On good nights, I climbed into bed around midnight and woke at five.

When my eyes popped open in the dark morning, I'd lie there as self-pity slithered through me. I had no passion for science, no care for the body's gory pathways. I didn't want to be a healer, but I thought about my parents and what they had gone through. My childhood hadn't been perfect, but they'd done the best they could. I was sacrificing for them now, as they had sacrificed for me. I'd roll from bed and turn on the hot plate. I'd tell myself, yes, I was tired. And yes, I hated science, but at least I finally had girlfriends who weren't my blood relatives. And true friends were important at Routledge, because the scrutiny of female students was ruthless.

Sisters had to be cautious with their reputations; each spring the guys released the annual "Dirty Thirty" list, which named the most sexually active sisters at Routledge. We had to be careful about what we did, what we said, when we checked into the dorm during the weekdays, and how many guys we'd been seen with during the academic year. Even if nothing sexual took place with any men, some young women would violate the sister code and turn on others: spreading gossip was the best way to knock out four or five females from that female-to-male ten-to-one ratio.

Keisha didn't worry about gossip. Her reputation was sterling: she turned down frequent male invitations to the Rib Shack, explaining without any embarrassment that she was saving her virginity until marriage, as was required by her Christian faith. "Jesus is my husband," she'd tell the guys who asked her out. She couldn't date because the Devil never slept. Especially, he suffered from insomnia on Saturday nights, the hours before God's faithful servants would convene.

Roz was bossy, but she turned out to be useful. She schooled me on the dating scene at our college, one of the topics Dean Walters hadn't mentioned in Freshman Orientation. Not only was there one male to every ten females, that one dude might be country and 'bama, if he was a local. Unofficially, Georgia was number four in

the 'bama category; the states of Mississippi, Alabama, and the entire city of Cleveland, Ohio, were numbers one, two, and three, re-
spectively. And since the pickings for non-'bama mates were slim,
female romantic anxiety ruled our campus. A few weeks into first
semester, Dean Walters sentenced two young women to behavioral
probation. They'd fought over the same homely guy who'd sported
a jagged S-curl. Even if the fights weren't physical, frequently, matters degraded into public shouting matches, which didn't make
sense to Roz. There was no need to fight.

"Because niggers ain't shit. And white boys ain't no better. You
can't trust a man."

Roz didn't tell anybody information about her vagina, but one
might imagine it was made of platinum as much as brothers had
begun to pursue her. On Sundays, brothers kept sitting on our
pew during mandatory chapel service. They stopped by our table in
the refectory, placing large candy bars on the table. They asked her
to the movies in Milledgeville and left urgent pink message slips for
her at the dorm reception desk. Curt Waymon, the president of
Gamma Beta Gamma, was particularly insistent, marking his territory with daily takeout from the Rib Shack. When that didn't help
him get next to her, he gave her his fraternity pin. Sometimes she
let Curt take her to the movies, though she only let him kiss her
with tongue and touch her boobs.

There were dance parties in the small student union, but the music was hit or miss. Or you could admit your nerd status and go to the
library on Friday or Saturday nights. The junior and senior women
had warned us never to hang out in the apartments of guys who lived
off campus, unless they were our official boyfriends. Because that's
how you got raped. Sets in one of the off-campus apartments were
even less safe, because the college rules didn't apply. That's how you
got raped. Under no circumstances were we to attend off-campus
fraternity parties, and don't ever drink hunch punch, which was a
homemade concoction of pure grain alcohol, red or purple punch,
and diced tropical fruit. Hunch punch was sneaky, and that's how
brothers got you blind drunk. And that's how you got raped.

There were no warnings about Pat Lindsay, though. Just like every young woman on campus knew who the rapists were, every sister knew the identities of the gentlemen. Pat was the latter, and you were lucky to be invited to a set in his room. He was safe, sweet, and he shared his supply of weed. In the refectory, he sat with Abdul Wilson and Steve Jefferson. They were known as "The Three Amigos," which seemed friendlier than the nickname my roommates and I had received.

The connection between the three wasn't clear. Abdul was from Philadelphia, and Steve was from Harlem; both were engineering majors, but Steve was in his mid-twenties. He wouldn't say what he'd been doing in the years in between high school and entering college, only that he'd gotten himself together. Pat was a sophomore and was majoring in French. Both his parents had graduated from Routledge, and he was the grandson of Robert "Rob-Boy" Lindsay, the late college friend of Uncle Root. In the refectory, he mostly ignored his two friends in favor of reading, usually Fanon or one of the Negritude poets. He put aside his book if a young woman stopped by the table, though, standing and kissing her cheek and hand.

There was speculation about who he was sleeping with, but Pat was secret with his sexual business. The sisters told it all, though: that he could control himself for hours in bed. He wasn't a selfish brother, either: he not only accepted oral sex from a woman, but performed it quite eagerly. A story had circulated that he'd gone down on someone for so long, she'd blacked out on her fourth orgasm; when she'd revived, Pat was between her legs, still licking away. No one knew the young woman's identity, and that only lent the story another layer of fascination.

———

One early October evening, Abdul let us into Pat's room, then sat on a twin bed by Steve. Roz and I perched on the other bed, but when joints were produced, she stood. Without asking, she opened the window on the other side of the room. Roz had been invited by Pat, with whom she'd attended high school, though he was a year ahead of her. She'd asked Keisha and me to accompany her, though Keisha had demurred. There was no way Roz was going to a dude's room by herself, even Pat's.

Pat offered me a red plastic cup and a drink from his bottle of Chardonnay, because he didn't play around with hunch punch. That shit was uncivilized. After he poured my drink, he sat against the closet, legs splayed on the floor. His curly hair was nearly the same golden color as his skin, and he was tall and on the heavy side. Freckles were scattered across his nose.

He was two drinks in and wanted to get deep, philosophizing on the uselessness of organized religion. I was relieved Keisha had turned down the invitation to the set.

"Black people, we need to ignore that Christianity shit," Pat said. "I'm an atheist, myself. No—Wait—I guess I would say I'm an agnostic. But if there is a God, He's not on his job, because this country is fucked up. So we need to stop praying and start thinking about the bigger picture."

"Like what?" I asked.

"Like Reagan was the Antichrist. And now his former vice president is his satanic minion. Bush is destroying our communities."

"Can I ask a question?"

"Sure, Ailey."

"Aren't you scared somebody is going to smell this weed?"

"Naw, I'm not pressed. My granddaddy's name is on this building. What they gone do, give back his million dollars?"

He passed the joint to me. I took a long draw and passed to Abdul, who sucked in smoke and was quiet. Steve had joined my roommate at the window, and the two of them politely refused their turn.

"This country is about to crash," Pat said. "Like, boom, goddamnit."

"You really think so?" I called to the window. "Roz, what do you think about *boom*?"

"I think you're high, and you don't need to shout." For the past half hour, she'd retained a bored expression as Steve whispered close to her ear, holding a hand to his chest as if defending himself.

"Are you sure *boom* means a crash, Pat?" I asked. "Are you absolutely sure?"

He put his hand on my arm, squeezing briefly. "Yes, baby. Can you lower your voice a little? If you're afraid I won't hear you, lean close all you want, 'cause you smell very good."

I spoke in an exaggerated whisper: "I'm sorry. But wouldn't *boom* sound like *rumble*, instead? I'm trying to get my onomatopoeia right."

"This jawn pulling out the big vocabulary words and shit," Abdul said. Of the three males in the room, he was the most handsome. He was dark brown and growing in an eighteen-year-old goatee. There was a crowding to his top front teeth, but the dimples made up for the imperfection. The muscles didn't hurt, either, but his being a complete asshole ruined the aesthetics.

He snapped his fingers.

"Ay, ay, Steve! This jawn right here says the word 'boom' is an example of onomatopoeia. Can you tell me what that word means?"

"Can't you see I'm busy over here?" Steve inclined his head toward Roz, widening his eyes. A lock of my roommate's long hair was stuck to his face.

"Answer the question, Steve."

"I don't know, Abdul. And you better stop tripping."

"Naw, that's you, son. You know that's Curt Waymon's jawn you talking to."

My roommate said she didn't belong to anybody, but her would-be suitor announced he had a test the next day. Yeah. A test. So okay, bye. He slammed the door in his haste to leave.

Pat returned his hand to my arm.

"The people won't put up with Bush's shit much longer. *Liberté, égalité, fraternité,* goddamnit."

"So you're talking about the French Revolution," I said.

Abdul clapped. "Oh! This jawn really thinks she's smart, don't she?"

"I am smart. And why do you keep referring to me in the third person when I'm sitting right here? And what in the West Hell is a jawn?"

"It's a person, place, or thing."

"Abdul, that word is not in the dictionary."

"It don't have to be, Ailey. That's what you call vernacular."

"Well, I never heard of it."

"You need to get out more."

Pat interrupted our bickering. He put out a hand and nodded in an exaggerated fashion. Let's have peace. Let's make love and not war. "And be more polite to this beautiful young lady. Don't scare her away. Because I want her to come back."

"See, that's your problem," Abdul said. "You can't be nice to these females. You gotta let them know who's in charge."

"Agree to disagree on that, my brother." When Pat pulled another joint from the front pocket of his shirt, Roz told me I could smoke my weed five more minutes, and then we had to get back to our dorm. She wasn't missing curfew.

IN THIS SPOT

❖

In Dr. Belinda Olufunke Oludara's classroom, a cone of incense burned on the desk. Her head was completely wrapped in blue-and-red printed cloth. She wore a dark-blue shift that skimmed over her very wide hips; underneath the shift, matching pants. Around her neck, several strings of chunky amber. There were gold earrings that hung nearly to her shoulders, matching the gold bracelets on her wrists. She sat down on the edge of the desk and waved her hands. Her cadence was dramatic, as if she were putting on a one-woman stage show. The bracelets clanged as she moved.

"Welcome, my brilliant scholars! I do have a doctorate, and you should respect that, as any Black woman who made it through seven years at Harvard has earned her propers. To paraphrase the great poet Sterling A. Brown, 'More Negroes have been ruined by Harvard than by bad gin.' Only he didn't say 'Negroes,' if you catch my drift."

The class tittered.

When I'd signed up for my spring classes, Uncle Root had advised me to save room in my schedule for treats. I didn't want to burn out in my first year of college. I needed a respite from premed classes, but when I'd handed him the college catalog, he'd put it aside.

"You need to take a class with Belinda. She'll definitely clear your sinuses."

Dr. Oludara had been the old man's prize student in history. She'd graduated from Routledge in 1972, gone on to Harvard for her master's and doctorate, traveled to Nigeria on a fellowship, and come back to the states with her African husband. Then, to the old man's complete shock, Dr. Oludara had returned south, bought a home an hour outside of Atlanta, and applied for a teaching job at Routledge.

"Call me 'Doctor,'" she said. "Or, if you prefer, 'Professor,' but never 'Miss' or 'Missus.' I love my Femi dearly, but I'm more than his wife and the mother of his children. I'm a scholar in my own right! And surprisingly enough I didn't go into teaching for the money. I do it for the love, since there is very little money involved. Femi's an engineer, so he makes the money in this family, which is how I can afford to teach and raise our children. And he gave me all this gold for my bride price!" She held up her arms, making the bracelets sing. "Be prepared to dive into the awe-inspiring history of our African American people! I'm amazed that I have the opportunity to be with you, and to be filled with your brilliance. My only prohibition is no cursing or name-calling. Our discussions might get a bit rowdy, but remember, everyone has a voice and there will be mutual respect. If not, I'll ask you to leave, and possibly drop you from the class. And if your behavior is very bad, I might refer you to the campus disciplinary committee for expulsion!"

She smiled cheerfully.

Though the required textbooks were in the bookstore, Dr. Oludara would give us additional handouts ahead of time for our units. She expected us to read the class materials, especially the seven extra students she'd allowed in the class, even though her load was supposed to be capped at twenty-two. But for this initial week, she had decided to do something she'd never done before. On Thursday, she was taking us on a surprise field trip.

In the second row, a raised hand. "Where are we going?"

Our professor stopped waving her arms. "Tell me your name, please?"

"Abdul Wilson."

"Thank you! My dear brother, a surprise implies a withholding of information, so that means I'm not telling you where we're going. However, be assured that you will be safe. All students need to wear something light-colored. No student wearing dark clothing will be allowed to join the group, and when we arrive at our destination, you'll be required to take off your shoes. What do you kids say? If your feet are 'jacked,' please hide them with light-colored socks."

Again, we laughed.

On Thursday morning, we met in front of our classroom building.

I was self-conscious in my yellow-and-white cotton dress. Even in the summertime, I preferred dark clothing; I hadn't brought any light clothing to campus, and both my roommates were much thinner than I was, so I couldn't borrow their clothes. So I'd driven to Chicasetta the day before and found a dress in my great-grandmother's trunk. My granny hadn't thrown out any of her mother's clothing, and the dress was from the '50s, when Dear Pearl had been smaller, though still on the chubby side. The dress was handmade, with tiny neat stitches in the seams. It had a narrow waist and a full skirt that fell a handspan below my knees. Thankfully, the sleeves were three-quarter; I was sensitive about my fleshy arms. Underneath the bodice, a thin lining. The skirt had a petticoat that whispered with my movements. Dear's feet had been larger than mine, so I stuffed toilet paper in the toes to make her beige high heels fit. I'd put on a pair of her clip-on earrings, and Keisha had loaned me some colorless lip gloss. I'd painted my toes and oiled the heels of my feet, but I didn't wear pantyhose. I was hot enough in the dress.

Pat walked up to me, followed by Abdul and Steve. The three were identically dressed in white button-down shirts and khaki pants. Pat had on tan-colored sandals, but the other two wore white sneakers.

"Damn, lady!" Pat said. "When you clean up, you really go all out! You got my heart beating so fast. Here, feel it."

He took my hand, squeezing. I laughed but didn't let go.

"Ain't nobody touching your chest, boy! You always trying to gas me up."

"Naw, Ailey, I'm for real! I see you at chapel, but I don't think I've ever seen you look quite this fine."

When Tiffany Cruikshank walked up in her cream-colored pantsuit with light-orange shoes, Pat told her, I didn't want to believe what men told me, but maybe I'd believe another incredibly beautiful woman. Didn't I look nice?

"Yes, you do look very pretty in your dress." Tiffany spoke formally, as if giving a speech, and didn't crack a smile. "That's a very ladylike ensemble."

"Thank you, Tiffany."

I crossed my arms; the attention was making me uncomfortable. Then, Dr. Oludara arrived, wearing a long white dress. Her hair was tightly wrapped again, this time in material that matched her outfit. She waved her arms and the bracelets jingled. Let's go.

I wasn't used to wearing heels, and once we stepped onto grass, I stopped and took off my shoes. The grass was warm against my feet. After about a quarter of a mile, our professor announced, we had reached our destination. My classmates and I looked around. There was nothing there. I'd heard that Dr. Oludara was rather eccentric, but I couldn't believe I'd dressed up and greased my feet to walk to the middle of an empty field.

"If you haven't done so already, my young scholars, please remove your shoes."

She closed her eyes and moved her lips soundlessly. When she opened them, she told us that this land had once belonged to other people. The Creek Indians, who had been driven from their homes. Think about it. Somebody making you leave your wonderful house and go some other place you knew nothing about. Think about how that would make you cry, as it had made the Creek people cry. And then think about how angry it would make you that the people who stole your house forgot it had ever belonged to you.

Dr. Oludara told us that after the Creek people had been forced off this land, it had been purchased by a slave master, Matthew Thatcher. Then the Civil War came, and afterward, Mrs. Routledge had traveled down south. Mrs. Routledge and Mr. Thatcher met and became friends. It was an odd connection, but somehow their bond was strong enough to compel Mr. Thatcher to leave Mrs. Routledge the majority of his estate in his will: one hundred sixty acres, his large, two-storied house, and nearly six thousand dollars—a lot of money in those days. But before his death Mr. Thatcher would build a one-room schoolhouse on that land for Mrs. Routledge. The small structure would eventually be named Georgia Institute for Colored Girls.

We'd already seen the old schoolhouse on our freshman tour; this spot where we were standing had once been host to a slave pen. Citizens in Milledgeville, only a few miles away, had come here, where the traders would have human merchandise waiting. When he'd bought the land, Mr. Thatcher had torn down the pen, but the debris—shackles and various torturous instruments from the slave trade—remained scattered in the place the pen had been, this very spot.

"Where you are standing is hallowed ground," Dr. Oludara said. "Our ancestors were taken from their families and brought to this place for slave auctions. They grieved as they were put in narrow enclosures, sometimes by themselves and sometimes crowded together. They were categorized according to the work they did. Field workers, who picked cotton. Artisans with special skills, such as blacksmiths and carpenters. House slaves, such as cooks and ladies' maids. But there was another kind of enslaved individual sold here. There was a euphemism: 'suitable for housekeeping.' That meant those females who would be used for bedroom purposes. Do you understand what I mean? Their bodies would be taken and degraded. Their children might remain with those mothers, or they might be sold as well. If they were daughters, they, too, would be used by white men, sometimes even as little girls."

I wrapped my arms around myself, buried my chin into my chest, and started rocking. I hoped no one was looking at me.

Then, Dr. Oludara told us, as a northern African American, Mrs. Routledge wasn't personally familiar with the slave trade or being hurt by white men, because she'd been born free. She'd been born lucky, but she had possessed a ministry to heal the pain of her people.

"Can you hear them? Can you feel that pain? Because Mrs. Routledge heard, across the miles, in Boston. And she answered that call."

Mrs. Routledge didn't need to have been a slave herself to know girls were endangered. They needed protection, and she handpicked twelve girls who were the children of formerly enslaved people. Along with her daughter, Violet, they were the institute's first class. They cleared off the land where the pen once had stood; they worked hard. They sweat. Their arms ached. The heavy skirts of the time made the work even more difficult, and the girls became fatigued—but, Dr. Oludara told us, Mrs. Routledge had put her hands on her hips. When she spoke, she rocked as if to her own, internal music, as she did when she instructed her girls to keep working. Do not faint and do not hesitate.

"Can you see Mrs. Routledge? Can you?" She began to clap softly. "Listen to her telling those girls, think of their people who needed their help. The other women. The other little girls."

When Dr. Oludara walked closer to us, something hit my chest. I caught my breath and when I exhaled, I began to weep. I thought of the little slave girls, and of the little girl I had been. The secrets I kept about what had happened to me, so no one would think I was dirty. I thought of the pain of my ancestors who'd been slaves, perhaps even sold in this very place. I thought of it all, and I put my hands over my face to hide my shame, but there was an arm around my shoulder. It was Pat, and I buried my head in his chest as he hugged me tightly. He kissed the top of my head, but my weeping would not stop, as our professor's clapping increased in volume.

"And let go of that hurt, that degradation of the past. That's what Mrs. Routledge told her students. Don't hold on to that madness. And then one of her students found the spot. The place where the blood of slaves had soaked into the ground. It was darker than the rest, even though this land is a red dirt place. After all those years that bloody spot was there. That was a horrible moment, and after Mrs. Routledge cleared this area, she decided, it was full of too much pain. Her schoolhouse needed to be someplace else on this piece of land. She left this spot alone, so it could heal. And that's why there are no campus buildings here."

Dr. Oludara stopped clapping. She released a large sigh.

"We have so much work to do, my young scholars! There is a reason for your presence, right here, right now. I am so happy to be your guide this semester, and I ask you, do not forget the blessing of this place. Don't you ever forget."

She was quiet for the next few minutes, as we students gathered our shoes. We laughed off our emotion, the embarrassment of the moment, until Dr. Oludara told us, let's head on over to the Rib Shack. It would be her treat for all of us! Communing with the ancestors was hungry work.

———

"Goddamn!" Abdul ejected. "You telling me Harriet Jacobs couldn't find no eligible brothers to get with?"

Dr. Oludara raised her finger in protest. "Brother Wilson, not cool at all. Apologize."

The antebellum review took place in the second week of Dr. Oludara's class, and Abdul fidgeted in his chair while she explained that, initially, scholars had thought a woman named Linda Brent had written *Incidents in the Life of a Slave Girl*, but in the late 1980s, somebody discovered the author's real name was Harriet Jacobs.

"My bad, Doc," he said. "I mean, I'm sorry."

"All right. I will forgive you."

"But Doc, look. If that jawn was in danger, how'd she find time to make not one but two half-white babies?"

"That's so foul," I said. "My cousins are mixed."

Abdul raised his hands, palms forward. "I didn't say a thing about your family. I'm talking about Harriet Jacobs. Did her children not have a white daddy? Thus, they were half-white."

He looked at Steve, who nodded vigorously. Behind them, Pat leaned back in his chair, but the annoyed look on his face told the real story: his friends were getting on his nerves.

"Are you saying we're supposed to feel sorry for this woman?" Tiffany Cruikshank asked. "Because I don't. Jacobs willingly had sex with a white man. Being raped by Mr. Flint would've been better than what she did."

"Wow, that's super harsh," I said. "How is rape possibly better?"

"Getting down on purpose with a slave master makes her a tramp, which is how white men viewed Black women anyway."

"That's, like, seriously old-fashioned."

"Yes, Ailey, and I'm proud to be that way. You went to some

private school with white folks, right? Is that why you think like a whore? Or are you one already?"

I caught my breath. "Oh my God, did you just say that to me—"

Our professor called for order and for kindness. "Sister Cruik-shank, you owe Sister Garfield an abject apology! Your insult of her is rude, cruel, and completely uncalled-for. In other words, it's not 'the jam.' Isn't that what you kids say nowadays?"

There was laughter at her attempt to be cool, and then Tiffany gave me a gruff apology, looking at the space over my head.

When I spoke again, my voice shook. "I'm as Black as anybody else at this school, and I'm not anybody's whore, either. I can't help that my parents sent me to a private school. Whatever to that. I was just saying I think Miss Jacobs might have loved that white man she had those babies with. And maybe he loved her back. Maybe he thought she was a lady."

Abdul and Steve erupted into outraged groans and then assaulted the air with their Public Enemy hand gestures. By 1992, PE had rendered Black male rage, with its attendant body language, fash-ionable again. Northern brothers on campus regularly quoted long passages from the group's lyrics. Even back in high school, Chris had urged me to listen to their albums, praising Chuck D's philo-sophical brilliance—even if his sudden Black identity hadn't kept him from attending Princeton instead of Routledge.

"How's a white man ever going to respect a Black woman?" Ab-dul asked. "Girl, where are you from?"

My mouth trembled as he swooped his arms around, compar-ing Jacobs's situation to "Who Stole the Soul?" from *Fear of a Black Planet*.

At lunchtime, my roommates and I sat in the refectory on the room's margins. The table in the center was reserved for members of Beta Alpha Beta Sorority. Even Roz, a direct descendant of a found-ing Beta Lily, didn't dare trespass.

Abdul placed his tray on our table, and Pat and Steve followed suit. It was an unseasonably warm January evening, but the Three

Amigos still wore their long-sleeved shirts and khakis. Abdul's chewing stick had disappeared. The gossips believed they were "Rocks," pledging Gamma Beta Gamma fraternity underground, which was rumored to be a months-long process.

"Who said you could sit here?" Roz asked.

"We always sit with y'all," Abdul said.

"I know, but you can't do that anymore."

"Girl, stop acting cute."

"I don't have to act. I am cute."

"Move your shit, Miss Siddity."

Roz looked around as if searching for someone. When she scraped back her chair and stood to go, Keisha shot me a pained look. As a social work major, she tried to get along with everyone. It was a professional requirement, and back in our room, she told our roommate her behavior hadn't been very nice. The Three Amigos were our friends. Even Abdul, with his rude self.

"Yeah, Roz," I said. "Why'd you leave?"

"Y'all know Abdul and Tiffany are kicking it."

"How you know?"

"Because I do."

"But who cares?"

"I care. I'm trying to pledge Beta in the fall." Roz began her tired harangue, that Beta Alpha Beta was a family legacy. As a fourth-generation legacy of the sorority, she couldn't be turned down for membership unless her grades tanked. Or if she had morality issues, which might come up if somebody on campus tried to start a rumor about her sleeping around. She had to be extra careful. She planned to be a lawyer and live in Atlanta, so she needed Beta membership, because there wasn't an African American city official in that town with any clout who didn't have Greek letters—

"Okay, already," I said. "But you know they won't turn you down."

"Maybe, but they can beat me when I get on line. They can beat you, too, if you apply. And if you don't leave Abdul alone, Tiffany's coming for you."

"Don't nobody in this room want to fuck that guy."

Keisha cleared her throat and I quickly apologized for using foul language.

"Watch," Roz said. "As soon as them two go public, every other sister gone want him. That's the way that goes."

But in the days that followed I refused to leave the table whenever our friends sat down, though Roz continually warned I might ruin my chances for Beta, or, at best, acquire a reputation as a gold digger. Pat's departed grandfather had donated that million dollars to build the male honors dorm. He drove his grandfather's old Mercedes, too.

None of our roommate's concerns swayed either Keisha or me. We kept sitting with the Three Amigos in the refectory. I still tutored Pat in math in the library carrels, and he still flirted endlessly.

FEMINISM, WOMANISM, OR WHATEVER

◈

"Abdul, you must not have read the essay," I said. "When W. E. B. Du Bois writes, 'The Negro race, like all races, is going to be saved by its exceptional men,' he incudes women implicitly. It's a rhetorical shortcut."

"No, it's not. He means it's the role of men to lead. Men, not women. You the one can't read."

Pat touched Abdul's shoulder. "What about the Negro women's club movements? What about those sisters who helped found the NAACP? That's leadership."

"No, that's support," Abdul said, as Steve made assenting noises.

"But what about Jessie Fauset helping Du Bois with *The Crisis?*" I asked. "*The Brownies Book* was her idea. And she published all those writers during the Harlem Renaissance, like Langston Hughes and Zora Neale Hurston. That wasn't Du Bois's work. He just took credit for it."

"But then Fauset wanted to run things," Abdul said. "Instead of her standing behind a brother where she was meant to be. And that's the problem, sisters wanting to be in front. Like I said, feminism is for white women."

"Are you kidding me? What about the handout on womanism and feminism Dr. Oludara gave us? And that essay on intersectionality?"

Tiffany raised her hand, and our professor asked, what did she have to contribute?

"I have a question. What does Jessie Fauset have to do with anything? She quit *The Crisis*, and we never heard from her again. The end—"

I tried to interject: "No, Tiffany, she published two more novels—"

"And when have white women ever looked out for us? I mean, I love my soror, Dr. Oludara, and everything, but I respectfully disagree that feminism is for us."

She smiled at our professor, who looked down at her dress and pulled off a piece of lint. The old man had told me that Dr. Oludara had pledged Beta back in her sophomore year at Routledge, but the next year, when she made the decision to stop pressing her hair, the chapter president had told her she needed to stop participating in sorority functions, because her nappy hair was an embarrassment.

Tiffany began pulling back fingers. "During slavery, they wouldn't keep their men from raping us. Then slavery was over and white men started lynching brothers. Then there's Frances Willard saying it's okay to kill Black men. She's one of your feminists, Ailey, isn't she? And then they didn't even want Ida B. Wells-Barnett walking in the 1913 march." She sat back in her chair, as if the case were closed.

"But Mrs. Wells-Barnett joined that suffragette march anyway," I said. "Even when they told her she couldn't, she was, like, no, y'all can't stop me. And other Black women marched, too. So feminism must have been important to them."

Tiffany rolled her eyes.

Abdul raised his hand again. "I don't get you, Ailey. Are you one of these lesbians—"

"What does that have to do with anything—" I raised my voice to gain purchase, but he began shouting.

"Naw, naw, let me say this! Women are supposed to be at home, not out on these streets! Y'all sisters need to understand your place—"

"Dr. Oludara, can't I talk?" I asked.

Our professor smiled, a brown Mona Lisa. "I'm not going to get in the middle, Sister Garfield. You know I like a free-flowing discourse, no matter how lively it is. But Brother Wilson, 'place' is an offensive term when talking about the roles of Black women. Further, there's absolutely nothing wrong with being a lesbian, either, and your implication otherwise is offensive as well. We are in the latter part of the twentieth century. Try again, please."

"Look, Doc, no offense. But I don't understand why our women"—
at this, several sisters erupted into yelling, but Abdul kept going,
again, raising his voice to a shout—"Yes, our women! Y'all belong
to us! And I don't know why y'all females need this feminism or
womanism or whatever. It's unnecessary if you got a good brother
paying bills and taking care of business."

Tiffany agreed with him, but other sisters threw "sexist" in his direction, until our professor raised her hand for quiet. "Sisters, please.
Brother Wilson has the floor. As obnoxious and sexist as he is, please
try to be respectful of his incredibly outmoded, offensive views."

There was laughter, but Abdul refused to acknowledge that he
was the butt of the joke. "Like I was saying, y'all women wouldn't
need feminism if you weren't lonely and mad. I ought to know. My
daddy left us, and my mama stayed pissed."

I raised my hand. "So because I'm supposedly lonely, I'm angry?"

"Are you going to deny you're lonely?"

"That's none of your business."

He exchanged a knowing glance with Steve. "You answered my
question, right there."

"I wasn't finished! You're saying if I had a man, I could be happy
in a patriarchal, sexist context, but it's clear you don't want to acknowledge my marginalized, intersectional identity as a woman of
the African diaspora!" I was very proud of my usage of all the new
vocabulary words I'd discovered in Dr. Oludara's handouts.

Abdul pointed his finger, Public Enemy–style. "See now, I didn't
say all that. What I said is, you wouldn't be angry if you had somebody to make some good love to you—"

At that, Dr. Oludara raised an objecting finger, but I cut in.

"If I'm so mad and lonely, what's your excuse? It's ten sisters to
every brother on this campus, which means you've got plenty some-
bodies to choose from. And yet you still got that funky attitude."

Other women clapped, urging me to tell it like it was. Pat covered
his mouth, but I could tell he was laughing.

"I got a right to be mad," Abdul said. "I grew up in the 'hood.

Your daddy's a doctor. Plus, a fine jawn like you with some meat on your bones, you could get a man, easy, if you calmed yourself down and stopped talking back to men."

Abdul leaned back and gave a smile.

"Talking back?" I shouted. "I am not a child! I'm grown! And this has nothing to do with you growing up in the 'hood! This has to do with you wanting a woman standing in front of a stove, barefoot and butt-naked, frying your chicken and dodging the grease."

"Naw, that's not it at all. You try getting stopped by the police every five minutes."

"Where, Abdul? On your walk down to the corner to get some fried chicken?"

"You can't get no chicken in Thatcher. There's only the Rib Shack." Abdul held out his hand, palm up, and Steve hit it loudly.

"You know what I mean, you goddamned male chauvinist pig!"

"Sister Garfield, please, let's not get abusive." Our professor's voice was serene.

———

There weren't many colors that Roz and I could wear to the Beta Alpha Beta spring rush. Other sororities on campus had their own colors. Along with being forbidden to wear Beta colors—orange and cream—we were barred from wearing the colors of any other sorority to the rush: no red, white, pink, green, blue, or yellow. I chose a belted gray dress, Roz a brown suit. We both wore black shoes.

Roz and I arrived forty-five minutes early in the faculty dining room. The rush was scheduled to begin at 7:30, but by 6:58 the Betas had already gathered. Each of the nineteen Betas wore orange outfits, like a human explosion of sherbet. Roz held me back, letting three others go before we went through the receiving line, shaking hands firmly. Then the line broke up, meaning it was time to mingle individually. My roommate left my side, and I stood there, veiled in awkwardness. I inched away when Tiffany approached but bumped into a Beta behind me; they'd tricked me with a maneuver from *The Art of War*.

"Hey there, Ailey."

"Hello, Miss Cruikshank."

She gave a grudging smile. As an aspirant, I couldn't call a Beta member by her first name, something only a serious Beta potential would know.

"Ailey, if you were a fruit, what would you be?"

"I don't like fruit, Miss Cruikshank." This was the safest answer. Choose an orange—a Beta color—and you were in trouble, because you would be presumptuous. But you had to be careful when picking another fruit that could be associated with a different sorority. Apples were red and white. Or watermelons could be red. But they also could be pink, and there was the green rind. Nana was a member of the pink-and-green sorority; in one of her monthly letters, she'd asked if I wanted her to arrange things with her organization, but I hadn't responded.

Tiffany's features were small and even. Her hair was blow-dried and pulled into a low ponytail that grazed her shoulders. Folks on campus talked about how fine Tiffany was, but I couldn't see it. She didn't have a hint of color in her white complexion, and as thin and bony as she was, she resembled a hungry vampire.

"Ailey, do you know who Violet De Saussure is?"

"Yes, of course. Violet Elizabeth De Saussure was the daughter of Adeline Ruth Hutchinson Routledge, one of two founders of this esteemed institution of higher learning."

"That's it?"

"Um . . ."

I'd become tipsy with cleverness, and now I'd missed something. I racked my brain for additional Freshman Orientation information that Dean Walters had made us memorize. I recited in a rush.

"Okay, okay, Routledge College was founded in 1873 as an institution to educate African American women, though it went coeducational in 1922. Our college is aligned with the American Missionary Association, an organization founded in 1846 for the abolition of slavery and the spread of Christianity."

"Nothing else?"

"Oh, wow . . . um . . . I don't think so."

Tiffany's face shined with sudden righteousness. Her thin nostrils flared, and she cupped her hands around her mouth.

"Calling all sorors! Calling all sorors! This young lady does not know who Violet Elizabeth De Saussure née Routledge is! Can you believe that?"

The Betas turned in unison and descended. The unseen sister behind me placed her mouth next to my other ear and proceeded in a menacing shout: "Do you mean to say that you don't know that Violet Elizabeth De Saussure née Routledge, along with fifteen other superlative African American women, known as the 'Lilies of the Nile,' founded the Alpha chapter of Beta Alpha Beta Sorority Incorporated on the campus of Routledge College on February nineteenth, 1912?"

Tiffany stepped aside, and Darlene Morris took her place, leaning into my face. Darlene was in my Organic Chemistry class, one of only three females, and, after me, she received the best scores on assignments. In terms of Routledge's historical color-struck standards, Darlene made the cut: like Tiffany, she looked white, but she was very heavy and well over six feet, and she had chronic acne, which made the pale skin of her face red and bumpy. She'd had to write to the Beta nationals to force the Routledge chapter to take her; the Nationals had decided there was no justification for turning down someone with a perfect grade point average. We'd heard that during underground pledging, the Betas had burned her bottom with live cigarettes, urging her to drop, but she hadn't. Now she had standing as the hardest Beta on campus: her line name was "The Grim Reaper."

"You're so pathetic," Darlene whispered. "I feel sorry for you, you know that? Really, really sorry."

I moved back from her pointing finger, but the unseen Beta dug her nails into my arm, as Darlene asked, could I recite the names of the sixteen Lilies of Beta Alpha Beta Sorority Incorporated in alphabetical order?

I could not.

And did I know the founding and guiding principles of Beta Alpha Beta Sorority Incorporated?

I did not.

Who were some of the most renowned members of Beta Alpha
Beta Sorority Incorporated?

I didn't know.

Then Tiffany and Darlene changed places again.

"Ailey, aren't you Lydia Garfield's little sister?" Tiffany asked.
"Lydia pledged here, didn't she? I believe it was the fall '86 'Eight Is
Enough' line. We're updating our chapter directory, and no one can
find her. Can you help us find her?"

She began to giggle, and Darlene and the other Betas joined her. I
hadn't told anyone about my sister, not even my roommates. They
didn't know I'd only come to Routledge because Lydia had gone
here. That I only wanted to pledge Beta for Lydia, who'd joined
the sorority in her sophomore year. I wanted the right to wear the
orange-and-white jacket that she'd left behind in our house. It had
her line name on back: "#7: Too Black, Too Strong." I'd kept her
downfall to myself, but someone must have found out, and while
my mother asked our parish priest to say special prayers for my sister, the Betas were mocking her. Laughing at my family troubles,
planning my downfall, and all because Abdul had sat at my table in
the refectory and argued with me in class.

The weight of my home training threatened to crush me. I imagined Dean Walters calling Mama to say that I had wrapped my
hands around the ponytail of one of Routledge's most distinguished
students, in order to imprison her, to keep her from running away,
while I punched the shit out of her with my other hand, because
Tiffany had implied, if not actually uttered, an insult against my
drug-addicted sister—though now, Tiffany and Darlene were whispering in my ear, calling me a whore. Telling me they didn't take
dirty girls like me into Beta. They had to keep their chapter clean.

When my tears began, I closed my eyes and beckoned a song:
"This Christmas," by Donny Hathaway, Lydia's favorite holiday

tune. I imagined the cheerful horn section at odds with the near sadness in Donny's voice. Mama played it every Christmas, just like she still made Lydia's favorite dessert from scratch, banana pudding with a custard base.

By some signal, the Beta mayhem ended. They walked away from me to the front of the dining room and formed a hand-holding chain. Moments later, an older alumna Beta walked to the lectern. She apologized for being late; there had been traffic on her drive from Atlanta. She informed us that guests should take their seats; the Beta Alpha Beta rush was about to begin. After another hour of games like "Name That Beta," and "Are You Ready for Beta?" the rush was over. I trotted ahead of Roz across campus. In the room, I ignored her obviously corny jokes.

———

I wonder how differently things would have unfolded if I'd had enough time to cool my temper before the intramural game the next night. Maybe I still could have joined Beta in the fall. In time, the cigarette burns on my bottom would have faded, with the help of cocoa butter and vitamin E oil.

But as Uncle Root liked to say, the women in our family were hot-tempered going back generations. Folks needed to get out of the way of his women when their blood was riding. He would laugh when he said this. To the old man, our anger wasn't a bad thing, and I let mine take control. I didn't care what happened after.

———

In the gym, Abdul was easy to spot. He sat at the far end of a top bleacher by himself. I climbed the steps toward him, pausing to keep from bumping into too many people. As I listened to the squeaking of sneakers, I didn't feel graceless about my inability to make conversation. Abdul and I sat together quietly, though sometimes he would clap for his team.

When Tiffany arrived with Darlene, they sat on the opposite side of the gym. Both were shooting me narrow looks, and it gave me a perverse charge. I'd upset the Sherbet Queens.

"Ailey, you want to take a walk to my dorm?" Abdul asked. "My roommate's gone to Atlanta for the weekend."

"Sure," I said. "Why not?"

When we crossed the yard, Tiffany shouted his name; she'd followed us. Even after what she'd done, I was embarrassed for her as she ran toward us. When she grabbed his sleeve, I turned my head and looked at the blackberry bushes instead. They were bare this late in the season, but I couldn't stand to see Tiffany's face.

"Come on, Abdul, let's go back to the gym," she pleaded. "Come on, let's get some nachos. My treat."

"Thanks, baby, but I'm not hungry. I'll call you tonight." He snapped his fingers. "No, wait. I got a test. Tomorrow, maybe. Or the day after. We'll see."

When he and I walked away, she lost her renowned composure, the reasoning behind the line name she'd been given while pledging Beta: "Portrait of a Lady."

"That fucking hoe better not write Beta in the fall! You hear me! That hoe better not come near any of my sorors, either!"

Not since Antoinette Jones had I been called out of my name, and I touched my head, remembering my bald trauma. When Abdul put an arm around me, Tiffany began screaming epithets about my crackhead sister.

In his room, I reached into my purse and pulled out a condom. I handed it to him, took off my clothes and underwear, and lay down on his bed. As he moved inside me, I began to cry. He asked, what was wrong? Nothing, I told him. Keep going.

V

The North, therefore . . . has much more than an academic interest in the Southern negro problem. Unless the race conflict there is so adjusted as to leave the negroes a contented, industrious people, they are going to migrate here and there. And into the large cities will pour in increasing numbers the competent and the incompetent, the industrious and the lazy, the law abiding and the criminal. . . . The crucial question, then, is: What does the black immigrant find to do?

—W. E. B. Du Bois, "The Black North: A Social Study"

THIS BITTER EARTH

❖

When Maybelle Lee Driskell began first grade, there was only one school for Negroes, the one at Red Mound Church. On Sunday, this was where she and her family worshipped, but from Monday through Friday fifty-nine Negro children sat in the two rooms of the church. The first room was in the church sanctuary, where the children sat in the pews and balanced their books on their laps. The other room was the fellowship hall, which had three picnic tables. That was the room for the middle and high school students, a group that thinned as the children of sharecroppers dropped out to join their families in working the land.

In 1954, when Maybelle Lee was eleven years old and told everybody she knew to call her "Belle" now, the principal of Red Mound Church School had walked into the second room of the church—the middle and high school room—and announced the Supreme Court verdict in the *Brown v. Board of Education of Topeka* case. Miss Rosalie McLendon was wreathed in triumph. She was a plump, brown-skinned spinster with short, neatly pressed hair. During the days of the week and on Sunday, her flesh was stuffed into an unforgiving girdle underneath the fashionable dresses a Negro seamstress in Macon made for her.

That day, Miss McLendon's second in command, Mr. Lonny Maxwell, stood beside her. His future ruin as an alcoholic was years away. That afternoon, Mr. Maxwell continuously nodded, while Miss McLendon explained what the *Brown* case meant: school segregation was over now, and Negro children could sit alongside white children in the same schools. No longer would the white children spit out of their bus windows at Negro children who had to walk through the countryside to school. And no cast-off textbooks with torn or missing covers and pages, either. One day, there would even be Negroes who taught white children—everything was going to change!

As W. E. B. Du Bois had prophesied, though, everything did not change in the aftermath of the *Brown* case. The Chicasetta School Board allotted money for one bus to take the Negro children in town out to Red Mound, but the schools in Chicasetta would remain segregated. The textbooks were still cast-off and filled with racist abuse, and it was beyond comprehension that Negro teachers would ever instruct white children.

Six years later, the newspapers would report about Ruby Bridges, the little girl who was the first Negro child to integrate an all-white elementary school in New Orleans, Louisiana. One would think that a six-year-old in pigtails wouldn't be so frightening to a bunch of adults; after all, what could she do, a child only recently liberated from infancy? Would she throw up or pee on somebody? Stick her tongue out and let it dance? Yet the segregationists in New Orleans acted as if Ruby was a dangerous animal. They gathered their defenses to resist her. Until they became used to seeing Ruby's small body encased in her fancy church dresses, Monday through Friday, climbing those endless-to-a-six-year-old steps, the whites in New Orleans who didn't want their children sitting next to a Negro girl broke fool in front of that learning place. Taunting Ruby. Threatening to charge through the phalanx of U.S. Marshals who surrounded her. One white woman promised to poison Ruby, and so Ruby's food always had to be carried from home, packed in a brown paper bag by her mother. Another white woman put a chocolate-colored baby doll into a coffin and shook it as the little girl walked along.

But even with these local and national disappointments, there was a sustained hopefulness in Miss McLendon. During monthly convocations, the fifty-nine students and Mr. Maxwell would crowd into one room, and Miss McLendon would talk about her responsibility to the race. She'd remind the students that though she'd attended Spelman College, a renowned school for the education of Negro women, there had been only three professions open to her: nurse, social worker, or teacher. Of course, Miss McLendon could have set her sights on lawyer or doctor, but those professions were difficult enough to pursue for Negro men, and Miss McLendon knew she didn't have the strength to chase those dreams. (Here, Miss McLendon would smile in a modest fashion.) That was how she settled on becoming a schoolteacher, and God had continued to bless her, elevating her to the level of principal. She didn't seem disappointed that her educational kingdom was a two-room church with a potbellied stove for warmth in the winter.

Miss McLendon's prize student was Belle Driskell, and she focused her attention on the girl, telling her how smart she was. That Belle had the intelligence to become a schoolteacher as well—even a principal. And Miss McLendon threw broad hints that she needed someone to teach in her place, once she retired. As a girl who'd grown up in Chicasetta, Belle knew the people and they knew her. Surely, Mr. Lonny Maxwell would take over as principal at Red Mound School, but Belle could be his second in command. They could do great things together, and Belle shined under Miss McLendon's attention. Belle was not only flattered, she was relieved that her life's work was decided for her, and that this work would not be like her mother's, the country wife of a farmer.

In her junior year of high school, Belle informed her mother that she intended to apply to Miss McLendon's alma mater, Spelman College, which was eighty-five miles away in Atlanta. Belle had not thought this choice would be a problem, as Miss Rose had known her daughter wanted to be a teacher for five years. Miss McLendon had discussed Belle's future with the lady. The principal had been to dinner at the Driskell household several times; always Miss Rose would send her off with a big plate of leftovers at the end of the evening.

Belle named her choice of college as she and her mother were sitting on the porch, snapping field peas. Her mother kept her eyes on her bowl of peas, as she told Belle, wasn't no way she was gone let her only girl go to Atlanta. It was over a three-hour drive from Chicasetta in Hosea Driskell's pickup.

"But Miss Rose—"

"—and why you gotta go to college anyway? You gone be done with high school next year. That's more than enough. Back in the day, all my teachers needed was eighth grade."

Belle would have been ready to fight somebody if they had called her mother ignorant, but that's exactly how she sounded right now. "Things are different these days."

"Well, I need you here."

"Why?"

"'Cause I said so. Unless you the mama now."

"But Miss Rose—"

"What I say? Go on and snap them peas. Supper in two hours."

The mother's fingers kept working, and it would be many years before she told her daughter that her heart had been thumping fast. Belle was her last child, and her second favorite. Her first favorite, Roscoe, had a birthday coming up, but he was serving twenty years on the chain gang for murdering another Negro man. All Miss Rose could thank God for is that Roscoe hadn't killed anybody white. Otherwise, he would have been smoke and meat in the state's electric chair. But that sentence might as well have been a lifetime, because Roscoe wouldn't let anyone in his family visit. He was too ashamed, and he'd sent Miss Rose away the seven times she'd tried to see him.

That year had been strange, unsettling. The season of peace that Chicasetta had experienced had broken: Tommy Pinchard Jr. had died. He'd been the last legitimate male heir of Wood Place, and the only stopgap to the Franklins' troublemaking. Since his death, they had grown bolder. Cordelia, Tommy's daughter, had neither the backbone nor the inclination to rein in the Franklin clan, and violence had erupted. Though the Franklins hadn't claimed credit for the incident, a young Negro man in town had been found dead, hanging from a tree on the land that the Franklins rented on Wood Place. The Franklins weren't afraid of Cordelia. She had a husband, though, and after the dead Negro's funeral, he drove out to Wood Place and informed the Franklins, that was it. They needed to find another place to live, and though the Franklins stayed in

Chicasetta, the clan scattered, renting pieces of land in the possession of other rich landowners who weren't bothered by their violence toward Negroes. And so another Negro who lived in Crow's
Roost had been beaten to within an inch of his life after failing to
step off the sidewalk for Jinx Franklin, who was almost an old man.
But instead of his benevolence emerging, Jinx's brutality had rip-
ened with the years. His sons and younger brothers were equally
mean. They had been known to corner Negro girls and women on
country roads, gang-rape them, strip them naked, and leave them
to be discovered.

Roscoe's crime hadn't been directed at the Franklins, however. It
had come as an odd cloudburst, a crackling of the rage he'd carried
since the day he was born. Miss Rose said that he'd come out of her
with a temper churning in his arms and legs, though he'd been a
pretty child, the first in a line of similarly beautiful children: dark-
dark with red underneath his skin, so that when the sun touched
him, he seemed to glow.

In the year since Roscoe had been sentenced, Miss Rose had begun to keep her daughter close. After her pronouncement against
Spelman, she walked the house at night and checked on Belle when
she hoped the girl was asleep. She began to say Belle had a gift for
fixing hair. Belle could start her own business, right in Chicasetta.
No need to leave, for there were plenty colored women who'd let
her touch their hair.

Miss Rose hadn't considered that, while she didn't allow Belle out
of her sight anymore unless her child was climbing in the truck
with Hosea to be dropped off at the new colored high school in
town, there was church on Sundays and at church, there was Uncle
Root. Her daughter's great-uncle had been saving money for Belle's
college tuition since she had turned three years old and had recited
her ABCs in front of the church congregation, before turning to
recite from the first Chapter of Genesis, to the amazement of everyone there. Looking at that tiny girl talking about, in the beginning
was the Word.

Throughout Belle's seventeenth summer, Uncle Root methodically plied his charm. On Saturday mornings, he drove to Chicasetta from the campus of Routledge College, steeling himself against the possible danger on the country roads. Twice, he had passed white men, but he did not show his fear. To his shame, he pretended to be a fellow white man, giving them friendly waves as he passed them by, instead of the frightened respect that a Negro man would. His great-niece needed him to listen to her mother's harangues, so he took the chance. He sat beside Miss Rose in the glider as she informed him she wasn't gone lose another child.

"I understand," he said. "I see what you mean, niece. Folks don't understand a mother's love."

"Naw, they don't!" Miss Rose said. "I carried that girl! Not nobody else!"

In the rocking chair on his other side, his sister watched him. Dear Pearl would snap her bowl of field peas. Or she'd peel tomatoes. Or she'd peel peaches. Or, in the sparse light of the evenings, sew scraps of cloth together to make quilt squares.

In the fall, before the weather broke into a chill, Uncle Root suggested to Miss Rose that if Spelman College was too far away for Belle to attend, maybe she could let Belle travel a short piece up the road to Routledge College, where he taught history, instead. It was only twenty-five miles away. And Dear Pearl rocked in her chair and gave her brother a sideway smile but kept her hands busy on her task. She was the big sister, had held that baby boy in her arms the day he was born, and after their mother had died in the 1918 influenza epidemic, Dear Pearl had raised him. It had been she who had given him the nickname "Root," because of that almost supernatural charm of his.

That next fall, in 1962, Miss Rose, Hosea Driskell, and Belle drove in the pickup truck toward Milledgeville, then took the turn off toward Thatcher, where Routledge College was. For the journey in the truck, Belle and her parents donned church clothes. Though he wore brogans for his corns, Hosea was in a suit with a white shirt and string tie. Miss Rose wore heels, stockings, an all-in-one girdle, and a light-blue dress over that. In the truck, they squeezed their daughter against the passenger window. Pine, wisteria, and cedars passed by, nodding to Belle, *Hey, girl, you finally got out your mama's house!* She didn't know what to expect, but the campus was covered in the same trees as her parents' farm.

A gravel road leading to the gates and beyond, until a grand structure appeared. A steeple reaching many feet: De Saussure Chapel, and the mother touched her daughter's arm. Since Belle had received her letter of admission, Miss Rose was grateful for bragging rights. Negroes in town had expressed their public sympathy about Roscoe's stint in prison, but word had come back to Miss Rose that folks were saying she thought herself above people, what with Uncle Root being a professor and Hosea and Miss Rose making such a good living on the Pinchards' land. Her son's crime was the Lord's judgment against pride. But now Belle would be a schoolteacher, the highest rank for a Negro woman, and that shadowed her brother's fall. Don't tell Miss Rose that God won't able.

They climbed out of the truck and Belle's daddy unloaded her boxes and walked them up the stairs of the dormitory. After the boxes were settled on the floor of Belle's room, he kissed the top of her head, but when the mother put her arms around her daughter, Miss Rose didn't want to let the girl go.

"I'm all right," Belle said. "Come on. Don't be like that."

When her parents left, she looked around. She wasn't used to sharing sleeping quarters, and the two beds in the room alarmed her. Belle's parents were country, but their house was big, with four bedrooms. She'd always had her own room, but when her large-eyed, brown roommate opened the door, Belle smiled brightly at her.

––––––

During Belle's first week on campus, she wondered if she had made the right choice of a college. Maybe she should have found some spunk and applied to Spelman anyway. The campus was in the country, but the students acted as if they were walking around their own private metropolis. The girls dressed in church frocks, heels, and stockings every day, along with wearing lipstick and powder. The boys wore starched pants and collared shirts with ties. And

Belle never had seen so many light-skinned folks congregated in one place. In particular, the sororities were filled with the fairest girls, whose curly, waved, or stick-straight hair definitely could pass a fine-tooth-comb test. Each of the sororities seemed to have a strict quota for members who were darker than brown paper bags, too, for there were no more than two girls per organization who could be characterized as "high brown." Belle felt like a fly in the proverbial buttermilk, though she was dressed beautifully. Dear Pearl had a fine seamstress hand; she had sewn all of Belle's clothes growing up, but her taste was old-fashioned. So Uncle Root had picked out a huge, modern wardrobe at Rich's in Atlanta, after driving there, passing for a white man, and befriending a widowed saleslady to whom he gave Belle's measurements.

Yet besides her great-uncle and her roommate, Marie Giles, Belle was very lonely. On Sundays, Belle walked with Marie to the chapel's "refectory," a fancy word for cafeteria. They passed by many light-skinned girls who threw haughty, unfriendly glances. After Sunday breakfast, a staid service in De Saussure Chapel. An uninspiring, quiet pastor who didn't shout to glory or even raise his voice, as he droned on about Sarah and Hagar.

Then, too, there were the distinctions made between the male and female students. There were strict curfews for the students, but only the females were punished for walking into the dorm lobby after ten at night. The males could roam the campus at will. Leaving through the gates of campus was an even bigger challenge for a young woman, for she was expected to be attired in a dress that was four inches below her knee, and she was required to wear a hat and gloves and carry a pocketbook—no matter the outside temperature. A young woman was not allowed to bring a car on campus or to leave through the campus gates without either two other female students or one of her parents, but male students didn't need a chaperone and were free to drive.

But there were a few respites that first year. Marie made friends easily, and wherever she went, she dragged Belle along. There were so few men to serve as romantic partners, Routledge seemed like a single-gender college, and the young women in Routledge Hall acted accordingly. They dressed up in cocktail gowns, put on music, and danced with each other. Those who didn't want to dance cheek to cheek with another female sat at card tables and played many hands of bid whist. Belle discovered she was good at the game. She had a competitive side.

And on Friday afternoons, her uncle Root—whom everyone called Dr. Hargrace—taught Freshman Orientation in De Saussure Chapel. He strode down to where the pews were located, instead of staying up on the stage. In his patrician drawl, he got in subtle digs at the unequal rules between men and women on campus, snorting that women had been allowed to drive since Mr. Ford had designed the nation's first automobile. In between his slight protests, he drilled the freshman class on the institutional history of the college, such as, the school had been founded during Reconstruction, when droves of white northerners had rushed south with their missionary zeal. They considered themselves friends to the Negro and worked as teachers at grammar schools built to educate former slaves, and colleges were started, too. But the Bostonian who had founded the college had not been a white woman. She had been a free Negro.

Before the Civil War, Adeline Ruth Hutchinson Routledge had lived with her husband, Coffee; their child, Violet; and her spinster sister, Judith Naomi Hutchinson. Then the husband died, and after the war, the sister died, too, and Mrs. Routledge and Violet traveled down to Georgia to help their newly emancipated people. Teachers were greatly needed to aid the masses of ex-slaves who didn't even know their ABCs, let alone how to read; it had been against the law, before the Civil War.

When Uncle Root sensed his charges' boredom, when they began to fidget and rustle on the chapel pews, he would spin them a tale or two. His favorite subject was the great scholar Dr. W. E. B. Du Bois, the first Negro to earn a doctorate from Harvard University. After he made history, Dr. Du Bois had come south to teach at Atlanta University. The color prejudice had been terrible, and the violence as well. Every year, there were tales of lynchings from the countryside, but the worst loss that he'd experienced was the death of his toddler son to diphtheria. Uncle Root didn't linger on the great scholar's feelings, though. He talked about what the man's wife, Nina, must have felt, watching her child die.

"I know some of you young men in the room think the Negro man makes the money for his family. If he dresses in suits, he leaves the house to go to work. If he's a farmer, he puts on overalls to work the fields. If the Ku Klux Klan shows up to the house, he stands in the doorway to protect his family, and, if need be, he's the one who swings at the end of a rope. And you think because of all that, the Negro man should get the glory."

Uncle Root raised a finger as the young men in the room shifted their seats. A few rolled their eyes.

"But when that Negro man leaves the house, he doesn't understand, he leaves his wife alone. She's the one who does the backbreaking work to keep his house clean. She raises his children. And that's only if he earns enough money to make sure she doesn't have to work. If he doesn't, she's leaving her children with her mother or grandmother, and dressing up, too, to make money, as a schoolteacher. Or, more likely, she's working as a domestic in the white folks' kitchen, or she's out there in the fields right beside her husband, helping him to plow, but then she's got to make sure the children are all right, and feed them, and feed him, too. And again, keep the house clean.

"So I want you to think about how Mrs. Du Bois felt that day her little boy died in 1899. There was a diphtheria epidemic in Atlanta that year, and because of how brutal the white people in that city were, the Negroes were afraid to give the vaccination to their children. Dr. Du Bois was afraid, and so he wasn't able to save his child. The little boy that Mrs. Du Bois had carried inside her body passed away. No man can truly understand a mother's pain."

Uncle Root walked closer to the front pews of the chapel. Briefly, he put a hand over his mouth.

"Lord have mercy, that lady must have grieved so badly for her baby boy! But Mrs. Du Bois continued to support her husband in his work. We don't see the written record of what she did, but rest assured Mrs. Du Bois labored right alongside him. And she bore him another child, though she must have been so afraid of losing another baby. I think that woman was so remarkable! If it weren't for Mrs. Du Bois, there would be no great scholar. And if it weren't for Adeline Ruth Hutchinson Routledge, another remarkable Negro woman, there would be no Routledge College. Make no mistake about that."

Uncle Root raised the finger again. He let the quiet muster, for his young audience was listening now. They'd forgotten their boredom, or at any rate, the female students had.

"I want every one of you to meditate on the importance of the Negro woman. Without her struggles, who would our people be? We'd be heathens, that's what we would be! We'd be stumbling around in the dark! The Negro woman is the best our race has to offer. My children, we must always cherish and love this woman. We must never leave her behind."

Beside Belle, her roommate giggled: Marie had a very big crush on Uncle Root. She was gossipy, too. In October, when a boy named Stanley Culpepper walked across the refectory, sat down at Belle's table, and asked her to the fall formal, Marie told everybody on campus the details about the young man. He was from Detroit and talked frequently about the many wonders of Motown. The word on campus was that Stanley only dated light-skinned girls, but something about Belle must have caught his eye, dark as she was.

For the formal dance, Belle wore a rose chiffon gown and Stanley cleaned up nicely for the evening. He bought her a carnation wrist corsage and gave her his arm to walk into the refectory, which was decorated like a ballroom with cloths covering the tables. But then he left her for twenty minutes inside the gym while he drank bug juice with his Gamma fraternity brothers outside, ignoring the danger of snakes that might be braided into the blackberry bushes a few feet from the gym's back entrance. After the dance, Stanley asked her to walk to his Buick, and Belle thought things might be looking up. Maybe they would drive for a late dinner. They said Paschal's in Atlanta had good fried chicken. The restaurant was owned by distant cousins of some folks in Chicasetta. But after Stanley stopped at the gate and paid the five-dollar bribe to the guard, he drove out to a country field. The car bumped along in the grass until Stanley stopped the car. Then he leaned over, and without kissing Belle, he shoved his hand up her dress.

She started kicking but couldn't do much damage: she was only five feet and not even a hundred pounds. But after pushing her down on the front seat of his car and throwing her dress and crinolines into her face, Stanley couldn't figure out how to pull off her merry widow.

"What's going on here?" Stanley leaned back on the seat, puffing air. "I thought you knew the score."

"What's that?" Belle asked.

"I take you to the dance and you put out. That's why I asked you."

"Well, that's not going to happen, Stanley."

"Look, kid, you'd be pretty if you weren't so black. But you are." Stanley's voice hardened. "And if I don't get me some pussy, you're walking back to campus."

It wasn't the first time Belle had been called that: "black" meaning "dark-skinned." It was an insult, but her father liked to say, these niggers with little color shouldn't be so proud. All light skin meant was that some cracker had forced his way up a poor Negro woman's dress, and what kind of prize was that? Naturally, her father didn't say that around Uncle Root and Dear Pearl, but it was no secret that Belle's grandmother and great-uncle were partial to darker-skinned folks, too. Look at the people they'd married.

It was a mystery to Belle why Stanley was so color-struck. He wasn't even fair-skinned. He was a meriney-toned fellow, and with that nappy hair, Stanley wasn't passing nobody's fine-tooth-comb test, neither—but she was sitting in this boy's front seat. She should be careful about making him mad. She didn't even know where Stanley had driven them, and these were the years when the white men in the area would drive up to the tall iron fence protecting the college proper. They would park and lean against their cars for two or three hours, watching. Just watching, before they climbed back in their cars and drove away. The college president was obsequious with the influential whites in the other towns, those worried something communist was happening on campus, so there was danger for Belle in the dark. Those white men might catch Belle walking back, her heels in her hand, her stockings ripped by snagging pebbles. Whatever they might do to her, she couldn't go to the police. No one would believe a Negro girl or even care, no matter what shade she was.

Belle shifted in a crunch of crinolines. "No, Stanley, I'm not walking. And if you keep on, I'm going to tell my uncle."

"You think I'm scared of some hick-ass farmer? Girl, I'm from Detroit!"

"You don't know Dr. Jason Freeman Hargrace? The history professor? He's my uncle, and unless you want him to get you expelled, you start this damned car and take me back to campus." Technically, Uncle Root was her great-uncle, but the details didn't matter. She was in a dill pickle here.

So Stanley started the engine and took her to her dormitory. Belle thought that would be the end of it, but some days later, she was in her room marcelling her roommate's hair. Marie was difficult; she was tender-headed and always accused Belle of trying to burn her.

"Ouch!"

"You know better than to be hopping up when I got these irons in your head." Belle pulled away and Marie turned around. There was a line between her eyebrows, the hurt of a scolded child.

"Why're you being mean, Belle, when I have a secret for you?"

"What's that?"

"Somebody told me something about you. Ask me who it is."

But Belle continued curling for the next twenty minutes, patting Marie's shoulder periodically to keep her from squirming. When she was done, she made swooping motions with her fingertips over Marie's hair.

"Go see how pretty you look!"

At the mirror, Marie started back up. "I bet you want to know what I heard. Stanley Culpepper said that a certain someone had relations with him out in the farmer's field. Twice."

"Really?" Belle's voice held no interest, but there was cut glass in her stomach.

"He sure did. You know who that certain someone is? You." Marie laughed, a sound with a hungry edge.

"That's what he told you?"

"No, he told Floyd. Floyd told Dennis. Dennis told Walter, and you know Walter and me are going steady."

Marie lifted a chain from underneath her blouse. On it was a gold ring set with the tiniest of rubies, but Belle kept a straight face when she told her roommate that she'd planned on losing her virginity to Stanley—yes, it was true—but when he'd pulled down his pants, his "boy" had been tiny, and worse, it wouldn't get up. She'd pulled on it for close to forty-five minutes while it flopped back and forth. Poor thing. Stanley was deformed, but even though he couldn't do the deed, Belle had promised him that they'd always be friends.

YOU MADE ME LOVE YOU

❖

By the fall of Belle's sophomore year, Stanley Culpepper had transferred to Albany State and Belle kept to herself. No other young men approached her for a date, and that was fine by her. She wasn't like her roommate; Marie Giles and her boyfriend, Walter Lipscomb, already had planned their wedding for after graduation.

Belle didn't have time for men. She'd decided that she didn't want to be a schoolteacher in the public schools; now she wanted to be a college professor. The work required to reach this apex, a master's degree and possibly a doctorate, didn't scare Belle. Whenever Belle walked across campus, there was a strut to her step. She might be too dark for her color-struck classmates to think she was pretty, but she had a perfect grade point average and was in the running for valedictorian of her class.

The first semester of her senior year, she took Medieval to Renaissance Literature. She was an English major, and it was a requirement for graduation, but the third week of classes, she tried to check out the translation of *The Canterbury Tales*. She wanted to get the jump on the final paper, but the librarian told her someone else had it, Geoffrey Garfield. Belle had spotted him in class. He was a senior, too. He'd given her appreciative looks, but he was much too fair-skinned for her tastes.

The day she walked over to the men's dorm, she dressed carefully as usual, in an orange cashmere sweater, matching skirt, and black shoes with a heel. Her hair was freshly pressed and curled, and she'd dusted cocoa powder on her nose to kill the shine.

She sent the dorm proctor to retrieve Geoffrey, and in the lobby, he told her he needed the translation for his paper.

"But we could share it, couldn't we, Belle?"

"I don't want to share. I want to read it all by myself."

She sighed, but he smiled and asked permission to walk her to

the library. He'd bring the book along, and maybe they could ne-
gotiate. She told him, all right, but she really needed the book, and
she didn't have time for all this back and forth. When they squeezed
into a carrel in the stacks, Geoffrey whispered an invitation.

"What?"

"I said, may I escort you to the fall formal?"

"Why?" Belle didn't whisper. She wanted to make sure he heard
her, but Geoffrey didn't miss a beat when he told Belle that she was
beautiful and smart, and he'd be proud to have her on his arm.

"You think I'm beautiful?"

"Of course, Belle. Don't you have a mirror in your dormitory?"

She searched for excuses to be rude, but this boy had thrown her.
"All right, Geoffrey—"

"—call me Geoff—"

"Fine, Geoff, let's say I agree to go to the dance with you—"

"—great!—"

"Hold on a minute. I didn't say I'd go. I said, let's say. Let me ask
you something: Do you know my uncle, Dr. Jason Freeman Hargrace?"

"Sure. Everybody knows him."

"Well, he gave me a switchblade, and I know how to use it, just in
case you try to get fresh."

The reference to possible violence didn't seem to put Geoff off.
He laughed and let her know he'd like to take her and the switchblade to the fall formal.

Her ivory gown and cape for the formal were duplicates of Mrs.
Jacqueline Kennedy's inaugural ball ensemble. Geoff wore a tuxedo
with a white jacket and bought her a pink rose corsage. When the
disc jockey put on "Reet Petite," he stood. This white-looking boy
had nerve, but on the floor, he twirled Belle around with rhythm.
After the dance, he wanted to drive to Paschal's in Atlanta, but she
put him off.

"Some other time. Could you walk me back to my dorm, please?"

"As long as there's another chance, I'm fine. And so are you, Belle
Driskell."

After the formal, Geoff began showing at her dormitory to walk her to breakfast, to sit with her at lunch and dinner, and to accompany her to the library. He insisted on carrying her books, too. There were stares and whispers, and Belle made sure to dress in her best everyday attire. She wanted those high-yellow girls who thought Geoff should be with them to get a look. He brought her the candy that his mother sent him in gift packages and copied out excerpts of his favorite poems for Belle in his neat cursive handwriting.

She already had received Marie's gossip, that he wasn't like others, those who only dated darker young women for sex. For some reason, Geoff preferred chocolate-toned ladies. He was a gentleman, too. Other young women had reported that when you said no, he was real sweet about things. As weeks passed, Geoff offered his own biography: he was from the north, from the City. His father was a doctor, and he expected Geoff to become a doctor, too. Geoff had wanted to be a schoolteacher, but his parents had vetoed that decision, and he wasn't sure he'd be able to make it on his own. But Geoff had refused to pledge his father's fraternity, the same one W. E. B. Du Bois belonged to—the only defiance Geoff felt he could get away with.

The day he asked Belle to go steady was the first time they kissed, on Violet's bench by the side of the library. If someone really wanted to spy, they could, but the bench that was named for Adeline Routledge's daughter was sheltered by a canopy of tall bushes. When Geoff leaned over, asking, could he have a kiss, Belle didn't expect much. There had been a boy in seventh grade who'd kissed her, but that had been wet and uninspiring, so she was surprised by the feeling that took her. She felt like she was drunk on her daddy's jar of moonshine, and she put her hand up to Geoff's cheek, then the back of his neck. She opened her mouth, letting her tongue travel to his.

He was the first to stop. There was a catch to his breath as he said, gee, she was wonderful. He hoped he wasn't being ungentlemanly, and Belle told him, no, not at all. She didn't know how to ask for more kisses, to tell him she wasn't satisfied with those few seconds. But she didn't want to be forward, so she folded her hands in her lap. He sighed, and then stood, reaching for her books. Halfway back to the dorm, he began to recite a poem by Langston Hughes, about Negro girls of various, beautiful shades, like chocolate.

"Listen to you!" She giggled. "You are something else."

"You bring it out in me." He jumped a bit off the ground. "You make me so happy, Belle."

They kissed the next day, and every day afterward, until it was time for the Christmas break. Before Geoff drove home for the holidays, he asked for her address, and until the break was over, she received long letters from him nearly every day. And when they returned to campus, there were more kisses on Violet's bench outside the library, and if Belle wasn't completely satisfied with necking a few minutes, she told herself, her restraint was for a purpose. She couldn't lose control, because Geoff might be nice but there was no way a boy that looked like he did could bring home somebody who looked like her. He was not her great-uncle Root, a pale-skinned man who had married a dark brown woman and adored her. No man was as good as her great-uncle—not even her daddy—and that was fine, because Belle was only having some fun until she graduated. But not too much fun. She didn't need to get pregnant; she had plans for her life.

That would have settled things, if it hadn't been for her brother Roscoe. He changed the entire course of her life, the night that Roscoe let his blood get up. That famous temper of his reared, even behind the bars of the regional prison where he was serving twenty years when Roscoe sassed a guard there. At least that's what the warden told Miss Rose and Hosea when they went to pick up their oldest son's body.

In five years, when one of Roscoe's friends on the chain gang was released, he'd tell the Driskells that the guard had tried something with Roscoe. Something like what a man wanted to do with a woman. He wouldn't say exactly what it was—not in front of Miss Rose—but the friend had hitchhiked to the farm of Roscoe's parents because he felt like he owed them something. After the friend sat awhile and drank some sweet tea and ate through the generously loaded plate that Miss Rose had prepared, Hosea Driskell gave him a ride to Madison. The friend had traveled a good distance, in order to do right by Roscoe, and the father wasn't gone let somebody who'd offered a powerful kindness wear out his shoe leather.

But that truth given by Roscoe's friend was five years away, and thus, when the warden told the Driskells they could pick up their son's bullet-ridden body, the warden didn't tell them he was sorry for their loss, only that if they hadn't shown in forty-eight hours, he would have buried their son in an unmarked grave. That was on a Wednesday afternoon.

Early Thursday morning, Miss Rose went into town to the home of Cordelia Pinchard Rice. She told Cordelia's maid what happened, and when the maid showed her into the front room (because Cordelia was "good white folks," a liberal type of lady), Miss Rose asked if she could make a long-distance phone call to Routledge College. They didn't have no phone out in the country. Cordelia said, of course, and so Miss Rose left an emergency message for Uncle Root with the campus operator, and after he received the message and called Miss Rose back, he walked over to the refectory and found his niece at a table, eating lunch with Geoff and Marie.

He wouldn't tell Belle what was wrong, only that they were driving to Chicasetta right away, and he ignored Belle's questions on the journey. It wasn't until he pulled up in front of the house of her parents that he cautioned her to brace herself, and told her what had happened. And then, Uncle Root held her as she screamed and cried. She smeared cocoa powder on the front of his clean white shirt, but he didn't complain. The funeral was held four days after that, and Mr. Cruddup, the family mortician, somehow made Roscoe look completely natural; that was remarked upon by those who attended the service at Red Mound Church. Three of those days, Belle would not remember, only that when her memory returned, she was coming to at her brother's funeral. She fainted again, and when she woke up, her mother was sitting on the side of her bed. Belle told her mother everything had changed. She wasn't going back to college. She would stay at home and be a beautician, but Miss Rose set her lips: she had waited too long to see her baby girl become a schoolteacher and she won't gone be disappointed. She needed something to look forward to, and she held Belle, patting her daughter's back. She kissed the top of the girl's head, as she hadn't since Belle had been very little.

When Uncle Root drove Belle back to campus, she told her room-mate that she'd experienced a loss in the family, and she didn't really want to talk about it. She repeated this every time Marie brought up the subject. She was numb, but when Geoff met her on the steps the next morning, Belle found that she had missed him. He looked very frazzled but relieved, and on the walk to the library, she looked around, making sure no one was close. Then Belle told Geoff what had happened to her brother. That she wasn't ashamed of him, but she knew what the campus gossips would make of Roscoe's life, if they discovered that he'd died on the chain gang.

And her brother had been more than a criminal. He'd been a nice young man, respectful of his mother and (mostly) helpful to his father in the fields. He'd been the best big brother ever, too, so protective and sweet. Nobody ever messed with Belle, because they knew Roscoe didn't play about his baby sister. Seven girls had shown up to his funeral—two of them married with children—and cried as if their hearts were broken, but that wouldn't matter to these snobs on campus, if they found out Roscoe had been on the chain gang.

"So please don't tell anybody," she said.

"I would never do that. You can always trust me," Geoff said, and the earnestness in his large brown eyes moved her. She asked, could they go for a drive somewhere that night? She'd meet him at his car. Throughout the day, she didn't make any plans. She only wanted to feel something other than sadness. That's what she knew, as she watched for the sun to give way to darkness, and she walked over to the male students' parking lot. Geoff was waiting for her, and when he paid the blackmail fee to the guard at the gate, she wasn't embarrassed.

Geoff drove his Seville to the same field where Stanley had tried to take advantage of her, but he was tender as a baby when he kissed her. After seconds, he tried to stop, but she told him, keep on. Please don't stop, and she leaned against the baby-blue front seat, took Geoff's hand, and placed it underneath her sweater, and inside her bra. His hand was so warm. So lovely as it found her skin and touched it to fire. She pushed the hand away, but only for a moment, because she found that she wanted him to put it someplace else. She really wanted that, and she told him again, don't stop, so he didn't.

———

Belle's dream told her that she was pregnant before her body did. She was rocking the most gorgeous brown baby she ever had seen. A little girl whose arms, thighs, and belly were ringed with fat. The little girl looked so much like her own mother that Belle was sure that she belonged to Miss Rose, who appeared in the dream. But when Belle tried to give the baby back to her mother, the little girl screamed until Belle put her to the breast that was instantly exposed. When she awoke, she was confused. She'd never been a dreamer, like her grandmother Pearl, who was known for the visions that either predicted or indicted.

It took time for Belle to catch on that the dream-baby was inside her. Miss Rose always had tracked her cycle, asking every month, had she seen the moon? There was no morning sickness, either, no weight gain, only full breasts. By that time, she'd received her letter that she had been accepted into Columbia's Master of Arts program. Uncle Root had told her he already had the money saved for her tuition, and he'd located a lady in Harlem who kept a respectable boardinghouse.

Belle had plans for her life, and so she was angry. Not at Geoff but with her brother. If Roscoe hadn't killed that man, he wouldn't have been sent away to the chain gang. If he'd only not sassed that guard and been shot. If he hadn't been dead and lying stiff and powdered in his coffin, Belle wouldn't have been at the mercy of her grief and she wouldn't have given in to Geoff.

Or rather, Belle had given in to herself, for Geoff had kept asking her until the moment he had slipped inside her, was she absolutely sure? Was he being a gentleman? And though there had been pain that first time and a bit of blood in her panties that evening when he returned her to her dorm after she had smoothed her hair and clothing—the second and third and fourth times had been free of everything except a glorious, wet heat. She'd calmed down enough after those few days to tell Geoff they should stop, and though he was disappointed—anybody could see that—he quickly agreed. He told her he hadn't meant to take advantage.

Belle was not only angry at her dead brother, she was angry at herself. Another, braver girl would be trying to collect money, the five hundred dollars that the gossips whispered it would take for a girl to pay a certain Negro doctor in Atlanta who could get rid of a baby. According to those gossips, the doctor was sage and clear, but Belle kept remembering the girl at her high school who had bled to death from a botched abortion. It had been the year that Miss Rose had pulled Belle close, trying to protect her daughter; as cranky as Miss Rose had been, she was a kind woman at her core. More than that, a godly woman who did not believe in speaking ill of the dead. She told Belle, that girl should have tried a different home remedy before the pregnancy took hold. Like drinking a tea made from wild carrot seeds, right after you lay with a man. Or ginger root tea, or even the more dangerous pokeberry wine, which only the truly desperate employed. The girl hadn't even consulted one of the euphemistic elixirs sold at the dime store that "helped to unblock menses" or "eased women's complaints." Instead, Belle's high school classmate had stuck a crochet needle inside her, which had caused her to bleed but didn't get rid of the pregnancy. And the girl had died from an infection.

Miss Rose would not attend the girl's funeral, because she was too upset thinking about that girl's mama crying over her child. She told Belle it was important to keep her wits about her, sure enough, but if Belle ever slipped up with a boy, don't be sticking nothing up her. And if the home remedies didn't work, Belle had people. She could come home, and Miss Rose would help her raise her baby. Anything was better than what that poor dead girl had suffered.

———

The night Belle told Geoff she was pregnant, she asked if they could drive to their spot. She felt badly for him. He'd be receiving sober tidings, instead of the loving she knew he was expecting. In the field, he reached for her eagerly, but she pushed at his chest.

"I've got some bad news, Geoff."

He leaned back. "Please don't tell me you don't want me anymore, Belle."

She touched his face. "It's not that. You're a nice guy. Real nice—"

"This sounds like you're about to break up with me—"

"Will you let me say what I need to, honey? Just wait. Just hold on."

When Belle told him that she was pregnant and he began to weep, she knew that she was on her own. She hadn't expected chivalry, but at least some offer of support. A monthly stipend for the baby. Something. She was nauseated by the odor of his Old Spice, which only a few weeks ago had driven her crazy with lust, so that she'd wanted to rub herself all over him. While Geoff had been inside her, he'd told her that he loved her. But along with the package of wild carrot seeds and the dried ginger that Miss Rose had given her—her daughter was too forgetful about one and too frightened of the other to use—Miss Rose had told Belle, men would say anything to get underneath somebody's dress. And God had made men that way, in order to keep the world full.

Geoff wiped his face and told her he was sorry. He hadn't meant to break down. But he was just so happy. They were going to have a baby, and then he asked her to marry him. She thought it was a joke, but he grabbed her, kissing her and rubbing her stomach. They should get married right away, he said. Tomorrow, even, and Belle lay against the seat. She should have felt relieved, but she was frightened. It was one thing to hug up and kiss with a boy you didn't know, but marriage was a lifelong pact. Her family didn't play, when it came to matrimony. Once she and Geoff married, something seriously bad would have to happen for them to accept Belle leaving him.

In a few days, she walked to the faculty building to see her great-uncle. She shut the office door but didn't sit down.

"Uncle Root, I'm going to tell you something. Please don't be mad."

In the roller chair, he twisted his knees back and forth. "Beloved, I could never be angry with you."

"I'm expecting a baby, and I won't be going to Columbia. I'm so sorry."

"All right, but who might be responsible? And is this situation voluntary?" He extended a surprisingly strong hand. His manner was refined, but his relatives knew the truth. If pushed, he could be a very dangerous man: Roscoe hadn't been the only one with a temper.

"The boy I went to the formal with, and no, sir, he didn't force me."

"That is very good, Maybelle Lee. Anything else?"

"Can you go with us to tell the folks? Geoff wants to get married."

"At least he's honorable. I'm sure you're happy about that."

"No, I'm not, but I made my bed."

He snorted. "I guess you did, but I won't ask where you made it."

"Uncle Root!"

He told her, don't be shocked. He'd once been young. He'd enjoyed that time thoroughly, and she should do the same. Old age was coming faster than she knew, and that weekend, he drove the young couple to Chicasetta and stood beside them in her parents' front room. At the house, Belle told her brother Norman, go somewhere. Leave, because she didn't want any trouble. It would be bad enough with their parents and the grandmother.

She had made sure her fiancé had gone to the bathroom before they left—twice—and she forbade him to drink anything before the drive. She didn't want him to have to visit her parents' outhouse, not before they got married, because he might change his mind. She had counseled her fiancé not to beat around the blackberry bush,

either. Just come on out with the news. Belle made like it was a tradition, a man asking for her hand, but she was scared of her parents,
grandmother, and even Pauline, though she was the same age as
Belle. If need be, Belle would put the blame on her fiancé, that he
had cajoled her to leave her morality aside. She wasn't above saving
herself.

"Mr. and Mrs. Driskell, I'm so pleased to meet you," Geoff said.
"And I'm equally happy to meet you as well, Mrs. Collins."

Dear Pearl looked at him, then made a farting sound with her
mouth.

The young man soldiered on. "Belle is expecting our first child,
so we're getting married Thursday morning at the Chicasetta courthouse."

At those words, Miss Rose gave a cry, and Dear Pearl stood. She
looked with disgust at her granddaughter and the boy who was
standing on the rug she'd braided. When she left, her steps were
heavy on the wood floor. Pauline followed to the room she shared
with her mother, after shaking her head dramatically; she was saving her body for the Lord.

"Say you is?" Belle's father asked.

"Yes, sir."

"Boy, what you say your name is?"

"It's Geoffrey Garfield, sir."

"A'ight, then. But I got me a shotgun to clean, in case you change
your mind. 'Cause I'm not fooling with you 'bout my baby girl."

Uncle Root put out a hand: come on now, give the young man a
chance. The damage was done, but Geoff was trying to do the right
thing. Then Uncle Root suggested that the three males in the living
room take a walk. See the property and chat a spell. So they did,
and they stayed gone for over an hour. When they returned, Geoff
looked very pleased with himself. Puffed up in some way, but Miss
Rose said nothing, other than to ask, had he eaten?

While the men sat on the porch, Belle fetched the bacon grease
can, then the skillet to fry the chicken her mother had been mari-
nating in garlic, salt, and onions overnight in the new refrigerator

she was so proud of. Some white flour. A spoon and some meal for corn bread. The bowl of fresh-gathered eggs. Baking powder. Sweet milk. A bit of sugar. Butter sliced and melted, because her mother didn't make her corn bread with lard.

Miss Rose issued instructions and not much else. It was her way when she was furious, keeping her words to a minimum. Her blows were rare, but dangerous when they arrived, and defense was never an option. Stay silent until the storm passed. Her children had learned that was best. The corn bread was out of the oven and cooling on the kitchen table before Miss Rose had her say.

"I was so proud. My child was gone be a schoolteacher. That was something I could finally talk about after church, 'cause I had one boy on the chain gang, and another always running after some fast-tailed gal. But I guess the Bible was right. Pride go before a fall, 'cause here you come with a big belly. Girl, don't you know anybody can get married and shoot babies out they ass?"

Belle reached for a clean cloth to wipe down the already clean table. Nothing she could say would make her mother feel better, and Belle had her own problems. A baby coming and a boy she hadn't planned to marry, but she knew one thing: soon as this baby came, she'd figure things out, and she still was going to be a college professor. Her life would be larger than this kitchen, that front porch, and even the field out front. She intended more for herself.

"I ain't never knowed you to be color-struck, though," Miss Rose said. "That why you change your name? The name I give you ain't good enough?"

"No, ma'am, that's not it—"

"That's why you gotta call yourself something else? So you could get you a high-yellow boy from the City and walk around thinking you better than me? Let me tell you, Maybelle Lee Driskell, yellow don't mean a thing. Yellow and some change will get you a orange drink down to the dime store. But the white peoples ain't gone let you sit at the counter, 'cause somebody yellow is still colored. And now you gone take my grandbaby up north, you and this boy. Lord have mercy."

Miss Rose sat down at the table and sighed, and then stuck the knife into the corn bread. As she cut generous, even slices, she told her daughter, go get her daddy and them. Food was ready, but be sure to tell Geoff, wash his hands at the pump outside. Just 'cause he was in the country didn't mean he could act any kind of way.

That Thursday, Geoff wore a black suit to the courthouse. Belle was dressed in a pink silk chemise purchased by her great-uncle, who had brought her a bouquet of white roses, and her father was the first to shake the hand of the groom, who couldn't stop smiling.

The ceremony had been a short event, a few words pronounced by a white judge, but there was a picnic back at the house. It was a big, noisy affair that included six chickens fried by Miss Rose, a hog barbecued by Belle's daddy, many bowls of potato salad and greens, homemade light bread, various cakes and pies provided by the other relatives and the sisters of Red Mound Church, and un-numbered quart jars of moonshine. The celebration lasted well into the evening, as if this weren't a shotgun wedding in the middle of the week, but a joyful something planned well in advance.

After a couple inches of moonshine, Geoff announced that it was the best wedding reception he'd ever been to, and he sure was glad it was his. Everybody laughed and talked their country talk with him, and he talked it right on back, in a cadence that was familiar, but that Belle hadn't known he possessed. Halfway through the evening, she saw him go around back to the outhouse, but she decided not to worry about his getting disgusted at the smell; they were legally man and wife.

Geoff even won her mother over, telling Miss Rose that she definitely knew how to fry some chicken, that it couldn't be beat by any restaurant, not even Paschal's in Atlanta. Miss Rose turned to her daughter and said it looked like Belle had herself a good husband. Make sure she did right by the man.

DON'T LET ME LOSE THIS DREAM

◈

After their hasty marriage, Belle and Geoff returned to campus as if nothing had happened, though he smiled broadly when he showed up to the dormitory to walk her to meals in the refectory. He drove her to their spot out in the field three to four times a week, and they made love with abandon. The worst had happened; why not take their pleasure?

There was graduation in May, and Belle walked across the stage as salutatorian, grateful that she still wasn't showing. Then they moved in with her parents at the farm. She spent two weeks sleeping with her new husband in her single bed at night, and during the day, listening to him showering her mother with compliments about her cooking, her kindness, her beauty, his gratitude to be part of this wonderful family. Miss Rose forgot her suspicion of proper-talking yellow boys; for fourteen days, she beamed and killed many chickens.

Then it was time for the newlyweds to leave for the City. Before he allowed Geoff to take his great-niece on their northbound journey, Uncle Root gave him a copy of *The Negro Motorist Green Book*, so they could find diners, hotels, and boardinghouses that would serve them, once they traveled out of family territory. Cut the journey into two or even three days, and only drive during daylight, Uncle Root ordered. Stay well under the speed limit, and Belle should sit in the back of Geoff's Seville. Mixed marriages were illegal below the Mason-Dixon line. If stopped by police, Belle should pretend to be a maid, because her husband looked white, and, well, obviously she did not.

When they arrived in the City, the young couple moved into a furnished two-bedroom in a neighborhood with one short tree per block. No trash in the streets, but there was a gritty, unclean feel to the area. No matter how hard Belle scrubbed the windows of the apartment, they stayed dingy. The glass made a vague outline of the sun, which already seemed fainter. Geoff's father had mailed him the address and key and paid six months' rent, but the young man didn't seem eager to see his own folks. It took three weeks to visit the elder Garfields, on a Saturday morning when the sun shined through rain. An omen of the Devil beating his wife.

Geoff wore a blue suit and tie, and Belle wore a white linen dress that skimmed over her midsection. A lady in a black dress and an apron answered the door, and Belle, surprised but pleased by the woman's dark brown skin, stuck out her hand.

"Hello, Mrs. Garfield! It's wonderful to meet you!"

The lady shook her head, but when she turned, Geoff was still back some paces.

"Baby, no. That's Delores. She's our maid."

In the living room, the pale, gray-eyed Claire Garfield chided her son for waiting to visit right before she was due to travel to the Vineyard. Minutes of that, then she pushed her nose right into their bedroom. Had Belle talked to her obstetrician about birth control, for after the baby? What had he advised? Belle tried to deflect with humor. When that didn't work, she turned to her husband, but he looked at his shoes.

It was the father who stopped the assault. He was a handsome, urbane man.

"Please excuse my wife," he said. "She doesn't realize that you aren't here for a medical visit." Zachary Garfield was as pale as his wife, only with brown eyes. His hair was trimmed neatly with silver at the temples. But though the elder Garfields were stylishly attired—Zachary wore a light, summer-weight suit with no tie, and Claire's pink silk shift came only to the knees, revealing shapely legs—they sat on opposite sides of the room. And unlike Belle's parents, there was no connecting vibration between her in-laws. They didn't throw each other secret smiles or exchange any significant glances. There was a chilly unfriendliness between them, which made Belle hopeful. It seemed they weren't united in their disapproval of her. Claire Garfield was on her own.

While Belle sat on the sofa, feeling like a dead cat on the line, the maid brought in new guests. The older brother, Lawrence, was on summer break from Amherst, taking his Volkswagen bus on the road. He'd popped up with his new wife, a long-haired brunette: a white girl. He and Diane had eloped, he announced. His voice was loud, a combination of *voilà* and *take that*, but his parents seemed fine with it, especially his mother, who had hugged Diane at the door, patting her back gently as if the white girl had the hiccups. His parents' lack of chagrin seemed to bother Lawrence.

It was 1966, and Belle knew about interracial couples. There was one who attended Red Mound, a white man and Negro lady who had lived as husband and wife for over twenty years, though they couldn't marry under Georgia law. And Belle's own lineage was mixed, though it wasn't mentioned outside of the family. But a white female with a Negro male? That just wasn't done where she came from. Geoff's brother would have been lynched for something like this, down in Chicasetta—he could be killed for even looking too long at this white girl. And why was she with Lawrence anyway? Was something wrong with her, something not readily noticeable? The mother-in-law was pleased, though. That was clear.

"Excuse me," Belle said. "Could you direct me to the powder room?" Minutes later, she flushed but lingered on the toilet, sighing many times. As she washed her hands, she looked around for a regular towel, but there was only one as fancy as the soap. This was a caution, washing all this money down the sink. When she came out, the white girl was waiting on her.

"Hi!" Diane said.

"Oh," Belle said. "Hey yourself."

"I've been so nervous! Lawrence told me Claire would be tough, but she seems really nice."

Belle noticed that the white girl didn't even think to put a handle on their mother-in-law's name. She'd automatically moved to first-name basis with an elder.

"Not to me," Belle said. "You know that woman asked me 'bout birth control? Here I am expecting, and she want me to stop 'fore I even get started." After her efforts to speak properly all morning, her speech now thickened into sap.

Diane blinked in confusion. "What woman?"

"Who the hell you think I'm talking 'bout? Besides you, me, and the maid, ain't no other woman in this house. I'm talking 'bout Miss Claire." She didn't care what this white girl did—she hadn't been raised to call her elders by their first names. Belle might be up north, but she hadn't left her home training behind.

"Oh my goodness! I'm so sorry!"

Diane's lower lip trembled. If this white girl started crying, Belle knew she would, too, so she laughed.

"I fixed that heifer, though. I said, 'Miss Claire, could you tell me what birth control is? 'Cause I ain't heard of such.'"

"Good for you! Give 'em hell!"

Diane put her arm around Belle, who tolerated the embrace only seconds before pulling away.

———

Regularly, Geoff drove her to her obstetrician, Dr. Moorhead. He was one of Zachary Garfield's fraternity brothers, and he approved of the advice of her mother, that walking would cut her labor time. In that year, the neighborhood was safe. Not fancy like the Gold Coast area, where Belle's in-laws lived, where well-to-do Negroes were lighter than brown paper bags and welcomed the sight of fine-tooth combs, but not dangerous, either.

Belle wasn't afraid to walk by herself, but she was lonely. There wasn't another woman to keep her company, an older female who could advise her about this and that. Not only did she long for her relatives, she craved the food, the offal of home: chitterlings side by side on a plate with collards. Peppers in vinegar, and a cake of hot water corn bread fried in bacon grease. For dessert, a slice of water-melon, a fruit that her mother-in-law forbade in her house.

One day on a longer walk, Belle found a corner store. There were bright turnip greens sitting outside in a bushel basket and an old lady behind the store's counter. She was walnut brown with pressed and curled white hair. There was a space between her teeth like Belle's, what everyone down home called "a lie gap," though Belle didn't know why. Folks with a gap didn't seem more dishonest than anybody else.

The old lady came from behind the counter and touched Belle's pregnant belly without asking.

"It's a girl! I can tell by the way you carrying." Her name was Martha Clyburn, and she was from Boone, North Carolina, but her late husband had been from Macon, Georgia. Pretty as all get out, but a no-good skirt-chaser dropping outside kids everywhere, and cheap with his money, too. She was grateful for the four boys that he gave her—all grown, alive, and not one on the chain gang— but she hadn't been upset when the husband passed away. That insurance money had come right on time. She'd bought the store with it.

Belle told her the husband's actions didn't surprise her. "I ain't try-ing to speak ill of the dead, but them Macon men got reputations."

"Child, please! You ain't said nothing but the word."

Whenever Miss Martha walked from behind the counter, the baby would kick excitedly inside Belle. Maybe it was the free food she gave them whenever the produce supplier drove in and brought in new stock. In late August, a slab of home-raised streak-o-lean. Early September, a paper sack of scuppernongs, which thrilled Belle to her soul. She didn't even wait to wash the grapes. She bit into one and sucked the inside from the skin, crunching the seeds.

Miss Martha smiled, showing her gap. "These colored folks up here don't like no scup'nons, but I knowed you would."

"I shole do. I thank you so much."

Whenever Belle tried to offer money for the gifts, the old lady told her, put that away. Don't be hurting her feelings. She helped Belle load her bags of fresh vegetables in the child's red wagon Geoff bought her, and Belle dragged the wagon home behind her, thrilled with her treasure. She'd bring what she could up the stairs to the apartment, leaving the rest in the hallway for her husband to de-liver when he returned from school.

When Belle's time came, Dr. Moorhead brought in a group of male residents, who took turns peering at Belle's shaved, gaping privates, and, oh, the pain that held her in its humiliating twist, because she was afraid to accept twilight sleep. And, Jesus, if this was labor cut in half, what was the full parcel? During those agonizing seventeen hours, fourteen minutes, and thirty-seven seconds, Belle prayed for her own death. Let that damned baby survive on its own, if it wanted to cause this much trouble. But Belle forgot her pain the moment she was handed the white-faced, blue-eyed ugliness. She loved this ugly thing. She loved her so much.

The next day, the nurse came to the maternity ward to demonstrate how to bathe the babies.

"How about we start with yours, Mrs. Garfield?" The nurse scanned the rows of infants. A finger pointed at a dark infant, born at a low weight. Belle shook her head. Another dark baby, a little girl. That went on for several minutes, with the other mothers laughing, already forgetful of their gendered agony, but the game wasn't funny to Belle.

The younger Garfields named their daughter Lydia Claire, and when mother and baby came home, Belle didn't want to leave the house. It was so cold outside; sometimes, it even snowed. Other days, the baby had an accident after Belle dressed her in one of the outfits that her grandmother had sewn and mailed to her. The baby would squirt shit through her cloth diaper, gurgling as if having accomplished a goal.

Other than visiting Dr. Clements, the pediatrician who shared Dr. Moorhead's practice, Belle only left the house on Sundays, to visit her in-laws. She'd hoped the parlor ambushes would end once a grandchild entered the scene, but the baby only became another weapon. Miss Claire constantly joked that if she kidnapped the baby, the police wouldn't return her. Lydia didn't look a bit like her mother, she told Belle, and she criticized nursing as old-fashioned.

Every time, Zachary Garfield would cut into his wife's harshness, talking over her.

"I'm very happy you're nursing, Belle." He smiled. "It's so healthy for the baby, and these modern women care far too much about high bosoms. You're such a good mother." He'd hold out his hands for Lydia, and she'd grab his silly tie, printed with a bear digging into a honey jar. The baby nuzzled into his chest as her grandfather rocked her, kissing the top of her head, saying Lydia was his favorite little girl in the world. His pretty, pretty girl, and there would be a serene interval before Belle's mother-in-law began her jagged criticism again.

After these visits, Belle would lie in her apartment bed, crying, as Geoff stood in the doorway. Whatever he'd done, he was so sorry. Please forgive him, as she covered her head with the spread. Throughout the week, she asked Geoff to go to Miss Martha's store with her list. Please give her apologies. Tell her friend that it was just too cold to go outside, and please don't forget his home training. Put a handle on that lady's name.

One Sunday, she found her nerve to confront him. "Geoff, I'm not going to your mama's this evening."

"What's wrong, baby? Are you not feeling well?"

"No. I'm sorry to say, your mama is mean. I can't take her anymore."

"I know that."

"You do? Then, why don't you say something?"

"Like what? 'Mother, you're a cold bitch, and always have been a cold bitch, but I need you and Dad to pay my rent and tuition'?"

"Lord Jesus!" Belle sat on the couch, hard. Where she came from, folks didn't talk badly about their mothers or let anybody else do it, either. She couldn't even imagine her baby calling her a name, once she learned to talk. Even an indirect insult would be insufferable. That's how her brother Roscoe had got sent to the chain gang: he'd sliced a man's throat open for calling him a goddamned bastard. The man had been insulting Miss Rose by association. He had been a stranger to the area; otherwise, he would have known to be careful with Roscoe Driskell. Everybody in Putnam County knew that boy had been crazy plus a full tank of gas.

"You don't need to call your mama out her name," Belle said. "Just tell her don't hurt my feelings. I know she's disappointed."

"You mean, about the baby?"

"Yes, that. But the other thing."

"What?"

She couldn't believe she had married this thick-headed boy. Not only didn't he have proper respect for his mama but he wasn't that quick, either.

"Miss Claire's disappointed because I'm dark-skinned, honey."

"Oh, that. I don't care what she thinks. I love your color, May-belle Lee Driskell." He kneeled in front of her, and she slapped at his shoulder.

"I told you not to call me that."

"But I love that name. And I love the girl with it." He put his hand in a certain place, but gently.

"Don't you get nothing started."

He stopped touching, but Belle told him, it was too late. She put her arms around him, squeezing him tightly. He better go 'head and finish. They'd see his mama another time.

When the weather broke, she toted the carriage down to the bottom of the stairs, then went back up for the baby. On the sidewalk, her stride was hurried. She didn't want anyone to stop her, to look inside the stroller, see the small, white face and the green eyes that had changed from the blue of a newborn. She didn't want anyone to think she was her own baby's nanny. At the store, she called a greeting and Miss Martha rushed over, making glad sounds. She pulled the baby out of the stroller. What a big, fine young'un! Look at all them chins, and Belle told her, the baby was so light because of her husband.

"I done seen your man a bunch of times," Miss Martha said. "I know what he look like."

"You think she gone get her color soon? It's been a while now."

"Child, this is her color! See the tips of her ears? See 'round her nails? See how they ain't no different from the rest of her? This baby ain't getting much more darker."

"Oh. Oh." Belle wouldn't cry. Not now.

Miss Martha moved the baby to her shoulder. "I been so worried 'bout you, child. You lucky you came when you did, 'cause I was gone ask your husband where y'all lived and come see 'bout you."

"I'm sorry. Don't be mad. I just been . . ." Belle wished she held the baby. She could have dropped her face into the sparse, brown hair and taken in deep breaths. That odor of purity made her feel better, if only for a few minutes.

"I might be old, but I done had four chirren. You ain't got to lie to me."

"Miss Martha, it seems like I lost something I can't get back. And it's been making me real sad."

"Oh, child, ain't nothing wrong with you. All womens be sad after they haves a baby. And you did lose something. You lost your freedom. You can't never go nowhere without thinking 'bout your chirren. You tied to 'em for life. Even when they grown you gone worry 'bout 'em, 'cause this world is a mean old place."

Holding the baby, Miss Martha walked to the door, shutting and locking it. She put up the CLOSED sign in the window, and told Belle she had some coffee upstairs, and some pound cake.

A CHANGE IS GONNA COME

❖

Saturdays were for sleeping in—if the baby let her—and for cleaning the small apartment and walking to the store. Not for shopping, but for visiting. Miss Martha brought down a rocking chair, so Belle could properly visit for a long time.

Sunday mornings were for feeling guilty that she wasn't attending church and praising the Lord. Belle had been startled when her husband told her he didn't attend church because he didn't believe in God. She'd never met such a human being before, and it rallied her to try her mother-in-law's church a few times. But the woman was Catholic and her parish mostly white. For Belle, church was not only for worship, but also for fellowship. She hadn't felt comfortable sitting among those whom she knew wouldn't welcome her into their homes. Then, too, later, there would be a bland dinner at her in-laws', where she'd be dodging Claire Garfield's viciousness. Church didn't seem to sweeten that woman's cup.

Belle's guilt over missing church was smoothed some when Miss Martha told her she hadn't yet found a church home, either. So on Wednesday afternoons, when Belle came to shop, the old lady put up the CLOSED sign. While the baby slept, the two women would have Bible study. Miss Martha picked the scripture, and then she and Belle would talk through the words. Such as, what did it mean when Isaiah spoke of "drawing water from the wells of salvation"? That moved them into practical territory: both of them had grown up with pumps in their yards.

And five days a week, Belle rose early and cooked breakfast, sending her husband off to medical school with a full stomach and a sack lunch besides. Every day, Belle nursed her baby and touched her cheek and gave her love. While Lydia munched on the full breast, making cozy sounds, Belle told her that things would be different for girls when she grew up. Lydia would be a smart lady and accomplish greatness. She'd make her mama proud, and after Belle put her daughter down, she'd sit in the kitchen, drink her coffee, and read a library book. She rubbed the table's edge. Sometimes Belle scolded herself. She had a good life, especially for a Negro woman. She didn't have the right to want anything else, so she should stop feeling sorry for herself.

She shouldn't hate the City, though it was full of strangers. It was her home now. She shouldn't look to her door, waiting for her mother or Dear Pearl to walk through without knocking, assured of a country welcome. She'd despised that violation of privacy as a teenager, but now she longed for it. And she shouldn't wake in the night and sit up, looking at the ghostly colored shoulder of Geoff, wondering how she'd gotten to this moment. Even Belle's own baby didn't look like her—that adored, tiny being that Belle would have died for, just to make sure Lydia was happy and safe and loved.

When the telephone rang one morning, Belle almost didn't answer: her family contacted her infrequently, and Miss Martha never called, so Belle suspected the call was her mother-in-law. She ignored the sound until it stopped, but then the phone rang again.

"Belle, hi! It's Diane!"

"Oh. Hey yourself."

"How are you? How's the baby?"

"She's good. Crawling now."

Diane chattered on, telling Belle that she and Lawrence had enrolled in graduate school at Mecca University, she in the psychology program, and Lawrence in English. Then she dropped the news.

"I guess you heard about Lawrence and me breaking up."

"Really? I'm so sorry." Belle hoped her insincerity didn't show, for she already knew about the separation. The usually composed Claire Garfield had been upset, but Belle had been secretly pleased when her mother-in-law disclosed the news at Sunday dinner. Belle hadn't liked Lawrence anyway: he'd never called her once to ask, did she and the baby need anything? Stuck-up yellow bastard.

"Yeah, it's heavy," Diane said, and Belle made an understanding noise, even though she didn't know what that meant. "I have a studio near the campus now."

"But that's a Negro neighborhood."

"No, it's integrated, because I live there."

"Diane, one white person in five city blocks does not mean integration. Who told you that? Lord, today!"

Belle heard her mother's voice in her head: Diane seemed like good white folks, like Cordelia Rice down in Chicasetta. Give her a chance. It would be the Christian thing to befriend her, because this girl didn't have one bit of sense. Clearly, she needed some people to look after her. Though Belle didn't exactly want to be bothered, she asked Diane over to dinner.

"Oh, goodness! Really? You don't need to ask Geoff?"

"Girl, I'm grown. And I run this house."

"Then how wonderful! I can't wait to see you! I hope this means we're friends, because you can't get rid of me now."

Diane burst into giggles, for seemingly no reason, and Belle was surprised when her heart squeezed in response.

Some nights, her husband didn't come in until late from the library, and she began inviting Diane over regularly. On those days that Diane wasn't in classes, she took walks with Belle and the baby. It wasn't hard for Belle anymore with someone to help. If the baby made an accident, Diane would sing made-up songs to her while her mother stripped off the soiled clothes.

Soon, Belle felt no shame telling Diane she'd "had" to get married, though she didn't regret her baby. In turn, Diane offered her own secrets: she hadn't known Lawrence was a Negro when they began dating. When he let out his secret after an entire semester, he gave the excuse that he hadn't found the right moment. It hadn't been an issue for Diane, though, and it hadn't upset her parents when she took him home to meet her folks. Mr. Murphy had given a surprised grunt. He'd looked over at Mrs. Murphy, and when she'd nodded her approval, that was that.

Diane's was a big Catholic family of eight children, and she was the youngest. Her mother hadn't wanted Diane to be a workhorse like she'd been, some man's wife toiling in rural Maine. She'd had higher hopes for her daughter, but when she found out Diane was moving to Massachusetts for college, Mrs. Murphy had wept for a month. It was funny, for she hadn't shed a tear over Lawrence. He came from a well-off family and belonged to the Church. And he couldn't help what he was, Mrs. Murphy said, no more than Diane could. Her parents were descended from Irish immigrants. They were supposed to be white but didn't live any better than many Negroes. Her mother told Diane that she should see the lesson in that.

"I don't believe nobody in your family cared," Belle said.

"What do you mean?" Diane asked.

"I think if you had brought a poor boy home who looked Negro, it might have been different. Your daddy might have tried to kill him, but then, if he had looked Negro and had been poor, I don't think you would have wanted him in the first place."

Diane sat up, her brown eyes wide. "Yes, I would have! I wouldn't have cared! Don't you think white people can be color-blind?"

"That's a medical condition." Belle looked down at her coffee. She hoped the baby would wake up, crying to feed, but leave it to that greedy child to stay asleep, for once.

In weeks, Diane had a key to her sister-in-law's apartment, in case of emergencies. She had confided something else, this time at dinner, right in front of Geoff: she'd left Lawrence because she'd caught him cheating with an undergraduate student at Mecca, a young girl no older than nineteen. Or she assumed they were cheating: she'd seen them laughing together in the stacks at the library. Diane had rounded a corner to see the girl running her hand down Lawrence's arm as he leaned over her, looking at her in a way that should be reserved only for his wife.

This conversation was women's territory: Geoff had hung his head, ashamed over his brother. In bed that night, he'd said he hoped Lawrence's misbehavior wouldn't harm his own marriage, because Belle was married to a faithful man. She could take that promise to the bank and cash it.

At that meal in the small kitchen, Diane hadn't identified the girl's race. And when Belle had asked, had the girl with Lawrence been Negro or white? her sister-in-law had blushed and said she couldn't remember. Belle knew then, even if Diane didn't suffer from a medical condition, she truly didn't care what race somebody was. Instead of pleasing Belle, this discovery made her furious, and she walked to the stove, though the burners were off and had cooled.

Belle stirred a pot of lukewarm greens to cover the noise of her loud breathing. Her outraged exhalations, as she considered that Diane was a white woman who could walk through the world and stay blessedly unaware of the color line.

———

The day of the first riot in the City was in fall 1967. Lydia pulled up on a chair and let go for several seconds. Belle was excited, and though she had visited Miss Martha's store only the day before for their Wednesday Bible study, she decided to walk there and give the good news.

She was standing at the counter, holding Lydia, when she heard raised voices outside. Miss Martha held out her arms. The baby went to her, and Belle followed the old lady outside. In the street, folks were clotted, grumbling. A police car had stopped behind a late-model Buick. The driver's door was ajar, and one of the cops, an older, short white man, had pinned a Negro man to the hood of the police car. The other cop, also white, was younger, taller and leaner. He had pulled out both his club and his gun.

The Negro was dressed in a shiny gray suit and his hands were interlaced behind his neck. His stomach rested on the front hood of the police car, and Belle could only see the back of his trimmed, neat hair.

"Um, um, um," Miss Martha intoned.

"What you reckon he done did?" Belle asked.

"Probably nothing, child. You know how these polices is."

"He shole look hot in that suit."

"Don't he, though? Bless his heart."

Belle wasn't sure what happened next, if the man in the fancy suit said something off to the white cop pinning him down, or if the steady, loudening rumbles of the crowd agitated them, but suddenly the younger cop hit the Negro on his head with the club. There were raw screams and blood poured, and Belle began to shake. She thought of her brother: what Roscoe probably had endured before he'd been killed.

Miss Martha told her she smelled trouble, and hurried with the baby inside the store. She returned shortly with a large sack. She placed Lydia inside her carriage and fitted the sack at the baby's feet.

"You be sure to call me when y'all get back home," Miss Martha said. "You got the number. And don't worry 'bout paying for no groceries. You can catch me next time."

When Geoff returned to the apartment that evening, he was breathing hard. For two days, there were sirens and screaming outside and lights flashing through the curtains. Belle called the store, worried.

"Miss Martha, you all right?"

"Child, yes. The windows got busted, but I put up some boards. I'm upstairs, listening to the radio."

"I don't like you being alone over there. I'ma send Geoff around."

"You leave that man alone. I got my shotgun in case somebody try to mess with me. And I done seen worse with the Ku Kluxers back home. At least ain't nobody hanging from that telephone pole 'cross the street. Thank you, Father God."

"All right, then. But I'ma check back on you."

After she hung up, Belle remembered her sister-in-law, and when the girl answered the phone, she ordered her not to leave her studio. "Do you hear me, Diane? Don't make me pack up this baby and come sit on you."

"That's not much of a threat, Belle. You don't even weigh a hundred pounds."

"I weigh one hundred and ten, for your information."

"Oh my goodness. Excuse me, fatso."

By the end of the week, the neighborhood had calmed, and Diane showed for dinner. But this time, she brought company: Lawrence.

They sat closely at the kitchen table, laughing at inside jokes while the other couple cut eyes at each other.

When her sister-in-law called the next morning, Belle was chilly: "Hey yourself."

"You think worse of me, don't you? I could tell at dinner."

"You said you thought Lawrence cheated on you. Now, if you want to be a fool like in some Aretha song, that's your business." Belle wanted to punish her sister-in-law. She'd gotten used to one set of circumstances, and now she was being forced to adapt.

"Everybody can't be as tough as you."

"I'm not, Diane. I just have me some pride, and clearly, you don't."

"That's a really, really shitty thing to say."

Diane hung up, but the next day, Belle called to apologize.

There was much news that winter. The reconciliation of her in-laws stuck, and Belle found out she was pregnant again. At first, she concealed the news from her husband, and didn't answer his concern over her new crying jags. She told him only when she'd broken down and tried down-home methods, which didn't work; scalding-hot baths and cups of fresh ginger tea did not bring on her bleeding. But Geoff was so happy, as he'd been with the first pregnancy. She remembered that night in the field when he placed his hand on her stomach. Only twenty-three, but Geoff already believed he could work miracles.

When Belle thought she might be showing, she sent him alone to Sunday dinner at her in-laws'. She was too tired. That's what she said, but really, she didn't want to face her husband's mother. Her diaphragm had failed her, and she was barely holding on. But soon, Belle's fears wouldn't matter. In her third month, she miscarried.

Belle hadn't wanted the new baby, but when she sat on the toilet that early morning and the large red clump dropped from her, followed by slick blood, she stayed on the toilet and wept for an hour, until Lydia awakened, making her hungry sounds.

———

In April, Uncle Root called. He had on his funereal voice, with many clearings of the throat, and Belle knew that somebody was dead.

She walked backward until her foot found a chair, and when her great-uncle revealed that Martin Luther King Jr. had been murdered, she said "no" repeatedly, sucking up her tears.

Uncle Root told her the story about when he had met the minister. He'd heard the young man was speaking in Atlanta. Uncle Root had lost his wife, and it had made him reckless, the way Death could wiggle his square toes. Reckless because his college president had begun to send out warnings on official letterhead that any faculty member suspected of involvement in "civil agitation" would be summarily fired. But without telling anyone—even his family members—Uncle Root drove to Atlanta anyway and sat in the pews of Ebenezer Baptist Church, where Dr. King's sermon gave him new life. Afterward Uncle Root felt optimistic about getting older: the world was in smoother, better hands, and in 1963, he attended the March on Washington for Jobs and Freedom. Before he drove his car north for the march, he told Belle and everybody else on campus he was going. He knew he was openly defying the orders of the president of Routledge College, and he no longer cared. The man was a hopeless toady to white people, and if Uncle Root was fired because his boss wanted to lick the boots of segregationists, so be it. Uncle Root had some money saved for the uncertain future; for the time being, he was going to enjoy himself, like a hardworking Negro man should.

He took the entire week off and stayed with his friend Freddy Hamilton, who was an English teacher. The two of them had met while graduate students at Mecca, and Freddy, a "confirmed bachelor," had adored Uncle Root's late wife. Freddy used to stock his refrigerator and pantry with gourmet food for Aunt Olivia: tins of caviar, pâté, and exotic fruits such as mangos and papayas, and his guest room had been filled with fresh flowers and gifts. Often, the items for Aunt Olivia had been very expensive, such as the French perfume, and that red silk nightgown hanging in the guest room closet. But Uncle Root knew Freddy's romantic interests lay with young men, so he had learned to put his jealousy aside.

At the march, Freddy kept sighing and declaring, things just weren't the same without Aunt Olivia, and, oh, how he wished she had lived to see this gathering! The march lasted all day, but then someone announced that W. E. B. Du Bois had died in Ghana at the home of that country's president. Uncle Root had tried to collect himself as Mahalia Jackson took the podium. She was the lead-in before King, who was the expected climax of the long march. She was resplendent in her grand, church lady hat, the spiritual she sang so familiar. And Uncle Root had taken off his own hat, using it to cover his face as he wept over the great scholar, someone he'd considered a father, if only in his fantasies.

On the phone, Uncle Root stopped speaking for seconds, while he cleared his throat ferociously. Belle was quiet, too, waiting for him to speak.

"I can't believe it, beloved. I can't understand the choices God makes."

Who was he grieving, Dr. King or the great scholar? Or Aunt Olivia? Maybe he was missing everybody he'd lost from the time he was a child, and that sadness was on him, a pulsing cloud, like Belle had felt after she'd had Lydia.

She hung up and turned on the TV, hopeful that her great-uncle had been mistaken, but there was Walter Cronkite looking forlorn. When the phone rang again, it was her mother, shrieking. For five minutes, one phrase repeated: *Lord have mercy.* Listening to Miss Rose, Belle's heart began to hurt. The phone sounded a third time: it was her sister-in-law, talking through her sobs. Belle told her to come on over. She didn't have to be alone.

"Okay, but . . . can Lawrence come, too?"

"What I say? Y'all both are surely welcome." In the kitchen, she pulled out pans and pots. Back home, Negroes would be killing chickens for the rituals of mourning. Dr. King had been a stranger to Belle, but every Negro she knew adored him. In her hometown, on her college campus, he was next to Jesus: Miss Rose kept a framed photograph of the young preacher on the living room wall. When someone died, mourners had to be nice to each other for a few days, too. The fourth call came: it was Belle's mother-in-law, and she consoled the woman, all the while thinking, Dr. King was the only brown person her mother-in-law had admired. Belle didn't invite Miss Claire to visit, however. Home training only went so far.

There was knocking at the door. She answered, and the young couple at her threshold looked a mess. Lawrence's hair was rumpled, his clothes wrinkled. Diane's face was puffy and pink. Belle opened her arms, and her much taller sister-in-law rushed to her, weeping violently as Belle rubbed her back, saying, it was all right. It was okay. Belle put two full plates on the table, and when she filled Lawrence's coffee cup, he grabbed her hand. Soon, her husband was there. Mecca University had closed out of respect, but it had been frightening on the way home. A Negro man had blocked Geoff's way, but he'd let him pass after Geoff recited a random poem by Langston Hughes. Despite her grief, Belle found the energy to stand over the stove. She boiled collards with a ham hock. Thawed and fried two chickens. Baked a pound cake and several pans of corn bread. Mashed sweet potatoes for the baby, and then decided to make a pie.

She put a stack of Aretha records on the player. Belle refused to call her favorite singer by her full name: where Belle came from, the last name "Franklin" was an insult. The two couples had a dance party in the living room and tried to shake off their blues. Belle taught her in-laws how to play bid whist, and Diane learned how to talk smack across the board. Unlike the young Negroes rioting outside, they obeyed rules and stayed inside: the governor had imposed a curfew. But after three days of forced isolation, tempers broke.

"I need to get out there with my brothers! I should do something!" Lawrence shouted, without rising from the couch. His wife kicked his foot and told him, lower his damned voice. She pointed at the baby's room, where Geoff was reading Dr. Seuss out loud.

Belle went to the kitchen and returned with a plate of food for her brother-in-law. He asked, were there any more biscuits? If not, he'd love some corn bread.

Diane erupted: "You just ate breakfast!"

"Maybe he could eat again," Belle said. "Could you let the Negro have some peace?"

Her brother-in-law offered thanks and shoveled into his plate. He didn't see the women exchange their mocking smiles above his head. Their rolled eyes.

———

Down south, the old folks liked to say, trouble don't last always. This was true in the City, too. The streets calmed, though sadness lingered. This time, however, when Belle showed up at the store, the plywood hadn't been taken down. Miss Martha announced, she wasn't gone bother because she was leaving the City. She had waited for Belle to come by; she'd wanted to see her and the baby before she left.

"What? Miss Martha, no!"

The baby squealed happily. When Belle handed her over, she slapped at Miss Martha's chest and received a kiss on her forehead.

"Yes, child. I got to go."

"But why?"

"Child, I'm too old for this foolishness. I'm going back home. Let my sons take care of me." She handed the baby back and reached into her bosom for a slip of paper. "Here my address. Don't you forget to write. And send me pictures, too."

"Yes, ma'am. I promise."

She sucked up tears, as Miss Martha hugged her, the baby between them. The old lady refused Belle's help in packing her things, saying it would only make her sad.

The store sold quickly, and by that next week, there was a new owner behind the counter. A young woman with a juicy behind that hiked up a dress barely covering her thighs. And she told Miss Martha's business easily.

"Me and my man got this store real cheap."

"Well, welcome to the neighborhood!" Belle was hoping for a new friend, a Negro friend. Maybe she could take the store owner shopping and help her pick out a proper dress that would cover her privacy. "Where you from?"

"Right here in the City," the woman said. "Born and raised."

"Oh, okay."

"You know that old lady Martha? I think she might have lost it."

The new owner touched her head, and Belle felt her temper bloom. She reverted to her college voice, the consonants cut-and-dried. The vowels not as long.

"That is not true. Miss Martha was incredibly sharp. What would make you think otherwise?"

"I mean, why go back to the country, as bad as those honkies are? Blowing up shit and killing people. When the brothers take over, they're going to change all that."

Belle didn't want to fight, but within a few weeks, she was further disappointed. The store had changed produce suppliers, and now the vegetables were wilted like at every other place. And the woman was "sometime-y": one occasion, she might be friendly, and another coldly indifferent.

As spring gave in to warmth, there was no violence outside. No streets cherried over with fire, but Belle wanted to be back home. She longed to sit on the porch with the women of her family. To talk about nothing special, until the fireflies came. When she told Geoff that she missed home, he said she should be glad to be away from the south, with its Jim Crow laws and dangerous white men. And Belle was safe, but her longings stayed with her.

Born in the City, her husband wasn't familiar with the taste of healthy, green food you had picked only hours before. The sight of earth not taken over by concrete. That in darkness, if there was no trouble, the only sounds came from small beings. He didn't know that you could ache for a place, even when it had hurt you so badly.

DO RIGHT WOMAN, DO RIGHT MAN

◆

In that same year that Belle's grade-school principal assured her Negro students the world was about to change, Belle had begun to tell folks she wasn't ever getting married. Her listeners would laugh at her and say one day she'd change her mind, because didn't she want babies? And the only way a good girl could have babies was to get married.

Belle had come to her decision after an insemination of one of her father's cows. It was in April that year, so Cross Eye was the heifer who needed to get pregnant. In the fall, Spot would be the one. That way, the Driskells would be kept in milk and butter and cheese throughout the year. When the calves got big enough, Hosea Driskell would sell them for meat, and that would make Belle cry, thinking about a cute animal being killed.

To impregnate his cows, her father had borrowed a bull from J.W. James, a tenant farmer who lived on the premises of the large farm owned by Cordelia Pinchard Rice. J.W. didn't work for shares anymore; he only paid rent for his land. It had been ten or more years since there had been sharecroppers on Wood Place. J.W. and Hosea Driskell were buddies, so J.W. didn't charge his friend money for the use of the bull, the way he did the other Negro men.

The insemination of the bull was a secret affair, and Belle's daddy had waved her away from the barn, telling her it won't no place for a little girl to be. This was grown folks' business. Belle walked away—her daddy didn't like to be disobeyed—but even yards from the barn, she could hear the loud cries of Cross Eye and her kicking the floor of the barn. The chuffing of the angry-sounding bull and Cross Eye being hurt some way. In a half hour or so, the men carefully coached the bull back into the metal cage on wheels, and then they enjoyed a picnic in the yard in front of the house. There were sawhorse tables set up and food brought by the wives of the other farmers, along with the chickens provided by Belle's daddy, who was known to be a wonderful host, and the men gathered in their own group, telling rough jokes about how big and long that bull's thing had been, and saying if they were Cross Eye, they wouldn't want no part of that, neither.

As the men ate their chicken and sipped their mason jars of moonshine, Belle sat quietly on the front steps of her house and eavesdropped. Her daddy had said, "grown folks' business," before prohibiting her from the barn. And whenever her parents used that phrase, it meant something between a woman and a man, after a bedroom door was closed. Belle wasn't quite sure about the logistics, but if whatever had happened in that barn with the bull and Cross-Eye was the same as between her mama and daddy, she wasn't going to do that. Ever.

She had witnessed other marital models that concerned her as well, such as J.W. James and his wife. While J.W. didn't appear to be any older than twenty-five, he was in his mid-forties. Jolene, his wife, while four or five years younger, was prematurely worn down and had let herself go. She was meriney with skin like red dirt before it's been rained on, or the shade of a ripe peach. Before her four children had been born, she'd been a pretty woman, especially by color-struck standards. And J.W. definitely had been a color-struck man: when he'd been courting Jolene, he'd announce to anybody who'd listen that he didn't like no dark woman, even though he was very dark himself. He liked to tell folks that he had some Cherokee in him, and he wore his curly black hair styled with grease and brushed until it lay down. As if that mattered, because when J.W. had been born, the midwife had written *Negro* quite clearly on his birth certificate, when she got around to registering the paperwork with the courthouse.

In church, Jolene followed behind her husband with her head down and her long hair was mostly gray in the old-lady bun she wore. She'd sit down on the pew with a sigh, but when the elder gave his sermon, Jolene was the first to start shouting. It was the only time anybody saw her with a smile on her face—maybe because J.W.

was a well-known cheater, even though he was a church deacon. Colored folks said he could have been head of the church, if he didn't have that other woman in town. After all, his granddaddy had been the very first elder of Red Mound.

J.W. even had two children with that mistress, who was much younger than his wife. The mistress who left her children alone in the house on Saturday nights so she and her children's father could be seen together at the juke joint out in the woods. Then J.W. got up on Sunday mornings, bathed, dressed, drove back out to Wood Place, and walked to Red Mound to praise the Lord. Unlike Jolene, the mistress hadn't let herself go. Her figure was slim in the tight-fitting, brightly colored dresses she wore at the juke joint. And J.W.'s tastes certainly had changed, because the woman was even darker than he was and wore red lipstick on her round, full mouth, as if to accentuate that not only was she was beautiful, she knew it. Her night-brown eyes were luminous and there wasn't a strand of gray in her straightened, gleaming hair.

The folks in town said J.W. wasn't the first man to step out on his wife, but the problem was, he didn't have no shame with it. That he acted like the mistress in her tight, bright dresses was in fact a second wife, as in the old ways of matrimony, back in African times. Because J.W. not only was with the woman at the juke on Saturdays; after a few years, he began to stay overnight at her house in Chicasetta's Negro neighborhood, Crow's Roost. Except for the few homes of Negro professionals, the residences in Crow's Roost were small and very close together. Thus, when J.W. came to visit his mistress, he was seen by everyone, and when he left her little house in the early mornings to drive his pickup back to the country to work his fields, he was seen as well.

But then there came that night when J.W. did not arrive in Crow's Roost. The morning when he did not walk down the steps of the tiny house of his mistress, who worked at the factory in town. And another night and another morning and those dark and light intervals added up to two weeks. The mistress could not call her lover, because in the late 1950s, there were only two Negroes in town who had phones installed in their homes, Dr. Thompkins and Miss Mc-Lendon, who'd become the principal of the recently constructed colored high school in town. Those phones were only for show, though, because if nobody else Negro had a phone, who was going to call the doctor and Miss McLendon?

It was a Saturday morning, but the mistress of J.W. dressed for the night, though this time she didn't leave her children at home while she rode out to the juke joint. Instead she packed the two children into the car that she had borrowed from a neighbor and drove out to the twenty-five acres that J.W. worked on Wood Place. She told her children, come on and get out the car. She had dressed them in church clothes, and the three of them walked up to the door of the house that J.W. had built his wife in the third year of their marriage, after they had moved out of the house with his parents.

Jolene would tell the story to Miss Rose Driskell, who was her best friend and whose first, Christian name actually was "Miss," so that white folks had to respect her, even when they didn't want to. When Jolene opened the door and saw the mistress, she wasn't mad. She didn't think about fighting this tiny-waisted, long-legged woman who didn't look as if she had labored to push two children out of a little bitty hole. Jolene had churned away her anger in the early years of her marriage, back when she, too, had a waistline. When her breasts had stuck out in expectation of the good-looking boy who became her husband. Even after her first child had been born, she and J.W. had sneaked in their love when the baby and J.W.'s parents went to sleep. Back then it had still felt like their courting days.

Jolene was pregnant again. This would be her fifth child, and she felt the mistress staring at her belly. There was a hurt look on the woman's face, but Jolene's newest pregnancy had been a mistake, though the loving hadn't been. At her age, Jolene had thought she was going through the change of life early, like her own mother had, so she'd gotten careless. She'd conceived this pregnancy in the aftermath of an argument with J.W., when he'd promised Jolene that he'd do right this time. He'd give up the fast life, and Jolene had laughed at him. She didn't care about what he did with his privates, she only cared that he was spending money at the juke joint when she needed to buy groceries for her children. She knew he was lying. He wasn't giving up nothing, but when he walked up with that way of his, she let him think he was convincing her to do something she didn't want to. She'd let J.W. beg her into bed, but she hadn't made him get up before he took his satisfaction, because she'd been so busy getting hers.

This mistress wasn't the only one J.W. had cheated with, neither. Beside her two "outside" children, he had three more children scattered across Putnam County. Surely the mistress had known this, but for some reason, she was fool enough to think she was special. Yet only as this dolled-up woman stared at Jolene's round belly was she learning what Jolene had known for a while: what J.W. was giving felt good, but it wasn't special, and neither was he. Pretty as he was, he was only a regular man.

At this point in the story, Miss Rose had sucked her teeth. "That hussy deserve what-all she got. Trying to break up somebody's home."

"You ain't seen it, girl," Jolene said. "A woman like that, getting gussied up to come to another woman's house. She must have been in a powerful bad way."

"You shole is a Christian, 'cause I would have whipped that heifer's tail."

But Jolene didn't propose violence to her husband's mistress. She told the woman and her children, come on in. Sit down. She offered everybody some pie, and cut her own self a slice, so the mistress wouldn't think somebody trying to put some roots on her.

Jolene's oldest daughter was already out the house, a married schoolteacher, and her oldest son was plowing the fields. Her two youngest were running around on the property somewhere, so there was room at the kitchen table. Jolene sat, and the mistress sat, and the outside children sat, and pie was eaten, and Jolene pretended this was an ordinary, nice visit, until the mistress asked about J.W. She said she was worried, because he hadn't been to see her two

Saturdays in a row, and this was the third one. The mistress was bold, meeting Jolene's eyes. Telling her man's wife that they had a steady thing going on, but Jolene told her that J.W. was lying in the back bedroom. The mistress could see him if she wanted, and there was surprise on her face.

When Jolene walked the woman back to the bedroom, Jolene was worried about whether she'd cleaned in the corners, those tiny spaces where the wood floor joined the walls. But she didn't care about what the mistress and her husband would say to each other, as J.W. lay in their marital bed, his entire chest covered with salve and bandages to help him recover from the steaming pot of stone-ground corn grits that Jolene had thrown on him. She left the mistress and her husband in the bedroom, as the mistress wept loudly, and J.W. croaked out his few words. She went back in the kitchen and told the outside children, she had some chicken left over from last night. Did they want some, and maybe some more pie?

It had not been Jolene's intention to kill J.W. If that had been the case, she could have done that so many nights. She could have poisoned him. She could have stabbed him in his sleep. She could have cut the brake lines on his pickup truck. It had not been Jolene's intention to stop him from going to see his mistress, either, for any man who wants to misbehave will find the time and energy to do so. Jolene had only wanted to bring wisdom into the carefree specter of her husband's Saturday nights, so that every time he took off his shirt in front of his gorgeous paramour, the woman would know that she wasn't dealing with an unattached, beautiful boy in his twenties, one who was at the beginning of his life, instead of in the middle. The mistress should know that she was sleeping with a tenant farmer who was the father of soon to be five children by his gray-headed wife, along with several other offspring he'd dropped by the wayside. And if Jolene had to deal with what her life had become through the years, then the mistress had to deal with that as well. No one in this situation could be free.

Until her husband died, Jolene would remain with her husband, whether or not J.W. decided to stop cheating on her. That's what Negro women did; they remained.

———

After Dr. King's assassination in the spring of 1968, Belle was forced to confront change. Though weeks had passed since the reverend's death—and there had been no more riots in the City, either—police sirens still rang through Belle's neighborhood. Cops were everywhere, hemming up young men on the sidewalks and beating them for no reason.

And there was an entirely new vocabulary, too. Within days of cleaning the riots' debris—sweeping the broken glass, towing away burned-out cars—the young folks in her northern neighborhood had decided they were no longer "Negro." Suddenly, they were "Black" with a big B. They began to proclaim themselves "Black *and* beautiful" and reference Africa at every juncture. Men and women began to refer to each other as "brother" and "sister," titles Belle only heard previously at her home church, down in Georgia. They let their hair travel on the metaphorical journey to Africa, too.

Brothers stopped going to the barbers every week, and sisters stopped pressing. Kinky defiance was in abundance, as was disgust over Patrick Moynihan's report, that ream of paper that white dude working for the Man's government had written, insisting that brothers had no power anymore in their own households. Sisters were in charge of families now, Patrick Moynihan had written in his report, though he'd still called Black folks Negroes. Sisters called all the shots and paid the bills. Even though Moynihan hadn't used the term "castration," he'd implied that sisters were running around with scissors pointed at the crotch levels of brothers.

Belle didn't understand the Black anxieties tripping through the streets. For example, she carried Geoff's last name, and her mother carried the last name of Belle's father, too. If somebody had asked both women, they would have said their husbands were the heads of their households. However, as Belle did for her small family, her mother handled the finances in her own home. Whatever her father made, he gave the entirety of it to Miss Rose, and she gave him back five dollars a week for gas and his walking-round money. This covered the cost of those peanut butter candy bars he loved, and the beers he drank with his friends on Saturday nights down at the juke joint. Other than that, Belle's mother didn't care what her husband paid for. She told her daughter, if her daddy could chase women with whatever change was left over from that five dollars, God bless him.

Though Belle really couldn't afford the long-distance charges, she began calling her mother several times a week, asking, how were things down home? She figured, if the country village where she was born was changing as well, maybe what she saw up in the City wouldn't feel so extreme.

Her mother didn't have much news. "They done built a new furniture factory, going toward Milledgeville. Your brother got hisself a job there. Good money, too."

"Are the folks down home calling themselves something besides Negro?"

"Like what, baby?"

"Like, Black?"

"Why they want to do something like that? That ain't a nice thing to call nobody."

Belle tried one more time. "What you think about me letting my hair go home? I mean, if I stopped straightening it."

"Belle, you ain't got the grade for that."

"I was just thinking."

Her mother let out a cackle. "You need to think about something else, 'less you want to be walking 'round looking nappy and crazy!"

———

Belle's husband did his part to embrace his heritage, as the neighborhood changed. Though he was very light-skinned, his acquired pimp stroll and serious kinship nod to other brothers carried the day. His hair couldn't go "home": it was straight as corn silk, but he began wearing brightly colored dashikis over his jeans, patterns that sang of Africa. And he was concerned about what he called "the movement," the progress of the Black folks that they lived around.

In June, Geoff brought Belle along to his Wednesday meeting at the community center, a few blocks from their apartment. At that first meeting, the attention was on the cops, who'd grown worse since the riots.

Belle nested into Geoff's side, trying not to fall asleep. The behavior of the police bothered her, but she was a young mother and too tired for outrage. She regarded the meeting as a sort of date with her husband. She was grateful for time away from the demands of her toddler, even if her rude, color-struck mother-in-law was the babysitter.

When Belle looked around the room, most of the women wore matching ensembles to the men's dashikis, though their dresses hid their ankles, a length Belle couldn't abide at barely five feet tall. The women sat in folded chairs in the back of the room and clapped their hands whenever male voices were raised. Sometimes they ejected, "That's right! Tell it, brother!"

The single woman who voiced a lengthy opinion was Evelyn Dawson. Long-limbed, cocoa brown, and with impeccable diction, she pointed her cigarette at the podium, where Zulu Harris stood. He was the founder of the community center.

"What're you going to do about these pig motherfuckers?" Evelyn demanded. "They are out of control!"

Belle looked at her lap, plucking nonexistent lint from her skirt. Down in her hometown, she wasn't used to hearing folks curse in public gatherings.

"We're working on that situation, sister," Zulu said.

"Apparently not, my brother. Last week, one of those bastards stopped me for street-walking! Then, he felt me up! I let him know I was in law school and he didn't even blink. So then I had to tell him my father was frat brothers with Thurgood Marshall."

"Sister, please be patient. In the meantime, my .45 and I would be happy to escort you wherever you want to go." There were knowing chuckles from the men, as three women in the audience cut each other glances and folded their arms in judgment. Their African cloth maxi dresses matched, and their heads were wrapped tightly in yards of the same cloth. These were Zulu's three common-law wives, who lived with him in a four-room apartment. He'd introduced them at the beginning of the meeting, asking them to stand.

Evelyn patted the side of her huge, sculpted Afro. "Keep your gun tucked. I'm not trying to start another riot. But when are we taking these pigs to court?"

"We have to be careful before rousing attention too early," Zulu said. "Remember what Chairman Mao said. 'When waking a tiger, use a long stick.'"

He introduced Belle's husband, saying, don't be fooled by Geoff's light skin, because he was as Black as they came. A brother, through and through, which the movement needed more of. Geoff was in his second year in medical school, and he was going to read them something encouraging.

Geoff walked up to the podium and pulled a paperback from the back pocket of his jeans. "I'm going to read a poem by the Black American poet Sterling A. Brown. It's called 'Strong Men.' I like this poem very much, because it speaks to me of the hardship I've seen in our neighborhood, but at the same time, it encourages me."

Belle saw folks poking each other. They didn't care what Zulu had said: Who did this proper, white-looking boy who couldn't even grow a real Afro think he was? She smiled when her husband cleared his throat: she knew what was coming. His voice climbed, the outraged baritone transforming him, and there was clapping, like when a preacher gave a Spirit-filled message, stomping of feet, and Belle was so proud of her husband, though her eyes were closing from exhaustion.

When the meeting ended, the folks rushed over to Geoff. How wonderful his reading had been! They raised fists or gave him the soul shake, but now that his performance was over, he turned into the modest young man that Belle had married. He dipped his head bashfully. It wasn't his poem; he couldn't take any credit.

And Zulu came over, his plate piled high with the food Belle had cooked, and for the next half hour, in between bites, he pontificated to Geoff on what he considered crises, such as the pigs who oppressed their people in their neighborhoods. Also, that outrageous report by Moynihan, who was trying to say, the Black man was useless in his own community. Obviously, Moynihan was a tool of white imperialism. Zulu was serious about making a change. That's why he advised the brothers to read the revolutionary classics: Malcolm X and Marx and Fanon. Even Du Bois, as old-fashioned as he'd been, but reading Chairman Mao was key. Read *Little Red Book*. It would blow the mind, what Mao said about class struggle and Black folks.

Days later, when Belle bought a copy of the slender manifesto from a street vendor, she wasn't impressed.

"This Mao man isn't saying anything special. And he doesn't even mention ladies."

Geoff told her that she didn't get the point. Mao was all the way in China, but he was thinking about Black folks. They lay in bed under the covers, and Geoff was trying to get something started. He'd kiss her neck, and she'd push him away. She didn't have the energy, after dealing with her toddler since dawn. Since Lydia had started walking, that child was a handful and a half.

"How's thinking going to do anything?" she asked. "I can think I'm the Queen of England, but that doesn't make it so."

"Woman. Please." He'd taken to calling her that, and it reminded him of older men from her hometown, how they laid claim to their wives with only one word.

"I'm saying, how is this Mao man supposed to be so profound? And why should I be grateful that he knows that over here we have Negroes or Black folks or whatever we call them now? I've been knowing about China, but nobody's calling me a revolutionary."

"Mao's showing the brothers how to lead."

"What about the sisters?"

"They're included, baby."

"Included where?"

"It's an implicit message. When brothers lead, we bring the sisters along. I mean, where could we go without our women?"

"Plenty places. My uncle and his boyfriend been living together for years. Whatever they doing, ain't no ladies involved."

Geoff sighed. "All right, woman. I guess I'm not getting any to-night."

"No, sir. You are not."

———

Belle's sister-in-law explained that Geoff was a male chauvinist. As a Garfield man, it was in his nature. Actually, chauvinism was in any man's nature.

Diane had learned that in her women's group, a gathering of like-minded individuals who met to complain about their husbands. She needed those regular meetings, too, because the women in her group kept her from stabbing Geoff's brother in his sleep. The marijuana they shared at the women's group was great, too, and Diane was going to smoke as much grass as she could, before she finally got pregnant and had to cast away her fun. Grass wasn't safe when you were pregnant.

It was a Monday afternoon, and Diane had a day off from classes in her master's program. Lydia was asleep in her crib, and the coast was clear for Diane to sit on the floor of Belle's kitchen, next to an open window. She took a bud of marijuana from her purse. She rubbed it between her fingers and sprinkled it into the folded cigarette paper.

"Our husbands are nothing alike," Belle said. "Geoff is sweet as candy. I won't say anything about Lawrence, because I'm not trying to be mean."

"You're not bothering me. Say whatever you feel like, but I'd be careful making assumptions. They're blood brothers. Also, both Black. That means they're alike."

"Diane, what have I told you about saying things like that? You're a white woman! You have to be careful, especially in this neighborhood."

"Why? I live here, too. I've been here for almost two years."

"Then I would expect you to know better."

"Are you saying I don't have freedom of speech, Belle?"

"Not when it comes to saying things like that around Black folks. You saying my husband is like yours because they're both Black is like me saying you must be like Bull Connor because you're both white."

"I'd kill myself if I was related to that fucking murderer." Diane finished assembling the joint and gestured with it. "Light this, please."

Belle went to the stove and turned on an eye. When the joint caught, she held her breath, turned her head, and handed it to Diane. She didn't want to accidentally inhale the smoke.

"And by the way, that Bull Connor shit is a low blow," Diane said. "Please apologize."

"I'm sorry, sister-in-law," Belle said.

"I forgive you. Now come to my women's group."

"With all those white ladies? Absolutely not. No, ma'am."

"I'll be there. And womanhood has no race, Belle. It's a universal class. And I'm white, so what are you trying to say?"

"You're different, Diane. You're my family member."

"Thanks, I guess."

"And didn't you tell me the last time a Black woman came to one of those meetings, somebody thought she was the maid?"

"Oh my God! They apologized! How many times are you going to bring that up?"

"Every time you ask me to come to one of those meetings."

Diane laughed, opening her mouth wide. "Why do you have to make me feel so guilty?"

"High as you are, I didn't know you could feel anything."

"You sure you don't want a toke?"

"Smoking reefer is not ladylike, Diane."

"I'm going to forgive you for that, too."

"I don't need your forgiveness. I've got Jesus on my side." Belle wondered if she'd caught a contact high, despite her precautions. She hadn't been to church since before Lydia started walking.

———

At the next community meeting, Zulu gave Geoff a passionate, complicated soul shake and introduced him around to some of the other brothers. It was rumored that Zulu was a Black Panther, but when questioned, he always denied it, though he smiled when doing so. He'd twirl a finger, saying, be careful. The FBI had spies everywhere.

"Brother Geoff, we want to talk to you about starting a health clinic here at the center." Beside Zulu, the other brothers nodded. Yeah, yeah. Right on. Speak on it. They kept their hands folded over their groin areas.

"I think that's a great idea!" Geoff smiled eagerly. "Gosh, I'd love that, Zulu. But I haven't finished med school yet."

"You still could help us. Give some talks on nutrition. Things like that. Maybe get our people off this swine. It's ridiculous how much we love barbecue. But it's dangerous!"

"That's the truth! You are so right."

Belle turned her head to the side: her husband loved bacon. He'd eaten three pieces that morning.

"Also, something else," Zulu said. "It's about that noodle thing you brought last time for fellowship. Do you think you could cook some more for next week?"

Belle discreetly elbowed her husband, but he put his arm around her.

"Oh, I didn't make that! My wife did. She calls it—what do you call it, woman?"

"Macaroni and cheese," Belle said.

"Sister, that dish was most delicious!" Zulu said. "Very rich and savory. Do you think you could bring an extra dish of that for the next meeting?"

The other men nodded again, making affirmative sounds. Yeah, yeah, that noodle thing had been out of sight. Right on.

"I don't know," she said. "I'm kind of busy."

"Please, my dear sister?" Zulu parted his full lips earnestly, and despite herself, she felt flutters: he was a dead ringer for Sidney Poitier, her favorite actor.

"Um . . . all right."

He clapped his hands. "Oh, thank you!"

At the next meeting, Zulu made satisfied noises as he gobbled down his second helping, telling Belle she was truly gifted. Not only a cook, but a chef. No, she was a griot of the stove, telling ancestral stories with eggs and cheese and spices—and by the way, wouldn't it be so wonderful if could she bring a third dish of macaroni and cheese for the next meeting? Could she fry a couple of chickens, too? The word had spread about the delicious refreshments provided at the meetings, and attendance had increased. Truly, she was helping the movement.

By July, Zulu was asking for pies—sweet potato, to be exact. Geoff bought twenty pounds of tubers and dragged them up the stairs. When he went back down and carried back up a huge sack of sugar, Belle decided this had gone on long enough.

That night, she made her husband's favorite dinner. She didn't complain that he was coming in late, meeting with Zulu and the other brothers.

"I need to talk to you about this food situation, Geoff."

"Woman, your cooking is so good! Everybody loves it."

"That's nice of you to say, but I don't have time to do that anymore. I have a small child and a husband."

"I thought you liked taking care of people."

"I don't know who told you that. It's my job to take care of my family. But cooking for some stray Negro who's screwing three silly women? That is not part of the deal."

"We're African people, Belle. Polygamy is accepted in the motherland."

"I don't believe we're in Africa no more. Matter of fact, I know your people haven't been there for quite some time."

"I can't help that I'm light-skinned, Belle. This is how I was born."

"Do you think that nasty rascal can please those three women?"

"Belle."

"Just tell me that and I'll leave it alone."

"That's none of your business."

"It's not my business, but you want me shaking a fanny 'round the kitchen for him!"

He put a palm down. A soothing gesture. "What you're doing is so important for the movement. And it's appreciated."

"Okay, Geoff. Fine."

"And I'm trying to help, too, along with providing for my family."

Actually, his parents were still paying his med school tuition and his living expenses, facts that Belle's mother-in-law made sure to broach at least three times a month. But Belle couldn't wound his pride. She had to stay on message.

"Is the movement why I don't even see you half the time?"

"Baby, all I'm doing is going to school and meetings. That's it."

He scraped up the last bits of food and held out his plate. She cut into the meat loaf and gave him another serving.

———

"It's not so bad, I guess," Belle said.

"Yes, it is! It's incredibly male chauvinist! You should threaten to leave."

They walked aimlessly through the neighborhood where the women's group met. Diane was telling her, wasn't this a nice place? Didn't she want to come to the next group meeting? But as Belle pushed the baby in her stroller, white people on the sidewalk stared at them, and she knew her sister-in-law wasn't catching on.

Belle laughed. "You want me to leave my husband over macaroni and cheese?"

"No! Because he is disrespecting your position as a woman in American society! I thought you said Geoff was nothing like his brother. But he is. I knew it. He's just as arrogant."

"No, he's not. He's an excellent husband. And he knows I'm not having our child become a welfare baby, like one of those kids Moynihan talked about in that report."

"That wouldn't happen to you, Belle. You've got a college degree."

"And no job experience. And no money, except my mad fund. I'd have to move back home."

"Better that than putting up with this foolishness. Don't you want to be a liberated woman, Belle?"

"Sure I do, just like my cousin. She's real liberated. Every month, the social worker comes by to lecture her about her illegitimate kids. Only thing is, my cousin used to have a husband before he got killed in Vietnam. Her kids have the same father, too, but she's scared to talk back because she needs that welfare check."

———

At the next community meeting, everyone was talking about Oscar Bradley. His friends had been with him when the police stopped them. They weren't even smoking weed, only drinking wine on the corner. The police let the other two go, but Oscar had been arrested and held for seven days so far, though not yet charged. They wouldn't even let him see his mother. Irma Bradley was too upset to come to the meeting and talk about her son, but she'd given Evelyn Dawson her proxy to make her case.

That evening, there was no cigarette in Evelyn's hand and no cursing. Instead of her usual dashiki dress, she was attired much more formally. Elegantly, and her purple jersey dress clung to her long frame, her unrestrained, firm breasts and hips.

"We need some donations for this young boy," she said. "He needs a lawyer, and I haven't passed the bar yet. But this is an outrage! Here we have a mother who doesn't know what happened to her child! Doesn't Mrs. Bradley deserve her son back?"

The other women nodded. A few dabbed at their eyes, and Belle thought of Lydia. She'd only been walking for a few months. What if somebody took her away?

After the meeting, Geoff told her he wanted to talk to Evelyn about building a neighborhood legal fund. Surely, they could gather some donations. Belle stayed at the table, serving folks who came up with their paper plates, but she kept looking across the room. The smoke from Evelyn's lit cigarette climbed around the two of them. Evelyn looked so fresh. Free, while Belle had to wonder, was there too much salt in the macaroni and cheese? Was the chicken done to the bone? Did the pies have enough spices? Belle's hair smelled like old grease, but there hadn't been time to wash and press it again.

Belle looked around. She was the only woman in the room who still straightened her hair. Instead of African garb, she wore a skirt and blouse with pantyhose and slip underneath.

After the community center cleared out, Geoff told her he needed to stop by the place of one of his classmates, to get notes from that week's lectures. Maybe Zulu could drive her to pick up the baby, and Zulu chimed in, saying it was no trouble. Anything to help his brother. The two men exchanged a soul shake.

At her mother-in-law's house, Belle told Zulu to wait in the car. No, she didn't need help with the stroller. But when she emerged with Lydia, he was standing outside the car with the passenger door open. Then, at the apartment, she told him she was fine. She was safe, but as she was putting Lydia down in her room, Belle heard Aretha singing. He had put a record on the turntable, and she wondered, who had raised this man? Where had Zulu learned to go searching through folks' homes, doing whatever he wanted?

Coming out of her bedroom, she yawned widely. She stretched her arms, but Zulu asked, would it be too much trouble for her to warm him up some food? He was always so hungry after the weekly community meetings. Something about talking in front of people took all his energy, and when he went home, sometimes he ate two or three plates.

"You sound like a preacher," she said. "Back home, our Elder follows folks after church into the parking lot. My mama always runs from him, 'cause she said she can't afford to be killing as many chickens as that man likes to eat on Sunday."

She laughed, hoping Zulu would take the hint, but he swayed to the music. He followed her to the kitchen as she prepared his meal. She made sure to put a huge portion into the baking pan: she didn't want him asking for seconds. She sprinkled water over the food before placing it into the oven to heat, and thought about the three women that he lived with. Did only one do the cooking or did they take turns? And how did the sleeping arrangement work? She was so curious, but it would be rude to ask.

Zulu leaned against the refrigerator, smiling. "Sister, do you know why I changed my name?"

"I didn't know you had changed it. I thought your mama named you that."

"Oh no! My slave first name was Tyrone, but I changed that last year. Now, I'm King Shaka Zulu Harris."

"Why'd you do that?"

"Because now I'm a warrior fighting for the revolution! 'We shall heal our wounds, collect our dead and continue fighting.' That's Chairman Mao. Heavy, ain't it, sister?"

"I thought he was Chinese."

"He is."

"But isn't the man you're named for African?"

Zulu nodded solemnly. "Exactly. This is a global fight. You getting it now, sister. Right on."

When his food was done warming. Belle sat at the kitchen table with him as he ate. Then she sat with him on the couch, listening to Aretha sing the same side of an album seven times. They talked about nothing in particular. By midnight, a dangerous comfort had sneaked up on Belle. That she could sit with a man other than her husband and feel so at peace frightened her.

She sat up, telling him she was real tired and her baby liked to wake at dawn. But at the door, Zulu lingered, and right when Belle was going to throw another hint, he told her he hadn't eaten cooking like hers since his mother had passed. She had been from the south, too. Alabama, and she'd had the same sweet ways.

Belle leaned against the doorway. She couldn't let a man tell her about such a great loss and immediately throw him out of her house. That wouldn't be right.

"I'm so sorry for your loss. And you know you're surely welcome to come back. Anytime."

"Thank you again, my dear sister," Zulu said.

He kissed Belle's cheek and left; as she closed the door after him, she trembled. When she finally lay down, it was two in the morning, and her husband had not returned home, and when light hit, he wasn't there, either.

Geoff didn't come back home until the next evening, and when she asked where he'd been, he told her he'd stayed over at Zulu's apartment on the couch. Thinking of how she'd lounged on her own sofa with Zulu, talking and laughing, she didn't confront her husband, or ask what had he been doing that necessitated his lying.

———

At the community center bazaar, Belle bought bolts of African cloth in tones of red, black, and green, and ran up minidresses on her sewing machine. And on her wash day, she decided not to straighten her hair after it dried. She couldn't stop touching it. It pleased her, how it sprang back from her fingers, and when Zulu saw her at the Wednesday meeting, his eyes widened. He showered her with compliments, praising her decision to no longer oppress her hair. He told her she'd already been a beautiful woman, but now she was a heart-stopper.

But Geoff said nothing about Belle's new dresses or her hairstyle. Soon, he stopped coming home after the Wednesday meetings, and then he stopped coming home several times a week. He claimed he was studying late at the library. He didn't want to wake her, so he was sleeping on Zulu's couch. When she assured him that it was all right to wake her—that she could hold his dinner—Geoff told her, no, but thank you. That was very kind of her. His cold politeness troubled her. Her husband always had been so warm, a fire she could stand next to.

The first night Geoff hadn't come home—her husband's first lie—Belle's guilt over sitting with Zulu had pushed her intuition into the road. Belle's mother would have told her she knew better. That when she'd opened her door and let Zulu in, she was allowing the Devil into the apartment.

But after several weeks of Geoff's lies, the truth sidled up to Belle: her husband not only was staying out nights. He was seeing someone else, for he no longer reached for her when he was home. This was the part of marriage that Belle hadn't been prepared for, despite what she'd seen back home. She'd convinced herself infidelity was only part of country living, brought on by boredom and old-fashioned women who didn't stand up for themselves. Even when the women in her small town threw hot grits on their husbands in retribution for cheating, that wasn't a prelude to leaving. That was simply an act of frustration—a sense of rage—that their lives would not change. Now Belle was becoming familiar with that infuriation. She and Geoff weren't playing house anymore. This was real. Even in the concrete strangeness of her new home, she couldn't pretend that she had other plans waiting around the corner.

She wondered who her husband was spending his time with. Maybe a girl who'd never had children. Who didn't have stretch marks on her belly and the sides of her hips. Whose breasts didn't tilt down, after a year's worth of nursing. And at the next community meeting, she watched her husband with Evelyn. His warm laughter as he threw back his head.

One rare night, Geoff came home late after a meeting. When he found her with Zulu at the kitchen table, he didn't complain. He hailed his friend with the usual handshake. Belle put his plate on the table beside his friend's, but there were no thanks, and when Geoff finished eating, he left his plate on the table, rose, and went to the bedroom.

"Well, I guess it's time to go," Zulu said. "Thank you again for the wonderful meal, my dear sister."

There was no cheek kiss at the door.

In the kitchen Belle wiggled her fingers in the dishwater, thinking of how, if this had been another night, Zulu would have kept her company while she cleaned up the kitchen, and then sat some more on the couch. And Geoff didn't even seem to notice Zulu was attracted to her. That he appreciated Belle, even if her own husband didn't.

She put off going into the bedroom. To lie down next to Geoff, who had turned into a stranger, but when she thought about it, she realized she had never really known him to begin with. There had been only a few months of going steady before Geoff had gotten her pregnant and they'd gone down to her hometown courthouse to marry. What had she known then? But she had to lie down, sooner or later, and when she did, Geoff reached for her, wanting. Their rhythms were off and she lay there underneath him, unenthusiastic. Waiting for him to finish.

In the morning, she rose and made breakfast and coffee. When Geoff followed the smell of bacon into the kitchen, she told him he needed to leave the apartment for good. Maybe he could stay with Zulu, like he always did.

———

Belle stopped showing up to community meetings. She was too embarrassed, watching her husband at Evelyn's side. And she didn't want Zulu's three common-law wives tossing their cloth-wrapped heads in her direction. Throwing her triumphant looks, because Belle had thought she'd had a man to herself. But see there? She was no different. And if Zulu's women had to get with the ways of Africa, so did Belle.

For a week, she waited for her husband to come back, begging. That was the ritual, down where she was from. When a man stepped out on his wife, and she discovered his indiscretion—when grits had been thrown or the tires of his pickup slashed—there always was a husband's contrition. And then, after the news had traveled through the Black part of town, there was the Sunday where the reunited couple would attend church, and the wife's triumphant look: what God had joined, let no hussy wearing bright lipstick and a tight-ass dress tear asunder. For it was always the woman's fault in Belle's hometown. Nobody really blamed the man; he was part of the weaker sex, one that couldn't control its urges.

So Belle waited, but Geoff did not return. And during those days, Zulu came by, knocking, even on days that weren't Wednesday. She only spoke to him through the door, her face resting against the wood. She was tired, she told Zulu. She didn't feel like company.

Another week passed, and she called her mother. "I might come home to visit. Would that be all right?"

"Girl, you know I want to see y'all! Come on if you coming."

"It's just gone be me and Lydia."

"What about Geoff?"

"He can't take off from school. You know, with studying and everything . . ." Belle's voice trailed. She'd never considered having this conversation. She was making things up as she went along.

"Belle, what-all's going on up there?"

"Nothing. I just miss y'all. I . . . I miss home."

"Uh-huh." Her mother paused. "Then you come on home, baby. You know you surely welcome."

The next afternoon, Belle dressed in the clothes she used to wear, before she'd been trying to recapture her husband's attention. One of her dresses from high school that came four inches below the knee. She washed and pressed her hair, which had grown down to her shoulders, because she didn't want to be a hypocrite. This was the way women in Chicasetta wore their hair. She had her own style of dressing, and it definitely wasn't anybody's dashiki, but she left off the hat and gloves. It was still summer; she didn't want to look ridiculous.

She left the baby with Diane and walked the several blocks to Evelyn Dawson's, and by the time she tapped on Evelyn's front door, she had blisters on the back of her heels. She told herself she shouldn't be ashamed of herself. She was only going to talk to the person who was trying to break up her family, woman to woman. Belle told herself she was doing this for Lydia, so her child could grow up with a father in the house.

She didn't have to search the neighborhood for Evelyn. She lived on the same block as the community center, in a two-story dwelling with a large covered porch and concrete steps bordered by short brick pillars. There were flowers everywhere, and Belle's heart drained to see a vegetable patch in a corner of the small yard. She recognized tomatoes and a basil plant.

Evelyn didn't act surprised to see her. She asked Belle inside and offered coffee or tea, but Belle requested water. Evelyn told her she knew why she was here, but she didn't mind the visit.

"I don't know what Geoff has told you about me—"

"Not much," Evelyn said. "And I haven't asked."

"All right. I'll tell you myself. I'm from a little town in Georgia called Chicasetta. And where I'm from, we talk straight. So I'm going to ask you, is this thing you got going on with my husband serious?"

Evelyn smiled. "Define 'serious.'"

"Are y'all in love? Do y'all want to get married? After he and I divorce, I mean?"

Evelyn reached to a side table. She picked up a pack of cigarettes and shook two out, halfway. When she offered one, Belle waved her hand. No thank you, and the woman lit the other cigarette. Evelyn wasn't nervous or stalling for time, only thoughtful, as she blew smoke.

"Marriage is a convention of the establishment," she said.

"What's that mean?" Belle asked.

"It means that I don't need a label to justify what I feel or what I'm doing. I care for Geoff, and I'm pretty sure he cares for me. But marriage is a white man's concept."

"Not when you have a baby."

"Look around, Belle."

So this woman knew her name. She wondered who had mentioned it, her husband or Zulu?

"There are plenty sisters in this neighborhood with babies and they aren't married."

"And they're not getting their bills paid, either," Belle said.

"That's how you define happiness? With money? Then you should be happy already. From what I know of Geoff, he's taking care of his responsibilities."

It was true. He had waited until Belle had gone to the grocery store and placed the monthly stipend his parents gave him on the kitchen table. When she checked inside, he hadn't taken anything for himself.

This conversation wasn't going the way Belle had planned. Evelyn didn't have one bit of embarrassment. Nor was she trying to stake a claim on Geoff because of love or another child. Instead Evelyn was speaking of Belle's husband from familiarity, when she knew nothing of what it meant to have a man's child inside you, to know that his seed and blood caused every bit of joy and heartache you were feeling right down to the moment when his baby split you wide open and you couldn't walk properly for weeks. When you were worried about pissing yourself, but still had to get out of bed to feed that man's progeny.

Belle put down her water glass. She smoothed her dress; it wasn't store-bought, but it was one of her favorites. A baby-blue cotton with tiny navy flowers. Her grandmother had made the dress for her, without taking any measurements. And by hand, too. Not a stitch had been sewn on a machine.

"I guess that's it, then," Belle said. "I didn't come to fight. But I can't share a man, neither. I'll cry, I know. I've shed a few tears already, but I have a baby to see about, so I can't cry but for so long."

Evelyn stubbed out her cigarette. "I didn't mean to cause you pain, sister."

"Oh, I don't blame you. Geoff's the one I married. But he's pretty charming when he wants to be. I guess you know that."

"He certainly is."

"All that poetry he recites!" Belle laughed. At least she had her memories.

"Oh, we don't talk much about that. We don't have time for frivolities. It's all about the movement around here. About the revolution coming. Geoff's a pretty serious man, and he has so many great ideas. He just needs somebody to listen."

Belle stood, holding out her hand. She'd never performed a handshake before, but she made sure her grip was firm. She told Evelyn, thank you for the hospitality.

––––––––

The next evening was the Wednesday meeting at the community center. Belle dressed Lydia in a romper and pulled on a plain shift and flat shoes. Nothing fancy, because she wasn't going to put forth too much effort. She pushed the carriage up the sidewalk and waved at folks in the neighborhood. She didn't know most of their names, but she wanted to be seen. She wanted them to carry the news that she wasn't crying. She was strong and with her baby girl.

In the community center, she saw Evelyn and Zulu standing with her husband. She didn't have to call his name because the baby did that for her. "Dada," she cried, and waved her hands. Zulu and Evelyn stepped in front, a shield as in ancient times, but Belle pushed the stroller toward them.

She told them this was between two married folks, and she didn't want no trouble. Belle didn't care that she sounded country; her temper was traveling.

Zulu stepped aside, leaving Evelyn to hold the field. The woman smiled, as if she knew the outcome of this scene. She was that sure of another woman's husband, and Belle gave a second warning.

"Evelyn, what I say? This ain't none of your business. But now, if you want to cut a jig, I can cut one right on with you."

A crowd had formed to watch. Some weren't even regular attendees of the meeting, but they'd come off the street because this was a new scene to them. There were used to the police getting rowdy and sometimes a brother beating on a sister and having to be pulled off, but they'd never seen a tiny woman with a very big voice getting her husband told. This was something else altogether. This was out of sight. Right on.

"Geoff, I know we young," Belle said. "And I know we both tired. But I'm the one taking care of this baby, and you the one wanted her. You the one wanted to get married, too."

There was clapping and cosigning from women in the crowd, even Zulu's wives. Go 'head, sister, they all said. Tell that brother how you feel.

Geoff stepped toward her, whispering, "Woman, do we have to do this here?"

Her tone was sarcastic. "Yes, *man*. We gone do this right here, 'cause you been messing 'round with her." Belle pointed in the direction of Evelyn, whose amused dispassion had flown; she was so alarmed her eyes were popping. "And it ain't no secret, neither. Everybody here knows it. So I'ma say what I came here to say, and then I'ma go. You see this baby in this stroller, Geoff? You keep on acting a fool and my baby and me going home to Georgia. 'Cause I'm not staying here without a husband. And I ain't sharing a man. I came to the City for you, and if you don't want me no more, I'ma leave you here."

Geoff spoke then, but not to his wife. He touched Evelyn's arm and told her he needed to return to his family. He had responsibilities, but he hadn't meant to do her wrong. Gosh, he was sorry, he called, as Evelyn strode away. Then he walked to a folding chair and sat down, hanging his head. A few of the men came over to him and patted his shoulder. Damn, brother, they told him. Your wife sure is loud.

Belle turned the stroller and pushed it outside, but within a few steps, Zulu caught up. It was too dark for her to walk alone, he told her. At the apartment, he held her sleeping toddler and followed as Belle walked the stroller up the stairs.

"Sister, you are such a good woman," he said. "My brother's so lucky to have you. The movement's so lucky."

"Ain't no revolution 'round here," Belle said. "It's just me and my child."

"I get that, sister."

"Do you? Would you want somebody treating your real sister like this? You knew what Geoff was doing, didn't you? Don't you lie to me!" Her chest expanded. She was feeling mighty and righteous and much taller than her sixty inches.

"I don't want to get in between the two of you, Belle. I'll only ask, will you forgive me? I sure wish you would."

Holding the baby between them, he leaned down, kissing her cheek. When he moved back, he hovered, his face only inches away. Looking at her. Waiting for permission, and it felt like he was Sidney Poitier in *A Raisin in the Sun* and she was Ruby Dee. It seemed he was sincere, picturing a future that included her.

Belle sympathized then with Zulu's three common-law wives. How they could discard their pride for a few unsatisfying morsels. She recognized the feeling, because she really wanted this man.

She could invite Zulu into the apartment and make him wait while she laid Lydia down in her crib. He could put a record by Aretha on the turntable. That would calm their sin as he took Belle on the couch, which needed the springs replaced. All night long, and maybe her husband would catch her with her legs wrapped around Zulu. And Geoff would understand what it felt like to be made a fool of, all while you were trying to keep a family together. To give a home some semblance of contentment.

But Belle couldn't invite Zulu inside, because she was pregnant again. Her freedom was dead. Her girlhood had soared away, without a voyaging word, and she pulled her child from Zulu's arms.

VI

The future woman must have a life work and economic independence. She must have knowledge. She must have the right of motherhood at her own discretion. The present mincing horror at free womanhood must pass if we are ever to be rid of the bestiality of free manhood; not by guarding the weak in weakness do we gain strength, but by making weakness free and strong.

—W. E. B. Du Bois, *Darkwater: Voices from Within the Veil*

THE DEBATE

❖

In the City, my mother had been a nuisance. Separated from her, I moved into deep affection. I ached for her voice, her questions about whether I was eating right and her urging me to take those vitamins she'd mailed, because I was a young woman and had to take care of my body for later, when the children came.

She sent me weekly letters—sometimes twice a week—filled with emotions I hadn't known she possessed. Lengthy missives about her staying in the house all day while my father was gone to his practice. She wanted to teach school again, and she knew it was wrong, but she was so jealous of Aunt Diane's counseling job. And my mother wrote to me about Lydia. Was she dead? And if so, shouldn't she feel it inside? Something ripping her open to steal her child's soul? But that feeling hadn't occurred, and not knowing what had happened to my sister was so hard.

I waited all week for my Sunday evening call from my mother, for the concluding endearments at the end of our fifteen minutes.

"I love you, baby."

"I love you, too, Mama."

Afterward, I'd stare at the phone.

That first year of college, I haunted Chicasetta, driving my car up 441 to Miss Rose's or to knock on Uncle Root's door after my afternoon classes. I never called to alert them. I was the descendant of countrywomen who showed up at the door and hollered through the screen. With the egotism of youth, I expected my kin to be thrilled, and they never failed me: they dispensed ardent kisses and hugs. After eating the meals my granny cooked or playing chess with the old man, I'd get back in my car and drive back to Routledge, feeling cheated and unsettled, only to return days later looking for a trace of home.

Miss Rose didn't detect my homesickness. To her, Chicasetta was my real home. Uncle Root told me outright he knew I missed my mother, but he liked having me to himself. He gave me extra gas money for my highway voyages. He assured me daily visits would be a joy. Maybe he was lonely, too. He was eighty-four that year, and many of his contemporaries had died, like Pat Lindsay's grand-father. Those who remained had progressed into fragility.

Uncle Root looked a younger man, but his vision wasn't as sharp, his reflexes not as spry. I became his chauffeur on Saturday road trips to Atlanta to the High Museum, or to his favorite art-film house in Buckhead, where he escorted me to my first Spike Lee joint. He dressed in a collared shirt, tie, and suit for these occasions. We'd attend the first matinee, and when the film was over, I'd drive us to Phipps Plaza. Most of the items in the stores were shockingly expensive—fur coats and leather suits—and we never bought any-thing, but the old man preferred walking in the tranquility of the empty, costly stores in Phipps as opposed to the push-and-shove of Lenox Square, just across the street.

"Look at this blouse, sugarfoot. Olivia would have loved this."

He'd hand over a piece of clothing, and I'd dutifully stroke the material, while a white saleslady looked anxiously in our direction. Once, a blond woman who'd followed us around Saks for twenty minutes asked Uncle Root if his "nurse" wanted to try on some-thing, just for fun.

"I beg your pardon. This young lady is my niece." The saleslady's expression of confusion as she looked from Uncle Root's pale face to my brown one tickled him, but he was kind enough not to laugh openly. He waited until we reached the car.

In late afternoon, our faux shopping would end, and the old man and I would sit on the bench outside the stores and chat until it was time to drive back to Chicasetta, where I'd spend the night at his house and make grilled cheese sandwiches, with sweet tea to go along.

That summer, I decided that I would stay south. Uncle Root and I made great roommates: he was entertaining enough when I wanted company, and when I didn't, he did not seem bothered. He always

had a book that he could read, or he would call my mother's brother
and ask him for a ride out to the farm.

Mrs. Cordelia Rice had arranged for a summer job for me in the
office of a doctor who was her late husband's kin, Dr. Rice. His assistant was Nurse Lansing, a heavyset sister with a baby face, who
had attended the old colored high school with my mother. My labor
at the practice was easy, only light filing, but it would add fat to
my future medical school applications. My employer was a sociable
gentleman with a boisterous comb-over, and sometimes he brought
in cinnamon doughnuts, my favorite. One July afternoon, when I
returned from work, David James was sitting on the claw-foot settee, drinking a cup of coffee. He'd changed so much since I'd seen
him the previous summer, at my family reunion.

In Uncle Root's living room, I sat in the wing chair farthest
from my ex-boyfriend, cutting my eyes in his direction. His haircut was neat as always. His handsome, chocolate face was smooth-
shaven, but he was no longer skinny. His chest was broader, his
arms thicker. He looked almost like a grown man. Even his voice
had deepened.

"You didn't bring what's-her-name with you?" I asked.

"It's Carla, and she's been my girlfriend for a while." David paused
and looked away. "Ever since you kicked me to the curb."

"Whatever."

"She's in Atlanta. She's at Spelman now. She has a summer job
there."

"Negro, I don't need this information! I really don't care. And
why are you here?"

"I'm visiting Dr. Hargrace. And why you always so mean?"

"'Cause I can't stand you, that's why."

The old man interrupted us: a snack was called for. He'd always
been hungry when he was young. He would warm up slices of the
pie he'd made, and could I help him? In the kitchen, he put the pie
on china plates with white linen napkins covering them.

"I make excellent desserts," he said. "My pie is much better than
Miss Rose's. My pound cake, too."

"But y'all both use Dear's recipe."

"That's not true. I add some special, secret ingredients." He poured coffee into a cup for me, splashing in some cream. Then a bit more. "You don't need your coffee black. You're already high-strung, and Ailey Pearl, could you please stop picking on that young man every time you see him?"

"I do not—"

"—yes, you do. But if you hadn't noticed, no matter how cruel you are, he never fights back. I'd like you to consider that beating up on a defenseless person makes you a bully."

He held the plates and backed out of the kitchen door. I leaned against the table, sipping my coffee. My granny had scolded me about how I treated David, too. She'd told me that I was mean as a snake to him.

When I went back out to the living room, the old man was telling his story about meeting the great scholar. When he came to his negative feelings about Booker T. Washington, I was curious: Why did everybody seem to despise that man?

"There was this dude in my Freshman Orientation class," I said. "And he called Mr. Washington an Uncle Tom."

"Indeed, that young man was right."

David put his plate on his lap. "Is it okay if I disagree with you, Dr. Hargrace?"

"Certainly, you may. You're entitled to your own opinion."

David flashed a smile: his teeth were sparkly as ever. "Well then, respectfully, I disagree. I think Mr. Washington was only looking out for poor Black folks. I mean, back in the day, white people didn't want us to go to college, right? My history professor told us they would punish us during slavery for even holding a book. Sometimes kill us."

I didn't want to agree with David, but even crotchety Dean Walters had defended Washington. That had to count for something. Still, I didn't want to seek peace with my former boyfriend. I wanted to hold my spear high, hopefully at throat level, since David not only had put on weight. He'd grown taller, at least two inches.

"Why aren't y'all talking about women?" I asked. "Weren't there any sisters who were concerned about Black folks?"

My ex-boyfriend said nothing. He cut into his pie with his fork, as the old man told me, I already knew there were Black women doing important work. Anna Julia Cooper, Mary McLeod Bethune, Ida B. Wells-Barnett, and so many others. As he remembered, I'd written a paper on this, back in high school.

"In Brother David's defense, I don't think he's trying to exclude women. I just think he's curious about why I have animus toward Washington. And that's because my mother didn't like him. You see that picture? That was taken in 1895, twelve years before I was born."

He pointed to the framed photograph of Lil' May, Big Thom, and Tommy Jr. on the credenza. I'd passed by that photograph so many times, I no longer paid attention to it.

"That picture was taken on the day Booker T. Washington gave his most infamous speech at the cotton exposition," Uncle Root said. "When he was still the Head Negro in Charge of the Race. Before that speech, he was a god among our people. His white patrons gave him money to fund Tuskegee. He even had dinner at the White House, but whenever a Negro man, woman, or child was killed, he was silent. He kept his peace, and that day at the Atlanta exposition, the event was segregated. They wouldn't even allow the rest of us into the event. The only reason my mother was allowed to hear Washington speak is because she was a servant tending to a white child. She was holding Tommy Jr.'s hand.

"My mother had a memory like nobody's business. It was miraculous. She could recall every word that someone spoke, and when I was little, my mother would repeat what she heard Booker T. Washington say to those white folks. He started out slowly, but then his message started getting good to him, like a preacher, don't you know, and when he came to the crux of the matter, the white folks cheered him on."

Uncle Root closed his eyes and folded his hands in his lap.

"He told them, 'You can be sure in the future, as in the past, that you and your families will be surrounded by the most patient, faithful, law-abiding, and unresentful people that the world has seen. As we have proved our loyalty to you in the past, in nursing your children, watching by the sick-bed of your mothers and fathers, and often following them with tear-dimmed eyes to their graves, so in the future, in our humble way, we shall stand by you with a devotion that no foreigner can approach, ready to lay down our lives, if need be, in defense of yours, interlacing our industrial, commercial, civil, and religious life with yours in a way that shall make the interests of both races one. In all things that are purely social we can be as separate as the fingers, yet one as the hand in all things essential to mutual progress.'"

Uncle Root opened his eyes.

"Can you imagine that? Here Booker T. Washington had the opportunity to change the hearts and minds of these vicious white southerners. He could have truly helped our people that day, and those despicable words are what he chose to deliver! He told those crackers that not only was segregation of the races perfectly all right, but he agreed with segregation! My mother didn't understand everything in that speech, but she got the gist. She didn't agree with what Washington said, not one bit, though naturally, Big Thom was just skinning and grinning, like he had seen Jesus move the Rock. My mother said, Washington was a well-spoken, well-dressed, red-nappy man with light eyes, and all he proved that day was he was a white man's nigger. Not because he was forced to be, either. But because he just loved pleasing the white folks so much. He just loved to kiss the white man's hind parts."

He held up his index finger.

"And now, Ailey, you ask me about women? My mother was the wisest individual I have ever known! And I have learned through much experience that when a wise Negro woman tells me something, I pay close attention. And now, Brother David, I hope you understand why I do not think much of Booker T. Washington. I don't even like giving him the respect of calling him 'mister.'"

"All right, I get it, Dr. Hargrace. You won today, but I'm going to be ready for you next time."

"And I eagerly await that opportunity."

Uncle Root rose from the couch. It was time for more pie, and he would bring out more coffee for us youngbloods, but not for himself. It was mere hours before his bedtime. Even though I hadn't yet gotten past my anger at David, I talked and laughed with them for another hour, until Uncle Root decided it was time for us to drive out to the country. David needed to visit my granny, and besides, the old man was missing his pecan tree.

———

I heard from Abdul only once, the summer after our freshman year, though I'd given him all possible contact information. One Saturday, he'd called the old man's house, asking me to meet him at a motel close to the exit near Madison.

When I left the house, I'd lied to the old man that I was driving to Atlanta to spend the night with Roz. In the motel parking lot, Abdul asked for my half of the room fee. Then we spent the day making love, in between watching cable TV and eating cheeseburgers and French fries. Sunday morning, I drove back.

In the fall, there were changes, as our public relationship had shifted. Now Abdul acted sometime-y. When I did see him, he'd call me after midnight, to come to the apartment that he now shared with Steve. He and Steve no longer sat at the table with us in the refectory, and whenever I saw Abdul, I held my breath, waiting. Would he speak? If he did, would there be a smile? Or would he ignore me entirely?

Pat's behavior had not changed, though. He kept sitting with Keisha and me in the refectory, smiling and making us laugh at his corny jokes. He and I kept meeting for our tutorial sessions in the library, and he still flirted shamelessly with me.

"Girl, you are so sweet. And beautiful, too. How come you're still single?"

"I'm not. I got somebody. I guess." I looked toward the stairs, nervous. I wasn't going to mention Abdul's name. In the library, the gossips hovered around each corner. They were worse than the rodents.

"Oh, that. But, girl, does that really count as a relationship?"

"Who wants to know?"

"I do." He touched my head. Let his fingers drag back and forth. "Um. Your hair is so damned soft."

I moved my head. "Pat, come on. You need to figure out these equations. You don't want to fail this class."

That fall, the Betas and the Gammas chose their new members. In the past the process had been called "pledging," and had been a public spectacle. Applicants wore identical outfits that they were required to purchase. My sister Lydia had worn those years before, when she'd pledged. All told, my parents had paid twelve hundred dollars for Lydia's fees. So much money in order for her to "cross the burning sands"—what the process of joining a Black Greek letter organization was called. Because of several legal suits that had been filed against the Betas and Gammas, "pledging" had become "intake," and hazing was supposed to be out. However, the Betas and Gammas just moved into underground mode, as they began to abuse their aspirants.

When Abdul became a Gamma "Rock," he stopped calling me for our late-night assignations. Pat was pledging Gamma, too; sometimes, when we met in the library, Pat was limping, though he claimed he wasn't being physically hazed by the Gammas. It was early onset arthritis, he insisted. But I wasn't fooled: I stuffed a cushion in my book bag and gave it to him to sit on.

And Roz became a secret Lily for the Betas. Like Steve and Abdul, she stopped eating at the table with Keisha and me. She sat on the other side of the refectory with the rest of the underground Lilies, who did not talk about their ambitions. I was decried as off-limits, since I had messed with Abdul and supposedly caused his breakup with an important Beta. Roz walked past me on campus as if I were invisible, looking forward intently as if she and the air had an exclusive appointment.

The Saturday after homecoming, the new Gammas and Betas "crossed the burning sands." When we heard the cheers, Keisha and I came outside our dorm to see Roz and the six others in their orange sorority T-shirts. Roz's line name was printed in white letters on the back: "Rapunzel." When the Betas finished their short routine, she headed for me, her arms wide. She hugged me tightly, saying we were girls for life. And don't be mad, okay?

The Gammas brought more excitement, when Abdul, Steve, Pat, and ten others gave their call throughout the yard. They stood like dark dominoes in a row, in their maroon-and-silver T-shirts emblazoned with their line names. They sang and stomped a few minutes, declaring their love of Gamma, but then they disappeared.

That night, while my roommates slept, I propped the door to our room open. At two in the morning, the hall phone rang. I ran to answer, nearly falling in my haste. It was Abdul. Come to the apartment, he whispered. He missed me, he needed me. I rushed back to my room to pack an overnight bag. It was filled with items that I'd leave in his apartment bathroom, to mark my territory. My blow-dryer and curling irons. A box of tampons. A bottle of nice lotion that men wouldn't use, because guys didn't mind being ashy. I remembered that Roz had told me that since Abdul and I hadn't made a commitment, I should be careful going over there: I didn't want to get a bad reputation. Yet I kept packing my bag.

At his apartment, I cuddled with Abdul naked in his double bed and watched television. That night, he and I made love twice. The final time, I was so close, as he went deeper. I wrapped my legs around him, and he whispered a growl as he ordered, call him by his line name, "Shotgun." Say it for my man.

"Shotgun! Shotgun!" I gripped him tighter and rolled my pelvis: I was almost there. But then, the moment was lost for me, and I lay there, disappointed, while Abdul climaxed inside me.

"Ooh, girl! Ooh! I love you, Ailey!"

Afterward, he didn't speak of feelings, but he told me he thought it was a good idea to meet my father. If Daddy wasn't coming to the reunion next summer in Chicasetta, Abdul could meet him during this Christmas break. Abdul and I could drive up together, and then, for New Year, we would continue to Philly to meet his family.

"Are you saying we're in a commitment? Like, boyfriend and girl-friend?"

"No, I'm not ready for that."

"We're not committed, but you want to meet my daddy? I don't understand."

"That's because you're not listening."

I sighed and rolled over, settling into my spoon. "Let's talk about this later, Abdul."

"What? You don't want me to meet your father? You just want to fuck?"

"Abdul, I'm naked. I don't think it's appropriate to talk about my daddy right this second, especially if we're not in a commitment. You're the one doesn't want to be my boyfriend."

"Ailey, you're not hearing me. My parents never were married. I got a brother three months younger than me. My daddy married Gary's mama, but that didn't do him a bit of good. He's in jail right now. Me? I was salutatorian, and my daddy wouldn't even come to my graduation. You don't understand what it's like. You come from something."

"Oh, sweetie. We'll talk about it another time. Okay? Please."

I rolled over on my side, and for the first time in years, I dreamed of the long-haired lady. I was walking through the field in front of my granny's house, heading to the creek. I didn't know the long-haired lady was beside me, until she touched my arm, asking me a question. But I couldn't understand her words, as she kept tug-ging my sleeve. She turned impatient, shaking her head, as I told her I didn't understand. The long-haired lady stopped walking and pointed to the bank. She spoke again, and this time, I knew she was saying, look. Over there.

Then I woke up.

FOUNDER'S DAY

◈

Uncle Root didn't like homecoming. To begin with, it was in October, when the nights started getting shorter. That meant it took place in the dark, and he'd been born during a time when Negroes didn't drive through the country after the sun went down. And there was too much noise and too many people, and if he was going to sit for a long period of time, so that his joints creaked and popped when he finally rose, he wanted it to be worth the sacrifice of his time and cartilage.

Founder's Day was different: it took place in March and during the daytime, so there was that. It was like a family reunion, too, because not everyone attended. Only the most devoted of alumni returned. And no matter how bourgie and accomplished they were, they were enthusiastic in their greetings. They repeated the sayings of their great-grandparents, those uneducated and hardworking folks who had suffered and worked and prayed to push their descendants forward.

"God is so good, isn't He?"

"All the time."

"I haven't seen you since Hector was a pup!"

"I know! It's been a month of Sundays!"

They hadn't moved so far from their origins that they couldn't enjoy the down-home repast, either, the one held each year in the faculty dining room. Fried chicken and greens and two kinds of quick bread. They tucked paper napkins into their necklines of the modest yet neat outfits they'd chosen for the day. There were no fur coats and tuxedos, as with October's homecoming. No need for all that, as they leaned bodies away from their plates but kept on chewing.

Founder's Day was the time for students to glimpse our future, or at least, that's what administration informed us on the handouts placed in our campus mailboxes. Classes were canceled, though we students were required to be in attendance. Junior and senior snitches were positioned at the front and side doors of the chapel with sign-in sheets. These same students blocked the doors if anyone tried to leave the building and directed us toward the bathrooms at the rear of the chapel if we lied about a full bladder's emergency.

In the very early morning, I drove to Chicasetta to retrieve Uncle Root for the service, which began at ten. I knocked before I let myself in with my key, and saw Mama and Daddy sitting in his living room.

"Oh my goodness! What are y'all doing here?"

As the old man smiled from his wing chair, my parents rushed to me. They gave hugs and kisses and exclamations that I had grown up, even since Christmas. Look at my pretty outfit, and my new hairstyle.

Mama stroked the edges of my pressed and curled hair. "Did your granny do this?"

"Yeah, you like it? All I have to do is roll it up at night."

"It's so pretty! I wish you'd convince Coco to grow her hair back. She's still baldheaded, bless her heart."

"We thought we'd surprise you, darling," Daddy said. "It was Belle's idea, and I took some time off from the practice. It's only two days, and aren't my ladies worth it?"

He put his hands on our shoulders, squeezing gently. My parents were dressed in color-coordinated attire. Mama wore a navy dress with a red belt. My father's suit was navy, too, and his tie was red. I touched his graying temples. When I'd visited for Christmas, I hadn't noticed that his hair had changed colors.

"Look at you, Daddy! You're all cute and distinguished."

"Your mama put this gray in my head, beating me every single day. This woman is so mean. She won't cook for me, neither. You see I'm nothing but skin and bone, don't you?"

He rubbed his round stomach and threw back his head, hooting. Mama and I joined in his laughter, as if my father's joke wasn't worn and frayed. I put my head on my father's shoulder, and when

I said this was a perfect day, my mother teased me. Don't be getting mushy, but she put her arm around my waist. She kissed my cheek.

The old man insisted I drive his town car to campus. He and Mama sat in the back, and Daddy was up front, marveling at how I took the road. Look at his baby girl, driving this big car. All right, now. Watch me go. When we walked into the chapel, I waved at my roommates across the pews, pointing exaggeratedly at my parents. I was going to sit with them, and when I passed by the pew where Tiffany and Darlene were, I slowed down on purpose so they could see my parents. What an attractive couple they made. How beautiful my mother was, tiny and neat and graceful. How respectful and affectionate my father was to her. That the three of us sat with the legendary Jason Freeman Hargrace. I didn't need to pledge Beta to be somebody. I was somebody already.

Students weren't allowed in the faculty dining room, unless they were escorted by a college alum, and after the program was concluded, I found my roommates, asking, did they want to sneak in with my family? They'd met my mother and the old man a few times, but never my father, and we three could be guests of alumni at the reception, since none of Roz's family had attended the program. I instructed Keisha to rush back to our room and get some aluminum foil. And bring a big purse like the one I had: not only were they serving fried chicken, there was a rumor that Mrs. Giles-Lipscomb had made several of her famous coconut custard pies. I'd brought some of my granny's Tupperware in my own purse.

"Are y'all two heifers gone embarrass me?" Roz asked. "Stuffing food in your pocketbooks?"

"Ain't nobody stud'in' you," Keisha said. "You gone be the first one begging for pie."

The dining room was crowded with alumni and their student guests. There was Pat, standing by a tall, brown-skinned lady with short, relaxed hair, and large-framed glasses. When I caught his eye and waved, he motioned that I should come over.

"This is my mommy!" Pat said. "Isn't she wonderful?" He squeezed his mother around her shoulders.

I shook Mrs. Lindsay's hand. "It is so good to meet you. Your son is a nice young man, and I can tell the fruit didn't fall far from the tree."

"Listen to you," she said. "So sweet and polite! My child can't stop talking about you. It's 'Ailey says this' and 'Ailey says that.' Now I can see why."

Pat nudged her with his hip. "Stop, Mommy."

"I'm sorry, darling." She giggled. "Was I not supposed to say anything?"

Abdul walked up to us, and I backed away several paces. The day had been perfect, but now I felt an awkward dread. Two weeks before, Abdul and I had been lying naked in his bed, when he told me someone on campus had referred to me as his girlfriend, but he had corrected them. They were sadly mistaken: I was not his woman. Abdul told them that we were just kicking it.

"Hello, Ailey."

I looked down at my patent leather flats. "Hello."

"Are you here with Dr. Hargrace?"

"Yes, and my parents. They flew in for Founder's Day."

"Oh, word? I'd love to finally meet them! Let's walk over."

"I'm sorry, but that's not possible. We have a very full day before they fly back to the City tomorrow." I turned to Mrs. Lindsay. I was standing so close to her, I bumped into her. "Excuse me! I'm so sorry."

"That's quite all right, darling," she said. "It's crowded in here."

"Well . . . um . . . I should join my family," I said. "I don't want to be rude to them. It was so lovely to meet you. It's been a sincere pleasure."

Mrs. Lindsay patted my arm. "The pleasure is mine. I hope to see you again, very soon."

———

Keisha tried to beg off from the spring step show, citing possible un-Christian behavior. Everybody knew the Gammas were going to show out, and anyway, she needed to study, but Roz dropped her tough pretenses. She tugged at our roommate's sleeve. Come support her; she was going to be in the show.

Keisha folded her arms. "I don't like the way them Betas did our girl. It wasn't right. And you didn't take up for her, neither."

"But Ailey, you know I wouldn't ever do you wrong on purpose, don't you?" Roz turned to me, her eyebrows pleated. This was as close as she would come to an open apology, though she'd made a tacit statement of her solidarity. Since she was an official member of Beta, she no longer sat with her line sisters in the refectory. She sat with Keisha, Pat, and me at our regular table. When we encountered the Betas on the yard and they gave their shrill call, she answered with a brief wave and kept walking.

"No, I'm not mad," I said. "It's cool. We're girls for life."

In the gymnasium, Keisha and I sat on the front row; she didn't care how much she loved Roz. If something happened that she didn't like, she was leaving quick.

The Betas filed in daintily in their matching orange high heels and orange jumpsuits. The members of the step team were an array of skin tones, from chocolate to cream, but all of them were slender and nearly the same height. Every woman's hair was at least shoulder length with an identical style: blow-dried flat with a part on the left side, and pulled back with a white satin ribbon.

Before the actual routine, a skit: Tiffany was the star of their show.

"Sorors?" she called.

"Yes?" The Betas answered.

"How hard did we work to become members of Beta Alpha Beta Sorority Incorporated?"

"We worked so hard!"

"And sorors?"

"Yes?"

"How much do we love Beta Alpha Beta Sorority Incorporated?"

"We love Beta so much!"

"I said, how much do we love Beta Alpha Beta Sorority Incorporated?"

"We love it! We love it! We love it!"

They began to hum, as Tiffany sang an a cappella cover of "Promise

Me," by Luther Vandross, the lyrics altered to allow for lines dedicated to their organization. After twenty minutes of pointless, ladylike prancing and a series of hand movements that always came
back to the Beta sign, the routine was over. The steppers headed in
the direction of their other sorors, who lauded them loudly, but Roz
walked to where Keisha and I were, across the gymnasium.

Then, the MC announced, were we ready for the nasty Gammas?

Only the neophytes stepped that night, the thirteen who had
joined the fraternity the previous semester. As the shortest, Abdul
was in front of the line. Pat brought up the rear. They all wore silver
boots with maroon pants and shirts, though Abdul wore his fraternity jacket, buttoned up the front. When the Gammas lined up, Abdul didn't give the signal for the routine to start. He looked around
the gym, and then walked toward where I sat. With each step, he
unbuttoned his jacket, until he slipped it off. Underneath, he was
bare-chested, and there were appreciative female shouts. When he
stood in front of me, holding out the jacket, there was more noise.
Roz poked me, take the jacket, people were looking, but on my
other side, Keisha whispered, don't do nothing I didn't want to.

I reached out with both hands. Abdul gave me the jacket, then
came in for a kiss. There were louder screams, and he walked back
to his space, and the routine began. I clutched Abdul's faintly funky
jacket as the Gammas pumped groins and stomped in unison. In
between nasty bedroom sounds, they chanted praises about Gammas and veiled insults about the other fraternities on campus.

From my seat, I looked around the gym at sisters tossing me envious glares and whispering to each other. But there were a few dot-
ting the audience who smiled at me. Those sisters had boyfriends
who had publicly claimed them, too, as Abdul had claimed me.
I was in an elite cohort: I had a man. I had beaten the ten-to-one
odds.

THE DIRTY THIRTY

❖

"Who y'all think gone make that Dirty Thirty list?" Abdul asked. "Freaknik is in two weeks."

Pat shook his head. "No comment. And this ain't respectful. Y'all see the ladies here."

"They can go in the kitchen, where they belong."

"I ain't going nowhere," Roz said. "And fuck you very much."

Even though Abdul and Steve had moved into their apartment in the fall, they'd been pledging underground. The Gammas had forbidden them to have any parties. So they waited until the spring to have their inaugural set. My boyfriend and his roommate had bought three cases of beer, the good kind. No weed, because they didn't want that smell in their new furniture. There were six pounds of chicken, which I'd fried for them, after calling Miss Rose for directions. I'd made potato salad to go along.

Roz and I shared a love seat and the four-pack of coolers that she'd bought. The Three Amigos half lay on the couch, bottlenecks resting on their chests, as the television blasted the Bulls versus the Knicks, a certain bloodbath. Nobody could win against Michael Jordan, but it was nice watching his aerial wonders.

"Precious Harmon, for real," Steve said. "She a natural-born freak."

"A freak like how?" Abdul asked.

"Like she had a three-way with Rick Bozeman and some dame from Atlanta. He said Precious ate that right in front of him."

Abdul moved into his patronizing tone. "Man, that girl is a dyke. That don't count for the DT. I'm talking about actual dudes that boned that jawn."

Pat sat up. "Y'all need to change the subject. Immediately. Like, post-damn-haste."

On the TV, Michael Jordan leapt through the air, his tongue out, and we clapped. How did he do that? It was some kind of miracle.

"Did Rick get in there?" Abdul executed a short air punch. "Or was it Precious on one end of that dame and him on the other?"

Steve put his red cup on the table. "Are you telling me a natural-born freak don't count for the DT just 'cause she ain't fucked—"

"—nigger, what did I just say?" Pat roared. "I told y'all, stop talking about this shit! Am I gone have to start busting heads up in here?"

I rose from the couch, and my roommate followed. We kicked male feet to navigate our way, but Abdul wouldn't move. He told us, step over, and tapped the side of his cup. Get him a refill. I snatched the cup from his hand, but in the kitchen, tossed it in the trash.

Roz leaned against the counter. She pulled on my shirt and I moved closer.

"Girl, what're you doing?" she whispered. "You're practically living here. And you cooking for him, too?"

"Only for special occasions."

"You lying."

"Why you so pressed, Roz? You the one told me I needed a man. Like you and Curt."

"He's in grad school, Ailey. You think I'm stupid enough to believe he's faithful in Virginia?"

"So why y'all still together?"

"Because he sends me a check every month. You know the deal. Ailey, you can't let a man treat you like this. Where's your backbone?"

"Why you gotta be so hard on Abdul? He's already had it bad. I told you how poor he was growing up."

"So that means he gets to be a jerk? Last I heard, home training don't cost a dime."

"Roz, I love him. At least . . . I think I do."

"You think you love him. Okay, just tell me this. Are y'all using protection?"

From the living room, there were shouts as the Bulls let go of the ball. They needed to call Jordan off the bench. Forget his rest. He could rest after they won the game.

"Not that it's any of your business, Roz, but yes, we use condoms."

"Can't you get your father to write you a prescription for the Pill?"

"You think I want my daddy knowing I have sex? That's disgusting."

"I hope you know if you end up pregnant, I'm moving out. I can't be roomies with somebody can't handle her business."

She left me there, leaning against the counter. I turned my back to the kitchen door and picked up a chicken breast. I didn't want Abdul to see me. He'd told me I needed to start watching my diet before I gained weight. He liked me big-boned, but fat and sloppy was another thing entirely.

"Hey, beautiful lady, what you doing?" Pat asked.

I dropped the breast on the floor. "Ooh! You scared me!"

He picked the chicken up, blew on it and bit into it.

"Pat!"

"Girl, whatever. God made dirt and dirt don't hurt. Ooh, this breast is so good and juicy. Mmm."

He smacked his lips loudly. Two more big bites, and he was finished. Then he looked around at the mess in the kitchen. The flour on the counter. The splotches of grease on the stove top. The mound of dirty dishes in the sink. He threw out the chicken bone and told me he'd be right back. When he returned, a large bath towel was tucked into the front of his waistband. He put the stopper in the sink and turned on the faucet. He asked, where was the dishwashing liquid?

———

When it came to men, Keisha was even more careful than Roz and me. The flesh was weak. Real weak, and the Devil stayed wide awake, she insisted. She didn't date or even talk to young men for more than a few seconds at a time. And the long dresses she wore announced her disinterest in anybody touching her, if they could even get past the waist-high panties, long-line girdle, full slip, and pantyhose she wore underneath those dresses, throughout every season.

But in April of our sophomore year, Keisha opened up to Roz and me. She told us she had something on her spirit she wanted to talk about. Keisha always had been honest with us about her poverty, that she'd grown up in the projects, and was on a full scholarship. She had no shame over that, but that night over cherry soda and ribs in our room, she confided that she wasn't truly a virgin. A cousin of hers had raped her when she was nine. Keisha had shown her mother the blood in her panties, but she was spanked for lying. Her mother told her that her period was coming in early. Puberty was turning her fast, and that's why she was musty, and making up lies on her own kin. Keisha's mother gave her cream deodorant to use and kept leaving her with the cousin to babysit, but then, just when Keisha lost hope, Jesus had appeared to Keisha in her dreams—the same dream for seven nights in a row—telling her she would be redeemed, and on the eighth day, the cousin was killed in a car accident, his body badly cut up by the impact of his going through the windshield, his penis and testicles mangled.

Her cousin's death was Keisha's sign to dedicate her life to the Lord and she was glad about that. Still the Dirty Thirty list hurt her. Because even if Keisha's name wasn't on a piece of paper—and even if she'd only been a little girl—she still felt nasty, no matter how hard she prayed. It was like her cousin had left all his filth behind.

"Do y'all think I'm bad, 'cause of what happened to me?" Keisha asked. "I tried so hard to be a good girl! I promise I did."

I held her as she wept. I told her she was as good as any person could get, and for once, Keisha didn't chastise Roz for cursing, for calling her cousin a low-down motherfucker. Roz told us that's why she treated men so indifferently. All they could do is pay her bills, because they weren't worth a damn. Doing this kind of shit to kids, and I was quiet. I held Keisha and smoothed her hair, hoping neither one of my friends would ask, had anything bad like that ever happened to me? I didn't want them to look at me differently. I wasn't religious like Keisha was, pledging herself to God.

A few days later, when the Dirty Thirty list appeared under our door that April morning, I couldn't even look at it. But Roz snatched up the list. She called the names out loud. None of us were on the list, but there were five young women in our dorm who were listed. Beside each name were the names of the brothers she'd slept with.

Other colleges had their own infamous lists, but they allowed those who smeared reputations to remain anonymous. At Rout-ledge, there was an honor code to the Dirty Thirty: if a brother wanted to drop a tarnished dime on a young woman, he had to give his name, either his government name or his fraternity moniker, which still identified him. Like "Serve," Steve's line name, which popped up next to six girls. And "Shotgun," Abdul's line name, which showed only once, next to Precious Harmon.

I skipped classes and meals in the refectory for three days, ask-ing Keisha to pick up my assignments from my professors. I walked to the vendors in the lobby, feeding change into the vending ma-chines to buy pop, packages of chips, and peanut butter cups. I let the sugar and preservatives console me, and I avoided Abdul's calls, until he paged me on the third day. The desk monitor who knocked on my door told me I had a visitor in the hallway. Knowing she was watching and would report back to the gossips, I gave Abdul a hug, and let him kiss me briefly on the mouth, before turning my head.

He led me out to the student parking lot. He told me he wanted to meet me back at the apartment to talk, but not with all these peo-ple looking. I climbed in my own car, though he told me he wanted me to ride with him.

In the parking lot of his complex, he was kind. Tender. "Is some-thing wrong, baby? You're not returning my messages. I'm ask-ing Keisha where my woman is and she won't tell me. I know she doesn't like me, but Roz won't say nothing, either."

He moved to touch my face and I stepped back.

"What's wrong? Abdul, you cheated on me!"

"No, I didn't."

"What do you mean? Your name was right there on the Dirty Thirty next to Precious! And now these bastards on campus are laughing at me! And you were just talking bad about her, too, right in front of me and Roz, when you knew you'd slept with her! How could you do that?"

"Oh, that. Baby, that ain't no thing. I didn't fuck that jawn. I only let her give me head."

"That's still cheating! And you shamed me! And Precious, too. How could you be so ungentlemanly? You don't see Pat putting his girls' names down on that list."

"That's cause that nigger soft. He probably gay." He put on his patronizing voice. "And head doesn't count as cheating. It only counts if I fuck her proper. Which I would never do with Precious. Everybody knows that jawn's a hoe. You're a good girl. That's why I made you my woman."

"That's supposed to make me feel better? That you had sex with somebody else, and now you're calling her names?"

He spread his hands. "Ailey, I told you, sex and head are two different things. And a man's gone be a man. A man can't help but say yes when a hoe with no morals offers to give him head. And anyway, you weren't officially my girlfriend when that happened."

"I was staying at your apartment all the time! We were sleeping overnight in the same bed!"

"But we hadn't discussed a committed relationship."

"You are crazy. You are loony tunes and low-down and ready for a bed at the Milledgeville hospital."

"No, I'm not. You just don't want to hear the truth. You want me to lie to you and say I don't like to get my dick sucked, but the truth is you need to learn how to please your man. Maybe if you did what I told you to, instead of always saying no, even when a brother begs you, I wouldn't need to—"

I turned around, and he told me, don't turn my back on him. He was talking to me. Didn't I hear him talking to me? He spun me around. Pulled me into a hug, though I was struggling, and I could smell that he'd had a beer earlier. When I pushed at his chest, he slapped me. I stumbled back, holding my cheek, and then I turned and ran to my car. As I drove away, I looked in the rearview mirror. He was still standing there.

Those final weeks of the semester, Abdul and I didn't see each other in private, but he played a game in the open. He acted as if nothing had happened. He blew kisses at me across the refectory. He touched my arm and used endearments when he saw me on the yard.

My roommates asked, what was going on? Abdul hadn't paged me and I hadn't left on the weekend with my overnight bag, either, and I lied to them that Abdul was studying. Or I was. Or both. I thought I was fooling them, but during finals week, Keisha told me she hoped that Abdul and I had broken up for good. It was clear that he wasn't living right.

Abdul's slap hadn't left any bruises, and I was grateful for that, but without the evidence, there could be no crime, at least not publicly. And though the campus gossips laughed about my humiliation over his cheating, I was the heroine. Abdul had behaved as men were expected to act, when confronted with his many female options. But I had been faithful. I was the long-suffering, good woman, and Precious was the villain, for she had gone after someone else's man. To everyone on campus, she was the Jezebel, the slut, the hoe, while I could cling to respectability.

In the weeks after he hit me, as Abdul blew kisses, I felt trapped by what I'd desired. I'd hoped to wound Tiffany for embarrassing me at the rush, for ridiculing my sister, so I'd slept with Abdul and made it impossible for her to stay with him. Then I'd wanted to be his girlfriend, to prove that I was a good girl, and not a whore who only sneaked out of the dorm to drive to Abdul's apartment. But the truth was I still felt dirty inside, even when Abdul had tossed me his jacket and everybody knew I belonged to him. I still felt ashamed.

When summer came, I took my old job back with Dr. Rice and stayed in town with Uncle Root. We took our trips to Atlanta to shop and see a movie, and one afternoon, when we returned, Abdul's voice was on the answering machine. He mumbled through his message, explaining, he'd found Uncle Root's number in the Gamma fraternity directory. And he was in Atlanta for the summer again. He had an internship.

"That young man sounds a bit forlorn," Uncle Root said. "Are you going to put him out of his misery?"

I walked to the answering machine and deleted the message, but the next day, there were two messages from Abdul, and even more messages the day after. One day in mid-June, I answered the phone and there was his voice. He sounded sad and disheveled. I pictured him on the other end, hair in need of a trim. A scraggly beard. Eyes red and bloodshot.

After a few minutes of his stumbling conversation, I told him I needed to go.

"Wait a minute, Ailey! Why you rushing me off the phone?"

"I know how much you need to save money. This is long-distance."

"But what if I said you were worth it?"

The next week, I received two insured packages, one with a depressed-looking pink teddy bear displaying a red heart, and another with gold earrings inside a velvet jewelry box. I held the earrings up to the light and located the 14k stamp. There was a card inside with a message about sincerity in the midst of sorrow: he'd bought me a card you give to someone who'd had a death in the family.

———

Abdul had been arrested once, back in high school. It was him and a bunch of dudes, coming out of a party. Teenagers, fifteen and sixteen years old. The cops had just grabbed them and started cuffing everybody. They wouldn't even say what the charge was. They'd denied Abdul a phone call, too, and for twelve hours, he'd done everything in that cell not to fall asleep. He'd stood, back against the wall, going over his homework in his head. Surrounded by all those hard legs, guys who looked tough enough to kill. Smelling them and trying to conceal his fear. That night, he hadn't known if he would make it back to his mother.

"Why are you telling me this?" I asked.

"I just . . . I wanted to talk to you, Ailey. Explain myself."

He'd asked me to meet him at the waffle place on the highway. It would be his treat, he'd promised, and I'd ordered more than my share. Steak, eggs, hash browns, toast, and unlimited coffee refills.

"But you're not explaining." I waited until the waitress poured my coffee. When she left, I leaned over my plate, lowering my voice. "Why'd you cheat on me?"

He turned his head to the plate glass window. There wasn't much of a view: the parking lot, and beyond that, the narrow highway.

I called his name softly. I told him to look at me.

"Don't try this, Abdul. You expect me to feel sorry for you?"

"You don't get it. You try working like a Hebrew slave with two part-time jobs for your pledge fees. Giving them Gammas money for their car payments or their rib plates or whatever shit they want, but it don't matter because they're still going to beat your ass. And now I'm supposed to belong, but I'm still not good enough. I just slipped up, Ailey. I just got stressed. I didn't grow up like you. I don't have a family to take care of me in case something goes wrong. It's hard out here for a young Black man."

"And so you're saying that's why you cheated on me?"

"I told you, Ailey. It wasn't cheating. I'm not going to argue about that."

"Okay, fine. But why did you hit me?"

"I just lost my temper, Ailey. I'm so sorry, but I was hurting, too. How you'd made me feel ashamed, not wanting me to meet your family. Letting me know I wasn't good enough."

"That's not true, Abdul!" I leaned over my plate, whispering. "I'd never in a million years say something like that. You were the one who told me I wasn't your girlfriend."

"But that was because you were ashamed of me. It really, really hurt me, Ailey."

Playing with the rest of my hungry man's feast, I told him I forgave him for hitting me, but I couldn't be his woman anymore. He said he understood, but that he hoped we could keep talking, because he needed someone to listen. He really needed a friend, and maybe we could talk some more, back at his apartment? I told him, no. I couldn't go back there. That was my final word, but he kept calling, and sent more presents. I began to meet him back at the waffle house, until one day, when he asked if he could kiss me, I told him, all right. Okay.

The next time he kissed me, he put his hand to my breast. I pushed him off, but then he began to cry. He was sorry, he sobbed. He loved me. He'd never put his hands on me again, and I let him touch me.

REUNION

❖

I'd never brought either of my roommates to the family reunion. Keisha would have fit right in, but I couldn't invite her and snub Roz, and I didn't know how Roz would respond to the barbecue in the field in front of my granny's house. To Uncle Norman laughing and drinking beer out of the can and calling our male relatives and friends "boy" and "son." Every once in a while, shouting, "What you talking 'bout!" and "Watch out there now!" The women of my family and community calling to me and tugging on my clothes and hair. Ordering me into the house to get some petroleum jelly, because I had an ashy patch on my knee.

But that summer, I decided to bring Abdul to meet my family. I didn't want him to think I was ashamed of him. For the family reunion, I wore my new lavender linen dress and my strappy sandals. Abdul was looking good, too; I'd called him the previous week and reminded him, be sure to get a haircut. I didn't want a scene like the summer before, when a cousin had brought her boyfriend down from Cleveland, where they'd had a revival of the pimp-inspired, Black male press-n-curl. As a joke, Uncle Norman had brought his electric clippers to my cousin's picnic table. The clippers had hummed and buzzed throughout the meal, like a Greek chorus.

My granny's brother decided to play his banjo. Uncle Huck sat in a chair on the porch, picking and singing the blues in a baritone. Down in the yard, there were cheers, folks shouting, play that thing, Huck! Play it! Mr. Luke looked on smiling and clapping, and everyone pretended they didn't know the two men were more than friends.

I leaned into Abdul's side, whispering I knew my family was 'bama, but he kissed my forehead. Don't worry. He was happy to be here. In the field, we sat with the old man and my mother. When I headed to the food table, she followed me.

"That's a lot of food for a second helping, Ailey. Aren't you full? You had a big plate."

"It's not for me. It's for my man. He's hungry."

"He can't fix his own plate? I thought you were a feminist."

"I am. I'm just being polite to a guest."

"I hope you know what you're doing, dating that boy. He's definitely no Chris Tate."

"Chris wasn't as nice as he seemed."

"At least he had some breeding."

"Careful, Mama. Your classism is showing."

"I had a dream about that boy Abdul. I saw his face and everything, but I didn't even know he existed until you brought him here. Don't you find that strange?"

"I'm supposed to choose my lovers according to your dreams?"

"Oh, you got lovers now? Excuse me, missy." She began spooning large portions of greens onto the plate I was fixing. "You want that boy to be constipated? If you going to serve somebody, do it right."

Along the road, the sound of tires, as a car parked far up the road, parking in front of the long line of others: it was David's Eldorado. I watched as he walked across the field and embraced my granny. He kissed her cheek several times as she fixed a plate for him. He greeted folks, making the rounds of the tables. Loudly told everyone, yes, he was starting his senior year at Morehouse in August, but then there'd be law school, too. That would take another three years.

When he set his plate at our table, my mother asked him, why hadn't he brought his girlfriend? She was surely welcome.

"Carla had to work," David said. "But I couldn't miss a chance at seeing you, Mrs. Garfield. Gosh, you're so beautiful. Do you even age?"

She snorted. "Boy, you're full of something, but I won't say what."

I ignored him and moved closer to Abdul, kissing his cheek. I fussed with the paper napkin tucked into his shirt, until he patted my hands, saying, all right, that was enough.

David began eating, but the old man wouldn't let him finish. He

began their usual debate: Washington versus Du Bois. Who was
the best leader for our people? Uncle Root cited the great scholar's
founding of the social work program at Atlanta University, proof
positive that he was the most devoted to our people. David countered with Washington's publication of *Up from Slavery*. It provided
history about the peculiar institution and a personal blueprint for
success. Definitely an important book.

"Yes, it was," the old man said. "But it was ghostwritten, like all
of his published work."

"What? Are you kidding me?"

"I am not, Brother David, and so you must try again. But that
trial is for another day, because it's time for a walk. Sugarfoot, are
you and your beau coming?"

We took our pilgrimage to the pecan tree and Uncle Root told
Abdul his story. On our walk back, David invited Abdul to the American Legion for a small get-together. That evening, Abdul told me
I couldn't join them at the Legion. This was a boys' night out, so I
had to stay back at the house. My granny had put him in my great-
grandmother's old room, and I'd propped the bedroom door open
with a stick. The floor wasn't level, and every time the door slammed
shut, Miss Rose would open it, declaring, respect her house.

Abdul silently rubbed his goatee with a hairbrush, then sniffed
under his arms. When he walked outside, I followed.

"But I'm wearing a cute outfit."

"And you look real pretty, Ailey. Go on back inside now."

"Come on. Please."

A supplicant's note slipped into my voice, but I wouldn't have
been ashamed if David hadn't been sitting on the porch steps,
watching me. He kissed his teeth and rose from the steps. When
he started the Eldorado, the strains of the Isley Brothers announced
he'd expanded his repertoire. I walked down the front stairs, still
pleading with Abdul, but he slid into the passenger seat, closed the
door and rolled up the window while I was still talking.

My voice rose into a shriek as I ordered David not to drive away.
He moved both of his hands from the steering wheel and put them

close to the ceiling of the Eldorado. Showed his teeth in that trade-mark "everything is everything" smile.

I leaned close to the glass of the passenger window, shouting. Banging on the window.

"Abdul, you better open this goddamned car door, or it's gone be some trouble! My heart don't pump no Kool-Aid!"

The screen whined open and my granny emerged, with my mother following behind. Neither were attired for bed. Over their jeans, they wore the reunion T-shirt that declared, WE ARE FAMILY! When my granny asked, why was I screaming? and I explained, Mama folded her arms. I knew she was thinking of her dream.

Miss Rose called to the car and David climbed from the Eldorado.

"Ma'am?"

"Baybay, what you and this Abdul boy done did to my grand-child?"

"Nothing, Miss Rose. It's just a misunderstanding. I'm gone fix this. I promise."

"You know you got to be careful with Ailey! You know she high-strung!"

"Yes, ma'am, I know, Miss Rose."

"Now, y'all take this girl with you to the Legion, and you better be nice. Don't you let me hear different. Don't make me call your granddaddy. You know J.W. don't play."

"Yes, ma'am, we gone be nice. You don't have to worry."

At the Legion, Boukie was waiting, and the four of us squeezed into a leatherette booth. My boyfriend sat with me, but his back was turned. He'd said nothing on the journey into town.

David put his hands on his slim hips. "Here she go: 'Open this car door or I'ma kill all y'all!' Partner, I was real, real scared."

When he threw back his head and laughed, Boukie joined in, saying he'd been knowing me for twenty years, and I came from a family of crazy, low-down women. "This girl got my ass whipped for nothing, back in the fourth grade. Her mama, she crazy on GP. Her grandma? Miss Rose the one who whipped me, plus, she threat-ened to cut my dick off in the summer of 1989. Her great-grandma,

Dear Pearl? She was crazy before she passed on to Glory, God rest her soul—"

"Boukie, are you gone talk about my whole family right in front of me?" I'd drunk two coolers, my anger melting away as the artificial fruit flavors hit my blood. "And you weren't in fourth grade when I got you whipped. It was the summer before third grade, though probably kindergarten for you, considering how many times you've been left back."

Boukie lit a cigarette, waving at the smoke. "You see what I'm saying? Ain't no way I'd sleep next to this girl. You might wake up wearing a pot of hot grits."

I slid from the booth. A quarter in the jukebox and an Earth, Wind & Fire slow jam. Back at the table, I told Abdul I wanted to dance. He jerked his hand from mine, so I turned to David, pulling him to his feet.

Abdul put his beer down. "Oh, so you just gone disrespect me, girl? You're not even going to ask my permission?"

"For what? Mr. Lincoln freed the slaves!"

I laughed, and David led me to the tiny dance floor, twirling me around slowly. When we settled into a slow drag, our hips fitting together, I remembered our summer. He whispered, I hadn't changed one damned bit. There was a sad-sweet chord to his words. I looked up and saw that he remembered, too.

I'M HUNGRY

◈

Abdul didn't call when he arrived back in Atlanta, though that was our custom. When I rang Abdul's rooming house, no one answered. His silence continued for the rest of the summer and when school started back, he ignored my waves in the refectory. When I'd knock on his apartment door, Steve would tell me, no, his sands wasn't home.

It took a month into the semester for him to page me, to meet me in my dorm lobby and ask me to walk to his car. In his apartment, he locked his bedroom door. He told me, there were some things I needed to know, such as, he didn't share his girlfriends. It was fine to share a hoe with a friend or a frat brother, but not somebody he was in a relationship with.

"Ailey, is something going on with you and that nigger?"

"Who?"

"That guy. David."

"What? No!"

"You telling me y'all didn't used to kick it?"

I didn't look away when I told him David was like my brother. And I took off my clothes, as Abdul directed me. I sat down where he pointed, but when he stood in front of me, unzipping his pants, I turned my head.

"I knew it. You lied to me."

"Abdul, no, I didn't. I promise."

"Open your mouth, then." He came closer—

I am four. I need to take a bath, Gandee says. If I don't I will stink like a nasty little girl. He pulls off the pretty dress Nana bought me and the matching panties with all the ruffles. He takes off all his clothes and his underwear and there is a red thing there. He tells me we're going to get in the tub together in the guest bathroom. We're going to have lots of fun and he'll put on my other clothes after our secret. I shouldn't tattle on him, because if I do, I will be a nasty little girl and he won't love me more than he loves my sisters and he'll kill everybody. I'll die and my mama will die and Lydia will die and Coco will die and my daddy will die and none of them will go to Heaven and do I want that to happen? In the bathroom, we get in the water. I'm between his legs and that red thing is poking me in the back and his skin is white and there's no ducky in the water. I have no friends in this water. Gandee comes at me and puts his hand down there. I start crying and I hit him on the arm and he says, be a nice little girl. Didn't I remember what he told me? Did I want everybody to die? Did I want him to kill me? I look at the squares on the side of the tub and Miss Delores and Nana aren't coming back but Mama is coming in a while to get me, after Gandee dresses me again. She's coming and I don't want her to die—

Abdul tugged my hair. I couldn't suck dick worth a damn, he told me, so he ordered me to lie on my back. He rolled on top of me, but I squirmed away, protesting, we had to use a condom.

"Like you and that nigger did?"

"I never slept with him!"

"Open your legs if you're not lying."

"Abdul! Quit!"

When I kicked and pushed at him, he slapped me. Again. Again. Again. I saw blue and pink sparks, but I kept kicking. He put his hands around my neck, choking off my air, until I stopped struggling. I was dry when he pushed into me, as he kissed my face, begging me, call him Shotgun, move around, do something, but I only lay there, my head turned. Through the walls, I could hear the sounds of Steve walking. He'd confided in me that he had nightmares; it frightened him to close his eyes after dark.

After Abdul was finished, he brought up the holidays, that he wanted to meet my father, like a man should. He wanted my father's blessing for our relationship, and then Abdul began his cherished story, that his parents had never married, that his father never had been in his life. I knew how sad his story was, but I wasn't going to comfort him. I let my breath deepen and he jabbed me with his finger. He called my name, but I didn't answer. When I knew he was asleep, I dressed and left.

———

Every day, Abdul called the dorm for me, but I took the pink message slips from the work-study student at the desk and dropped them in my purse. In the refectory, he waved, blowing kisses. The gossips were watching, but I didn't return his gestures. I didn't care who was watching, ever since I'd returned from my appointment at Dr. Rice's office, where Nurse Lansing had told me I had gonorrhea.

I'd called her at home, asking if I could take a pregnancy test. She'd said she'd open the office early on Friday as that was Dr. Rice's late morning; he wouldn't be there, in case I wanted privacy. Nurse Lansing said she needed to do a pelvic examination. When she finished, she told me I wasn't pregnant, I didn't have a yeast infection, and there were no warts. But my cervix was very red. I had a sexually transmitted disease.

As I cried, her voice gentled. She put her hand on my shoulder, and told me she knew privacy was important, so she was phoning in a prescription for the antibiotics to a pharmacy in Macon. And birth control pills, too. I didn't have to take them, but the option would be nice, wouldn't it?

"Don't forget to call me back," she said. "You have to get your HIV and syphilis test results. And when you finish the antibiotics, remember to start using condoms, okay? Carry your own, if you can, in case you go back to this boy. Don't you be embarrassed, neither."

I'd driven to Macon and picked up my antibiotics, but I hadn't confronted Abdul. When I called after Nurse Lansing's deadline, she told me, fortunately, I was negative for the rest of the diseases, but she repeated, don't forget to use my condoms.

A month later, when she examined me again and gave me the all clear, she gave me the same warning. But I didn't need it. I continued to ignore Abdul's waves. I laughed uproariously at the table with my roommates, even when Roz asked, what the hell was wrong with me? Nobody had told a joke. I ripped up Abdul's pink message slips in the front of the desk monitor, knowing the word would get around. I didn't open my door when I heard my name in the hallway, telling me somebody was calling. It took a while to tell my roommates what the gossips already had surmised: I'd broken up with Abdul.

One day Abdul paged me. I came downstairs and walked past him as he shouted my name. He didn't know that day was Lydia's birthday, that I had awoken with her on my mind. How she would have made me feel better about the mess I'd made of my life. Growing up, my big sister had made me feel as if I was perfect. Nothing ever had harmed me in her eyes.

———

At Thanksgiving dinner, my granny told me my face was as long as her arm. She tried to get me to talk, and so did Uncle Root. I left early, even though I'd promised the old man that I'd spend the weekend and do some window-shopping in Atlanta. I didn't lie when I told him I had a test on Monday but omitted that I'd been studying for three weeks.

In the student parking lot, I sat in my car, listening to the radio. Lydia's favorite Christmas song came on, and I felt sorry for myself. I considered driving back to Chicasetta, but my people would be lingering over dinner. My granny would hover, then offer her only solution: more sweet potato pie.

When I walked across the yard, there was Pat, sitting on the bench smoking a joint. What a pleasant surprise, he told me. He patted the bench: come sit with him.

"I thought you'd be in Chicasetta. Did you come back to see Abdul?"

"Don't nobody want to see that asshole. I have a test on Monday."

"Aw, damn, girl. Shit. It's like that?"

I plucked the joint from his hand, taking a draw. "Why aren't you in Atlanta? And how you just sitting in the open, smoking weed?"

He put his arm behind me, on the back of the bench. "I got a test, too, and you know I share with the security guards. How they gone drop a dime when I'm getting them high?"

We passed the joint, smoking it down to the roach, and he lit another. There weren't many words: we expressed thanks when the joint moved from one hand to the other.

"Ailey, can I ask something?"

The second joint made my throat raw. I had swallowed instead of exhaling, bringing on a coughing fit. I gave Pat a thumbs-up and a backward wave. *Go ahead. Keep talking.*

"What's going on with you and Abdul?"

"How is this any of your business?"

"I'm concerned, Ailey, that's all. You don't seem very happy."

"So, you some kind of premarital counselor now? What? You want to listen to me bad-mouth your sands?"

I knew I should be annoyed at Pat, but my high was kicking in. He took the joint when I gestured, smoothly inhaled, then handed it back.

"Yeah, all right, Abdul is my sands, and I guess I love him. You can't pledge on the same line with somebody and not have love. Especially not for Gamma. We got our asses beat together."

"Which is, like, a real stupid way to get friends, but I'm not gone criticize. We all have our needs for human companionship."

He laughed and put his hand on my nape, stroking.

"I don't understand something, Ailey. How did a gorgeous, extraordinary woman like yourself end up with this hood-rat two-timing you? Can you explain that, please?"

Whether I was high or struck by his candor, the question was hilarious. I was overcome with giggles. I touched his face, pushing gently.

"You're so snobby!"

He grabbed my hand, rubbing the tips of my fingers over his lips.

"You misunderstand me, Ailey. Nothing's wrong with being poor. My mama was poor before she met my rich daddy. I'm talking about who Abdul is. He can't help being poor, but he can help being an asshole. N'est-ce pas?"

I wanted to stop giggling. I wanted my granny's sweet potato pie, because I was no longer sad, but I did have the munchies. I wanted Pat to keep kissing my fingertips.

"And if that nigger mentions his deadbeat father one more time." Pat lifted his voice into a childish singsong. "'My *daddy* tried to get my mama to have an abortion when she was carrying me. My *daddy* didn't pay the child support. My *daddy* didn't come to my high school graduation.' This nigger always talking about how mean his daddy was, then he kicks dirt in the face of every sister he gets with. But y'all women? Y'all just flock to brothers like that! Mon Dieu! C'est incroyable!"

He had entered a reefer-smoking trance, the arena of deep thought, at least until the high comes down. "What kind of hold does this dude have over you, Ailey?"

"I mean . . . I don't know . . ."

He scratched the side of his face with his thumb. When he laughed, it came out in nearly soundless puffs. "Oh. I guess he's laying some serious pipe."

"You are so nasty."

"Girl, look. We're out here smoking marijuana on a bench during a holiday weekend because you're mad at your cheating man—"

"—I'm not mad! And he's not my man anymore—"

"—and I'm the one who's nasty? I tell you something, Abdul might not know how to treat a gorgeous individual such as Ailey Garfield like the queen she is, but I certainly do. Je t'adore, ma reine. C'est vrai."

I wasn't so high that I couldn't recognize a pass when I saw one, the meaning in his French compliments, the touching of my hair, the kisses of my fingertips, or his refusal when I tried to offer him the last of the second joint: "No, baby, it's all yours, if you want it."

An hour later, when Pat offered to walk me to my dorm, I invited him to sit inside my car and listen to the radio, but in a few seconds, I pulled him to me and began to kiss him. I was no longer high. I knew exactly what I was doing. I couldn't get close enough as he whispered how beautiful I was, how sexy. How perfect. I put the brake down to give us more room, but my car was too tight. He apologized for being a big dude, and I asked him, did he want to go to a motel? We could split the cost, but he insisted, no, no, he had it. What kind of gentleman asked a lady to split the cost of a room? Just drive, baby. On the highway, he leaned over, kissing my face. When car lights passed us, I checked myself in the mirror. Was I going to do this? Was I really this brazen?

In the motel room, I reminded him, we couldn't stay until morning. We had to be careful, because of the campus gossips, but when I clicked the bedside lamp, he turned the light back on.

"I want to see you, Ailey. Please."

He asked me to sit down, and for seconds, I was afraid. Maybe Pat would hurt me, like Abdul had, but he kneeled. Took off my shoes, one by one, and then my socks. He pulled at the bottom of my jeans and slipped off my panties. Slowly spread my legs and touched me. Exclaimed how wet I was, and, oh, I was beautiful. He'd been wanting this for so long.

"You like me dreaming about your pussy?"

"Yes, I do, Pat."

He opened me further and began licking me as if there were no tests on Monday, anywhere in the world, and brought me to climax twice before producing his own condoms. When he took his time entering me, saying, if he ever hurt me, don't be afraid to let him know, because he never wanted to hurt me, never in his life, I decided that Patrick Bertrell Lindsay didn't need to lose any weight. Not at all. Those extra fifty pounds fit him perfectly.

And when I decided not to worry about the gossips and we spent that night, and then another, in that motel room, my mind didn't change.

———

The Monday after Thanksgiving, Abdul was waiting for me on the steps of the refectory. When he saw me, he smiled. His face was calm, guiltless. I was with Keisha, and she tugged on my arm. I motioned that it was okay but stepped back when he moved in for a kiss.

"What do you want?" I asked. "I'm hungry."

"You seem to be mad about something. I don't know why. But whatever I did, baby, I'm sorry."

I said nothing. I was afraid, if I allowed myself to become angry, I'd blurt out what he'd done. That he'd raped me and hurt me. That he'd given me a disease and made me feel even dirtier than I already felt.

"Uh-huh. Okay. Can I go now?"

"This is kind of public, Ailey. Can we go somewhere? I'll buy you dinner at the waffle place."

"No thank you."

"Ailey, please."

"Fine. I'll meet you at the apartment. Give me fifteen minutes."

"Okay, baby. I'll leave the door unlocked. I love you."

I waited until he walked out of earshot before I told Keisha I'd buy her dinner at the Rib Shack, because I needed her to ride with me to Abdul's apartment. In the car, she advised, forget about the stuff I'd left at that boy's place. I could buy another curling iron and blow-dryer. When we pulled into the parking lot of Abdul's complex, she wanted to go inside the apartment with me.

"I don't trust him, Ailey. He's not a good person."

My heart was pounding, thinking about going into his apartment. But I couldn't help but laugh at her wise tone.

"Okay, Keisha. Like you know so much about men."

"Just because I go to Bible study don't mean I'm stupid."

"I'm okay, girl. It'll only take a few minutes."

She climbed out of the car. "I'll wait by his door."

"Keisha—"

"—What I say? I'm giving you five minutes. After that, I'ma start banging on the door and screaming and somebody gone call the police. Five minutes, so you better make it snappy."

The sound of her voice, the stern set of her lips made me wonder, how much did she know? Maybe I hadn't been as good at concealing my troubles as I'd thought.

Inside the apartment, I called out a greeting, and from the back, he answered. Come on, he missed me. He lay on the bed naked and hard: he was that sure of himself. After I put my keys on the top of the television, he reached for me. I told him, let me go freshen up. It had been a long day. In the bathroom, I pulled out the milk crate holding my blow-dryer and curling iron from underneath the sink. In the brand-new box of tampons that I'd purchased, I noticed only two were left. Jesus. Not only had I been sharing a man, I'd been sharing feminine hygiene products.

When I left the bathroom, I told him I was leaving.

"Come on, Ailey, don't be like that."

"Like what? Like I don't want some girl's sloppy seconds—"

"—Why you bringing up that bitch? That's in the past—"

"Or I don't want you to hit and rape me—"

"Man, whatever, Ailey. You don't know how to forgive. That's your problem."

He picked up the remote from the bedside table and turned on the TV.

"Abdul, did you know I fucked Pat?"

He dropped the remote and pulled the sheet over himself: he wasn't hard anymore.

"I sure did. After I took the antibiotics and got rid of the gonor-rhea you gave me, I fucked Pat. And let me tell you, I have never had such an incredibly satisfying sexual experience."

He swung his legs to the floor, and I stepped back quickly. If I had to, I'd drop my stuff and run. Or Keisha and I could beat him up: he was naked and defenseless.

"I also sucked Pat's dick. Unlike some people I could name, he did me first. Oh man, did he do me! Talk about 'Sweet Lick Papa.' Wasn't that his Gamma line name? A very accurate description, and I thought, *Hey, why not be polite and return the favor to that brother?* So I did." I shifted a couple of my belongings to the crook of my arm and picked up my keys from the television. "You know, fellatio is surprisingly yummy, especially when somebody's not slapping you upside your head and trying to choke you with his penis."

"You're lying, Ailey. You're just mad and making up stuff. You're not like that. You're a good girl."

"I am? Why don't you ask your sands about that? Tell Pat I know what a true gentleman he is, but I give him permission to spill the beans, this one time."

At the bedroom door, I paused.

"Who's the bitch now, Abdul?"

ALL EXTRAORDINARY HUMAN BEINGS

◆

When Pat called me at the old man's house, he apologized for tracking me down, but he was worried. He'd looked me up in the student directory and called my parents' house and had a wonderful conversation with my mother. Initially, she'd been suspicious, until he told her his parents had been freshmen during her senior year. She'd given Pat my granny's number, and Miss Rose had kept him on the phone for a half hour. Before they hung up, she'd invited Pat to visit the farm, any time he liked. Miss Rose had told him I was probably at Uncle Root's. Here was the number, and don't be no stranger. He was always surely welcome.

"Ailey, I haven't seen you since . . . Thanksgiving . . . and everything."

"Pat, I just saw you on the yard."

"You know what I mean, girl. Let's meet up at the Rib Shack. You were looking like you had fallen off some. You need a good meal."

"Pat, I'm not anybody's skinny. And we can't be seen together."

"Why not?"

"Because people would talk."

"Ain't nobody thinking 'bout them niggers."

"But what about Abdul? He's your sands."

"Ain't nobody thinking about him, neither! You know he tried to get up in my face about you."

"I shouldn't have said anything to him. I'm so sorry."

"Don't apologize, baby. I'm glad he knows, but I told him, if he tried to dog you out in public, he'd be the one looking bad, 'cause he couldn't keep his woman. Plus, I'd beat him up."

"You're so sweet. I mean, not that I condone violence, even toward assholes."

We laughed.

"Don't you miss me, too, Ailey?"

"You know I do. I'm . . . I'm crazy about you, Pat."

"Oh, girl! I want you, and not just like that. I want you to be my lady. I've been trying to tell you that for three years, Ailey. I'm dead serious."

"I want you, too, Pat. I can't stop thinking about you."

"Oh, baby, et moi aussi! And I'm not trying to hide that shit no more! Let's do this."

I wanted to see him so badly. To have him kiss my forehead and my fingertips. To hold me, whisper his tender, pretentious French phrases, and have sex with me, leisurely, for hours. But I told him I had to think about making us public. Give me a while to get myself together.

That evening, Uncle Root needled me into a chess game, though my skills hadn't improved. I refused to protect my queen, the most powerful figure on the board, whom Uncle Root called his "Lady Love." Shortly, he castled me, his hands blurring. On my side of the board, I moved my knight out of harm's way.

"Ailey, are you going to introduce your new beau to me, or are you keeping him a mystery?"

"Who told you I had somebody?"

"No one. But I assumed it was Rob-Boy's grandson, because you lit up like a Christmas tree when I called you to the phone. So tell me, is he your beau?"

"Maybe. Maybe not."

"All right, you're entitled to your secrets. You are an adult."

"I am?"

"Yes, you are, and if the sound of Brother Patrick's voice is any indication, he thinks so, too."

"We're not a couple. Not yet."

"And why is that? Is he not a gentleman?"

"Uncle Root, he totally is. He's, like, so nice and so wonderful and just perfect. But the way we started seeing each other . . . it's kind of scandalous."

"My favorite! Do tell."

I kept my eyes on the board when I reminded him, I used to go out with Pat's fraternity brother. Not just his Gamma fraternity brother. His line brother, his sands.

"I remember now. This is that rude boy you brought to the reunion last summer? Raheem or something or other?"

"Abdul."

"That's right. I didn't like him, not in the least. And as I recall, your mother and Miss Rose didn't, either."

"I thought you took to him."

"I just have manners. But if you two broke up, what's the problem? These intrigues happen all the time. I'm sure that Raheem is pining for you—"

"It's Abdul—"

"Whatever his name is, I'm sure he's devastated. You're a prime catch, but it is not for him to decide your romantic future. That decision is up to you."

—————

Keisha didn't blink when I told her that Pat was courting me, though I was trying to keep it secret. Even with the reefer smoking and the wine, she'd always thought he was a nice guy. And Keisha acted as go-between when he gave her notes in French in the refectory, whispering to her to pass them on to me. She giggled, "Ooh, girl," when I pulled out my dictionary and translated for her. I was glad Pat kept his messages Christian-friendly.

Though my other roommate had approved of my dismissing Abdul, she was less than excited about my new romantic direction. She rolled her eyes at the increasingly tall stack of Pat's notes I kept on my desk.

One Wednesday, when Keisha was away at Bible study, Roz warned me, this was dangerous. If I wasn't careful, I'd get a bad reputation. I knew how vicious the gossips could be.

"You can't be dating two Gammas on the same campus," she said. "And definitely not line brothers."

"I'm not," I said. "Abdul and I broke up."

"You know what I mean! Ailey, you have to leave Pat alone."

"No, I don't. I can do whatever I want to. I'm grown, and this is America."

"All right, then. Keep on with it, with your American ass. You gone be at Bible study with Keisha and the rest of them Jesus-freak bitches who can't get no man."

"Keisha is gorgeous! She can date whenever she wants to!"

"But the rest of them heifers can't. They ugly, and that's why they saving it for the Lord."

———

On Valentine's Day, Keisha handed me a red envelope. Inside, there was a fancy card covered in velvet and a snippet of a poem by Léopold Senghor. She whispered, Pat was waiting for her in the library stacks, in case I wanted to respond. While she giggled, I scrawled quick, English words on notebook paper, and handed it to her.

Thirty minutes later, Pat and I met in the parking lot of the waffle place on the highway. When Pat drove up, he rolled down his window, signaling me to follow him. After another forty minutes driving toward Macon, he pulled off to a dirt road.

The trailer in the clearing belonged to his family, and so did the surrounding twenty acres. Pat's grandfather used to go out there to clear his head. Since his passing, the trailer had sat there, unused. Inside was dusty, and though there weren't any roaches, a few large, anonymous bugs of the woods had found their way in. But the baby-blue sheets on the double bed were clean. They were the thick, all-cotton kind you used to see in homes of the elderly, before they gained popularity with the wealthy.

I pulled him to the bed and stripped off my pants and underwear. Closed my eyes when he began to rub his face between my legs. He licked and hummed, and whispered, he wanted to live down there. I tasted so sweet. I tasted like candy. Then I watched as he pulled on a condom. His look of joy, his startled laughter as he entered me. When he declared that he loved me, I told him that I felt the same way. When he asked, was I really sure? Please don't play with his feelings. Please, and I reassured him: I loved him so much.

Afterward, there wasn't a television to keep us company, but we wouldn't have watched anyway. We cuddled tightly, as Pat recited from memory the poem by Léopold Senghor he'd slipped into my Valentine's card. He'd told me that it was supposed to be political, about Africa's independence, but every time Pat recited the line in French about the nude Black woman, I'd get a naughty thrill. The way he rolled his *Rs* elated me.

My fears were not dispersed, though. That if I was seen with Pat in public, shame would be splashed on me. That I would be called a frat freak, hopping from one Gamma to the next, though Abdul had moved on since early January. He was dating a sophomore girl, but for weeks, I spent far too much on gas money, following Pat down the highway, instead of riding along in his car.

When Mrs. Stripling confronted me one morning, asking where had I been sleeping nights, I told her I was experiencing a family emergency. I produced a teardrop to lend my story veracity, and she took my hand. God was able, she assured me. He would work everything out.

One morning during spring break, I woke up in the trailer to find Pat lying beside me, a troubled look on his face. When I nudged him and asked what was wrong, he asked, was I embarrassed by him?

"I know I'm not like Abdul, all diesel and everything."

"I don't want him, Pat. You are way cuter than him, and you make a great cup of instant coffee. The coffee is actually why I dig you so much."

"Don't you make fun of me, Ailey. You want me to eat you out in private, but you'll pretend you don't know me in public."

"That was such a rude thing to say!"

"You're the rude one! You hurt my feelings, Ailey! You really do!"

Before we headed back to Thatcher, I told him, don't turn right off the highway. Keep going and follow me. Since he thought I was ashamed of him, I had something to show him. At the front door of Uncle Root's house, I introduced Pat as my new boyfriend, and the old man exclaimed, this was a lovely surprise.

There were lots of smiles, and when the two exchanged their

Gamma fraternity handshake, I turned my head to preserve their mystery.

"Patrick, it's so good to see you! You are the spitting image of your grandfather!"

"Everybody says that, Dr. Hargrace."

"Rob-Boy would be so proud of you. I haven't seen you since his homegoing. That was a lovely funeral." He nodded his head for a few seconds. "And now look at you! How you've grown."

"I'm fatter than him, though."

"Not at all! That's just good living! Isn't that right, sugarfoot?"

"Uncle Root, I keep trying to tell him how handsome he is."

Inside, we young folks sat on the sofa and the old man brought us cold sweet tea. We caught him up on campus doings, which buildings needed alumni donations for repairs, and which were holding up, and he asked, what did we think about the new president, that fellow that used to work on Wall Street? The old man didn't approve of these corporate types to run colleges. They didn't understand the classroom, let alone the moral and spiritual work of teaching. It was only about the money to those people, but if the new president could track down where half the school's endowment had gone, then bless that man's journey.

Then he dived into Frantz Fanon with Pat. It had been some years, but Uncle Root was working his way back through the postcolonial canon. He liked to read things at least three times, and now that he was retired, he had his leisure moments. But he hoped Pat knew that so much of Fanon's ideology was stolen from Du Bois. It was true, and when the old man turned to his ancient story about meeting his hero, the tale changed. This time, the great scholar had entered Miss Fauset's room as Uncle Root sat there drinking his tea.

"Uh-uh," I said. "That's not right."

"This is my story, Ailey," he said. "I think I know how it goes."

"You've told me this story six times, and you never said you saw him again. You only said he was an asshole."

Both men shouted my name.

"What?" I asked.

"You can't call him that," Pat said. "That's like cussing in church."

"Last I heard, W. E. B. Du Bois was not Black Jesus," I said. "But I see the two of y'all are getting along."

"And why wouldn't we?" the old man asked. "This young man comes from very good stock. Now let me get back to my tale. You didn't hear all the facts, Ailey, because you were barely a teenager when you first heard this. I didn't want to shock you. But yes, indeed, the great scholar walked into Miss Fauset's room, without knocking. He called her 'Jessie.' And she called him 'Will.' And then . . ." The old man mustered a longer-than-usual dramatic pause, before flinging his arms wide. "They both began speaking in French!"

"Um . . . what's so scandalous about that?" I asked.

"Brother Patrick, your young lady has told me that you are a Francophile. Will you explain the significance of that exchange to her?"

Pat put his arm around me. He kissed the top of my head. "I sure will. See, Ailey, two Americans didn't need to speak in a foreign language unless they were trying to hide something from the other people in the room."

I leaned away and looked up at him. "Maybe they were being fancy."

"Or maybe they were having an affair. After all, baby, French is the language of love."

My cheeks warmed as the old man told us, there were more than enough tidbits about that affair in the latest biography of the great scholar. All one had to do was put the clues together.

"So, wait," I said. "You really think them two were messing around? But Dr. Du Bois was married!"

The old man shrugged. He sighed. He had never wanted to speak ill of the great scholar when I was younger, but now I was old enough to hear the truth, that Dr. Du Bois had been a well-known Lothario. So many mistresses—so many—all over the country: white women, Negro women, young and old. He'd given Mrs. Du Bois such trouble over the decades, causing scandals. And imagine how Miss Fauset had felt, when she'd really been his junior wife! Or would have been, over in Africa. Those two poor, long-suffering women. It was awful, the way the great scholar had mistreated them, all the while writing essays about the need to protect the equal rights of Negro women. Such rank hypocrisy, but still, Dr. Du Bois had been a brilliant man who'd labored in the service of our people. And all extraordinary human beings had their faults.

———

For Easter, Pat coaxed me down the interstate to meet his parents at St. Anthony's in the West End, their family parish. He didn't need to play on my guilt, though. I wanted to meet them.

He and I slipped into the pew at nine forty-five for the morning Mass, and I put my purse on the pew to save two extra seats. I told him, we should have come the night before for vigil, because the holiday sinners crowded out the regulars on Sunday. Look at that line for Communion. When we returned to our pew, I was supposed to kneel like my mother had taught me. I should think on the goodness of the Lord, but I cheated by half sitting on my haunches. I ran through my calculus homework. My eyes were closed when I heard Pat's whispered greeting to his parents, and I kept my head bowed, wanting to impress them. When I finished my fake prayers, they were sitting on Pat's other side.

After Mass, we lingered in the pew until the church emptied. I leaned over Pat and shook the soft hand of Mrs. Lindsay, who wore a paisley blouse tucked into a black skirt.

Clothed in a blue linen suit, Pat's father was a handsome man, though much fairer than his son. His pate was bald, the sides cut low. Though his remaining hair was curly, not straight, Mr. Lindsay was a dead ringer for my grandfather, when Gandee had been a much younger man. My breath caught. In my spotty memory, I saw the picture, framed in silver and hanging on Nana's red-painted wall.

"Young lady, it's so good to meet you," Mr. Lindsay said.

I couldn't speak, as Pat's father held my hand. I smiled and nodded at Gandee's brown eyes ringed with Gandee's salt-and-pepper lashes. I thought of those times with my grandfather in the bathtub, his showing me how to touch his red penis, how to put my small mouth on it. My heart trotted as I tried to swallow. It was the Communion wafer. It wouldn't go down.

"This boy has nothing but praise about you," Mr. Lindsay said. "And now I can see why."

"Yes, sir." That was all I could manage, but everyone laughed, before Pat's parents left the church to walk to a lot down the street, where the latecomers parked.

It was a long drive on the interstate, out toward Cobb County, where the Lindsays now lived in a McMansion. They'd finally given up their smaller house off Cascade, where they knew everybody. They'd loved southwest Atlanta. They'd raised their children there, and the schools couldn't be beat, but they were getting older now, and southwest was turning bad. So now they were surrounded by wealthy white folks who didn't speak or invite them to Saturday barbecues, but on the plus side, they didn't have to worry about some crack fiend breaking into their basement.

Pat's older sister, Collette, was in the living room. Her husband was with his parents at their Baptist church. Collette was a plump, shorter version of Pat. In her arms, a sleeping baby girl in a lace bonnet, white satin dress and shoes to match. The other child, a toddler in a pastel blue Easter suit, white shirt, and bow tie, ran around like a lunatic.

"Look how pretty you made them," Mrs. Lindsay said. "Why didn't y'all come to Mass?"

Collette shifted the sleeping baby.

"Mama, you know I can't take that boy to church. I can barely get him in the car seat. Stop now, R.J.! Before you get dizzy."

Her little boy ignored her, spinning in circles. Then he tired of that and tugged at my boyfriend's cuff until he was lifted and turned upside down several times. When his uncle put him down, R.J. began to shriek. He wanted to be picked up again.

"Not now," Pat said. "And quit that noise. You embarrassing me in front of my company."

"Don't be mean," I said. "He's just a little boy."

I kneeled down and held out my arms.

"He doesn't like strangers," Collette said, moments before R.J. moved into my arms. When he kissed my cheek, there were approving sounds. A check mark for me in the "pro" column.

"Well, I'll be dog," Mr. Lindsay said.

"I told y'all she was sweet," Pat said.

I sat R.J. on my thighs and cut my food into tiny bits and fed him, glad for the distraction, that he ate my dinner when I couldn't. But then he fell asleep in my arms, and when Mrs. Lindsay took him upstairs to the guest room, I had no shield, nothing to defend me from the attention of Pat's father. I moved my chair closer to Pat and continually drank water to wet my closing throat. I cut the one slice of Easter ham I'd asked for, using my excellent table manners to move the meat around the plate.

Mr. Lindsay kept approving of me, by praising my origins, and his wife agreed, when she returned. They loved my great-great-uncle; what a brilliant man Dr. Hargrace was. What a fine teacher he'd been. Routledge had been so lucky to have him for so many years. They'd met my parents, though they'd been three years behind Mama and Daddy at Routledge. And they made broad, rueful hints about a wedding, hopefully in not too many years.

When we left, Mrs. Lindsay hugged me in the foyer. Mr. Lindsay did, too, and I gave thanks to the resurrected savior that he didn't wear the same hair oil as Gandee, because I would have vomited in the foyer, instead of waiting an hour, when Pat turned onto Highway 441. I told him, stop the car. Right now. Stop. I threw up only water.

———

There were only forty days left until Pat's graduation when he told me it was time to come out as a couple.

"Everybody knows already. The other day, somebody called you my girlfriend."

"But you're graduating. How is this supposed to work?"

"I'll be right in Athens at the University of Georgia. I can come see you all the time. Or, you know, we could get an apartment there and you could drive to classes. We could get out this funky trailer."

"What are you saying? I love our trailer."

Every day, it circled: his pressing me, and my excuses. I don't want to remember his face when I told him I'd had my fun. It had been great, but it was time for me to move on. I cried myself when he started weeping.

We made love that last time, and inside me, he begged, don't do him like this. Don't leave him. Didn't I know how much he loved me? I was his whole world, and I almost changed my mind, until afterward. When we lay there and Pat reminded me that his parents were coming for the graduation ceremony. Since Easter, Mr. Lindsay had talked nonstop about me.

My fears about Mr. Lindsay weren't real. I knew that. The man couldn't help looking like my monster of a grandfather, but I couldn't help casting my gaze down the road of years, either. If I joined Pat's family—if we married—there would be no logical excuse to avoid holidays with his people. My memories wouldn't be dust, but animated flesh sitting across the table. I'd try not to vomit as I looked in the face of a man who resembled Gandee. I'd relive old outrages. I'd rush from the room as Pat tried to justify my bad manners. I'd lock myself in the bathroom while he tapped on the door, begging me to come out. Asking, Girl, what's wrong? But I couldn't tell him: *Pat, your perfectly nice father disgusts me.* And what of our offspring? How long could I keep them away from Atlanta? And when Pat insisted it was time for them to meet their grandparents, what could I say to Mr. Lindsay? What explanation could follow, after I shouted at him, don't you dare touch my children?

———

In the morning, Pat asked me not to go back to Abdul. He had a feeling Abdul might be trying to come back around. It wasn't only jealousy, either: something was wrong with that guy. He couldn't be happy or treat a woman right. I deserved better. I gave Pat my promise. And I hoped he would forgive me, for hurting him. He deserved better, too.

NGUZO SABA

◈

Sometimes, when a person is dying of a terminal disease, he rallies for a short period. His cheeks fill with color. There's extra elasticity when he rises from the couch. He wants to buy Christmas presents himself, not send someone else out to the department store with his list. This is what happened with my father, when he was recovering from surgery after his second heart attack.

There had been the dozen bottles of pills on the dresser, but my mother hadn't bothered to look up the names of the medicines. Her job was to take care of him and cook heart-healthy meals. Even Coco hadn't been aware that my father would not recover. Usually she was sharp, but she was in the second year of her residency at City Memorial Hospital and she was exhausted. Daddy had deceived all of us about his grave prognosis.

It was Dr. King's birthday when my mother found my father dead in their bedroom. They'd been planning on going to church; our priest had planned a special service. After her shower, she'd dried herself and was taking her hair from the curlers when she noticed Daddy wasn't moving. I was her first call. She reached me at the dorm.

"Ailey, I was telling him that I'd cook him bacon, since it was a holiday. He'd been begging for months, and the one time I was going to let him cheat, he couldn't even enjoy it. I feel so bad."

To keep from pushing her grief forward, I wept with no noise, as her voice altered on the phone between her usual alto and a high, tormented soprano. I closed my eyes and saw her story.

It was my senior year. There was a special convocation in the chapel that morning, but I can't tell you who the speaker was or what they said. After, I went to the refectory but didn't reveal to my roommates what had happened. If I didn't utter that my father was dead, he wouldn't be. And I wanted to call Pat, so much. He was only ninety minutes away in Athens, but nothing would change, no matter how I felt about him. It wouldn't be fair to use him, just because I was grieving.

I drove to Chicasetta and then back to campus. I looped the journey five more times before driving to the old man's house. It was dark, but the porch lights were on and he was sitting on the glider. He'd poured some liquor in a glass for me.

"He's really dead, isn't he, Uncle Root?"

"Yes, he is. I'm so sorry."

"How could he leave me? How could Daddy do that?"

As I cried, scotch dribbled out of my mouth and I wiped it away. I moved down and laid my head on his shoulder.

"I know, I know. It's all right, sugarfoot."

We drank the whole bottle that night, the beginning of many times that I'd share a drink with the old man. I wished I hadn't had to lose my father to earn my rite of passage.

Down in Chicasetta, it was a pretty time. A sharp, goose-bump wind was the only indication of winter the day God got in His laugh—the way my mother had let her hopes rise, that my father was going to beat his illness. And the Lord was slapping us blind when He made sure that my father stayed in a cooler for a week up in the City while my mother drove around unsafe neighborhoods, Aunt Diane riding shotgun, as they looked for Lydia.

My other sister had refused those drives. She wasn't going out there with them. They both needed to forget about Lydia. Pray for her and let her go. But Coco didn't have a mother's love. Until a woman births her own, she can't know what it feels like to have her breasts ache with milk, years later, after a dream, when there is no suckling child. Mama knew that marrow-filled affection, but finally, she let go of her hope that Lydia would return and shipped Daddy's body to Chicasetta. She laid him to rest in our family cemetery, behind the charred plantation house. Throughout their years together, he'd told her he didn't care what happened, so long as he was buried where she would be buried. He wanted to sleep beside his woman.

I suspected Nana Claire would have been upset about the loca-tion of my father's grave. That she might have objected, saying she wanted her son buried up in the City, but the previous autumn, she'd had a stroke. The day after my father had died, Mama told Nana her son was gone. Nana cried, but the next morning, she couldn't remember what had happened. So my mother reminded her, but again, my grandmother couldn't hold on to grief, and my mother wouldn't tell her a third time. She couldn't take the sadness of that daily knowledge, that Nana's tears were temporary.

———

After my father's funeral, I stayed nights in Chicasetta, driving to campus only for classes. I didn't think of graduation or what my future would bring. All I could think about was my father, hoping he wasn't lonely in his casket.

I still hadn't told anyone on campus about my loss, for fear of breaking down. My roommates kept asking, was something wrong? But I told them, leave me alone, and in the afternoons, I'd drive back to the old man's house. He'd stand in the doorway of my room, and ask, could he get me anything? I didn't seem to be eating. Maybe a slice of pie, and I told him I wasn't hungry. I just wanted to sleep.

Then, Mrs. Stripling left a pink slip for me under my door: *Come see me. Urgent.*

When I knocked on her door, she demanded to know where I had been sleeping nights.

"Ailey, this is unacceptable. You can't just be staying out like this—"

"It's my daddy, Mrs. Stripling," I said. "My daddy died."

I began to shake, unable to continue, and she opened her arms to me. Every time I tried to speak, a new wave of tears, as she held me, whispering, oh, baby. Oh, I'm so sorry. She told me I needed to be with my people. Sleep in Chicasetta as long as I liked. She would make an exception, and we would keep that between us.

Four months later, when my mother came down for my gradu-ation, I told her I'd decided to defer my first year of medical school at Mecca University, based upon family emergency. Classes for med school were supposed to start in June, but I thought deferral was a better option than flunking out. We were in my dorm room, packing up my belongings. I'd asked my roommates to clear out so I could have some time alone with my mother.

"What about Morehouse in Atlanta? You could go there instead. It's probably not too late to contact them, and you could be close to Root. I know you'd like that." Her back was turned as she filled a box with books.

"Mama, it's too late to apply. And anyway, I'm not sure I want to be a doctor. I don't think it's going to make me happy."

"Is that all? Girl, nobody's ever happy working! That's why it's called a 'job' instead of 'pleasure.' But you know what would make you happy? Making a lot of money and having good credit. Buying yourself some nice things. Finally driving a new car."

"I've already contacted Mecca. The deferral is only for a year, until I get myself together."

She kept packing boxes, and on our journey back to the City she was quiet in the car. That only lasted a few days, though. Soon, she began telling me I needed to go to med school. Several times a day, she brought it up, unless Aunt Diane told her, stop haranguing her niece. She and my youngest cousin were living with us, now that my aunt and uncle were divorced. But Mama only would stay quiet for a while, before she started up again: Sure, take the year off, but be sure to contact Mecca University and let them know I would be ready to start medical school next summer. And if they told me that I had to reapply, then do that, too. Whatever it took to get my life going.

———

Over the months, to speed my progress, Mama popped her head into my room and offered daily, curt clichés: "Quitters never win" and "Put your best foot forward" and "Rise early and keep your hand on the plow." Mornings, if the sidewalks were clear, Mama took her own advice. When the light appeared, she put on her tracksuit and took up her pepper spray. She would not miss her morning walk. Daily sunshine was important.

Sundays, she took a rest from talking about medical school, but still, she knocked on my door. "You sure you don't want to go to Mass, baby?"

"No, I'm good."

"But Father Dan keeps asking about you."

"That's nice of him. You tell him to pray for me."

"Ailey, you better not get smart about God. You gone need Him one day."

After church, she'd invite me to dinner at Nana's, where everyone now collected. The stroke had come as a surprise. She'd always eaten sparingly and watched her weight, but when Coco had moved into the house to take care of Nana, she'd found the stash of Gauloises, along with the jade holder. When Coco ordered an MRI, the consulting doctor told her this hadn't been our grandmother's first stroke; she'd had some mini-strokes as well.

Nana needed the support of her family, my mother told me. That's why I should come to dinner, and besides, I should meet Melissa. She was my grandmother's caretaker, now that Miss Delores had retired. If I ever came to Sunday dinner, I could see what a nice girl she was. Melissa was real pretty. Big-boned, too, not one of them skinny types. Also, she was my sister's girlfriend.

I'd suspected that Coco was a lesbian. To my knowledge, she'd never had a boyfriend, and back when we'd spent summers in Chicasetta, whenever boys had approached her, she'd spoken to them rudely. "You're bugging me," she'd say. But I acted surprised when my mother revealed her big news about what was going on with my grandmother's at-home nurse. And I nodded when my mother warned, don't be prejudiced about your sister's lifestyle. Times had changed: I had to keep up.

When she recounted her discovery, Mama had emphasized she was not a snoop. She only went upstairs at Nana's house to use the bathroom. Nana's personal toilet was downstairs, but it was too small. My mother liked to have space to move around, and once there, she reasoned that it was totally acceptable to examine the toiletry articles inside the medicine cabinet. She wanted to see how the rest of the upstairs had changed as well, and after checking the closets and bureaus of the other bedrooms, she didn't see any evidence that another person slept in those rooms, which seemed strange to her since it was clear Melissa slept there—there were perfumes and lotions in the bathroom, and Coco didn't like all that. Soap and water always had been plenty for her. Mama hadn't thought herself nosy, either, for turning the knob of the closed door of her daughter's room, the one that had been Nana's. On the wall of the now-white anteroom, she saw several framed photographs of Coco and Melissa embracing, among the family pictures. (My mother was pleased to see three photos of herself on the wall, too.) And when she inspected the closet of the bedroom—okay, all right, yes, at this juncture, it was a complete invasion of privacy—one half of the walk-in closet had contained female clothes too tall and wide to fit her petite daughter.

"But isn't this nice?" my mother asked. "I gotta tell you, Ailey. I thought something was wrong with your sister. She never had anybody. Lord, I'm so relieved. To God be the glory."

The Sunday that I gave in to her nagging and attended dinner at Nana's house, I noticed the house was smaller than I remembered. Her bedroom had been moved downstairs to the maid's quarters, the walls of which were painted red and displayed her pictures. There was a bathroom a few steps from the bed, which was no longer a four-poster. The pill containers were kept on a shelf inside the carved armoire that was wedged into the corner.

My sister's girlfriend was tall and plump and cinnamon-colored. She tried to serve, until my mother sweetly scolded, she better sit right down. Sunday was the Lord's day, and Melissa needed some rest. Then Mama asked her, what did she want on her plate?

"You know I wouldn't mind some greens, Miss Belle. Your greens are so good."

After dinner, we moved to the living room and Coco turned on the VCR. None of the Black classics were out on videotape, so we watched my grandmother's preferred movie, *The Lion King*.

"I'm bored," my cousin Veronica said. "I've seen this movie, like, a thousand times. I'm ready to go home."

My mother told my cousin she had a secret. That was her code for a hug, and the girl rolled her eyes. At twelve, she was too old for foolishness, but Mama held out her arms, and finally, my cousin sat down, snuggling into her. Our grandmother swayed to her movie as she sang about the circle of life.

Coco had told us Nana's larger stroke hadn't left her completely debilitated, but she'd never be the woman she'd once been. I looked at my grandmother, wearing the expensive housedress she'd called "a lounging outfit" in her stronger, acerbic days. The embroidered satin slippers on her feet. All my grandmother's memories might not be present, but mine were. And I didn't want to feel sorry for her.

I retreated to the kitchen, rambling through the fridge. Looking at the snacks that Nana never had kept in the house when I was younger. Individual containers of chocolate pudding, pound cake covered with plastic. Times had certainly changed.

Then, a tap on my shoulder. "Hey girl."

It was my sister, sneaking up on me. She had our mother's light, terrifying step.

"Coco!" I put my hand over my chest. "Girl, you scared me! Damn, you walk like a cat."

She laughed. "Melissa tells me the same thing. Listen, I'm worried about you."

"Me? I'm fine."

"But you need to do something with yourself, Ailey. When med school starts back up next summer, you don't want to be used to sleeping in every morning. You need to be able to hit the ground running, or that schedule will kick your ass."

"Okay, I'll look around for something. I think Worthie's might be hiring."

Coco put out a calming hand, like our father used to do. "Don't be upset."

"What did you do?"

"Nothing bad! I only set up an interview for you at that free clinic where Daddy worked. They're on Mecca's community network."

"How'd you know that?"

She looked away for a few seconds. "Just show up to the interview, okay? If you don't like it, you don't have to take the job."

"How much are they paying?"

"It doesn't pay, but it looks good on your résumé."

"Volunteer work? How many days a week?"

"Two."

"Two days a week and no damned money, Coco?"

"It would make Mama really happy, Ailey. And she's been having a really hard time. She's really sad."

I sucked my teeth. "Fine, Coco."

"You mad?" She bumped me with her hip. "Don't be mad, okay?"

"I won't be mad if you stop being creepy, sneaking up on folks. Wear a bell around your neck or something. Shit."

The clinic where Coco had scheduled my interview was in my parents' old neighborhood, over in the northeast quadrant of the City. My mother called the neighborhood a ghetto; we'd lived there when I was small, but I didn't remember. After we moved, Mama never returned to that part of the City. She'd told me she was grateful she'd made it out, and she didn't want her daughters going there, either.

My father's practice had been in a nicer part of the City—that's how he'd made his money—but Seven Principles Clinic was the legacy he'd helped to build, with the help of a friend, Mr. Zulu Harris. The clinic used to be called "The People's Nguzo Saba Afya Center" but the name had changed, once the federal government began to give community grants.

That clinic had been my father's passion, but I'd never met Zulu Harris. He and my father had been good friends, yet he'd never visited our house. I got the feeling that Mama never liked him much: whenever my father mentioned him, she would say, don't let that nigger get him in trouble. He knew what she meant.

As I drove to that neighborhood, I saw that every fifth or six building was empty. Addicts with concave eyes sat on the steps, smoking and talking. But there were other houses with front lawns of blossoming pink and purple flowers and trimmed hedges. Only the bars on the windows let me know, this was a place to be careful.

On the clinic's front steps, a handsome, goateed man stood. His head was shining bald and he wore a Cuban shirt, linen pants, and sandals on his feet.

"I cannot believe this is Brother Geoff's baby! When I found out you were volunteering here, I said, I was going to meet you!"

When I stepped back a few paces, he laughed.

"Aw, darling, I didn't mean to scare you. I'm Zulu Harris."

I joined in his laughter.

"Oh, okay! All right! My daddy used to talk about you all the time."

"I hope so! We were best friends. I miss that man. He was my brother. And now, how your mama holding up?"

"She's keeping, Mr. Harris. You know. It's a little hard for her."

"I understand."

We sat on the stoop and he gave me the rundown of the neighborhood. Don't forget the ten dollars for the group of little boys. They would protect my car in front of the clinic. The police ignored them, because Mr. Harris had a friend on the force. But the ten dollars was important, because if I did not gain a reliable reputation with the little boys and pay them, the more dangerous grown men would take over.

"Otherwise, come outside and no car!" He snapped his fingers. "I pay fifty dollars a week myself. You're on a sliding scale."

And don't mind the addicts at the clinic, neither. They were terrible, coming in with their fake coughs, trying and trying to get the drugs. They scared the new doctor, the guy who'd taken over for my father. When Daddy was alive, all he'd give them was three ibuprofens apiece. No matter how they cried. And finally, don't lecture the teenage mothers about birth control. These girls were just doing the best they could.

"All right, the director of the clinic will show you the rest of the ropes next week, when you start. I've got a community meeting, but don't forget to go 'round to my restaurant. Zulu's Fufu. Your money's no good there. Anything you want, just order."

"Thank you, Mr. Harris."

"And you tell your mama I asked about her. You tell her my brother wouldn't want her needing anything and not getting in touch with me. Make sure you tell her." He pulled a folded piece of paper from his pants pocket. "Here's my number, just in case."

Back at home, I let myself in, and Mama ran to me.

"Are you all right?"

She stroked my face, and I pulled from her onion-perfumed hands. "I wasn't fighting in the Gulf War. I was across town."

"You were in the ghetto, baby. Why can't you just say it?"

"Because 'ghetto' is a politically incorrect term. It's called an 'inner-city neighborhood.'"

"It's impossible for Black folks to be politically incorrect."

I followed her into the kitchen, telling her I'd finally met Daddy's best friend, Mr. Zulu Harris. He seemed really nice, and I thought he was well off. He owned a restaurant and some apartment buildings.

"I haven't seen him in years," Mama said. "What he look like? Is he all broke down and his teeth gone?"

"No, not at all. I mean, I don't know what he used to look like. He had some gray in his beard. But for an old dude, he's actually kind of fine."

"Oh—Okay."

"Mr. Harris asked about you, too. He said, if you needed anything just give him a call."

Mama touched her collarbone. "Did he, now?"

———

That next week, there was a band of little boys blocking my way to the clinic, one so young, his two front teeth had fallen out.

I spoke to the tallest boy. "What's your name, sugar?"

"What's it to you?"

"I'd like to know who I'm giving my money to."

"Maurice Bradley. What's your name, lil' mama?"

He stroked his hairless chin, and I resisted my urge to yank his ear. It was either ignore this child's bad manners or leave my car at home and take the bus. My mother would never allow me to take the bus to this neighborhood.

"My name is Miss Garfield, and why do I have to pay you ten whole dollars?"

"'Cause we said so."

"Where're your parents while this is going on?"

Maurice stood taller and adjusted his baseball cap. He looked back at his miniature cosigners, and they nodded their heads.

"Who're you, the social worker? All you need to know is your car will be here when you get through. That's what you call a contract."

"Here's the deal, Brother Maurice: I don't have but five dollars today." I raised my hand. "I forgot my money, but I'll have fifteen dollars for you next week. So how about I give you this five dollars, and as a good-faith gesture, you can have this?"

I pulled out a large pack of Now & Laters from my purse. I liked to tuck them in my jaw and let them disintegrate throughout the day.

Maurice's cosigners made happy noises, and he snatched the money.

"All right, then. But I can buy my own candy."

It was a day filled with trouble. After my exchange with the Colored Lord of the Flies, I'd tried to get an elderly patient to fill out a new questionnaire. She had been fully clothed but pointed her finger at me.

"What you think this is? I don't know you!"

I clutched my clipboard to my chest.

"But Mrs. Bradley, this is just a new questionnaire we need you to fill out. We have to maintain statistics for the government."

"I don't give a good you-know-what about no statistics! Just cause I'm poor don't mean I gotta to tell all my damned business to the whole congregation!"

I backed out of the room, but as I turned the corner, I heard a familiar sound. Lydia's laughter, the free huskiness rising.

Disbelief gobbled my air, and I knew then, I'd never expected to see my sister, outside of my own memories. But there Lydia was: alive. There she was, a miracle standing at the desk, talking to the receptionist. My sister had that same charm, the ease of our Chica-setta women.

When she turned around, I rushed to her. The clinic was sched-uled to close, but patients were backed up, staring as we held each other and cried. As Lydia called my name, rocking me in her arms. She called my name again. She called it one more time.

◈

SONG

◈

How a Man Becomes a Monster

The fault of how Samuel Pinchard, the man who would be known by the Negroes on his land as "Master," became an atrocity, a devil clothed in beautiful skin, bright hair, and the strangest of eyes, instead of a human being with a soul that listened to God calling in dreams, began with a woman. Or at least Samuel would fault this woman. She was the one who had thrust him out of her perfect, warm place and into a cold container that was not a true world but a hell. This woman was Samuel's mother, who bore him by a father whom no child deserved.

Her name was Joan, and like all of her children, she was a woman of incomparable beauty, in the time and place where Samuel was born. She and her husband, Adam, had lived on the land the English called Virginia. That land had been taken from its original inhabitants, as all the land in this place on this side of the water had been taken, and Adam had built a farm that was not wealthy, but was not poor, either. There was a house of one level with two bedrooms, and a kitchen that served as a parlor. This house was built of split, sanded logs. A porch and two chairs that rested upon it, where Adam and Joan sat in the evenings and shared very few words. In the distance would be the lights coming from the cabin that seven of their Negro slaves shared. Adam and Joan thought little about these Negroes except to take their respect and (presumed) affection for granted, like all owners do for that which they consider things and creatures. As Adam took the wood of the chair that cupped his buttocks for granted. As he took the meat on his plate for granted and did not weep over the spilled blood of the animal who had crossed from the side of the living over to death. And why would he? He believed that Negroes were the children of Cain, the least favored son.

Adam was handsome, though of dark hair and eyes. His children with Joan had inherited her fair looks. Had it been this lack of resemblance, the blond hair of his children, that caused Adam to leave Joan's bed in the night without a backward glance? To never consider if she was warm in the cold or if her stomach was full of supper? To consult the hole in his chest where his soul should have been, and then walk to the other room, which was on the left side of the large kitchen? The Bible lent him absolution, for there were stories of men who abused women, even their own children, as Lot had ravished his own daughters, in the days after the destruction of Sodom. Maybe Adam thought of Lot, that bearded, self-righteous man, when he chose one of his two daughters from the children's room. Yet there was no justification for him on the nights Adam chose one of his four sons.

The six children of Adam and Joan were beautiful, and when the family arrived at church in their town, the only place where the eight of them visited together, it seemed acceptable to the congregation that the building where God lived should house such splendor once a week. The Pinchards sat in a row up front. Their Negroes sat with the others of their tribe at the very back of the church, as there wasn't a balcony.

Sunday nights were a reprieve in the life of Samuel and his siblings, for the other six days a week, that light would be followed by the demon-filled darkness. In the room that he shared with his brothers and sisters, his rest was never deep, for he waited for his father's candle to appear in the doorway, and for Adam to pull the covers off one of the three beds and select the child he would take away and remain with that night. Each night the candle appeared, Samuel would suck in his breath and hold it. He would pray, and two or three times a week, his prayer was answered, for Adam's hand would reach across Samuel to his twin brother, and Samuel would be saved. Or Adam would not approach Samuel's bed at all, and he would pull the covers off one of the other two beds. And rarely, there were nights when the door to the children's room would not open, and Samuel wondered, was his father at rest, or had God answered his prayers and killed the man?

Yet there were the nights when Samuel was chosen and led through the kitchen and outside to the barn, where a blanket lay on the alfalfa hay. A Negro man slept in the barn and Adam did not bother to tell him to leave as Samuel was hurt in the darkness. Often, he hoped that the Negro would save him, that the Negro would strike Adam on the head with a horse's whip or the shovel used to clean out the stalls of the horses and the mule, and then Samuel would be free. He did not ponder what would happen to the Negro upon his father's death, as surely the Negro did. He did not care that perhaps this Negro would be sold to cover the taxes of his father's thirty-five acres. Samuel only wanted not to lie facedown on a blanket in a barn.

Once, on a night that Samuel was chosen, and Adam's hand steered him through the kitchen, Samuel began to scream for his mother. He cried Joan's name, he begged her to make it stop, he surely howled as long and loud as an animal soon to be transformed to meat, and Joan appeared at the door that opened from her bedroom to the kitchen. Her face was utterly perfect, lit by the candle she held. Samuel reached his hand toward that light. He cried her name—*Mother*—and Joan stepped back and shut the door.

That next morning, after Samuel had slept away his pain and wretchedness, he felt Joan's hand on his shoulder, tender and sincere. She told him she had cooked griddle cakes for his breakfast, with cane syrup and butter to go along. Joan's odor drifted above him, an aroma as only a child knows, the perfume that would invade his memories and make him weep, long after this time. And he hated his mother. And he loved his mother. And he wished that he would no longer be weak and a little boy. And Samuel made promises of what his strength would accomplish, once he became a tall and powerful man.

The Monster Roams the Countryside

When Samuel was sixteen, his father died, carried away by a fever. Adam lay in bed, shaking with the heat that emptied his bowels and shaved meat from his bones. Throughout he held his Bible close to his chest. He was a righteous Christian to the end, as was Joan, who read to her husband from the biblical book for the prophet for whom Samuel had been named: "And she said, Oh my lord, as thy soul liveth, my lord, I am the woman that stood by thee here, praying unto the Lord. For this child I prayed; and the Lord hath given me my petition which I asked of him: Therefore also I have lent him to the Lord; as long as he liveth he shall be lent to the Lord. And he worshipped the Lord there."

The week after his father was buried in the small backyard, Samuel took a horse from the barn and rode away into the night. He cared nothing about his brothers and sisters, not even the twin with whom he had shared a womb. He had planned his escape and had packed a leather satchel with clothes, hiding it in the corner of the barn under hay. It was the same corner where his father had assaulted him. Samuel hadn't slept the day of his leaving and tipped into the kitchen that served as a parlor as well. He took a loaf of bread that was covered with cloth, and a small dish of butter. He uncorked a jug, sniffed, and was happy it was water. As he walked past the room where he knew his mother lay in the same bed where his father had died, Samuel did not knock or call a greeting. He continued out the door to the barn. When Samuel took the horse, he did not care if the Negro who lived in the barn would be punished for his theft. He did not care about his siblings. He did not care about the land. Care was a flaw that burdened the weak. He meant to be strong now: brutality was his traveling companion.

His journey to our land was roundabout. For three years, he traveled south and east through paths that had been cut through trees by our people. He rode up to cabins where men had seen their youth depart, in their quests to make fortunes on our land. He smiled and used deference and his beautiful face as weapons, for fading men want to be reassured that their shoulders haven't narrowed, and their bellies haven't sloped. A few times, when Samuel rode his horse up to homes, he encountered widows, and after charming a meal from these women and a night's worth of sleep on the porch or barn, he rode off with no warning. Samuel had no use for grown women; he despised these bleeding, musty animals. In their weakness, women wanted to dump a burden in a man's lap.

He had thought himself free of the nature of men, until one day, many months into his journey away from his homeland, he saw Negroes working in a tobacco field. It was midday and a time of rest, but children everywhere are the same and though the day was warm, the small ones ran around the tobacco, laughing. Among their number Samuel saw the prettiest little brown girl, with her hair in short plaits. She was playing a game of tag. Her milk teeth were very white. Her eyes large and brown. Samuel felt a rush, such as a man feels heat for a woman. He knew he wanted to stay at this farm, simply to be around this little girl.

So he stayed three months and had not imagined he would leave until one day his passion ruled him. He was returning from the outhouse and came upon the little girl. She was throwing corn to the chickens and calling to them. An animal overtook Samuel. He grabbed the little girl, placed his hand over her mouth, and ran with her back to the outhouse. Afterward, he did not try to dry her eyes or keep her from weeping. No one would believe a Negro girl's accusations of a white man. And even if she was believed, no one would care. The next morning at breakfast, Samuel's happiness was overwhelming. He had slept dreamlessly and deeply, and when he awoke, he conducted himself as if nothing had happened.

Samuel did not feel morally bankrupt. To the contrary, he believed that he had been seduced by the child he'd assaulted, that the little girl had flaunted her beauty before him and that as a man, he had been helpless. Her Negro status was even more to blame, for hadn't his father taught him that Negroes were descended from Cain? Though a child, the little girl belonged to an inferior group, and Negresses were known purveyors of temptation for white men. Samuel had not dragged his own daughter or even the child of someone white into the outhouse—he would never do such a thing. Samuel had taken a Negress and he was a white man. He was the surveyor of a kingdom that God had given him, and he was a white man. In fact, Samuel had honored the little girl with his seed: he was a white man. And Samuel was certain that the little girl felt honored—after all, he was a white man.

No consequences occurred after that day, and Samuel watched the little girl for weeks, stalking her, so that he could capture her and steal her away to the outhouse again and again. It was a source of such great pleasure, until the afternoon when she turned limp in his hands. He did not fill with panic. His sense of power had inebriated him, coddling him in tranquility. He left the little girl slumped in the outhouse, not caring whether she was alive or dead. In the dwelling of his host, he sat for a delicious supper, and then regretted to inform him that he had strayed from his home too long. Samuel confessed that his mother was sick, and though she had been in the fine care of his other siblings, it was time for Samuel to return. He'd neglected his filial duty. A few weeks later, he arrived at the large plantation of a man who lived outside of the city of Savannah.

The Monster Finds a Sanctuary

Samuel was twenty-one and living on a vast establishment on an island off the coast of what was now called Georgia. There he was overseer for nearly one hundred slaves who grew tobacco for their owner, a man named Ezekiel Waterford, who owned a second property as well. The other place was a far more lucrative plantation where rice was cultivated; it had five hundred slaves, and three more overseers. As Samuel had done at his previous appointment, he had knocked on the door of the plantation house—this time on the back door—and shown his lovely face. As usual, his charm and beauty had resulted in his welcome. It was at this rice plantation that Samuel had heard about the lottery for land in the state, that parcels of a bit more than two hundred acres would be granted to lucky white men and white widows who won.

Ezekiel was a man whose wealth had been inherited. He dressed as if for visitors every day, only to walk down to the small, whitewashed building that was designated the plantation office. There, Ezekiel sat in a chair at a walnut desk that his grandfather had imported from England and moved papers from one side of the desk to the other. He stood at the window and surveyed his property, though he could not see his slaves because the land where they worked and were overseen by Samuel was some great distance from where he lived and worked himself. Ezekiel was not a hardworking man, and yet Samuel longed to model himself after him—to wear shirts of fluffy whiteness and close, dark breeches that never were stained with sweat or dirt, with shiny black shoes that made impressive noise when Ezekiel walked upon the floor of his house or office. But such a noise would not be made if Samuel remained an overseer. He could not earn enough money to own even one Negro, let alone build a big white house with outbuildings surrounding it. Samuel would not have a cot in his office upon which he could assault the slaves that he owned. He needed to make something of himself.

Ezekiel was a married man who regularly attended Sunday services at the church that he had built on his island. He gave the excuse of piety or work to his wife, whenever she knocked on the door of his bedroom and he did not answer. She may have known that he was not in his separate bedroom, but lying on the cot in his office, pressed on top of the back of a muscled young man. Before Samuel had accepted the position of his overseer, Ezekiel had forced one of a group of handsome Negro men, which the previous overseer had culled for him from field slaves. That overseer had left a few days before Samuel had knocked on the back door of Ezekiel's kitchen house. Ezekiel never had known congress with any man who had not been forced to comply; he had ignored the grunts of pain, the leaking blood and bowel effluvia of his Negroes. Thus, when Samuel did not shrink from Ezekiel's searching hand on his shoulder, and then his open mouth and tongue, Ezekiel quickly fell in love. He was unaware that, while he was ecstatically pressing himself inside the slim blond-haired man with the aid of a generous slathering of lard, Samuel was fantasizing about murdering Ezekiel in torturous, inventive ways.

After Ezekiel had finished with his passion, Samuel would pretend he could not bear to part with his older lover. He clung to Ezekiel, and in a matter of weeks, Ezekiel had told him many important pieces of information: about the running of the plantation; the yearly expenses and profits; the buying of slaves; the selling of slaves; the tending of the land; and how a man of property did not merely own that property, but must make sure that he paid taxes on this property. A man who did not pay taxes could not retain what he had worked so hard to possess.

While Ezekiel spoke, Samuel kissed him with flutters. He touched Ezekiel's lips, his cheeks, his collarbone, and more often than not, Ezekiel became capable again, this time in Samuel's mouth. While Samuel tried not to choke, he no longer fantasized about Ezekiel's death. Instead, he calculated what he would purchase that would require taxes. Within two years, and with the benefaction of Ezekiel, Samuel owned a secondhand two-wheel carriage, on which he paid taxes, as well as other goods that required the same. When the lawmakers in the (then) capital of Georgia, Milledgeville, passed the act announcing that each county should submit the names of the white heads of households, single white men, and white widows who had paid taxes for at least one year into a land lottery through which Creek lands would be distributed, Samuel's name had been written down many times in Ezekiel's record books as a respectable white man. And it was Ezekiel Waterford's love, his grateful, sacrificial feeling, that persuaded him to write a letter certifying that one Samuel Edward Pinchard of legitimate, white birth had labored in his employ from March 1801 to September 1804, so that there would be no doubt that Samuel had a right to our land stolen from the Creek. When the announcement came that Samuel's name had been drawn, that he was now the owner of a parcel of two hundred and two and a half acres, Ezekiel gave Samuel three hundred dollars and a better, younger horse than the one Samuel had taken from his dead father's farm, and Ezekiel sent the younger man on his way with tears, well-wishes, and prayers.

The day Samuel rode away, he was not only proud of his status as a landowner; he was proud that he had suppressed his own tastes for little girls. Ezekiel had been devoted to Samuel, but also jealous. On certain days, he had ridden down to the tobacco fields unannounced to see if Samuel was standing too close to large, handsome Negroes. He had watched from a distance for a time, never climbing down from his horse, then ridden back the mile to his office. Samuel did not know if his jealousy would extend to children, but he hadn't wanted to take the chance. Thus, Samuel spent four years in agony, watching little Negro girls carrying water out to the fields he supervised. The sound of their laughter was like knives in his flesh, but he was patient.

The Monster Makes His First Friend

Aidan Franklin was not as young as Samuel. His eyes were not Samuel's strange, ever-changing color, only a pedestrian blue, but he was still a very handsome man. Aidan had scrambled for a living since he'd been a young boy in his parents' one-room cabin. When Aidan married, his wife had given birth to five children, before she died in the blood of the childbed. Aidan married again, and that wife had given him seven children, so that children seemed to hang everywhere. Yet life's misfortunes had not stolen Aidan's optimism. When Samuel met him and his very young, tired wife along the way to the new town called Chicasetta in the middle of Georgia, Aidan quoted to him from Romans: "And we know that all things work together for good to them that love God, to them who are called according to His purpose." Aidan and his wife rode one horse. His children walked beside it.

Samuel parted ways with Aidan, and shortly he was knocking on the door of the cabin he discovered on the land that was now his in the eyes of the United States government. It was the cabin where Micco lived. Samuel was pleased to see this farm up and running, but when he knocked on the door of the cabin to evict the occupants, something about Micco gave him pause. Samuel knew nothing about Micco's lineage—about the red hearts of his ancestors—but the younger man's heart had no color. He had never used a weapon and he did not know how to kill. His only resources were his beauty, charm, and ability to manipulate. So he smiled and introduced himself and decided to wait to act.

That next morning, Aidan arrived at Micco's cabin as well. He introduced himself and asked, could Micco help him to build a cabin? Samuel greeted Aidan as if they were just meeting for the first time, giving him a quick wink. There was a general air of friendliness, even when Aidan said he owned the parcel of land to the north of this cabin. Samuel corrected him, telling him no one owned anything, except this man Micco, right here.

Aidan tilted his head in confusion. "Well, now, that's not right at all—"

At that, Samuel cut him short, and asked him if they could talk outside. When Samuel returned, he told Micco that the other white man had been confused, and he had set him straight. Micco had not smiled, but his face had softened at the loyalty of the strange-eyed newcomer who sat at his table, not knowing that when Samuel had walked Aidan outside, he'd told him, don't talk about ownership. Not yet. Samuel needed to ease this Indian inside the cabin into the notion that the land wasn't his anymore. They didn't want any trouble and have to kill these savages in their sleep. It was fine to kill the man, but there was a woman and little girl in the cabin. That wouldn't be Christian, now, would it?

When Aidan returned a couple of days later, he was still friendly, and labeled himself a squatter. Micco seemed completely at ease, and, as usual, Mahala brightened in the presence of a white man—until Aidan mentioned that he was planning to build his cabin with a view of territory, right on top of the flower-covered mound. Mahala gasped, and Micco reached behind himself, clutching for a chair. He took a breath and informed Aidan that he was so sorry; he could not spare his time. He offered Aidan tools, though. They were a gift, Micco said. Don't bother bringing them back, and he smiled and nodded again, when Aidan said, that was right neighborly.

When Aidan left, Micco invited Samuel to sit longer and poured more coffee. He leaned into the ways of his people, carefully talking. He told Samuel that he learned the manners of white men and had adapted. In fact, Micco's own father was a Scotsman. Instead of only hunting for his meat, he now kept cattle and pigs. He wore clothes of cotton and wool, instead of deerskin. And Creek towns had changed, too, for now there were many places that no longer contained women-lined clans, but rather, clans that traced lineage through the men. Yet Micco told Samuel that what Aidan was suggesting— building upon the mound—went beyond adaptation into a matter of the grotesque. The mound was sacred, Micco said. Long ago, high-status people had lived on the mound, but no one who was alive, nor their parents nor their grandparents, remembered that time. In the village, the mound was untouchable. One did not climb upon the mound or pick its flowers. One only revered it from afar. To break that taboo was to court death.

Throughout Micco's quiet speech, Samuel was silent. He wanted to laugh at this savage's superstition, but he couldn't tip his hand.

As Aidan Franklin began to build his cabin on top of the mound, he was cheerful. This optimism would remain some months, as the finished cabin was a fine structure. Within two years, however, Aidan would set fire to the cabin, after his wife and eleven of his twelve children died of a contagion that did not touch anyone else in the territory. Along with his family, Aidan's cheerfulness died. He became a bitter man, as he tried to eke out a living on the other acres in the shadow of the mound. The day that he set fire to his cabin, the red and blue flowers of the mound shriveled in the heat, as the wood of the cabin popped and sang. When re-counting to Samuel, Aidan would say that, when he woke in his lean-to shelter with his remaining son, the flowers and grass on the mound had grown back overnight. This only living son was named Carson, and his father's loss of optimism in the face of trag-edy would transfer to his son, and his son's offspring, along with a resentment of the mound.

Before Aidan died, he would not be able to make a living on the two hundred and two acres that he had won in the Georgia land lottery. Over the years, Aidan would sell acres to Samuel piecemeal, for half of the usual price per acre. It gave Samuel pleasure to dupe another white man, as if he had dug up his father's bones, animated them, and spelled them back into dust. He bought twenty-five of Aidan's acres, and then forty of Aidan's acres, and so on, until Aidan did not own any more land. Then, with a smile, Samuel offered Aidan and his remaining son the use of their own cabin, the second one they had built, far away from the mound. Samuel told them they could live in this cabin gratis, if Aidan would serve as his overseer. He needed a white man to keep his slaves in line.

The Place Where the Monster Will Play, The Place Where the Monster Will Harm

Samuel became a man of ingenuity as he slowly took over Micco's farm. In addition to Samuel's thriving cotton harvest, he built a general store where poor, middling, and wealthy white men came together to buy their supplies. There were only two of the latter in the territory. The rich men mostly kept to themselves, though along with Samuel, they had invested in the town's only cotton gin.

Samuel considered himself a happy man, except for his hungers, which he had difficulty feeding. He would mount his horse and ride through the countryside, until he found a yeoman farmer who would accept money for the use of a little Negro girl. Samuel learned that he couldn't be choosy during these times. He paid the dollar or two for these moments.

Darker-skinned children had been his favorites at first, but he began choosing bright-skinned girls after he'd expanded his body of scholarly knowledge. He had been surprised to learn that, as Ezekiel had patiently explained to him, the majority of mulattoes were sterile, except in extraordinary cases. Samuel had also examined the works of Petrus Camper, Immanuel Kant, and David Hume from the eighteenth century, how they'd measured the skulls of Negroes and compared them with great apes' and found them very similar. In his own century, he'd found the treatises of Samuel Morton to be immeasurable—and was very pleased that this brilliant scientist had carried his same name—but if Samuel Pinchard were honest (and not at all arrogant), these learned observations were not earthshaking, only logical. Samuel's regret was that he had no inclination for the written arts himself, for if he had, he believed he could have given the scholars a run for their money. And he read the Bible, learning that, along with Cain, Ham, the son of Noah, was responsible for the cursed color of the Negro. God had placed them on the earth to carry burdens, the Negro men and boys were ordained to exhaust themselves in brutish labor, and Negro women and girls to tolerate the weight of white men on their bodies, and if it pleased God, to nurture the seed of their white masters within their wombs. That was the prescribed order of this world, and even in Heaven, Negroes would be expected to serve cheerfully.

And thus Samuel had bought Mamie, the beautiful dark girl whom he chose to work in his kitchen. But he'd forgotten Ezekiel's teachings and so miscalculated: Mamie was not a sterile mulatta, as his past mentor had talked about. She was a full-blood Negress, and she conceived; though her frame had been thin and she'd given every appearance of not having yet bled, Samuel's assault had made her pregnant. Yet her hips had been too narrow for labor, and she died after giving birth to a baby boy. So much miscalculation: Mamie may have given the impression of childhood, with her short height and minuscule frame, and the high-pitched octave of her voice, but in fact, Lancaster Polcott, the trader, had no provenance for her birth. When Samuel had discovered Mamie's pregnancy, he'd estimated her to be around twelve. Yet she was older, though her exact birth date had not been recorded by her original owner. There were many stunted slave girls and women like this: in their early years, their growth was abridged by a lack of hearty mother's milk, and then a lack of proper food.

The death of Mamie had cast a pall over the plantation. Work slowed, even when Samuel allowed Carson Franklin, the overseer since his father had passed, to use his whip. Samuel ignored the accusatory looks thrown his way from the Quarters-folks. He was the master of this plantation, and as Micco had in times past, when Samuel walked the earth of his plantation, he whispered that this land belonged to him, as did everything that grew upon it. The blossoms, the greenery, the trees, the peaches and other fruit. The creatures: the horses, the cattle, the pigs, the chickens, the Negroes. Under the law, Samuel could do as he willed with any of his creatures—even kill—and no one would take him to task. Thus, any little girl he wanted was his to ruin as he saw fit.

Yet Mamie's death threw permanent shadows into Samuel's life: Nick, the child she would bear, and the wrath of Aggie. Nick would become the only person that Samuel would ever love, and Aggie the only person who would acquaint Samuel with shame.

He had been shocked by both emotions that morning when Aggie had brought the baby out to him, wrapped in clean cloth. She'd told him only the Lord could save Mamie. She'd described the girl's condition, how she was weak and in pain and couldn't stop bleeding. Her frown had accused Samuel, though her words had been devoid of expression, and suddenly, shame had assaulted him. He'd thought he was suffering from a bout of indigestion, for his stomach lurched. Then he felt weeping coming on, and a feeling he'd never experienced before: self-recrimination. For several seconds, he'd known himself to be a bad person. To push the feeling aside, he'd pulled the cloth off Nick. The baby was white-skinned and blond. His eyes were tightly closed, but in six months, they would change from a newborn's blue to the eyes of his father. Samuel made a sound—an "oh" of marvel and gratitude—and tears stung his eyelids.

He wanted to protect this child. It was an unsettling yet pleasurable emotion. Yet the feeling he had in Aggie's presence—the shame she called instead of offering him obeisance—roused something in Samuel akin to terror.

The Building of the Left Cabin

After Mamie's death, Samuel began to stalk his own fields for child victims, but within three years, he decided that was not for the best. He didn't feel badly for using what he owned, but conducting his pleasures with his Negroes' own children led to a slowdown of work. And Samuel was a businessman; he could not allow his inclinations to affect his fiscal ventures.

When Samuel would visit the Quarters to seek out the only lasting happiness in his life—Nick—sometimes he would run into Aggie and her deepening frown. And that same ugly feeling would coat Samuel's skin: Aggie believed he was a horrible person, a man hidden from the glare of God. Thus, he began to avoid the Quarters entirely.

For a time, he again sought out yeoman farmers in the territory and paid to assault their little Negro girls, as he had done in those years before choosing Mamie. Yet within another two years, these moments had stopped satisfying Samuel. He had become a cultivated, rich man, and he decided to act accordingly. He directed Carson to pick strong Quarters-men from the fields to cut down trees, and their labor didn't take long to build a new structure on the left side of the big house. A beautiful one-room cottage, which Samuel had copied from a picture in a book of Brothers Grimm tales. He ordered new furniture and toys. A hobbyhorse, a dollhouse with tiny furniture of its own, and porcelain dolls dressed in elaborate clothing that matched the children's dresses he had ordered as well. And he stocked up on infusions of poppy flowers and mixed them with cane syrup, for children loved the taste of sugar.

The day Samuel purchased a mulatta child at Lancaster Polcott's auction, he was the happiest he'd ever been. Since the government had outlawed the transport of slaves over the Atlantic Ocean, an equally thriving trade for Negroes had erupted along the federal road. And since the expansion of the federal road, the southern transport in slaves was much easier, and the choices in humans were dizzying. The little girl Samuel would buy was a specialty item of Lancaster, who had begun to hold auctions the next county over from Chicasetta. His Negroes were quite expensive: the little mu-latta cost Samuel seven hundred dollars, but Samuel was pleased to know she was only nine years old. He thought he'd have several years of use until she blushed into maturity. Lancaster Polcott al-lowed Samuel to enter the tiny pen where the child was kept. In the corner, a blanket was pulled over a cot fitted neatly with sheets and a pillow: she was special and did not sleep on straw. The child was bright-skinned with long, wavy hair pulled back in a woman's bun. She wore only a sheer, clean chemise. When Lancaster ordered the child to completely disrobe and turn around slowly, there no marks anywhere on her body. Samuel became quite agitated, as his need came upon him—even though the child was weeping—but Lan-caster warned him, he could only look at the child, until money for their transaction exchanged hands, and he delivered her to Wood Place. Samuel told him he wanted to take possession of the child right now. Right this second—he had cash and he had his wagon outside—but Lancaster refused. He gave the excuse that he wanted Samuel to gain control, but really, he wanted to dangle the child over the other man. Lancaster was a churchgoing soul, and though slave trading was an honorable profession—wasn't it right there in the Bible?—Samuel's particular appetites turned his stomach. Yet Lancaster reasoned with himself: he had a family to support.

In addition to ordinary field hands (and such), Lancaster offered a variety of specialty merchandise, such as the little girls and young women for boudoir purposes. He was open in this selling of fe-males, and when he put them on the block, ribald in his language. Yet—though he didn't dare to speak the words out loud—at other, discreet, unadvertised auctions he also traded boys and young men as expensive "butlers and valets" for the use of white men who paid three times the price for a field slave. Lancaster smelled a life-time of money, if he could keep Samuel Pinchard—and others like him—on the leashes of their desires.

Samuel would purchase a tall Negro for a discount. He had been the slave of a liberal type in Milledgeville, a minister who had taught his slaves to read so that they would know the Bible. Yet this minister had been in defiance of the new law that forbade anyone to teach slaves to read. The minister had been jailed and could not pay his five-hundred-dollar fine. His two slaves had to be sold to cover the cost. That Negro Samuel had bought, though young and strapping, had only cost one hundred fifty dollars because none of the other white men at the auction wanted a Negro who could read. He was very homely, and his name was Claudius. Samuel would put him in charge of his garden and his barn animals, as well as tending to the landscaping around the cabin he built for his little mulatta. Similar to Rappaccini's garden in that tale by Mr. Nathaniel Hawthorne, lush plants had been trained to grow near the gate and between its spokes, obscuring her view. Claudius kept the plants growing in all seasons. Along with studying the science of Negroes, Samuel studied horticulture and would instruct Claudius what he wanted him to plant or cultivate.

In two days, Lancaster Polcott delivered Claudius and the mulatta child to Wood Place. The child was taken inside by his cook, Tut; fed, bathed, dressed again in fresh clothes down to the skin; and settled into the little cabin to await her owner's visitation. Claudius would begin to trim the flowers and pluck the weeds. He would sleep in a lean-to on the side of the barn and eat his meals in the kitchen with Tut. Samuel didn't want the man to develop any friendliness with his fellow slaves, in the same way that Tut had no allies, because she had allowed Mamie to be abused in the kitchen house by Samuel, and even lied to protect her master. Samuel wanted no loyalties forged between the ordinary slaves and the caretakers of the little girl he would call his "Young Friend."

The Quarters-folks eventually discovered the terrible purpose of the little house Samuel had built to the side of his big house. They called it "the left-handed cabin," or, more simply, "the left cabin," as the Devil favored that direction. When Samuel overheard his slaves talking about the structure, he would not comprehend that they were calling it a place of evil: soon, he would call it the left cabin, too, and smile at the simple ways of Negroes.

VII

Consequently, though we ordinarily speak of the Negro problem as though it were one unchanged question, students must recognize the obvious facts that this problem, like others, has had a long historical development, has changed with the growth and evolution of the Nation; moreover, that it is not one problem, but rather a plexus of social problems, some new, some old, some simple, some complex . . .

—W. E. B. Du Bois, "The Study of the Negro Problems"

FOR YOU TO LOVE

◈

If Lydia Garfield's life were a song, it would have been a blues, like her uncle Huck sang down at the family reunion every summer. Plucking his banjo, crooning in a baritone, while Mr. Luke, the man who was the love of Uncle Huck's life, clapped his hands and patted his feet. And everybody in the yard urged Uncle Huck to sing, sing that song, but they didn't pay attention to the words, that Uncle Huck sang the pain of his life. That he had to call Mr. Luke his "best friend," though Mr. Luke and he were joined forever, as tightly as if they'd stood in front of a preacher and said vows.

The folks ignored the tender, bold touches between the two men. The pats on the shoulder, the forehead kisses. The folks called out praise instead. Boy, that Huck shole could sing. Got that voice smooth like butter.

Maybe that's what Lydia had done when she'd picked up her habit. She was trying to sing her pain, knowing that for the rest of her life, she had a burden to tote. She couldn't ever put it down. It didn't matter how pretty people said Lydia was. Pretty wasn't shit. Pretty didn't mean a goddamn thing. When people called Lydia that, they might as well have spit in her face. Because the man who'd first called her pretty had been the one who'd handed her this load.

There were other names she was called at school. *Redbone. High yellow. Light-skin-ded. Siddity heifer. The-one-who-think-she-cute.* But Lydia was never called ugly. Her beauty was assumed, because of her paleness, her hair that reflected light. Her eyes that changed colors, depending on her outfit. *Pretty, pretty girl.* Her grandfather had called her that, when she was six years old. Back when he used to hurt her. She didn't remember when it started, only that when she emerged into memory, the hurting already was a fact of her life.

She was in the station wagon with her mother and Coco. They were in the City. Lydia knew that much. Her mother was driving to

Lydia's grandparents' house, because Mama and Daddy were taking a trip to New York. She'd finally convinced him to take her on a honeymoon, after all this time of being cooped up in the house with two children. A woman needed more than housework, she told Lydia. She talked to Lydia a lot, as if a child were a short, small-boned girlfriend in a pinafore with ankle socks and Mary Janes. As if a little girl could understand the trials of motherhood and being a wife.

Mama would turn to her daughter and ask, "Darling, do you understand what I'm saying?"

"Yes, Mama. Uh-huh." She knew that she had said a pleasing thing. That her mother would be satisfied: she would receive a pat on the knee.

Mama didn't trust a babysitter for her children. Where she came from, mothers relied on other women they knew to take care of their children. So she drove her daughters to Nana's house, that big place in the neighborhood where the high-class, wealthy Black folk lived. She deposited her girls and a pleather suitcase with Miss Delores, a brown-skinned lady with skinny legs and a soft bosom that was smaller than her belly.

Coco was asleep that day. She was an early riser, waking in pre-dawn darkness to stand in her crib and bump it against the wall, until Mama came into the room and picked her up. I'm hungry, Coco would say. She knew exactly what she wanted. Biscuits with butter. Or cheese and grits. Whatever she asked for, she demanded it immediately in sentences free and clear of baby non sequiturs. The only indication that she was a toddler were her sudden, long naps, after the day was high.

In the hallway, Miss Delores balanced the sleeping Coco on her hip, then took Lydia's hand. In the kitchen, she gave Lydia half of a peanut butter and jelly sandwich with the crusts cut off. They watched *Sesame Street* while she washed the breakfast dishes.

"That Cookie Monster gets on my nerves," she said. "He acts like he's drunk." But when *The Electric Company* came on, she turned appreciative of the brown Dracula. "He needs a haircut, but it's easy to fix up a good-looking man. My husband is like that. A fixer-upper, but he cleans up nice. I have to watch these fast-tailed heifers around him."

Coco roused. "A heifer is a female cow." Then she went back to sleep.

"Lord, this child!" Miss Delores whispered. "She's too smart for her own good!"

After *The Electric Company*, there was *Mister Rogers' Neighborhood* and the cardigan-clad white man. He talked to puppets as if they were real people in his patient, whispery voice. He made Lydia believe they were real people, too. Then they headed upstairs to the guest room, where two fancy dresses lay on the bed, a sign that there would be company soon. Lydia knew how to dress herself and fit the fancy frock over her head. She took off the days-of-the-week panties her mother had put on her and pulled on the ruffled bloomers. Coco had ruffled panties, too, only with plastic sewn inside. She stayed asleep throughout her outfit change; when Miss Delores laid the little girl on the bed, she tucked her legs under her bottom.

Then there was her grandfather calling, girls, girls, where are you?

"Hello, Dr. Garfield," Miss Delores said.

"Hello, Delores. Did you have a good morning?"

"Yes, sir, I sure did. And you?"

"I suppose."

"I believe I'll wake up the little one from her nap. We should take a walk in the park. She likes that. Mrs. Garfield has gone shopping already."

Lydia grabbed her hand. "No! Don't go! Please don't!"

She pulled away. "Child, what has gotten into you? Your granddaddy took off the afternoon, just to take care of you. Dr. Garfield, I'm so sorry. She must be having a bad day."

"Oh, I'm not mad. Not at all. You're my pretty little girl, aren't you?"

He chucked Lydia under her chin, and Miss Delores left the kitchen.

Then it was time for a reading lesson in the study with Gandee.

They sat together on the dark, shiny couch. She knew her colors already, as well as her ABCs. Her mother had taught her not to rush though the middle part, LMNOP, but it was Gandee who'd tried to teach her how to read in his study. At first, short words, like "cat," "rat," and "dog," but it was hard for Lydia to grab hold. So Gandee gave up, and read to her from *The Brownies' Book*, with Black children in the pictures, and Gandee began to read: "'When Blanche was a boy, he had to work as a slave on a plantation in Mississippi. Like many a slaveowner, his master needed him too much to allow him any time to get an education. But young Blanche made up his mind he was going to learn his abc's the best way he could . . .'"

When Gandee finished reading, he led her to the guest room, closed the door, and pulled off the fancy dress that Nana had bought her. Then he took off her bloomers, because she needed to take a bath. If she didn't, she would stink. And they would bathe and play together in the water, and wouldn't that be fun? He liked to bathe with her because she was so pretty and special. The most special little girl. Her hair was so shiny, and he loved her more than anybody else in the world. But despite all her specialness, Gandee still threatened to kill Coco, Mama, Daddy, even Nana, if she ever revealed their secret, what he did to her in the bathtub. Gandee was a doctor, he told her. He could kill everyone with poison, and no one would ever know.

And every Sunday at dinner, he was charming and smiled at Lydia, calling her his pretty, special girl, as if he hadn't threatened to destroy her life.

―――――

Lydia wouldn't know it right away, but when her mother returned from New York, she had a baby inside her. In a few months, Mama's dresses were tight around the middle. She was sick a lot, too, and she lost weight from the frequent vomiting. Daddy began to take the children to his parents' every weekend. Some days, Lydia went shopping and her younger sister stayed back.

There was nothing but boredom, walking beside Nana at the department store, but Lydia was relieved. That it was a day that Gandee wouldn't probe her with his fingers and teach her how to touch and kiss him or make her look at pictures of men and women doing the thing her parents had done to bring her into the world.

When the new baby was born, Mama was even more tired. She argued with Daddy, shouting, every time she turned around this dingy-ass apartment, there was nothing but children pulling on her. Was this all that she could expect in life? He was the one who'd wanted to have a third child. This hadn't been her idea. She was supposed to be an educated woman; she wanted to do something more with her life. Lydia found this out by eavesdropping on her parents talking, and one evening, when she was supposed to be in bed, she learned that her father had killing on his mind as well.

Her mother was complaining about the long hours Daddy worked, but he assured Mama he wasn't cheating on her. He wouldn't do that to her. He swore on everything he had. Daddy was only working for his family. He was trying to save for them to get a house. And he never thought he'd love anybody as much as he did his children.

"Woman, I don't know what I would do if a man hurt my girls. I'd murder him and go to the electric chair."

"How can you even joke about that? You know my brother died on the chain gang."

"I'm not. I'm serious."

"I'm not asking you to kill nobody. All I want is for you to help me with these kids. I'm tired, Geoff. If it wasn't for Diane coming to babysit, I couldn't even go the grocery store. Do you know I have to take the baby with me to the bathroom?"

"I'm sorry, woman. I'll try to do better."

Those years were tense, insecure, for a little girl, as Lydia considered what death meant. What Gandee had said, what her daddy said, and what telling of her pain would mean. No, not pain. Pain wasn't a big enough word. Lydia had no vocabulary to capture what was happening to her. She only wanted it to stop. Once, when Lydia was seven and her new baby sister had started to crawl, Lydia had tried to find the words to tell her mama what her grandfather was doing, even though she didn't want him to kill everybody in her family. That Gandee wasn't like Mr. Rogers on the television, who was kind and calm and made Lydia feel safe. Like he was the real relative and not Gandee, even though Mr. Rogers was a white man. She loved Mr. Rogers, and she knew he loved her back, even though they had never met. She wished he could come visit her and tell her what to do, and she knew Mr. Rogers would never make her get naked in the tub. He was her friend, and his love made her strong enough to go into the kitchen that day to tell her mama what Gandee had been doing.

Her mother was at the stove, stirring a pot of greens. It smelled funny in the kitchen, but that funny smell meant that dinner would be good: Lydia loved her mother's greens.

"Mama?"

"Yes, baby?"

Her mother looked over her shoulder, and her face was streaked with water.

"Why you crying?"

Her mother let go of the spoon and wiped her face. "It's all right, baby. Grown ladies get sad sometimes. You understand, don't you?"

"Yes, ma'am . . . Mama?"

"Yes, baby. What is it?" Her mother sighed. She had picked up the spoon again. In her other arm, she bounced Lydia's baby sister, Ailey. Ailey was always crying. She seemed sad, too, and Lydia set aside her own feelings. The despair of her mother and her baby sister added up to more sadness than Lydia could contain, and her courage left her. She couldn't hear Mr. Rogers in her head anymore. And so Lydia set aside her own feelings and asked to hold her baby sister, who was fat, with many rolls. Mama quickly handed her over, saying Lydia was her good girl. Her good little helper, and Lydia balanced the baby on her bony hip. She carried Ailey into the living room and sat with her. She put her nose at the top of Ailey's head. It smelled good. Like peace or something near to it.

From then on, Lydia liked to hold her baby sister on her thin thighs. Rocking, until the baby's crying stopped. Her first word was to Lydia, as she grabbed hair: *Mama.* Lydia held on, dirging her way through the fall and winter and spring. Then in the summer, Mama's father died, and Daddy drove them down to Chicasetta in his Cadillac because Mama wanted to see her father in his casket before they put him in the ground. In Chicasetta, everyone was crying, but Lydia wasn't sad. She hadn't ever met Grandpa Hosea, and there was quiet down south, peace like the perfume of her baby sister's curls.

Each year after that first one, her mother drove them south in her station wagon, and Lydia looked forward to those summers, to the playing in the heat that didn't seem to tire her. To the laziness of the time. At the height of the day, when the sun was too hurtful, Lydia would sit on the living room floor. She cut out dresses for her dolls as her great-grandmother gave her instructions. Dear Pearl sat on the couch because her knees were bad. They wouldn't let her get up again if she got down that low.

As summers passed, Dear Pearl showed Lydia how to make clothes for real people. She took an old dress, plucking at the thread. She mixed up the pieces and told Lydia to close her eyes. Could she see how to fit the pieces back together? And somehow, yes, Lydia could. The old lady was grouchy with everyone else, but she told Lydia that she was a real smart girl. Dear Pearl's own mama had taught her the trick of taking a dress and pulling it inside out. To look at the seams and how each piece joined together and figure out how to make another one. Dear Pearl's own daughter and granddaughter couldn't master that trick, but see how Lydia could do that? And soon, she learned how to cut out her own dress patterns from brown paper bags, because her great-grandmother insisted a woman who knew how to sew could always make her own money, selling to another woman who didn't know. And that meant Lydia would never go hungry, not one day in her life.

There was dinner in the evenings, and Mama had to take Coco into another room and whisper to her that it was not nice to make faces at the pinto beans and corn bread and greens someone had kindly prepared for us. It was polite to eat whatever was placed before us, so eat it, damnit, and don't say another word about it.

And now that Mama thought about it, don't be looking around at the wallpaper while somebody asked the blessing, like Coco didn't know any better. Bow her head instead. After the meal, the peeling of peaches and tomatoes, then helping the older women piece together quilts in the evenings. Or there was a long walk. Dear Pearl stayed back at the house while Miss Rose and Mama and Lydia and her two sisters headed off, until Ailey got tired and wanted to be carried. Lydia let her mother tote her baby sister, though, because she liked to run in the open spaces. She was unaccustomed to not having to look both ways and watching out for cars and having Mama tell them, come back here right now.

"I sure wish you would move into town with Uncle Root," her mother said one night. "It's too quiet out here."

"I like it out here," Miss Rose said. "This my home."

"There's too many ghosts on this place for me. Dead Indians. Dead slaves. And what if somebody comes out here to mess with you and Dear Pearl? Norman don't even live in yelling distance."

"Then I got something for them. They gone get a chest full of what's in my rifle. I ain't scared of nobody. I'm grown. And I like my ghosts. I like looking up and seeing the same sky my people seen all them years before me. It kinda make me want to pray. Don't you laugh at me."

"How you mean? I'm not laughing at you."

"I love this place, even if my own child had to run away."

"I didn't run. I went to college, and I married Geoff. You make me sound like a fugitive from justice."

"You went to college right down the road. You coulda came back here and married somebody else."

Mama snorted. "You mean, if I hadn't gotten pregnant?"

Miss Rose laughed. "You know what I mean! You had plenty boys you coulda married. Like that Wilt Monroe. Remember him? He sure was sweet on you."

"That's who you wanted me to marry?"

"He came from a decent Christian home."

"Mm-hmm. Christian enough to try to get me to go in the bushes with him, behind school. You didn't know that, did you? And he was ugly and had that funny-shaped head, too."

Miss Rose tapped her daughter's arm, but playfully. "You the Devil, Maybelle Lee Driskell!"

"No, I ain't, neither!"

They laughed and nudged shoulders, and in the darkness, Lydia had looked up at the sky. She thought she could see every star there was. Was this the same sky her daddy could see, up in the City? Somehow, her granny's sky seemed bigger. If she stayed here, if she hid in the woods, she could sleep under this sky. It would keep her safe, but then her mother was calling.

"Y'all girls come on. It's time to go inside and go to bed," and the little girls made sounds of protest. They weren't sleepy. Then Miss Rose was saying they should mind they mama. But take her hands and walk with her. She didn't want them to get lost out here.

THE NIGHT I FELL IN LOVE

◈

When Lydia met the young man who would become her husband, he made the mistake of commenting on her looks. He'd almost lost his chance with those three words she'd heard too many times.

"Hey, pretty girl."

"Don't call me that." She'd turned her back on the young man, flipping her hair over her shoulder. Most Black folks didn't like that gesture, and she didn't use it often. Only when she wanted to be rude on purpose. To make a point that she knew what people thought of her. *High-yellow girl. Siddity heifer.* She felt her anger rise, like a bear moving in a cave, ready to come out. Ready to attack.

It was Lydia's sophomore year of Routledge College, and she'd ridden in a car packed with her sorority sisters to Atlanta for the Morehouse basketball game, but none of them wanted to see who won. They'd crossed over for Beta the week before and were anxious to show off in their orange-and-white jackets with their line names printed on the back. To make their Beta call to their sisters from the Spelman chapter and maybe score some numbers from cute Morehouse dudes.

Lydia was excited. It was her first trip to Atlanta without her family. She was feeling grown, until she walked into the humid brew of the gym. A November night but hotter than July in that gym. She made a move to pull off her jacket, and her line sister put a hand on her arm.

"Leave it on," Niecy said.

"But I'm hot, girl," Lydia said.

"Soror, everybody else kept theirs on. You want to look ashamed of Beta?"

Niecy was her roommate, too. When they'd pledged for Beta, they'd had a hard time avoiding their big sisters, because she'd opened the door every time a Beta member knocked, even when Lydia told her, stay quiet. Don't move. Since they'd crossed "the burning sands," Niecy used every excuse to mention their new status in conversation. It was "soror this" and "soror that," and it was getting on Lydia's nerves, because her roommate barely had squeaked into the sorority. Her grades had been high, but Niecy was short and chubby, and the Betas were notorious about uniformity on their lines.

Lydia sat on the bleacher, sweating. The air was so thick, it felt like a hand on her throat, and her curls were falling, too. She'd done a wet set with gel, but the steam was attacking her look. She tapped Niecy's knee. She was going to get a hot dog. Did Niecy want one? As soon as Lydia left the gym, she took off her jacket.

At the concession stand, there was a guy trying to flirt. Saying the wrong things, though he was good-looking. Tall, very slender, a chocolate brother with real smooth skin. Too handsome and well groomed for Lydia's taste, like he spent a lot of time in front of the mirror. He wore a blue velvet tracksuit with the jacket unzipped to reveal his white T-shirt. A white Kangol cap like he thought he was LL Cool J. Those gold chains around his neck: 'Bama with a capital B.

When Lydia flipped her hair, the guy told her, be careful. She didn't want that wig to fall off.

She turned back, outraged. "This is my own hair!"

"Yeah, it's yours, if you bought it." He looked so serious, she didn't know he was teasing, until he asked her, could he have one of her hot dogs? She let him move closer. She guessed he was all right.

"You got a dollar?"

"Aw, that's cold, woman! They don't cost but seventy-five cents apiece."

"I'm trying to make a profit. Times are tough these days."

"You kinda skinny to be eating four hot dogs." He lifted her wrist, but she didn't pull away. His touch was warm.

"I'm a little piece of leather, but well put together."

He threw back his head, laughing. He told her his name—Dante Anderson—and wanted to know, where was she from? She sounded proper, but didn't nobody say stuff like that, unless they were from the country. Lydia told him, she was from up north, from the City, but her mother's people lived in Chicasetta. She gave him her name but wouldn't give him her phone number.

"Chicasetta? So your people from the country, then. I bet you can burn. You know how to fry pork chops . . . Lydia?"

"Damn, brother, you must be hungry! First you want my hot hogs. Now you looking for a home-cooked meal."

He laughed again, and moved forward in the line with her, though his friend was motioning, it was time to leave. That was his partner over there, Tim. His ace boon coon—but let him get back to her. Dante liked her style, the way she carried herself. Tough but sweet. Couldn't nobody put nothing over on her, and Lydia smiled, finally. They kept talking, even after her order came, and he asked for her phone number again. He wanted to talk to her some more, and so she gave him the number to her dormitory, plus her last name. By that time, the hot dogs she'd ordered were cold, so she went to the back of the line, and he walked with her. They talked some more.

He didn't wait long to call her, only a day. She heard her name called on her floor.

"Lydia Garfield, telephone! Lydia Garfield, telephone!"

She didn't answer, though she'd already dreamed about Dante. That they sat together on her granny's plastic-covered sofa. Laughing and talking, like familiar home folk. It scared her, the vividness of that dream.

Dante called again that weekend, but she ignored her name. The Monday after that, she returned from dinner at the refectory, and the desk monitor handed her several pink message slips. She told Lydia, she must have put something strong on that guy, because he'd called the dormitory's main number three different times. That night when she heard her name on the floor, Lydia went to the phone, but he didn't sound urgent. Just happy to hear her voice. He'd been thinking about her. Had she thought about him, too?

"No, I've been too busy."

"You lying, Lydia, but I'ma let you slide." He laughed, an easy sound, and she leaned against the wall, cradling the phone. She forgot the time until he told her he should stop running up his mama's

bill. But he called a few days later, and in two weeks, they had settled into a rhythm: he called every night, and they talked for ten
minutes. He told her how much he had been thinking about her,
and she avoided saying the same.

Another two weeks after that, he offered to drive to campus and
visit her, but she refused. People were nosy. She didn't want the
campus gossips all up in her business.

"You shamed of me, Lydia?"

"For what? You're not my man."

"Not yet. Wait a minute. I'ma be right back. Don't go nowhere,
okay?"

There were the strains of Luther Vandross, singing about the
night he fell in love. Dante sang along, and his tenor wasn't bad.
Better than Mr. J.W.'s singing, down in her family church, though
that wasn't saying much. Mr. J.W. sure was an awful singer. At the
end of the call, Dante invited her to his mother's church in Atlanta.
He went to church every Sunday, and he could drive to fetch her,
and take her back. He wanted his mama to meet her, but Lydia told
him, no, she could drive herself. Give her the address. She would
meet them there.

That Sunday morning, when Lydia drove down the highway on
the way to the interstate, she wore a dress she'd sewn herself. A
modest frock that covered her arms, bosom, and knees. She was
nervous: the road that led to the highway went right past the turnoff to her granny's house. She hoped she wouldn't pass anybody she
knew along the way. A friend or relative, who'd want to know, why
wasn't Lydia attending her family church that morning? Couldn't
she praise the Lord among her own?

Dante's wasn't a big church. It was in a storefront in a strip mall
in southwest Atlanta, but his mother was dressed as if it were already Easter. Miss Opal was tall and slender like her son, and wore
a purple print dress, and an ostentatious purple hat that looked to
be a foot tall. Dante had on a black suit; his tie matched his mother's
hat. When the collection plate came around, he put a twenty on top
of the single bills. Weeks later, when Lydia would laugh, accusing

him of showing off, he'd quote from scripture. That Genesis said you were supposed to tithe. Second Corinthians, too.

After the service, they went to the apartment he shared with his mother. For dinner, Miss Opal had put on a spread. There were greens and candied yams and macaroni and cheese. None of the dishes had enough seasoning, and the fried pork chops were too greasy. But Lydia praised the food and ate her fill, after Dante said a lengthy grace. His friend Tim was there, in his jeans and sweater and tennis shoes.

After dinner, Lydia offered to wash dishes, and Miss Opal smiled, flashing a gold incisor. No, Lydia was company. Maybe another time, and the three young folks sat in the living room and watched *Sixty Minutes*. During a commercial, Dante slid over, nuzzling her neck. Come to his room, he urged. Spend the night, so he could make her feel good. Tim was looking at them, smiling, and Lydia flushed. Her temper rose: she could feel her bear shifting in its cave.

"I don't know what you think this is," she said. "But this ain't that kind of party."

He tried to shush her, a finger to his lips. His mama was right there, keep it down. When Tim laughed, Lydia picked up her purse, and walked in the kitchen.

"I'm headed out, but I just wanted to say, I appreciate the hospitality, Miss Opal."

Before she took Lydia's hand, the older woman wiped her hands on a dish towel.

"We gone see you next Sunday, baby?"

"Um . . . no, ma'am. I got to study."

Miss Opal held out her arms, and when Lydia hugged her, Miss Opal whispered, don't pay her son no mind. He was just trying to show off for his friend. Lydia knew how men could be when they got together. Come back another day, when Dante was by himself.

He tried to walk Lydia to her car. It was dark out there. It wasn't safe, but Lydia told him, that was all right. She'd been taking care of herself for a long time. She didn't need a Johnny-come-lately. That evening, when the hall phone on her floor rang and her name was called, Lydia opened her door and hollered out, tell that guy on the phone she wasn't in. Then it was time for winter break, and Lydia drove her car up to the City. She kept dreaming about Dante but tried to put him out of her mind.

————

When Lydia was almost twelve years old, her grandfather lost interest in her. It was the day that her period began, which occurred during one of their bath times.

"What did you do?" A look of disgust on Gandee's face. Her bleeding wouldn't stop, and he climbed out of the bathtub and left Lydia there, as the water turned pink. She climbed from the tub and put on her clothes, and when Nana returned from shopping, Lydia told her, she thought something was wrong. She couldn't stop bleeding, and her grandmother informed her, this was the burden of being female. She was surprised that the girl's mother hadn't told her what suffering meant.

The next morning, Lydia's baby sister asked, why was there blood on her pajamas? Before Lydia could stop her, Ailey had run crying from the room. Calling for their mother. Something was wrong. Lydia had hurt herself. Her mother came into the room and saw the sheets. Wait just a minute. In a while, she came back with an aspirin and a glass of water. She brought a bulky pad with adhesive and pulled new underwear from Lydia's drawer. She should go to the bathroom and wash up, but don't ever try to flush a pad. That would be a sure enough mess.

Mama spoke to her daughter in a low, sad voice. When Lydia came out of the bathroom, her mother told her she was sorry she hadn't talked about this before. It was her fault. Mama had thought she'd have more time. In an hour, Ailey was crying again, because her mother and eldest sister had dressed up to go to the department store, and she couldn't come. This was a ladies' trip.

"But I want to go!" Ailey held on to her sister's leg, and Lydia stroked her head. Don't cry, please. Don't cry.

"You'll go some other day," Mama said. "Soon enough. Lord have mercy."

She was dressed in church clothes and so was Lydia. They drove in the station wagon to Worthie's to pick up some brand-new lingerie. Daddy was back home, watching her sisters, because he needed to do something other than sleep on his one day off from moonlighting in the emergency room. He needed to know there were no servants in his house.

In Worthie's, Mama didn't say much as she pulled through the lace panties, camisoles, and small-cup bras. It was only when she rode with her daughter on the elevator to the basement café that Mama brought up boys.

"This is your period, Lydia. It's going to happen every month, like it does with every woman. I get these, too. And what this bleeding means is, you have to start watching yourself. Don't let boys get too close to you. Because a boy can put a baby in you now. Do you understand?"

"Yes, Mama." Lydia wasn't paying much mind to what her mother was saying. She was eating ice cream and thinking about what her new panties would look like when she tried them on, in a few days, when the bleeding stopped. Mama had warned her, don't wear her good underwear when she was on her cycle.

For a time, Lydia hadn't needed her mother's advice. She was still in junior high school, and she wasn't interested in the gangly boys who tried to talk to her. And up in the City, her mother didn't let her date—not until she was sixteen, Mama said—so Lydia didn't need to watch herself. Her mother did that for her. But there was a relaxing of the watch in Chicasetta, during the summers. There weren't expanses of concrete and police lights constantly flickering, and her mother wasn't as careful of Lydia. She didn't hover in Chicasetta, and so, three years after her period started, when Tony Crawford had caught her that Sunday as Lydia was leaving the outhouse out back of Red Mound Church, she didn't think about any warnings. Tony seemed so nice, and he told Lydia he liked her.

Lydia said, thank you, sir, and Tony said he was only thirty. He wasn't nobody's sir, not yet, and he talked to her. He wanted to hear about her life. For six Sundays he managed to catch her alone, when she came out of the outhouse. For three Sundays, it had been a surprise, but then, when he told her she had the body of a full-grown woman, she made his nature rise, Lydia caught on. Their meetings had been planned.

The next Sunday, he asked to kiss her, and jammed his tongue in her mouth. It didn't feel good, but she liked the attention. How, when she returned to church, and then, after a long time, Tony did, too, he watched her. The following week, he put her hands on the place at the front of his pants, put his hands over hers, and what she touched began to move and lengthen and grow, and she remembered when her grandfather Gandee's penis had done the same. But Tony didn't force her to keep touching him. He didn't threaten to kill her and her whole family. Tony begged, please, girl, please, he was crazy about her, and Lydia felt powerful. People always told her what to do, even when they loved her. She liked that she had a choice of what she wanted to do. Nobody ever was going to tell her what to do, not again, and it made her want to see what else she was capable of.

She knew enough to keep Tony a secret. Even though he wasn't a boy, he was in the male category, and her mother had warned her to be careful. Even more, he was much older than Lydia, and Mama was fond of pointing out men in Chicasetta who chased behind young girls, because they couldn't handle a woman their own age. She didn't know why Black folks in the country acted like that was okay, when it wasn't. It was nasty and against the damned law and they needed to put those niggers in jail and throw away the key.

So Lydia began to make plans with Tony in their short time in the church outhouse. She would wait for him at the creek on Sundays, after church, and then every day after that, until that afternoon when he begged her to let him stick it in. Just the tip, he said. Not the whole thing. He wasn't good-looking, but his begging made him handsome. When she told him yes, he changed from a tender, begging man. He put his full length inside her, ignoring her cries, and then shot a white stream onto her stomach that she remembered from bathing with Gandee.

But afterward, Tony told her he loved her, and she felt strong again, and she consented to ride with him in his truck, crouching down on the seat so nobody would see her as she left her granny's farm. He drove them up the highway to a motel, and got a room, and Tony begged her again. Even when she said no, he begged, and she relented, and soon it was early morning. Lydia was scared to go home to her granny's home and face her mother, but she didn't have anyplace else to go.

When Tony dropped her off in front of her granny's house, he kissed her, and then Mama was down in the driveway and screaming and crying. A few days later, she overheard her uncle Norman tell her mother, he'd fixed that sumbitch Tony Crawford. He'd beat his ass good, and if Uncle Norman weren't scared of going to the chain gang, he'd have cut that bastard's dick off and let him bleed to death. And before Lydia and her sisters rode back north to the City, she pleaded with Mama not to tell Daddy, and her mother said, of course she wasn't about to tell. Did she look like somebody's fool? Even in a few weeks, when Lydia discovered she was pregnant, Mama kept the secret from Daddy. And after the abortion, Mama said she hoped her lesson had been learned about what men and boys would do, and now, it was time she got on some birth control.

Even with the pills her mother gave Lydia and the daily, private reminders to take them, Mama kept up with her cautions about men and boys, but her warnings no longer carried a bite. Lydia already had been pregnant, had traveled the same road as a grown woman, and when she came to Mama in winter after she turned sixteen saying a boy had asked her to the movies, and was that all right, Mama said, okay. She guessed that was fine. She looked defeated as she told Lydia she hoped he was nice. Before the boy had rung the doorbell and introduced himself to Mama, she'd slipped Lydia a handful of condoms to put in her purse. The pills would keep her from getting pregnant, but the condoms were to keep the worst from happening.

Lydia had her own condoms, and she'd already slept with her movie date. He seemed to really like her, though that didn't matter to Lydia, only that she felt a power when he'd climbed on top of her.

How his face had changed when he was inside her, and he made his weak noises, and she moved fast to get it over with. She was strong, like a bear that had awakened during a barren, cold season. She could hurt somebody. She could destroy, like she did her movie date when she told him they'd had a few nice times, but she'd moved on to someone else.

The bear only roared for the time somebody was inside her, or when she was discarding them. When she hurt their pride. But that only lasted a short while. And then she was ashamed of herself. She hated herself, so every time a boy asked her, she let him climb on top of her, so she could feel powerful again. She didn't have orgasms with anyone but herself. She faked and moaned with whoever was on top of her. They asked, you like that, baby? and she told them, yeah, yeah, that was nice, but really, she felt nothing. She thought sex wasn't her thing, like how Aunt Pauline ignored the flesh in service of the Lord. She'd had a hysterectomy in her early thirties. The doctor had said the growths inside her were benign. Just leave them alone, but Aunt Pauline made him take her whole womb, and then she hadn't felt the Devil's urge anymore. What a blessing, she liked to say.

The boys she screwed would pass Lydia in the school hallways or they'd see her on the bus and whisper to their friends that she was a whore, a slut who'd do anything. They gave her sly looks, but she acted like the stuck-up yellow heifer everyone thought she was. She flipped her long hair and pretended she didn't know her betrayers' names. Lydia asked her friends, did that Negro look like anybody who was good enough for her, who'd she even let sniff her drawers?

Lydia knew how to make other girls love her, to tell them exactly what they wanted or needed to hear. What the lines around their eyes and mouths craved: girls needed love more than anybody else. She was popular at Toomer High, with plenty friends, and they protected her with their words, and in college, she never ended up on the Dirty Thirty list. One guy in her freshman year started a rumor that Lydia was a freak, but Lydia told her girlfriends he had an incurable disease. He'd even shown her the sores. No way would she get close to that guy. When she saw him again on campus, he looked at Lydia like he was a beaten dog, and she smiled at him and tossed her head. She was the bear, big and strong and wild. And he was only a dog who couldn't keep his mouth shut.

Lydia thought she was fooling her father, too, that Daddy didn't know she was having sex, and though she loved her father dearly, that made her feel powerful, too. Her lovely, harmless daddy who worked so hard to provide for his family. He thought his oldest daughter was innocent, but one early morning in high school Lydia had crept into the kitchen, after a late night when she hadn't even made it to the movie she'd been invited to. Her date had told her, he forgot something back at his place, and then propositioned her in the driveway of his parents' house.

Daddy was sitting at the kitchen table, eating a bowl of banana pudding.

"Hey, darling."

"Oh! Daddy, you scared me!"

"I bet." He looked at his watch. "It's a little late, isn't it? I thought your mama gave you a midnight curfew."

"Yeah, I'm sorry. My girls and me were studying. I forgot the time."

"Studying. Huh. Okay."

Lydia walked to the cabinet and pulled out a bowl. At the table, she scooped up a portion of pudding and pulled up a chair. Then she felt silly that she hadn't seen what was coming, when Daddy told her, it was fine that she wanted her own personal life. He wasn't going to pry. She was at an age where she wanted to explore, and as long as she wasn't doing anything she didn't want to do, he was happy. But also, he was going to write her a prescription for birth control pills and give her some money to buy some condoms at the drugstore. Lydia didn't tell him she already had her own pills and condoms, as Daddy kept on. She needed to protect herself, and next time she wanted to study with her girls, she might want to take a brush along. Get her hair together before she headed home, because it was all over the place.

Daddy told her that he was tired. The emergency room had been busy that night. Some crazy brother had come in there bleeding but didn't want treatment. He only wanted painkillers. People were truly something else, and Daddy should get some sleep. But he stretched out his legs under the table and spooned up another bite of pudding. Daddy laughed and said he never thought he'd see this day. His little girl staying out half the night. He remembered his salad days of staying out. That's how Mama and he had made Lydia. So please be careful, darling, and then Daddy laughed some more.

———

Spring was Lydia's favorite time. Up in the City, the few trees on her block would whisper into buds. Waiting, defiant of the lingering chill, but in Georgia, spring shoved winter out of the way. *It's my time now*, spring insisted. One night you could go to bed and the trees were plaintively bare. The next morning, every branch was sassy. Full of green and red and pink, and one spring afternoon, when Lydia returned from classes, there was Dante Anderson, sitting on the couch in the lobby of her dorm.

When he'd stopped calling, Lydia had dreamed about him. There was no romance in these nightly reveries, only mundane events that they'd never experienced in reality: she and Dante shopping for groceries. She and Dante on her granny's farm, walking up the road that led to her family church.

But Lydia had not expected to see him again, not while she was awake. When she tried to treat him like she had boys that she'd discarded—cold, contemptuous—Dante only sat there. He looked different from the other two times she'd seen him. There was no church attire or expensive velveteen tracksuit. He looked ordinary, in his collared shirt tucked into ironed jeans. On his feet, penny loafers.

"I was trying to say I was sorry," Dante said. "But you wouldn't take my calls."

"What you sorry for?" Her voice was harsh.

"For not acting like a gentleman. I knew I was wrong already, and then my mama, she was so mad when you left. She told me she'd raised me better than that. I thought she was gone whip me. I really did, and the last time I got a whipping, Lydia, I was five foot three and in the seventh grade."

Lydia wasn't going to forgive him that easy, but she sat on the couch beside him. They said nothing, until it was dinnertime, and then she stood. She held out her hand.

"Come on. Let's get some chicken. I know a place."

He reached into his pocket and pulled out his keys. "You drive."

"You sure?"

"Yeah, I trust you."

On the way out of the dorm, there was her roommate. It was a warm day, but Niecy wore her Beta jacket. Lydia tensed and then slowed. She told Niecy this was her homeboy, Dante. She'd known him for a long time, and Niecy held out her hand. Any friend of her soror was a friend of hers.

Dante's car was an old one, a metallic green deuce and a quarter, but it was clean. The seats were uncracked, and he'd replaced the radio with a cassette deck. A fragrance card in the shape of a Christmas tree hung from the rearview mirror. He wedged against the passenger door, watching as she drove, then rolled down the glass. Gusts of warmth touched Lydia's face as she headed toward Chicasetta.

At the Cluck-Cluck Hut, he insisted on paying for their dinner. No, he had it. They sat at the only picnic table in front of the stand, and every minute or two, somebody stopped to speak to Lydia. She returned their greetings: *Hey, y'all. What you know good? How your people doing?* She introduced Dante to each person who approached the table. This was her friend. She didn't know why she wasn't afraid. Soon, her granny would hear the news that Lydia had been eating fried chicken with hot sauce, biscuits, and French fries with a handsome young man, though he shole was skinny. Looked like he needed some home-cooked meals, or at least more dark meat in that chicken box. Or maybe, the boy hadn't yet put on his "man weight." And then Miss Rose would call Mama in the City, and tell her, you know your daughter is courting.

Yet Lydia sat there and kept raising her hand as people approached. She laughed and let her proper grammar slide away. She'd never let a male see her as she truly was. That it didn't matter how light her skin was or how shiny her hair, she wasn't really siddity, and Chicasetta was her town. These were her folks, and anybody who wanted to know her, needed to know that. But because she hadn't planned this afternoon, she wasn't ready to take him the few blocks to the house of her mother's great-uncle or on the longer drive out to her granny's farm.

Lydia didn't know why she didn't drive back to campus, why she drove to a motel instead. It had been an afternoon of surprises and lessons, but here she was ruining a perfect day. It was twilight when she pulled into the parking lot. She told him, wait, and Dante touched her hand. If she was sure, if this was what she wanted, he had the money. They bantered back and forth about who would pay, and underneath the teasing was the knowledge that this would lead to a change. They didn't speak about what was to come, and finally, Lydia said she would compromise. Dante could give her the money, but she would go get the key.

At the door to the room, he said they didn't have to do nothing, but she thought he was lying. That she would rest underneath him, making false sounds to speed him along, but she wanted to get this out of the way. To see if what she hoped for would come after, but when she took off her clothes, Dante stopped her from unhooking her bra. He had taken off his shirt and pants but left on his underwear and T-shirt. Let's slow this thing way down, he said. They slid underneath the covers and he held her, her head to his chest.

"Lydia, I love you."

"Already?"

"Yeah, woman, and I'm scared."

She shifted away, and then sat up. Put her feet on the carpet. She didn't know why she started talking about Gandee, what he'd done to her in the bathtub when she was little. She didn't like to think about it, how it made her bear crawl back into its cave. It weakened her to return to the memory, when everything she'd done afterward was about trying to be strong. Lydia started crying. Her arms and legs went numb. Even her blood was too tired to crawl through her veins, and she couldn't tell Dante the rest. There was too much: Tony and the abortion. All those other guys, how she couldn't remember most of their names. She was afraid that if she confessed everything, Dante would make her feel even worse.

He put his hand on her back. "Lay down with me, baby."

She shook her head.

"Please, Lydia. Come on."

She couldn't face him: she was too ashamed, so she curled on her side and he held her that way, his belly to her back. His breath moving the hair on her neck, while he told her somebody did bad things to him, too. His uncle, a man that he had loved like a daddy, because Dante's own father had killed himself after he came back from Vietnam.

Uncle Warren had helped to raise Dante. He taught him how to play basketball and fix a car, but then Uncle Warren had pounced and raped him when he was ten. He said that Dante was the faggot, taking it while his uncle was giving it. The raping kept happening, over three years' time. The only reason it had stopped was Dante's friend Tim, when they'd been in junior high school. They'd known each other since kindergarten, and he had protected Dante growing up. When the other boys at school had called him skinny and soft, Tim had beat them down, and told them, don't fuck with his friend. Because Dante was more than Tim's friend. He was his brother, and he showed it, too. One night in junior high, when his uncle was watching Dante while his mother was at work, Tim and his friends let themselves in with the key that Dante had slipped them. They whipped this uncle's ass good, and Tim told the uncle they'd kill him next time.

"You think something's wrong with me 'cause I couldn't fight for myself?" Dante asked Lydia. "'Cause I let Tim do it for me? Tell me the truth."

"No, you're just fine," Lydia said.

"Ain't nothing wrong with you, neither."

They didn't make love. That would take two more weeks. That night in the motel, they only held each other tightly. They talked until they fell asleep, and when Lydia woke up, Dante was still there. That was enough for her.

———

The semester ended in May, and Lydia had a month before her mother and sisters came south for the summer, time enough to get her story straight. To think about what and how to tell her mother about Dante. For Lydia to explain that their love was different from anyone else's. She knew something that other women didn't, and Dante was different than other boys and men. He was good and kind and she couldn't let him go.

Lydia packed her belongings from her dorm room, placed them in her car, and hugged Niecy. She drove to her granny's house, unloaded the boxes onto the back porch, and gave her the story she'd worked out with Niecy, that Lydia was staying with her roommate in Atlanta. Niecy's parents had a big house and didn't mind company, but she didn't want to bring all her junk to Niecy's house. Here was the number, in case of emergency. Lydia would see her granny in June.

Dante had moved into a smaller apartment, further down the road from where Miss Opal lived. He told his mother, please don't be mad, but he was twenty-two. He needed his privacy, and business at the convenience store was good. He was working more hours. Dante told Lydia he didn't want to hurt Miss Opal's feelings and make Miss Opal feel like he was trading her for another woman. That was his mama and he'd always love her. But Miss Opal wasn't mad when she came by one evening in the middle of the week, after Bible study, and there was Lydia cooking dinner. Miss Opal laughed and told Dante she understood that her son was a man; this is what she raised him for. She didn't want him living up on her until he was fifty, and besides, her sister wanted to move from Macon to Atlanta. And she told Lydia, come hug her neck, when Lydia asked her to stay for dinner.

By then, Miss Opal was calling Lydia her daughter-in-law. Teasing her every time Lydia came to church and ate dinner at her apartment after services. Miss Opal's sister and Tim joined them, but there were no more ungentlemanly displays. After dinner, Dante would bid his friend and family goodbye, and he and Lydia would leave. He wanted to spend some quality time with his lady.

In the new apartment, there was a plaid couch Dante had found by the side of the road. Two television trays made a coffee table. A TV rested on an orange crate, but Dante had splurged for cable. In the bedroom, sheets covered a mattress and box spring. Beside the makeshift bed, another crate topped with a pillowcase and a lamp. Lydia used some of her emergency money to make some purchases. A see-through shower curtain with fishes, and a fluffy mat and toilet cover and towels in bright pink. A visit to the thrift shop, where she bought a scarred chest of drawers and used pots and pans that reminded her of Mama's, streaked with the residue of grease and soot. Metal already seasoned, used in a happy kitchen.

"Woman, keep your money. I can take care of you." He'd started calling her that regularly—"Woman"—and it gave a thrill. Her father called her mother that, and hearing Dante say it made Lydia feel solid in her love.

"This is to keep those other girls away."

It had been scary when they'd stopped using condoms weeks earlier, because that meant a real commitment to Lydia. Dante told her he wanted to feel her. And she was his lady. He trusted her—he loved her—and didn't she trust him and love him, too? She told him that didn't have anything to do with her protecting herself. But they went down to the health clinic and got tested for all the diseases, including HIV. They both were nervous, waiting the two weeks for the tests to come back. And then euphoric when they found out it was okay. The test results were mailed to Dante's apartment during the week, and when he called her at the dorm, she told him she was skipping classes that day. She wanted to see him right now, and when she arrived at the apartment, Dante had put on his Luther Vandross cassette and had candles lit, though it was the middle of the afternoon and the sun was still shining.

When they made love, Dante stopped Lydia from pleasing him before she took her own satisfaction. He would withdraw and say, slow down. It was her time. He wanted to make her happy, and he would move his mouth down and lick slowly and touch her with his fingers until she shivered. He'd watch her face, begging her, please don't lie. Was she satisfied for real? Once when they were finished, she asked, how had he learned all that? What to do with a woman, and he kissed her. He smiled and said, let him keep a few secrets. He couldn't tell her everything; otherwise, she'd stop loving him. Then he asked her to marry him, as he'd done several times before, both in and out of bed, but no, Lydia didn't want to spoil things. They could talk about that another time.

There was a month of playing house and settling in. Making love until the early hours, so that Dante only had three or four hours of sleep. Cooking for him in the morning and packing him an equally big lunch, because she didn't want him eating fast food during the day, or worse, chips, candy, and soda from the convenience store where he worked. At the door, Dante couldn't bear to part from Lydia. *I love you, woman. Give me a kiss. I'll call you on my break. Just one more kiss.*

The time without him snailed along. She read her favorite book, *The Color Purple* by Alice Walker. Her English professor had urged her to try Toni Morrison, but it was too complicated for Lydia. She couldn't yet grasp what she was reading. If she was feeling annoyed about what she'd seen on the news, she read an essay in her James Baldwin book. That man always seemed mad, but in a smart kind of way. It took Lydia longer to read than other people did; her teacher had told her mother that, when Lydia was in second grade. She was good at speaking, but she had to go back over a page twice and sometimes three times to catch the meaning. The letters raced from her until she caught them, but she still liked to read. When she finally understood what was happening, it was a puzzle she'd solved, and Lydia felt proud of herself.

When she was finished with her book, she rolled a joint from the stash that Dante kept in the top drawer of the dresser. Then she watched public television. She didn't want Dante to tease her, so she concealed that she loved the shows from her childhood. She waited for Mr. Rogers to relax her, while she enjoyed her weed high. His voice that told her the world didn't matter. Mr. Rogers told Lydia that she could make it; every human being could.

Sometimes Tim would come by and interrupt her reverie. He would sit on the couch and change the channel from Mr. Rogers and ask for Lydia to prepare him a sandwich. Tim wanted some red Kool-Aid with plenty sugar, too, and a squeeze of lemon in that special way she made it. He followed Lydia into the kitchen, watching as she pulled bread from the refrigerator and dropped it into the toaster, giving her additional directions. That was too much mayonnaise and mustard on the bread, and next time, maybe Lydia could fry his bologna. After sitting on the couch for a while, Lydia would tell him it had been nice of him to visit, but she had to go to the grocery store now. Dante would be expecting his dinner, and Tim would tell her, his partner had a good woman. But Tim never smiled when he said that.

At the store, Lydia would pull out the coupons she'd clipped from the Sunday paper she'd subscribed to in Dante's name. She'd pick up meat and smell through the plastic. She'd turn fruits and vegetables in her hand. Look for the smallest imperfection marring the colors. When Lydia returned, she would sit and watch more television. She would hear Dante's key in the door, and she would run to open it. They would kiss and she would lead him to the bedroom, and they would make love, as if they hadn't only hours before, and while Dante slept, Lydia started on dinner. Cutting onions and garlic and green peppers. Turning on the television to keep her company again. Then calling for him, as Lydia's mother had called for her father on the nights that he wasn't moonlighting in the emergency room. Dante, your dinner is on the table, and he would sit down to his plate and smile at Lydia. Woman, this sure looks good. Thank you so much for taking care of me.

This was what she had been born for, to be with somebody who needed her love. There didn't have to be sorrow or fearsome excitement, only a daily presence. This is what her parents had, even when they argued, and maybe what Miss Opal had with Dante's father, before he had gone to Vietnam and come back saddened and shot himself in the head. This was what the Bible had failed to explain to Lydia. Because the Bible didn't say, loving a man in the flesh took more devotion than loving a heavenly promise. And if you really loved somebody, they became greater than a god.

Her month with Dante went too quickly, and then Lydia drove to Chicasetta to join her mother and sisters. She didn't want to tell anyone about her love. She wasn't ashamed of Dante, his bad grammar, his high school diploma but no years of college. But she was afraid of Mama and her prescient dreams, of what they might reveal about the man Lydia loved. Dante was too important to her. Lydia couldn't give him up.

And she couldn't keep still, those summer days. In the garden, the weeds weren't enough for her hands. She rushed through plucking her rows, and then asked her granny, was there something more she could do? Miss Rose set her to snapping beans for dinner, but Lydia would finish those quickly, too. So she'd sew a dress for Ailey to wear to church, because her baby sister was complaining that she wasn't a little girl anymore. She was almost an adult, and she didn't want to wear pinafores and puff sleeves, and that was Lydia's excuse to drive to Macon to the fabric shop. On the way back, she'd stop at a pay phone and use her phone card to call Dante at work.

"When you coming to see me? I need you, woman."

"It's only been two weeks."

"You telling me you don't miss me?"

"You know I do, but I can't come. Mama's here."

"Baby, you grown!"

"Not to her. I told you how she is."

They talked until their ten minutes were up. She wanted to save the minutes, because her mother would be suspicious. What had taken Lydia so long? But Dante wanted to know, was Lydia still his lady? Was she trying to break up with him on the sly? Was some nigger in Chicasetta trying to beat his time? Then Lydia had to spend three more minutes to tell him there was nobody else but him. She couldn't think of another man touching her, not anymore, and she and Dante talked naughty for a few moments before offering their love to each other. *You hang up first. No, you hang up. I love you. I miss you so much.*

When Lydia returned to the farm, Mama would ask her, had she been standing in the sun? Her face looked so flushed. Was she coming down with something? She would put a hand to her daughter's forehead. Maybe Lydia needed to go lie down.

What made her ache the most was Dante's absence at her great-grandmother's funeral. He should have been there when Dear Pearl was laid to rest. Dante had plenty church clothes, and he owned his own Bible. He would have fit right in with these people she'd grown up with. He would have put his arm around Lydia as she cried over the old lady who hadn't smiled much and had always seemed in a bad mood, but she had made Lydia feel smart. Dear Pearl had taken away her shame without even knowing, before Lydia had to return to her grandfather's abuse and suffer the shame all over again.

It was Dante's idea that they marry at City Hall, when the semester started in late August. He'd been without his woman for three months, and though Lydia spent the weekends with him, he missed her during the week when she was away at school. He wanted to make this thing permanent, and was happy when Lydia told him she felt the same way. She cut class and visited the Fulton County courthouse to fill out the forms.

For the ceremony, she wore a green silk dress, and he wore a black suit he'd bought out of the trunk of somebody's car. It would have been perfect for Lydia, if her family had been there. But she hadn't been able to bear to tell them—not when she knew how disappointed Mama would be.

And perfect for Dante, too, if his uncle and his wife hadn't come. Uncle Warren was retired and had plenty time on his hands. When Miss Opal had called him, Uncle Warren had declared that he wouldn't miss this wedding for nothing in the world.

There was almost a scene when the man insisted that he stand beside his nephew, as a witness. Miss Opal and her sister agreed. Family should do this.

Dante pulled his mother by the arm, and Lydia followed.

"This ain't about y'all," he said. "This about me and my lady. This our day. And why you bring him here? You know I don't like that nigger."

"Boy, watch your mouth! And I don't know why you acting like this. My brother ain't never been nothing but good to you. You loved him when you was little."

Uncle Warren wandered over, an unlit cigar in hand, asking what the problem was. And Lydia looked at him, assessing him like she would a dress. How to take this man apart and put him back together in the way she wanted.

She put a hand on Dante's arm. "You know what, baby? Everybody's going to Restaurant Beautiful later, and didn't Tim say the best man should pick up the tab? And then we're picking up that cake I ordered and some liquor, too, right? If your uncle wants to pay for all that, why don't we let him?"

Uncle Warren backed away. He told them that was all right. He didn't have to be no witness, but he'd come to the after-party. At Restaurant Beautiful, he piled up his plate, and when he passed the cashier, he pointed at Tim to pay. When he sat, he smirked at the head of the large table the women had made by pushing several together. He called to the other end.

"Nephew, you sure you can handle a fine redbone like that? That girl look too much for you."

Tim whispered, "This nigger here." Dante kept his eyes on his short ribs, but his uncle kept on.

"I'on't know if you man enough. You always had a little sugar in your tank."

Uncle Warren gestured with his cigar, and his sisters laughed: he played too much. But Lydia called back, her husband was more than enough for her, and she could handle whatever he was putting down. She channeled her granny and the church sisters at Red

Mound. The ridicule they heaped on men, when they moved into a whispering circle. How they talked underneath men's clothes.

"Talk about soft," Lydia said. "How many years you got on you, Uncle Warren? 'Cause ain't nothing softer than an old man. Now, me? I like me a young, hard man with a young, hard back. And that's why I got me a real strong bed at home."

Lydia stroked Dante's shoulder and he gave her a long, deep kiss. He said he couldn't wait for the honeymoon, but he might have to buy a new bed. 'Cause the way he was feeling, he was gone break that box spring tonight.

When Uncle Warren headed outside to smoke his cigar, his wife followed. The two did not return.

———

When Lydia's mother had attended Routledge College in the 1960s, it had been against the rules for a female student to be married. A male could have a wife back home, along with children, and he was applauded for wanting to make something of himself, to push his family forward. But a young woman was admonished that her place was in the home. She needed to be there for her husband, to tend to his needs. Mama had scoffed at such male chauvinist nonsense. Women worked harder than men, she said. Most women could do anything they set their minds to, and for the rare woman who couldn't, that fact was for her to find out. It wasn't for a bunch of male administrators at the college to decide.

Yet the week after Lydia married Dante, she didn't want to go back to campus. It wasn't right for her, walking on the yard, headed to one building and then the next. Attending sorority meetings and deciding who would make it onto the new Beta line. Sitting in the refectory, eating the food that other hands had prepared for her while Dante was at home eating a hamburger and fries that probably had sat under a heat lamp because Lydia wasn't there to cook.

She felt guilty for not being with Dante and guilty for not caring one bit about how Niecy was getting pushed around by the Betas, though she was already a member. Niecy was her friend, but Lydia wasn't concerned about her fight to include more girls with high grade point averages on the new line, how Niecy had gone to Dr. Oludara to complain about how the Betas were too color-struck. Dr. Oludara was the oldest sorority sister on campus, and she didn't believe in excluding young women from membership based upon the length of their hair, their weight, or their skin shade. But the problem was, Dr. Oludara hadn't paid her sorority dues since the seventies. Her word didn't carry much weight with Beta.

"I think I'm going to write a letter to the national chapter," Niecy said. "I'm tired of this shit."

Lydia flipped through a sociology textbook. She was behind in her lessons, but she couldn't concentrate. The letters skipped around.

"What do you think about that, soror?"

"About what, Niecy?"

"My writing nationals about the Beta line."

"That sounds good."

"Will you sign the letter, Lydia?"

"Yeah. I mean, sure. But Beta has been color-struck for years. That's why I didn't want to join this shit in the first place. I only did it for you."

"I know, soror. But this is important. We have to make a stand."

"Okay, you do your thing. But you gotta type the letter."

Lydia hardened herself to Niecy's concerns. She couldn't worry about children's games acted out on campus. Routledge wasn't the real world. It was a giant playground, but Lydia was a woman now. She had higher matters to attend to, like making sure to remind Dante to pay the rent and the electric and water bills. Calling up an insurance company and making an appointment for an insurance man to come by the apartment, so she and Dante could have burial policies. They were young and had years ahead of them, but every married couple needed those policies. Paperwork was proof of life-long commitment.

Her suspicions that marriage was not child's play were confirmed that weekend, when she went to Atlanta to see Dante. When she returned from the Laundromat and folded his clothes. Other than cooking, doing laundry was her favorite chore. Lydia made Dante clean the bathroom and wash dishes, but she actually liked folding clothes. It had been the only time that she'd had peace with her mother growing up. She and Mama used to sit in the basement together, saying nothing, only moving their hands, while the washing machine and dryer rumbled softly beside them.

Lydia's contentment was broken when she opened the top drawer of the dresser—Dante's drawer—and saw the cluster of cellophane packets. They were filled with what looked like cloudy diamonds.

TILL MY BABY COMES HOME

❖

Lydia was fifteen, going on sixteen, when Mama had talked to her about what it meant to be a woman. How Mama had been in college, headed to graduate school and planning to become an English professor, before she found out she was pregnant by Lydia's father. Mama had set aside her dreams to become a wife and a mother, and she hadn't regretted her choice, not for one second. But she told Lydia that she wanted her to understand that once a woman had a child for a man, he could come and go in a woman's life, exactly how he pleased. He could decide if he wanted to get married or stay single. He could pay child support, or make a woman track him down every month or take him to court to buy formula for her baby or groceries once his child had teeth to chew proper food. And even if a man did pay child support, that wouldn't be enough to cover the bills for a house he wasn't staying in. Even if he did want to get married and live with a woman, her child would be a red wagon to pull behind her, not the man's. A mother couldn't ever be free of her child.

And while Mama loved all her daughters dearly—God knows she did—she wished somebody had told her what a woman's life truly was before she and Daddy had gone down to the Chicasetta courthouse and married. That when the women in her family had talked about the evils of men, they hadn't been so specific, naming this man or that man. Pointing at random, troublemaking men in the community as exceptions and not the rule. They should have told her every man has got some serious faults.

"But Daddy is nice to you, isn't he?" Lydia asked.

"Oh, yes, baby, your daddy is a real good man! I don't want you thinking I'm trying to bad-mouth him. I love that man strong. But as nice as your daddy is, Lydia, I want you to know that I got lucky. I'm saying, if he wasn't nice, it wouldn't have mattered, because I had you. And having a child with a man ties you to him for life, even if you're not married. Even if he doesn't even want you."

That day would have been the time for Lydia to tell her mother, no, she didn't understand. To sit in the car with Mama and talk it out, but that morning, Lydia was pregnant. It was early September, and they were sitting in the car in the parking lot of an abortion clinic outside the City. When Lydia had returned from the south in August, she hadn't known that she was pregnant by Tony Crawford. She hadn't noticed anything at first, until her mother asked her, how long had it been since she'd seen a period? Had she been feeling sick? And were her breasts hurting?

Her mother made the appointment for the abortion without even asking. It was for eight in the morning. Aunt Diane would take her sisters to school, because Lydia and her mother left the house at six forty-five. If she missed that appointment, she'd have to wait six more weeks to get a new appointment. By then, she'd be in her second trimester, and an abortion would be a complicated affair. Perhaps a hospital stay and general anesthesia. If that happened, Daddy would have to be told that his daughter was pregnant, instead of given the lie that his wife and oldest child were going on a shopping trip for school clothes because Lydia had hit a growth spurt.

At the clinic, she was given a pregnancy test that confirmed what Mama already knew, and after the abortion, Lydia was occupied with the memory of what had happened. That her mother had not asked her, did she want to keep her baby? Though Lydia definitely hadn't wanted to bear Tony Crawford's baby, she thought her mother should have asked. Instead, when her name had been called in the lobby, Mama told her, it was time now. She asked Lydia if she wanted her to be in the room with her, and her daughter said yes. Then Lydia had lain on the table and a nice but businesslike white doctor had pricked a needle inside her while Mama had held her hand. There was a sucking noise, and the slight cramps that the doctor told her to expect were more than that. The pain nearly overwhelmed her, and she wanted to piss herself. But in a few minutes, it was done, and Lydia only bled normally, not the clots that would have been cause for alarm. The relief would come days later, but before that, there were the familiar feelings of self-hatred and shame. She wasn't a good girl anymore; she was tainted. And because Lydia was busy nursing both of those emotions as if they were twin babies she'd birthed, she forgot to ask Mama about what else went on in a marriage. What else should she know?

Five years later, Lydia went down to the Fulton County courthouse and married the man she loved. By then it was too late. Nothing her mother could say would push Lydia from her path, even after Lydia found those cellophane packets in Dante's drawer.

She wanted to let go of her panic, and then anger. She'd grown up with drugs. Not in her parents' house, naturally, but there had been drugs in her high school. Everybody drank beer. There was weed, too, which was harmless, a plant that didn't do much, unless you were drinking while you smoked. A few bold kids stole Valium from their parents' medicine cabinets, but those were very rare treats.

Like the stolen pills, cocaine was for special occasions. Once in a while, somebody at a party had a packet of powder but kept that confidential, only sharing it with a chosen number, and Lydia was always asked, did she want a line? And she'd smoked primos, too, joints with coke sprinkled inside. She really liked those, how the coke sent you flying, but the weed chilled you out. She and her high school friends had agreed that primos and even straight powder cocaine were completely different from smoking crack rocks.

Crack was ghetto and trashy. You didn't bring rocks to a party or smoke them when you were kicking it with your friends. It was like a tacky outfit that you hung in the back of your closet, because you never wanted people to see you with it on. And anybody who smoked rocks went downhill rapidly, like the miserable souls who frequented the crack house three blocks away from Lydia's high school. The neighborhood had once been a nice, middle-class area, and the house had been a showpiece, but something happened at the beginning of Lydia's sophomore year. The kids at school said the people who had lived in the house had died and their only child, a son, smoked rocks. Within weeks, the house had turned into a residence haunted by addicts struggling up the steps and hanging outside. And it hadn't mattered how many times somebody called the law. The police would raid the house and the addicts would scatter, but forty-eight hours later, the smoking would begin again.

Lydia thought of what smoking crack would do to her husband. His lips constantly dry from the chemicals. An empty stare to his eyes, and her heart contracted, but that Sunday, when she called him to let him know she had arrived back on campus safely, he sounded his usual self. He only missed her, he said. He had a hard time sleeping without her.

"Do you want to tell me something?" she asked.

"Why don't you ask me what you want told?" he asked.

Lydia liked her husband's openness. She hated somebody beating around the blackberry bush, too.

"Dante, we need to talk."

"Uh-oh. What'd I do?"

"I saw something in your dresser drawer. I was just putting your underwear in the top drawer, like I always do. I promise I wasn't snooping."

"Lydia, let's talk about this on Friday when you get here. Okay, baby?"

"But Dante—"

"Woman, what I say? We'll talk about on the weekend. Good night, okay?"

On Friday, her classes were over at noon, and she already had her bag packed in the trunk of the car. She stopped in Chicasetta at the Pig Pen and picked up pork chops, several bunches of greens, two plump ham hocks, and a package of frozen lima beans. For dessert, she wanted to make a pound cake, and also bought eggs and butter. There was already rice in the apartment; she made sure to buy five pounds every month.

A good meal would lull him into a compromising moment, but when she opened the door, she noticed changes in the apartment. In the living room, a bright red leather sofa and a coffee table. A white bed frame with a shelf and mirror as the headboard and matching end tables for each side. On one of the end tables, there was a phone; no longer would Dante have to drive to Miss Opal's house to call her. In the bedroom, the scarred chest of drawers had been replaced with another dresser, also white. Everything gleamed.

At dinner, when Lydia asked Dante where the new furniture had come from, he told her he got it on sale.

"So, Dante, you going to tell me what's going on?"

"What you mean?"

She lost her temper, shouting. "Dante Alexander Anderson, don't you play with me! I spent two hours making this goddamned meal!"

"Aw, baby, thank you. It was delicious." Her raised voice didn't rattle him. He took a toothpick from the holder—this was another new item on the dining room table. A table that was no longer an unsteady place for playing cards. This one was a sturdy, oak piece of furniture. "I ain't want to tell you about this, but they cut my hours at the store. So what you saw? I'm selling that part-time, till I can get back on my feet."

"So you're saying you're not smoking crack?"

Dante shifted the toothpick to the corner of his mouth. "Oh, naw, baby. You know I try to keep it light. I mean, weed is one thing, but that other? Naw, I ain't going out like that."

"And what about the police kicking down my door?"

That was funny to Dante. This wasn't some big deal. It was only a side hustle, and nothing more. Tim was fronting him, to help Dante out, and it was easy money. Tim was the one who had to be careful.

"I'm just trying to take care of you, woman," he said. "Like a husband should. I'm head of this household. I got responsibilities now."

"No, we are the joint heads of this household. I don't play all that male chauvinist mess."

He removed the toothpick. "Wait a minute. The Bible says the man is the head, and I'm—"

"The Bible don't say nothing about you selling crack, though. So you can hush up with that bullshit."

Dante laughed, and asked, could he have another pork chop? Hers were better than his mama's, but don't tell Miss Opal. He didn't want to hurt her feelings.

She wanted to keep talking, to let her husband know, the matter of selling drugs was serious, but that evening, there would be no further discussion, because Tim knocked at the apartment door. He'd brought a couple of his other boys, too. When Lydia offered them dinner plates, Tim pulled out a roll of cash from his pocket. He declared he didn't want no regular dinner. He felt like some pizza, and Lydia placed the leftovers in the refrigerator instead. Then Tim demanded, who was gone make a run to the liquor store? Don't bring back that clear liquor, though. That shit fucked him up. Unlike his boys, he had brought a date to the set, a brown-skinned young woman with not enough flesh on her curvy frame. Tim gave the girl abrupt orders: Pour him a drink. Come sit on his lap while he played his hand of bid whist.

At midnight, Lydia tried to give cues to let these men know they needed to leave. They'd been there since eight p.m. Lydia asked, what time was it? though she knew: she wore a watch. She sighed loudly when Tim began to make a homemade pipe from materials that Dante found at his request. The pipe was for Tim's date. Her full lips were painted a glossy wine, and she bit at the color as she watched Tim poke an extra hole in the side of an empty soda can. He took a cheap pen and pulled the insides out until it was a shell, placing it into the can's side. He molded foil on the can's top, poked smaller holes into the foil, and carefully placed a crack rock on top. When Tim lit the rock, the date sucked at the smoke, making satisfied noises. Then she went to the couch and sat. She didn't seem to mind that she was by herself. Somebody pulled out some weed, and Tim had a packet of powdered coke and used some to make a joint. When the primo came Lydia's way, she reached for it, but she slid a glance at the girl, staring blankly on the couch. Without taking a hit, Lydia passed the primo to the left.

After playing a couple more hands of bid whist, Tim put his cards down on the table. He called to his date, come get some more, and he set her up again and he laughed as she sucked greedily at the smoke. Then he announced that he had to take a piss. He pulled his date from the couch, and she walked meekly behind Tim into the bathroom. No one said anything, until Dante asked, Lydia, you want to play the hand? Let me teach you how to play. She sat in Tim's chair, and when the cards were dealt, she proceeded to run a Boston. She patted the table, crowing, and the other two guys at the table said, man, you said she couldn't play. And Dante smiled: his wife had been keeping secrets.

As the game continued, no one commented about the sounds coming from the bathroom, as Tim could be heard ordering his date to turn around, take this shit, take it, and get down on your knees. It was a long time before the bathroom door opened. The date came out, her hair a mess. Tim followed, zipping up his fly. He tapped Lydia's shoulder and said, I'll play this hand, if you don't mind.

She looked at the couch where the date sat, continually biting her now-bare lips, eyes staring blankly. Lydia wanted to say something to that girl, like, I've been there. Don't let this asshole make you feel small. But if she said that, if Lydia aligned herself with a girl who had fucked a dude in a bathroom in a stranger's apartment, then Tim and his two friends would turn on her, and then they'd turn on Dante. They'd wonder why he'd chosen Lydia for his wife. Why Lydia would defend somebody Tim had treated like a whore. And if that's who Lydia would defend, they'd think she was a whore, too. And maybe Lydia was a whore. She'd slept with so many boys and young men, and her husband didn't know. She couldn't let Dante know that she was the same as that girl sitting on his red leather couch.

Tim tapped her shoulder again, and she threw her cards on the table. She walked back to the bedroom and slammed the door with all her might. When Dante came in hours later, she squeezed her eyes closed. In the morning, she didn't make his breakfast.

The next evening, Tim came by himself, and told a story about the brown girl that he'd brought as his date. She was a geek monster, but in high school, she'd walked around with an attitude.

"Tay, you remember her?"

"She was a cheerleader, right?"

"Yeah, but that was back in the day. You give that bitch a rock now, she real compromising."

Dante touched his friend's arm. "Hey, partner, watch your mouth. You see my wife sitting here."

Tim let a few seconds pass before he apologized, saying he meant no disrespect. He knew Lydia was a good woman.

She went to the stove and fixed Dante's plate. She set it on the table and walked back to the bedroom. She didn't know she'd fallen asleep until Dante put his arms around her.

"I put a plate for you in the oven, baby."

"I'm not hungry." Her stomach growled, and he hugged her tighter.

"I think you lying. And I believe you mad at me, too."

She turned around. "I don't like how you act around that guy."

"You mean Tim?"

"Yeah, him! That guy's got you selling drugs!"

"Aw, woman, don't be like that. I'm just making money for the house. And you know it's temporary, till I get enough for my mechanic's license."

"It's not just that, Dante. You act different around Tim. Like when I met your mama that time and you were rude to me? And we had just come from church, too."

"Lydia, please don't throw that up in my face. I know I was wrong, baby. You didn't deserve that, but I thought you said you forgave me."

"I did, but what I'm saying is, you turn into somebody else as soon as he knocks on the door. And then he brought that girl in here and shamed her and you didn't say one word. I never thought I'd see you act that way, and then he came back today, laughing at that girl. Like, just in case we didn't see what he did. He's not a good person, Dante."

"Yeah, he is, Lydia! Don't say that! He's just had things tough. His daddy beat on his mama all the time, and Tim used to run away to my house. And you should have seen his clothes. I mean, I was poor, but Tim was real poor. And the kids would pick on him. That girl he brought over? She was one of them."

"Okay, so what she did wasn't right, but y'all graduated high school six years ago! He didn't have to humiliate that girl. If he wasn't over how she did him, he should have cussed her out in private. I don't want to see him no more. I mean it."

Dante started weeping. His shoulders shaking with coughing sobs, as he begged her, please. He didn't have another friend. Tim was like his blood. Please don't do this, and she hugged his head to her chest and rocked him. Don't cry, she whispered, as his sobs subsided into hiccups.

"All right, now. It's okay. All right. But no more of his nasty stories. He needs to keep that shit to himself. And he better not go with nobody else into that bathroom, either."

"I promise. Thank you, baby. Thank you."

He kissed her cheek and then tried to fit his lips to hers, but she moved her head. She didn't feel like it tonight. Maybe her period was coming on. Dante didn't care what time of the month it was. They could put down some towels, but she rolled over, turning her back to him.

In the morning, though, she rose early and went to the kitchen. By the time he had finished showering, there were pancakes and sausage waiting for him on the table. And Lydia was dressed for church.

———

There were days of Lydia trying not to worry, of her reading pages in her textbooks, only to read them again. Concentration eluded her, and in her classes, she doodled in her notebook, her knee jiggling. She thought of Dante. Maybe he was being arrested as she sat here, listening to her professor lecture about statistics. She should be home with him. She should get a part-time job. She should do something so her husband wouldn't have to commit a crime to support them. She couldn't even share her worry with anyone. No one knew she was married. She hadn't told her family or her roommate, and they would turn against her if she told them, not only did she have a husband, but he sold crack. And Lydia couldn't share her worry, either, when she realized she'd skipped three of her birth control pills. That she was anxious that she might be pregnant, because she didn't use condoms with her drug-dealing husband.

In the middle of the week, she drove to Atlanta. When she let herself in the apartment, there was a new picture on the wall: a huge velvet portrait of Jesus. She snapped at Dante for the rest of the evening, when he returned from work. He touched her, and she shrugged him off, saying she didn't feel like it. And when he inquired about dinner, she told him he was making enough money to feed himself. He could pick up a chicken box around the corner.

"Lydia, why you acting so hateful? What I do to you?" His forehead was wrinkled: as easygoing as he was, she'd hurt his feelings.

The next morning, she felt guilty. She cooked him a big breakfast, but he was gruff. She put her hand on his, and he put his fork down.

"I know I was real mean yesterday," she said. "I'm so sorry."

Instantly, he forgave her: his smile was wide. "That's all right, baby. Everybody got they days."

She squeezed his hand, then put another sausage on his plate.

"Dante, I need to talk to you about something."

"Okay, but let's do that tonight."

"I thought you didn't work today."

"Not at the store. But I got that . . . other thing."

"You told me that was just on the weekends."

Dante leaned in and kissed her forehead, then wiped off sausage grease. "If you need me, just page me."

"You got a pager now?"

He went to the coffee table, where her notebook lay. He ripped out a piece of paper and wrote down his number, along with instructions. Page him anytime, he told her. Even every hour. He always wanted to talk to his wife, and here was Tim's pager number, too, just in case.

Another kiss on her forehead, and Dante was gone. She busied herself cleaning. Washing the breakfast dishes and mopping the kitchen floor. She used the new vacuum that Dante had bought, running it over the carpet. She even cleaned the bathroom, something she hated, but she noticed that Dante had been slacking on that job. So she got down on her hands and knees and used an old toothbrush on the linoleum. Then it was time for public television, but Mr. Rogers didn't make her feel the same.

That evening, she let Dante eat in peace. She didn't want to upset the man in the middle of his meal. She waited until he sat back, toothpick in his mouth, before telling him she had slipped up. She'd forgotten to take her pills for a few days, and she was scared she might be pregnant. She didn't yet know. Her period was due early next week, so it was wait and see.

"I'm sorry, Dante. I didn't do this on purpose. I hope you believe me."

"What you sorry for, woman? It take two to make a baby. And we already married, so it ain't nothing to be ashamed about. It'll be tight for a while, but I'll be in mechanic's school by next year, so—"

"Dante, I love you for being so honorable, but I don't want a baby. I'm still in college—"

"But it don't matter what neither of us want now, Lydia. If you pregnant, that's the blessing God gave us. And we got to deal with that—"

"Are you serious—"

"Hell yeah! Ain't gone be no abortions 'round here! The Bible say, thou shalt not kill—"

"Why are you always bringing up religion to make a point—"

"Woman, you know who you married! You know what I believe! Our first date was at church, Lydia! And I don't care how I make my money. God always been at the head of my life. Now, I'm telling you, I intend to be a man about this situation, and I'm expecting you to be a woman. Like I said, we married. We love each other and we gone make this work. Case closed."

Before she could say any more, to tell him this was her body, not his, and not God's, either, his pager went off. When he left the apartment, she put her clothes in her overnight bag and drove down the highway to her family's farm. She wasn't worried about talking to her husband: he didn't have the number to Miss Rose's house. She didn't want to talk to him, because she needed to prepare herself. If she was pregnant, she'd need to put distance between herself and him. And then Lydia would lie that she'd had a miscarriage and hope he believed her, but on Sunday morning, when Miss Rose started to sing hymns, Lydia woke up with cramps. She waited until Miss Rose went to church and called Dante to tell him the news. He sounded disappointed, but told her, it was like he said, God was in control.

That Friday, they were stiff with each other. They barely greeted when she let herself in. Lydia slept so close to the edge of the bed she was afraid she might fall on the floor. In the morning, Dante's pager went off just after dawn. He was out the door before she could start frying breakfast sausage. He returned, but only for a short while, before his pager went off again. He kept going to their phone and calling, talking low into the receiver, and he didn't look at her or give a farewell when he stepped out the door. Each time he left, Lydia would sit on the couch and change the channels on the television. She couldn't make herself busy, she was so sad about him. In the afternoon, she crawled back into bed, willing herself to sleep. She awoke when she heard voices and music. She wrapped a robe around her and peeked out the bedroom door. There was a house full of people. She saw someone crushing a rock to powder beneath a glass, but they placed the entire small hill into the joint, sprinkling it on top of the marijuana bud.

Lydia closed the bedroom door. When she emerged fully clothed, someone she didn't know asked, did she want to hit this? Lydia held out a hand. Sure, she might as well, and within seconds of smoking the primo she felt a glitter. A sparkling alertness, and her worry disappeared. She loved her husband and they had made vows for life. She walked to the table, where Dante was playing cards with Tim and two people she didn't know. She peered over Dante's shoulder, plucked a card from his hand, and threw it on the table. Tim called,

"Book!" Lydia kissed the top of Dante's head. She touched the place at the side of his neck that only she knew about, saying she was going to lie back down. She'd see him in a while.

In the bedroom, the glitter still clung to her. She closed the door to the bedroom, pulling off her clothes and then her underwear. She put her husband's cassette of Luther Vandross on the boom box, and when she touched herself, she was already wet. She brought herself to climax once, twice, biting the pillow to keep from screaming. She kept touching until she heard Dante call to everyone, "Y'all niggers got to go."

The bedroom door opened, and Lydia told him, take off his pants. Luther sang as she said, Come on right now, don't worry about the rest of his clothes, come on. Dante moved inside her with his usual tenderness, but she bit his shoulder and told him, make her feel it. Do it hard. It had been so long since she'd felt him. She needed to feel him, and she turned on her stomach, spreading herself, as Luther sang. Do it, she said, and Dante was slamming inside her, saying he didn't want to hurt her. Give him a sign, say something if he wasn't treating her right, because he loved her too much to hurt her, but she pushed back against him as Luther sang. Her husband moaned, damn, he'd missed her so much. Oh, she felt so good inside, and she hadn't ever let him go this far before. Was she sure he wasn't hurting her, but Lydia was climaxing and couldn't stop. It kept coming back around, as he slammed into her and called, oh, there it is, oh, Lydia, I love you, baby. He collapsed, his lips on the back of her neck, but she told him she wasn't done. She wanted some more, because it had been too long. When he rolled off and lay on his back, she took him in her mouth, and in a few minutes, he was ready again. And he laughed, shuddering. Saying, Lord, woman, what has gotten into you, as Lydia climbed on top.

———

After that night, she started looking forward to Saturday nights, when the house would be full of strangers, and then somebody would crush a rock beneath a glass and roll up the powder with leaves inside a cigarette paper. When the house cleared, she would be waiting for Dante in their room, wet and ready. And after, she would curl up on his chest while he caught his breath. She was wearing him out, he told her, and he didn't mind one bit. And she would smile, all of the worries and shame and sadness gone in those moments.

She told herself smoking primos was different than sucking on a crack pipe. She just needed to relax, that was all. She just had pressures: she had a test and she hadn't studied hard enough. Or she hadn't yet gotten over her pregnancy scare. Or she felt sad about keeping her marriage from her family. She wanted to share her joy, but she couldn't. She started to become impatient for Saturday nights, waiting for the primo. She had to wait, though, because she didn't want to ask and have one of Dante's friends think she was needy. But there came a day when she didn't want to wait anymore until the following Saturday. She wanted more now, though she told herself her want wasn't truly a need. She wanted to smoke a primo before the seven days were through. So one Saturday, after she had loved Dante into an exhausted sleep, she went to his drawer and pulled it open. There were the little cellophane packets. She looked back to make sure that Dante was asleep before slipping a rock from a packet. She carefully closed the drawer, then went into the kitchen and retrieved a glass and a plate. In the bathroom, she crushed the rock into powder, and distributed it into four joints.

When Lydia drove back to campus Sunday night, she waited until dark to smoke half a primo in her car in the student parking lot, but then she quickly wanted the other half in the morning, and she crouched down in her car in the early morning while she sucked in the smoke. On the fifth day, she ran out of primos and couldn't concentrate in classes. She felt sad for no reason, and sick, and she didn't wait until the next day to drive to Atlanta. She skipped Friday classes and surprised Dante at the apartment. When his pager went off, and he left her, she went to his drawer. She stole two more rocks so she could make it through the entire next week.

She thought she had fooled him, that he hadn't noticed she was borrowing from his supply, but the following Saturday morning, he told her he wanted them to take a drive. She thought he'd pull onto the highway, but he only turned onto several streets, and they stopped in front of the convenience store where he worked.

Dante pointed out a guy who stood in front. His name was Marcus. Nigger used to be the one the girls chased, back in high school. An offensive guard and rope-a-dope like a motherfucker. When Marcus had walked through the halls, he hadn't looked left or right. He'd known everybody would give him room, and he'd dressed sharp, too.

It was winter, and Marcus wore filthy sweatpants and a T-shirt with no jacket. In front of the convenience store, his smile was a shade of dun as he held out his hand to customers, pleading. Those who were polite only shook their heads. The flesh had been stolen from his bones, but his broad chest spoke of laureled days.

"Him?" Lydia asked.

"Yeah, that nigger," Dante said.

"You sell to him?"

"He gone get it someplace. Might as well be me. But that nigger is too far gone to ever come back, Lydia. And that's why I'm cutting you off."

She pretended she didn't know what he was talking about. She kept her face immobile, but he told her he knew she had been slipping rocks from his supply to make her primos. And that was gone stop, right now, because crack was dangerous. Even when you put it in weed, it could sneak up on you. And Dante wasn't going to be married to a crack fiend.

That night, when the house crowded, Lydia sat by Dante. She was timid and didn't say much. When the primo came her way, she quickly said no, she was cool. And Dante patted her knee: he was proud of her. After everyone left, he came to their room, ready for loving, and she had to pretend she still liked him to get wild with her. She didn't want him to know he had provided only half of her pleasure. She faked her moans, urging him to go deep in her, to go hard, while she gritted her teeth at the pain. In the morning, she was sore, and she looked at him sleep. So content, like the baby he had been prepared to force her to have.

That Monday, after Dante left, she called Tim's pager number and asked him, could he come by the apartment? When he knocked, she made his sandwich and poured his special Kool-Aid. She asked, could she buy something from him? He couldn't tell Dante, though. Sure, he told her. She didn't care that he smirked and lidded his eyes. When he told her he'd give her the pipe for free, she said she didn't need it. She only smoked primos, but he still put the pipe on the counter.

———

The week before Thanksgiving, she rang her parents' house. Ailey was near tears as she demanded, where had Lydia been? Didn't Lydia love her anymore? She soothed Ailey, offering her the secret of her love, if not her marriage. A secret would make Ailey feel special, make her forget all about her hurt feelings. Mollified, Ailey put their mother on the phone.

"I'm sorry I haven't called, Mama," Lydia said. "It's just been real busy. My sorors and I are practicing for a step show."

"Baby, listen. Is something going on? Are you in trouble again?"

A slight clutch in Lydia's chest. The first moments of fear nibbling at her, but she trilled a mortified laugh. "Oh my God!"

"Lydia, are you taking those birth control pills your daddy prescribed? We don't want another accident like back in high school."

Niecy came up the hall, calling Lydia's name. They had step show practice. Come on. They were going to be late.

"I gotta go soon, Mama, but I wanted to know if it was all right if I came home for Thanksgiving. I know I usually wait for Christmas—"

"Child, how you sound? It's your home! Of course you can come. And any guest you'd like to bring is surely welcome, too. Like this young man you're keeping company with. Miss Rose told me y'all went riding through Chicasetta. You know you can't keep no secrets in the country."

"Um, yeah, Mama. I want to bring that guy. His name is Dante. I guess he's my boyfriend."

"Y'all come on, if you coming. I'll set out an extra plate."

It would be a short trip, only two days. Dante couldn't take off more than that. Not with his hours at the convenience story already cut off, though he'd started fixing cars in the apartment complex, too. Only small tasks, such as changing oil and flushing carburetors. He couldn't do engine work. He had to find a space and a lift for that.

The Monday before Thanksgiving, Lydia gave Mrs. Stripling a sad face. Her family was continuing to have a hard time, and she was going to drive to the City early to see what she could do. Instead, Lydia spent Tuesday washing clothes. Frying chicken for the journey, though Dante told her they could just stop somewhere to eat. It was only an eight-hour drive. On Wednesday night, Lydia packed their bags, then went into the bathroom to smoke her magic joint. She didn't know Dante was in the apartment until he knocked on the bathroom door. When she came out, he told her she'd have to leave her weed behind, in case the cops stopped them on the interstate.

They drove through the night. When they arrived in the City, it was broad morning. They parked on the street in front of the house, and Lydia let them in with her key, calling. Dante put their suitcase down. He stood fidgeting by the staircase, until Lydia took his hand and led him into the kitchen. Her father was at the table, eating his breakfast. Her sisters were there, too. Ailey hopped up and hugged her, and Lydia held on to her, rocking.

Mama told everyone, move over and make room. They had a guest. In an hour, she was testing Dante, saying he had to sleep in the basement. He was a worthy opponent, though: he didn't mind at all, and Mama nodded. At least this boy had manners. And Lydia was relieved. It would be fine. She'd made the right decision. She relaxed as her aunt and uncle arrived with her cousins. Lots of hugs and kisses, though whenever someone tried to start a conversation with Dante, Lydia interrupted with her charm. His grammar wasn't the best, and while Lydia didn't care, she knew her mother would notice.

Then Nana arrived. She had a key but refused to use it. She rang the doorbell once and then twice, and Lydia let her in.

"Hello, dear." She handed her granddaughter her purse and that damned plate of cookies. After so many years, you'd think she would have learned to make something else.

"Hey, Nana. How are you?"

"I'm very well."

Such a short exchange, but the anger roused in Lydia. The rage she forgot was there, her bear asleep in its cave. Lydia tried to coax the rage back to a darkened, calm place. She almost succeeded, until dinner was served, and Nana began telling stories about Gandee. What a kind man he'd been, when he'd been alive. She went on, extolling Gandee's virtues, and Lydia started trembling ever so faintly, remembering her times with her grandfather in the tub. How he had pushed her head down to his groin, and when she cried, he'd reminded her of what would happen if she didn't do what he said. That death was the result of disobedience.

"Excuse me," Lydia said. "I'm sorry to interrupt you, Nana, but I have an announcement. Dante and I are married, and I've moved to Atlanta! And I transferred to Spelman so I could be with him, across the street from Morehouse!"

Under the table, the husband tried to grab her hand. This wasn't what they had discussed, but Lydia pushed him away. She went into her charming routine: she was back in control. Her bear was awake but that was fine. She was the bear, but no one else knew it. She watched Nana's displeasure as no one paid attention to her anymore. How Nana plucked at the edge of her napkin and grew smaller in her chair.

Nana was easy. She had been vanquished. It was Mama who frightened Lydia when she lost control, shouting about how she hadn't wanted to marry Lydia's father.

That night, Lydia told Dante she had to take a shower. But she took her purse with her. After she locked the door, she pulled out the pipe that Tim had given her. She couldn't smoke a primo in her parents' house; everyone would smell the weed. So she turned on the shower and sat on the toilet seat. When she lit the crack rock and pulled the smoke through the pipe, the happiness filled her veins.

She didn't care about what her mother thought about her husband. Or what Dante thought about her. She only wanted to sit on this toilet and inhale this smoke. When she finished smoking, she put the pipe back in her purse, stripped, and took a shower. She rinsed her mouth out with toothpaste.

Her mother was pleasant to Dante in the morning. She made him a big breakfast and handed him two plastic containers filled with Thanksgiving leftovers. She had wrapped an entire pie for him, too, but no banana pudding for Lydia. That was the only indication of her mother's hurt feelings.

At the door, she pulled Lydia aside and held out a spiral notebook. Write down her new phone number and address. Then Mama leaned in and whispered, she was putting a little extra money in Lydia's mad fund. Every married woman needed something, in case she ever had to leave. Lydia thanked her but was insulted by the implication. The bear roused in the cave, but Lydia gentled it back to sleep: she'd given her mother the wrong contact information.

———

In Georgia, the weather chilled permanently. That December, Lydia packed up her belongings in her dorm room, but she didn't tell Niecy that she wasn't returning in January. She didn't want to provide any explanation. She didn't want to be away from her husband anymore. When the holidays arrived, as Lydia decorated a tree and bought presents for Dante, she thought of her grandfather. How Christmas used to be the worst time of the year, back when she was a little girl. During the holidays, Mama would drop her children off at her in-laws' house nearly every day. Gandee would take off time from his practice, and Nana would go shopping for her granddaughters. She would splurge on beautiful dresses for them, frocks made from satin and taffeta with many ribbons, and tell them to act nice and be pretty.

Thinking about her daily holiday baths with Gandee made Lydia sad. She craved her rocks even more: since her trip to the City, she had given up the pretense of primos. Now she paged Tim twice a week. She smoked a rock after Dante was sleep, which lasted her into the morning, when she tried not to show her impatience with him as she sent him off when his own pager buzzed.

But there was the night when she sneaked into the room where Dante was sleeping. She picked up her pocketbook and gently closed the door behind her. In the bathroom, she slipped the rock and the pipe from her bag, and there was nothing between that cloudy diamond and her. The smoke. The smoke. The smoke. The smoke. Yesyesyesyesyesyes. She was putting her hand in her panties and touching herself and she was coming. She was the bear in the cave and she was standing on her hind legs and nothing could kill her but there was a roaring and it was Dante. He knocked the pipe from her hand, but Lydia wasn't angry. She had sucked up all the smoke.

She tried to speak, but the words in her mouth didn't match what was in her head. She couldn't fit the understanding to the movement, but she didn't care because there was pleasure and she was alive and by the time she came down, Dante was pulling the blanket off the bed and telling Lydia he would sleep in his car.

When dawn came, she was back to herself and feeling ashamed. Her husband had found her smoking crack and touching herself. She didn't know how to make that better, but she showered and washed her hair. She wanted to be squeaky clean, a different woman from the one he'd seen the previous night. And she prayed, too. It had been a long time for her since she'd sent up some words or given gratitude. She and Dante hadn't been to church since he'd started working for Tim. Those long Friday and Saturday nights had tired him out; he didn't have the energy on Sunday morning.

Lydia was standing at the counter with her eyes closed, begging God to save her marriage, when Dante came up behind her. He hugged her, and whispered, sit down with him. Eat some breakfast, but her appetite was gone. Her plate turned cold.

He touched her hand. "This is my fault, baby."

"Dante, no—"

"Yeah, it is. I brought this to you. You not used to this life. This ain't you. And really, it ain't me, neither."

"I don't know what happened, Dante. It just got away from me."

"That's what happens, baby. I tried to tell you, but we gone stop this, right now. I been saving, and I almost got enough for mechanic's school. A couple more months is all I need. And I think you should go to the City to your family—"

"What? You want me gone?" So her prayers hadn't been answered. He didn't want her anymore. Her words sent above had been returned with ashes.

"No, Lydia, I don't want you gone. I love you, baby. But you can't be around this kind of life no more. So what we gone do is, you going home, and you gone get yourself together. And then I'm gone save, and I'm gone get another place in another neighborhood—"

"Dante—"

"No, woman. I'm not changing my mind. I'm gone take this weekend off. We gone drive your car up to the City and I'm gone take the bus back. That's what's gone happen."

He was no longer the soft boy that she had met at the basketball game. His voice had deepened. Even his face had changed, with lines that had not been there before. Perhaps he'd never been that boy, but always a man with the bitterness of strength, taking charge of the weaker beings in his sphere. And Lydia was weak. Once, she'd dreamed about being taken care of by this man. But this care didn't have the sugared taste she'd imagined.

When he left, she tried to spend her day as she had before, in the mindless months when Dante and she had played house. But time had sped up, and the apartment was clean and there was nothing else to do. She tried not to think of the cloudy diamonds in her purse, the ones that called to her. She rode the minutes until they became an hour, and she was suffering. On the second hour, she broke.

She went to her pocketbook, but there was nothing there. She searched the compartments, pulling out the lining. Then she went to Dante's drawer, moving the clothes she had neatly folded. She ran her hands inside the edges of the drawer, but there was nothing. And she shook and cried and thought of what she would say to Dante to make him give her a rock. Just one, but he did not return, and Lydia didn't know which was worse, Dante leaving her or that she had torn up the apartment and found no rocks.

He was gone all night, and in the morning, there was a knock. She ran to the door. She hadn't slept. Every time she'd dozed, her heart had pounded, and she would cry out and she was afraid of sleep. But now Dante had come back. He would make things better, he would give her a rock, and she would do anything he asked to get it. But it wasn't Dante knocking because he had forgotten his key. It was Tim, and he was telling Lydia that her husband was dead. And Lydia was wailing as she slipped to the floor. As she beat her fists against the carpet.

Tim kept talking over her cries. He had seen the whole thing. He'd been coming to the back of the convenience store, where the owner didn't have cameras, and that geek monster Marcus had pulled a gun on Dante. He had been begging, just give it to him. He didn't have any money, but he would soon. So just give it to him, please, brother, please, he was good for it, but when Dante shook his head, Marcus shot him. He'd been searching Dante's body when Tim had walked up. There wasn't anybody around, so he shot the geek monster in the head.

Tim pulled a wad of money out of his pockets. "Here you go. This all my boy had."

When she didn't take the money, he started for the door. She was still weeping, but she couldn't stop herself. She'd gone too long without. She needed something.

"Wait," she said. "Did Dante have anything else on him?"

Tim turned. "Say what?"

She wiped her face. "You know. Like . . . you know?"

At least Tim didn't smile when he reached again into his pocket for the cellophane packets. And there was another pipe, if she needed it. He was grim as he said he'd get at her. He'd come back and check on her soon.

Before calling Dante's mother, Lydia smoked a rock, but Miss Opal already had heard the news. She was screaming, her only baby dead. Why, Jesus? Why? And Lydia told her she was sorry, but Miss Opal didn't have to worry. She had enough to bury Dante.

"We had policies, just in case. It's only four thousand. I got a little bit more in my emergency fund, though."

"Baby, that's all right. That's more than enough. I just thank you so much."

"Don't say that, Miss Opal. It's what I'm supposed to do. I'm his wife. Was . . . his wife."

After she hung up, she smoked another rock, and another one that night, because she couldn't be high in the morning when she drove to the apartment of her husband's mother and signed over the policy to bury her son. And she'd have to sit there for a while, too, and hold Miss Opal's hand and listen to her cry. Lydia couldn't allow her own grief to take over, because the woman who had carried him needed to be honored. That was the old way, and besides, Lydia had to find the words to tell Miss Opal she wouldn't be at the homegoing. She couldn't see Dante in his coffin. She'd been to enough funerals in Chicasetta. Lydia didn't want to see Dante powdered and stiff, maybe even with a grin on his face, as some bereaved families requested for their departed. They wanted their loved ones to look jolly on their way to meet Jesus.

She stayed in the apartment, smoking up what Tim had given her, and when that ran out, she called Tim and gave him her gold wedding band as payment. In two weeks, the furniture was gone, carted out in pieces by Tim. The television. The stereo. The pots and pans because she didn't feel like cooking and Tim would bring her candy and pop when he came by. She kept her clothes. She couldn't walk around naked, but finally, she offered Tim the car. That should buy her enough for a month, but he told her he didn't need that. He already had his own.

"What do you want? Oh! I got the cassettes!"

She ran to the bedroom closet and pulled down the shoe box. She came and set it on the kitchen counter.

"It's some good stuff in here. I got Shalimar—old Shalimar, not new Shalimar—and I got Cameo." She put the Luther Vandross tapes aside.

Tim put his hand on hers and curled the fingers around. She slipped her hand from his, and pulled more cassettes from the shoe box, but he told her, he wanted her for his woman. She was a lady, not one of these crack hoes, sucking dick for anybody with five dollars. That's why Dante had married her, and Tim wasn't even mad at her for coming between him and his partner. That Dante had cussed Tim out, saying he'd gotten Lydia hooked on crack.

He pulled the plastic bag from his pocket and opened it. He shook a rock onto the counter. She told him, leave that, and come back in a couple of hours. But then he picked up the rock from the counter, and she knew her gamble hadn't worked.

When he came in for a kiss, she pushed at his chest.

"I'm not my best right now. I need to take a shower. I'll see you tonight, okay?"

"That's why I like you," Tim said. "'Cause you say things like that. Dante was right about you. You're a real good woman."

After her shower, she dressed and braided her wet hair. She was grateful she still had a working phone: when she called her granny, there was no scolding or yelling about where Lydia had been, all this time. Miss Rose only told her granddaughter, come on, if she was coming, and Lydia took down her suitcase from the closet. She put her clothes and cassettes inside the suitcase. When she walked out of the apartment, she left the door unlocked. It was dark as she turned off toward Chicasetta, but she wasn't afraid of the country roads.

At the farm, the porchlight was on, and Miss Rose was sitting on the porch. Lydia went to her and sat by her feet. She put her head on the familiar, fleshy leg, and her granny touched her hair. Then, she told Lydia, it was time to call her mother. She had been worrying herself sick, but Lydia shouldn't be scared. Everything was gone be all right.

MY SENSITIVITY GETS IN THE WAY

◈

Though no one used the term, there had been folks in Chicasetta who could be called "addicts." For instance, there was Mr. Lonny the Wino. When he stood in front of the liquor store, sweeping the same patch of sidewalk, he was usually placid. But if he'd imbibed more than his share, Lonny's personality would turn. He would block the entrance of the liquor store, snarling.

"Got-damn bastards! I'm coming for all y'all! You better watch out! I got something for you!"

Mr. Hurt, the owner of the store, would come outside, waving a baseball bat. "Go on, now," he'd say. "I can't have that mess 'round here. Go on." And Lonny would amble down the street to return the next day, smiling affably, revealing toothless gums. He'd been a schoolteacher once, at Chicasetta Colored High School. A quiet man who dressed neatly, he'd taught math to his students, trying to explain the concepts of proofs and oddly shaped geometrical figures. It was a woman who had caused his fall, or rather, a girl. One of his students in eleventh grade who'd been too pretty for Lonny to resist. That's what the men in town had said when the girl had reported Lonny to the principal. He'd touched her hair, before grabbing her and tearing her clothes. She'd kicked him in the privates before running away.

Too pretty, the men said, and what man could resist such a female? Skin so smooth and a body tight in all the right places. An ass you could set a drink on, and it would never fall. Big old pretty brown eyes with shiny whites. But the women said, Lonny was a pervert who couldn't keep his hands off underage girls. Nasty bastard, and him with a wife at home, though soon, the wife packed up her children and left town. Lonny started drinking, and the rest of the story tumbled out, along with his teeth each passing year.

Crack was different from liquor, though. It was irresistible, and those who smoked it quickly became shameless in their need. At first, it was in the northern cities, like at that house with boarded windows around the corner from where Lydia had attended Jean Toomer High School. The people who walked in and out of that house looked awful. Their lips chapped and eternally ashy. Their eyes bugged and staring at something that they could only reach once they had smoked another rock or two. When crack traveled from the urban Sodom to the country, it began holding its own with liquor. Folks who'd kept to themselves, avoiding the fast life, couldn't get enough of it. The pull was legendary: once you smoked it, you couldn't turn it down. But the danger only made it more seductive.

You could smell it on the skin, that metallic odor. That's what Miss Rose had remembered, the day a stranger came by the farm. She shouldn't have opened the door for him, but the man looked awful. Skinny, clothes not clean. She took pity on him, offering him a meal, but made the mistake of leaving him in the kitchen while she visited the bathroom. It didn't take that long for Miss Rose to do her business, and she had sense enough to take her purse with her. When she returned, that man had run off with the plate she fixed him, and he'd stolen two hens out her deep freezer, too. Miss Rose wasn't angry at the man. She prayed for him that evening, because she could see that he'd had some pain in his life. Something pushing him to the edge.

Yet Lydia's fall was a mystery to her family. A girl like her, provided with every necessity, a mother and father, plenty love. Educated at college and on her way to becoming a social worker. A good girl like that. What had gone wrong? And when Lydia reflected on her life, meditated on it, the way Elder Beasley at Red Mound told his flock that they should meditate on Jesus, think about His suffering, how He toted the troubles of the world so the rest of human beings didn't have to, Lydia couldn't have told you how she had ended up in the thrall of a white rock that looked harmless. The pellets like cheap jewelry, cloudy diamonds that somebody tried to pass off as priceless. They didn't look like something that could ruin

Lydia's life. That could make her family ashamed to call her name out loud in polite company, make her mother feel as if her heart had been stolen and carried off to Hell.

It had been frightening for Lydia, phoning her mother. Ringing the house at nine thirty, so there would be no harmless chitchat. A call that time of night could only mean a death or an emergency. Lydia took it as a sign when her baby sister answered the phone, though there were only seconds of hearing Ailey's voice before Mama snatched the phone away. Lydia told her she was in trouble. She'd gotten in with a bad crowd. And when Mama pressed her, she admitted, yes, it was drugs. By that time, Lydia was shaking. She only wanted her need to stop. Her grief to stop. Only her granny's hand on her shoulder was keeping her from screaming.

But it was a relief, knowing Ailey was still there, waiting. Loving her. Lydia closed her eyes and kept Ailey's face in front of her, as she lay in the bed that she had shared with her baby sister only the summer before. Tried to remember that when her mother arrived at Miss Rose's house the next evening. Her uncle collected her mother from the airport in Atlanta, and at dinner, Lydia knew there would be no respite.

"I knew something was wrong with that nigger," Mama said. "I had a dream."

"This ain't the time to be bringing all that up," Miss Rose said. "Let the child be. She already upset."

"Don't you think I see that? She's my daughter, not yours!"

Lydia sat at the kitchen table. Her plate untouched. An old quilt of her great-grandmother wrapped around her shoulders. When her mother asked, where was that boy, now that he'd gotten her hooked on drugs? Lydia trembled in her misery. She lied that Dante had broken up with her. She lied, because if Mama kept low-rating Dante even after she found out he was dead, Lydia definitely would hate her.

For the next few days, Lydia walked over the wood floors of her granny's house. Her mother would call her name, a noise Lydia didn't truly hear, because she was focused on getting from one minute to the next. She couldn't stop shaking, and her heart raced, like she had drunk too much coffee. She wanted to scream: she bit her lips to keep the sound in, until she tasted blood. Then she told herself, lie down. Maybe some rest would do her good, but when she closed her eyes, a strange dream—

Always, the same handsome white man in old-fashioned clothes. A man with eyes like Uncle Root, but the man was a stranger, who led her to a gingerbread house like in a fairy tale. Lydia could even smell the gingerbread. It made her mouth water, but when she walked inside the fairytale house, there was nothing but claw-foot tubs, and little girls standing beside them. Little, light-brown girls dressed like the dolls Lydia's granny kept on her bed. Little girls wearing dresses with lace and petticoats, and grown women's buns fastened at the back of their necks, and then the little girls stepped into the bathtubs and lay back and closed their eyes and the water closed over their heads—

"Lydia, baby, come on now. It's time to get up."

Her mother was calling her name, telling her she should take a bath and get herself cleaned up. Lydia hesitated at the door, until Mama told her she'd sit in there with her, right on the blue fluffy toilet cover. She thought her daughter might want her privacy while she bathed, but if she didn't that was all right. She was Lydia's mother. She'd seen everything she had already. Mama laughed. After Lydia's bath Mama helped her dress in clean underwear and a bra and then a shirt and jeans. She kneeled down and slipped socks and tennis shoes on her daughter's feet. She weaved Lydia's hair into four long braids.

Uncle Root was with them for the drive to Atlanta, past the city and out to one of the counties where only white folk lived. A building that sprawled, and a white lady at the front desk who said that Lydia had to sign the forms herself. She was an adult, and Mama was hugging her, and Uncle Root was hugging her, and the white lady at the front desk was taking her back through the doors. She introduced herself as Dr. Fairland, and apologized for patting Lydia down and told her she had to go behind that curtain and take off all her clothes, so they knew she wasn't bringing drugs into the facility. Please forgive her, and Dr. Fairland had to search through Lydia's suitcase, too. But she had a smile in her voice as she stuck her hand through the curtain with Lydia's clothes and underwear. She told Lydia that she was so proud of her. No contraband. This was a great first step! And she sounded even happier when Lydia asked, could she have some juice or maybe something to eat? She was really hungry.

—————

In their early days, when the patients came into the center and were detoxing, some wept, giving over to depression. Others wanted to fight, and they jumped at the television, the only valuable object in the room. When days passed, their shame would tip into the space. In group therapy, the patients would repeat their apologies to the counselor. "I'm sorry" and "I didn't mean it," and Dr. Fairland would nod sympathetically. She was in charge of Lydia's group, one of four in the center. She was Lydia's personal counselor, too. It wasn't enough to have a daily group therapy. There had to be one-on-one confessions as well, and she listened to Lydia's issues for sixty minutes every day. The lack of sleep. No privacy. That strange, red-haired chick who was Lydia's roommate and asked her throughout the day, did Lydia want to hear about her soul, in that candy-coated southern drawl.

About halfway through her monologue, Dr. Fairland would ask, "Why do you think you did it, Lydia? Why'd you start using drugs?" Lydia envisaged her trying not to look at her watch, calculating how much money this crack fiend was providing for her mortgage and car note. The facility was nice. She knew her parents were paying plenty money.

After her cravings and panic attacks stopped, she was relieved. But when she was forced to confront her feelings, her cravings started again. So Lydia kept quiet in group therapy, and watched the other patients, a passive witness. Except for one Black guy, the rest of the patients were white, and open with their agony, their anger, though Lydia had been raised to keep her composure around white people, to never drop her guard. Just because she was addicted to crack didn't mean she had an excuse to forget her home training and act any kind of way in front of these people. It had taken her five days in the group session to admit that she was an addict. On that day, she quietly stated, yes, it was true. She had been far gone, after only a few weeks of smoking primos, before she moved on to rocks.

There was approval around the circle, even from that one Black guy whom Lydia had nicknamed "Brother Patient" in her mind. When Lydia had casually called him "brother" during the snack break, letting her cadence move into a rhythm, he'd looked at her, his eyes surprised, then assessing. The look of recognition: he saw it now. That she was a Black woman and not Puerto Rican, or maybe from the southern part of Italy. Then his eyes moved past her to another spot. He wasn't interested in communion. He'd thought he'd bumped into something strange, but now he wanted to get away from the familiar. But Brother Patient did give her a grudging smile. A quick nod. That's right. Lydia was doing the work. Good for her.

————

In her second week, Dr. Fairland asked her, had something happened? Lydia picked up the pillow and sat it on her lap. She picked at the corners; the seams weren't reinforced. In a year, maybe less, the stuffing would start to come out.

"My parents, they had to get married," Lydia said. "Because of me. My mama got pregnant in college. She had wanted to be an English professor. She was supposed to get her master's and then her doctorate."

"Okay." Dr. Fairland's hair was a mess, a wild brown perm that went everywhere. Her eyes were pretty, even though Lydia rarely liked light eyes, even her own.

"And my mama was headed to Columbia," Lydia said. "But then she couldn't go. So she couldn't get her doctorate and be a professor. It was even a long time before she started teaching elementary school. And when I was little, she was mad a lot. Like constantly."

"What about your father?"

"He's a doctor. And he's gone all the time, working. I know he had to work to support us. I know that's what a man is supposed to do, but when I was little, I felt like I was all by myself. Except for my baby sister."

"Did you think that was your fault, Lydia? That your mother was mad?"

"Yeah, it is." Lydia sat up. She corrected her diction. "I mean, yes, of course, it's my fault. If it hadn't been for me, Mama would be a professor right now. And now, here I am. In here." Lydia waved her hand. "Her whole life was ruined because of me. She married Daddy because of me."

"But you didn't ask to be born. Your parents were adults when they conceived you. All right, yes, they didn't plan you, but they knew that having sex might result in a baby. And how can a baby be responsible for her parents?"

"I didn't say that."

"Essentially you did, Lydia. You said it was your fault they had to get married. Why do you think you feel so protective of your parents, especially your mother?"

"I mean . . . you know . . . the Bible says, honor thy mother and father and all that."

Dr. Fairland smiled. "Uh-oh! I'm not stepping into that mine-field."

"I'm not trying be religious. I'm talking about how I was reared."

"And how was that?"

How to explain what it was like to be Black to this white woman who wasn't even southern? That a Black child didn't have a right to hate their Black mama? Hatred was not allowed against your parents, no matter what had happened. You had to forgive your parents for whatever they had done even if they'd never apologized, because everybody had to stay together. So much had been lost already to Black folks.

———

In her third week, Lydia told Dr. Fairland what Gandee had done, the things he had made her do. She didn't want to—she couldn't even understand why she'd told—but she began weeping, and Dr. Fairland let her cry it out, her face sympathetic.

Gently, she asked, had Lydia ever told her parents?

"Oh, no. I could never."

"Why not, Lydia? Why do you think that is?"

"I don't know. I just couldn't."

"Do you think you've never told because you feel responsible for them, especially your mother?"

Lydia wiped her face. "I don't want to hurt Mama even more. How am I supposed to tell her, that man molested me, when I'm already here? That's bad enough."

"So instead, you have to carry all this by yourself? That's a lot for somebody who's only twenty-one years old. Doesn't that get heavy for you?"

New tears surged. "It does! I'm so tired, Dr. Fairland."

"I bet. And you have a right to be. You have a right to be sad, too. Do you know that? You have every right to every feeling that you have. You don't have to feel guilty or apologize."

They talked some more, until the sixty minutes were up, but still, Lydia didn't confess that her husband was dead.

———

The rehab facility let Mama visit in the fourth week, and Lydia confessed she'd lied about Dante being in college, because she'd been sure he'd enroll in college at some point. She came clean that she hadn't transferred to Spelman, though her mother already knew that. They sat on the couch in Dr. Fairland's office, half facing each other. Lydia with the pillow on her lap, and her mother hugging her pocketbook. Dr. Fairland was quiet, waiting for them to begin.

"I'm sorry. I know I'm supposed to talk this whole thing through, but I don't even like hearing that boy's name." Mama used her schoolteacher's tone. Proper, faultless. "It's his fault my child is on drugs. Was on drugs."

"Please tell that to your daughter. You're here for her."

Mama put down her pocketbook. She slid closer to Lydia, pulling her hands away from the pillow. She told Lydia she was sure it was that boy's fault. That Lydia was a good girl.

Lydia wanted to take up for her husband, to say, he'd done the best he could. Like anybody. Like Lydia's parents. He'd been planning to drive her back to the City when he'd been killed. But since Lydia had called her mother to say she needed help, there'd been nothing but hostility whenever Dante's name had been spoken. There was no use trying to defend him. He was dead now, and she didn't have the energy to debate her mother. Nobody ever could win with her.

"Mama, I'm sorry," she said. "I didn't mean to cause trouble."

"Don't you worry about that, baby," her mother said. "I'm here now."

After a few more days, Belle came to retrieve her. They spent a month in Chicasetta. Then, Mama drove them in Lydia's car, and on the way to the interstate, she stopped at a fruit stand, buying peaches and watermelons from a fat white man in bib overalls. As Mama busied herself with slapping the side of the melon, he watched her, spitting brown tobacco juice into a tin can. He was dour, until Mama exclaimed, "Oh! Brunswick stew! My mother never makes this anymore." The man smiled a stained grin as she bought all five jars in the display.

When her sisters had ridden with them in summers past, the trip had seemed shorter to Lydia. Even with stopping every two hours so she could take Ailey to a bathroom at a fast-food restaurant. On this journey, both the women in the car had stronger, larger bladders, and there was only one stop. After they used the facilities, they sat in the parking lot outside the restaurant and ate their fried chicken and cold biscuits. There was a quart of sweet tea for each of them, taken from the cooler in the back of the car.

Lydia was apprehensive, thinking about her father. Would he be disappointed in her? Would he, too, disparage Dante? But at the house, after she hugged Ailey in the foyer—how tall her baby sister had grown—and laid her cheek against the wild curls that smelled like blue grease and a peaceful yesterday, Daddy had nothing but kindness for Lydia. His face relaxed, though he had put on so much weight. He hugged her closely, telling her she'd scared him. But she was home now. His girl was home.

A few days later, Mama accompanied Lydia to the registrar's office at Mecca University, standing beside her as she filled out the forms for the summer classes. Mama whispered, did she need to take that class over? Be honest, and Lydia whispered back, yes, she'd failed the entire fall semester. She had to take those over, and her mother told her, take only two classes. She didn't want Lydia to overwhelm herself. The classes were half-full, the professors easygoing. They dressed casually and flipped past pages in the textbooks, declaring, six weeks wasn't enough time to cover some of this material properly. So there'd be a multiple-choice test instead of a paper on those pages.

Lydia received As in both classes and spent her free month sleeping in and making preserves with Mama in the kitchen, though there wasn't the same pleasure in peeling fruit and vegetables as down in Chicasetta. After the jars were boiled and cooled, it was Lydia's job to carry them down to the basement. She'd take a few moments to rest on the stairs, enjoying her brief solitude. Then she'd remember those mornings and early afternoon hours in the apartment that she shared with Dante. When she'd been free and a woman, not a child again in her parents' house, though Mr. Rogers still had been her good friend. Lydia smiled, recalling how he talked to those puppets as if they were real people. Then Mama would call down to the basement. Was everything all right? She hadn't fallen down the stairs, had she? And Lydia would climb back up.

In August, she returned to classes at Mecca, taking up her same major, social work. In her classes, everyone talked about the readings, but they were too distant from the people they needed to help. They looked upon poor folks as if they were experiments. Lydia didn't care about the case studies in her textbooks. She'd had real family living in the inner city of Atlanta: Dante's mother and aunt. She'd lived with Dante on Campbellton Road. That hadn't been in the projects, but it had been rough. The roaches bold until they'd swallowed enough boric acid. The people who'd lived in her apartment complex had real blood moving through their bodies. Not statistics. They drove old cars that always needed fixing, and they would knock on her apartment door, asking, was Dante in? Could they get a battery jump? Or, how much did he charge to look underneath the hood?

Lydia missed those folks, the children or grandchildren of migrants from the country towns only an hour or two away from Atlanta, but which they referred to as if those places were in faraway lands where English wasn't spoken. They struggled on a daily basis to make rent and buy groceries, so they took their fun on the weekends, playing cards with their friends in their small dining rooms. When you passed their doors, you could hear the blues or the rap music thumping. On Sundays, it was gospel music, before they emerged in church finery, headed off to praise the Lord. To receive the Word that would sustain them throughout the week while they labored at their minimum-wage jobs. They didn't have enough money to worry about the bourgeoisie matters that occupied the large, comfortable house where Lydia lived now with her baby sister and her parents. When her grandmother came to Sunday dinner, Nana wasn't filled up with the Holy Spirit, because nobody got happy and shouted during a Catholic Mass. Maybe that was Nana's problem: she hadn't made the acquaintance of a colored people's god.

———

Mama had been full of apologies since Lydia and she had driven up from Georgia. She was sorry she hadn't kept a closer watch on Lydia, that Tony Crawford had taken advantage of her daughter. She was sorry that she hadn't paid more attention to Lydia's reading. She was sorry she hadn't caught her daughter's difficulties, that it had taken a school counselor to inform Mama that her daughter wasn't lazy. That, in fact, Lydia was a brilliant child with a near-photographic memory; however, Lydia also had a mild learning disability, and thus, it would require more time for Lydia to absorb information. So her mother needed to make sure that she was patient and sit with Lydia, so that she could compete her homework.

These apologies were useless to Lydia, because her mother wasn't apologizing for the right offense. Lydia didn't blame her mother for her learning disability. Her great-grandmother had the same problem, and the counselor had told Lydia that sometimes, these issues were inherited, like high blood pressure, or the tendency toward diabetes. And she didn't blame Mama for what had happened with Tony Crawford. That was on him. He had gone behind every adult's back to cajole Lydia into meeting him at the creek. Even if Tony had lied to himself that Lydia had been a willing participant, he should have left her alone. Fifteen going on sixteen was still a child.

What Lydia blamed her mother for was the thing that had been right in front of her all those years: Gandee's abuse. It hadn't happened once. It had happened at least a hundred times over the years, and somehow, her mother hadn't thought to notice. But Mama had been too enamored of Gandee's status, his high education and good grammar, to be able to see who Gandee really had been. She couldn't understand that a man like him—a doctor dressed in suits and ties and who spoke with a perfect, bleached-to-whiteness accent—could have been capable of hurting little girls. Such a fact couldn't even occupy a hidden place in Mama's skull. It could not even penetrate the bone. Yet because Dante had been from a bad neighborhood, her mother could make him a villain.

Dr. Fairland had urged Lydia to have the conversation with her mother, to confess what Gandee had done. Maybe the past could be reconciled, she'd said, but Lydia wasn't willing to step on that darkened road. She'd already disappointed her mother. Even if Lydia carried hurt, she didn't want to hand her mother even more.

And she was better now. She'd gotten past her addiction. It was time to move on, to look ahead. To try to be normal again, to find that place where Dante had led her. To try to find some joy, and she was so happy when Mama finally relented and let her leave the house one October evening for a party Niecy had invited her to. The onus wasn't on Lydia to convince her mother: Coco surprised everyone by catching the bus down from New Haven. The family was back together. All the daughters under one roof, and Mama was happy, too. She told Lydia, maybe being around young folks would bring the color back to her cheeks, but she had to take her sister as chaperone.

The party wasn't at Niecy's house, but at another soror's, one from Howard. Out in the country, where the rich folks lived. There were signs placed along the long driveway, leading to the house, but it wasn't hard to find their way. People were outside. The music was blasting. Lydia parked on the lawn, far from the house.

"I'll just stay here in the car," Coco said.

"But you're supposed to be watching over me."

"I am. So don't do anything stupid, and don't get in trouble. Oh yeah, and go with God." She rolled up the window.

Inside, Niecy waved and rushed over for a hug. She held on, rocking. She'd missed her line sister so much, but beside Niecy was a guy who inched steadily closer. Whispering in her ear, and she smiled sheepishly at Lydia.

Lydia went and held up a wall, drinking a can of orange pop. Dante and she had gone to clubs together, before things had gone bad. He'd taken her to a couple places in Buckhead, but she'd preferred the funky joints, like the Royal Peacock and Charles on Simpson Avenue. She felt an ache thinking about him. How when they slow dragged, they fit together. Each of Dante's hands on her hips while he moved her against him. When the DJ in the basement slowed it down with Luther, playing "Superstar," Lydia was afraid she might cry. She squeezed past the folks on the stairs and headed to the bathroom. There was a line for the one in the basement but the house was huge, so she decided to sneak upstairs. Coming back, she got turned around and opened the door she'd mistaken for the basement entrance. It was a large supply closet. Inside was a guy sitting on the floor. He had an album on his lap and was pulling apart buds.

"Come in or stay out," he said. "But make up your mind."

The door across from the closet opened and the music drifted out. The DJ was still playing Luther. She stepped inside the closet.

The guy pulled out rolling papers and a bag of white powder from his jacket. She watched as he layered the weed on the folded paper, then sprinkled it with the powder. He rolled everything to-gether. Briefly, he held a flame underneath the joint. She shook her head when he offered: ladies first. When he lit the joint, it took some minutes for the glittery smell to emerge through the cover of mari-juana. A perfume as familiar as a Gospel word.

If she left the closet, she'd be safe, but then the guy lit another, and there was no denying her need. When Lydia took in the smoke, there was gratitude. When he held out the primo, there was Dante again, in Lydia's head. A memory of that night, when Dante had thrown everybody out of their apartment and come to her. How wild their love had been—but she didn't want to think about that anymore, to hurt anymore, and she took the primo and put it to her mouth. She held her breath for a long time, until the back of her throat protested. But the bitterness on her palate was like the embrace of an old friend, one who knew you better than anybody else.

"What's your name?"

"Lydia."

"Lydia what?"

"Garfield."

"I'm Ray. Not Raymond, but Ray. I'm a fourth, too."

She settled back as he told her he was selling to put away money for after college, and when he graduated, he was changing his name. Ray the Fourth didn't care about pissing off his dad. He couldn't stand that nigger, always talking about how he'd grown up poor and made himself from nothing. How he was from the ghetto, and his sons needed to get tough. They were too soft, just like their mother. Since Ray the Fourth was supplying his drugs for free, Lydia shared as well. She told him she used to be married, young as she was. But she was a widow. Her husband had been mur-dered.

"Baby, I'm sorry. That's some heavy shit."

She laid her head on his shoulder, and Ray put his hand on her hair. It was so soft, he told her, and she was pretty. Real pretty, but Lydia ignored his saying that, because he rolled up another primo.

The party was in full effect when Lydia exited the closet. She saw everyone as if for the first time. They were happy, like she was happy. And young and alive and life was all right. The music was inside her, like the smoke was inside her. She visited the basement bathroom, splashing water on her face. She slathered on the fragrant lotion that her hosts had provided, letting the perfume cover her sin. She found Niecy, gave her a farewell hug, and said she'd call her, but at the car, Coco wasn't anxiously searching the crowd for her. She was outside the car, pressed against the passenger side while a girl kissed her deeply on the mouth. She didn't see her sister, and Lydia walked away some distance. She sat on the lawn and waited. It was after one in the morning, but at least the DJ had switched to Cameo. She waited through three more songs, until the girl and Coco parted, and Coco opened the passenger door.

Lydia went to the car, tapping on the window.

"You ready?"

Her sister looked at her, and Lydia knew she was wondering. How much had she seen? but Lydia only smiled back. She asked, did Coco want to drive?

That night, Lydia dreamed. She'd come upon the cave where her bear lived, but the cave was empty. And she'd stood at the mouth of the cave and screamed. She'd called the secret name of the bear, but she knew it was dead, and she woke up with shame. There was so much shame, but she knew that she'd be expected to come down for breakfast. She had to pretend that she was still walking a good path. At the breakfast table, her mother told her Coco already had gone, though Mama had hoped she'd stay another day. Coco didn't even have classes on Monday, but she'd been in such a hurry. Throughout breakfast, Ailey sulked about being left at home while Lydia and Coco had gone to the party. She flopped around and sighed, and Lydia pretended to ignore her, but she felt even worse. Her baby sister loved her, and she'd hurt her feelings. Lydia was a horrible person. Despair clawed at her throat, the spot where only the night before, her happiness had rested. After breakfast, she went upstairs and moved her clothes from the room she shared with her baby sister. She didn't want to face Ailey anymore.

Lydia was shaking when she dug in her purse and found the number that Ray the Fourth had given her. She called him and asked to meet at Mecca University's library. And bring what he had brought last night to the party.

A HOUSE IS NOT A HOME

◈

There was a familiarity in moving to a memory that included Dante. Lydia felt remorse when she met Ray the Fourth on Mecca's campus and went to his car. She gave him money and he discreetly handed her the small plastic bag. And then there was joy in sneaking to a bathroom in one of the buildings and waiting until the bathroom door closed and she was alone. Joy in pulling out the pipe Ray had given her and smoking the rock. Oh, the forgetting Gandee's hands and Dante's death! Oh, the euphoria, the smoke in her mouth! There was no rousing of Lydia's bear, though. Her animal refused to wake in its cave.

But there was such shame after her high came down, though she was doing everything else right. She attended classes and submitted her homework. She only got high twice a day: in a campus bathroom before classes, and at night, when she closed herself in the small closet of what used to be Coco's room.

And then everything ended. Her parents sent her baby sister to Nana's house. They wanted to have a talk, but Lydia was counting the minutes. Ray the Fourth was supposed to meet her in front of the library at noon. He liked her and wanted her to be his girlfriend, he'd told her, and that's why he gave her a discount for her rocks. Lydia had run out of money, and she planned on walking to the pawnshop to see if she could get some money for the opal neck-lace her father had given her a few years ago for her birthday. She was grateful she'd left her keepsake box in the City. Otherwise, she wouldn't have anything to barter.

Then her mother told her Daddy was taking her to rehab, and Lydia sat up.

"No, ma'am. Uh-uh. I'm not going back there."

The shaking, the detox hadn't been so bad, but traveling through pain was horrible. They acted as if once you understood what was tormenting you, you could get rid of the memories. But you couldn't. The memories always would be there, hurting you. Lydia couldn't talk about those with no respite in sight.

She couldn't soak herself in that again. With no promise of smoke hitting the back of her throat and the high drowning out the pain.

But Daddy told Lydia, go upstairs and pack. Get her things. He'd wait for her outside. He wasn't playing with her. In her bedroom, she made sure to empty her keepsake box into her suitcase. She might not have another chance. They would take her things in rehab, until she finished the program, but she could get them back. She hesitated, then crept to her parents' room. She opened her mother's jewelry box and pulled out two heavy gold bracelets that her mother never wore, except at holiday dinners. She didn't have a plan. She just knew she would find a way out of rehab. She couldn't stay there again. That's what she told herself. But in the car, Lydia learned, her father had lied to her mother, but he wouldn't lie to Lydia. The insurance wouldn't pay for more rehab, and her parents had run through half their savings. He was taking Lydia someplace else, and telling Mama her daughter had run away. Lydia would have a roof and food and he'd buy her a bus pass every month. He was doing this because he was her daddy. It was his job to protect her, but he had to protect his wife as well.

"You can't come back to this house, Lydia. I can't see your mama's heart broken, not again. I'm not giving you money, either. Whatever shit you want to smoke, you get on your own. I'm giving your car to Coco."

As they drove to the other side of the City, Lydia recognized the streets. They'd lived in this neighborhood when she'd been a little girl. Her father pulled up to an apartment building. He got out and headed toward a handsome, dark man who rose from the stoop. The man kept her daddy from falling as he began to sob.

————

When it was pitch black, when no one could see, Lydia took the bus from her new neighborhood to the places where she would find her rocks. When her father first moved her into the apartment, she had called Ray the Fourth, and taken the bus to Mecca's campus. She'd pawned some of her keepsakes, but he had stopped wanting her money. He wanted something else, and she just wanted to smoke in peace.

She didn't want to buy the rocks in her own neighborhood. Zulu Harris was watching her. He knocked on her door to check on her and didn't want anything more than that: Lydia knew enough about men. So she boarded a City bus, looking for sad, hollow-eyed passengers. It took her two days of riding the bus to overcome her fear, and by that time, she was sick and determined. When the sad people left the bus, she stalked them to their sources. She followed her instincts. If she got a bad feeling about a dealer, she didn't listen to her need. She'd walk away and hop the bus again, following new tragic-faced people. Lydia brought her bounty home, hiding it behind the armoire that her father was proud to have bought at an estate sale. Rich people gave away such nice things, he'd said.

She was supposed to be part of this community now. The despised, the pathetic, but Lydia rejected this connection. She was different from these people. One day, she was going to stop using drugs. Even when the police arrested her coming out of a crack house, she didn't feel a kinship. She called the only phone number she was allowed to use, that of Zulu Harris. As she waited in the holding cell surrounded by sullen female strangers, she dreaded his arrival. But when Mr. Harris paid her bail and retrieved her, he only said, try to be more careful. And it was probably best that they didn't share the episode with her daddy.

Mr. Harris was an old friend of Lydia's father, from way back. In his mid-forties, bald, and with a hint of a paunch, but so handsome. He called Lydia his niece and told the waitresses at his restaurant that she could eat for free. The waitresses had started out with attitudes, but eventually she'd won them over. Now they shouted Lydia's name when she walked in. They tried to give her pie.

On Friday evenings, there was her father. He'd knock on the door of the apartment where he'd installed her. He'd put a sack of groceries on the small table in the space next to the kitchenette. There wasn't much time that elapsed before he would begin asking, what had he done? What hadn't he done? And what could he do for Lydia now?

"It's not your fault, Daddy. It's mine."

Weeks passed, and she became weary of his routine, especially the part where she'd ask him, when could she come back home? Then his tender nature would congeal. She couldn't come home. Let's not talk about this, he'd tell her, and they'd sit quietly on the corduroy couch.

For a gift, Daddy brought her the sewing machine her granny had given her. He'd sneaked it out of the house while Mama was out. An antique, a Singer 66, purchased by her great-grandmother Pearl; before that, Dear Pearl had sewn on her hands. Her father made Lydia swear on her Bible that she wouldn't sell it. He'd brought one along.

Lydia laughed. "Daddy, are you serious? You're an atheist."

"That's not true."

"Yes, it is! You don't have to pretend with me. Mama's nowhere around."

He sat down on the couch with a low grunt. Mr. Harris and he had found it at a thrift shop out in the country, where the rich white folks lived. At the same estate sale where he'd bought the armoire, there had been an antique coffee table and dining room suite, china plates, flatware, and a four-poster bed, all of which her father had acquired for nearly a song. The apartment was cozy, not thrown together. Lydia wondered, how long had her father been planning to exile her from the family?

"Fine, darling. I'm an atheist. You caught me. But you aren't, so put your hand on this book." He picked up the Bible from the coffee table, and she sat beside him, putting her hand on the cover.

"I swear that I will not sell the sewing machine," she said. "In Jesus's name, Amen."

"Very good! Let's go get something to eat down at Zulu's place.

Belle thinks I have patients, but I have Fridays off now. You don't think less of me for lying, do you, Lydia?"

"No, of course not."

She asked if he could bring her some fabric. She wanted to keep her skills up. He brought her back some pin-striped linen, making her put her hand on the Bible again.

It was a lady named Irma Bradley who noticed her dress in Mr. Harris's restaurant. That dress was too fancy for this neighborhood.

"Where you get that?" she asked.

"I made this myself, Mrs. Bradley."

"Shonuff?"

"Yes, ma'am."

When Mrs. Bradley wore a dress that Lydia made, she told the other, older ladies that Lydia's prices were more than reasonable. If someone brought a pattern, that was nice, but if not, tell Lydia where to find the dress. She'd take the bus down to the store, carry the dress into the dressing room, and turn it inside out. She could make her own pattern out of brown paper. That girl had a gift.

It was passed down from her great-grandmother, Lydia told Mrs. Bradley. The lady hadn't learned to read, but she'd had a photographic memory. Though Dear Pearl been a white man's daughter, she was still Negro, and the stores in town hadn't let her try on clothes. But those white folks hadn't bothered her; she could see a dress in the store window and make an exact copy.

"Them white folks," Mrs. Bradley said. "That's why I left Mississippi. But I wish I could go back for good. I still got people there."

Lydia took the pins from her mouth. "You should, Mrs. Bradley. I bet it's not as bad."

"I can't leave now. Not with Maurice." He was her grandchild, the son of Sondra, whose boyfriend had refused to marry her. But when they'd broken up, he'd thought his court-sanctioned child support of Maurice gave him a say-so. The judge thought he had a say-so, too. Two years later, when Sondra was diagnosed with early breast cancer, she'd moved back in with Mrs. Bradley. When

Sondra died, Maurice's father still wouldn't let anyone take his son out of the City, though he had a new woman and a new baby, and said that the apartment they lived in was too small for Maurice. So here Mrs. Bradley was, trying to raise a badass little boy at her age. But she couldn't leave him for his father to palm him off on some stranger or maybe even foster care. God would never forgive her, would he?

"I don't know about that, Mrs. Bradley. I pray, but I don't hear too much these days. I do know this: the Lord knows you're just doing the best you can. And whatever you decide, it'll be all right."

"Thank you, darling. Sometimes I need me a good word," and Mrs. Bradley's face cleared of discontent. She was soothed, and Lydia sat back on her heels. She'd known what had been expected of her, but she had been glad for it. Somebody needed her, for once, and there was a near happiness. Almost as if it was only an extended holiday she was taking, in her small apartment decorated with charming odds and ends.

That weekend, she violated her father's orders. She called her parents' house on a Sunday, when she knew Mama was in the kitchen. Lydia listened for that southern, musical sound, and then hung up.

———

Christmas was the hardest that first year. The time she'd hated the most as a girl, but there was a longing for the familiar. Mr. Harris didn't celebrate Christmas, and Lydia didn't want to feign an interest in his Kwanzaa celebration. Her mother had made fun of that holiday, saying, Black folks always wanted to make something up, just to be fancy.

Lydia missed her baby sister the most, the child who thought her unsullied, even in her lowest time. The baby she'd held for comfort, and Lydia was lonely. She told herself she didn't have a right to feel that way. She'd messed up her life. Still her husband was dead, and Chicasetta was an impossible distance away. She needed her baby sister. And she took the bus to her grandmother's street, watching as Mama pulled up in the station wagon. It took some time for Ailey to exit the car: their mother was talking with her hands.

There were a couple weekends of observing, and Lydia decided she would get clean. She wouldn't see her baby sister high. She cut the days into pieces. Into hours and then minutes. The need kept coming down, and the day Lydia took the bus to Nana's house, she went a whole day and a half without a rock before she rang the doorbell.

Miss Delores answered and ordered her to stand in the hallway, and Lydia waited, sending her mind different places while she timed the minutes without her rock. She looked at the stairway, waiting for Ailey. The need was worth it, because her baby sister was coming, but Miss Delores sent down Nana instead, who called Lydia a disgrace to the family. Certainly, she hadn't inherited these weaknesses from the Garfield side of the family.

Lydia had dropped her head, waiting for the tirade's conclusion. It would end, and then she could see her baby sister, but her grandmother told her, it was time to leave.

"Please, Nana. Let me see her."

"No, this is for the best. You cannot ruin that child."

If she had pushed Lydia toward the door—forced her outside—that might have been the end, but Nana told her, maybe if her mother had raised her children properly, this wouldn't have happened, and then Lydia told it all, every offense of Gandee, how he'd hurt her. Even when Nana's self-righteousness turned to horror, to contrition, to weeping, to denials, Lydia kept shouting. She wasn't going away without burning down a forest and salting the dirt to ruin.

When she left, she headed around the corner to the bus stop, and when the bus came, it wasn't her line, but she got on anyway. She watched the faces of people until she saw the needed misery. Her comrades. Her new family.

THE OTHER SIDE OF THE WORLD

◆

There had been terrors in the seven years that Lydia had lived in the neighborhood. Times that she had been hurt in the places where she went to buy her drugs. Twice, her father had disappeared for weeks, until Mr. Harris had passed on the news that her father was fine. He told her don't be upset, but her daddy had a heart attack. When her father returned to his daughter's apartment, he told her his doctor had made him cut his hours on account of his health. Mama didn't know that, however, and Daddy hated to lie to his woman. But a brother didn't want to be tracked constantly, even when he wasn't misbehaving. Some nights when he told Belle he was working the emergency room, he really was at Mr. Harris's house, just hanging out. Sometimes they took a sip or two of brown liquor, too, and Daddy would fall asleep on his friend's couch.

In the years since he'd put her out of the house, Lydia's father had lost his severity. He left envelopes of cash on her couch, without a word. He was direct with Lydia, too, as he'd never been before her own troubles, and it occurred to her that he had no fear of judgment from her.

Two weeks before her father died, he gave her his usual lecture, which always occurred after the new year. They'd sat at the small table in her kitchen, eating out of takeout containers from his friend's restaurant. Her father had asked her to fry him some pork chops, but she'd refused.

"Daddy, you know you're not supposed to have pork."

"Who's going to know?"

"Mama will! She'll smell that grease on you. And you're supposed to be dropping weight. Now, you eat that baked chicken like your doctor told you."

"If I drop this weight, you need to walk behind me and pick it right on up. You're too skinny."

He put one of his corn muffins in her container, and Lydia nibbled it as he gave the family news. Veronica was showing out, with her rotten, spoiled self. Uncle Lawrence was trying to get back with Aunt Diane, as usual. Malcolm was making good progress on his doctorate, up in Amherst. Her baby sister was getting high grades. And Coco was coming back to town. She had a residency.

"I know Nana must be happy," Lydia said. "She finally got her doctor."

"Don't you dare be jealous," he said. "Coco isn't any smarter than you."

"Yes, she is, Daddy! She tested as a genius."

"Yeah, well, her social skills are damned awful. She and my brother are two peas in a pod. Not that I don't love all my girls equally."

"She's okay with folks when she's comfortable." Lydia wasn't going to tell her sister's business, that she was charming indeed, in the presence of a pretty woman.

"I'm just saying, all you have to do is apply yourself," he said. "Your whole life is ahead of you."

He'd had such faith in her, that her kicking drugs was like studying for a test.

When her father died, she found out from Mr. Harris, weeks after the funeral. He swore he hadn't known. If he had, he would have taken her to Georgia. Surely, his brother would have wanted it that way.

"Who told you, Mr. Harris?" she asked.

"Your sister," he said.

"Ailey?" She pictured a girl, tall but with baby fat. Her wild curls going in all directions.

"No, your other sister, Coco."

"Did she ask about me?"

He took her hand. "She did, Lydia. She's very worried about you. She wants to get you back into treatment."

"How'd she know?"

"Don't be angry, darling, but your daddy told her."

"I'm not mad, Mr. Harris. And I'm gone get myself together. I promise."

"I believe you, darling."

She slid her hand from his. He was a nice man; he'd never tried anything with her. There wasn't even a funny look trained on her. He was like an uncle, like Uncle Root or Uncle Norman, and she knew he meant well, but with her father dead, sobriety occupied a distant land. It made Lydia's legs tired, thinking of walking there.

Spring arrived. She would wait until the long light gave way to darkness, before taking the bus to places she knew she shouldn't go. Neighborhoods that were extremely dangerous, and there were things that happened to her. Bad things, but when she was high, she reasoned, it wasn't as if anyone cared. Perhaps she would die in one of those houses with shutters like missing eyes. Infrequently, she ate candy bars. She stayed like that for many days, ignoring Irma Bradley's knocks. She put a note on the apartment door, that she'd suffered a loss in the family.

When the phone rang, it shocked her. Her father had paid the bill. Since he'd died, she hadn't gone near it. She hadn't wanted to pick up the receiver and hear silence.

"Lydia, it's your sister, Carol Rose." She sounded so much like their mother, it struck Lydia in the chest. The throaty alto. The catch at the bottom of a phrase. "Say something, girl. I know you're there. I hear you breathing."

"Hey, Coco."

"Hey. I got your number from Mr. Harris."

"Okay."

"So how are you doing? How's your health these days?"

If her sister hadn't sounded so graceful, Lydia would have laughed. Before Dear Pearl had died, she'd hated folks asking after her well-being. She'd tell them, none of they damned business. They won't no doctor. But the irony was, Lydia's sister was a doctor. She had a right to ask.

"I'm fine, Coco. Thank you so much for calling."

"So listen—"

Lydia hung up abruptly, and when the phone rang seconds later, she did not answer. She spent a lot of daylight sleeping, until the summer came one day. The sun coaxed her out of bed. Like a friend who won't give up on you, no matter how many times you tell her, *leave me be. Just let me be miserable. Girl, I'm grown.*

There weren't many trees in the neighborhood, but the sky was pretty when Lydia emerged from her building, blinking. She kept her head down, embarrassed, but her neighbors loudly greeted her. In the clinic, Gretchen, the receptionist, came out from the reception cubicle and hugged her.

"Girl, where you been?"

She caught Lydia up on everything. Not much had changed. There hadn't been enough heat in the winter, but at least the air conditioner was working now. And the clinic director was trying to convince Irma Bradley to let a new volunteer help her fill out a questionnaire.

"Dr. Pillai should know better," Lydia said. "You know Mrs. Bradley's particular about her business."

"Ain't she though?" Gretchen said. "I was scared for that volunteer, 'cause Mrs. Bradley don't play!"

They grabbed hands and laughed real loud. Then someone called her name, and there she was: Ailey. Her baby sister, all grown up. Curly hair cut to her shoulders and blow-dried. Still big-boned, but the plumpness had settled into curves.

Lydia was ashamed of what Ailey saw: a young woman who'd aged tremendously. Lydia's eyes shot through with red, skin riddled with acne, one tooth missing from the front. She raised a hand to cover her mouth, but Ailey pulled it away. She placed her sister's palm on her cheek, and Lydia was grateful she wasn't high.

———

When Ailey found her, even the ghetto seemed cleaner. There was hope now. And love and family and company. The kindness of others who weren't her blood was no longer a burden. She had introduced Ailey to the people she spoke to in the neighborhood. The waitresses at Mr. Harris's restaurant, whose suspicious expressions gave way to surprise. This was Lydia's sister, for real? They didn't favor at all, but as time passed, people in the neighborhood began to remark, they held their mouths alike. And when they talked, it sounded like the same person.

Seven years away from Chicasetta was a long time, and though Daddy had relayed some of the information, he'd never remembered the same details that Ailey did about Chicasetta, the family drama and chronicles that occupied Lydia's imagination. Who else had died since Dear Pearl had passed away? Who was married? Who had given birth? She smiled when Ailey confessed that she'd had a summer fling years ago with her old playmate, the boy everybody had called Baybay, though her sister referred to him by his government name. They hadn't gone all the way, but it had come close.

"I bet that guy's still sweet on you, though."

Ailey laughed. "Oh, I doubt it! That's been so long ago. We were just kids, and he's engaged now."

"That don't matter. Who could ever get over you?"

On the days that Ailey volunteered at the clinic, they met for lunch at Mr. Harris's restaurant. They squeezed into the same side of the booth and ate from the same plate. After the clinic was closed for business, they would sit on the stoop, and Irma Bradley would sit with them. They'd listen to her stories of the husband who had cheated but not deserted, who'd come north with her from Mississippi, accompanied by cardboard suitcases and brown paper bags stained by the grease of fried chicken. But those two deep southerners had been disappointed by the coldness of people and weather. That the bugs in the City weren't as large as the ones in Mississippi, but seemed more sinister because nobody had said, y'all they got roaches up in the City, too.

Autumn, and a chill that settled into the tailbone, and Lydia told Ailey, don't be sitting out on those steps, freezing her ovaries. Somebody had to give their mother grandkids, and Mr. Harris let the two sisters sit in the lobby. Technically, it was still the man's clinic, and since he vouched for Mrs. Bradley, she came inside as well.

Ailey balanced a takeout container on her lap. She moved a large piece of meat loaf in Lydia's direction. "Girl, eat that. You see I'm getting big."

"No, you ain't. That's just baby fat." Lydia took a morsel with her fork. "Um. That's good."

"How I'm gone have baby fat when I'm twenty-two years old?" She pushed Lydia's shoulder gently.

"'Cause you my baby."

"Hey, y'all." Mrs. Bradley sat down in a chair across, making a huffing noise.

"Good afternoon." The sisters spoke in tandem.

Lydia gestured politely with the fork. "Have some, Mrs. Bradley?"

"No thank you, darling. The doctor say I'm not supposed to eat no beef. Say it run my pressure up."

"You sure?"

"You go on 'head and eat that."

Mr. Harris came through the door. "Look at this! I need to take a picture! My brother's girls. Man, I miss Geoff." He began to talk about the old days, when he and the sisters' father had worn dashikis. He clapped his hands in mirth. "Geoff tried everything to get his hair nappy! One time, he washed his hair with Ajax and it turned green. He had to shave it down to the scalp."

"Oh, Jesus," Ailey said.

"I remember that man," Mrs. Bradley said. "I thought he was white, but then I seen him with your mama. When did he pass?"

"Last winter," Mr. Harris said. "It was sudden. He didn't suffer. Your sister called me and told me about the funeral. I didn't know until then."

"Coco called you?" Ailey asked.

"Yeah, but it was too late," he said. "I hate I—we—missed the service."

Ailey listed the attendees at the homegoing, saying the service had been lovely. The family from Chicasetta. Some folks from Red Mound. Her old playmates, Boukie Crawford and David James.

Nana wasn't there, though. She informed Lydia that their grandmother had had a stroke and couldn't travel long distances. Lydia didn't say anything.

"But it was a real nice service," Ailey said. "And there was a barbecue for the repast."

"Ooh, girl!" Lydia said. "Daddy would have loved that!"

"Yes, my brother was hung up on that swine," Mr. Harris said. "And it's just not good for you." He began quoting from a medical journal he'd borrowed from their father when he'd still been alive. Daddy had told Mr. Harris he was in excellent health, probably because he'd become a vegetarian.

Mrs. Bradley snorted. "You probably gone die early from all that lettuce. And ain't nothing wrong with pork. You just got to drain the fat, that's all."

Whenever the two elders debated, the sisters would lean back, exchanging discreet pokes, and back at Lydia's apartment, they marveled, older Black folks were the same everywhere you went, weren't they?

It had taken months for Lydia to let Ailey into her apartment, to the two rooms, the kitchenette, and bathroom. The thrift-store odds and ends. An old TV with an antenna. There was no cable for the television, but there was a bookcase filled with books. The antique sewing machine in its cabinet, covered by a length of blue satin, and Ailey asking, where had she found it? It looked just like Dear Pearl's.

"I know, right?" Lydia said. "I couldn't believe it when I found those at the thrift shop! White folks throw out the nicest things." She didn't want to tattle on their father, even though he was dead. That he'd sneaked out the sewing machine from their house and brought it to Lydia.

"Girl, this is cute!" Ailey said. "It's all, like, arty and stuff."

She could have anything in the refrigerator that she found, Lydia told her. There wasn't much, but she always kept water because she liked it cold. The same as Miss Rose, in a quart mason jar with a piece of plastic wrap over the top.

The bedroom was off-limits, unless Ailey had to pee. The first time she'd walked toward the closed door, Lydia had jumped from the couch and asked, where was she going?

When Ailey came out of the bathroom, Lydia was standing next to the bed. She knew that her sister had checked the medicine cabinet, that she'd lied about her bladder, and then flushed the toilet and ran the water while she did a quick search. Wasn't she a Garfield woman? But there was nothing in there but off-brand tampons up top, and some bleach and washing powder in the lower cabinet, along with a hot water bag and sanitary napkins the same brand as the tampons.

Lydia saw her sister scanning the living room and the kitchenette. She was wondering, where could the drugs be? But Ailey couldn't turn the apartment upside down, not right in front of her big sister. She didn't know that Lydia's hiding place was behind the armoire.

———

Some evenings, Lydia tried to teach Ailey to sew. If she learned a skill, it was hers forever. She'd never need to buy clothes again.

"What about my drawers?" Ailey asked. "I need to buy those, don't I?"

"Don't make fun. And you can make your own out of T-shirt material. Or you can get fancy and buy some silk."

"Like I'm really gone be whipping up some silk panties in my spare time."

"You are incorrigible." She pulled the test skirt from her sister's lap. "And that zipper is grinning."

"I'll do better on my drawers."

They laughed some more, and then Lydia pulled out *The Color Purple*. It was Ailey's turn to read aloud. There was nothing that had changed about Ailey's love, though she was no longer a girl. She still wanted to lie next to her sister on the couch, her feet resting in Lydia's lap. She still giggled at the portion in the book where Celie and Shug became lovers.

Then it was time for Ailey to leave. Their mother would be waiting, but she held on to Lydia tightly. Don't go away again, she begged. She stuffed a twenty-dollar bill into Lydia's hand. Just for emergencies, and Lydia tried not to clutch the money. Mr. Harris slipped money under her door every week, but it was starting not to be enough. Long ago, she had run out of keepsakes to pawn, and there were only so many dresses she could make.

But Ailey wasn't content with the two of them spending hours together in the tiny apartment. She wanted to bring Lydia home. She thought her strategy was subtle, but Lydia had helped to raise her. She knew every one of Ailey's tricks, like how she wiggled when she had a secret.

"Lydia?"

"Yes, baby?"

"I was just thinking. "

Lydia shifted on the couch. In a while, her need would come down. She didn't want to lose sight of the time.

"You know Christmas is coming up," Ailey said. "I just don't want you to miss it. Thanksgiving is already gone."

"We'll see."

The holidays came and went, but in the New Year, Ailey didn't surrender. She began to speak of Easter. There were three months to prepare for that season. Her sister should have some new clothes for the Resurrection. When the sun shone, but the air was still cold, Ailey drove them to Worthie's. She had insisted on their dressing up, like when their mother had brought them there as children.

Ailey flipped through the racks. "What size do you wear?"

"A four."

"How about this?"

"No, that's too expensive."

"I told you, I got it. And we're in the sale section." Ailey pulled out another dress. "What about this?"

Before Lydia reached out to finger the material of the dress, she wiped her hand down the seam of her suit pants. She touched the collar for the price tag.

"Unh-uh. No. This is way too much."

There were two white ladies a few feet away, touching dresses under the watchful gaze of an anxious-to-please saleslady. She had flicked her eyes to the sisters as they entered her sales zone minutes before, and then turned her back. The security guard perched on a stool in the corner was watching.

Lydia placed her pocketbook on top of a stack of shirts. In the corner, the guard put one of his feet on the ground. She withdrew her purse from the stack, clamping it in the space in her armpit, and the guard settled himself back on his tall stool.

"Please let me buy you something," Ailey said.

"Okay, baby sister, but I don't like it here. Let's go to the fabric store."

———

As the weeks passed, Ailey kept talking about Easter.

"Mama was talking about you the other day. About how much she missed you."

Lydia didn't speak.

"I didn't say I'd seen you, though. I wouldn't do that."

"That's good."

"But you know Easter is coming up," Ailey said. "I just don't want you to cancel, like with Christmas."

"I didn't cancel, baby. I never promised you I would come."

Politely, they had talked around it, the subject of her addiction. Lydia told her she wanted to be perfect for their mother. Clear her skin up. Put on some weight, and she tried to cancel Easter, the special day that Ailey had planned for her, buying the expensive jersey from the fabric store out in the suburbs, and a Vogue pattern for the new dress.

"Ailey, I'm not well. You know that."

"It doesn't matter. She won't care. Don't cancel again. Please."

Lydia shifted, pushing at her feet. "I gotta work on Mrs. Bradley's dress. You know how particular she is."

Ailey didn't respond, and settled in, though her sister's foot tapped nervously. She didn't want to go, to lose her sister to whatever was calling to her, but Lydia began shaking. She needed to answer that call. She had to, but at the door, Ailey dawdled. Covered the hand that stroked her face, the same way their mother touched.

"I'll see you next week, baby," Lydia said. "I love you."

"You sure?"

"How you sound? Of course I do."

"And I'll see you, for real?"

Lydia tried not to shake. She tried so hard, her teeth felt see-through.

"You sure will," she said.

"All right, now, don't have me looking for you like Celie at that mailbox."

Lydia laughed and gave a teasing push to Ailey's shoulder, a movement to steer into the hallway. The door closing in her sister's face, and then she ran to the armoire, reached her hand behind it, and pulled out her plastic bag.

———

On Easter Sunday, Lydia sat on her couch as Ailey knocked on the apartment door. She called Lydia's name, the hope leaching from her voice. She knocked a long time before she left.

Three days later, she appeared. She was sulking, like when she was a little girl. Lydia had stood her up, and that hadn't been nice. And Easter dinner had been real good. Their mother had made a big ham and so many sides and banana pudding for dessert, but Ailey had been too mad to bring leftovers by.

Lydia turned to her dependable tactic: she offered a secret. When Ailey had been a little girl, that had always chased her anger away. Lydia confessed that she hadn't run away. Their father had placed her in the apartment, and when Ailey turned her anger on him, Lydia told her, no, it wasn't cruelty on his part. Don't be mad at their father. He had done his best.

And Ailey should feel the same about Dante. She tapped her feet while she talked to Ailey about the love of her life. His kindness, how he had tried to protect her. That he hadn't broken up with

Lydia, but had been murdered, and he hadn't been the one who'd gotten Lydia hooked on drugs, either.

"I know you want to think that. But is that really true, Lydia? I mean, I'm sorry Dante died, but that doesn't make what he did right."

"No, listen! It's Gandee's fault, not Dante's!" Lydia hadn't meant to say it, but she couldn't let her sister talk bad about her husband. Maybe if Lydia finally told the truth her family would stop demonizing Dante. Their bad opinion of him hurt her almost as much as his death.

Her baby sister touched her hand. "No, you're confused, darling. Gandee has been dead for almost twenty years."

She spoke to Lydia as you did to a small child. Or an invalid. Or a dangerously insane person who was wielding a knife. There was no one who respected Lydia anymore. Not even this woman whom she'd taught to swim and taken to the bathroom as a toddler, and wiped her messy behind.

Lydia moved her hand. "I know Gandee's dead. I might smoke crack every day, but my memory is just fine." The old bear stirred in its cave. The animal she'd thought had frozen to death during that hard winter years before. "What I mean is, Gandee did something to me when I was a little girl. Something real bad."

"I know." Her sister's voice was gentle. "I heard you downstairs that day, when you came to Nana's. It happened to me, too."

Lydia shook her head, no, that couldn't be true, though the dread crawled through her. She had finally told the truth, as Dr. Fairland had counseled her to do, back in rehab, assuring her that telling the truth wouldn't be so bad, but here was Lydia's most beloved person in her small world, saying her sacrifices as a little girl had been useless. No longer a child, as Ailey smoothed her big sister's hair. Don't cry, this woman said. It would be all right.

"But he told me I was the only one!" Lydia said. "He told me I was special! And now you're telling me that I was quiet for nothing? That he hurt you, too? Oh my God. Oh Lord."

The light was dimming, the sign that her sister should go home.

Lydia didn't want her to leave, but her need was coming on, and strong. She didn't want to lose herself to what called her, but she couldn't help it, and she put on a smile to quell Ailey's concern. She told Ailey she would see her in a couple of days, and watched as her baby sister reached into the pocket of her jeans and pulled out a twenty. Lydia wanted to say, don't give the money this time, but she couldn't. She held on to the bill.

After Lydia closed the front door, she went to the armoire and pulled out the plastic bag, pipe, and lighter. She turned the ancient heater higher, but she was still cold, so she went back into the living room and pulled out a blanket from inside the armoire. In the bathroom, she piled towels on the fuzzy mat, sat on top, and wrapped the blanket around herself. She didn't feel anything with the first rock, so she smoked another, and then another until her supply was gone. But she wasn't frightened. Her sister had left the money on the table and Mrs. Bradley was coming the next day, so Lydia could fit her for a dress.

She lay back against the tub. She felt so nice but was annoyed that she'd left the cassette player on. She didn't remember turning it on. Something with drums was playing, and it kept running past the same loop. She got up, stumbling, and went into the living room, but she was wrong. The cassette player was unplugged, and now somebody was knocking at the door and they wouldn't stop. Calling her name, and she walked to the door, reminding herself, don't be rude to Mrs. Bradley. You couldn't yell at an old lady, not if you had home training.

When Lydia opened the door, there was a woman standing there in a ragged dress. And so much hair, well past her knees. How did somebody fix all that? Lydia didn't even want to think about this lady's complicated wash day.

"Yes, ma'am. May I help you?"

The long-haired lady didn't answer, she just took Lydia's hand. She led her to the staircase; Lydia looked down. Below her on the steps, she saw her great-grandmother, but Dear Pearl wasn't carrying her cane. She was young and her hair was black and pulled into a bun. She wore a yellow dress with buttons down the front and yellow shoes to match. Dear Pearl shimmied in the dress, giggling. She said she'd sewn this on her hands, and wasn't she looking fine?

At the bottom of the staircase, there was Dante in church clothes, saying, hey, baby, I missed you, and Lydia gave a cry. Her husband put his hand on the shoulder of her father, who had on his doctor's scrubs. Daddy waved at her, apologizing. He was sorry that he'd left so suddenly. But he was here because he'd missed Lydia so much. He'd come back to get his darling girl.

VIII

. . . need I add that I who speak here am bone of the bone and flesh of the flesh of them that live within the veil?

—W. E. B. Du Bois, *The Souls of Black Folk*

KEEPING THE TUNE

❖

My mother didn't feel it when her child died. There was no dream, no prescience in her spirit, and when the police informed her that a woman named Irma Bradley had found Lydia at the bottom of the stairs of the apartment building where she'd been living, the surprise hit my mother so hard that she fainted.

Lydia hadn't died from the fall down the steps, but from the series of seizures from the cocaine in her system, which had moved her into a short coma before her heart had stopped. Coco would explain that to us, after she went to the hospital and identified our sister's body. Lydia had kept a card in her bra with our parents' address, number, and names printed neatly on it. At some point, she had added my name beneath theirs in red ink: *And my youngest sister, Ailey Pearl Garfield.*

It was a spring morning when Lydia passed away, a morning that I was sleeping in. I didn't have volunteer work at the clinic, but I was planning to see my sister later in the day. I was sleep-logged, and when I came down the stairs, I was disappointed I didn't smell coffee. Then I saw my mother's head on my aunt's shoulder; her eyes were closed. I joked that the both of them were goofing off so early in the day, but my aunt shook her head.

"Darling, it's Lydia. She's gone, Ailey. She passed away."

I made a loud cry, and my aunt put her finger to her lips. She shook her head again and pointed at my mother. Not now. When we half carried Mama upstairs, she awoke, and I supported her while Aunt Diane pulled off her clothes, dropping them into a pillowcase. I held Mama steady as my aunt tugged a fresh nightgown over her head. Before she fell back asleep, Mama promised me she would be better tomorrow. Her voice was faint. She shuddered between words.

No mother expects to bury her child, and there was no funeral policy for Lydia, the daughter everyone had prayed would get better. Coco told me she'd solicited donations to bury our sister. It happened quietly, she said. Our Chicasetta relatives called each other behind Mama's back, and that collection paid for shipping the body down south. The pink casket, the flowers, and the repast. The gravestone, though no plot had to be purchased. Lydia would be buried in the old cemetery out on the farm, on the left side of our father's grave.

Miss Rose made the funeral arrangements with Mr. Cruddup, our family mortician. He'd been the one to bury my father and so many others in my family. He made Lydia look like a girl again, dressing her in the Easter outfit she'd made from the fabric I'd bought her. It was a small homegoing, with only relatives and friends: David was there with his fiancée, Carla. Boukie and Rhonda came, too. They had three children now. I'd called my college roommates, but only Keisha attended. I sat between Coco and her during the service. Melissa didn't come. Somebody had to stay in the City and be with our grandmother, because Aunt Diane wanted to attend the homegoing. She had loved my sister like her own daughter.

In our church, the men spoke, but I was too grieved to care about the sexism. I was happy I didn't have to say anything. I held Coco's hand throughout the service, as my mother's brother spoke for the family, tears streaming down his face. When it was Uncle Root's turn to speak, he pulled out index cards from the inside pocket of his jacket. But then he only stood there, clearing his throat, before abruptly stepping down the two steps from the altar. When he sat down on the pew, he covered his face with a handkerchief.

At the cemetery, I was surprised to see my other roommate's ancient hatchback: Roz hadn't been at the church. Another car had pulled up behind hers, and four more behind those. Women began to climb out from the cars, all of them dressed in white, with gloves and shoes to match. Dr. Oludara went over to the old man, and he moved into her arms. Roz headed right to my mother. She whispered something, and Mama nodded a few times. Then Roz and Dr. Oludara returned to the group of women in white.

Elder Beasley recited the final remarks, and then, a young woman I'd never seen walked to the grave. She was light-skinned, short and plump.

"God bless you all," she said. "I am so sorry for your loss. My name is Crystal Lightfoot—they called me Niecy back in college— and Lydia was my line sister and my best friend. When I heard the news about Lydia passing, I knew . . ." She paused. Took a few breaths. "I knew I had to be here with the rest of my sorors, to tell y'all that I loved Lydia so much. She was a good friend and a hard-working girl. You could always call on her in a time of need. We are Lydia's sisters of Beta Alpha Beta, and we want to honor her today."

Niecy reached for Roz's hand, and Roz reached for Dr. Oludara. The handholding continued, until the white-garbed women made a large circle. I'd kept my composure through Elder Beasley's words, but as these women began to sing of lilies and never-ending sister-hood, I emitted loud, guttural wails.

In my stupidity, I'd refused to wear black, thinking my sister might look down from Heaven and smile at me in my pretty pink dress and pink shoes. If it hadn't been for Coco and Keisha, I would have fallen in the red dirt and been stained, but they each held an arm. They whispered it was okay. It would be all right, as I fought their holding hands. Others began to scream: my mother, my granny, and Aunt Pauline. The noise ascended, but the women in white kept their tune.

The light shuttered: my sight dimmed, though it was a sunny day. I heard my sister's voice. It was Lydia, speaking to me. She was here, she told me. Don't worry, baby sister. She'd never leave me alone.

WHATEVER GETS YOU OVER

❖

I didn't stay long in Chicasetta after the burial. Only two days, before I climbed into Coco's car with my aunt and mother and headed up the interstate.

We didn't say much on the drive. I was afraid that if I began talking, I'd stumble into a story about years past, when a woman and her three daughters would pile into a station wagon in the early hours of the morning. The radio turned to a station that played Aretha, or if not, at least Earth, Wind & Fire. How Lydia would be sure to point out the Peach Butt in Gaffney, right around the time I would begin to hunger for the chicken that my mother had packed in a brown paper bag.

In the City, I called the clinic and left a message with the receptionist, who spoke to me tenderly. Everyone in the neighborhood had heard about my sister, and they were real, real sorry. Lydia had been so sweet; everybody had been hoping she'd get herself together. I tried not to cut the receptionist off. Already my heart was beating fast, and I huffed through my mouth for seconds. I told her I was taking a break for bereavement. I hoped I wasn't leaving them in the lurch, and she told me don't even worry. Take as much time as I needed.

Each night, I made to-do lists of what had to be accomplished the next day. I fueled myself for future purpose. I'd take a run on my father's funky treadmill, down in the basement. I'd clean my room, change my ripe sheets, and finally unpack my suitcase from Chicasetta—but each morning, I'd lie in bed frightened about greeting the day. I'd think about what I'd see when I unzipped my suitcase, the pink dress and pink shoes I'd worn to Lydia's funeral. I'd pull the covers over my face, so I wouldn't see the bed on the other side of the room. The place where my sister used to lie.

But I couldn't sleep. Not with Mama rustling through the house, asking my cousin Veronica, did she have her book bag? How many times had Aunt Diane told her if she put it in the big basket by the foot of the stairs, she'd always know where it was? And didn't Veronica know she should listen to her mother sometimes?

My only escape was when the phone rang. It would be the old man calling during the day, even before the rates went down. He wasn't worried about running up his telephone bill. What future was he saving his money for? He was going to spend like there was no tomorrow, because actually, there wasn't one for a man who was almost ninety.

"Sugarfoot, you should come down for a visit. You can stay as long as you like."

"You don't have to feel sorry for me."

"I don't, Ailey. I'm feeling sorry for myself. I really miss you."

"Uncle Root, are you turning soft on me?"

"I'm in my dotage. It makes me very emotional."

"You're going to live longer than me."

"No, I'm not, child. My time is coming. That's the cycle of life."

"Permission to speak freely?"

"Permission granted."

"Uncle Root, the cycle of life can kiss my natural, Black ass."

"There's the spirit!"

We'd talk for a few minutes until he told me, he guessed he should stop wasting my time. I was a young person and didn't want to spend all day talking to a senior citizen. He knew I had things to do.

The morning I finally came down for breakfast, Mama didn't make a big production. She handed me a cup of coffee, and asked, did I want grits? It was Aunt Diane's late morning at the counseling center. She'd already taken my cousin to school, and her first client wasn't until noon. She and my mother had their heads together as usual, but this time, it was their regular argument.

My aunt believed in deep breathing to dissipate anger. That's what she counseled her clients. She'd found that over the years, keeping one's mind calm really helped with anxiety, but Mama had different ideas about rage. You had to allow your anger to have its way, and cuss out folks who got on your nerves. Now that she was in her fifties, she was tired of being nice. So anybody that messed with her needed to know, it was the cuss-out or the get-run-over. And that's what my aunt should have done last Saturday, when she and Mama saw my uncle at the community flea market with that girl that was young enough to be his daughter.

"Diane, did I not tell you these nonconfrontational strategies don't keep a man in line? You should have cussed Lawrence out, like I told you to. And then kicked his ass right there in the flea market."

"Honestly, Belle, it wasn't that upsetting. I can't even remember her name."

"It was Cherise."

"Thanks for that."

"You need reminding because Lawrence is disgusting. That girl looked like she had her first period last year."

"She was of age, Belle. I'm pretty sure."

"Did you see that girl's birth certificate?"

"Belle, he's a free agent. We're divorced. Lawrence can do whatever he pleases."

"Y'all have two kids together. Two." Mama held up the peace sign, jiggling each finger. "That man won't ever be free of you. Plus, you're the best woman he's ever had."

Aunt Diane laughed. "Now, I can agree with that!"

"And you don't act free, going out to dinner with him. Coming in all times of the night. I hope you're using condoms with that hound dog."

"Belle, you're being inappropriate in front of my niece."

"She's a grown woman. She ought to know what a condom is, and if she doesn't, we got trouble."

"You know, I do feel sorry for Lawrence. A middle-aged man like that, rubbing against someone so young and pretty. Just imagine him putting on a condom in front of her."

"Imagine if his thing couldn't get hard in the first place." Mama laughed. "The man is over fifty years old!"

"Don't I know it?" My aunt giggled, holding her stomach, and I marveled at their rhythms. They were each other's true life mates, not like the husbands to whom they'd once pledged themselves, one dead and the other exiled.

"Ladies, I hate to break up an important discussion, but I've got a busy day. I'm back at the clinic today." I twirled in the dress I'd pulled from the back of my closet, a pastel blue that my mother had given me for Christmas. "How do I look?"

"Fierce!" Aunt Diane snapped her fingers, a gesture she'd learned from me.

"So nice, baby!" my mother said. "You've always been such a beautiful girl. I'm so proud of you."

As I left, I looked over my shoulder, hoping she wouldn't follow me. No, I was safe. She and my aunt were continuing their debate. I picked up the overnight bag I'd placed at the foot of the stairs.

At Zulu's Fufu, I picked up my free breakfast from a waitress who gave me sad looks. I hoped she wouldn't say something about Lydia. To distract her, I asked for more grits. Oh, and more turkey sausage, too.

The door to the café jingled, and Mr. Harris came through.

"Hey, Ailey!"

"Hey there, Mr. Harris."

"How your mama doing?"

"She's good."

"So when do you think you might give me the apartment keys?"

"Soon, Mr. Harris. Real soon. I just want to make sure the place is completely clean."

"I have a crew, Ailey. They can get all that."

I stepped to the door, calling, I would let him know. I'd call him, and it was so good to see him.

In the living room of Lydia's apartment, I pulled some clothes from the overnight bag. I changed my clothes and lay down on the couch, then remembered that I needed to hang up my work dress. I couldn't get it wrinkled. That would require an explanation, when I was supposed to be volunteering at the clinic two times a week. I put in my earphones and turned on my Walkman. I had three hours before my mother expected me to return home. As I lay there Lydia's voice came to me again.

Lying to your mama is wrong, baby, Lydia said. *You weren't raised that way.*

"I'm going to start back volunteering soon," I said. "So then it won't be a lie."

If you say so. Whatever gets you over.

"Leave me alone, please, Lydia."

I didn't talk out loud to her, only in my head. But I did turn up the music.

————

On the days that I didn't leave the house, I helped Mama with the housework, dusting the banister and using the special oil soap to mop the hardwood floors. I asked for the grocery list and drove to the farmers' market. There was a stall run by a young white guy with a waist-length ponytail. My mother told me he sold the freshest greens in town.

I thought my ruse was slick. I'd certainly fooled my mother, who smiled brightly the mornings I met her in the kitchen dressed for the clinic. She didn't approach me with accusations, to tell me her dreams had informed her that I was a lying, pitiful excuse for a daughter. But at a rare Sunday dinner at Mama's house, Coco cornered me in the kitchen, walking soundlessly behind me.

"Listen, how's everything going? I'm concerned about you."

I scraped my plate into the trash can. "No need for that. I'm fabulous."

"Ailey, no, you're lying to Mama."

"What're you talking about?"

"I know you're not volunteering. The director of the clinic called me looking for you."

I ran a soapy cloth over a plate. "I just haven't seen him. I guess he doesn't come in on the same days I do."

She pushed my arm roughly. "Do I have 'Boo-Boo the Fool' stamped on me?"

"I know you better stop putting your hands on me, unless you want a fight. I'm not scared of you."

In the dining room, our mother was telling a story about her brother Roscoe. How one morning their father had tried to make him get up early to work the fields, and Roscoe told him he didn't want to smell the ass end of no mule.

"Okay, Ailey. Okay. I'm sorry." Coco made our father's palms-down gesture. The nails on her small fingers were short and very clean. "It's just . . . it's been a month since Lydia passed. I'm just worried about you, girl. That's all."

"Worry about yourself! Worry about your own conscience. I know what you and Daddy were doing. Paying Lydia's rent. Keeping her away from us."

She blinked at me and screwed up her face. For once, I'd thrown her. "Ailey, is that what you really think of me? Daddy and I weren't keeping Lydia away. We were just giving her some time to get herself together, until she could come back home. And Mr. Harris let her stay in that apartment for free."

"Daddy told you that?"

"Yeah, he did. Said he'd wanted me to take care of Lydia if he ever got sick again, but she needed to go back into rehab. Get herself together. You can't enable an addict."

"So you left her there? Fuck you, Coco!"

I whispered my rage. Through the kitchen door, Mama's story voice was loud and holding laughter. She was still talking about Roscoe, before he'd gone to the chain gang. That boy had been a caution.

My sister's physician's reserve, the coldness, always seemed to fit her, but now her face was wet. "Fuck me, Ailey? No, I didn't leave her! I was paying her utilities, even though she wouldn't talk to me—"

"That's because you're so judgmental—"

"When have I ever judged either one of y'all? Why do you think

I sent you to that clinic when I knew Lydia lived in that neighbor-hood? I was hoping you would bring her home! I mean, it's not like you have a job or care about anybody but your damned self. I fig-ured I'd give you something useful to do, but of course, you fucked that up—"

"That is so mean and low-down—"

"You know what else is mean and low-down? That you don't do a goddamn thing for this family but take! Do you even know what I do for y'all? No, because you don't ask! I'm working thirty-six-hour shifts for my residency so I can pay for Nana's care! You think Med-icaid covers everything? Shit. My girlfriend can't even work a real job, because she's looking after that woman full-time, and who do you think paid for Lydia's funeral? I don't have a cent left in savings! And if it wasn't for Mr. Harris giving me the money to ship the body, we couldn't have even buried her down home! He wanted to pay for the funeral, too, but I was too embarrassed—"

"—you said you took up a collection—"

"—what else did you want me to do, Ailey? Ask you for six thou-sand dollars, plus shipping costs, and you don't even have a job?"

When I said nothing, she snorted.

"See? This is what I mean. You just took it for granted that the money would be there. And you know why? Because you're selfish—"

"That's not true! I was trying to bring Lydia home. I was giving it some time. Things were hard for her."

"Don't you think I know that?"

"No, Coco. Really hard. Like, Gandee hurt her. He molested her, like he did me."

I watched her face.

"You think that motherfucker didn't mess with me, too? Well, he did."

"Oh God, Coco."

"Don't you dare feel sorry for me! I'm fine! And you don't see me using Gandee as an excuse to sleep late and be lazy and eat up somebody else's groceries. And before you feel the need to trot around telling folks, you keep this shit to yourself. How you think it would make Mama feel? What's she supposed to do, go to Gandee's grave and cuss out his headstone?"

"I didn't say I would tell. I'm just telling you."

"Okay, so you did. Now get on with your life. Just try to make something of yourself, like I did. Not that anybody cares about me. You and Lydia, that's it. That's all Mama has ever paid attention to."

She picked up a plate from the counter, dumping bones and bits of greens into the scrap bowl. I walked quickly out of the kitchen, almost jogging. At the dining table, I filled my plate a second time. When I finished, I wanted banana pudding.

I kept eating another plate and bowl, one after the other, until I couldn't hold anything else inside. In the bathroom, I vomited in the toilet bowl. When the first wave came, I pissed through my under- wear. After I wiped down the floor of the bathroom, I sprayed some cleaner, leaned back from the fumes, and wiped again. I stripped off my clothes and underwear and looked in the mirror. My cheeks were red underneath the brown, my eyes puffed with tears. I started running the shower.

———

The next morning, I poked my head in the kitchen to tell my mother and aunt I was headed to work. No rest for the weary, and my mother smiled. She told me she was proud of her baby.

At Zulu's Fufu, I ordered my food. I just wanted to hurry back to Lydia's apartment. Eat my food quick, but Mr. Harris called my name from a booth in the back.

I gave him a neutral wave and he walked up to me.

"Ailey! What you know good, girl?"

"Hey, Mr. Harris."

He leaned in for a side hug. "And how your mama doing?"

"She's keeping, Mr. Harris."

"Come on back when you get your food. Sit with me a spell."

The waitress called my number and I went up to collect my

takeaways. I checked the path to the door, but knew there was no escape. I couldn't take a man's free food and dash.

I sat down in the booth, sighing. "Well, Mr. Harris, I should go soon—"

"And so, how are you doing?"

"Me? I'm doing great!" I scrunched up my mouth in what I hoped was a perky manner. I flicked a glance over at his food. There was a pool of melted margarine in the middle of his cheese grits. Mr. Harris made humming noises in between bites. I heard his foot tapping under the table, like a baby tasting his first solid food.

"This is so delicious, Ailey. You should eat."

"I just came to pick up something."

I patted the top of my plastic bag. I hoped he caught my drift, but Mr. Harris began to talk about the past, when my father and he had worked for the movement. My mother was young then, and so beautiful. And although she was a new mother, she had volunteered in the early days, before the center had become a clinic. Boy, she sure could cook! Mr. Harris never tasted food so good before or since. He'd looked for a woman like that his whole life, but never could find one. God broke the mold when He made Belle Garfield. That was a good woman, right there.

"Your father was my brother, Ailey. And I love you and your sisters like you were my nieces."

"And we appreciate you, too, Mr. Harris." I tried not to sound impatient.

"You don't understand. Your father brought your sister to me when things got bad. I was supposed to look out for her, but I failed my brother, Ailey. I failed your mama, too, and she doesn't even know it."

He put his fork down. Turned his head briefly, recomposing.

"Mr. Harris, it's all right. You did your best."

"No, it's not. But I'm not going to fail your parents again. Ailey, it's been months now, and you haven't packed up that apartment. I'm giving you another week, and then, I'm changing the locks—"

"But Mr. Harris—"

"And it's not about the rent, either. I don't need that money. I got plenty, but Ailey, this neighborhood is not a good place for you. And I don't want to see you leave like your sister. Lydia was a sweet girl. A good girl. She was just caught in a bad situation." He reached into his back pocket, lifting his hips. When he put the money in my hand, I saw the top of Benjamin Franklin's head peeking out. I tried to give it back, but he pushed my hand away. "Go on, now. You take that. And if you ever need anything else, anything at all, you got my number. And the same goes for your mama. You tell Belle I'm always here."

Mr. Harris picked up his fork and dug back in. He had a blob of grits on his chin, and it moved up and down as he chewed. I sat back and thought of the cold food I didn't want to eat anymore.

When I walked over to Lydia's apartment, I don't believe I wanted to die. I only was tired of not sleeping, lying in the dark cuddled against the old childhood comforter that no longer fit. I just wanted to close my eyes and have it count.

But I did take the switchblade Mama had given me out of my pocketbook. She'd wanted me to have it when I started volunteering at the clinic. Just in case, she'd said. Uncle Root had given it to her long ago, back when she was in college. I lined the tub with towels I'd found in Lydia's corner armoire and took two codeines saved from the last prescription my father had written me for my period. I pulled the bedspread off my sister's bed and dragged it to the living room. When the high kicked in, that would be my signal to head to the bathroom. To start.

On the TV, a daytime talk show. There was a debate between Ms. Talk Show Host and Today's Guest, one of those paramilitary types who wore a jacket with epaulets on each shoulder. He insisted that we were under siege from illegal outsiders. If deported, they would return to the U.S.A., so the government should capture them. Relocate them to less populated areas of the country. That way, the jobs they were stealing, picking lettuce and tomatoes and other sandwich fixings, would be freed up for real Americans.

Ms. Host had on the red silk-linen suit I'd seen on sale at Worthie's.

Or, it looked exactly like it, marked down from fifteen hundred dollars to two hundred ninety-nine. Had Ms. Host bought her suit off the rack? Wealthy as she was, did she shop for sales?

"The American government has planned this sort of endeavor before, but they tabled that proposition," Today's Guest said. "Now it's time to reconsider."

Ms. Host was silent, raising her eyebrows in her customary *I'm listening* expression.

Today's Guest took out a laser pointer, aiming the red dot at the large map that appeared in the space behind the couch. The dot settled on what seemed to be Montana.

"This area up here isn't that heavily populated. Big-sky country and quite beautiful. With a bit of maneuvering, this could be an enclosed living area for those groups I'm talking about. Of course, there'd have to be peacekeeping forces on-site."

In the audience, people murmured as Today's Guest sat onstage, wearing a beatific smile. Before the break, Ms. Host reminded everyone that tomorrow's show featured chefs from three-star Michelin restaurants. One would be cooking seafood crepes. Ms. Host had recently returned from the Caribbean, where she'd bought an entire island, and let her tell you, the ocean was so blue and the seafood had been fresher than fresh!

The screen went to a commercial for laundry detergent. Another for disposable diapers starring a baby so adorable, my womb hurt looking at her crawling across a wood floor. The woman hired to play her mother urged her on.

"And we're back!" Ms. Host said. "Before the break, Today's Guest explained his plan to relocate all undocumented immigrants to Montana."

There were thirteen minutes left, minus commercials. Ms. Host went in for the kill.

"I believe your so-called relocation plan is a redo of the Trail of Tears, which didn't work too well for the Native Americans, now did it? And President Lincoln's initial idea for shipping all the slaves back to Africa was scrapped as well. Don't you understand this is a ridiculous proposal?" The noise coming from Ms. Host could be a laugh. She tussled it into subjugation, but the audience was her chuckling proxy. As ever, they were on her side.

Today's Guest looked at Ms. Host severely.

"No, I don't. This is an excellent plan. I would think you of all people could see its merits. I can explain, if you keep an open mind."

By the time the credits rolled, I was whirling from codeine: it took a few attempts before I could rise from the couch. In the bathroom, I stripped down to my underwear and sat in the empty bathtub. I opened the straight razor, but then I dozed off.

When I awoke, I was standing in the creek, down in Chicasetta, and the long-haired lady sat on the bank, my friend from my bed-wetting days. She spoke, but I couldn't understand her, until Lydia appeared beside her.

"She says, 'My, you've grown, my daughter.'"

"Is that you, Lydia?" I asked. "Or is the codeine just that good?"

"Yes, baby sister, it's me. I'm here."

I hurried out of the water toward her. We embraced, and she touched my face. Don't cry, she said. Sit with her a spell, and I settled on the creek bank, between my sister and the long-haired lady. The plantation house was in the distance, tall and ghostly and unburned.

A basket appeared in the creek and floated up to the bank. It was filled with corn. The long-haired lady passed us the ears. She began to shuck, and my sister and I mirrored her, our fingers making a trance as we filled the basket.

There were catfish swimming in the water, fat, bold with switching tails. The long-haired lady walked into the water and began to throw the creatures upon the bank.

"I'm so hungry," I said. "When can we eat?"

"Don't you remember?" Lydia asked. "We have to clean those catfish first. Do you have a knife?"

I showed her the switchblade.

"I can let you borrow it," I said. "But I'll need it for later."

"No, Ailey. Once I take the knife, you can't have it back. Are you sure you want to give it to me?"

I was craving fish, fried and crispy. I wanted to swallow until I split open. I handed Lydia the switchblade, and she passed it to the long-haired lady, and then my sister told me wake up. Open my eyes and step out of the tub. Come home.

I NEED MY OWN CAR

◈

That June morning, Mama and I sat on the corduroy couch in the basement. She was preparing for our annual trip to Chicasetta and gossiping about our family. She'd made her two piles of laundry, one for clean and one for dirty. One the other side of the basement, the washing machine was humming.

"Mama, I'm taking my own car to Chicasetta."

"What kind of sense is that? Two folks driving separately to the same place? That's just a waste of gas money."

"I have some emergency funds. And Uncle Root told me I could stay with him. He needs somebody to drive him."

"You're only going to be there two months. I can take him if he needs to go somewhere."

"What if you're gone visiting?"

She looked at me. Her eyes narrowed. "Ailey Pearl, what is this about?"

That's when I let her know, I was moving down south with Uncle Root. He'd already invited me, and I'd already said yes. And before she brought it up, I'd quit my volunteer job at the clinic and the old man had sent me the money to get my car serviced.

Without sniffing, Mama threw a shirt in the clean pile. Then she stomped up the basement stairs. For the rest of the week, she barely spoke to me. She placed my breakfast plate on the kitchen table and took her oatmeal and coffee to the dining room, where my aunt and cousin would join her. Saying, I'm sorry, please excuse me, when she encountered me on the stairs. She didn't go on her morning walks. Instead of the tracksuits, she wore a series of clean housedresses and slippers. She took the curlers out of her hair but didn't comb the rows.

Her usual allies stayed out of it. Aunt Diane wore a disappointed expression but said nothing, and if my sister detected a skirmish, she didn't show it when she stopped by the house. Since our argument, Coco and I had only given each other the barest of greetings. Sometimes less than that: we only raised our eyebrows at each other. But the day before I was due to leave, she cornered me again.

"Hey, girl," she said.

I threw the sponge in the kitchen sink, spraying water. "Here we go—"

"No, wait! I don't want any trouble. I just wondered if I could take you out for coffee tomorrow morning?"

"I can drink coffee here, Coco."

"I know, but I'm buying. Please?"

———

The place where I met my sister was only a few blocks away from Nana's house. It was a new establishment, and semi-fancy. Their version of breakfast consisted of muffins of all kinds. It was the kind of place that Aunt Diane would have loved.

My sister and I sat there with our giant blueberry muffins and cups of overpriced coffee. Coco brought up the weather. It was hotter than usual. The electric bill at Nana's would be sky-high at the end of the month.

"Look," I said. "I'm headed out early tomorrow morning and I still need to pack. Say what you need to say, so I can go."

"You're mad at me, aren't you?"

"Hell yeah, I am." I took a bite of my huge muffin. It was free and delicious, so this wouldn't be a total loss.

"I'm really sorry. I didn't mean to talk that way to you. I just snapped when you said what you did about Lydia. And I'm always going to be hurt over what Gandee did. I tell Melissa that all the time."

"You told her about him?"

"She's my lady. I wasn't going to keep it from her. She had to know, sometimes, I'm gone flip out. Other shit, too. And I went into therapy."

"I still don't know how you stand living with Nana. I can't even go to Sunday dinner at her house."

"I guess being a doctor helps. You get used to putting things into boxes. I look at Nana like a patient. Her long-term memory is shot, but sometimes, yeah, I do want to cuss her out."

I laughed. "You did a pretty good job of that with me. I deserved it, though."

"No, you didn't. I was taking stuff out on you, like I'm really broken up about Lydia. Melissa was so mad at me when I told her. She said, we should be coming together, not cussing at each other."

"I knew I liked her."

Coco smiled. "She'll do."

My sister wasn't a big talker, so I thought that was it. I was reaching for my pocketbook when she told me, wait a minute. Let's stay awhile longer.

"Ailey, I'm so sorry about back in the day. When we were little, I mean. How I hit you when you told me what Gandee did."

"You were just a little girl, Coco."

"I know, but I should've been taking better care of you. I don't know why I believed him when he said I was the only one."

"It wasn't up to you to take care of me. Our parents should have done that—"

"—they didn't know, Ailey—"

"—I know they didn't. I know that. But still, they were the adults in charge. You act like you were grown back then, but you're only four years older than me."

"My therapist said the same thing. And I was getting up the nerve to tell Mama what Gandee did, but then Daddy died. And then Lydia died, too. I just don't want Mama to hurt anymore."

"I know. I feel the same way. But at least you took back something. You went your own way. I feel like my whole life I've been watching this family from the outside. Just trying to stay out of trouble, but I never knew what I wanted. I mean, besides being a good girl. I just didn't want to be bad. I just didn't want to feel dirty."

"Who cares if you're a good girl, Ailey? Or nice or moral or whatever? I know I don't. If there's anything I learned from what happened to Lydia, it's that you never know the hour or the day."

"You sound like Miss Rose."

"She's right."

"You don't understand, Coco. You're the perfect one. You've always been that way."

"Ailey, I'm a dyke! I sleep with women!" She leaned over the table. Lowered her voice and chuckled. "Let me stop being so loud before these white folks call the police. But yeah, I hid that shit for years, thinking about, what is Mama gone say if she finds out I'm a lesbian? I knew Daddy wouldn't care, but you know how religious she is. So I was scared of my personal life. Even scared of the dark. You know that until about a year ago, I couldn't even sleep with the lights off? I could cut somebody's chest wide open, hold their heart in my hand, and not even tremble. But I couldn't lie in my own bed and sleep in the dark. Does that shit sound perfect to you?"

"I guess not."

"But I just had to say, fuck it. I gave Gandee the first part of my life. I'm not gone give him the rest."

Coco inched her hand toward the middle of the table. Then some more, until she covered my fingers. We didn't say anything for a while, until I told her, all right, now, let's not get mushy. Too late, she said. She smiled and held my hand some more.

————

The next morning, the ritual started off familiarly. I woke earlier than the rest of the house. But unlike times past, my mother had not beat me to the kitchen. The kitchen was dark and there was no breakfast on the table, no pot full of fresh-brewed coffee in the machine. I took my time fitting my bags into the trunk of the car, but she did not meet me outside, clutching her housecoat. I was on my own as I drove off.

On the interstate, I was afraid, though I had the credit card Uncle Root had ordered in my name, with a line of five hundred dollars. A calling card, too, with fifty dollars' worth of minutes. I'd memorized the journey south, but it was dark, and before the dawn cracked, I put in a CD and sang along with Chaka Khan. She assured me that I was a woman. Anything I wanted to do, I could.

I stopped for a long lunch, ordering twice as much food since I hadn't eaten breakfast. I drank a pot of coffee. Hours later, in Gaffney, I heard my dead sister's voice.

"It's the Peach Butt!" Lydia said.

There was no one in the car but us, so I spoke to her out loud: "I know! We're almost to the Georgia state line."

"Don't forget to stop for a watermelon for Miss Rose. And be sure to thump it on the side. You know she can't stand bad fruit."

When I pulled into my granny's driveway, I tooted the horn. Then I struggled out of the car with the watermelon. Miss Rose and Uncle Root stood and waved. The old man didn't hop down, but his step was still spry, and he held my granny's hand as she huffed down the steps.

My mother remained on the porch in the rocking chair: somehow, she had beaten me to Chicasetta. At dinner, she didn't say much, and when her brother stopped by, he gave me only a quick hug, before telling me, he'd heard I wasn't working.

"Ailey, you can't be living up on people," Uncle Norman said. "If you ain't got no husband and no children, you need to be working. Post office always hiring. That's a good job, too. Benefits and everything. But you need to go to med school. That's what you need. It's some good credit in doctoring."

Mama nodded along, unbothered that she was joining with her brother to shame me. She was my mother. She was supposed to be on my side, but the way her head bobbed, she seemed to have forgotten that.

The old man balled his paper napkin and placed it on the table. He grunted as he rose. His joints were so angry, he told us. He could feel his age today.

"Sugarfoot, can you walk me to my pecan tree? It's still light, but I might need a young shoulder to rest on. I don't want to trip on anything."

Uncle Root walked slowly through the house, but when we closed the screen door and walked down the porch steps, he strode ahead. Stop dawdling, he called. I was too young to be so slow. At the pecan tree, he told his story, which had changed. This time, Jinx Franklin had punched him first, before Uncle Root pushed him to the ground.

The next morning, my mother called the old man's house, and I told her he and I had plans. I'd call her later in the week, but the next morning, she called again. I told her I didn't have time to see her. I stopped answering the old man's phone when it rang, and when he called my name, saying my mother was on the phone, I'd tell him I was reading.

I never did call her back, though I'd see her in church. After service, I'd hug my granny and then walk to the other side of the fellowship hall to avoid Mama. She'd look over at me, her face painted with an aggrieved expression, as if I'd done something awful. I'd breezily wave at her, and she'd turn her back.

In July, I drove the old man out to the farm and dropped him off at the family reunion, though he asked me to reconsider. Didn't I want to see anybody? My mother had been asking about me, and David and Carla were coming. Surely, I wanted to sit with the young folks a spell.

"No, I'm good," I said.

"Ailey, this thing between you and Belle has got to stop. The both of you are still grieving. You need to cling to each other, instead of fighting."

"I don't know what you're talking about. She's the one spreading my business around the family. Telling Uncle Norman I'm some kind of derelict. I'm tired of her bad-mouthing me."

"She's just worried about you, Ailey. You know, she's lost one daughter. Can't you understand her being a little overprotective?"

"More like over bossy. She doesn't need to worry about me! I'm twenty-four years old! I'm grown."

Uncle Root sighed. "All right. I'll call you when I'm ready to go. Do you want me to pack you a plate?"

"Yes, and can you put me some ribs in there? Like, five? Oh! And some sweet potato pie and pound cake? And some greens? And some macaroni and cheese."

"You could pack your own plate if you came to the party."

"No, I'm not even that hungry."

All summer, I avoided my mother, but in August, she didn't call the house before she stopped by. The old man called up the stairs. There was somebody to see me, and there was Mama, in her T-shirt and jeans, looking almost like a girl. She'd made a pie. Did we want a piece? and Uncle Root said, hot dog, he was never going to turn down pie. She stayed a long time, until the sun went down. Then the old man said he believed he'd go upstairs and do some reading.

Mama and I stood there awkwardly, until I said, did she want to go sit outside? I picked up two church fans from the foyer table, and we sat on the glider, waving at mosquitoes. She told me that she had gotten reconciled. Every child needed to be independent, and she knew that the old man and I were thick. He needed somebody and so did I. We could keep each other out of trouble.

"I'm leaving tomorrow, baby," she said.

"You can stay a little longer," I said. "You can even stay, like, forever. You know you're surely welcome."

"No, I can't leave Coco by herself."

"She's got Melissa."

"You know Melissa's people are in Detroit. So the both of them need me. And maybe I can convince one of them to have a baby."

I laughed. "How didn't I see this coming!"

"Somebody gone have me some grandkids! Now, y'all need to decide who gone do it."

Mama nudged me, and I giggled.

"But can I call you sometimes, Ailey? I mean, I know you don't want to be bothered and everything."

"Aw, Mama, don't say that! You know I always want to hear from you."

———

When the summer ended, the days crawled, even slower than when I was a child. I had no sisters to keep me company. My former playmates were grown and had mates. Even the town seemed smaller, the sides of the streets pushed together.

There was only so much visiting that one could do. The walks over to Miss Cordelia's house. The drives out to the country to see my granny. Church on Sunday at Red Mound. After I made our simple dinner of baked chicken or warmed-up leftovers from Miss Rose's big Sunday spread, the old man and I would talk quietly in the evenings, discussing the news or the books that we were reading. There was a peace that I didn't know that I'd craved.

On odd Saturdays, I drove with the old man to Atlanta and met up with David. Carla and he were married now, and they had an apartment in Buckhead. While David studied for the bar exam, she was the breadwinner, working as a high school teacher. She'd be on maternity leave soon, though: she was pregnant with their baby. The neighborhoods in the southwest area of the city had more Black folks, and the real estate was cheaper, but the crime was too much. The thieves had become too bold.

David would ask his wife along to our arty film, rubbing on her round belly.

"I don't like to leave you alone," he said. "What if something happened?"

"Nothing's going to happen," Carla said. "Y'all go on. I'm going to put my feet up. Enjoy my quiet time while I can."

But she would extend an invitation to the old man and me for a late lunch. After the movie, simple sandwiches, potato chips, and dip, all that David knew to make in a kitchen. David offered to barbecue chicken on the hibachi on their patio, but Uncle Root told him, don't go to all that trouble.

The old man and David would banter through their debate on W. E. B. Du Bois and Booker T. Washington, laughing and teasing. I'd crunch on my potato chips and look at Carla in her classy maternity outfits, her fingers long and elegant, even in pregnancy. Her brown face roundly angelic. She always wore lipstick and eyeshadow.

Carla didn't seem threatened by me, and I was relieved, instead of resentful. I was over David now. My childhood really was past, and he had indicated the same. He didn't act uncomfortable around me, but he was no longer flirtatious. At the movies, the old man sat between us. And in the apartment that he shared with his wife, David didn't avoid speaking about the past, but he always included a third person in his narrative. Remember that time I got him and Boukie whipped? Or, remember that time we three went to Dr. Hargrace's pecan tree and he told us he was almost lynched?

David's little girl was born in October. If the weather was fine, he'd take a break from his studying and drive his small family to Red Mound. The baby—Brittany—decked out in her lace dress with petticoats underneath. She was good-natured, either sleeping or cooing through the first half of service. It was only in the second hour that she started protesting, and Carla would take her outside. I would sit on the front steps of the church, talking to Carla as she breastfed the baby, covering herself with a light blanket. I'd ask, did she need anything? Was there something she wanted from her car? Then there would be the strains of the final hymn, the signal that service was ending. We heard David's grandfather singing off-key, and always, Carla and I would laugh. Mr. J.W. couldn't sing worth nothing. When he died in January, I felt guilty for making fun of him.

Like my great-grandmother's homegoing, Mr. J.W.'s funeral was held in the gymnasium of the old high school that my mother had attended. The difference was that Mr. J.W.'s obituary listed a colorful account of his life, such as when he'd been a younger man, he had run the road. He'd chased women and drunk more than his share of liquor. Even after he'd been a deacon, his behavior had been disgraceful. But that was when he'd been "in the world," before the Lord had spoken to Mr. J.W. and he'd truly been saved, not just by the words of his mouth, but by his deeds.

I was familiar with this testimony; Mr. J.W. had been giving it in church since I was a little girl, though I hadn't understood the significance of it back then. Someone had written down one of his testimonies, presumably word for word. It appeared beside a picture of him in his golden years. He had worn his hair on the longer side, though it was pure white. In the picture, it flowed from underneath his favorite stingy brim, the one with the blue feather in the band.

At the service, there were no shocking revelations, as I'd seen at other Chicasetta funerals. No secrets decked out in scarlet, because Mr. J.W. didn't have any mysteries. He had five grown children with Miss Jolene, but also five outside children, from the times he'd stepped out, before following the Jesus-lit path. His widow was a forgiving woman. Miss Jolene made no distinction between any of her dead husband's outside progeny: they were listed on the obituary, along with their three mothers. These women were labeled "beloved friends of the deceased."

I sat two rows back from the family, and my heart loosened at the sound of David weeping. He had been his grandfather's close companion, learning to fish and hunt with him. My mother had flown down, and at our small repast table, she and my granny whispered about Mr. J.W. Look at all these kids he had, and only half of them by Miss Jolene. She sure had been a patient woman, and sweet, too, inviting these heifers he'd cheated with to the funeral.

Like that one at that table across the room. Hadn't Miss Jolene burned Mr. J.W. with grits over her? That woman sure had gained some weight. Remember that fine frame she used to have? That body had gone to Glory, same as Mr. J.W. And no wonder: the woman was on her third plate. Looked like her arches had fallen, too.

They tried to include Uncle Root in their gossip, but the old man said his name was Bennett, and he wasn't in this mess. He kept his eyes on his plate while he munched the repast.

"Goodness, this chicken is delicious! Somebody stuck a foot in this, right up to the ankle."

"Root, you know I fried that chicken," my granny said. "You just trying to change the subject!"

Indeed, he was, because he was too old for gossiping about folks. Thus far, in his ninety years, Uncle Root had escaped catching a pot of grits, and here they were, trying to get him killed, when he was past his prime. And could somebody get him some more chicken, please, put a roll on the plate, and then let him eat it in peace?

My mother and my granny giggled, holding hands, and I tried not to laugh. I put my arm around his shoulders, and he said at least he had me. I would keep him safe from these two troublemakers.

SHOWER AND PRAY

◈

A few days after Mr. J.W.'s funeral, Uncle Root received his annual invitation to Founder's Day at Routledge College. It had been two years since I graduated, and Roz had kept me up on the news about my classmates. Some had continued their studies, while others were working full-time jobs. A third of my graduating class were married, and when I thought about running into any of them, my extended vacation didn't seem so wonderful anymore.

I tried to talk the old man out of going to Founder's Day, but he put his foot down. He told me I had nothing to be ashamed of. I was grieving two deep loves. People needed to understand that, and as for him, he wasn't a young man anymore or even middle-aged. He'd promised himself not to miss another Founder's Day. He didn't know how much time he had left, and the last time he'd skipped had been the year that Rob-Boy Lindsay had died.

"You know I hate when you talk about dying," I said.

"Are you feeling guilty?" he asked. "Because that is the purpose of this macabre conversation."

On campus, nothing had changed. At the gate, the pots of camellia shrubs burst with pink blooms, and as I steered around the long driveway, the sprinkler system, timed to waste water, kept the grass thick and green. We parked and walked past students in their jeans and T-shirts. I was only twenty-four, but I felt ancient. Had I ever looked this unfinished? This new?

When we arrived in the chapel, the old man wouldn't stop waving. There were his former students. His colleagues. He was the only one left in the class of 1926, but he'd taught so many who sat in the pews. Dean Walters. Mrs. Giles-Lipscomb. Dr. Oludara. Half the history department and a third of English and biology. I'd forgotten that he was more than my great-great-uncle. He'd given three-quarters of his life to this college, to most of the people sitting in this room, and I'd tried to keep him away from his other kin. All because I was unemployed and embarrassed.

Dr. Oludara didn't hide her joy at seeing me. In the faculty dining room, she trotted over. I tensed, then tried to fix my face. To get my lie straight, in case she asked me, what was I doing these days? Was I going to make something of myself? But she only hugged me, and I sniffed the familiar, smoky odor of her incense.

"Belinda, have you finished that book yet?" the old man asked.

"Dr. Hargrace, you know better than to ask. My nerves are so bad!"

"You better get on it," he said. "I heard through the grapevine that Yaw Abeeku person is shadowing your every move, trying to get his book finished before yours."

"Yes, he is! Fortunately, he has no manners. Do you know when he was on St. Simons Island, he tried to haggle over prices with the basket ladies?"

"No!"

"Dr. Hargrace, yes, he did!"

"Does that man not understand that we Negroes don't haggle on this side of the ocean?"

"Well, you know, Abeeku is from Ghana, but he was trained in the British system. And that sense of entitlement is so strong. I have the same problem with my Femi, though I've almost broken him down."

"Belinda, you're so funny!" The old man threw back his head.

"But I don't know what to do in the fall, once my sabbatical is over. I can only threaten to leave so many times to get a course release. I'll be back teaching and still running the department. I really need a research assistant. It's just too much."

"That is such a coincidence. Because Ailey was just telling me the other day, she really needs a job. Weren't you?"

"Sir?" I asked. "Excuse me?" I had only been half listening. Scanning the room and making sure none of my former classmates were here. Roz had told me the gossips reported that Abdul Wilson had showed to campus to haze Gamma hopefuls. The last thing I needed was to run into him.

"I said, Ailey, I was just telling Belinda here that you were look-ing for a job."

"I am?"

"Yes, sugarfoot. You are. You said you really need a job because you're bored." The old man patted my shoulder, his smile sweet. Ca-joling, but I'd seen his charm on display enough times to know that I was being played.

"This is such luck!" Dr. Oludara clapped her hands and the brace-lets sang. She couldn't pay me too much, she told me. Only gas money plus fifty dollars a week, and Uncle Root told us he thought he saw some of his former students across the room. He would leave the two of us to work out the details.

As he walked away, I threw invisible darts at his tweed-covered back. Damn that old man's time. I should have known this was a trick.

————

As chairperson, Dr. Oludara had access to two offices. Her adminis-trative office was large and neatly pristine. The other, smaller office was down the hall, and that's where she kept her research materi-als. When we'd talked on the phone, she'd told me that, as her re-search assistant, it would be my job to organize the books and articles that she'd collected.

Early that Monday, Dr. Oludara gave me a key to the smaller of-fice, and told me she'd check on me at lunchtime. She'd paid for a semester meal ticket in the refectory, in case I didn't want to bring lunch from home.

When I opened the door of the office, there was a space about three feet square that was free of clutter. I walked inside and shut the door behind me. The clean portion of the floor was sparkling with sunshine that came from the window. As for the rest of the floor, it was taken over by banker's boxes. Many, many banker's boxes. On one wall, a tall bookshelf coughed out stacks of books and papers. Along the adjacent wall, a table covered with other stacks, along with small wooden boxes filled with blank index cards. I was being paid less than minimum wage to organize all this shit.

There was a phone on the table, and I picked it up. Uncle Root was going to hear about this, but when I dialed "9" to get an outside line, I was informed that I needed a code to make a long-distance call.

Dr. Oludara knocked on the door. When I didn't answer, she opened the door slowly.

"I'm very sorry. I know it's a mess. You're not going to quit on me, are you? Please don't quit." She sounded like a little girl.

"This is a lot. Like, a whole bunch."

"Can I buy you a plate of ribs for lunch? Would that help?"

"Sure. Okay."

I didn't do any work that day. I stuffed myself with too many ribs, French fries, and white bread, and then I drove back home early.

At the old man's house, he raised his eyebrows and made a production of looking at his watch, but I sighed as I flopped beside him on the settee. I complained for an hour, until Uncle Root stopped me. Every job had its problems, but I'd committed to Belinda Oludara, and I couldn't back out now. He'd promised her that I'd stay on for six months, and if I did the math, that was twelve hundred dollars plus the money for my mileage. Think of what I could buy for myself with all that money. Also, I would embarrass him greatly if I quit, and it might cause him to have a heart attack and keel over from stress.

The next morning, I was sitting in the middle of the office floor when Dr. Oludara came in. She made enthusiastic noises—how happy she was, how grateful she was—but I didn't answer. I made a show of dumping boxes of their contents, until she told me she'd let me get back to work. As I made my way through the mess, I was amazed to realize that the woman that I'd been in awe of back in college had horrible organizational skills. There weren't any file folders, only uncollated pages inside the banker's boxes. When Dr. Oludara made copies of articles, she threw them in a box. Ditto for the books.

Each day, I cleaned in two shifts of three hours each. I'd sit on the floor sifting through piles of papers and books and decide which of them corresponded with each of the nine chapters of Dr. Oludara's book. Then I labeled banker's boxes for each set of materials. The materials I was unsure of, I placed into boxes with no label. For each article, I made a file folder. I turned the radio on low, singing inappropriate rap songs as I worked, skipping over the curse words. After my first shift, I'd break for lunch, head to the refectory, and sit in the corner reading my own book, a mystery or romance.

At the end of my day, I'd knock on the door of Dr. Oludara's other office and give her a neat stack of unassigned materials. I'd ask her to make a handwritten list of the proposed chapter that each article and book corresponded to, and to fill out an index card with the bibliographic information for each source. I'd already begun filling out cards for the materials in the banker's boxes, and placing each one in the little, wooden box.

Every time I gave her a handful, she told me I was amazing. I didn't know whether she was flattering me or not, but my first four weeks of work, she bought large rib plates for me at least a couple times a week. I would set the grease-stained bag aside and walk over to the refectory to eat a free lunch. The ribs and French fries would be for the old man and me that night, and I'd pretend to make it healthy by putting together a large salad to go with. Uncle Root would tell me I sure was helping him save grocery money.

The day I cleaned off the office floor, I decided to celebrate by eating lunch early. I walked over to the Rib Shack, ordering extra ribs and French fries. I had ripped open the bag when I remembered there was a closet in the office. When I opened the door, I saw another stack of banker's boxes in the closet, as tall as I was, and I decided it was time for a walk, before I began to cry.

When I returned, I was relieved that none of the boxes in the closet contained research materials. Instead, they were filled with office supplies: Paper- and binder clips, file folders, accordion folders, small and medium index cards, reams of copy paper, and brightly colored rubber bands, which were wrapped around each other, until they formed a ball.

That afternoon, Dr. Oludara came down to the office. She wanted to sit a spell. She grabbed a rubber band ball and threw it against the newly clean floor.

"Don't you just love these?" she asked. "They bounce! Isn't this fun?"

"Yes. Totally. So cute." I caught the ball and put it on the table. "Dr. Oludara, may I make a strong suggestion, as your new research assistant? With the greatest of respect?"

She sat up. "Yes, Ailey. Of course."

"This might be a time for you to take a break from buying office supplies. You have enough for now."

"But, Ailey—"

"Dr. Oludara. Please." I lowered my voice, the way my father used to. I put out a hand, in his signature style. "Look at this office. Are you happy with what you see?"

"Oh, Ailey! You just don't know! I never thought—"

"—I have cleaned this office from top to bottom. And it was a lot of work. I cried, several times. Like, sobs."

"I'm so sorry, Ailey."

"It's fine. But now that I've gotten everything clean, please don't come back with more office supplies. Please, Jesus. My nerves can't take it."

She cackled. "Ailey, you sound like an old lady!"

That was the day she paid me. She placed my monthly check in a cream-colored "Routledge College" envelope, sealed it, and handed it to me, telling me, be sure to leave early so I could catch the bank. I didn't want to open it in front of her, so I waited until I was in my car. Inside the envelope was a personal check for four hundred and sixty-four dollars. On the enclosed note, she'd written that she didn't know how to calculate a half cent, so she'd rounded up the mileage reimbursement to thirty-three cents a mile.

When I arrived back in Chicasetta, I stopped first at the bank and deposited the money in the account Uncle Root had opened in my name. Then I drove to the Pig Pen and used my checkbook to buy groceries: a raw chicken, instant oatmeal, a head of garlic, soul food seasoning mix, two loaves of whole wheat bread, butter, lettuce, tomatoes, cucumbers, salad dressing, and a quart of chocolate-chip ice cream. I carried that out to the car, then decided to go back and buy a gallon of milk, a pint of heavy cream, a half gallon of orange juice, and a twelve-pack of toilet paper.

When I walked into his house toting my plastic grocery bags, the old man was on the settee, reading. I told him that I'd be buying groceries every week. I knew I couldn't cover everything, but I wanted to contribute something. He nodded, inquired about our dinner menu, and went back to reading his book.

After four months of working for Dr. Oludara, her research office was finally organized. No longer were there unlabeled boxes with unfiled articles tossed inside, books sitting on the floor, or plastic bags of unopened office supplies crowding the closet, but she hadn't gotten used to the sight of order. Every time she knocked on the door and entered, she marveled at what I had done. How I had helped so much, because her book project was so complicated.

She hadn't intended to write a book on the largest slave auction in the history of the United States, an event that had taken place in Savannah, just a two-and-a-half-hour drive away. Scholars called it "the weeping time," because of all the enslaved Black families that had been separated. Initially, Dr. Oludara's project had been for more personal reasons. She'd only wanted to compile a family history on her ancestor, the slave woman her father had named her for. All anybody in the family knew was that the ancestor had been called Mother Belinda, and that she'd talked about the weeping time auction until the day she died. When Dr. Oludara had started doing her research on her ancestor, she'd become interested in the four hundred other enslaved folks who had been sold during the auction as well. She'd known about that auction since graduate school. But now it was personal.

It made Dr. Oludara curious about where those other folks had gone, especially since her ancestor's two children had been sold from her at the auction. And though Dr. Oludara knew her search for those children would be fruitless, she hadn't stopped looking. She'd framed her book outline as a story of her own family, interwoven

with the larger, public history of the auction and what became of
some of the other enslaved folks sold there. And maybe another pair
of eyes could help her. And since I'd been so great at organizing
her research, could I stay on and maybe reread some of the materials? She'd already done the reading herself, but after seven years
of research, she was so close to the material; she wanted a pair of
young, fresh eyes.

I looked at her bookshelves. There were at least seventy books on
those shelves, and at least a hundred articles that I'd filed.

"Um . . . I'd have to think about that. I'm not trained for this kind
of work. And, you know, I might be going back to the City soon."

"Really? I thought you were staying here for a while. That's what
Dr. Hargrace told me."

At home, I told the old man I was not an indentured servant. He
couldn't loan me out to his friends however he felt like it. And those
articles were too dense for me. I'd cracked a couple open, and they
were worse than my college biology textbooks.

"There's a way to read them, sugarfoot. I can show you, if you
like. It's a magic trick."

"You mean, how you tricked me to take this damned job as a
research assistant?"

"Oh, no, sugarfoot. That was basic manipulation."

The next morning, I called Dr. Oludara's office on campus. If she
still wanted me to work for her, I could start on reading her materials. But with respect, I would need a raise. She asked, how about
twenty-five more dollars a week? I told her that sounded fine to me.

———

During the summers, Routledge didn't offer classes. The campus
was closed to students from the third week of May until the first
week of August. I let myself into the faculty office building and listened to the quiet. I knocked on Dr. Oludara's door and told her that
I was headed to work. She answered that she was working herself. I
whispered, afraid to break the quiet. She told me she would let me
work in private, but when I got back home, don't forget to shower
and pray before bed. Put on something white or light.

"Don't forget, okay? And if any research ideas come up, call me, even if it's late. Don't worry about the time. If you don't want to call, just write it down. Remember, I need fresh eyes."

She had left typed notes for me, telling me where the white side of the story had started. It was easier to start with that side; unlike African Americans, white people had decent records. Their names, their birthplaces and dates. Sometimes even the color of their hair and eyes. Dr. Oludara had put a copy of a diary on the office table, written by an actress known as Frances Anne "Fanny" Kemble. She was the Englishwoman who had been married to Pierce Mease Butler, a slaveholder who'd been so wealthy he'd owned an island that carried his last name.

When Mrs. Butler aka Fanny went to live with her American husband, she was so appalled and disgusted by the way he'd treated the Black folks of Butler Island she'd left him, but she'd also kept a diary of the human offenses she'd witnessed. Mr. Butler wasn't only cruel to his slaves: after his divorce, Mr. Butler sued for and gained custody of their daughters. He thought that would be the end of his trouble with his English ex-wife, but in 1863, fifteen years after their divorce, his ex-wife published her diary during the Civil War, under her maiden name. But even before its publication, manuscripts of her diary had privately circulated for some years. Mr. Butler's reputation in the north had been permanently damaged, as the news of his brutality toward his slaves spread among abolitionist circles. Abolitionists added Mr. Butler's name to the growing pile of evidence of slavery's evils, a hill already built by narratives published in the north by escaped slaves. But Mr. Butler's name was damaged even further: he'd been very bad with money, and in 1859, he sold at auction over four hundred of the enslaved Black folks who'd lived as one community on Butler Island. One village on an isolated island off the coast of Georgia was destroyed in the auction called "the weeping time."

Beside the diary, Dr. Oludara had included a copy of the original newspaper article about the auction, written by a dude with the most ridiculous name ever, Q. K. Philander Doesticks. And though

Fanny Kemble's journal hadn't yet been published officially—that wouldn't happen until four years later—apparently, Mr. Doesticks had seen a private copy of the diary, because he called his article "a sequel to Mrs. Kemble's Journal." He had been at the auction and had witnessed the group of over four hundred enslaved people waiting for their fate. At the auction, these people had been broken into parcels of four or five enslaved folks. But Mr. Doesticks had focused on individual, personal stories of the Black folks who would be sold, like that of Jeffrey and Dorcas.

> *Jeffrey, chattel No. 319, marked as a "prime cotton hand," aged 23 years, was put up. Jeffrey being a likely lad, the competition was high. The first bid was $1,100, and he was finally sold for $1,310. Jeffrey was sold alone; he had no encumbrance in the shape of an aged father or mother, who must necessarily be sold with him; nor had he any children, for Jeffrey was not married. But Jeffrey, chattel No. 319, being human in his affections, had dared to cherish a love for Dorcas, chattel No. 278; and Dorcas, not having the fear of her master before her eyes, had given her heart to Jeffrey. Whether what followed was a just retribution on Jeffrey and Dorcas, for daring to take such liberties with their master's property as to exchange hearts, or whether it only goes to prove that with black as with white the saying holds, that "the course of true love never did run smooth," cannot now be told. Certain it is that these two lovers were not to realize to consummation of their hopes in happy wedlock. Jeffrey and Dorcas had told their loves, had exchanged their simple vows, and were betrothed, each to the other as dear, and each by the other as fondly beloved as though their skins had been of fairer color. And who shall say that, in the sight of Heaven and all holy angels, these two humble hearts were not as closely wedded as any two of the prouder race that call them slaves?*
>
> *Be that as it may, Jeffrey was sold. He finds out his new-master; and hat in hand, the big tears standing in his eyes, and his voice trembling with emotion, he stands before that master and tells his simple story, praying that his betrothed may be bought with him. . . .*

On my drive back to Chicasetta, I stopped at the Cluck-Cluck Hut and bought a family-size bucket of chicken with biscuits, and three orders of fries. Uncle Root didn't fuss at me when I ate too much at supper. He only laughed, saying I sure was going to sleep well with all that food in my system. I was so hungry that I ate until my stomach hurt. As the old man had predicted, I went to bed early.

In an hour, I awoke, heart jumping. I felt my stomach roil. I ran to the bathroom, closed the door, and quickly stepped out of my pajama pants. I didn't want to piss on them when the vomiting started. The next wave of nausea came over me, and then another, and when I kneeled in front of the toilet, the air rushed out with a high sound. Another wave, and a scream hit, before I hurriedly covered my mouth.

I don't know how long I stayed on the floor, waiting for vomiting that never came. Rocking and patting my arms. I don't know what time it was when I called Dr. Oludara.

"I know it's late, but something's wrong—"

"—you didn't shower and pray, did you, Ailey?"

"No, ma'am."

"But I told you to do that."

"I know, Dr. Oludara. I'm so sorry."

She told me, no need to apologize. But go ahead and take that shower now, and if I had some light-colored pajamas, put them on. She'd hold the line. She promised she wouldn't hang up. Then we'd pray together.

YOU CAN BE PROUD

◈

In late July, Dr. Oludara asked, did I want to take a road trip? It was her last week of freedom before she had to start prepping for classes. She'd visited the site before but wanted to hear my impressions.

When I hung up the phone, I pretended to Uncle Root that I was annoyed by the intrusion on my free time, but I was excited. I went through my clothes and found Dear Pearl's old yellow-and-white dress but left her heels in my trunk. I found some white flats, dusting them inside with baby powder. Then I called Miss Rose's and asked for Mama, who had come back down that summer. Could she come to town and stay with the old man, in case I was held up overnight? I had to take a business trip. I felt so much satisfaction as Mama repeated that phrase, raising her voice in a question: Business trip?

It was a three-hour drive in Dr. Oludara's car from campus to the plantation, one that had housed three enslaved women who had been sold at the weeping time auction. The highway narrowed as we drove away from campus. We wouldn't be taking the interstate, Dr. Oludara told me. We'd have to take the back roads.

About an hour into our journey, she stopped to get gas and returned with a packet of peanuts and two grease-stained packs. Did I want a fried pie? She had no intention of starving me, she said. We'd eat on the way back, but there were some sandwiches she'd made in the cooler. She reached in the back seat into the small cooler and pulled out a bottle of cola. Before she opened the door of the car, she told me, don't judge her, please. Then she held the cola out of the door and dropped half of the peanuts into the bottle. The liquid bubbled up, and she slurped at it.

The plantation that we visited was small and separated from the rest of the town. The guide told us that the owner's descendants had sold off all but twenty-five acres of the land. The property was owned by the state of Georgia now, including the house. It was huge and built in the Greek Revival style. The guide was an elderly white man with a thick head of white hair that would have made the old man envious. He was tall and thin, with a blue polo shirt tucked into khaki pants that were pulled up several inches above his natural waist. He told us that he was a retired history professor, and an expert on antebellum architecture.

There were no other guests on the tour, only Dr. Oludara and me, but our guide's voice was loud, his laughter timed with the amused tone of his statements. This house had been built in 1841. The original size of the property had been seven hundred and fifteen acres. Then the owner had sold off five hundred of his acres to a Yankee carpetbagger after the Civil War. Don't be fooled by the thick green lawn at the back of the house—right there had been a man-made pond that the owner had stocked with trout. And the columns on the front of the house? They had been chiseled out of whole trees and painted to look like stone, because the owner lied to his neighbors about the columns and told them that's what they were made of. It was only a hundred years later, when the state took over the plantation, that the truth of the columns was revealed.

"Thank goodness the termites hadn't eaten through them," our guide declared dramatically. "There was some chemical in the plaster and paint used to cover the wood that poisoned the termites. I can't tell you what it is, though. I've been trying for years, but nobody knows what it was. Probably some secret of the Indians!"

I'd brought a small notebook and scribbled my impressions. I leaned close to but did not touch the shiny emerald-green fabric that covered the walls of the plantation house. I counted the number of steps to the second floor. I noted that the portraits of the master and his children showed dark hair and eyes and wrote down that perhaps that meant Native American blood. I leaned and peered at the furniture in the parlor. What kind of wood? Cherry or walnut? It was too dark to be oak.

The tour took an hour. By the time it was over, the pits of my sundress were soaked with sweat. The house had not been altered, and there was no air-conditioning. And I had several mosquito bites, one in the middle of my back. Our guide thanked us for coming and led us to the front hallway, where our tour had started. He invited us to sign the guest book and offered to sell us postcards with scenes from the plantation as it would have looked before the Civil War. Also, there was a booklet with information about the architecture, and how the plantation had escaped Sherman's March to the Sea during the Civil War. The original property was located too far inland and surrounded on three sides by a river that the soldiers had not wanted to cross. The owner had burned the bridge that crossed the river.

"Are there any other buildings on this property?" Dr. Oludara asked.

"There's the old kitchen house, but it's closed for renovations. That will be opening next year for tours."

"Any other buildings?"

"Well, there's the quarters." Our guide waved his hand. "But those are further back in the woods."

"Aren't they part of the tour?"

"Technically, yes, but I refuse to go back there. They're practically falling down. I don't know why the state hasn't destroyed them. They're a real safety hazard."

"I know how busy you are, so just a couple more questions. Who was living here before the owner took over the property?"

"Oh, nobody! He was the first owner."

"But what about the Indians?"

"Oh, them. Well, they left. After the Removal and all that."

I made a noise, and Dr. Oludara grabbed my hand. She asked, how many slaves were owned here? After a long pause, our guide told her, there had been thirty-nine people who labored on the plantation. They all had been treated exceptionally well.

"This house was built by slave labor, no?" Dr. Oludara asked.

Our guide's blue eyes twinkled. "Oh yes! And you can be very proud of that, can't you? That your Negro people built this wonderful place!"

I caught my breath loudly, and Dr. Oludara squeezed my hand several times, an emotional Morse code: *Keep it together*.

"Is it all right if we walk to the quarters?" she asked.

"Surely, but I must warn you that any injuries incurred are your own responsibility. Thank you so much for visiting Moss Road Plantation."

Our guide smiled brightly, and then he left us at the entrance.

Dr. Oludara and I didn't have that long of a walk. The quarters weren't deep in the woods, only fifty or sixty yards away from the plantation house. The three cabins were huddled together, a few paces between each. There was a plaque in front, telling us that the thirty-nine slaves who had worked the fields of Moss Road Plantation had lived in these three cabins. Perhaps as many as fourteen individuals had crowded into each structure, living and sleeping in one room.

The first and second cabins were empty. Nothing on the walls or the floor, though light peeked in through tiny holes in the wood planks. The stone fireplace took up most of the north wall. The third cabin had furniture, such as it was. There was a rope bed with no mattress, and a chair with the bottom missing. Propped against the stone hearth was a large pot that would have been black, if it had not been covered in rust.

When I pulled out my notebook, Dr. Oludara told me, put that away. Just stand here awhile and look at this place. Think about the people who had lived in this one room. That's all I needed to do. She'd been to this cabin four different times, though the guide didn't remember her. She'd even taken pictures.

On our return drive, we stopped at a homestyle diner. The meal was on her, even after I told her I was really hungry. I ordered a whole catfish and hush puppies. Four sides, and I took two rolls out of the basket and smeared margarine on them.

"Gosh, I'm starving. I don't know what's wrong with me. I had that fried pie. And I ate a huge breakfast before that."

"Don't you even worry, Ailey. I'm about to grub myself, when my plate comes. The catfish is outstanding here."

We didn't talk much on the rest of the drive. I was sleepy from all the food I'd eaten, and Dr. Oludara didn't start a conversation. It was evening by the time we arrived back on campus, though the summertime sun was high. She wheeled the car into the parking lot, but when I opened the door, she asked, could we sit a spell? She'd keep the car running so we could sit in the cool air.

"So, what'd you think, Ailey?"

"You want me to tell you the truth?"

"Definitely."

"I hated that tour guide! He was so rude. No, not rude"—I tilted my head—"something else I can't put my finger on."

"He was dismissive."

"Yes!" I bounced in my seat. "That's it! It's like, he didn't even care about the Indians or the Black folks. And when he said we should be proud that slaves had built that plantation? Ooh, I wanted to choke him!"

She laughed. "I know! I'm glad I was there. You were about to catch a case."

"You said you've visited four times. How many of these other plantations have you toured?"

"In the past five years? Twelve. And I've gone to each at least twice."

"Oh God."

"That dude back at Moss Road is one of the nicer ones. I've had other guides stop the tour when I asked about slavery. A couple of the plantations, they've literally whitewashed the quarters and put in furniture and throw rugs, like a slave cabin can be gentrified."

"How do you deal with that?"

"You get used to it. But there's something about the sadness I feel, whenever I go those places. It's all on my skin. But you must know what I mean. Your family lives on a former plantation. You must feel those people every time you step on the land."

I moved my purse onto my lap. I liked this lady, but I wasn't going to tell her my business. I didn't want her to think I was crazy, and she would, if I told her my dead sister talked to me.

"I guess I don't really think about it much."

"Really? Dr. Hargrace took me on a tour of the place a few years back. None of the original cabins are still there, but there's the old general store and the plantation house ruins."

"Did he take you to his pecan tree, too? He loves that tree!"

She didn't join in my laughter. "He did take me, Ailey. And I was very respectful. Dr. Hargrace tries to entertain people with that story, but one can only imagine the trauma of that experience, that he narrowly escaped a lynching. I'm sure he has nightmares about that."

"You think so?"

"Of course he does! And the fact that a Black man of his generation stayed in the deep south and had to struggle with that memory? And then continued to do such important work for his students, even for the Black community in Chicasetta? How he's kept your family church intact? Do you know that the original wood floor of that church is still there, from back in 1881?"

"No, I didn't."

"And now he's trying to stop it from becoming a historical site."

"But why? That would be a good thing, right?"

"Usually it would, but he wants to keep it private property. Otherwise, the city will want to have tours up there, and then people will want to visit that mound behind the church. He has an attorney helping him, to make sure the state doesn't try any shenanigans. A family friend, he said. A young brother named James something. He just passed the bar."

"David James?"

"That's him. Dr. Hargrace wants to make sure people won't walk on that mound and erode it. Like what happened to Rock Eagle. People came through there stealing bits and pieces of the monument."

"This is the first I've heard anything about this. Uncle Root didn't tell me one thing."

"Ailey, hasn't your family lived on that land for over a century?"

"Yeah, I guess so. It's been a long time."

"You have all this history in your actual backyard and never were curious about it? That's surprising." Her bracelets clattered. "What do the kids say? Girlfriend, you're slipping."

When she pulled up to the old man's house, she told me, don't forget to shower and pray. Remember what happened last time.

———

In the days that followed, I began to talk about our family church, hoping Uncle Root would reveal what he and David had been working on, but he never took the hint.

One night at dinner, I told him that it hurt my feelings that he was keeping secrets from me. That Dr. Oludara had told me all about what he and David had been doing, to make sure the church didn't become a historical site, unless the state agreed to Uncle Root's terms.

"I wasn't being intentionally secretive, Ailey. You've never seemed concerned with family history."

"That's not true! I love your stories. Didn't I ask you to tell me your Du Bois story last night?"

"That is for entertainment. This issue with the church is a serious legal matter that involves Brother David. He owns the building."

"But I thought Elder Beasley owned everything. He's been the preacher for, like, forever."

"He was appointed by our congregation, back in the sixties, but that building was in the name of David's grandfather, and when J.W. died, he inherited it. This is why David didn't leave the state for law school. He promised his grandfather and me that he would look after the church, because I own the land the church sits on. And that includes the mound."

"But what about the cemetery? Miss Cordelia is old. Won't her relatives try to sell the farm?"

"Oh, I'm not worried about that. Not at all. Cordelia and I have an understanding."

I tried to salvage my anger. "You still could have told me. That's not cool."

"Sugarfoot, I'd be happy to share any information about our family. All you have to do is ask. You know I love talking to you. Now, I think I'd like a cup of real coffee for a change. What about you? Why don't I put us on a pot?"

That Sunday, after church, I walked through the fellowship hall and out the back door of the church. I hadn't been back there for a long time, ever since I'd been stung by the wasp. The outhouse had been torn down, once the inside toilet was installed in the fellowship hall. Now nothing obstructed the view of the mound and pink and blue wildflowers that had erupted on its surface. Behind me, I heard the old man ask, wasn't it beautiful? He touched my shoulder, and I nodded. I laid my cheek on his hand.

On the walk back down the hill, he wanted to visit his pecan tree. He had a feeling it was lonely without him. When we walked through the tall weeds, the old gray cat came up to me, mewling.

He leaned against his tree. "I'm not young anymore, either, Ailey."

"Here you go with that—"

"—stop, sugarfoot! Would you just stop?" His voice was transformed: he was nearly shouting.

"I'm sorry, Uncle Root. I didn't mean to be disrespectful."

"You have to listen sometimes! You can't cut folks off or talk over them every time they say something you don't want to hear."

"Yes, sir."

He sighed, and when he spoke again, he'd lowered his voice. "Ailey, an old person needs people to take care of them, no matter how independent they want to be. But I didn't know that as a young man. I promised my mother I would leave, when I was a little boy. I didn't even know what she meant when she told me, leave this place. Olivia wanted to come back south, so we could help my family, but I hated this place. I hated the white folks for being so brutal, and I hated the Negroes for being so afraid. And once I came home, I hated my brother, Tommy. I was furious all the time."

He stayed quiet for a time. He broke off twigs from his tree, but I didn't say anything. I waited. I wanted him to know I had paid attention to his words about listening.

"One Sunday, I was sitting on the porch and my brother walked up and sat down. Tommy liked to come and visit Pearl on the Lord's day. She always had a plate for him, and they would sit and rock on the glider. As he sat there, I listened to him talk. He was so sweet and friendly, and my sister and him got along like a house on fire. He was ten years older than her, old enough to be my father, and he thought he was a fair man, what we used to call 'good white folks,' even though every Negro family on his farm was barely scraping to get by. All the Negroes except my family, that is. But Tommy had lied to himself that he was an honorable man, and my sister was lying to him, and all the Negroes on the premises were lying, too. Acting like he was another breed from the other white men in town, but they never knew when he'd turn on them. Those turns were rare, but they had happened, and so the Negroes on Wood Place held their breath. Pearl wasn't scared of him, but everybody else was. That was the truth, Ailey. And the truth can be both horrible and lovely at the same time. It seemed like I was the only one who would say that out loud. I was the only Negro that Tommy knew who would tell him what was what. And you're like me, Ailey. You tell everybody the truth."

"Not all of it, Uncle Root. There're things I just can't say out loud. Not now and maybe not ever. I'm tired sometimes. And I'm really, really sad."

"I know you are, sugarfoot."

"I was sad before Lydia died. Even before Daddy died. I didn't want to admit that to myself. It seemed like I was just holding on, and now I just don't know if I'll ever not be sad."

"But it's good that you can say how you feel, Ailey. And you don't have to tell all the truth if you don't want to. But it's important to know what the truth is, even if you only say it to yourself."

I walked the few steps to where the old cat lay in a sunny spot. She probably had fleas or worse, but I leaned and stroked her head. She purred and rolled over on her back, exposing a belly that had bits and pieces of leaves stuck in the hair.

I spoke with my back turned. "Lydia is still gone, no matter what

I say. Why couldn't I save her, Uncle Root? I wanted to, so bad. I wanted to make her better."

"I know. That's the way I felt about my mother, Ailey. She died and left me when I was just a little boy, and for years, I blamed myself. If I could have taken her away from this farm, from my father, from all this racism and oppression, she might not have caught influenza. That frustration will probably be with me until the moment I leave this earth. But once she was gone, it took me years to see that I had to live for the both of us, because she loved me so much. Like Lydia loved you. Anybody could see that, Ailey. She was crazy about you. She probably loved you more than even I do, and I love you very, very much. And that's why you have to carry on, Ailey. Wherever Lydia is, she's asking that of you. She wants that for you."

I kept scratching the cat's tummy, and she wiggled around on her back. Purring, eyes closed into green slits.

◆

SONG

◆

⊙ ⊙ ⊙

The Growth of a Family

Even in a place of sorrow, time passes. Even in a place of joy. Do not assume that either keeps life from continuing, for there are children everywhere. And children are life, for they keep their mothers' beauty. Sometimes, even when their mothers are lost to death or distance, these women urge their young toward survival. This is what happened after the girl Mamie died in labor giving birth to Samuel Pinchard's son, who had been named Nick. Even in death, Mamie looked after her child.

After Mamie's death, the newborn Nick needed milk, and there were only two women in the Quarters who were nursing. These two women shared the bald, white baby between them. They walked between their cabins to exchange him. Yet while they were feeding Nick, they did not touch his face or make the sounds that babies crave. Neither woman wanted to raise the baby as their own; he looked like his father, whose transgressions had killed Mamie. Though Nick was blameless, it did not matter to these women. They had no affection for him.

After his nursing time, when Nick could tolerate mashed sweet potatoes and finely minced greens, and did not wake in the night, screaming for milk and absent love, the women approached Aggie. They asked her to take Nick for her own child. Ahead of time, the two women had worked out the argument, that they had five children between them and husbands and field work. One woman was holding Nick, and when she put him down, the child crawled to Aggie. She picked him up and he twined his arms around her neck. Her breasts began to ache, and she heard Mamie's voice telling her, don't abandon her baby. He could not help that he looked like a slave master. He was only a motherless child, and Aggie should know how that felt.

Aggie took this baby in without asking Midas or Pop George, but they did not reject the child's arms, either. Before he was old enough to walk alone, Aggie carried the baby on her back, wrapped around her in a cloth. In his third summer, Nick let go of Aggie's hand and joined the other Quarters children in their play. The child listened to Pop George's stories and, despite his pale skin, blond kinks, and cat's-eyes, he was accepted by the other little ones, for the very young do not take on prejudice the same as adults.

Nick was enough for his now-mother. Aggie did not want another baby. It was one thing to take care of a little boy who had no one else in the world, but to bring another child into it was too much for Aggie—for after the death of Mamie, Samuel's ugly appetite had increased. The first time, he'd knocked on the door of one of the cabins, asking for a darling dark-skinned little girl by name. She had an infectious laugh and dimples; in the fields, the grown folks could not help but return her smile. The little girl's father had refused to send his child out, and that next morning, the father had been found dead in the fields, his broken body a brazen image, and Carson Franklin had ordered two Quarters-men to drag the corpse to the small cemetery allotted for Negroes. The next night, Samuel knocked on the same cabin door. The little girl's mother tried to refuse—her face was lined with tears—but Samuel pushed past the mother and sought the child. The mother screamed, and holding on to the child, Samuel kicked at her legs. As he headed out of the cabin, the mother called after her child, Mama shole was sorry.

Thus, Aggie listened to her body; remembering the lessons of her grandmother Helen, she resisted Midas's quiet embraces in the front chamber of the two-room cabin during the times when her womb wanted to conceive. If she gave in to her own desire, she made sure to drink a tisane from wild carrot seeds steeped in boiling water, which would make her body inhospitable to pregnancy. Yet, when two years passed and Samuel had not snatched any more little girls from the Quarters, Aggie relented. With a monster like her master, she couldn't be sure that all would be well, but she let Midas court her womb the same as he had done her heart. During her sad times, he took Nick upon his knee, to the boy's delight and his wife's reluctant smiles. And Pop George did his part as well. He told Aggie he wanted as many grandchildren as she could give him. They could sleep in his room. And when her womb filled, Aggie relented to gladness. She was fat and hungry through her ten moons of pregnancy.

At Aggie's labor, when the Quarters-woman who'd urged her to strain and push told her she had given birth to a girl, Aggie was touched with fear. The woman placed the baby to the mother's breast. Apologetic, she pointed to the red-tinged birthmark on the baby's forehead, but Aggie laughed in pleasure. Though her daughter was perfect in her mother's eyes, the baby would be flawed to her master.

Samuel ordered Pop George to bring the child to the kitchen house, in order for him to inspect the baby Aggie had borne, whom he called his "new property." He didn't want to see Aggie for those few minutes, for he couldn't abide her presence. Pop George reported that when Samuel saw the angry red mark across half of the baby's forehead and left eyelid, he shrank back with disgust. And Pop George whispered that this child was a blessing, and Midas whispered that God shole was good. And Aggie agreed and held out her arms for her baby, and said she wanted to name her Tess.

Nick clapped his hands at the adults' joy. He went to the bed where Aggie lay with the baby in her arms and kissed his sister on the cheek.

The Place Where the Young Friends Live

During the time that Aggie had been pregnant with Tess, Samuel had begun the building of the structure on the left side of his house. And only weeks before Tess was born, Lancaster Polcott's wagon had pulled up to the yard. A bright-colored little girl had been lifted from the back of the wagon by Polcott's Negro helper. The girl had been adorned in an exquisite child's dress with many ribbons— the skirt only a bit below her knees and ruffled pantaloons down her legs—but she'd worn a grown woman's severe coiffure. Aggie's unborn baby had listed within her, a sad prophecy, as she'd

watched the left cabin from afar. She'd seen the new Negro, Claudius, grooming the flowers from afar, but she did not see Samuel.

Aggie suspected what was happening in the left cabin, but she
was determined not to let it spoil her own happiness. She cultivated
indifference: she was a woman and a slave, and she could not control
everything. The little occupant in the left cabin had not been born
on Wood Place. She was a stranger. When Aggie stopped nursing
and began to have women's cycles again, she returned to the moon
house. Yet she did not reveal Samuel's actions to Lady, the same way
she had been silent about Lady's Negro heritage. Lady already knew
about Mamie, but not the other little girls. It wasn't Aggie's responsibility to cause trouble in order to keep others informed.

The crack in Aggie's ice began one evening, during the time of
cotton chopping. She was sitting in the yard, while Pop George told
stories to the very young children. Tess was asleep and tied with a
cloth to Aggie's back, but her other child had been patient for too
long. She hadn't played with Nick for many months, since before
the new baby was born. He spotted Aggie and began their old game,
"See and catch me." Nick ran very fast, and, sighing, Aggie rose and
called after her son, she was gone get him. She laughed to herself:
she hoped this activity would tire him out, as much as she was tired.
It was more than a notion to care for a little boy and an infant, as
well as the Quarters-children besides. She began to walk, but Aggie
came upon Nick sitting in a red dirt puddle. His child's linen shift
and face were wet with mud and he was shrieking.

Aggie saw that they were nearly upon the left cabin, and she
hissed at her son, quick, give her his hand. Yet Nick sat in the puddle
and refused to rise. Suddenly, Samuel appeared. He'd watched his
child from afar, but because Nick was in Aggie's care, Samuel kept
his distance. He didn't want to get within even a few feet of that
woman, but he knew to harm her would be to hinder the life of his
child.

Yet that day, Samuel's love overcame him: Nick was his only seed,
he told himself. And Samuel was not a young man anymore. He
was near forty years old, though there was not one line on his face.

His blond hair wasn't even silver at his temples; he seemed to be both a young and never-aging man.

Samuel pulled the child into his arms, unconcerned that the mud on Nick would ruin his clothes.

The mother snatched her son away.

"Don't you be touching him," Aggie said. "Don't you never put your hands on this chile again."

At her words, fear seized Samuel: he quaked throughout his entire body. He turned on his heel, opened the leaf- and flower-covered iron gate of the left cabin's fence, and walked inside. In moments, there was the high-pitched sound of a child screaming.

The Day of the Selling

After the scene at the left cabin, Samuel decided he'd had enough. He was tired of deferring to Aggie, who was nothing but a nigger and a woman. Until he'd encountered her, he'd only felt shame over his long-dead father's assaults. Not when he read his Bible, for Samuel only pulled out those scriptural pieces that assured him, as a white man, he was next to God. Not when he heard the screaming of his Young Friend, for the more he hurt her, the more powerful he felt. Yet the sense of power he had felt that evening in anticipation of hurting his Young Friend had leaked out of him when Aggie had snatched Nick from his arms. He'd wanted to punch her, but the strength had left his bones when he'd tried to raise his arm.

His night with the Young Friend had ended too quickly, and when he returned to his own bedroom in the house, Samuel decided he would have to sell Aggie. He could tolerate her no longer, and once Aggie was gone, all would be well, no matter the potential demonstrations among the Quarters-folks. If they wanted to slow down their work, he would allow Carson to use his whip. No one would stand in the way of Samuel and his son. He sat down at the desk in his parlor and wrote two short documents: a letter to Lancaster Polcott and a pass for Claudius.

Samuel expected to sleep well that night, but he had nightmares of someone's lips touching his ear, whispering, giving him instructions, though he couldn't remember what they were when he awoke in the dark, sweating. He heard footsteps over his shiny pine floor and saw the outline of a small figure, though he couldn't see the face. And when Samuel lit his lantern, there was no one in his room. The door was tightly closed as before. In the morning, Samuel was uneasy, as he walked to the kitchen house, and had Tut send for Claudius. The master gave him the two notes, and told him, make haste. He held out the pass, explaining what it was—as if Claudius couldn't read—and said, if he encountered white men on the road, to give them this paper. Not the other. And don't lose his pass, because a nigger on a horse was bound to be challenged. It was twenty-five miles to where the trader lived—too far to travel quickly on foot.

Lancaster arrived four days later, with his Negro helper. Beside the wagon, Claudius rode the horse. The trader got down to business quickly, saying he might be able to get a prime price for Aggie, since Samuel had figured her as in her early twenties, but with the bad birthmark that Samuel had described on Aggie's baby, that would surely diminish the baby's price. He and Samuel stood in the yard. Though the sun was high, and Samuel had drunk three cups of black coffee, he was groggy and rubbed his eyes.

"That's not right," Samuel said to the trader. "That's not right at all. I said I had a buck to sell . . ." In his confusion, he couldn't remember the words from the note he'd written to Lancaster, nor what he'd intended it to say, only what had been whispered in his ear from the night before.

"No, sir," Lancaster said. "With the greatest of apologies, I fear you are mistaken. Wait . . ." He patted his breast pocket. He reached inside, searching. "I don't know what I did with that paper, but I distinctly recall what this nigger gave me." He gestured to Claudius, who had climbed down from his horse. Asked, boy, what did that paper indicate? And don't pretend he hadn't read it.

Claudius looked from Samuel to Lancaster. He was caught like a catfish on a line. One of these white men was his master, and a nasty sumbitch at that. Yet he could not accuse Lancaster of lying, either—this would assure that he'd be whipped at the least. So Claudius looked down at his shoes, until Samuel said to him, go into the fields and tell Carson Franklin to get his son, Jeremiah. And then bring back a Quarters-man. Anyone, as long as he was strong.

A half hour passed, and Carson and Jeremiah walked to the yard. They had taken hold of the struggling Midas. Aggie was sitting in the small yard in front of her cabin and saw the braided head of her husband. She began to run toward the big house, but Samuel made a gesture, and she was caught by Claudius. He whispered that he was so sorry. He was only doing the best he could, as she called him a white man's nigger. Samuel urged Claudius to hit her. Make her shut up, but Claudius only held her arms and rocked her. He pulled Aggie closer and pressed her face into his chest. He whispered, look away from her man, 'cause it was too much. Just look away, and she fainted in Claudius's arms.

In the wagon, the overseer's two sons held on to Midas, who yelled and kicked as the trader's helper locked him in chains. He screamed Aggie's name. Pop George's name. Then, repeatedly, the names of his two children, Nick and Tess.

"Papa love y'all!" Midas cried. "I won't never stop! Y'all 'member me! Papa love his babies!"

His voice could be heard as the trader drove off. Hours later, it seemed as if his voice screamed still, like the ghost of somebody who had died.

A Family's Grief

We do not need to tell you that Aggie and Pop George grieved after the selling of Midas. That evening after he was taken away, Aggie was senseless in the bed she had shared with him, where Claudius had carried her and laid her down. Outside, the Quarters-folks had congregated and sang their sorrow songs around a fire. That night, no one in the Quarters slept. Even the children refused to lie down on their pallets in their cabins. In their mothers' arms, the babies cried throughout the night. Sadness was a wounded animal crouching in every corner.

In the years after her father's selling, Tess would not remember him, but she would withdraw into quiet, except when she sat underneath the large pecan tree that was feet away from the general store that Samuel had built. Then she talked to herself, laughing, and sometimes jokingly hitting the pecan tree. Tess insisted that the tree and she had long conversations, and Aggie left her in peace to her fantasies, the way she'd left Mamie to the same tree. Aggie reasoned that life was long and full of suffering; let children have their scant happiness.

Yet Nick would not forget his father, and in the days and weeks after the trader's wagon had pulled away, he would ask Aggie, where was his papa? Where had he gone? Aggie would cry and hug herself, and Nick would ask her, why ain't she say where his papa had gone? Until the day that Pop George took the child aside, saying that he needed him to be a big boy now. Didn't nobody know where his papa had gone, and his mama was sad about that. And every time he be asking about Midas, Nick be making his mama even more sad.

Thus, Nick hushed his questions and became stoic, but one morning, he announced to Aggie, "I know where my papa be. He be gone to Jesus." His mother asked, where'd he get that notion? and her son told her the Good Lord had told him in a dream. The child was so serious that Aggie did not have the heart to correct him. And when Nick said he wanted to put a rock in the graveyard for his papa, so he could pray, Aggie assented.

Then came the day when Nick was put to work. This was a ritual in the life of every Quarters-child: in their seventh summer (or rarely, their sixth or eighth year), the top milk teeth of the Quarters-children fell out, leaving the empty homes as the marker of a new time. Most of the children that Aggie and Pop George tended would go to the fields, but some would help Claudius work the two large vegetable gardens, one supplying the House and one the Quarters. These same children would help Claudius tend the hens and the milk cows, which supplied the butter, cream, and cheese to the House. They would not be allowed near the left cabin, however, to trim the flowers that wound through the spires of the fence that imprisoned the Young Friend.

When it came to Nick's labor, Samuel decided that the child he loved would not be a field hand. He wanted to keep Nick close in the big house. The little boy didn't yet know that Samuel had sired him. He was not yet of an age to consider logic, that Midas's skin had been dark-dark, and Aggie's only a few shades lighter. The brown eyes of both, while Nick's were like a light-eyed cat's. That both had black hair, while their son's was blond, though tightly kinked like any Negro's. When Quarters-children had tried their hand at teasing Nick, Pop George had scolded them. They was a family at Wood Place, and that made Nick they brother. And they was supposed to take a brother to they bosoms, not make him shame over how he looked. 'Cause didn't nobody make theyselves. Only the Good Lord did all that.

When Nick was assigned as Tut's kitchen helper, he displaced another little girl, who was sent back to the fields. That evening, when Nick tried to settle with the other Quarters-children in his own years, to listen to Pop George's stories, they moved away from him. He didn't like the feeling, and he asked his mother, why couldn't he work the fields like the other children? And Aggie said, she didn't know, because their master did all that. That next morning, when Nick approached the cook, saying, please put him back in the fields, she told him the same.

In the ways of children, Nick began a protest. When sent on an errand, he went the other way and stayed absent for a long stretch. When he returned, Tut said nothing, for she'd been instructed by Samuel not to whip Nick. Even if he hadn't spoken to her, any fool could see the boy was this man's son. Except for the wool on Nick's head, he was Samuel's spit. Yet when Samuel came to the kitchen with smiles and candy for the child, Nick did not act as another slave child would. He was sullen and looked at his new shoes, which had been given him when he started working in the kitchen. The shoes hurt his feet. When Tut pushed him forward, saying, didn't he hear Massa talking to him? Nick was quiet. And when Tut was questioned by Samuel, who asked, had she done something to this child to make him so unhappy? she hasted to tell Samuel, oh, nawsuh! She loved this child just like her own. She fed him well, and spoke soft-like to him, but it seem like the boy didn't know his blessing. He kept crying to go to the fields with them other pickaninnies.

The next morning, Carson Franklin came to the kitchen, bringing Tut's previous helper. He told her he'd come to take Nick to the fields.

Though the labor was difficult and the days long, Nick was happiest with the Quarters-children, whom he'd won over again, when he exchanged his privileged place to be near them. He won their respect further when he shielded them from Carson Franklin's whip by taking credit for what Carson perceived as misbehavior. Nick didn't know that the overseer was forbidden to whip him, only that whenever he took the blame, nothing happened.

In four years, when Tess was assigned to the field—for her birthmark still covered half her face, and Samuel did not like to look upon imperfection—Nick worked even harder to fill her cotton sack as well as his own.

Lady's Desire for Children

Lady desperately wanted to feel the smooth, fat hands of a child on her cheeks. That would be her only consolation in life, since she despised her husband, but Samuel did not visit her bedroom, no matter how she arranged her hair or how elaborately she dressed. Lady consulted her own mother about how to draw her husband closer, but Mahala never took her daughter's side. Mahala told her she knew nothing about superstitions, and if Lady would learn only to submit to her husband's every wish, he would seek her out. Mahala had become old and petulant before her time. Her trust and adoration of white people had gained her nothing, and she was jealous of her daughter. She refused to see her daughter's unhappiness.

So Lady sought out Aggie about the means to conceive. The two continued meeting in the moon house, for they were still linked in their bleeding, and through the years, they had become friends.

Aggie's grandmother had not taught her how to urge seed into a womb, only how to keep it from taking hold and how to expel it. One night in the moon house, however, she considered that Samuel depended upon women for his food. And she remembered her grandmother's story of the Creek warrior who had been felled by a maiden. The next morning, Aggie headed to the kitchen house, though she was still bleeding. She smiled at Tut, telling her, she must be so tired. Aggie would watch her pots and pans while Tut sneaked to the keeping room of the kitchen house for a nap. The cook sighed in gratitude and disappeared, and Aggie shooed away the child who was the kitchen helper. Go outside and play, Aggie told the girl. Go on, now. Then Aggie began to stir the bubbling pots on the stove, and spit in the pots. She pulled a small jar from her skirt pocket and poured blood into each pot. She did this every day, until the blood was gone.

By the time Lady ended her monthly interval in the moon house, Samuel was greatly weakened. His attention to the farm's business was blurred. His strength had waned, and he slept later and went to bed earlier, neglecting his visits to the left cabin. At night Lady would slip into his room and nudge him, but he would not wake. She would reach under his nightshirt to rouse his manhood, as Aggie had instructed her. Then Lady would quickly climb on top of her husband, swallowing her pain and disgust.

By the time he discovered Lady was expecting, Samuel was confused as to how his wife had gotten with child. He had no memory of her climbing astride him and was dumbfounded when he discovered her condition. He accused her of infidelity with one of the farmers in the territory, but she assured him that was not the case. How would she meet anyone? she asked. He did not allow her to leave the plantation. And Lady feigned shyness when she asked Samuel, did he not remember their nights together? She had enjoyed those times very much, and Samuel decided, however these children were conceived, he was a white man. He needed legal heirs, even if they weren't of his own seed.

Assisted by Aggie, Lady gave birth in the moon house. She bore a set of twins named Gloria and Victor. Both were golden-haired like their father, and Lady wept. Thinking her friend was upset by the white appearance of her newborns, Aggie told her, do not blame these babies for their blood. After all, Nick was Samuel's seed, too, but she loved the boy as her own.

Yet Lady told her she was weeping for joy, for her children had no appearance of Indian blood. She had lived in fear during her pregnancy. And Aggie was silent, considering that her friend still seemed unaware of her African line. In her heart, she was sympathetic, however, that a burden had been lifted from Lady.

Of Warriors and Prophets

The love of our land was a fever that would not be chilled. It called white man after white man to our place, which they labeled a "frontier." To these men, our people weren't even as good as animals, because our people could not feed the hungry or keep others warm with their hides. They were inconveniences, sitting upon spots that these men coveted, and as more treaties were signed by more self-appointed leaders of our people giving away our land, more white men came. They came with the rights they had given themselves and the rights they had taken away from others. They sent word from mouth to mouth that our earth was free. Come and split down the pine, the cedar, the pecan. Come and shoot the deer. Come and bring your pigs and cattle that trample the earth. Here is a place where a white man can make himself a king.

There had been skirmishes and battles between the Creek people and white men. And there were traitors to the Creek people and there were loyalists and a civil war fought between those factions: the Red Stick War. Our people fought against each other, one side supported by the British and the Spanish, who wanted to get back at the Americans, who held up the other side. Yet whichever side the white men were on, they urged our people, turn on each other.

Then there came warriors, such as Tecumseh of the Shawnee, a tribe in the north of the continent. And there were prophets, such as Tecumseh's brother Tenskwatawa. Together these men were the Shooting Star and the Open Door, and they rode down to our land to unite our people of the south with our people of the north. Tecumseh held a weapon and Tenskwatawa held a dream, and the dreaming brother's sights led him to tell the Creek, unite against the white man. Abandon eating his cattle and pig and chicken and wheat and return to the bison and the deer and the corn, as should be the way. And give up the white man's god—his ugly god, his lying god, his torturous god, his thieving god, his tricking god, and rebuke his missionaries who had one set of rules for white Christians and another for Christians among the people, and who, when asked, talked crossways, so that one word followed the next down a line leading to a place where buzzards roosted and called out beaked noise.

Yet some Creek did not heed the warrior. They paid no attention to the prophet. And our people kept fighting each other, and an American murderer was able to win the Red Stick War. His name was Andrew Jackson and he and his soldiers murdered many hundreds of Creeks, so that his name would become a curse among our people. Indian Killer, he would be called, but somehow he would become a hero among white men. In a new century, statues of him would be built, and his face would be printed upon money.

And his name was praised after he brokered a new, treacherous treaty with the Creeks, the Treaty of Fort Jackson, in 1814.

And more land was taken from our people.

And there was a traitor, a mestizo named William McIntosh, who presented himself as a leader of the Creeks in 1825. McIntosh signed away the rest of our land in Georgia. In that year, this was the Second Treaty of Indian Springs. And McIntosh would be found guilty by our people and executed, but his damage was done.

And in time, Andrew Jackson the Indian Killer became the president of his white man's nation. And in 1830, this murderer signed the Indian Removal Act, after which the Creek people's hope turned to the mud after a heavy rain, for this law decreed that all Creek people were ordered to leave their homes permanently. Many tried to resist and hide in the forest and in the hills. And many of our people were hunted and killed.

The Departure of Micco and Mahala

When Samuel Pinchard read in the newspaper about the new law that forced all Creeks to leave Georgia, he laughed as if this was welcome news. He told Lady it was time for all savages to leave. And he laughed again when he invited her to walk with him to her parents' home to say goodbye.

Lady was ashamed, imagining her place beside her husband as he told her parents they had to depart the land they'd once owned. Even Carson Franklin, a mere tenant, had been allowed to stay. It was not right, but Lady was deprived of gumption. She was a woman and an Indian, and the law placed Samuel above her, in both categories. She was quiet as she walked to the small cabin where her parents had been exiled. Her parents had set aside their disappointment in Samuel when Lady gave them grandchildren. It had been a moment that Micco had never expected. Though Micco didn't speak of his son-in-law's perversions, he'd seen enough to know they existed. Yet his power was gone, and he was only happy that his family would continue, blond-haired and strange-eyed as his grandchildren might be. As always, whiteness in others pleased Mahala, and she had spent many days stroking the light-colored hair of her grandchildren, and telling them how beautiful, how special they were.

In his in-laws' cabin, Samuel spoke directly: the two of them had to leave. They were Indians, and according to the laws of Georgia that had been in place since the previous century, neither the Creek nor the Cherokee were in amity with the government of Georgia. Mahala began to weep. Micco was completely beaten, his shoulders slumped, his frown apologetic, as Samuel advised him that it was time to go west. He would provide a covered wagon and money to get his in-laws settled. Then Samuel slipped the knife in further: he reminded Micco that he was a Negro, because of his grandfather's African blood. His body was a crime, his presence against the law, and Micco placed all of them in danger. If anyone found out about his blood, not only would Samuel's marriage to Lady be voided under the law, but her children would be documented as Negroes.

At these words, Mahala shrieked: in their years of marriage, she had never guessed her husband's secret. She began to flail, her eyes widened, and then, she fainted on the dirt floor.

"Papa?" Lady whispered. "Is this true?"

Micco held out his hand. When his daughter moved toward him, Samuel grabbed her arm, digging in his fingers. He asked, was she a nigger or was she a white woman? She better make her choice, and Lady turned and left the cabin.

And so, in 1832, Micco left his youngest child in the care of her husband. He took Mahala and left the home that had cradled him. They headed west, crossing the Mississippi River. Micco's heart was sibilant when he settled in the ultimate destination of the Journey-Where-the-People-Cried, a place called Oklahoma, a land that originally was the home of the Kickapoo, Wichita, and Osage tribes.

The earth was red in Oklahoma, but there were no trees worth praising. Though Mahala and Micco found their three sons (for they had been required to leave Georgia as well), Mahala still could not find the happiness that had eluded her all of her life. She was surrounded by Indians of all nations out in Oklahoma, including the Creeks, who spoke a language Mahala had avoided since memory. She did not respect them or their ways, but she would never be the white woman she'd aspired to be, either. And she had been betrayed by her husband, whom she now regarded as an African animal.

Soon, she tired of the stunted pine trees that Micco had planted from saplings he'd taken from their original homeland. Those trees never would grow half as tall as those of her youth. One day, Mahala lay down on the cot that was provided by the American government for the removed Indians, underneath the rough blanket that had been given by the same. She closed her eyes and would not speak to anyone, not even her three sons. She ignored the quiet words of her husband, who had asked her forgiveness for his lies. In six years after leaving Georgia, Mahala would pass away.

The End of a Bond

When her parents had prepared for their journey west, Lady had not helped them pack. Nor would she take the days before their departure in early summer to spend last moments with them. When her children whined to see their doting grandparents, Lady spoke sharply to them that she did not have time. It was only after Micco and Mahala left that Lady informed her children that their grandparents had gone on an adventure out west. They had wanted to be near her brothers, she explained. When her children cried, Lady hugged them to her breast, but she did not weep. Her anger at her father was a coal within her, relentlessly bright. Micco had placed her—and her children—in jeopardy, by his inability to keep quiet. How could he not have seen that Samuel was a dangerous man?

Except her children, everything Lady looked upon was tinged with filth. Even her only friendship was ruined, for though Lady had loved Aggie, she felt diminished to her level. And when Lady next met Aggie in the moon house and confided what she had discovered about Micco, Aggie's blank expression revealed her lack of surprise. So Aggie had known! That though Lady slept in the big house, wore beautiful clothes, and was served by dark beings, all along she had been the same as these slaves. Lady was no longer superior to Negroes. She suspected that Aggie had been laughing at her over the years. Another month passed, and when she and Aggie met in the moon house, she was cold to her friend. And Lady left her children in the care of Tut, instead of bringing them along. Lady did not want any more contact between her children and Aggie, and when Aggie brought up her years-long disquietude about the Young Friends in the left cabin, Lady replied, they weren't her concern. They were only pickaninnies, and her husband's property to do with as he wished. She saw Aggie's shocked expression and felt pleasure. She hoped Aggie was hurt.

The next month, Aggie did not appear at the moon house, and Lady did not send for her, either. Lady told herself her life was only about her children. They were her charge, and her only focus. If they succeeded, then her loneliness would not have been in vain.

Lady had been frightened when she'd given birth to a little girl. She was terrified Samuel would pounce on Gloria. She would not let the child from her sight, for Gloria had no marks that would make her imperfect. Lady placed Victor in his cradle, but she slept with Gloria at her breast. Once, Samuel had tried to lift the baby girl from her body, and Lady let out a powerful, sustained scream until he let go. It was Lady's idea to find Gloria a maid, a Quarters-girl named Susan who had been sent from the fields to serve as chaperone until Gloria started to bleed. Lady was equally concerned about Victor, though for other reasons, for while she had seen Samuel's eyes rest lovingly on Nick, he had no such affection for his white son, whose face was identical to Samuel's father's. And Victor did not turn to Lady, though she adored him: he was a boy and white and would one day be master of Wood Place. He would be her salvation and her protection in her old age.

It had been confusing to Victor when his grandparents disappeared. After they left, he felt all alone. His mother was kind, but he'd watched Samuel treating her as if something was very wrong with her, and so Victor began to draw away from her.

As a young child Victor had played with Quarters-children. But when the front teeth of those in his age cohort were shed, he had to play by himself. He pined for playmates, but the other two planters ignored Samuel's invitations. At the general store, he warned his son, the children of the yeomen were not of his class. Victor finally found a companion in the season of chopping, when the weeds are stubborn around the cotton plants. The Quarters-boy

was chopping with his hoe when Victor appeared, carrying a basket of cheese, biscuits, and sweet potato pone, which he had ordered
Tut to prepare. The meal was nothing fancy, but to a field worker,
a feast.

Victor pulled back the cloth in his basket. "I like you," he said.

The other boy had been reared to return kindness from a white
person; if he received violence, he was merely to beg for mercy.
He nodded his head and smiled. Carson Franklin watched the exchange. He called to the Quarters-boy to get back to work, and,
after some confusion—which white male would he obey?—the
Quarters-boy followed after Victor. At the creek, he ate quickly,
and then he saw no reason to refuse Victor's handholding or cheek
kisses. In five years, Victor would wield more power with this same
boy. That would be the year he turned fourteen, and when Samuel
would discover his son's appetites.

Samuel was walking through the peach orchard. Since the day,
years before, when Micco had given him that first delicious peach,
Samuel had not lost his craving for the fruit. During the summers,
he liked to pass among the trees. He cradled the fruit gently, whispering words of encouragement, and on this day, at a distance, he
saw Victor. His trousers were unbuttoned, and he held himself,
pushing closer to the face of the kneeling Quarters-boy.

"Kiss it for me," Samuel heard his son say.

The boy shook his head, and Victor slapped him several times,
shouting, do it, do it, until the Quarters-boy opened his mouth, and
Victor pushed himself inside. After the act was complete, Victor
plucked a peach from a tree and took a bite. He walked away from
the other boy, who was spitting furiously on the ground.

Thereafter, Samuel planned to kill the Quarters-boy. He drew
up notes for the act, but he was saved the exertion by a rock wielded
by another. Emboldened—or anguished—by his relationship with
his master's son, the boy in the peach orchard had taken to bully-
ing other Negro children until he'd picked on the wrong one. This
bullied child picked up a rock and bashed in the skull of his oppres-
sor. The mother of the rock-wielder was terrified, but nothing came

of the event. Samuel only told Carson, choose some men from the field to dig a grave in the Negro side of the cemetery. Bury the Quarters-boy, and then quickly get back to work.

A Marriage, a New Set of Twins

Nick had been discontented, ever since the selling of Midas. Though he worked among his comrades in the fields and sometimes smiled, he was largely a stoic child, who became a brooding young man. In the privacy of his family's cabin, he expressed his desire to run away from Wood Place, from Samuel, whom he finally understood was his father. Aggie would ask, did he want to break her heart into pieces? Hadn't she lost enough? How much more did he want her to cry?

And so Aggie was glad when he approached her and told her he was a man. He wanted to marry. This pleased Aggie—marriage would settle him down—until Nick told her he planned to marry his sister. This change in her children—that they had moved from siblings to sweethearts—distressed Aggie. She turned her gaze upon Nick, looking for signs that he carried the distorted cravings of Samuel Pinchard. Yet he was a good son, always respectful and helpful, after his labors in the cotton fields. Pop George reminded Aggie that her children were not actually blood kin, so she should not feel disgusted. In fact, she should be grateful, since Tess was a curious girl with odd behaviors—the talking to trees, the staring into space. Nick assured his mother that there was a side to Tess that only he knew. And that he would love Tess until the end of his days. She no longer was his sister. Now she would be his wife, and after weeks of stony frowns, Aggie finally gave her consent. She moved into a narrow bed on the other side of Pop George's room, and gave the newlyweds the front chamber, along with the bed that she had shared with Midas.

The twin girls of Tess and Nick were born near the Lord's Resurrection, a holiday that Samuel celebrated in his white man's generosity, giving two days of rest to the slaves. It wasn't Easter yet, however, and that morning, Tess's birth pains began in the field. She walked slowly to her cabin. Some hours passed, and a baby girl was born. Moments later, another baby girl. A week went by, and Tess returned to the fields, leaving her unnamed babies with Aggie, who would carry them to her at nursing time. Aggie would be followed by the other children, two or three of the smallest ones holding on to her dress or her long braid, which fell to her knees. As Tess nursed her babies, she would weep. When her babies opened their eyes, she longed to keep holding them, one in each arm, instead of returning to her work.

Samuel was no longer afraid of Aggie. He had watched her for seventeen years, since he had sold off her husband. He saw that the sparks in her spirit had died. Thus, two weeks after the twins were born, he walked boldly into Aggie's cabin without knocking. He took his time in inspecting his newborn property, pulling the quilt off the babies. The baby on the right was very fat and healthy. She had a head full of black hair and was a pretty cradlesong: though bright-skinned, she had the features of the beautiful, dark-dark Mamie. She was born perfect.

Samuel named this baby after his wife. "Since your mistress is the first Eliza, this child will be Eliza Two."

Small and poorly, the other baby was wrinkled, completely bald, and looked only like herself. Unlike her twin, she had no passed-down magnificence from Mamie. She twitched her limbs as if taken with palsy. Samuel decided to give this twin the name Rabbit.

When the twins lost their front teeth, they were given jobs in the big house, which had changed in its occupants: Victor had gone to the university, accompanied by the much older Claudius, and Tut the cook had died. A new cook had taken over, Venie, a young woman who had been drafted from the fields to replace Tut. With her move, she had been placed in charge of the left cabin, along with Pompey, the young man who had taken over as gardener.

Because they took care of the Young Friends, and thus, were involved in Samuel's perversion—despite being compelled to do so—both the cook and gardener were friendless. The Quarters-folks avoided Venie and Pompey, and so, the two were grateful for the attention of Aggie. Along with other Quarters-children, Pompey had been raised by Aggie, before he had gone to the fields. He was devoted to her as much as to his own mother. As for Venie, the bond the two women shared would not have been likely, had they not been lonely. Aggie was twenty-five years older than Venie, but she was equally friendless. Living for years in "the yard" had distanced Aggie from the other women in the Quarters, though they revered her and were grateful for her careful tending of their children. She and Venie had more in common with each other, as both were connected in their different ways to the big house. Venie was a rare individual: she had been purchased as a Young Friend, but when Samuel tired of Venie within only a month, he could not sell her: Lancaster Polcott told him, if Samuel wanted to get rid of a child so quickly, he must have damaged her irreparably. And there were no refunds for human merchandise. So Samuel had purchased another Young Friend, and had cast Venie into the fields. He reasoned that, in time, he would find someone to breed her with, from among the Quarters-men. That way, he could recoup his financial loss when she gave birth to valuable babies.

Now, Venie was in the kitchen, and it was she who told Aggie that it hadn't been Samuel's idea to move her granddaughters to work in the big house. It had been the mistress's notion. And Aggie was confused: Had Lady meant this as an overture to repair their friendship? Yet when she traveled to the moon house and knocked, Lady answered with a cold mien, informing her she did not wish for company.

Aggie wasn't afraid, however, for she knew how much Samuel loved Nick, and these girls were his own blood. More than that, Samuel had only recently purchased a new Young Friend and had stopped using the children of the Quarter-folks ever since the left cabin had been built. She was certain that her granddaughters would be safe. Eliza Two became the maid for Gloria, and Rabbit was assigned to Venie.

For these little girls, the days were pleasant enough. In the kitchen,

Rabbit was given as much to eat as she desired; she was a tiny girl, but her appetite was unending. And Gloria treated Eliza Two like a live doll, dressing her in cast-off dresses, and Eliza Two learned to be patient with Gloria's repetitious stories and her childishness, even though technically, her mistress's daughter was a young woman. Gloria's former maid had grown too old to listen to the Grimms' Fairy Tales. Susan's body had strained at the bodice and her hips flaunted in the outlines of her dress. Yet her age was not the reason she had been replaced. Susan had convinced Gloria to teach her the ABCs, by encouraging her repeated recitation of the letters— which Gloria was more than happy to do, given her fondness for repetition—and then asking her to write them on dozens of sheets of paper. Susan had progressed from small words, sounded out from *Peter Piper*, which Gloria had kept from her early years, as she had all her dolls and anything else given to her, to longer words and finally to reading. Although Susan had no paper when she returned to her pallet in the attic, because of Gloria's need to travel the same rutted road in her mind, Susan had memorized long passages from the plays of Shakespeare and from the Bible. At night, when it was dark, Susan would close her eyes and see the words moving. Her mistake was that she took a book that she wanted for her own. When she was discovered she was cast back into the fields.

Aggie had made sure her granddaughters knew that neither should take the same liberties as Susan. They were never to look any of their masters or mistresses in the eye. They were never to forget a "sir" or "ma'am." They were never to take something that had not been offered first. They were never to touch anything in the rooms of the big house, unless they were ordered to do so first. Especially, they should never touch a book.

The twins worked in the House during the day. Eliza Two slept alone in the attic, in case Gloria needed her in the night, but Rabbit would return to her family's cabin in the evenings. Their coverlets were child-size quilts that Aggie had made. Rabbit's quilt was pieced together of red squares, with a few dark-blue scattered among the red. In the middle was a big five-pointed star made from yellow flowered gingham. Her sister's quilt was pieced together of blue squares and a scattering of a few red. Her star was yellow as well.

The Death of the Young Friend

The year that the daughters of Tess and Nick turned ten marked a sad milestone: that was the year that the tenth victim to be imprisoned in the left cabin died. She had caught a fever, after walking in her sleep. It had not been the first time she'd been found by Pompey, standing next to the tall iron spokes of the left cabin's gate, her eyes staring and vacant. Yet this time, the Young Friend's fever would not chill, no matter how many bowls of hot soup or glasses of dark elderberry wine Venie fed her. It was a blow to Samuel, losing a Young Friend after only a few months of ownership. He'd planned on keeping her for three—maybe even four—more years before selling her back to Lancaster Polcott at a discounted rate. Other than Venie, the trader had always accepted Samuel's merchandise cheerfully, as Samuel took great care of the little girls. And besides, there was a thriving market for child prostitutes down in New Orleans. But this time, Lancaster would not answer Samuel's queries for four months, and finally Samuel would receive correspondence telling him Lancaster had been inconvenienced with a long illness and only had just recovered.

In the meantime, Samuel resorted to past behavior. He visited the yeoman farmers in the area, paying a dollar for two or three hours of time with a slave child. Yet he felt the same past dissatisfaction creep in. These little girls were not beautiful or cultivated. They had not been trained. They were rough-hewn, with lint in their hair and clothes in rags. They did not even know to curtsy in Samuel's presence. And despite himself, Samuel found that a beautiful child in his own household had caught his eye: it was Eliza Two, the daughter of Nick.

Counter to Aggie's assumption, Samuel did not consider this child to be his kin, no matter her connection to Nick. To himself, he denied that she was the progeny of his own action. She was light-brown-skinned, not white, and thus removed from him. This lack of filial consequence was normal to Samuel, for he did not even love his children by Lady; not only did Victor look like Samuel's despised father, but also, Gloria was very odd, and this made her damaged in her father's eyes.

Samuel only loved Nick. He only craved his return of affection. He did not know why, but it was so. And since he made his own rules and own shining moral circle to shield himself, he decided that Eliza Two was a random Negro child. Yet Samuel was not completely senseless: he knew that Nick would feel differently. Though he had the power over his son, he did not want to test Nick's hand, for Samuel had seen his son and Tess and the little girls walking on Sundays. The way the girls ran and skipped before returning to the parents. Sometimes Nick would pick up the girls and carry one in each arm, no matter how large they were becoming, and kiss each child upon her cheek. And Samuel would smile, not at this show of paternal warmth, but rather marveling at the strength in Nick's arms.

Samuel kept his intentions quiet: he didn't move Eliza Two into the left cabin as his Young Friend. Rather, he kept her in the big house, sleeping under his own roof. Between this and the lies and manipulations he planned to use to control her, he believed that these things would maintain his secret. And he began stalking Eliza Two, coming upon her in the hallways, as she ran errands for her young mistress. She would curtsy and keep her eyes to the floor—as she had been taught—and Samuel would pull one of Eliza Two's long braids in a teasing way. He gave her candy and each Saturday, a half dime to save, telling her she was born to greater things, for she was the most beautiful girl he ever had seen. After each compliment or gift, Samuel reminded Eliza Two not to tell anyone of their conversations. Because they weren't as special as she was, no one would understand the bond that she shared with her master.

Eliza Two had been reminded by her grandmother to obey the white occupants in the big house, and so the child did not report their interactions. She'd heard that Samuel was a cruel man as well, so his behavior confused the child. He seemed so kind to her. So gentle, and he was very handsome. Up close, his resemblance to her father soothed her, and yet it was confusing, for she did not know that Samuel had sired Nick. Even more intoxicating than the gifts of food, candy, and money, Samuel dangled freedom above Eliza Two's reach, promising her that if she served him well, and fulfilled all that he required of her, one day he not only would free her, but he would build a great house for her to live and raise her family in. He repeated, never tell anyone of his gifts, and especially, she should not tell her father; otherwise, Samuel would change his mind and Eliza Two would never be free. Eliza Two believed there would be happy endings for her, as in that book Gloria read aloud, showing her the tower where a girl with long hair lived. Her hair was even longer than Aggie's, and Gloria would ask, "Do you see her hair? Do you see her hair? Do you see her hair? Do you see her hair?" And every time, Eliza Two would answer, "Yes, Missy. I sees it."

Yet Samuel had not calculated the closeness between twins, that children who had shared a womb, had shared a unique language even before they were born, had a connection that others could not grasp. Thus, whenever Samuel caught Eliza Two in the hallway and plied her with candy and promises, Rabbit would have a stomachache, though she was a distance away that spanned the length of the big house, through the outside walkway, and into the kitchen house. And one Sunday evening when the twins were playing their hand games alone in the yard, Rabbit asked Eliza Two, did she have some secrets? It had been a common question between them, since they had been little. Remembering the warning of her master, Eliza Two tried to evade, but her twin pressed on, and soon, demanding Rabbit's confidence, Eliza Two began to prattle about Samuel's promises and her dreams for a better day.

And the next day, she came down to the kitchen house and motioned Rabbit into the pantry. She pulled Samuel's candy from the pocket of her dress, offering it to Rabbit. Eliza Two told her there was a store of half dimes that she had buried, and these were Rabbit's as well. As their grandmother had many times, Rabbit lectured

Eliza Two about eating food that had been prepared by hands she did not know, hands that might have been unwashed or in service to the Devil, who knew many languages spoken in many tongues. Eliza Two laughed, insisting that she had eaten of Samuel's candy many times and had not been struck ill or dead. Finally, Rabbit took the offered candy but protested that she was too full of the midday meal to eat it then. She said she would eat the candy later, when her appetite returned. When her sister left the kitchen house, Rabbit threw the candy in the scrap bucket that Venie kept for Pompey; the contents of this bucket was used to feed the hogs. Then Rabbit washed her hands several times in the bowl of clean water that Venie kept in the kitchen. Later, when Eliza Two would ask, had Samuel's candy been to her liking? Rabbit would assure her how delicious it was and that she was grateful for Eliza Two's kindness in sharing. She would rub her belly so that Eliza Two would believe she was telling her the truth. They would embrace and kiss cheeks, these little girls who had held hands in Tess's womb.

Samuel put off his satisfaction with his granddaughter, letting it build. Then came the night when he visited Eliza Two in the big house attic, where she slept. Samuel brought his bottle of poppy syrup and fistful of candy. He told her that she was pretty and that was why he loved her more than anyone else. Why she was so special. That is all she remembered when she awoke in the morning to find herself wounded and confused. After several of these visits, she reported her injuries to Rabbit, who, in turn, reported them to Aggie that next morning. The child did not know the implications of her sister's injuries, only that when Eliza Two had spoken, Rabbit's stomach was in agony, as if she had been stabbed repeatedly.

A Terrible Decision

When Rabbit came to her, Aggie was stricken with remorse and self-loathing. She awakened from the fog that had obscured her life. Not slowly, but as if someone tossed night water in her face. Or shouted at her in the middle of a meal. Or slapped her without warning after offering her a compliment. She had been warned, hadn't she? For years, Samuel had announced his crimes in the open. Every adult on the premises knew about the Young Friends in the left cabin. Samuel was a monster, and Aggie knew that. Yet she had dropped her guard and placed prey right in front of him. She had thought herself and her family above harm. And more than that: she had borne witness to grievous sins against other children as well and turned her back. In exchange for the safety of her own progeny, and those of the Quarters-folks, she had ignored the suffering of the most helpless. Yet this safety was an illusion, for every Negro—in the big house, in the Quarters, and in the left cabin—was a slave. And all of them were at the mercy of a capricious, evil man. God was punishing Aggie; this she knew. And hopelessness tightened its grasp, until a message from above arrived.

It was a Tuesday evening when Rabbit came to her with the information about her twin. The next morning, Aggie put away her guilt and began to prepare. She only had five more days. She could not alert Samuel that anything was amiss. Though Rabbit was only a child, Aggie told her, do not tell anyone else about the injuries to her twin. Yet also, she told the girl that she could trust her grandmother. Aggie would ensure that all was well.

On Sunday afternoon, Aggie closed the door of her cabin after gathering her family. She told Nick it was time for him, Tess, and the children to leave Wood Place. She looked over at Pop George, who did not seem surprised. Nick was squatting on the braided rug; he only raised his eyebrows. Tess and her little girls were sitting at the table, and Tess began to weep. The twins were silent for different reasons. Eliza Two had been groggy for days, as Samuel had continued to ply her with his poppy syrup. As for Rabbit, in that same time, she had become steely and grim—too mature for a little girl of eleven.

"Mama, what happen?" Nick asked. "Why you done change your mind?"

Aggie lied, saying nothing had occurred. It was only time for his children and grandchildren to leave. Yet when Nick questioned her again, she relented, his girls didn't need to be working in that house around that evil man. Nick's eyes widened. He leapt up, and his mother blocked his way to the door. Pop George called his name. Sit down, boy, he said. Listen to your mama. It's time for you to leave. It seemed when Pop George spoke, all sound stopped. Unless he was telling his stories, he was a man of few words. Perhaps this was why Nick turned from the door.

Time slowed as Pop George and Aggie prepared Nick. As they told him which star he should follow, that if he were in the right position the star would keep in front of him, and that the green moss needed to grow on the front side of the trees, too. If he had those two guides, that would serve him. But no, she did not know how this knowledge came about, only that she had been told by her grandmother Helen, and she had been told by somebody else, and so on, and yes, it might have been the star that came up the night Jesus was born, but then again, it might not have been, but that wasn't important, and Nick should listen to what she was talking about, so he could remember. She didn't see that her son was gulping down her words. They were keepsakes. Aggie gave him light and corn breads given to her by Venie, along with a large portion of a ham.

Pop George had joined into the preparations as well. He warned Nick to retain his wits, that when he heard wagons, he should keep to the trees, but if he kept his distance, he would be unnoticed even if seen. His white skin and his light eyes would be his protection so long as he made a shaving foam with a portion of his drinking water and soap and used his razor to keep the kinks on his head at bay. He needn't worry about his beard, which was a vibrant, golden color and not that much differently textured from white men's. He should be careful about talking, though: his speech would give him away. From afar, others would assume Tess and the twins were his property.

Then it was time. The plantation was asleep, and all lights in the Quarters and the big house were extinguished. Yet through the hours, Rabbit clung to her mother, and Eliza Two had shaken off her poppy fog. Both twins were weeping. Aggie hissed, hush that fuss now. They had to go. Aggie's resolve was crumbling, but she knew if her son remained, Nick would kill Master, and then he would be killed in turn. And Eliza Two might be sold down the river to New Orleans for even more abuse.

Aggie could not bear such losses. She turned to Rabbit, telling her, go with Nick. Yet Rabbit said, if Eliza Two and Tess would not leave, then neither would she.

And so, that night, only a young father would leave the plantation. And Aggie would be forced to make a terrible decision.

The Power in the Field

Since Nick was a little boy, he had added stones to the grave site he'd made for his father. Even after he was old enough to understand that Midas had not died, rather he had been sold away, Nick would carry a handful of stones to the place he had chosen in the slave cemetery. In time, he made a pattern with these stones, a symbol of his loss.

The night that Nick escaped Wood Place, he crept to the cemetery and chose a stone. He placed it in his pocket. Then he began to walk the road that passed the big house, the left cabin, and further on, past the general store. At that point, the road narrowed to a path. After some distance, he saw the mound rising, and the ramshackle cabin where Carson Franklin lived with his family in its shadow.

Then someone called Nick's name. He turned, and there was Pop George, saying he'd come to lead him awhile. He'd lived on the plantation for so long, he knew the place pretty good. Pop George's back had straightened, and in the dark, he looked to be a much younger man. His hand was strong and sure as he touched Nick's shoulder. When they passed closer to the Franklins' cabin, Nick tensed, for someone was sitting on the porch of the cabin, smoking. The ember was flickering red. Pop George touched Nick again, and whispered, stop. As they waited, the figure on the porch walked down the steps. Closer, until Nick could see the cigar that he took from his mouth, and that the figure was a man, but no taller than Nick's twin girls. He bowed to Pop George, who told Nick he would leave him here.

We don't lose track of Nick at this point when he leaves our land, but this is where we will finish telling his story. There were others in the south who escaped from slavery, who wrote the tale of their triumph in books commissioned by their abolitionist friends. They would recount the fear of cramming into boxes, enfolded by their excrement, as in the instance of Mr. Henry "Box" Brown. Riding in trains, passing for the white owners of slaves, if they were light enough, as the fair-skinned Mrs. Ellen Craft did, accompanied by her much darker husband, William. Running through the woods, the North Star above and moss and grass and leaves, tiny apertures of the journey stuck in their hair. We won't tell you whether Nick lived or died, or whether he learned to read, or if he knew about Mr. Frederick Douglass, a former slave who found power in a root, the magic dug up from dirt.

Back then, Mr. Douglass's name was Fred, and that root allowed him to resist. There were such battles in the Bible, where a root was not solid, but made of Spirit, given by an old man who had learned of it in his dreams. Or in the stories told by a mother, when a prophet flung his stone at a monster's forehead and the monster fell. And the Word was changed. And the Word was knowledge. And the knowledge was a sound within the flesh, which may have been the Good Lord, or may have been dead ones in Africa talking across an ocean, or our people here on this side. Yet we know that in one of those tales, a man did rise tall in the field. And that man was renamed Mr. Frederick Douglass.

IX

It is a peculiar sensation, this double-consciousness, this sense of always looking at one's self through the eyes of others, of measuring one's soul by the tape of a world that looks on in amused contempt and pity. One ever feels his two-ness, an American, a Negro; two souls, two thoughts, two unreconciled strivings; two warring ideals in one dark body, whose dogged strength alone keeps it from being torn asunder.

—W. E. B. Du Bois, "Of Our Spiritual Strivings"

WHICH NEGROES DO YOU KNOW?

◈

I'd moved to the right side of a duplex, a place I'd rented sight-unseen in Acorn, North Carolina, when I decided to enroll in graduate school. The place was in the historic district of my university town, on a street of cozy, cute houses that approached shabby. My duplex was large, with tall ceilings, but with none of the bed-and-breakfast flavor I'd expected from the university mail-out I'd received before moving to town.

A few moments after I walked in, I realized that "historic location" meant "old as hell." The kitchen had a stained porcelain sink and no dishwasher, and when I opened the top of the tiny gas stove, there appeared to be twenty years of grease caked on the burners. The hardwood floors were scarred, and there was only one tiny air-conditioning unit in the living room; it rattled and kicked out dust when I turned it on. When I saw the ancient radiators, I had a feeling it'd be bad in the wintertime. And to be on the safe side, I'd need to visit a hardware store and purchase boric acid to sweep in all the corners, before I was rewarded with roaches.

I heard my dead sister's voice in my ear.

Now, what did you learn from this experience? Lydia asked.

"I learned never to trust some fucking pictures in a university mail-out."

That's right, baby, she said.

I held out my hand and pretended Lydia was there to give me five. Then I turned my palm down, this time on the Black-hand side.

There were two linebackers living in the house across the street from me. Big, fine, pea-fed boys, their skin gleaming in the tank tops they wore. They walked slowly, as if it took effort to cart that much prettiness around. They were sophomores, both from Louisiana. Eddie Thibideaux was Creole and shy with dark-blond hair. He had better manners than Mike Corban, a brown-skinned honey who gave me hound-dog glances, saying he liked him some older women. But the day I moved in, they rushed to help me unpack the car, though it was July in full blast. As a gesture of gratitude for their help moving, I cut up and fried a whole chicken and baked biscuits for Eddie and Mike, which they dispatched in around ten minutes.

The next week, Mike showed up begging for a meal. Eddie peeked from their doorway, hopeful, and then disappointed, as his teammate ran a slew-footed jog across the street, shaking his head. But they were generous, too: Mike would knock on my door, inviting me over to share their five large meat lover's pizzas, just delivered.

"Have some, Miss Ailey? It's gone be real, real good."

I would wave him out of the doorway as he reassured me that I didn't need to be on no diet. I was thick and super fine in the right places.

Other than athletes, there were very few brothers on campus, and even fewer in the graduate programs. Scooter Park was tall and slim, and other than my neighbors, he was the finest Black man walking around North Carolina Regents University. A lean runner type, he concealed whatever muscles he had under his rotation of business suits. My first semester in Acorn, we met at the annual Black graduate students' association reception, two weeks after classes had begun.

I almost hadn't gone to the reception: my social awkwardness had returned with a vengeance, along with my homesickness. That year, there was a heat wave in North Carolina, and each morning I urged myself to get out of bed and face the day. Telling myself my ancestors had been through worse summers than this, and I should get up and take a shower, with my twenty-first-century, lazy self. I'd turn the water to lukewarm, just enough to clean the funk off, because hot would make me sleepy. Or make me a coward.

The night of the Black graduate reception, I stood in front of my bathroom mirror, chanting self-affirming mantras at my reflection. I could survive without my family and my college roommates, the only non-kin girlfriends I'd ever had. I was twenty-eight years old and a grown-ass woman. And look how captivating I was in my red linen dress (with girdle underneath) and Italian leather pumps (that I'd bought on sale). My courage lasted about twenty minutes, around the time I drove up to the multicultural center. I made the mistake of using the wrong entrance and ended up right behind the refreshments table. Worse, when I entered the room, I forgot to catch the door, and it shut with a loud bang.

Dr. Charles Whitcomb, associate graduate dean and full professor of history, was in the middle of his remarks, and everyone looked back at me, glaring. Then someone else arrived, using the same entrance, but I feigned concentration as Dr. Whitcomb told our gathering that we were "the future of the African American race," even when I felt a tap on the shoulder. At the second tap, I turned around and a tall brother leaned down.

"Hi, I'm Scooter Park."

Small wisps of warm air hit my cheek. The wing tips were shiny, the suit a lightweight gray, and the tie a nearly matching shade in silk. He was a darker version of Denzel Washington, his cheeks smooth-shaven. I felt myself stirring, even after I saw his wedding band, and while Dr. Whitcomb continued to give his racially uplifting remarks, Scooter and I whispered to each other. We played the "Which Negroes Do You Know?" game and found out his aunt and my father's mother were in the same sorority. Like me, Scooter had attended a private high school, though his had been a boarding school in Massachusetts.

We left after the last of the speeches, carefully closing the door so it wouldn't slam behind us. Outside, it had settled into full darkness, and Scooter insisted on walking me to the car. He held on to the door handle and talked in a concise baritone, while I sat with my keys in the ignition.

His family hadn't forgiven him for eloping after college graduation, during his internship. Two years later, he'd turned down Wharton for business school at North Carolina Regents University, because his wife wanted a change of scenery. His family was sending him a generous monthly stipend, and he hoped they would come around to the marriage, because Rebecca's family wasn't going to accept him. Her parents hadn't cared where she attended graduate school, or whether she eloped, but they were absolutely pissed she'd married a Black guy. Scooter's family wasn't too happy, either. His father had tried to roll with things, but his mother had held out hope that he'd marry a sister, even though his other girlfriends had been white, too.

"What did Mom expect?" Scooter asked. "She sent me to Phillips Academy and Brown. There weren't that many Black girls to date. And now what? Am I supposed to divorce Rebecca?"

"I get it, brother," I said. "You don't have to convince me. I'm good."

We laughed, and I told him that after I turned down medical school, I'd needed a job, so I took one as a research assistant for one of my college professors, and I caught the historian's bug. My mother had wanted me to reapply to medical school, but my father wouldn't have minded. That is, if he hadn't died.

Scooter placed his hand on the edge of the car door. He told me he was sorry about my father. His face was open, so full of emotion, like Denzel Washington's in the whipping scene in *Glory*, when that single tear had traveled down his cheek. It was the drop of water that had soaked every pair of Black woman's panties in the United States of America. I raised a hand to put over Scooter's, but let it fall away: I had to defuse this situation, before it went too far.

"May I ask you a personal question?"

"Shoot."

"Youngblood, did your mama really name you after a motorized toy? I've heard some strange handles before, but yours has to be the absolute worst."

Take that, you beautiful, married bastard.

He only laughed, opening his mouth wide enough for me to see the pink of his throat.

"No, woman. My mother did not name me Scooter. My name is Quincy. I am not a junior and I am not a third." He reached into the breast pocket of his jacket, pulled out a card, and wrote his phone number on the back and gave it to me. On the front, there was only his name: Quincy X. Park.

I asked, did the X stand for Malcolm?

He told me it most certainly did not.

———

No one had suggested graduate school to me—not the old man, and not my mother. I'd come to the decision of grad school on my own, after nineteen months of working for Dr. Oludara. I'd been so reluctant to reach into the bookshelves lining the walls of her second office. To explore the articles in the banker's boxes I'd stacked in the office's closet, but when I'd begun to dive into the materials, the stories of the people had spoken to me.

No matter how dry the prose of the books and articles, I could see the people in my imagination. Their old-fashioned clothes of heavy wool, and boots that buttoned up. I poured voices into their mouths and rounded the words that might emerge. But they weren't characters. They were real people. I couldn't turn away from them. I didn't even try, and frequently, Dr. Oludara told me I'd caught something she hadn't seen in her reading. She'd stop by before it was time for me to leave for the day, sit down, and we would talk about her project. Many times, the building would empty, and it would be dark when I pulled up to Uncle Root's house. He didn't complain, though. He'd tell me he already had made himself a sandwich.

It had been an early September day when I knocked on the door of Dr. Oludara's main office, asking, did she have a second?

"Ailey, I don't mean to be rude, but I need to make this grant deadline. "

"Oh, okay. I didn't mean to bother you."

She looked up from the computer screen. "Can you give me a couple hours? Hold that thought, all right? Don't forget."

It took until the end of the day, because I had to drive to Milledgeville and mail off her fellowship application. I was afraid that she'd be gone by the time I returned, but she was still there. She had a while, she said, because she was not about to drive back to

Atlanta into that afternoon traffic. I fidgeted, and she told me, don't be afraid to speak my mind.

"I'm a little nervous," I said. "I feel kind of silly. Um . . . okay. Do you remember when you asked me what my dream was, a while back? And I said I didn't have one? Well, I did, when I was a little girl. But I thought it was a stupid dream. And then my sister got in trouble, and my family was worried about her. And then she passed away, and then I guess I made a mess of everything."

"You seem fine to me, Ailey. A little long-winded, because I still don't know what this is about."

When she smiled, I knew she was teasing.

"I'm sorry. So . . . um . . . it's like this. I want to be a history teacher, or maybe a history professor, you know, like you. And I was wondering, you know, if I applied to a graduate program in history, if you could write me a letter of recommendation. I wasn't a history major, so I'd need to take some more undergraduate classes in the field, but Uncle Root told me he'd pay for those, and—"

"Is that all? Ailey, I already have a draft of your letter of recommendation on my hard drive. Dr. Hargrace asked me a year ago, but when you never said anything, I didn't want to be in your business."

"For real?"

"Listen, sister. Do you think I kept you on because you were cheap? Ailey, you're my fourth research assistant! Everybody kept quitting as soon as they saw that mess in the other office. But you just rolled up your sleeves and got to work! And then all those excellent notes you took on those research materials! You really are brilliant, Ailey. Surely you must know that."

"You think so? Oh, gosh. Oh, thank you so much." I put my hand over my face. I didn't want her to see me crying, but she tugged at my hand.

"Bless your heart. Don't cry, sweetie."

"You just don't understand. I never thought I'd find something that made me feel this way. I've never been happy before in my whole entire life. I thought I never would be."

"Oh, sister, I understand completely! Why do you think I work at this school for peanuts? It's so I can feel how you do right now."

I thought I was done crying, but another wave shook me. She stood up and hugged me around my shoulders. Tomorrow, we'd start to plan out which extra undergraduate classes I needed to take, but this evening, we were going to eat us some ribs. Lots of them, because we needed to celebrate.

She had celebrated with me again when I'd been accepted to the graduate program at North Carolina Regents University. She'd run checks on every professor in my department, putting out their names on the Black historian grapevine. But she assured me I'd have no problem with her former Harvard classmate Dr. Charles Whitcomb, whom she called Chuck. He wasn't just Black on the outside. He was a real brother, through and through.

Then she'd warned me: just because I was a brilliant researcher didn't mean I could easily acquire a doctorate in history. The next few years were going to be brutal. I'd be exhausted, existing on very little sleep. I'd be drinking coffee like it was water. Even with the minority fellowship I'd won, I'd be poor as a church mouse at a Devil worship convention. Most of all, I needed to get my mind right, because I'd be lonely: there never had been a Black doctoral candidate in history at my university. But I'd assured Dr. Oludara that I was ready for whatever came my way. I'd finally found my briar patch. My purpose in life, and she'd told me, I had her home number.

———

That night of the Black graduate reception, I didn't tell Scooter that I already knew his wife, after a fashion. I'd been quiet when he talked about Rebecca, but I saw her at least once a week in the history department. Like me, she was a first-year student in the master's program. We were in the same seminar class, Southern Reconstruction and the New South. Rebecca wouldn't speak to me, but rather teased with an eye-slide: she'd lock eyes with me for a split second before altering her gaze and fixing it on some spot beyond me, as if I was no longer there. It was like a movement you might make after casual sex, but without the orgasm, or the hopefully free dinner beforehand.

Our class met for three hours every Thursday, where Dr. William Petersen terrorized us Socratic-style. On the first day he told us, he would ask questions. We would answer. We would not raise our hands or interject with comments. He was like that mean fat man in *The Paper Chase*, only Dr. Petersen was from Mississippi.

But I was ready for him, because the nights before his class, I wouldn't sleep. I'd take reams of notes and memorize the order in which I'd written them, so I didn't have to flip through the pages.

"Miss Garfield?" he asked. "Was the Reconstruction era a failure or a success? You have three minutes. Make your case."

"Well, Dr. Petersen, that depends on who you ask. W. E. B. Du Bois believed that Reconstruction was a long game. But he makes a moral case that it was a failure because Blacks and whites did not join forces against the white ruling class. He was disappointed about the loss of enfranchisement, and the rise of Jim Crow made civil rights impossible, but ultimately, Du Bois was optimistic. Should I go on?"

"Absolutely."

"If you ask C. Vann Woodward, it was not only a failure, it was a tragedy, and the tragic hero was the white male aristocrat, who had tried to preserve a dying way of life instead of accepting that death."

"I see you've read ahead."

I smiled and nodded my head modestly.

"But you still haven't answered, Miss Garfield. What do you think, personally? What is your opinion?"

"I would have to agree with Du Bois. I think it was a balanced achievement for African Americans."

"Excellent, Miss Garfield! My goodness! Aren't you surprisingly articulate?"

He smiled at me, and my own smile froze. "Oh. Um . . . thank you so much, Dr. Petersen. That's so wonderful of you to say."

"You watch that Petersen cracker," Uncle Root said.

"Oh, he's harmless," I said. "He's a liberal. A Marxist, too."

I wasn't going to mention my professor's "articulate" compliment. Uncle Root hadn't wanted me to attend graduate school so far away. He'd told me, several universities in Georgia had fine programs. But I'd wanted to prove I could make it on my own.

The old man snorted. "A liberal, Marxist cracker from Mississippi! There's a phrase I never thought I'd hear. I believe I can die happy now."

"Uncle Root, please stop using that word."

"What word?"

"The C word."

"I'm unsure what you mean, Ailey."

"'Cracker.' You're being prejudiced."

"I am not. I simply have common sense. That's why I call you every week."

"I thought you called because you loved me."

"I do, sugarfoot, and it's because of my love that I'm telling you, I don't care what that white man calls himself. A cracker from Mississippi can never be trusted."

Those initial weeks, I only read books and articles and wrote reviews of both. There was a lot of reading, though, more than I'd anticipated. I was taking the full load of graduate classes. With those three classes combined, I was required to read between three and five hundred pages a week. But I used the magic trick that Uncle Root had shown me, when I'd been a research assistant. The old man had told me, reading scholarly articles wasn't like reading a novel. There was no joy in the language, no delicious anticipation of lyricism. It wasn't like reading original documents either, where you had to read everything and in order. For an article, I only needed to read the first and last paragraphs followed by the initial sentence of each remaining paragraph, writing down pertinent dates and facts as I went. Finally, I had to make sure to read the foot- or endnotes to the article and circle back, because those would point to important information in the text.

I was disappointed that none of my three classes required visits to the Old South Collections, the archives at the university. That was what I had been looking forward to the most about the program, and within days, I telephoned Dr. Oludara. Did she want me to look through the Georgia plantation portfolios? Just to see what I could find on the weeping time auction that she was writing her book about?

"My goodness, are you kidding me? Ailey, yes! But are you sure? Do you have time?"

"Yes, ma'am. I need the practice."

"How much do I owe you?"

"Oh, it's my pleasure, Dr. Oludara! Don't you even worry about money."

But within a few days, a package from her showed up on my front porch. Inside, there was a check for fifty dollars and several copies of journal articles. When I saw the thick stack of brand-new legal pads in the package, I called her back, lecturing: do not return to that office supply store, under any circumstances.

My three classes were on Monday, Tuesday, and Thursday afternoons. Weekday mornings—Monday through Friday—I drank coffee and studied at Shug's Soul Patrol, the only Black restaurant in town. At noon, I drove to campus and parked. If I had an afternoon class, I walked in one direction, to the history department. If not, I walked in the other direction to the Old South Collections, where I did research for Dr. Oludara. When I arrived, puffing from the stairs—the elevator was only for staff or patrons who were disabled—I waved at Mrs. Ransom, the head archive librarian. She fixed her glasses on her nose. Smiled in recognition. She handed me white cotton gloves, then the document request forms.

The oak table was the closest to the reception desk, in clear sight. I waited for Mrs. Ransom to deliver my manuscripts, and when they were set down, I dipped my head in gratitude, said, "Thank you, ma'am," and got to work, writing on my legal pad with the fancy

pencil David had given me, that long-ago summer. Once she'd mistaken it for a forbidden ballpoint pen, until I'd screwed off the top,
showing her the lead inside.

I was careful with Mrs. Ransom, who hovered near my table. Who
watched me. In this modern day, the collections weren't barred
from a person of my color, not like during the era of Terrence Carter
Holmes, the old man's professor at Routledge College. While researching for his dissertation at North Carolina Regents University,
Mr. Holmes had been forced to sit in a separate, secluded room, far
away from white female librarians, and wait for men to bring him
his plantation records, lest Mr. Holmes give in to the much-feared
rapist tendencies of Black men that southern white people in 1929
believed they knew all about. A natural fact, despite Mr. Holmes's
daily suit and tie; his timid, near whisper; and his ten letters of introduction from W. E. B. Du Bois, Mr. Holmes's white professors from
Yale, and other renowned white historians throughout the south,
liberals of their time. It had taken six months of constant telegraphs
and letters by his patrons to gain him entry to these collections.

At my oak table, I'd ignore Mrs. Ransom's careful eye and move
through plantation journals, fascinated yet horrified by the inventive punishments of enslaved African Americans. All of it recorded
in elaborate, cursive writing.

One imaginative owner had written a letter to another owner,
noting that it was important to provide torture that did not disable
the slaves' hands and feet: those were needed to work. But teeth
were not needed, and neither were ears.

I'd get so engrossed in my readings, I'd lose track of time, until
Mrs. Ransom came over to my table.

"Yes, Mrs. Ransom?"

"It's time to leave."

"But I just got here a little while ago. Did I do something wrong?"

"Ailey, it's five thirty. You've been here five hours. We're closing
now."

As I walked the mile across campus to the parking lot, I tried to
shake off the horror that I'd read about in the journals. When I'd

lived in Georgia, doing this research for Dr. Oludara had been emotional, but I'd never felt lonely in my grief. Or foolish: trying not to
cry over the sufferings of folks who weren't even alive.

But when I opened the door of my duplex, I wouldn't wait. At
the door, I'd drop my bag on the floor. I'd shower, put on my white
nightgown, and kneel on the rug next to my bed. I'd stay a long time
there on my knees, praying. I'd lose track of time again.

MAMMIES, OR, HOW THEY SHOW OUT IN HARLEM

◈

In September, I saw Scooter again, out at Shug's Soul Patrol. When I'd arrived in town, I'd driven to Shug's on a Saturday, but it had been overrun by whites, with a line that stretched a quarter mile. I stood for an hour, tolerating openly hostile looks from white customers. When I got inside, Miss Velma, the cashier, whispered enough to let me know that weekends were for "them." Monday through Friday, Shug's was for "us." The system had been worked out during segregation, when Mr. Shumate, the original "Shug," ran things, before he turned it over to his son. His daughter-in-law owned the barber and beauty shops next door, the only places in town Black folks could get our hair styled. The other places claimed no one was trained in "Ebony textures." Miss Velma wore black brogans with thick soles, used endearments, and asked about our days when pouring the coffee. She smiled when I never failed to say, thank you so much. I appreciate you. Sometimes when mornings were slow, Miss Velma would come and sit with me, and I'd put aside my books and papers and we'd chat.

When Scooter walked in that Monday, he was in another suit, a black pin-striped one this time. He carried a brown ostrich brief-case. He looked preposterous and sexy, but I didn't regret not calling him. I didn't need some married man poking a stick through the bars of my cage. When he spoke my name, I returned a dry half salute. I left it at that.

Two days later, I saw him at Shug's again. When I went to the counter, Miss Velma told me my refills had been taken care of. I looked around and Scooter lifted his cup of coffee. He was semi-casual: the suit and shirt were a tan linen, and there was no tie. He came over to my table with his briefcase, sat down without asking, and removed his jacket. I had my papers and books spread out, and he pushed them to one side to make space. He looked amused, as he had that evening in the parking lot.

"Ailey, I'm very hurt. You promised you would call."

I looked at him over my new horn-rimmed glasses. "I don't remember saying that. And anyway, what was I supposed to say to your wife when she picked up?"

"Easy. Just ask for me." He pulled out one of his cards from his breast pocket and flipped it over to the blank side. "Okay, then. Give me your number."

"Why?"

"I thought you could come over to the house and have dinner with Rebecca and me."

"I don't do dinner, Scooter."

"Everybody does dinner."

"Not me."

"Don't you eat?"

"No, Scooter, I don't. Look me up. I'm in the *Guinness Book of World Records*."

I looked down at my notes, expecting him to leave, but he pulled his briefcase onto his lap. He clicked the locks and pulled out some papers. We sat there together for two hours, reading. Like Daddy and I used to, him with his patient files and me with my novel.

Whenever Scooter and I met for coffee, he paid. And even though he didn't like down-home fare—he preferred fruit in the mornings—he'd cover the cost of my grits and sausage links, too. And by early October, he'd invited me to dinner at his house seven times. He'd say that Rebecca was grilling tuna or salmon or shrimp. I should come to dinner that weekend, and I'd told him, no thanks, I was too busy. He'd ask for my number and I'd change the subject.

Some mornings as Scooter and I got wired off coffee, Dr. Charles Whitcomb would stop by Shug's. During the week, Black folks from the university would offer each other friendly nods. We were family, even when we didn't know each other. But when Dr. Whitcomb came through the door, bald head shining, he'd smile and loudly call out, "Hey, brethren! Hey, sistren!" It seemed like he knew every-body in town with melanin.

Dr. Whitcomb would stroll through the tables in his pimp-cool, '70s way, giving out soul shakes to the men and courtly bows to the women. At the counter, he held out his arms for Miss Velma. He gave a delighted noise when she came from behind the counter, squeezing him tightly. And his many different suits were impecca-ble. Scooter and Dr. Whitcomb dressed like twins, eternally pre-pared for an important job interview.

This was what I'd taken for granted in Chicasetta and at Rout-ledge: other Black people. Their warmth, the greetings they gave each other, peacocking their bonds. Even as awkward as I was, I'd been so comfortable with my natural self. I hadn't realized how lucky I'd been, not having to look over my shoulder for white ap-proval.

———

The week before midterms, Scooter showed up at Shug's with Re-becca. He only gave me a nod as they headed to the line. He'd flung his tie over his shoulder in preparation for a meal.

The sister at the next table tried to whisper. She wasn't good at it.

"I drive out here on a Wednesday so I can eat in peace. And now these honkies are coming during the week, too? This is just like Harlem. They're taking over."

"Gayle, one white person doesn't mean gentrification," the other sister said.

They were about my age, graduate students. I didn't know which program, but I recognized them from the multicultural center. Aside from Shug's, that was the Black folks' regular haunt.

"I will give him this: at least she's good-looking," Gayle said. "Usually they pick the homely white chicks, and then you're think-ing, *Did that nigger need to go outside the race for that?*"

"Shh, they can hear us."

"Yvonne, I don't give a fuck. What's that white girl going to do? Bring the Klan up in here? Where'll they get their ribs, then?"

Rebecca and Scooter stood in line. I hoped they hadn't heard the conversation, but her face was dark pink, and he turned my way, frowning. He raised an eyebrow at me, and I shrugged. I wasn't going to lecture two Black women over a white woman who barely acknowledged my existence.

"Honey, I'd just like a salad," Rebecca said at the register.

"All we got is potato salad and coleslaw." Miss Velma spoke slowly, her hands folded across the front of her apron.

"That's not real salad." Rebecca let go of Scooter's arm and batted her hands about: the extra-large diamond in her ring reflected sparks. "And it's dripping with mayonnaise."

"We got some collard greens. You might like those."

"But you make those with pork. That's not any better, now, is it? You know what, honey? Let me have some dry lettuce."

"Ma'am, we don't have none of that."

"Are you telling me you don't even have plain iceberg?"

Scooter had told me she was from Atlanta, but she hadn't ever sounded southern in class. Now, though, I thought I detected the accent, but I couldn't be sure. It might be her tones, which were muted as if she never had to raise her voice to receive plenty.

"No, ma'am, I'm so sorry. We don't have no lettuce."

"Why don't you go back and check, honey? I'll wait." Rebecca gave a smile so broad I swore I could see her jaw teeth. Her husband rubbed her arm.

Miss Velma spoke carefully. "Ma'am? All we got is coleslaw, collard greens, crowder peas, black-eyed peas, sweet corn, baked beans, macaroni and cheese, potato salad, French fries, and candied yams. Them's all the vegetables we got. And then we got light bread, but that's with the ribs. If you look up over my head on the wall, there go the whole menu. Ain't nothing else in the back."

Rebecca started to say something else, and Miss Velma held up both hands. She closed her eyes and several moments passed. As she moved her lips, I heard what sounded like *Lord Jesus*.

"I know just how she feels," Gayle said. "'Honey'? Miss Velma is old enough to be that white girl's grandma! See what I mean? No manners. That's just how they show out in Harlem."

That afternoon, Rebecca showed up at Old South Collections. She was by herself, and when she waved in my direction, I swiveled and looked behind me, but there was no one there. She walked to my oak reading table and pulled up a chair. She set a stack of blank legal pads on the table. Rebecca was dressed in a female version of her husband's uniform. A severe suit, but with a blouse in luxurious fabric. She had that self-aware manner of a very pretty woman: she knew someone was watching her and, sooner or later, coveting.

"Hey, how's it going?" she asked. "I love that blouse. That salmon color is fabulous."

"Thanks," I said. "I got it from the thrift shop. Two dollars."

"Gosh, it's nice. I don't think we've been introduced. I'm Rebecca Grillier Park."

I tilted my head: I'd sat at a seminar class table with her since August. Was she really going to pretend she didn't know me? I stuck out my hand, giving her a strong grip so that she would know my strength.

"Good to meet you, Rebecca. I'm Ailey Garfield."

"What do you think about the program?" Rebecca asked.

"It's fine," I said.

"I just love it already! People told me that graduate school was hard, but I'm having a wonderful time."

"Great." I picked back up my magnifying glass. I bent over my plantation records, but after a few moments, I stopped. "Oh. You're still here, Rebecca. Hey, thanks for introducing yourself. You know, finally, after over a month of seeing me in Dr. Petersen's class. But I've got to get back to work."

She rose from the table. "Okay, I'll see you tomorrow."

The next time Rebecca showed in the collections, her hands were empty. She sat without papers or reading materials, lazily pulling her blond ponytail through her fist.

"I heard that you've been looking at plantation records. What're you planning to do with them?"

"Who told you that?"

"I'm friendly with Mrs. Ransom." She waved at the head librarian, who touched the glasses that were suspended by a chain and sat on her chest. She fixed them on her nose and smiled.

"This isn't my research, Rebecca. I'm doing this work for a colleague, so I really don't feel comfortable sharing." I liked the way that sounded: "colleague."

Her brow wrinkled. She looked down at her folded hands. I knew I'd hear something from Scooter the next time I saw him.

"I can tell you where some of my own interests lie," I said. "But why don't you tell me what you're working on first?"

"Okay!" She bounced in her chair. "I'm interested in doing research on mammies."

"Mammies?"

"Yes, mammies."

I searched for humor in her face. Or irony. Anything. There was nothing. "Um . . . great."

"See, people talk about how there was so much animosity between masters and slaves, but I want to prove there wasn't. I want to talk about family."

"You mean biracial people?"

"No, I mean slaves. Slaves were family, too. Living in the house, taking care of their masters' children like they were their own. And there were some kind slave masters, although nobody wants to talk about that. God forbid anyone would want to be politically incorrect." A hand in the air, the diamond shining. "You know, I was raised by this wonderful Black girl, Flossie? She's worked for my family since before I was born."

"How old are you, Rebecca?"

"Twenty-four."

"Wow. Miss Flossie has worked for your family over two decades? That's a really long time for someone to remain a girl. She must use some high-end moisturizer."

"Yes, Flossie's very beautiful, and so loving. She fed me from her own breasts. She used to say somebody wrote the Book of Ruth just for us: 'Whither thou goest, I will go.' Okay, I told you my research, now you've got to tell me yours."

She gave me a flirtatious look, wiggling her shoulders. I told her that I was interested in slave life.

"Why slave life?" she asked.

"I guess it's personal for me, because my family is descended from slaves."

"Well, of course they were. You're Black."

"Thanks for noticing that, Rebecca. Because do you know that, dark as I am, sometimes people actually think I'm Puerto Rican?" I looked at her seriously. I willed myself not to laugh in her confused face.

"Oh. Really? Okay."

"So anyway, Rebecca, after my family was freed, they were tenant farmers. They still are."

"Sharecroppers, you mean."

"No, I mean tenant farmers."

"Which is the same thing as sharecroppers, Ailey."

"No, Rebecca, it's not. And nobody works for shares anymore. It's the twenty-first century."

"If you say so, honey."

Rebecca pulled her shiny ponytail and looked away from me. I watched her glance around the room, blinking her eyes slowly. I hid a smile at her uppity shenanigans: this chick could stroke her hair all she wanted, but she still didn't know the distinction between tenant farmers, who'd rented land but owned their own crops, and sharecroppers, who'd worked for shares, borrowing against their crops. Knowing her ignorance gave me a nerdy frisson.

"Ailey, I need to say something. Scooter needs a friend who's like him. You know what I mean. And I'm so glad he has you. I really am."

"No problem. He's like my little brother."

"And Scooter and I want to invite you over to dinner. He knows loads of cuties over in the B-school. Not that you need fixing up, but I'd love us to hang out."

"Thanks, that's so nice of you. I'm so busy right now with my research, but when things calm down, I'll think about it."

———

"You're going to end up cussing that woman out," my mother said. "You might even have to fight her."

"Mama, please stop tripping."

It was on a Sunday, on what had become our regular phone date. She'd had a phone installed in her bedroom, so she could relax while we talked. And now she allowed me a few "girlfriend" moments.

"Ailey, she's . . . what do you call it? Stalking you. That's what she's doing, because she thinks you're going with her husband."

"I told you, Scooter and I are only friends."

"But hasn't he been paying for your coffee? And your breakfast, too? I know I'm out of practice, but that shole sounds like foreplay to me."

"Lord have mercy."

"I'm not judging you, baby. I was young once with a hot tail."

"Mama, please. This is so nasty."

"And if you use condoms with the man, what's the problem?"

"What's the problem? He's married to that girl!"

"So? I'm supposed to feel sorry for Miss Anne?"

"Her name is Rebecca."

"Her name is rude, insensitive white woman. And I still can't get over that mammy thing. Done, Jesus."

"Wasn't that crazy?"

"Why you think that boy married her in the first place?"

"I've wondered the same thing. She is very pretty."

"You can't find you another Black friend in town?"

"No, I can't. It's real hard to make friends here. And before you say I should have gone to medical school, please don't."

"I wasn't going to say that, baby. Give your mama a little credit."

———

On Dr. Petersen's syllabus, there was a week in late October labeled "TBA," with no readings assigned. But there were flyers pasted throughout our building, with his picture, as well as the information that he would be delivering a public lecture, "Race Relations During the Cotton Boll Weevil Plague in Mississippi." The morning of the lecture, he sent an email to my class, saying that we'd be required to attend the lecture. It would take place in the common room located on the second floor of our building.

When I arrived thirty minutes early, the common room was crowded already with faculty and graduate students. I had planned to sit in the back, but then I heard my name: Dr. Whitcomb was waving and pointing at the seat beside him in the front row. Though I'd seen him frequently, I'd never conducted a lengthy conversation with him. Yet here I was, the only Black grad student in my program, sitting next to the only Black professor. I felt the stares from around the room and reached into my book bag. Maybe if I took notes, I wouldn't feel so uncomfortable.

It was a dry lecture, during which Dr. Petersen discussed how Black people in Mississippi had been lynched during the years of the boll weevil plague from 1889 to 1929. That this violence was a result of white anxiety, which always spiked during times of economic duress. As Dr. Petersen dispassionately rattled off the many different kinds of lynching—the hangings, the dismemberings, the castrations, and the burnings of still-living African Americans—I quietly panted. I wasn't sure how long I could sit there, when Dr. Whitcomb pulled out a little notebook from his jacket pocket, along with a fancy black-and-gold pen. He nudged me, nodding toward the notebook, where he'd written *I know, this is very, very sad, sistren!*

I looked at Dr. Whitcomb, nodding, and he patted my shoulder. Then he wrote down something else: *It's almost over! I've heard this lecture several times before! Smile!*

Afterward, Dr. Whitcomb and I stood in the receiving line together. I shook Dr. Petersen's hand, telling him, as the granddaughter of Georgia tenant farmers, I'd found the lecture quite rousing and elucidating. Dr. Whitcomb looked on, smiling, as I offered another superlative about the lecture, before saying I looked forward to class next week.

I walked to the second-floor ladies' room, where I sat on the toilet, rocking.

Could I actually keep this going? If I was lucky, I'd do well in the master's program, which would last eighteen more months after this semester. Then five to six years for the doctorate, depending on what I chose to write about for my dissertation. But if the scene in the common room was any signal, I'd be spending the better part of a decade with only one Black person in my department to keep me company.

The door to the ladies' room slammed open.

"Jesus H. Christ, that was boring."

"Oh my God, there was not enough coffee in the world to keep me awake during that."

It was Rebecca and, from the sound of her voice, Emma Halsey, another grad student from Dr. Petersen's class. Carefully, I leaned back.

"And did you see the way she was pretending how exciting it was?" Rebecca asked.

"I know! Sitting there cuddled up to Whitcomb! Taking notes, even. What a kiss-ass."

"That's what Ailey has to do, I guess. Everybody in the program knows the only reason she's here is affirmative action."

"It must be so nice to be Black."

"Yeah, nice and easy!"

"That's so mean, Rebecca."

"Stop feeling sorry for her! You sound like Scooter. He's always taking on these charity cases. Bless his heart."

They laughed, and the door slammed again: they'd left.

UMOJA, YOUNGBLOOD

❖

At Shug's, Scooter had taken over the table with his belongings, and I pushed his papers back to his side. I was cranky: he'd just told me how he'd fallen for Rebecca in his junior year of college.

They'd met in Cancún over spring break. She was a sophomore, only from the University of Alabama. Scooter had known she was the one when he saw her walking on the beach. Her bikini had been the tiniest thing, barely decent. He'd asked for her address, and after that week, when they'd returned to their respective universities, he'd written her nearly every day.

I hadn't worn a bikini since I was eight years old.

Now he was back to his tired refrain of asking me to dinner.

"Ailey, you're something else, you know that?" Scooter asked. "It's not nice to turn down invitations. What are you, some kind of racist?"

"I'm a racist because I don't want to eat shrimp at your house?"

"No, Ailey, you're racist because Rebecca says you're barely friendly. And she doesn't know why, because she's so nice to you."

"Really? That's what she said about me?" The corners of my mouth twitched, but I knew if I told the truth about his wife, he'd only take her side. That was how marriage worked: a couple was a united front. I'd learned that from my parents. "If your wife wants me to come to dinner, why doesn't she ask me herself? I see her every week in Petersen's class."

Scooter sucked his teeth. "That's your defense for bad manners?"

"I will have you know my home training is immaculate." I glanced around the room, blinking my eyes. It was the uppity move I'd cribbed from Rebecca, but when I looked back at Scooter, he glared at me, his lips in a grim line.

"We both know why you don't like my wife, Ailey. You think I don't notice these looks around campus when Black women see us together? And here I thought you were different. I can't believe you call yourself a feminist."

He stood up.

I pulled some papers from the middle of my stack and began to read.

He sat back in the chair, but I made him wait an entire minute before I looked up. I sang the "Happy Birthday" song in my head five times.

"You're still here, youngblood? Oh, no, please leave! Go 'head and make your dramatic exit. Have your moment. But before you do, tell me, are you gone accuse me of hating your wife because she's white, when I told you about my white aunt?" My voice was loud, and I'd moved into my mother's southern drawl. At the counter, Miss Velma was leaning on her elbows and laughing at us. "Are you really accusing me of that, Scooter? Tell me right now, so you can find somebody else to drink coffee with three days out the week."

I took in air and let my jaws fill up. When Scooter leaned his long frame into his chair and crossed his legs at the ankles, I let out the air in tiny puffs.

"No, I'm not saying that, Ailey."

"You sure? Because it sounded like that to me."

"I'm sorry. I didn't mean to insult you."

"I accept your apology. And stop being so sensitive."

"I'm not the sensitive one here. Don't put that on me."

He wanted to bluster. We both knew I had won, but I switched to a near whisper to save his pride. "Listen, Scooter. Let me explain something."

"Like what?"

"Like there are two African Americans in the entire history department: Dr. Whitcomb and me. That's it. And Dr. Whitcomb? He's convinced himself that he can save the Black race, one history class at a time, even though ninety-nine-point-nine percent of his students are white."

"And what about you, Ailey?"

"Me? I'm the sister who's pretending not to care whether my

white schoolmates think I could be at this university for a reason other than affirmative action. But I have to prove them wrong, and that means earning a perfect grade point average. So while I'm sorry that you think I'm being rude on purpose refusing your kind offer of a seafood dinner with you and Rebecca, I'm not. I'm studying, okay? And I really don't have time for anything else."

"Come on, Ailey! Rebecca's really nice!"

"Sure she is, Scooter. Uh-huh."

"And that's why I want you two to connect, Ailey. I know she doesn't always get, you know, the race stuff, but she's trying. And maybe you can help her with that. Teach her."

I sighed and moved in my chair.

"Ailey, look. I know Rebecca's hard to read, but has it occurred to you that she just might be intimidated? You're so smart, it's kind of scary."

"We have coffee, Scooter. How do you know anything about my brain?"

"Anybody who talks to you for five minutes knows you're brilliant. Plus, you're so damned beautiful. And you know how you girls get jealous of each other."

I snorted. "Don't you mean 'women'?"

"Sorry! I don't mean to be politically incorrect! Anyway, I think Rebecca's just jealous. And no, that's not cool, but a gorgeous creature can get away with anything, right? Or in this case, two gorgeous creatures." He put his hand on my arm, rubbing lightly.

I scraped back my chair: the next round of coffee was on me. When I returned, Scooter asked for my phone number again. I was a woman alone, he told me. I needed someone in town to check on me. It wasn't safe, and finally, I gave him my number. I warned, it was only for emergencies.

That Saturday, he called. He was in the middle of leaving a long, rambling message on the answering machine when I picked up.

"This better be an emergency," I said.

"It is, kind of. Can I come over? I really need a friend—"

"—Scooter—"

"—please, Ailey. Please."

He always seemed so collected, but now his voice was wavering. A half hour later, when I answered the door, he was wearing a sweat suit and tennis shoes. He carried a six-pack of imported beer. I tried to joke, saying I hadn't known he owned casual clothes, but he didn't smile. He asked, could we watch the game? but I told him I didn't have cable. My little thirteen-inch television only received the public station. Not that I had time to watch, anyway. I was too busy studying. I told him to wait, while I put the beer in the freezer.

When I came back from the kitchen, he had his head in his hands.

"Scooter, what's wrong with you?" I hesitated. "Is Rebecca all right?"

"She's fine. Whatever."

I sat down beside him, waiting. I had a book review due in three days, but I didn't want to seem impatient. If you cared for somebody, you were supposed to be there for him. And I guess I cared about Scooter, after a fashion. When he didn't talk, I asked, was he hungry? All the chicken I'd bought at the grocery store was in the freezer. But I had some leftover pizza in the fridge. He asked, could I get him one of the beers? I tried not to be annoyed, but I sighed. Sure, and went back to the kitchen. After he drank that beer, he asked for another one. When I told him this wasn't a bar and I wasn't his waitress, he caught me off guard: he started crying. That's when the story came out.

Like me—like nearly every African American graduate student on campus—Scooter was the only person of color in his department. He'd been recruited by the business school, and was on fellowship, and when he arrived, he'd made every effort to fit in. He wore suits and ties to his classes, like his peers. He studied hard. He'd made As on his individual projects for the first modules of his three classes. And he'd joined a study group. One of the guys in the group was even a past member of the fraternity he'd joined at Brown University, where he'd attended undergrad.

"I thought you said you were the only brother in the B-school here."

"I am."

"So this dude, he joined a Black fraternity?"

"No, Ailey. It wasn't. It was integrated. And why does that matter?"

Scooter looked around, as if he'd brought anything but beer over. Maybe he should go, but I stroked his shoulder.

"I'm sorry, sweetie. I didn't mean to judge."

When he leaned back against the couch, he told me that the members of his study group had told him that they'd decided to disband. That's why he'd started studying on his own, out at Shug's. But yesterday morning, he'd found out that his study group had been meeting three days a week without him, instead of breaking up, like they'd told him. Then they'd the nerve to ask for his individual study notes. And Scooter had handed the notes over. He'd wanted to take the high road.

I was prepared to tell him, what did he expect? That's how these white folks rolled at this university. But then Scooter started crying anew. I looked at him, sobbing like a kid, and opened my arms. When he laid his head on my shoulder, I told him, it was all right. It was over now. And when he fell asleep against me, I didn't have the heart to wake him. I gently pulled my arms away and found a blanket for him. And in the morning, I acted as if nothing had happened.

———

At the end of that semester, I held my breath when I saw the envelope from the registrar's office. But when I opened it, I'd received an "A" in all three of my classes. When I called up Uncle Root, he didn't seem surprised. I'd been brilliant since I'd been born, he calmly said. Even as a baby, my facial expressions had indicated intellectual profundity.

My next call was to Dr. Oludara, who showed far more excitement. Then I called my mother, who said she guessed this meant I wasn't going to medical school. But then she said her baby girl was still going to be a doctor—now she'd have two kinds of doctors in the family. So folks in Chicasetta could put that in their pipes and smoke it.

For winter break, I drove up to the City, but only stayed two days. The house still made me sad, without Lydia there. But I didn't want to bring up her name and remind Mama of her. I left the day after Christmas; that evening Scooter called: could he come over again? At my front door, he carried a huge box, his muscles straining through his cashmere sweater.

"Merry Christmas, Ailey!"

"Scooter, I regret to inform you that you've missed half of the holidays. We are in the Kwanzaa portion of our celebrations now. Today is 'Umoja,' youngblood."

I gave the Black Power salute.

"Ailey, don't you see me holding this big-ass box? Let me in before I have a heart attack."

I tried to say what was required when receiving an inappropriate, wildly expensive gift from a married man. I told him a television was too extravagant, and damn, I didn't get him anything in return, even as I picked up the little TV off the cherry dresser I'd bought at the thrift shop and set it on the floor.

Scooter didn't even give me a chance to ask why he was in town, instead of at his parents' house in D.C. with Rebecca. He began talking about his marital problems, saying he'd spent the holiday alone. Rebecca's family had invited her to come home, only without him. He couldn't believe that she would accept the invitation, but she'd wept and told him that she needed it. Scooter had been too embarrassed to go back home. He didn't want to hear his mother's mouth.

I patted his shoulder. "It's all right, youngblood. You two will make up."

"You think so?"

I told him, if he was patient, I'd fix him some coffee. There was sweet potato pie, too, but my mother had baked it two days before. I was hoping a sugary dessert would keep him from crying, but when I returned from the kitchen, he didn't seem upset. There was a playfulness to him, as there'd been the evening of the graduate reception. And I found myself relaxing as I had then, but this time, I didn't disrupt the ease. I smiled when he told me, my mother sure could burn. This pie was fantastic.

He asked me about my life before I'd moved to North Carolina.

Why wasn't I married yet, a great catch like myself, and I laughed. I told him about the boy I'd desperately loved in high school, David James. Then the rebound Negro I'd settled for, Chris. Then Abdul and Pat. And after I'd moved to Chicasetta before grad school, I'd had several flings with country brothers, but I never allowed anything to get serious.

Somehow, I wasn't embarrassed, talking to Scooter about my sexual history. He was a married man. I didn't need to impress him, or pretend to be a good little virgin. And I didn't turn away when he moved closer, or when he kissed me. Even when things got heated, I didn't stop him. In my bedroom, he begged to make love. I told him I didn't have any condoms, and was surprised when he assured me he'd brought his own.

I pushed at him, ordering him to lie on his back, and when I settled on top of him, he started moaning. I was so wet, so tight. I leaned down, whispering in his ear. How long had he been thinking about this? How long? And he confessed, since the very night he met me. When I hadn't called, he'd driven all over town, looking for me. That's when he found me, out at Shug's. He couldn't get me out of his mind.

We made love twice, and afterward, when his eyes started to close, I shook him. He needed to leave. I didn't want anybody to see him in the early morning. God forbid Eddie and Mike came back to town early and saw him creeping out my door.

The next night, he came by without calling, and I told him this wasn't a good idea. This couldn't continue when school started back up, and he kissed me, pulling at the band of my sweatpants.

"Whatever you want, Ailey. Whatever you need."

I didn't mention his wife's name or ask when she would be back in town, because Scooter's hand was already inside my panties. I tugged at his belt, ordering him, go into the bedroom. Get ready for me to fuck him. When he reached for me, I reminded him, pay attention to me. Go in the bedroom and wait.

◆

SONG

◆

The Worthy Lineage

When Aidan Franklin settled his second wife and his many children in the cabin he built on top of that flower-covered mound, he continued a legacy that had been established by his grandfather, a man by the name of Gideon Franklin. In 1733, this man had found sea legs on a ship baptized *Anne*, along with one hundred fourteen others, including James Oglethorpe, the founder of the Georgia colony. It was the ship that had been anointed by Oglethorpe's lofty prayer of the worthy poor.

In England, Gideon Franklin had been in jail, in anticipation of his hanging. He had been a young man with opinions about the monarchy; he was angry King George the Second had allocated property for rich men, carving it out from the land that common people had freely roamed in centuries past. These commoners had picked fruit from trees, fished in ponds, and hunted deer that roasted deliciously on spits hovering above fires. Then the king had taken this land, parceled it into gifts for his noble friends, and the common fellow—and his family—was expected to scrabble or starve, even as he stared at food that hung over his head, or that swam or ran within his sight.

The king not only forbade, he enforced: there were laws passed that made it a death sentence to be caught with a rich man's property, but Gideon Franklin was tired of hearing his mother and siblings whimper in hunger. His father rubbing his powerless hands. One night Gideon took a bow and arrow to the lands of a rich earl who delighted in serving his equally rich friends venison, for it had become more succulent with the knowledge that it was forbidden to the poverty-stricken. When Gideon was arrested two days after he killed the earl's deer, Gideon was consoled that at least his parents, brothers, and sisters had already eaten the meat. The bones had already been buried. The only evidence had been the skin that his mother had begun to cure, in hopes of making rough coverings for the feet of her children. When the earl's men burst through the weak-hinged door of his home, Gideon had readily stepped forward. Even after the justice of the peace had sentenced him to death, Gideon did not believe this was how it would end. He was a cheerful, optimistic lad of nineteen, and he believed that God watched over him. And indeed, five days after his sentencing, the justice gave him a choice: execution for theft, or transport to His Majesty's lands, over the ocean. Naturally, Gideon chose the latter.

On the *Anne*, James Oglethorpe had brought others of his own elite class. When he emerged from his cabin in his extravagant clothes and shiny boots, he smiled vaguely at his own cohort, and ignored those his project had saved from death. Yet Gideon met other new colonists like himself. Like him, they vomited over the side of the ship, or in buckets below in the tight, filthy quarters, and ate the sometimes-spoiled food. But when Gideon arrived in the land that was called Georgia, he discovered that, after his seven-year term of indentured servitude was up, he would be given his own parcel of fifty acres of land. Our land.

Gideon did not question whom the land had been taken from. He saw it as a free boon, as free as the deer, and Gideon had developed a permanent taste for roasted venison. The master who owned his indenture was mild-mannered, and not a nobleman. For him, Gideon performed menial labor, clearing off land, and helping to build a cabin that he was not allowed to sleep in—Gideon slept in a lean-to shed—but he was proud that he had work to do. And the master allowed Gideon to make a bow and arrow and kill as many deer as he wished, so long as he shared a portion of the meat with his master. In his first year, Gideon glutted himself on the venison and learned to sew clothes from the cured skin. He found blackberries in the forest during the summer and picked buckets for himself and his master. And by the end of his indenture, Gideon had gained weight, and had forgotten his outrage at men in power, for he was now a white Georgian with property of his own, instead of a hungry lad gaping at the well-fed rich. And the people—our people—whom the English called Indians were now be-

neath Gideon. Finally, Gideon Franklin could look down on someone else, instead of being the most despised himself.

As a landowner, Gideon was no longer close to power, he possessed it, and even more so when Oglethorpe's wish of a colony
without slavery was violated. And as the years passed, and enslaved
Negroes were brought into the colony, though Gideon remained
poor, he had pride in his freedom. His optimism grew, as well as his
belief that God had blessed him with special grace. And why not?
On our land, which the English had stolen from our people, Gideon
was a white man. And even the poorest of white men was better
than the Indian and the slave.

This optimism was transferred to Gideon's children, when he married and propagated with a young woman who had been accused
of prostitution, a charge that she'd spiritedly negated. His youngest son would marry another young woman who'd been forced to
choose between debtors' prison in England and transport to Georgia. But by the time this youngest son's children reached adulthood, the original parcel of land allotted to Gideon had been sliced
into mere strips. And one of Gideon's many adult grandchildren,
the man named Aidan, decided to make his own way. Aidan entered
the Georgia land lottery, won by the grace of his god, and took his
second wife, his many children, and his inherited optimism across
the Oconee River. Along the way, he met Samuel Pinchard.

Yet that Franklin optimism would die with Aidan. Only the sense
of superiority would remain, that being white was a blessing in
Georgia. And this superiority would combine with the hopelessness
of poverty to breed a distinct ruthlessness. And it would be so with
other white men who had arrived in the years of Oglethorpe's worthy project as well. Those who killed too many deer and stuffed
themselves with the meat.

A Hunter of the People

These would be the men who hunted our people in the time of Andrew Jackson, one hundred years after Oglethorpe's ship anchored

in what would become Savannah, Georgia. And Jackson would be called Indian Killer. And in the time after all those broken treaties with our people, there was the final Removal Act. When our people were forced from our land in the 1830s.

We don't want to remember how our people looked back as they walked away.

How they mourned us, while drinking in the beauty of the pine, the oak, the pecan, the cedar. The heaviness of plums and peaches that contained a solacing flavor. Blackberries enticing snakes from their hiding places. The deer that watched with large eyes that seemed to understand. When someone or something dies, at least there is an ending, a resolution, no matter how mournful. Yet with our people, there was no ending, for as the last groups began to walk west to Oklahoma, they knew that our land was alive. And so their longing would never abate.

Yet there were a few of our people who remained on our earth. And the white men who were hungry for our land began to seek out the people who refused to leave on wagons, and the descendant of that worthy Franklin was one of these men. This was Jeremiah, the oldest son of Carson, who was the great-grandson of Gideon.

During the time after the Removal of the Creek, Jeremiah became a hunter of our people. Whatever Jeremiah found, he claimed as his own, and either kept it or sold it. Yet the plunder and the bounties weren't the only pleasures for him. He loved the viciousness of the people hunt.

In a neighboring county, there had been a stubborn Creek mestizo who refused to leave during the Removal. He'd stayed after things became dangerous, and hearing about this man, Jeremiah had snuck up on the man in his field of vegetables, hitting him with a large staff. The mestizo staggered about, recovering enough to charge Jeremiah with his hoe, but Jeremiah managed to beat the man to unconsciousness with the staff. He used the hoe to chop the mestizo's body into pieces, and then walked to the cabin. However, the mestizo's wife had spirit. She charged him, but he hit her with the bloody staff, then struck at her throat with the hoe, killing her.

This turn of events annoyed Jeremiah, for he considered himself an honorable man. Jeremiah enjoyed killing men, but not women. He didn't like rape, either; his brothers did, but they weren't with him that day. When the wife fell, her two daughters looked at each other. One could escape Jeremiah, but the other would fall. Thus, Jeremiah feigned breathlessness and sat down on the dirt floor. He did not pursue the daughters when they ran out the front of the cabin, though he could have grabbed at their long skirts. After they were gone, he bounced up quickly. After that, he went through the cabin's belongings: a teakettle, a pot, two pans, three petticoats, a set of colorfully beaded boots made from the skin of deer. Also, the dead man's rifle and a horse and pig in the barn.

Soon, the few remaining Creek people hid themselves in the woods. If they were mestizos, their white skin could often hide their lineage. If mulattoes, they were enslaved as Negroes. Jeremiah's appetite for blood had not been sated, however, and he became a slave patroller for Putnam County, the new boundary that had been established after the land lotteries. This patrolling gave Jeremiah an income, since he made no money as a farmer, as he owed everything he made to Samuel Pinchard, who owned the land. Jeremiah lived in a small cabin next to that of his father and four other cabins populated by his brothers and their wives. All were built in the shadow of the mound, the landmark that was despised by his family.

So when the only beloved person in Samuel Pinchard's life ran away, Samuel sent word to Jeremiah, saying he wanted Nick returned, but he did not want him hurt. It was the morning when Samuel sent word, and Jeremiah arrived promptly with the hound dogs he had raised from pups, who heeded his voice and signals. The men working with Jeremiah were his younger brothers, and they admired Jeremiah's coldness when dealing with Negroes and his lack of obsequiousness when standing in the dirt in the front of the steps of a wealthy, condescending white man's big house.

"Your nigger might be in the area. Then again, mayhap not. But if he is, we gone find him. You best believe it." Yet it had begun to rain, and Jeremiah failed to say that would hinder Nick's retrieval. He was not about to educate his landlord on hunting slaves, for he was being paid ten dollars up front to find Nick.

But even before the rain, the trail had been lost. For in the daylight before the evening that Nick ran away, Aggie and her gaggle of Quarters-children had walked into the woods. She'd carried a burlap sack and a large jug. After telling them of her game, she reached into a sack of wild onions and passed them out. She told them, run and throw. Run and throw. And they did, with enchanted calls.

Before they returned, Aggie uncorked the jug and began to walk, sprinkling along her way. She saved her nighttime water for many purposes. This time, she hoped that when Samuel sent word to the patrollers, their hounds would run in confusion. The scent of wild onions and night water were obfuscation enough, but the rain was the final blessing.

A Marriage

Samuel was disappointed that Nick could not be found, but he kept Jeremiah Franklin on a monthly retainer of ten dollars; perhaps there would be a breakthrough. Jeremiah warned Samuel that the trail was gone, but he took the money with no contrition on his trips to Samuel's store, where he picked up supplies for his farm. Often times, he brought his baby sister. Approaching seventeen, and exceedingly buxom, Grace Franklin was too mature to catch Samuel's eye. Grace was unremarkable in looks, but Samuel spoke to her as if she were most splendid. He gave her an extra yard of calico for free on one of her visits and a small package of candy on another. He advised her to place strips of linsey-woolsey inside her shoes. The extra layer would warm her feet in the wintertime and keep her soles from blistering. Confused by his employer's conduct, Jeremiah reminded his sister that Samuel was a married man. She could take his calico and candy, but she should stop letting him hold her hand for so long.

Like his father, Jeremiah knew about the little girls that Samuel imprisoned in the left cabin. He did not feel sorry for the little girls, however, any more than he felt sorry for a pig, a dog, a horse, or a cow. He had very little compassion to begin with, and certainly he could not waste it on a Negress, and a child at that. So neither Jeremiah nor his father were bothered when his landlord proposed to his overseer there should be a marriage. Carson readily agreed.

Though it was walking distance, Samuel had ridden his horse to Carson's cabin, sat down to accept the barebones hospitality of the overseer's wife, and then quickly offered the proposal. His son was back from the university. Victor was of an age to marry, but too shy for sparking. Perhaps Carson might speak to Grace on his behalf?

"I'm gone have to ask her," Carson said.

He was lying. Grace would do as she was told. Carson had his eye on buying back his father's original parcel of land, and what better way to do that than to marry his daughter to his landlord's son? And after he bought back the land, he would attend to the destruction of the mound. Not only did Carson not warn Grace about the goings-on with little girls in their landlord's left cabin, he didn't tell her that her intended groom didn't like to lie with females: Carson had seen Victor in the midst with the now-dead Quarters-boy.

Samuel was unaware that his son's secret was known. He thought he'd been careful by sending Victor to the university in North Carolina. There hadn't been any romantic scandals, however. Claudius had started a business at the university, amassing a nest egg by writing poems for Victor's classmates to send to their (female) sweethearts. They'd paid Claudius a dime apiece to write his quixotic verses, and before Victor had graduated, Claudius had slipped away in the night, never to be heard from again, aided by his store of dimes.

As for Grace, she was thrilled about the prospect of being married into the Pinchard family. Her life was not fearful. Her brothers did not abuse her or try to catch glimpses of her as she undressed in the one room her younger, unmarried siblings shared. Yet like Gideon, her long-ago ancestor, Grace saw how the rich men in her sights lived, how their wives were dressed in finery when they visited Samuel Pinchard's general store. Even the wives of the yeomen who patronized the store were better off than the Franklins, for they had somehow hung on to the acres they'd won in the land lottery and owned one or two slaves.

The wedding of Victor and Grace was unimpressive, much to Samuel's dismay. He had invited the two other richest men in the county, along with their wives, but both couples had sent their social regrets along with two silver platters, beautiful and redundant. The only guests were the region's yeomen, their wives, and the Franklin clan, all of whom were dressed in church clothes a mere step above their daily rags. However, Grace was ecstatic, in the green everyday dress and matching shoes that Samuel had purchased, which was fancier than anything she'd ever owned.

After her wedding, Grace began to comprehend that she'd been given a pig in a poke. One fine day, when she sat alone in a rocking chair on the second-floor gallery, she caught a look over the left cabin's fence, where she saw Samuel bend down and kiss a luxuriously clothed pickaninny full on the mouth. And most nights, she slept alone in the bed she should have shared with Victor, if he had not made a pallet elsewhere. Yet Grace was reconciled, in part because her mother-in-law embraced her with fervor.

Although another woman of Creek lineage might have been upset at her son marrying the baby sister of a hunter of our people, Lady was happy to have new friends and flattered that her affections toward Grace were returned. Even more: Grace was obsequious to her mother-in-law. In various ways, she would seek Lady's counsel on her manners, dress, and speech. When Grace sat in the parlor of the big house and her sister-in-law Gloria made her usual blunt statements, Grace would not seem surprised or act with condescension. Rather, Grace would answer with a warm smile, which endeared her to her mother-in-law; for many years, she had feared that Gloria would be a source of ridicule. And though Lady was certain that Grace's grandfather and father had been aware of her Creek heritage—if not her African blood—Grace did not speak of this lineage. And Lady was grateful to finally sit in her parlor and be treated as the white wife of a wealthy man. If someone had reminded her that she had taken on the desires of her mother—Mahala's lifelong craving to throw off her Indian history—Lady would have been adamant in her denials.

Yet indeed, Grace was aware of her mother-in-law's Creek background. This information had been bandied about many nights in her parents' tiny cabin. But Grace didn't care about Lady's heritage. Grace lived in the big house now, and if her husband slept someplace else, at least he did not force himself on her. She was content when she lay on the feather mattress on a four-poster bed that took up all but a few inches of space in her bedroom, a bed that, when Samuel passed on, would be given to her children after she and Victor moved into the extra-large bedroom. For now, she had a fireplace in her room, which she'd never imagined. On cold nights, she did not have to pile quilts on her bed to keep warm.

And Grace began to take on airs. When she sat on the gallery with Lady and Gloria, she began to ignore the waves of her father and brothers when they walked to the yard of the Pinchard big house. If they shouted her name, Grace would shut her decorative fan, telling her in-laws she believed she would go inside and rest.

Though a woman, Grace had more power than any male in her family, for she was no longer a Franklin, forced to scrabble in the dirt and hunt runaways. Grace was a Pinchard now. She'd come up in the world.

X

We can only be interested in men by knowing them—knowing them directly, thoroughly, intimately; and this knowing leads ever to the greatest of human discoveries,—the recognition of one's self in the image of one's neighbor; the sudden, startling revelation, "This is another ME, that thinks as I think, feels as I feel, suffers even as I suffer." This is the beginning, and only the true beginning, of the social conscience.

—W. E. B. Du Bois, "The Individual and Social Conscience"

THE PECULIAR INSTITUTION

I'd done well my first year in the master's program: I earned As in all my classes, and unless I choked, I was pretty sure I'd continue to excel. But before my second year began, I had a decision to make: whether I'd continue on to the doctoral program and stay where I was or apply elsewhere. Before I made my decision, I called up Dr. Oludara. She told me if I wanted to attend another university for my doctorate, she had my letter of recommendation already written. And when I finished my doctorate, she'd be ready to support me on the job market, too.

"I mean, unless you do something crazy, Ailey, I have your back for life. And I've known you for a decade, so I don't think that's happening."

"Thank you, Dr. Oludara. But you know . . ."

"I told you it would be lonely, Ailey."

"It's not that. I mean, I have a Black friend."

"Well, that's great! Look at you!"

"But what I want to study, Dr. Whitcomb would have to be my advisor."

"Even better!"

"But would they respect me here, if all I do is stick underneath the only Black professor in the program?"

On the other end, Dr. Oludara heaved a sigh.

"Ailey, why are you making things harder than they have to be?"

"I'm not. It's just—"

"Ailey. Let me ask you something. Do any of your classmates invite you to their study sessions?"

"No, ma'am."

"Are they even friendly to you?"

"I mean . . . no. Not really."

"Then why do you give a good goddamn about what they think? You could have nothing but white folks on your dissertation committee, and your classmates still would have something to say. I'm sure they've passed around that you're there on a quota. They love to accuse Black folks of taking their place. Even when it ain't but one of us, and fifty of them, they don't even want us to have that one spot."

I stayed quiet.

"You know how I know, Ailey? Because when Chuck Whitcomb and I were at Harvard years ago, that's what they said about us. And it didn't matter that we both worked like dogs to get our grades. We weren't ever going to be good enough for those bastards. If you want Chuck as your advisor, great. If not, choose somebody else. Or go to another university. It's up to you. But instead of you trying to please some white folks whose names you won't even remember a decade from now, how about making your own decisions?"

———

Dr. Whitcomb's The Peculiar Institution in the Archives was a requirement for any master's student concentrating in early American history. But that first class, it seemed as if he was pitching his lecture toward the most untrained of students.

At the front of the room, his dimples were on constant display. He spoke in his lulling tenor, explaining that we would spend a lot of time in the archives. He wanted to train us early, because some of us would be continuing for the doctorate. The secondary texts would supplement the original documents, because the point wasn't just to read letters or wills or what have you that somebody else had found. The point was to learn how to become academic detectives.

Class time would be for presentations and for discussing sources, he told us. There were several class requirements: five one-page book reviews, a twenty-five-page paper due at the end of the semester, and two oral presentations on what we'd found in the Old South Collections. And we'd be responsible for the background reading, which would guide us in the archives. We had to choose which family we wanted to focus on, from a list of thirty slaveholding families that he gave us. Each of these families had papers located in the Old South Collections, and we would be reading their records with an eye toward three themes: kinship, resistance, or economics. We could select one theme to focus on, two, or all three.

"Now, I know this is a lot of reading, but before you deep dive into archival work, I want you to fully comprehend the cultural and emotional contexts of the documents that you'll encounter in the Old South Collections. This is not a course where my intention is to cut you off at the knees. The work is hard, I cannot lie, but please know that you can come to me anytime and talk these texts through. I'm here for you, and I mean that sincerely. If I'm not teaching, I'm in my office five days a week, nine to five. I can take lunch meetings with you as well. Just so you know, I really like potato chips. The super-crunchy kind."

There was laughter, and, it seemed, relief in the room.

After Dr. Whitcomb had passed out the reading list, along with the list of families in the Old South Collections, he used that entire class period to give an elementary African American history review that reached back to 1619. He spoke slowly, as if the whole class couldn't understand English. And Dr. Whitcomb was very patient when Rebecca Grillier Park asked, what was the premise of the Fugitive Slave Acts of both 1793 and 1850? I looked across the table at her, trying to fix my face. Rebecca was supposed to be specializing in early American, like me. She briefly met my eyes, and then looked away, inspecting the walls. Stroking her blond ponytail.

In the corner of the seminar room, there was a record player with an album fitted on top. He turned on the player, and a soft group of voices began to sing as he talked about Olaudah Equiano, his favorite abolitionist. In the eighteenth century, someone had caught Equiano and his baby sister and taken them into slavery, split them up, and sent him across the Middle Passage by himself—if you don't count the other folks by themselves, too, there in the hold of that ship.

If you get there before I do
Coming for to carry me home
Tell all my people I'm coming too
Coming for to carry me home

Dr. Whitcomb sang along in his passable tenor, completely un-embarrassed, as his students exchanged glances. I looked down at my notebook, avoiding anyone's eyes. Just because the man was Black didn't make him my relative. I didn't have to claim him.

"Does anybody know what those lines mean?" After a couple of beats: "Ailey? What do you think?"

The other students turned and looked at me.

Aw, shit.

"Um . . . well, I'm not sure, Dr. Whitcomb . . . you know . . . but I've read that whenever a slave was planning to run, he or she might sing that song to alert the rest of the quarters that an escape was taking place soon. Those stories might be apocryphal, however."

"Exactly! Wonderful, Ailey!"

After class, our professor smiled again, zipped up his old-fashioned doctor's bag, and left us looking through the syllabus.

"I really like him," Rebecca said at the far end of the table before calling down to me: "What about you, Ailey?"

"What about me?"

"What do you think of Whitcomb? Don't you just love him?"

"He's fine." I packed up my books as Rebecca moved closer to Emma, whispering.

But the second week of classes, Dr. Whitcomb was no longer the sweet man who had spoon-fed us. His personality had completely changed, like that character in a psychological movie that you learn has been the serial killer all along.

When he walked in that Tuesday, Dr. Whitcomb was wearing reading glasses, and his large, white teeth did not flash in a smile. When the dimples appeared, they seemed ominous. He told us that he didn't like dead air in a class, so he'd be using the Socratic method for the rest of the semester to call on us randomly. This would be the structure of classes from now on, except for the days that we gave our presentations on the research we'd found in the Old South Collections. And by the way, we needed to give him the name of the family that we would be researching for the rest of the semester.

There were fourteen students around the seminar table, our books and notebooks in front of us. My classmates sat there, giving each other painful glances of confusion. What had happened? They'd thought Dr. Whitcomb had been so nice.

Everyone was confused but Rebecca, that is. In the space in front of her, her book wasn't even open. She stroked her ponytail confidently as she told Dr. Whitcomb, she'd decided upon the Paschal family of Georgia. They were her mother's family, and I maintained a flat expression: I was almost positive Rebecca didn't know about the African American branch of the Paschals, the ones who owned the restaurant in the West End of Atlanta. My father had loved their fried chicken, back when he'd been at Routledge.

"I thought we'd have some more time to make our decision," Boris St. John said.

Our professor looked over his glasses. "Is that right? Including this class, we have fifteen more weeks. How long do you think it takes to excavate important information in the archives?"

Boris turned red. He pulled out the list of families; with his pen, he traced the list.

I raised my hand.

"Yes, Ailey."

"Yes, sir. I wanted to choose the Pinchard family, but I didn't know if that would be ethical. I mean, my family is from Chicasetta, Georgia, and I've heard stories and everything about the Pinchards."

"Unless you've already written a paper on them in another class, you're good."

"No, sir. I mean, I've avoided Chicasetta altogether."

"Why's that?"

I looked over at Rebecca and Emma. "Um . . . I didn't want anybody thinking I was taking the easy way for my archival research."

"As long as you retain some professional distance, Ailey, I'm sure it'll be fine. So I'll circle the Pinchard family for you?"

Then it was time for us to discuss the reading for that week, Du Bois's *The Suppression of the African Slave-Trade*. Our professor called on Emma Halsey first, and she gave her summation of the reading. I'd been in four classes with Emma already. I didn't like her, but I had to admit, she didn't play when it came to preparation.

"Rebecca?" our professor asked. "What did you think of the reading?"

Stroke, stroke, stroke on the ponytail. "I loved it! It was really interesting."

"And?"

"Du Bois didn't like slavery. Not at all."

"All right, can you expound?"

"Um . . ."

Dr. Whitcomb took off his reading glasses and set them on the table. "That's what you have to say, Rebecca? You have spoken fourteen inadequate words, which provide no substantive information about this text."

Rebecca's hand dropped from the ponytail. Her cheeks colored.

Our professor put his glasses back on. I braced myself: I had a feeling I knew what was coming.

"Ailey? What are your impressions of today's reading?"

I flipped through a legal pad. During Emma's comments, I'd put a red check mark by anything that she'd already discussed.

"Okay . . . well . . . I'd like to talk about Du Bois's social justice project in the book."

"Go ahead."

"It's clear that he really is outraged about slavery, as Rebecca has noted"—I turned in her direction, and she gave a begrudging nod—"but what's obvious, at least to me, is that he is making an argument about how we were mistreated by European powers since the eighteenth century, if not before—"

"—excuse me, Ailey. Have you ever been a slave?"

My stomach lurched at the laughter of my classmates. They were relieved he'd found another target.

"No, sir, Dr. Whitcomb."

"Well, then, it isn't 'we.' It is African American, Black, etc. Please retain your professionalism."

"Yes, sir, I'm sorry."

"Continue, please."

"Okay, um, um, well, as an African American, Du Bois takes that mistreatment very personally. Though his writing style is dry and data-based, his points are cumulative. For example, when he presents that large section on Toussaint L'Ouverture leading the Haitian Revolution, Du Bois seems to be commenting about our potential progress . . ."

Dr. Whitcomb raised his eyebrows.

". . . I mean, the progress of Africans around the globe—even though L'Ouverture was eventually tricked by Napoleon and imprisoned until his death. After all, Du Bois was a Pan-Africanist, and at the end of his life, he left the United States and moved to Ghana at the invitation of President Kwame Nkrumah."

"I see that you're actually familiar with Du Bois's biography."

His expression was stern, but it seemed like a tiny bit of praise. Silently, I sent gratitude to the old man for his stories.

———

The day I received my first book review grade I decided I needed to call up Uncle Root personally to thank him for those reading tips he'd given me; I'd received an A+.

After class, Rebecca lingered. "What'd you get, Ailey?"

I pulled my glasses down until her face was cut in half between clear and blurry. "And why would you need to know that?"

"Gosh, you don't have to be so rude." She moved her chair away from me and huddled with Emma.

I wasn't able to even enjoy my grade, because the next morning at Shug's, Scooter wanted to talk about his wife.

"What did you say to Rebecca? She came home crying."

I took a sip of coffee. "I didn't say anything, Scooter. I mean, we got our papers back and she wanted to see my grade."

"And did you show her?"

"No, Scooter, I didn't. First of all, my grade is none of her damned business. And second of all, she doesn't even talk to me. She barely looks at me in class. And this was going on way before . . . you know."

He and I never spoke about it during the daytime: what had happened between us. What was continuing to happen, at least once a week.

"Ailey, she doesn't talk to you because you frighten her. And not just her. Everybody in the history department says you're very angry and dangerous. Like you might attack someone."

I raised my voice. "You cannot be serious!"

"Don't shoot the messenger. I'm only saying, make more of an effort to be friendly. And smile more. You have a beautiful smile, Ailey." He squeezed my hand. "Another piece of advice? Stop always whining about being Black. It's not attractive."

I pulled my hand away. "Is that how you fit in, Scooter, by being pretty and pretending you just have a super-dark tan?"

"Why are you projecting, when I'm trying to help you?"

"I don't need a shrink, Scooter. I need a friend. That's supposed to be your purpose in my life."

"Then, as a friend, let me ask you this. Has it occurred to you that when people in your department don't like you, it's about you and nothing else? No, it hasn't, because you use that race shit as a crutch."

"So that's what you told yourself last year, when you were crying at my apartment about those white boys at the B-school?"

"Now, see, this is the attitude I'm talking about," he said. "This is why you're so isolated. Look within, Ailey."

He collected his things and left early, saying he had things to do. But that evening, he rang my bell. When I answered, I stood in the doorway, asking, what did he want?

"I'm sorry, Ailey. Can I come in?"

He sat down on the couch, but I kept standing. I didn't want to sit close to him, to smell his aftershave. The scent he left on my sheets, every time we slept together, but he reached for me, saying, sit down. Please let him explain: after a year, Rebecca wasn't suspicious. It had never occurred to her that he would cheat on her, but she had accused him of always taking my side. That's why Scooter had promised Rebecca that he'd talk to me. And that's all he'd meant to do at Shug's, but I was so bossy. He'd never met a woman like me before, and though he knew I was older—

"Scooter, I'm not Methuselah. I'm four years older than you."

"I know, but you always have to be in control. And sometimes that pisses me off."

"So this is about you wanting to be on top in bed—"

"No, that's not it—

"Oh, okay. You want me to give you blowjobs. Well, that's not happening, youngblood. You can let your wife do that for you—"

"Ailey, stop! Damn! That's not even what I'm talking about."

He inched toward me, tugging at my hand, but I moved away. I told him I had to study, but he should feel free to watch the game. After all, he was paying my cable bill.

Three hours later, he was on the couch asleep. When I woke him and walked him to the door, he leaned in for a kiss. But when he tried to pull me to the bedroom, I pushed him away and walked to the couch. I stepped out of my sweatpants and panties and leaned over the couch with my back to him.

"Is this how you want it, Scooter? You want to be in control? Then take it."

He didn't leave my apartment until dawn, but I didn't ask what he would tell Rebecca.

———

No matter how tough I'd acted with Scooter, he'd upset me. That Sunday, when Mama called, I asked her, did I seem like a bad person? Scary, even?

"I have it on good authority that everybody in the department of history says I'm hostile and possibly dangerous."

She blew a loud raspberry. "Oh, please. That's because you have some pride. You just don't want to hang out with a bunch of un-friendly so-and-sos. And I bet I know which white girl started that rumor."

"I barely say a word to Rebecca. And now I'm this female Bigger Thomas?"

"But that's her problem, baby. You're supposed to be lying awake nights, obsessing about her blond hair, and wondering why she's got a Black husband and you don't."

"I do think about being single."

"Child, you want to get married, ain't no magic to it. Get you a man, a license, and go down to the courthouse. But first you got to get out the library sometimes and meet somebody, 'cause it ain't legal to marry books."

"You know what I mean. I'll be thirty next year. Who's going to want me then?"

"What are you talking about? I had you at thirty, so apparently, your daddy wanted me. Otherwise, you wouldn't be here."

"That's different. Y'all were already married."

"Baby, listen. You aren't seeing what's really going on. Rebecca's scared her husband is trying to sleep with you. If he isn't already, because I had a dream about you and that guy."

"No, Mama! I told you we're only friends." I had a right to my secrets. I was grown now, or at least professing to be.

"All right, if you say so, baby. In that case, she's just suspicious."

"But maybe Scooter was right, Mama. I guess I could smile more."

"You could tap-dance like Mr. Bojangles, too, but that wouldn't make a difference. Not with those low-down white folks."

"You just love me. You have to say that."

"Just because I love you doesn't mean I'm not right."

PLURAL FIRST PERSON

❖

Sometimes, while Dr. Whitcomb was drilling one of my classmates, I'd look around the table. Indulge in tiny amusements, playing private games such as, what would we all have been?

With his patrician air, Boris St. John would have run his own plantation. Him with the fraternity pin stabbed through his tie. Though he was past the age of beer keg parties, on Southern Heritage Day, he joined the undergrads in dressing up in Confederate uniforms to parade around the campus main square. After that, they'd come back to their fraternity house and eat an old-style breakfast prepared by the African American cook, who'd dressed up like an enslaved person. She insisted that she was happy to do it, according to the article in the student newspaper. It was so much fun.

Harvey Dixon—how like *Dixie* his name was—would be a yeoman farmer, which Whitcomb had explained was basically a synonym for "white trash," though that was a prejudiced term, like "cracker" or "nigger." We needed to remember that.

"Our yeoman farmers, with their cherished one or two slaves apiece? We can't say they kept the economy flourishing, but we can say they did their best. We had those good ole boys doing their part, fighting for the Lost Cause, and killing those disloyal and ungrateful runaway Negroes."

You could hear the contempt in Dr. Whitcomb's voice, as Boris and Harvey shifted in their chairs. They probably weren't used to such language from a brother. Our professor was safe, though, no matter what they wrote on the student evaluations at semester's end. He was the only African American faculty member on campus with an endowed chair. Out of all the history professors, he had the most books: five edited texts and seven monographs, two of which had been finalists for the Pulitzer.

Rebecca, she would have been the master's daughter. Or maybe the wife of the master's son. Certainly, with her beauty, someone's prize. Emma would have been her nearsighted, spinster sister.

Whitcomb and I, we'd have been enslaved. Maybe he would have had the courage to run, but I was a coward. I would have stayed and suffered, but I couldn't yet decide whether I would have been up at the big house or out in the fields. The hard life or the soft. It might have depended on whether my master thought I was pretty or not. It wouldn't have mattered if he believed in God.

[Pinchard Family Papers, Boxes 1–12, circa 1806–1934.]

6 JAN 1814 Ahgayuh purchased frm Lanc. Polcott

(450 DOLLR)

2 JAN 1816 Mamie purchasd from Lanc. Polcott

4 JUNE 1817 Nick (b) born Mamie (Ahgayuh Nurse)

6 JUNE 1817 Mamie dead

7 MAY 1821 Tess (g) born Midas's Ahgayuh

29 JULY 1822 Midas sold Lanc. Polcott

The year before, I'd been so anxious to do research in the Old South Collections. The archives had fascinated me. Made me happy for the first time in my socially awkward life. But there was a catch when you did research on slavery: you couldn't only focus on the parts you wanted.

You had to wade through everything, in order to get to the documents you needed. You had to look at the slave auctions and whippings. The casual cruelty that indicated the white men who'd owned Black folks didn't consider them human beings. When I began doing research in the Pinchard family papers, I wasn't reading about strangers anymore. These were my own ancestors, Black and white. Samuel Pinchard was the great-grandfather of Uncle Root and Dear Pearl.

When I'd done research on the weeping time auction, I'd felt so saddened, but now, when I left the Old South Collections, rage joined my sadness. Every white person who crossed my path made me want to scream so badly, it seemed my flesh burned with the effort to maintain control. And to make matters worse, on my walk across campus from the collections, I'd be forced to go past the statue of the colonial founder of my university, Edward Sharpe. The students called his statue "Quiet Ned."

Sharpe had owned forty-three enslaved Black folks, but had caught religion during a sermon by a Great Awakening minister. After hearing the sermon, Edward Sharpe had decided he was against slavery. But instead of freeing the Black folks he owned and giving them a plot of land to work, he'd sold them for a profit, and bought land and started a university with the proceeds. In the university mythology, Edward Sharpe was lauded as a moral hero, and no information was given on the people he'd traded.

Every time I passed Quiet Ned, I thought of the hurt he'd caused those forty-three Black folks. I'd get so angry, it would make me sick, and I couldn't eat for one or sometimes two days. I could only drink coffee to keep me awake. I'd tremble, unable to sleep. I'd whisper curses toward flesh-peddling white men, hoping my words could travel to the past.

1 Oct 1824 Nick sent kitchen

6 Oct 1824 Nick sent fields

16 Sept 1828 Tess sent fields

11 April 1840 Eliza Two & Rabbit born to
　　　　　　Nick's Tess

5 Jan 1843 Venie purchasd frm Lanc. Polcott (990 Dllr)

11 Oct 1847 Rabbit sent kitchen

11 Oct 1847 Eliza Two sent maiding

3 Oct 1851 Nick gone (Ran)

4 Oct 1851 Jeremiah Franklin patrol (10 Dllr)

3 Jan 1852 Leena purchasd frm Hez. Polcott (1100 Dllr)

3 Sept 1852 Grace Bless Franklin & Victor Pinchard married
　　　　　　(Rev. Dalton 2 Dollr)

For the fourth week of his class, Dr. Whitcomb had assigned two big books, John Blassingame's *Slave Testimony* and Eugene Genovese's *Roll, Jordan, Roll,* what our professor called classics in the field. In addition, he'd compiled a homemade reader that we'd bought at the campus copy shop. The reader contained copies of the Federal Writers' Project slave narratives, interviews with then-living Black people who had survived slavery. These narratives had been commissioned by the government back in the 1930s, when President Roosevelt was trying to put the country to work.

"Ailey, what are your impressions of our readings?" Dr. Whitcomb asked.

I flipped through my notes. "Okay . . . um . . . I hope it's all right that I comment on the narratives since nobody else has."

"I'm waiting with bated breath."

"All right . . . well . . ."

"We don't have all day, Ailey."

"I could be wrong, but there is a lot of pro-white bias on the part of some interviewers. And I found this bias extremely problematic."

"Go on. Expound."

"Those particular white interviewers clearly are invested in downplaying the brutality of slavery and the trauma suffered by formerly enslaved African Americans. They appear to be steering their Black subjects to say how great they were treated by their former masters, and I thought—"

When Rebecca raised her hand, I expected Dr. Whitcomb to ignore her. I wasn't yet finished, but he surprised me.

"You have something to add, Rebecca?" he asked.

"Yes, I do. Maybe we should consider, just maybe, that the interviewers for these narratives weren't racially biased. Maybe these former slaves were telling the truth and their masters really had been kind to them. Maybe they had been happy."

I raised my hand. "Can I rebut?"

"I don't know," Dr. Whitcomb said. "Can you?"

I cut him a glance, and thought I saw a brief smile, but I couldn't be sure.

"If slavery was so great, why did the Civil War happen?" I asked.

"Because the north was infringing on our southern states' rights," Rebecca said.

"Are you seriously going to bring up that old chestnut?" I laughed, and our professor tapped the table with his knuckles. *Keep it professional here. Don't be derisive.*

"Sorry," I said. "But I would like to ask Rebecca, exactly who is this first-person plural in 'our states' rights'? Is it white people? And are you referring to the fact that only whites were citizens in this country until the Fourteenth Amendment in 1868 granted citizenship to African Americans, or are you thinking of the 1924 Indian Citizenship Act, when Native Americans were granted citizenship? Which one, Rebecca?"

"Our southern identity is not about race," she said. "It's about the fact that we lost the Civil War—"

"And again, you are using a plural first-person pronoun," I said. "What 'we' are you referring to? Because my Black family didn't lose the war. We won it."

"I would expect a Yankee to take that attitude, Ailey."

"My mother is from Georgia, and her entire family is, too. Further, 'Yankee'"—I made air quotes—"does not describe African Americans. It is a term that is specific to whites from New England."

"How did this become a racial debate, Ailey?"

"Rebecca, how is the Civil War not about race?"

"Because the Civil War was about states' rights."

"Yes, the right for southern states to hold African Americans in slavery!"

Dr. Whitcomb tapped the table again. "Okay, that's enough. This discussion has become circular and borderline impolite."

After class, I waited as he packed his books. "Dr. Whitcomb, I wanted to apologize sincerely for my disruptive behavior. I hope you can forgive me."

"No harm, no foul." He zipped up his old-fashioned physician's bag. But when I began to express gratitude, he cut me off. He told me, have a good afternoon.

But I didn't want to leave things on an odd note: the next day, I showed up to his office in the multicultural center. I hadn't made an appointment, and when I knocked on the door, Dr. Whitcomb had a submarine sandwich and chips on his desk. He had rolled up his sleeves, and his cuff links and tie sat on the desk a few inches away from the food. His large-screen television was turned to the sports cable channel.

He waved his hand at me. "Hey there, sistren! I was just watching the playoff report."

Dr. Whitcomb pressed a button; there was a flash of dark limbs silently running up and down a court. He smiled at me and the dimples flashed. But when I told him I had come to apologize again, the temperature in the room chilled.

"Sistren, I told you it was fine. But now that you're here, let me give you some advice from an elder with gray in his beard. You need to stop engaging in petty arguments over inconsequential issues. You aren't here for that foolishness. You're here to get at least one graduate degree in the discipline of history."

The rage suddenly overtook me as he put another chip in his mouth. Did he know what it was like, struggling up those steps to the collections to do that research? How I'd lost weight because my appetite had basically disappeared, ever since I'd been reading those journals written by Samuel Pinchard, that asshole of a white man who had the nerve to be one of my blood ancestors? Or the humiliating exercises I had to perform to get those journals from the research librarian? *Yes, ma'am, Mrs. Ransom, I'ma be shonuff careful with these here papers.* Dr. Whitcomb had no idea how that librarian watched over me, waiting for me to pull out a bucket of fried chicken and start munching on it over her precious original documents.

What did Dr. Whitcomb know? Him and his six-figure salary, his endowed chair, and his fucking cable in his university office.

"Is that all?" His hand hovered over the remote. "Did you need something else?"

I put extra cornpone and molasses into my voice.

"No, Dr. Whitcomb. I understand what you're saying, and I hope you know I really appreciate you. I appreciate you so—"

"Ailey, stop. That 'southern belle' bullshit don't work with me. Girl, I got regrets and kids older than you." He put a chip in his mouth, then began to laugh. He was still laughing when I gave my excuses and left.

14 MAY 1855 Holcomb Byrd James hired as overseer

24 DEC 1857 Matthew Thatcher in Guest Cabin

4 FEB 1858 Matthew in Guest Cabin

4 MARCH 1858 Matthew in Guest Cabin

1 APRIL 1858 Matthew in Guest Cabin

6 MAY 1858 Matthew in Guest Cabin

3 JUNE 1858 Matthew in Guest Cabin

1 JULY 1858 Matthew in Guest Cabin

5 AUG 1858 Matthew in Guest Cabin

2 SEPT 1858 Matthew in Guest Cabin

7 OCT 1858 Matthew in Guest Cabin

4 NOV 1858 Matthew in Guest Cabin

24 DEC 1858 Matthew in Guest Cabin

4 FEB 1859 Matthew in Guest Cabin

27 FEB 1859 Leave for Savannah w/ Matthew

10 MAR 1859 Return frm Savannah w/ Matthew

10 MAR 1859 Gloria dead, Sunday last

2 JUNE 1859 Peach blighting

10 JULY 1859 Fire in Left Cabin

11 JULY 1859 Rabbit & Leena dead (Monday last)

11 JULY 1859 Pompey & Sugar & Cletus gone (Ran Monday last)

At Shug's, Scooter tried to start a conversation, but I told him I couldn't chitchat. I had eight hundred pages to get through. But I thanked him for the coffee, and no, I didn't want any breakfast. I wasn't hungry.

"Ailey, I've got a favor to ask."

"No, youngblood, you can't hold twenty dollars. I'm light, brother. It's the middle of the month."

"Very funny. No, I need you come to dinner with Rebecca and me."

I looked over my glasses. "You're kidding, right?"

"No, I'm not. Rebecca really wants you to come over."

"That's not going to happen, Scooter."

"Why not?"

I rose and walked to the counter. It was a slow morning, and so I stood there for several minutes, talking to Miss Velma. Did she have any new pictures of her youngest grandbaby? And she leaned down and brought up her purse, saying, she shole did.

I returned to my table but didn't speak to Scooter. I gathered my books and papers and headed toward the door. When he called my name, I didn't turn around. That evening, he came by my apartment. He stood on the porch, ringing the bell and knocking, but I didn't open the door. I sat on the couch, listening as Mike scolded Scooter, he didn't live on this street. So he couldn't be standing on a lady's porch, causing a ruckus like he didn't have no sense. Somebody might call the police, and Scooter was a Black man. He should know better: he had to be careful in this town.

June 26, 1868

Dear Master Samuel

I trust this letter finds you well. I write to inform you that I have been living happy and FREE these last seventeen years. I shall not reveal the names of my benefactors or the city in which I dwell, only that I have been aided by righteous people who are very kind. They ask that I worship the Lord in exchange for my roof, bed, and many good meals and I am happy to do so. Surely God is deserving of my praise. Yet my benefactors have asked me all these years to consider my salvation. They have reminded me that the Good Lord requires our forgiveness of even the most grievous of sins. Master you have surely trespassed against me, my grandfather, my mother, my father, my beloved wife, my children and everyone else at Wood Place who occupy my affection but after much prayer I now write to you and offer my forgiveness. I forgive you Master of your many thousands of evils. I forgive you for being the left-handed comrade of the Devil who whispers his desires in the dark and who you follow without hesitation. Truly I forgive you Master though you are a creature worthy of disgust without mitigation. Daily I pray for your ugly, miserable and tarnished soul. May our most merciful Savior redeem you before you pass from this earthly vale and are sentenced to Satan's fiery depths.

Your former slave
Nick Pinchard

THE THRILLA IN MANILA

◆

By midterm, I'd made my way through the earliest records of the Pinchard family. I'd walk across campus and huff up those stairs. I'd wave at Mrs. Ransom and she would fix her glasses on her nose then give me the inevitable white cotton gloves.

Those early records coincided with the first land lottery in Georgia in 1805, when white men over twenty-one and white widows were given a chance to each win a plot of land of a little over two hundred acres, with the odds of winning were approximately one in ten. In this way, the territory became Putnam County. Treated as an empty space, instead of the home of the Creek who had already lived there. This was how Samuel Pinchard had come to own Wood Place Plantation.

Samuel Pinchard's journals were so boring, they made me drowsy, even with my years of training. There were accounts of his bargaining with suppliers for feed and livestock and for lumber—and there was much bargaining, because Samuel was an exceptionally cheap man.

But my persistence was rewarded when I realized the date of Samuel's visit to Savannah, which I'd seen in his journal, placed him there in early March 1859, during the weeping time auction. Not only that, Samuel somehow had also made the acquaintance of Matthew Thatcher, the benefactor of Routledge College, who'd accompanied him to the auction. When I called Dr. Oludara to let her know what I'd found, she told me, hang up. She would call me back, because this was going to be a very long and expensive conversation.

Indeed, 1859 had been a very eventful year for Samuel Pinchard. In addition to the weeping time auction, there was the death of his daughter, he'd received the letter from Nick, an enslaved man who had run away, and then in July, two more deaths had occurred. Leena

and Rabbit, two enslaved girls, had died in a fire that destroyed a
structure Samuel had called "the left cabin" in his journals. I read
and reread those entries in Samuel's journal: "10 July 1859 Fire in
Left Cabin. 11 July 1859 Rabbit & Leena dead." Two short entries,
that's all he'd recorded of the death of those girls. Rabbit had been
the twin sister of Eliza Two, the girl who would become my direct
maternal ancestor.

Burning was such a horrific way to die. I couldn't even imagine
that kind of agony, both for the girls who perished in the fire and
those who couldn't save them. The loss of a sister was a grief that
never waned. This is what Eliza Two must have experienced, after
Rabbit died. Samuel Pinchard didn't have to write that down in his
journals. I understood that grief already. I still dreamed about Lydia,
and when I awoke, I still felt cheated that she wasn't alive.

———

For my presentation on the archives in late October, I took twenty
minutes to detail the initial records that I'd found in the papers of
Samuel Pinchard. I focused on the descendants of two women, Mamie and Ahgayuh, specifically on Nick, who'd been born on Wood
Place in 1821, married Ahgayuh's daughter, Tess, and sired twin
girls with her, Rabbit and Eliza Two. In 1851, Nick had run away,
but sometime on or around June 26, 1868, a letter had been mailed
to Samuel, signed by Nick. He'd written Samuel on the older man's
birthday, though that milestone hadn't been mentioned—perhaps
the timing of the letter had been a coincidence. But the tone of the
letter was quite rancorous, as Nick described in generalities what he
termed Pinchard's "thousands of evils." In another folder in the Pinchard papers, I'd found a flyer offering a reward for Nick's return.
The sketch and description of Nick indicated he'd been of mixed-
race heritage, though he did not identify his probably white father
in his letter. Therefore, it wasn't clear whether Samuel Pinchard or
another white man had sired Nick.

Though I wasn't sure how Dr. Whitcomb would respond, I outlined
my kinship to Nick, that he was the father of Rabbit and Eliza Two,
that the latter girl would become my fourth great-grandmother. Dr.

Whitcomb only nodded at this information; I couldn't tell whether I'd made a mistake or not, talking about my family connection. I ended by noting that the Old South Collections librarian had told me no one had examined the Pinchard family papers since 1934, the year Thomas Pinchard Jr. had donated them to the university. His daughter, Cordelia Pinchard Rice, was the last legitimate descendant of the family, although there were plenty African Americans in the Pinchard line.

Rebecca raised her hand. "How do you know there are Black descendants of this family?"

"That's a really great question," I said. "I know because Pearl Freeman Collins was the daughter of Thomas Pinchard Sr. This is common knowledge in Chicasetta. And Thomas Sr. was the grandchild of Samuel Pinchard."

"But what proof do you have of that? Did Pearl take a paternity test?"

"No, Mrs. Collins didn't, but—"

"—then how do you know?"

"We have the word of Mrs. Collins's mother, Maybelline Victorina Freeman. We have the long, close relationship between Thomas Pinchard Sr. and his two biracial children, even after their mother's death. There was a second child with Maybelline, Jason Freeman Hargrace. And we have the word of the white male sibling of Dr. Hargrace and Mrs. Collins, who publicly acknowledged them as well. That would be Thomas Pinchard Jr."

"But that's not real proof."

"Rebecca, has your father ever taken a paternity test to prove you're his child?"

"I can't believe you asked me that!"

Quickly, I cut a glance toward our professor. His eyebrows were raised.

"Excuse me, Rebecca, I definitely didn't mean to insult you, and I sincerely apologize if I've offended you. But I'm simply making a point. None of the white descendants of the Pinchard family have had paternity tests, but no one ever has questioned their lineage in over a hundred and fifty years. Their paternity is an a priori assumption, and we can only conclude that was because the so-called legitimate descendants were white."

She turned her gaze from me, casting around in her gorgeous way.

"Ailey, let's bring this back to your records," Dr. Whitcomb said. "How long did it take you to find this information?"

"Not long. A month for this particular information, but definitely, I have more."

When I finished my presentation, I sat down at the seminar table. Dr. Whitcomb didn't give me any compliments. Instead, he suggested that I look at some more sources on Georgia state history and see what I could find that intersected with Wood Place Plantation. Right now, my research was not complete.

Then it was Rebecca's turn to present. Before detailing what she'd found in the Paschal family of Georgia, she started with an anecdote about her Black nanny. Rebecca recounted her earliest memory: she'd awoken with Flossie's nipple in her mouth.

I sighed and lowered my head, looking at my legal pad.

After class, Dr. Whitcomb told me he needed to talk to me. I was putting away my books, but when he spoke to me, his voice sharply stern, my heart pounded. I looked over at Rebecca and Emma, and they were smirking. He waited until everyone left and walked over to me. When he put his palm out, I looked at it, perplexed.

"Come on, now," Dr. Whitcomb said. "You gone leave me hanging?"

He smiled, his dimples in merry action. I tentatively touched his palm, and he told me I could do better than that. Give him some dap like I meant it. When I hit his hand with force, I felt a charge.

"Ailey, that presentation was out of sight!" He jumped on the tips of his shiny shoes. "Now, that's what I'm talking 'bout!"

"So I was okay?"

"Okay? Sistren, you were brilliant! And now, are you going to continue here next fall? For the doctorate, I mean?"

"Definitely, Dr. Whitcomb."

"Yes!" he said. "That is fabulous news! You have made my entire week."

"And I was hoping . . . maybe . . . do you think you might be my doctoral advisor? I know how busy you are and everything—"

"Of course, Ailey! I don't care how busy I am! I will make the time for you."

"Really? Thank you so much, Dr. Whitcomb!"

"I guess you approve of me now, huh? I'm pretty good at reading people, Ailey. I was almost positive that you didn't like me."

"Oh, no, Dr. Whitcomb. I've loved this class since the very beginning."

He laughed, putting his fist to his mouth. "That is not true! But I appreciate the home training."

I smiled and looked down at the table.

"Ailey, I can understand why you didn't like me. This is one of the highest-ranked programs for early American history in the country, and there I was, giving an overview of basic information to grown folks in graduate school. But that's what you must do with certain individuals, Ailey. Slave history is inconsequential to them. They can recite the Mayflower Compact by heart but haven't even heard of partus sequitur ventrem. You know who I mean by 'certain individuals,' right?"

"Yes, sir. I think so."

"And they aren't used to working as hard as us, either. They don't have to. But that's the Black tax at work. No use in complaining. You know I used to have an afro this big, back in the day?"

He cupped his hands around his completely bald head, and I grinned.

"I came here in the eighties, Ailey, after teaching at Howard. They gave me a lot of money here, and I wanted it. I'm being honest. But that money came with a price. I thought about leaving, but then more Black undergraduates came in, so I thought, *Before I go, I'll get a multicultural center built for these kids.* And after that, I said, *Well, the history program has never graduated an African American on the master's level.* So I recruited Jamari Brooks, and he earned the master's two years ago, but he decided he was going someplace else for his doctorate. And then when Belinda Oludara sent you my way, I thought, *Maybe Ailey is the one. Maybe she'll be the first African American to get the doctorate here in history.*"

He walked to the door, looked outside, and then pushed it closed. He lowered his voice to a whisper.

"You need to know something, Ailey. Nobody in this department ever says they don't want African Americans in the doctoral program. They say it's a coincidence that there haven't been any. Or they say they can't find one that's qualified. Okay, well, now you're here, full of qualifications, and taking the hardest classes and making the highest grades. But they just happened not to give you the mentoring you'll need to continue to the doctoral program. And that's how that goes, Ailey. When we come to these all-white spaces, we have to be tough. We can't show any weakness. I know that's difficult, but that's the way it is, and that's why I'm so hard on you. And I will continue to be hard on you, Ailey, because I want to prepare you for what's coming. It's gone be the Thrilla in Manila when you enter the doctoral program. They will throw everything they have at you. If you fail, they'll say, oh, that's too bad. You just weren't smart enough. If you succeed and earn the degree, despite all the obstacles they put up, they'll take credit for your success and congratulate themselves for fostering a nonprejudiced environment. But, Ailey, you aren't going to fail, because I am going to help you with every ounce of power that I have, all while pretending that I'm not helping you. For example, you and I never had this conversation. Do you understand me?"

He raised his eyebrows.

"Yes, sir."

"I have faith in you, Ailey. We're going to get you to that promised land, and then I'm gone find a tenure-track Black faculty member to replace me, and then I'm gone retire and take myself back to D.C. to a chocolate-covered neighborhood! Nah'mean?"

We laughed, and sat there for a long time, talking. He told me, when I spoke again with Uncle Root, please let him know that his book on African American families in the City had been life-changing. Dr. Whitcomb must have read that book five times, back at Harvard. When I gave my apologies, saying I needed to get back to making notes on my research, he told me no apologies were necessary. Dr. Whitcomb understood my obsession. And please keep him updated on my progress in the archives. He especially wanted to hear about my Wood Place kin.

————

At four thirty, I returned the documents I'd been reading to Mrs. Ransom, flipping the pages of my legal pad to prove I hadn't stolen anything, as a Frenchman five years previously had done. The international market for historical documents was surprisingly brisk.

"I notice you've been looking at those Pinchard records. What are you writing about?" She patted a wayward curl into place with the rest of her bouffant.

I stood at the counter, trying not to dance: I'd skipped a pee break.

"I'm not sure. Just doing research for Dr. Whitcomb's class."

"Oh, Charles! He's such a nice man. We've helped him with his books over the years. He always puts us on his acknowledgments page. Did he assign this family to you?"

"No, ma'am. My mother's people have lived on that land for generations."

"In Chicasetta?"

"Yes, ma'am."

A sudden smile; the teeth unusually white for someone her age. She placed her hand on top of mine.

"Oh my goodness! My daddy's people are from Milledgeville!"

We remained at the counter almost an hour, chatting, though the collections were supposed to be closed. I confided that I didn't ever want to live in the City again. I regularly traveled to Georgia to see my family and wasn't the countryside so pretty and peaceful? And since Mrs. Ransom had roots in Milledgeville, which Flannery O'Connor story was her favorite? Had she ever been to Andalusia? The house was fallen and musty, but the grounds were beautiful. The pond, the old barn, that old mule that refused to give up the ghost. The smell of wisteria.

I had turned to leave when Mrs. Ransom remembered the daguerreotypes—one of them was the only image of slaves in the Pinchard papers.

"Photographs?" The excitement hit my bladder with renewed force. I tried not to run, calling over my shoulder that I'd be right back. I needed to visit the ladies' room. Please don't close the library on me. When I returned, she'd set me back up at my table, along with a new set of gloves and two rectangles of folded paper, each about five by three inches. I sat down, pulled on the gloves, and carefully touched one of the papers. When I opened it, there was an image of five white people. I immediately rewrapped that image and turned to the other paper, which had writing on it—what I assumed were the names of the picture's subjects: "Leena, Eliza Two, and Rabbit, April 1858." It was dated fifteen months before the fire Samuel Pinchard had recorded in his journal, the one that he'd noted had killed Rabbit and Leena, two of these girls.

I opened the paper and touched the edge of the daguerreotype inside. It was a picture of three girls who seemed more than solemn. All three wore frowns so deep, they seemed to be scowling. My breath caught—one of these girls was Eliza Two, my great-great-great-great-grandmother. They represented three different skin tones: on the left, the darkest and shortest girl, whose clothes were hidden by a long, white apron. Her face appeared chiseled from a rare metal, her hair a coiled mass puffed high. On the right, a tall, plump girl in a shabby dress, perhaps sewn from "linsey-woolsey," the cheap cloth used to make slaves' garments. She had a braid that fell over one shoulder and what appeared to be keloid scars on her cheeks. The fairest girl stood in the middle. She had hoops in her ears, and her hair was brushed into ringlets. She was dressed in an extravagant frock with many ribbons and buttons.

"Is the one in the fancy dress the master's daughter?" Mrs. Ransom asked.

"No, ma'am," I said. "I don't think so."

I could see why Mrs. Ransom would think the girl in the middle was white. There was her skin color and then her undoubtedly expensive attire, which didn't indicate enslaved status. But there was something else that pulled at me and made me answer in the negative: I was certain I'd seen this girl, and the one on the left, before.

———

I'd never skipped a class in my program, and I wasn't going to start. But for two days, I couldn't sleep, thinking about the daguerreotype that I'd seen in the collections.

On Thursday, my class was over at four thirty, and my car was already packed. I drove by the gas station to fill up. Then I headed south. When I passed the sign for Gaffney, South Carolina, I heard Lydia's voice, squealing at the Peach Butt on the horizon.

At Uncle Root's house, I let myself in with my key. It was late, almost midnight, but he was sitting on the couch, waiting for me. He smiled, bemused. Was something going on? My face was shining like a new penny, but I wouldn't tell him what I'd found.

"I can't tell you. Not yet. I'll let you know tomorrow."

"All right, Ailey, you're allowed your privacy."

"No, no! I'm going to tell you, but you have to wait! It's so exciting!"

"Ah! A mystery."

I wanted to be certain. That was the requirement of my profession, to lay my own eyes upon the proof, before I told anyone. Like my Aunt Pauline might say, I didn't want to shout until I got happy.

In the morning, I drove to Routledge. I parked in the lot by the library. Mrs. Giles-Lipscomb still remembered me. Hug her neck, she ordered, and she wasn't a bit surprised that I was going to be an historian. She'd been waiting for me to follow in Uncle Root's footsteps, but when I asked to see the old documents from the college archives, she was reluctant. Those papers were very fragile, she told me, until I reminded her I was the former research assistant of Dr. Oludara.

"You can call her. I don't mind."

"No, Ailey, I'm going to trust you."

But when Mrs. Giles-Lipscomb brought the box out, she reminded me, please be careful. This box contained an original portrait, not a reproduction. She laid down a cloth on the table, then several layers of acid-free paper, and finally—reverently—the daguerreotype on top. She kept whispering, careful, careful, but when I reached into my purse for white cotton gloves, she smiled.

"All right. I see you know what you're doing. I'll leave you to it."

I looked inside the box, and there were two other items in the box: a cameo brooch framed in tiny pearls, and a linen handkerchief embroidered along the edges with blue thread. Before placing a finger on both sides of the daguerreotype, I fitted a glove over each hand. If Matthew Thatcher had wrapped this image in fabric or paper, that covering was long gone. There was damage to the edges, little chips and tears, but the center was clear. It was an image that I'd seen many times, in my four years in college, on the first floor of the library. This small daguerreotype that had been reproduced into a much larger image. It was the portrait of our college founders, Adeline Ruth Hutchinson Routledge and her sister, Judith Naomi Hutchinson.

The two young women were probably in their twenties. They clung together, surrendering no space, and wore matching dark dresses—maybe black or gray—with voluminous skirts. There was lace around their necks as well, collars that draped over their bosoms. The smaller woman was strikingly beautiful, very dark, with prominent cheekbones and full lips turned upward. There had been an attempt to restrain the coils that sprang around her face: she wore a crocheted or knitted snood, but her hair sneaked out. A brooch was fastened at her collar, but I couldn't be certain it was the same one from the box. The much fairer-skinned woman beside her was pale with a thin grimace, and hoops in her ears.

Except for the clothing and the ages, these women were identical to two of the girls in the first daguerreotype Mrs. Ransom had shown me from the Pinchard archives: it had to be Rabbit and Leena, who had supposedly died in the fire in 1859, according to Samuel Pinchard's journal. Yet here they were in another daguerreotype. I knew from my college's history that this image was dated around 1866. Rabbit and Leena must have somehow survived the Wood Place fire, made it to freedom in Boston, and changed their names to Judith and Adeline Hutchinson. We'd been taught in college that Judith had passed away early, but Adeline had gone south after the war and founded a school to educate Negro girls. I was sitting in the very library that she had built.

But the third girl, the girl with keloids on her cheeks who'd been in the Wood Place daguerreotype, wasn't in this picture I was holding. For some reason, that girl had been left down south: Eliza Two, my direct ancestor. I wanted to be grateful that she'd remained behind. If she hadn't stayed in Chicasetta—if she'd had no descendants— I wouldn't even be alive. But this meant Eliza Two had endured six more years in slavery, until it was abolished, and all the other crimes against southern Black folks that would come afterward. How much more had Eliza Two suffered on that plantation, after she'd already lost a father and a sister?

I covered my face and began to cry.

I don't know how long I sat there, but the librarian must have taken me up on my offer and called my former professor. Before I heard the other chair scraping the floor, I smelled the incense. Dr. Oludara didn't even ask me what I'd found. She only touched my shoulder, telling me, it was all right. It was okay. Sometimes it hit her like that, too, thinking about our people and those sad days. She patted my shoulder as I sobbed.

WITNESS MY HAND

❖

[From the Routledge Family Papers, Freedom Library, Property of Routledge College, Matthew Thatcher, Box 1, Single Folder]

December 25, 1859
Boston Mass

Dear Matt,

Happy Christmas! Our <u>sisters</u> in <u>Christ</u> are learning their ABC! I am <u>trying</u> to teach Adeline to keep house but I am of the mind she <u>never</u> will cook or be a seamstress. I can <u>rejoice</u> that she is <u>clean</u> as Judith's side of their room is cluttered. But O the <u>lightness</u> of your Judy's <u>biscuits</u>! Surely the Lord <u>provides</u>, as Luke counsels, "<u>Seek the Kingdom of God</u> above all else, and he will give you everything you need." We take daily walks for their <u>constitution</u>. Adeline is <u>hail</u> but your Judy <u>needs</u> fattening and coughs at times. She eats too <u>little</u>. (Do not worry! I am taking great care of her!) Yet how <u>blessed I</u> am in these girls when I despaired of <u>never</u> having children! Like <u>Sarah</u> I have my Isaac and <u>another</u> in my heart. Surely <u>God</u> is <u>merciful</u> and great!

> Your loving sister,
> *Deborah*

[Undated journal entry by Judith Hutchinson (?)]
dis evenin debrah brung the ink an papar she say my salvasun lay in the pin she say o judi it is yor duti to yor bredrin to rit it doun cant yu see she say my swet judi doan call me miss call me debrah an yor mat wud wont you to rit it down he love you so veri much shorly you no that an I drop my

hed she swet an so kin i no i can rit now an i can so an cook but ~~teena~~ addie
be cleenin an debrah say wat on cant do the udder can an god provid i is wel
prase jesus but i com down wit the crup an scar me orful i thank on how i
wont be seein my matt no more an i love him so much but then i thank on
jeesus he be up there waitin an ~~teena~~ addie put her hans on mi hart aftur
dockar say no she ant gitin up an ~~teena~~ addie pray an the lord heel me an
i fil so bless

January 1, 1866

My Dearest Matthew

I hope this letter reaches you! We have despaired of the mail
during the War and now I wish to hear from you every single
moment of every hour! Today Addie and I walked having been
given an errand to visit some folks and deliver good tidings of
the New Year. I baked cakes for two of the elders. I do not tell
Deborah that one of our charges is the grandmother of a very-
very handsome Negro gentleman of the last name Routledge.
The old woman has no teeth and no taste for sweets. Addie
brought Mr. Routledge my cakes and told him that she baked
them tho you know she cannot even scald milk! As we walked
I felt the Spirit come strongly upon me lifting me up—if I did
not know myself to be one of God's lowly servants I would
have thought my feet would take me straight to Heaven. I had
to cease walking and clutch my basket so happy was I of that
memory. I wanted to sanctify His name and began to weep and
laid my head on Addie's shoulder. It was she who'd heard the
cry first on the day of Mr. Lincoln's tidings. The gladness in the
notes—the sweetness—caught me that day and then I knew.
When I came to the main fare the folks were thick outside.
Some were shouting with joy others weeping—it was Freedom!
It was Jubilee! That night I could not sleep and when I lay my
body down ingratitude visited me that I could not share this
preponderance of God's mercy with the folks back home. It

has been so long! How I miss them! I miss the trees! I miss the brightness when I had a small creature's name! I look for Father every day and ask at the Meeting House but none have seen him. I wish I could write him and tell him the news you wrote us about Granny and Mother passing to Heaven. I keep a stout face to Addie and Deborah for if I begin to weep I shall not stop. I miss them all but more than anyone I miss my sister. There is never joy in a circle only half. I am cut from my sister and it is a terrible feeling. It is near daybreak and I have labors in too few hours.

My Matthew, I miss you terribly. Please come to your darling soon.

My whole heart for you & the Lord,
Judy

Boston
June 23, 1866

Dear Matthew
I take my pen in hand to write that I am now a married lady! Deborah and Judy were in a flurry over my wedding and trying to make me learn to cook in time but all was lost. I have learned to sew a bit but do not favor the work. My husband tells me he did not marry me for food and clothes but for my kind nature and because God wishes it. Judy says she is his sister too and will cook for us all. She has taught my husband to read the Bible and I cannot help but remember how Deborah taught Judy and me ciphering and letters. The constitution of all is fair and there is much happiness.

We miss you. Visit soon.

Affectionately,
Mrs Coffee Routledge (Addie)

Thatcher Farm
Baldwin County Georgia
April 19, 1867

My Darling Judy
Tho I've not written please do not be angry with your sweetheart! You are ever in my thoughts. The planting season is
done and the men are hardworking. I hope to get a high price
in the fall for my crops. I bought two beef cows & put up five
hams. Thank you for the blue shirt you made me. Your hand
is very fine and when I wear it I always think of you. Well that
is all.

Please write soon. I miss you so much. I shall be traveling to
Boston soon my love.

Yours only,
Matthew

Thatcher Home
Baldwin County Georgia
July 30, 1868

My Darling Judy
That man is finally dead and in the ground since Sunday past.
Please come home my love. There is always a place for you in
this house. There is no need for worry. Please come home.

Yours only,
Matthew

Boston
February 9, 1869

Dear Matt:
I know no other way to impart this news. Your Judy is gone

to Glory. She came down with a fever and never rose again. Her last words were of love for you and for the Savior but I could not be glad at her passing. If not for Sister Deborah and Brother Winfred I fear I could not last. I have not their cheerfulness in the presence of trials. There have been too many. I cherish my sweet Violet but already miss Judy! My only hope is that I shall know her face in Heaven. I am so angry at what I have endured! What God would take my sister from me so soon after my husband passed away?

I am so very sorry to give you this news.

Affectionately,
Addie

Thatcher Home
Baldwin County Georgia
March 5, 1869

Addie
My heart is breaking to pieces.
    If God wills I will see my darling Judy again in Heaven.
    I cannot say more. These words are not enough.

Matthew

Thatcher Home
Baldwin County Georgia
August 20, 1871

Dearest Addie
Please come home. Please Addie.
    I am very lonely. This house needs laughter. Please.
    My Judy would want you and Violet to come home. Please.

Matthew

Boston
October 23, 1871

Dear Matt,

My child and I shall be coming by train to Macon in a week's time. Please wait for us at the station. I fear my heart will shatter when I step foot upon that earth again, but I shall withstand, as there is much work to be done for my people.

Affectionately,
Addie

This is the last will and testament of Matthew John Thatcher of Baldwin County, Georgia, a servant of Christ in whole mind and body. All other wills composed heretofore are null.

I appoint Winfred Hutchinson of Boston, Massachusetts, as my sole executrix and any thereafter as seen fit by him.

I bequeath the following to my servants and fellow travelers in Christ:

To Mungo Thatcher, cash in the amount of $50 and two acres in Baldwin County.

To Quaco Thatcher, cash in the amount of $50 and two acres in Baldwin County.

To Juno Thatcher, cash in the amount of $50 and two acres in Baldwin County.

To Caesar Thatcher, cash in the amount of $50 and two acres in Baldwin County.

To Athena Thatcher, cash in the amount of $50 and two acres in Baldwin County.

To Obour Thatcher, cash in the amount of $50 and two acres in Baldwin County.

To Matilde Thatcher, cash in the amount of $50 and two acres in Baldwin County.

To Orpah Thatcher, cash in the amount of $50 and two acres in Baldwin County.

To Simon Thatcher, two suits of clothes, my leather shoes, my shotgun, cash in the amount of $100, and my dog (and any litters), and two acres in Baldwin County.

To Dori Thatcher, all my kitchen utensils, my butter churn, three bolts of calico cloth, one lace wedding veil, ten mother of pearl buttons, cash in the amount of $100, and two acres in Baldwin County.

The remainder of my estate is bequeathed to my family members:

To my sister, Deborah Thatcher Hutchinson, I bequeath my Bible and my gold watch and chain.

To my niece, Violet Elizabeth Routledge, I bequeath my gelding, one gold ring with lapis stone, and cash in the amount of $750.

To my sister, Adeline Ruth Hutchinson Routledge, I bequeath all my remaining cash in the present amount of $5887, one hundred and sixty acres (and any harvests planted) in Baldwin County, Georgia, my remaining books, my house, all outbuildings, all furniture, all farm tools including my plow, one wagon, one mare, four milk cows, one bull, two calves, fourteen (and counting) chickens, one rooster, three pigs, one mule, and one goat. Further, any of my possessions not mentioned herein shall be the sole property of Adeline Ruth Hutchinson Routledge.

Witness my hand and seal at Thatcher Home, Baldwin County, Georgia, this third day of October in the year of our Lord one thousand eight hundred and eighty.

May God have mercy upon my soul.

MY BLACK FEMALE TIME

◈

In early December, Scooter called me. It wasn't a shock: he'd been calling every day, leaving messages on my machine. He'd stopped coming by without calling, though, and knocking for long minutes. The second time it had happened, Mike had told him, show up again making a fuss, and Scooter would get his ass beat. Won't nobody playing with him.

I'd stopped going out to Shug's for our standing coffee date. I'd gone to the grocery store to buy ground coffee. My brew was strong, though not as smooth as Miss Velma's. But it powered me through my long nights of studying. I wasn't as lonely as I expected to be, either. I was working so hard in my classes, I had very little time to feel sorry for myself.

On the phone, Scooter asked, could he watch the basketball game at my house? I waited for his reminder that he paid the cable bill, but it didn't come.

"Sure, youngblood. Come on over."

Within minutes of his arrival, he asked, could I get him a beer? I went to the refrigerator and pulled out a six-pack that had been there since October. I put the pack down on the floor, hoping he would take the hint to drink a beer and leave, but after he drank one, he still sat there.

"Can you make some wings, Ailey? I'm a little hungry."

"No," I said. "I'm too busy for that."

I waited for him to broach what had happened. But he only settled on the couch and clicked the remote. He let out a small cheer when his team made a free throw or a grunt of disappointment when the ball turned over. He finished one bottle and wordlessly held out his empty bottle to me. Shaking it, but I didn't take the bottle. I watched his face for something. A change, yet there was nothing.

I stepped in front of him, blocking his view of the television.

"Scooter, are you only my friend because of my fried chicken wings and innate sense of rhythm?"

"What?" He looked away from the screen. "Is this some sort of riddle?"

I walked to the dresser and turned the television off.

"Scooter, I didn't appreciate what went down the last time I saw you."

"So you really want to talk about this? I would think you would be embarrassed. You walked out on me at Shug's—"

"After you invited me to your house, when we've been sleeping together—"

"Okay, here we go—"

"Here we go? You actually expected your Black mistress to eat dinner with your white, racist wife—"

"Oh man! Really, Ailey? This is you apologizing?"

"Wait. Is that what you expect? An apology?"

"Yes, I do!"

"Well, youngblood, if wishes were horses, assholes would ride."

"See this? This is precisely why I'm not with a Black female! All you sisters want to do is yell and scream and roll your necks. You love all this unnecessary"—he waved his hands—"all this drama."

My voice rose to a shout.

"Oh, it's like that? I'm so damned repulsive, and yet, you fucked me for almost a year! You couldn't get enough of this! And apparently, you still can't, because here you are at my Black female house, taking up my Black female time, and hoping for some more of this Black female pussy!"

He put the beer bottle on the table. "Look, Ailey. I'll see you next week for coffee. Okay? Try to calm your nerves between now and then. Maybe eat something for a change."

I took several deep breaths. Lowered my voice, channeling the serenity of my dead father.

"Scooter, listen very carefully—"

"Ailey, I don't want to keep fighting—"

"—wait a minute. Let me finish. I was very lonely when I came to

North Carolina, and I will always thank you for being there for me. But whatever this is?" I drew a large circle with my index fingers. "This is over. I did not leave kith and kin to come to Acorn, North Carolina, to do whatever this is with you. I came here to be the first African American at this university to get a doctorate in history, and nobody is getting in the way of that. Now, you need to go, because I've got two essays due in seven days. And I'm not messing up my perfect grade point average."

When I walked to the door and opened it, he began pleading. What happened the last time we saw each other was a misunderstanding. Couldn't we both forgive and forget? Please? I could tell he was hurt: there was water standing in his eyes, and I closed the door. I didn't want a big scene playing out while cars passed on the street, or, God forbid, while Mike and Eddie watched from across the street. For a few moments, I let him beg. Let him ask, let's sit down and talk this out. He had all night. He didn't have to rush home because Rebecca had flown to Atlanta for the weekend, to see her parents, who still hated Scooter. They kept trying to make her divorce him.

When he tried to kiss me, I turned away. A feeling came over me. Not desire anymore, but comprehension. He had counted on my rancor, that I wouldn't feel guilty about sleeping with him, because of the beautiful racist he was married to. And I hadn't felt guilty, either: I'd put the blame squarely on her. It had been so easy to make her the monster of my nighttime tale, and yes, Rebecca was a complete bitch. But I wasn't in high school or college anymore: I couldn't blame my bad behavior on somebody else. I was a grown woman. I opened the door and told Scooter to leave.

He called the next morning. I picked up the phone in the middle of the message he was leaving on my answering machine. His husky whispering: God, he missed me so much. Please let him come over. Whatever I wanted to make things right, he'd do it.

"Hey, Scooter."

"Ailey, hey! I'm so glad—"

"Don't call me anymore, youngblood. Okay? Don't call me again. And God bless you."

I couldn't afford cable, but I wasn't going to offer to give back the big-screen television he'd bought me, either. It was too late for Scooter to get a store refund, and I was too spoiled to watch thirteen-inch people.

———

I returned to Shug's, too. I wasn't going to lose my Black oasis, and when I came through the door, Miss Velma rushed from behind the counter, arms outreached. After we hugged, I confided that she hadn't seen me these past weeks because I'd been avoiding Scooter. I talked around what had been going on, but I knew she was wise.

"He's a married man, Miss Velma."

"I know, baby. I know."

"And so I decided it wasn't right for me to spend time with him. I hope you don't think less of me."

"Aw, baby! I ain't here to judge you."

"I appreciate you saying that, Miss Velma. I really do."

She told me that, while I'd been gone, Scooter had come looking for me. He'd tried to pay for my future coffee refills, in case I returned, but Miss Velma wouldn't take his money. Instead, she offered him some free counsel, based on thirty-nine years of marriage: he should go home to his wife and try to work things on out.

And he needed to leave me alone, too. Miss Velma told him, I was a pretty girl, but it wasn't fair for Scooter to keep wasting my time. So he should let me walk on. That's what he needed to do, because it looked like I didn't want to drink his free coffee no more.

◆

SONG

◆

⊙　⊙　⊙

The Terrible Decision

Yes.

We know you are impatient to hear what happened the night that Nick ran away. We know, and we have waited to tell you.

We have waited, sipping our own grief, before recounting the rest.

That Aggie didn't want another child hurt by anyone, and especially by Samuel Pinchard. And her hopelessness tightened, until a message from above arrived. She heard the voice of Nick's birth mother, as clear as if Mamie was standing next to her. This was no time to turn back.

And Aggie prayed, after Nick left the cabin. He went to seek his freedom, after he had cried over who he was leaving behind. And Aggie had turned to Eliza Two, a mere child, and told her what would be required. And Eliza Two squared her thin shoulders, as her grandmother wiped oil of cloves on Eliza Two's cheeks. Aggie's own cheeks were wet as she took a clean, sharpened knife and cut three lines on each side of her granddaughter's face. Marks made near the bones. Signage of unknown tribes across the water, a place of which Aggie only had dreamed. After the marks were made, Aggie used the same knife to cut her granddaughter's hair to the scalp. Then she sent Eliza Two back to the big house, under cover of darkness.

This is the tragedy of slavery. These are the grains of power. There isn't a true innocence for children whose parents are shackled.

It was very late that night, when Samuel crept up to the attic. He carried the poppy syrup with him, to drug Eliza Two again. If Samuel had left his lantern on the first floor, his misshapen happiness could have lasted a few more hours, but he was afraid of falling down the staircase. When he cast his light on the scrawls of blood on Eliza Two's face, her shorn hair, he began to scream. Not her name, but that of Nick, his beloved child. He made his way down the steps of the attic, and out the front door of the big house. He ran to Aggie's cabin, banging on the door. When she answered, he shouted, where was Nick? as she pretended to wipe sleep from her eyes. She told her master that Nick had not come back that night.

And Samuel held his head and cried. His plans for Eliza Two had been dashed: he could not abide ugliness or imperfection in any being.

And Samuel's affection had been cast aside: Nick, the only human being he'd ever loved had run away, and before that, he had arranged Samuel's defeat. This is what Samuel would believe for a very long time: he would be unaware of who actually had crossed him. Samuel didn't know that Aggie had been his opponent. Her woman's spirit had reawakened, even in the bleakness.

The Aftermath of Scars

In North Carolina, a territory far from our land, there lived a woman named Harriet Jacobs. She was the daughter of two mulattoes whose parents had been mulattoes in turn. Such proximity to the blood of her masters had been considered a gift and would be touted as such in the next century, by male thinkers and writers who did not understand the plight of women. Who considered themselves experts on the rivalry between "the house" and "the field." The ability to place brown paper next to a hand or face and remark on the skin's light victory. The pulling of a fine-tooth comb through hair with ease, instead of an encountering of resistance.

Yet when Harriet Jacobs would write about her life as a slave, how, like Frederick Douglass, she would eventually escape bondage, how before her freedom, she had hidden for seven years in the small space of an attic—space that was only rivaled in its misery by the hull of a slave ship—Harriet would describe the labor of those Negroes who lived next to the mouths of plantation big houses. The girls and women who would be forced to bear their master's light-skinned children. And those children could not claim their masters as fathers, and sometimes were sold. And should we speak of what is tapping at the back of logic's skull? That enslaved boys and men were not safe from their masters' reach, either?

Thus, Harriet would alert her readers that there was no difference between "house" and "field." Though daytime labor might have been easier in the master's kitchen or in his laundry, when night fell and the Quarters-folks laid their exhausted bodies on floor pallets, those slaves who tended to the masters slept with fear. And those women and girls—and sometimes boys and men—had aching bodies as well, not from cultivating rice or tobacco or cotton, but from withstanding the weight of their masters—and sometimes mistresses—on their bellies or chests or backs. And these slaves turned their heads toward walls to keep from breathing the conqueror's air.

When Eliza Two was shorn and scarred, she was eleven years old. Her father had begged her to run away, but she did not want to leave her mother, and the only home she'd known. Yet she had acquired an adult's knowledge.

As a very small child, Eliza Two had been proud of her bright color and her long, glossy hair, which had been remarked upon by the Quarters-children she had played with, before she shed her front teeth. And if she didn't guess that her lighter skin separated her from her playmates, the larger, two-room cabin where her twin, her parents, Aggie, and Pop George lived announced superiority, for Eliza Two's playmates were jammed along with thirteen or fourteen other Quarters-folks into a one-room structure. When her front teeth fell out, Eliza Two was not sent to the field wearing a ragged tunic. She was dressed in a linsey-woolsey frock sewn by Tess. Shoes were put on her feet, cast-offs from her master's daughter. There was food of varied kinds in the big house kitchen. And Eliza Two had begun to take on airs of superiority, though she had been lectured against this by her grandmother. Eliza Two even had felt superior to her twin sister, because Rabbit was dark-skinned with coiled, wooly hair.

The realization of her past foolishness would take some time for Eliza Two to grasp. Yet before that era of wisdom, there would exist in her a sadness and anger toward her master and her grandmother. Eliza Two would feel ugly and ashamed, and she would retreat into quietness, where before, she had been a sparkling, charming child.

The one blessing in this hooded time was that Samuel Pinchard pretended that Eliza Two did not exist. He removed her from the big house, but did not throw her into the fields, for he still believed that Nick would return, and Samuel did not want Nick to leave again in anger over Eliza Two's mistreatment. She became the only Negro on the premises without a purpose: silently, she sat in the yard in front of her cabin, listening to Pop George tell stories to the littlest ones. She ignored the apologetic glances of her grandmother, who asked Eliza Two's forgiveness every day. Yet the girl did not yet have sympathy for Aggie. The memory of the knife was too fresh, especially when the scabs fell from her cheeks and were replaced by wormed scars.

The Monster's Continued Appetites

You should not expect a monster to change, even at the end of a fairy tale. For in a children's story, the monster must be killed. If he remains alive, his nature will be limned. There is no gentling of an abomination.

In the months following Nick's absconding, Samuel made a flyer on a small press he had acquired for his general store. The press had been idle, as there were no new goods that needed advertising. Seed was seed. Cloth was cloth, but Samuel had been proud of his runaway flyer, offering a reward for Nick, until he had overheard some of the yeomen laughing at the sketch of Nick, the white skin, the blond hair, and the light-colored eyes. The yeomen had chuckled that Master might as well have put up a runaway flyer asking people to return his own self, as much as the sketch resembled him. After he heard the phrase "nigger by-blow" tossed about, Samuel took down the runaway flyer that he'd placed up in the general store and sent through the region.

He began to mope about, and when the New Year arrived, he

wrote to the son of Lancaster Polcott, Hezekiah, requesting information about purchasing a new Young Friend. By then, Lancaster
had passed away. Of the men that Samuel had known in the county
during the time of the land lottery, he was the only one still alive.
He was in his sixties but felt vigorous and energetic. He did not
think of death. Indeed, Samuel believed himself to be akin to one of
those men in the Bible. He would live hundreds of years, for wasn't
he blessed by God? A modestly rich man, Samuel did not have to
worry about the upkeep of his slaves, who were self-sustaining and
increased his wealth. Nor did he fret about the size of his family, now
that Victor had taken a wife. Samuel expected legitimate grandchildren, sooner or later. Even with Victor's hesitance with Grace, it
would only take one or two instances of congress: one thing the
Franklins actually did right was fill a house with offspring.

The child Samuel purchased in the New Year was named Leena.
Her skin was the color of a French crust made with butter. Shiny
black ringlets the width of a garter snake fell down her back, and
she had large, dark eyes. Generations of breeding had made her a
testament to rape, compulsion, and smudged currency. The child's
mother, a quadroon, had succeeded in compelling miscarriage four
times, but before the fifth, her owner had said that any living new
issue would be freed. The owner's true intentions toward the quadroon were unclear, for he died. To satisfy the codicil of his will, the
quadroon was mortgaged for a loan, and by the time the owner's
wife, a lady who was irritated with Negresses' siren magic on decent white men, began preparation to sell the quadroon, the wife's
son had taken a shine to his father's leftovers. Thus, the quadroon
decided it was time to slit her wrists.

When Leena's front teeth fell out, she was sold to a man living on
a country plantation deep in the Louisiana bayou. This man used
children, and he gave her to a slave woman, a caretaker who tutored
her in finding that internal place that countless other enslaved folks
had cultivated, a pleasant numb location in the mind. That owner
died, too, and his wife sold Leena once more, though that particular
wife had no rancor against Negresses. She just wanted the money.

Leena was sold one more time after this as well, before Hezekiah Polcott sold her to Samuel. And at each auction, no one questioned why a child would be sold at all, let alone for such despicable use, instead of nurtured and loved.

Like her predecessors, when Leena became a Young Friend, she was denied contact with other slaves, except those responsible for her comfort and imprisonment. Near dusk, Venie would come to the left cabin to feed, bathe, and dress Leena a second time in fresh clothes down to the skin. After evening fell, Pompey came to trim the flowers and pluck the weeds inside the fence. He carried a lantern to light his way. Another gardener would have come during the daylight hours, but Pompey did not like to see the Young Friends. Their presence made him feel guilty and he did his best to never interact with them. Yet in the year that Leena was purchased, Aggie had spoken to Pompey and told him to engage Leena in conversation. And Pompey, a man whom Aggie had tended when he was a child with a mouth full of milk teeth, began conversing with Leena through the gate.

The Love of Rabbit

Nick's other child had been grieving his absence, too, in the five years that passed since he had escaped. Rabbit was the more sensitive twin, born smaller, with a tender shell and a feeling heart. Her limbs shook with revulsion of the outside world. Her bald head had shined with just a few strands of reddish-brown hair, and her skin had darkened to match her mother's.

In her first years of life, no one would have called Rabbit an attractive child, taken beside Eliza Two.

At the age of sixteen, however, her woman's blood arrived—on the same day as her twin's—and Rabbit's beauty emerged. She remained tiny, but the curves of her body began to form. Her dark-dark skin stretched over sculpted cheekbones, with a reddish cast beneath. Her full lips turned upward, even when she wasn't amused. Her hair, so sparse when she was a little girl, had deepened in color, and grew into a tall, thick mass of kinks. Young Quarters-men smiled to see her on Sunday, walking to visit her family's cabin. *There go that purty Rabbit girl*, they'd say.

Yet Rabbit hadn't cared for her looks as a child, and she did not care for her looks at sixteen. There were no mirrors around her, and the adults she'd lived with hadn't made a fuss over such things. Rabbit only cared for her family and their suffering touched her.

Her mother had gone deep within herself. Always a strange woman, Tess now mumbled about messages imparted to her by her favorite pecan tree. She claimed to have a dream vision where Nick had landed safely in a place with many buildings, with white folks and Negroes walking on hard-packed streets. There were carriages crowded onto a road and such noise as no one on a plantation ever had heard. Tess claimed in another dream she saw Nick reading a book with two white children painted on the cover. When Tess woke up from that particular dream, she waited until the plantation had awoken, then sent her mother to the kitchen house to tell Rabbit what she'd seen. She hadn't wanted to wait for her child's Sunday visit. And solemnly, Aggie had communicated Tess's wish, her frown deep, and Rabbit knew the older woman was withholding her own sorrow.

Rabbit did not worry about Aggie or Pop George, however, for with her sensitivity, she knew that her father's departure had not broken these two. Still, she felt their pain. She saw how they ministered to the Quarters-folks and their children on the plantation. How they felt it was their responsibility to keep everyone safe, and that "everyone" now included the Young Friend in the left cabin. How, when Jeremiah Franklin had taken over for his father as overseer, he had freely used the whip, in addition to abusing the field workers with mean, careless words. And on her Sunday visits, Rabbit heard her grandmother and Pop George whisper their concerns for victims who had been striped in the fields.

Yet Eliza Two was another matter. To Rabbit, her twin was still the most beautiful girl she'd ever seen. Eliza Two's hair had grown and fell down her back again. Her eyes were large and expressive.

Even her scars made her striking, but when she told her twin this, Eliza Two looked at Rabbit, wounded. She believed her twin was ridiculing her. Thus, Rabbit, the kindest girl with the most sensitive spirit of anyone who lived on Wood Place, could do nothing for the person she loved more than anyone else.

And so the only thing that she craved was the comfort of Nick. That was the year that Rabbit decided that she would run away from Wood Place and find her father. He would make Eliza Two all better. Rabbit didn't know what freedom was, but she knew love. It was a gift that she craved to bestow on others. This ability to love was her resistance to the cruelty of the plantation.

The Cook's Helper and the Young Friend

When Samuel purchased Leena as his Young Friend, he was un-aware that Venie began giving him food and drink designed to cut his vigor using substances that had been provided by Aggie.

In the morning and midday, Venie prepared Samuel large, steam-ing cups of sugared spearmint water. These tisanes were lovely for older women going through their change, but they would reduce desire in men. The homemade licorice root candy that Venie made and that Samuel absolutely loved did the same. Then, too, there was the richness of the food that she prepared. The breakfasts of new bread slathered in butter, along with thick slices of ham, grits sit-ting in cream, the eggs, and peach preserves. The midday meals of meat and root vegetables. For supper, more meat with greens and corn bread topped with bacon grease. And desserts of cakes and pies. When summer came, Venie would bake a cobbler of sugared peaches and spices and topped with a latticed French crust. Samuel began to put on weight, which diminished his vigor even further, so that when he went to visit the left cabin, he had no interest in abus-ing Leena. He only would sit and hold her hand for a few minutes, then return to his big house.

When Samuel purchased Leena, he'd assumed she was a child, when in fact, she was already reaching puberty. So shortly she journeyed into womanhood: oddly enough, her blood had shown in the same year as Nick's twins'. When she revealed this to Venie, the cook told her to keep that information to herself. She gave Leena rags. When Venie reported the event of the Young Friend's blood, Aggie gave instructions, and Venie began saving and adding this blood to the portions of food served to Samuel. This weakened him further. And though time passed, he did not contact the slave trader to buy back the girl at a discount, as he had with Young Friends in the past. His lack of desire made him undriven to do so. Thus, Leena stayed among the children's furniture and toys in the left cabin. Though she matured, she wore the clothes of a little girl.

The day that the link between Rabbit and Leena was forged occurred a week before Christmas. Samuel walked back to the kitchen house to discuss the special menu for the left cabin and found Venie ill. He called to Rabbit, ordering her to cook the meals for the left cabin. And he sent Venie to the place where she slept, the tiny cabin out back of the kitchen house.

When Pompey let her through the left cabin's gate, Rabbit found Leena outside, sitting on the grass, where the sun warmed the chilled air. She had dressed herself in her winter frock and pantaloons, cap and bonnet, as if she were still a child. Over these was a fur-lined blanket that Samuel had ordered from the north and for which he had paid far too much money. Rabbit carried a silver tray supporting small crockery wrapped with gingham. The other girl sat on several layers of quilts. Her hands and head were visible, and, covered as she was by the dark fur blanket, only her pale face kept her from looking like Tar Baby, as in the funny story Pop George told.

Rabbit spoke a greeting, but receiving no answer, she placed the tray on the quilts and turned.

"My doll's name be Agnes," the girl called.

"Is that right?"

There was no doll in sight, not on the quilt or on the ground.

"I got three more inside my cabin. One be name Beth. One be name Amy. The last one be name Sally. But this one be name Agnes."

A rustling. She pulled a doll through the narrow enclosure of the fur blanket.

The doll had an ivory bisque face, with golden curls and blue-painted eyes. She was clothed in a maroon dress with blue ribbon fringe, a waistcoat of the same material, and under layers of petticoats trimmed with ribbons, white pantaloons. The tiny shoes were made of silk the same color as the dress. Because the Young Friend was hidden, Rabbit could not know that underneath the fur blanket, her outfit was identical to the doll's.

"And what might be your name?" Rabbit asked.

"My name be Leena. That's what my mama name me, but she dead."

She offered the doll, but Rabbit told her she could not take it.

The girl pulled the doll back under her dark cover. "But I ain't got nothing else to give you."

"Why you got to give me something?"

"'Cause I want me a friend. And I ain't got nobody else but Pompey and that white man. And I doesn't like that white man. You ain't g'wan tell on me, is you?"

Rabbit lowered herself to the quilts. There was one napkin, and that contained a spoon but no fork or knife. She offered that to Leena, who emerged from her blanket to take the napkin. Rabbit untied the gingham from around each of the little pots. Inside one were chicken and dumplings, another held sweet potatoes cooked down with butter, and the last contained greens and ham hocks cut up in tiny pieces as if to feed a toddler. There was no dessert or bread, nor would there be. Samuel did not like his Young Friends plump.

The girl took a bite. She gave the spoon to Rabbit and pointed at a pot. It was an offering, and because of the girl's clear loneliness, Rabbit did not tell her she needed no bribing. If she'd wanted to taste a dish, she could have used her own cook's spoon.

At the end of the meal, the girl asked once more: "You ain't g'wan tell on me, is you?"

"Ain't nothing to tell."

Rabbit gave the spoon back.

The Death of Carson Franklin

A year after Nick had run away, Carson Franklin died, bringing more change to Wood Place. It was astounding that Carson lasted as slave overseer for so long. He had been working for Samuel for decades.

Carson was buried in the Wood Place cemetery, in the area designated for whites. Although Samuel did not think Carson was worthy of this place—after all, he was a tenant farmer and owned no slaves—it would not have been proper to bury him in the area for Negroes. Carson's son Jeremiah took over his father's position and had assumed he would continue permanently as overseer. To his surprise and hurt, Samuel would hire another man, an itinerant traveler who would inquire about the job.

And Jeremiah's pain would feed the resentment, which had traveled through his blood. The Franklins despised Samuel: he had taken advantage of Aidan in a difficult time, dangling pennies for Aidan's land, instead of helping him like a friend should. Yet there was a grudging admiration of Samuel, too, for here was a man who had come up from two hundred and two and a half acres to own a thousand acres. And if a man such as Samuel could evolve from a common, working man into a wealthy landowner, there was hope for anyone, provided he was white, for Negroes didn't count, and Indians were dead men walking.

It was this hope for his own land that fueled Jeremiah, along with his hatred of the mound that shadowed the cabins where his extended family lived. He nursed an obsession to erode the mound one day. This hatred was like milk, bread, and meat to him.

The New Overseer

The man who would be hired as the new overseer of Wood Place was not what he appeared, but few on the plantation would know this, as he was a quiet man who kept his thoughts to himself. His name was Holcomb Byrd James and he would sire a family with many descendants on our land. But we are not in that time, not yet. We are only at the day of his romantic undoing.

Holcomb hadn't been seeking a job, only passing through Chicasetta, when he saw a flyer advertising for an overseer at Wood Place at the general store. He inquired of the young man standing behind the counter, Victor, who pointed to his father's office in the back of the store. Samuel hired Holcomb right on the spot, offering him the top pay of fifteen dollars a month, three dollars more than the going rate: Samuel liked the man's sturdy, upright carriage, as well as his dark-haired handsomeness. And he liked the fact of hiring someone else other than a Franklin. We already know that hurting people gave Samuel much satisfaction, feeding his mean spirit for weeks to come. However, Samuel also wanted to alert the Franklins that the privilege of Grace's new, elevated position as the wife of Victor did not extend special favors to her natal brood.

Samuel told Holcomb to head up to the big house he had passed on his journey to the general store. In the kitchen house, the cook would give him a proper meal.

While speaking to Samuel, Holcomb didn't let the white man know that he didn't like to stay in any one place too long. He did odd work here and there for his survival. He definitely wasn't going to inform Samuel that he was a Cherokee man. His mother had not given him a middle name, but Holcomb honored her by taking the name of her clan—she was of the Birds—though he changed the spelling to keep from attention. Yet when he entered the kitchen, there was Venie. She appeared to be crying, and something in her face paired with the tears that streamed, touched him, even when he noticed that she held an onion in her hand. And then the first crack in his façade: he doffed his hat, pressing it to his chest.

Venie leaned back. She'd seen other white men perform the same ritual, but never with a Negro woman, slave or free.

"Did you eat yet, suh?"

She wiped her face with her forearm, as Holcomb worriedly

watched. The forearm was attached to a hand that held a knife, which was hovering close by her eyes. He touched her hand softly, then took the knife away.

"No'm," he said. "I have not ate. Much obliged for the meal."

Venie had been a child, perhaps twelve or thirteen, when purchased by Samuel—not a "young woman," the way some would describe slave girls in a future time, calling them hastily into a realm of knowing.

Her previous owner had given Venie, a child mulatta and the byblow of his older brother, as a present one night to a close comrade. It had been the comrade's birthday, coming two weeks before his wedding. The comrade was not repelled by her thin child's body: Venie's owner had assured him of her precocity. By grace, Venie's ordeal had lasted but a short while. The comrade had passed out after minutes into the painful act, but not before vomiting on the nightgown and several locks of Venie's hair, which the maid of her owner's wife had loosed from her braids. She did not know what was worse, the sharp pains when she walked or her forgetting to wash the blood and vomit from her nightgown. She was punished by her owner for her inability to please his comrade and for ruining the nightgown.

When Samuel had purchased Venie, he'd been bothered by her crying, when it would have pleased him with another child. After a month, he'd thrown her into the fields, but when Tut had died, Samuel remembered that Venie's skills as an apprentice cook had come recommended by the trader. Thus, Samuel relocated Venie to the kitchen, bringing in a boy to carry the water and bigger pots. Upon tasting her peach cobbler made with a butter crust, Samuel congratulated himself for his unexpected boon.

Venie was a grown woman when Holcomb Byrd James was hired, and in her twenty-some years, she'd never known a man in the voluntary sense, or loved one, and she had no desire to do so. Yet here she was, concerned for Holcomb: He needed training to break him of chivalry toward Negro women. If Samuel heard him "ma'am-ing" her, the man would be sent on his way. And she had taken a liking to the new overseer, seeing his fear for her eyes.

She served him leftovers from Samuel's lunch, but she made him fresh biscuits with butter pats inside. On the pine table, the other meal she'd made for Rabbit, Pompey, and herself. Rabbit was in the corner of the kitchen house, busy plucking a scalded chicken for supper. Neither of these three ate rich food during the day, as that courted drowsiness: there was only a pan of corn bread, a bowl of greens revealing hints of pork, and slices of red tomato on a tin plate. The greens and tomatoes had been picked by Pompey from the garden only hours before.

In weeks, when Holcomb would ask permission for and receive a kiss from Venie, he would bemoan his missed corn bread that day. And Venie would tell him that he should have asked. There had been plenty, and she would make it for him every evening, and in the mornings, hominy porridge, if he were so inclined.

That first day Holcomb had looked to Venie like a white man who'd want high-toned food. Yet the day of their kiss, Holcomb would tell Venie that his parents were pale mestizos who'd insisted on holding on to their old ways. As proof of his love, he'd shown Venie the medicine pouch he wore around his neck covered by a shirt. It was the most precious thing he owned.

The Taking of a Side

Though Jeremiah Franklin remained obsequiously respectful to his landlord, he continued to be angry that his position as overseer had been usurped, even after a year, and then two, passed. And he noticed that Samuel Pinchard did not seem vigorous anymore, but instead was settling into his dotage, putting on weight, and losing his mental sharpness. Yet this diminishing of the man did not give the Franklins an advantage, for Samuel's son began to take on the master's mantle.

When the new overseer had arrived, he had taken up residence with Pompey in the barn. Holcomb washed at the pump, along with the Negro, and ate his meals in the kitchen house. The overseer did not voice any complaint about this situation. However, within a year—and without asking his father—Victor had ordered the Franklin clan out of their cabins. Then Victor had ordered Quarters-men to burn all but one of the cabins—and he moved the overseer into the remaining structure. Thus, the entire Franklin clan—men, wives, and their many children—relocated to the south side of the plantation, with only a stingy twenty-acre plot to farm. They had to build new cabins from the ground up. There, they were far away from the big house, which relieved Victor's wife, for Grace was tired of the many machinations required to avoid her poorer relatives; their presence now greatly embarrassed her, and she had voiced these feelings to Victor. He did not love Grace and never would, but he tried his best to make her happy within reason, since he rarely visited her bed.

But Jeremiah and his brothers were not about to let things go that easily. At night, they began to watch the Quarters, waiting for one of the folks to visit the community outhouse. They would catch someone coming out after relief, grab them, and beat them. Because the Franklin brothers wore cloth masks with holes for the eyes and mouth and did not speak, none of the folks who were assaulted could identify their attackers, but in the Quarters, it was assumed who the nighttime predators were.

If Jeremiah and his brothers had kept to the night, their actions might have been tolerated. When Quarters-men limped to the fields in the morning with bruises on their faces, and when Quarters-women wore the tragic expressions of those who had been ravished—and later when their wombs swelled with Franklin seed—the folks would keep their own sad counsels. This was the lot of Negroes, and they didn't expect any better, though their resentment fumed in the sun. Jeremiah and his brothers' mistake was bringing their violence out into the open. It was on a morning when the weeds were to be chopped in the fields. Instead of tending to their own patch of cotton and vegetables, the Franklin brothers walked the long distance from the south side of the plantation up to the master's fields. The Franklins were a group of six, but because they were white men confronting Negroes, they believed their strength to be magnified. Each Franklin moved into the huge cotton field, grabbed someone at random—a man, a woman, a child—and began to choke and slap.

Holcomb was on his horse that day, riding slowly around the fields, and he clearly saw the Franklins' melee. He shouted, but the Franklins didn't stop. When he turned the horse around and headed back to the north side of the plantation, the Quarters-folks despaired: they were on their own. White men always took each other's side. Yet in a few minutes, there was the sound of a gun blasting as Holcomb rode the edge of the field close to a Franklin brother. Holcomb was an excellent shot: when he pointed the gun again, the ground beside the Franklin brother's foot exploded. He did this another time, and like skulking animals, Jeremiah and his brothers ran away back south.

Not only was Holcomb expert with his gun, he didn't let time pass: that very evening, after eating the dinner Venie had prepared (with an extra pan of corn bread for him), Holcomb waited for his landlord. When Victor came back to the kitchen, instead of his father, Holcomb looked at Venie, who nodded. Then he explained the situation, what the Franklins had done that day, and what he suspected had been happening at night for weeks as well. Holcomb insisted this wasn't his taking the Negroes' side. This was about growing cotton. And the Franklins were getting in the way of that. As overseer, Holcomb couldn't have a ruckus in the fields slowing down work. Victor nodded and left the kitchen house, and within moments, Holcomb apologized to Venie. He hadn't meant to hurt her feelings, with what he'd said about Negroes. And Venie told him he needed to hush. She knew where Holcomb stood already— didn't she bake him corn bread every day? Venie kissed the top of his head.

The next day, the Franklin brothers were absent in the master's fields, and when night came, the dark path to the outhouse in the Quarters had become safe.

A Kind of Peace

In his first year at Wood Place, Holcomb bonded with Aggie. His beloved Venie already adored her, and Holcomb had come to feel the same. Though the Creek and the Cherokee had been enemies at times, the new overseer was grateful that some of the people of our land had remained there. On Sundays, after the light died down, he and Venie would slip through the back door of Aggie's cabin. There, they would speak quietly, and the woman would have a bit of joy at speaking with one of the people.

This man came at a necessary time, for even Pop George had not been able to console his family of women over the hurting of Eliza Two and the loss of Nick. Aggie had turned grim, her lips pressed into a forbidding road. In the cotton fields, Tess stood on her row with no interest. Often, Holcomb found her sitting on the earth, gone somewhere in her mind. He left her there with no bother. At night, Tess would walk to the pecan tree that stood a few feet from Samuel's general store. She would sit under the tree and talk for long hours, crying and wrapping her arms around the thick trunk.

And though Rabbit had found the company of Leena, her twin continued to ache. Eliza Two still grieved for her face, her lost beauty, and her lost innocence. This girl might have disappeared into blood, a new trail made by the edge of a second knife cutting open a vein. So many slaves like her were lost in these ways. Eliza Two might have traveled into madness or sorrow, had it not been for Holcomb. Though he was nearly as quiet as Eliza Two, he was as watchful as Rabbit. And he saw Eliza Two's disharmony up close, on those Sundays when Venie and he joined the family at dinner.

One of those evenings, Eliza Two sat in the yard in front of her cabin alone. Her twin had taken a tray to the left cabin, for Leena didn't have anyone to spend this day with. There, Rabbit and she would sit on a quilt in the grass with a lantern, for Leena was afraid of the dark. Holcomb came outside and sat on the log with Eliza Two. He wasn't frightened of being seen, for the occupants of the big house were in their place, and the Quarters-folks liked him enough to put off curiosity. The girl was perched on one of the logs upon which the smallest children would sit during the days when Pop George and Aggie tended them.

Holcomb sat down, and he didn't speak for a while. Then he began to tell Eliza Two about his brothers and sisters. He had been the youngest child, and every Sunday the seven of them would enjoy a dinner with his parents and grandmother. He had a great-aunt who lived deep in the woods, so connected was she to the land. As the descendants of white men, this mixed-blood Cherokee family had enjoyed a measure of financial security. Their house had four bedrooms, and a kitchen structure out back, on twenty-five acres. They lived adjoining the farm of their full-white relatives, yet in spite of having white men's blood, Holcomb's family kept to many of the old ways of their people. Alongside their Christian beliefs that had come from the white men, they had their stories of how the earth had been formed, how corn had been gifted to the people. They wore clothes like their white relatives, but deerskin moccasins on their feet. And here, Holcomb Byrd pulled at the pouch from inside his shirt: all members of his Cherokee family had a pouch like this, filled with medicine, meant to keep the wearer safe.

Eliza Two was silent, but she was listening closely to this gentle-spoken man. Months before, her twin had reported about the day Holcomb arrived on the plantation. Rabbit had been in the kitchen watching, her sensitive nature attuned. She liked this man. Though she had thought he was white, she knew immediately he was not like the others. She had never seen Venie smile at a man before, not even Pompey.

Holcomb was confiding in Eliza Two dangerous knowledge, for even she was aware that Indians were despised in Georgia; only the Negro was lower than the people. Holcomb was trusting her to keep his secret. He thought her worthy of keeping it, despite the scars on her face. He didn't view her with pity, but as someone he could talk to. His kindness reminded her of her father's and Pop George's.

Then he told her of the saddest night of his life, when white men had given his family a choice: die or leave their land. The group of men had included Holcomb's white relatives. They had grim faces—like the Franklins—and when Holcomb's grandmother had called to their white kin with the authority of an elder, one of them had walked up to her and slapped her to the ground. His parents had asked to pack belongings into the wagon, but the white men would not give them that chance. They went into the house, tossing things outside. Holcomb had been hiding and watching this scene, but at this, he had run to his great-aunt in the woods. He only had been six, and he was afraid that he would get lost, but finally he saw her cabin. There he lived with her for ten years until she'd died. He believed she'd been covered by a blessing, and that this had extended to him as well, for white men had come through the woods many times, but never barged into his great-aunt's little cabin. When she passed away, he burned the cabin to the ground as she had asked him to do, and began a life of travel. And for years, he had roamed, unable to settle, until the day he'd ridden his horse to Wood Place. Until he'd met Venie in the kitchen house. Yet Holcomb never had forgotten the pain of seeing his family loaded onto a wagon by those white men and sent on their way out west. Every morning that he rose, he thought of his family. Every night before he went to bed, he did the same. He knew that he would not stop missing them, for kin was a line that never snapped.

From his pocket, Holcomb pulled a leather pouch like the one from around his neck. He told Eliza Two that he had made this pouch for her. It was filled with tiny things, and he had said a medicine prayer of healing over this pouch, in both the old words and those of Jesus, and it would give Holcomb much happiness if Eliza Two would wear it. When she placed the tied strings over her head and tucked the pouch inside her bodice, there was no miraculous feeling. She did not experience instant joy, but when she looked in the distance toward the direction of the left cabin—when she saw the light of Rabbit's lantern—she experienced a longing to be with her sister, one that she had not felt since the night their father had left. She rose, looking down at Holcomb, but he told her, go ahead.

And Eliza Two walked toward the left cabin until she was at the fence and called through the spires. At the sound of her twin's voice, known from within the womb, Rabbit gave a cry. She ran to the fence and unlocked the gate. They held each other for some time, and then Rabbit led her to where Leena sat on the quilt.

The Arrival of the Yankee

In the years before the Civil War, cotton was the dominant crop in the south, and some northerners had relocated to the region to partake in the wealth. Many did not flourish, and the customs were foreign, especially the holding of slaves, which had fallen from style in the north. The weather was oppressive in summers, a punishment to make up for the benevolence of the glorious springs and mild winters.

One such northerner was a young man named Matthew Thatcher, who, in 1856, had traveled to central Georgia to make his fortune. He was twenty-five years old. While in college, Matthew's mentor had encouraged him to travel there, where the problem of his mediocre lineage and lack of inheritance would not pose impediments. His mentor was a Harvard graduate but not put off by the younger man's awkward manner. The mentor staked Matthew one thousand dollars, a chestnut gelding, three tailored suits, and gave him the deed to one hundred eighty acres. Matthew would be required to pay his mentor back within twenty years—so it was really a gift, because the mentor was in his sixties, and most men did not live long in those days.

"I know you'll find your way," the mentor said. "And don't carry all your money on your person."

They were sitting in his library, each on a sofa facing the other. Matthew puffed on a cigar, as if he was used to smoking.

"Yes, sir," he said.

Unknown to the mentor, Matthew had his own money saved; he was good at cards, and several of his wealthy classmates were not. It would be enough to hire three white hands until he could buy his own slaves. The property his mentor had purchased was located on a parcel that abutted Putnam County. The place had formally been owned by the Polcott family, a line of slave traders who'd held auctions out in the country. Yet that family sought to come up in the world, and when they wanted to move their business out from the country, they wanted quick cash. This is how Matthew's mentor had acquired their land in Baldwin County, paying the Polcott family enough to expand their slave-trading business to the capital city of Milledgeville, as well as to Macon and Augusta.

When he longed for company, Matthew Thatcher read the books that he had carried on his journey in a small, wheeled vehicle tied with two ropes to his horse, and he went about his business, trying to push away his loneliness, until Samuel showed up one day at the hideous, flat front of Matthew's abode, riding in the back of an open-faced carriage.

Before he formally met this Yankee, six months after his arrival, Samuel had seen him at the general store that he owned. Samuel was lonely, too. He reasoned that, at his age—for he was now elderly—a man needed more than female flesh to satisfy him. He needed other men to complete him. Yet the yeomen were not of his rank, and he had failed in his attempts at friendship with the two other wealthy planters in the county. Samuel could understand the social issues of Mr. Benjamin, who was a child of Israel. Perhaps that man's religion prohibited him from making relationships with those outside his worship circle. But Mr. Sweet was a different matter. He was Christian and from older money than the others in the region; his family was from Savannah and reasonably placed. When he visited Samuel's store, Mr. Sweet was polite. He shook hands upon entering and upon concluding his business, but he never took off his gloves to do so—cotton in the warmer months, leather in the colder. Once, when he was not aware of being watched, Mr. Sweet had rubbed his gloved hand down the side of his pants after shaking Samuel's hand.

Under other circumstances, Samuel would not have sought camaraderie with the likes of Matthew. The young man's house was built in that tragically ugly New England style known as the "saltbox." The absent front porch discouraged visitors, even those eager to marry off unattractive daughters. Where were people supposed to sit when they came? How could they take the air? Where was the veranda, for Heaven's sake?

In Matthew's family's saltbox in rural Massachusetts, Matthew's parents, siblings, and he had taken the air on the back porch on those summer afternoons when they were not completing chores. And no one took the air in the wintertime in Massachusetts, or not anyone with sense. As a New Englander, Matthew didn't understand that well-bred southerners craved stories. That's why they liked front porches. The back of the house was for concealing things southerners did not desire to look at or smell—the realities of a backyard chicken house and hog pen, a vegetable garden, and a green-painted fence that shielded the owner's privy from the public, but whose color announced something important lay beyond its boundaries.

The day of his visit, Samuel hopped down without any help from Pompey, and approached the front door that was just stuck out there with no artifice to help it along. It was not the first time Samuel had won over a reasonably well-off man. And even at Samuel's advanced age, his beauty and charm were worthy matches to the sternest of opponents, but there was no resistance to speak of. The young, white man who answered the door—not even sending his Negro housekeeper to do it—stumbled an eager greeting.

Samuel graciously accepted the invitation to enter the house, empty of but a few pieces of furniture, walked through to the back porch with no complaint, and sat down in a hard chair that wasn't even a rocker. As someone who had not attended any university except that called by life's clarion, Samuel perked up the day the young man mentioned that he was a graduate of Harvard College. And when Samuel left his plantation with Pompey driving the carriage, he somehow felt stronger and clearheaded, and he began to crave the company of the younger man from the north. Samuel liked sitting on the back porch of the ugly saltbox house.

And he had other purposes for Matthew, for though time had

passed since Nick's running, Samuel had not given up on finding him, and hoped that, with the aid of the Fugitive Slave Law passed years before, he could still recover Nick. He had taken down the runaway flyer, but that did not mean Samuel had given up the ghost. He gave several flyers to Matthew to mail to his acquaintances up north and the younger man made the mistake of sending them to his sister.

It was a distressing time for slave owners, for, above and below the line drawn by Messrs. Mason and Dixon, tendrils of abolition had thriven. Matthew's sister Deborah was a reader; she'd gotten ahold of a privately circulated diary written by Fanny Kemble, the former wife of a man in Georgia who owned over a thousand slaves. Mrs. Kemble's diary detailed gross violence toward Negroes, and Deborah had mentioned it in her letters. It did no good for her brother to explain that growing inland, short-staple cotton was far different—requiring slave labor but far less cruelty—from growing long-staple, because based upon a few words his sister had read in an almanac, she thought herself an agricultural expert. Matthew had not told his family that he owned Negroes, but he assumed they had guessed, as Deborah prodded him in letters, asking him to explain how one man could cultivate nearly two hundred acres of cotton "all by his lonesome," an unfeasible task, even with his Congregationalist guilt about sleeping late. His sister had digested chunks of the Bible, even more now that, at an age when her parents had despaired, miraculously, she had married Winfred Hutchinson, one of Matthew's classmates at Harvard who'd since become a minister.

According to the gossips at the college, Winfred had not been ashamed to visit a brothel (or three), but Matthew was too shy to parry his sister's veiled attacks with a query about her husband's proximity to syphilis, or to note that his parents had not refused his bank drafts, sent from his own bank to the one in Boston. But he did his second best to otherwise incense his sister: he sent her a handful of Samuel's runaway flyers. She was furious and threatened him with the wrath of his parents: "How Mother and Father would grieve to know your <u>fall</u> in the world but I shall <u>keep</u> it from them! I am <u>aghast</u> that you are unaware <u>your soul is in sore peril!</u>"

Matthew's feelings were wounded, but he knew he wasn't a bad man. Abolitionists knew nothing about building a house in southern climes, about growing crops in uncultivated ground. He did not waste his strength or dignity arguing outright with his sister; he was settling into his new home.

The Joy of the Season

Since the infancy of their friendship, Matthew had told Samuel that the distance from his family increased his loneliness. He was startled by his feelings, for he had not been close to his brothers and his sisters previously, and his father had been a difficult man, overly fond of parts of the Bible that struck his mother as cruel-natured, as she went in for merciful devotions herself. The Psalms were the favorite of Matthew's mother. She was kind, but tired from the tedious work of women on a farm, as well as from a last baby—a girl—who had been born to her after she believed the burden of children had been lifted. (At this point in Matthew's monologue, Samuel had interjected that the book of Genesis dictated that women should bring forth children in pain. After a few beats of silence, Matthew replied that during his mother's last lying-in, his father had been fond of quoting from that same portion of Genesis.)

The winter holidays were an especially black-clouded time for Matthew. A week before Christmas, when his brown-skinned maid, Dori, had walked through the kitchen into the back room that Matthew called a parlor and announced Samuel, the younger man nearly wept with appreciation. Samuel carried a large straw basket of delicacies: airy, risen, light bread; two kinds of cake, pound and fruit; a smoked turkey; a small portion of sugar-cured ham; two crocks of cloth-sealed blackberry preserves; head- and milk cheese; and scuppernong brandy.

After a year of visits, Samuel asked Matthew if he would do him the honor of spending the twelve days of Christmas with him. He advised that Matthew should hire a patroller to oversee the property in his absence, to keep his Negroes in line. The younger man speedily answered that he would do so, but when he didn't expound on his plans, Samuel suggested Jeremiah Franklin, the sharecropper and part-time slave patroller. He had a heavy hand with Negroes, and was a rough-hewn sort, but he was reliable.

Though he knew it was a day early, Matthew arrived on Christmas Eve. Matthew appeared laden with his own gifts of food prepared by his housekeeper, who had not traveled to New England and had not seen the much more practical amounts of food put on tables. Matthew brought several hams that Simon, his head Negro in charge, had smoked, after respectfully chiding his owner over giving all that meat to a man that he'd heard tell had four times as many hogs as anyone in the region. Matthew was in a good mood and had not chastised Simon, only said that he wanted to be neighborly. It would not have been seemly to admit to a slave that he wanted to impress Samuel. It was because of this same good mood that when he hired Jeremiah as temporary overseer during his absence, Matthew admonished him that he did not want to come home to find his male slaves sporting bloody stripes, nor his females crying as a result of molestation; if that was the case, payment would be withheld from Jeremiah. And Matthew ignored the man's expression of contempt over concern for Negroes. Nothing was going to ruin Matthew's good mood.

Samuel installed Matthew in the guesthouse to the furthermost west side of the plantation. The guesthouse was charming, with a parlor, two bedrooms, a sturdy front porch with railings, and polished wood floors throughout. There was an inside privy closet containing a cabinet with a hole cut into the top; when opened, a flowered chamber pot sat inside on a shelf. In the back of the guesthouse was a white-painted outhouse for the use of any slaves. What everyone else on premises knew was that this structure was the former moon house, where Aggie and Lady had spent their bleeding times in years past, renovated and expanded since then.

Samuel had made sure the guesthouse was very far away from the big house—and the left cabin—as some of his prospective guests had wives. He did not want to offend delicate female sensibilities. Samuel had hoped that rich planters of good breeding, their families, and their slaves might visit, but that had not happened. Matthew was, in fact, his first guest.

When Matthew had arrived at Wood Place, he'd had no idea that he was the subject of much female speculation. For example, at Christmas Eve dinner, Grace looked at him and then at her husband, who smiled in fawning admiration of the green-eyed Yankee. After five years of marriage, and only four instances of conjugal congress—and after pulling a succession of nine attractive Negresses from the fields to serve as maids, and making sure to place each in Victor's path, and Victor paying absolutely no mind to any of them—Grace had concluded that her husband's interest might not lie with women. And now here he was, smiling and offering Matthew Thatcher glasses of port wine.

Then there was Lady, who, with a mother's intuition saw that her husband intended to somehow beguile Matthew into marrying the strange Gloria, who was thirty-one years old and never had a beau, despite her bountiful beauty. Lady's consolation was that Samuel had never abused his daughter. Despite her pure state, however, time had wasted for Gloria—in a decade, she might already be entering her woman's change. Matthew Thatcher seemed nice enough. And if he wasn't Lady would find a way to kill him. Though she and Aggie had not been friends—or even on speaking terms—for many years, Lady was certain she would find a way to seek Aggie's help in killing this Yankee man, if the need arose. If the crime were to be discovered, she would place the blame on Aggie.

At Christmas dinner, after Venie's turkey and one of Matthew's huge hams were served to exclamations, Gloria turned to him. She announced that though he was not as handsome as her father and brother, she wanted Matthew as her beau. And what did he think about that? With his characteristically dark blush, Matthew smiled and shyly dipped his head.

The Delivery of Meals

The women of the kitchen house and the yard were not only curious about the Yankee named Matthew Thatcher, they were also anxious, for white men could not be trusted. Yet they were trapped, for they had been ordered to serve him his morning and midday meals, way out at the guesthouse.

After assuring Aggie and Venie that she would be careful—and after receiving instructions from Pompey that he had placed extra firewood in the guesthouse, which could be used as weapons—Rabbit headed through the woods with her large basket of food that early Christmas morning. She placed the basket on the porch, knocked sturdily, and walked away in case the Yankee liked to sleep late. At midday, she brought another basket. She noticed that the basket on the porch was gone, so she knocked again, but this time Matthew immediately opened the door. He wasn't a tall man. Even a petite girl like Rabbit could see that. And like Gloria, Rabbit didn't think he seemed so good-looking, either, though she was prejudiced. Her father and Pop George were the two most handsome men in the world, in Rabbit's opinion. Yet with her keen sensitivity, she could see he wasn't dangerous. He was only gawky, and though he was white, she felt rather sorry for him.

Matthew assessed the tiny girl in front of him as well. To his eyes, she was strikingly beautiful—the most beautiful person he'd ever seen—and he blushed darkly: he knew he should not be thinking about a Negress this way, but already, he had surrendered to his appreciation. And when he smiled at her in his self-conscious way, Rabbit smiled back, and the entire porch was lit with her empathy. And he invited her inside to share the meal in the basket that she'd delivered. After she pointed out the cupboard in the corner, he brought out the china plates and she served his food, but he refused to eat until she had prepared a plate for herself. At first, she demurred: this man was not from this place. His foreignness was apparent, the dark and unattractive winter clothes that were far too heavy for the mild Georgia winter, the blunt accent of his speech, his smiling at a Negro girl and asking her to sit at the same din-ing table and eat along with him. Yet Matthew was aware that he held the power here, and when he insisted, Rabbit had no choice. She sat at the table with him, her small feet dangling above the shiny floor. Though her sensitivity told her that he was harmless, she was cautious. She kept her chair partially away from the table and trained her sight on the firewood that Pompey had strategically arranged. In the pocket of her dress, there was a razor-sharp kitchen knife, just to be on the safe side.

There was no need for her precautions, however. Matthew and she only sat together and shared the meal. When that was over, he thanked her and bowed. At supper that evening, he was disap-pointed to see that Rabbit was not there, serving at the table. And the next morning, the food basket was placed on the porch: she had knocked so softly, he hadn't heard. The hours between breakfast and lunch dragged for Matthew, as he waited and hoped to see the petite Negro girl again. At midday, he tried not to show too much happiness when he opened the door and saw her there, but failed in that endeavor. Again, they both stood on the porch smiling, until they were aware that they had not moved. And so Rabbit walked inside, and he insisted that she share his meal again.

A Reluctant Courtship

When the twelve days of Christmas were over, Matthew didn't want to leave Wood Place. Back at his saltbox house, he thought of Rabbit constantly. He smiled, remembering her tiny perfection, her feet dangling above the floor. He was afraid to call his constant thoughts infatuation, much less love, for Rabbit was a Negress.

Unofficially—for not even white men would write such rules down—if Matthew wanted to take Rabbit by force, no one would challenge him. It was not even against the law in Georgia for a white man to ravish a slave woman. If the woman was a white man's own slave, it was his right. If he ravished another white man's slave, it was only a crime against property, such as hurting a horse or dog that belonged to another. Yet the thought of violence toward a woman that he cared for filled Matthew with self-disgust. He would rather cut his own throat than to hurt one of the coiled hairs on Rabbit's head. His gallantry was unusual for his new home: among his own slaves, there were Negroes whose skin color announced that they had been the product of ravishment by white fathers. Though he was the owner of slaves, Matthew considered himself upright, but his sudden feelings for Rabbit fell outside the boundaries of southern society.

After those twelve days of Christmas, Matthew was uncertain, but he knew that he could not abide another year until he saw Rabbit again. And he made a choice that was admittedly immoral: he continued to visit Samuel's plantation, under the pretext of seeing Gloria. As young men in love will do—during one tormented night when Matthew touched himself and pictured Rabbit's exquisite, stone-chiseled face, he finally admitted that he was in love—Matthew reasoned that the rules of society were made to be broken. There were no rules, except those he made in pursuit of his affection. Thus, he did not flinch when Samuel suggested that he begin to formally court his daughter.

Matthew didn't know where this deception would end, but he didn't care, either. He only knew he had to be with Rabbit again. Each visit with her was a chaste one, and he was proud of this. They sat at the table in the guest cabin for an hour and ate the food she prepared. Matthew took out his pocket watch to be careful of time. By his fourth visit to the plantation, they had begun to share secrets, but these two were bound by more than their feelings. Rabbit was a slave, and thus, she would not tell Matthew about the stories every Negro on the premises except the smallest child knew: that Samuel Pinchard was a monster who kept a series of little girls to harm in the cabin on the left side of the big house. That her own sister had been scarred in order to protect her from Samuel's abuse. Or that her father had run away from Wood Place with her grandmother's help. And Matthew did not talk about how he could not imagine an honorable future for them, because she was a Negro and a slave.

Or that he had become more sensitive to his role as someone who owned human beings.

The First Lover's Sin

You should know that Matthew and Rabbit mightily tried to avoid consummation during the times that Matthew visited Samuel's Wood Place three days each month on the false pretext of courting Gloria. That Matthew and Rabbit continued to sit at the table together or outside on the porch, chaste yet burning for an entire year.

They shared more secrets. Matthew confided that he still missed his youngest sister, a baby who had emerged dead from his mother, but had been so loved that Mrs. Thatcher had insisted on naming her and refused to speak to Mr. Thatcher until the man had paid for a gravestone for the dead baby. The little girl had been named Judith and was buried on the family farm. Rabbit finally revealed to Matthew that her father had run away from the plantation—though she still withheld the details—and that Tess had dreams about Nick, as if they were together, instead of separated by distance, and even perhaps death.

And Matthew committed the first lover's sin: he didn't admit that he had tried to help Samuel retrieve Nick from wherever he had run to. He was afraid that Rabbit would despise him for a betrayal that had taken place before they'd ever met. And this was a valid concern, for even Matthew's own sister had scolded him all the way from Boston.

And then we know that these two sweethearts finally gave in to each other, after a year. Sitting closely led to handholding. That led to brief kisses. Those led to longer embraces, and the warmth of need, and that next winter holiday, Matthew crept one night and met Rabbit at the barn where she waited with a lantern: he hadn't wanted her to trek the long distance to the guesthouse. They walked together to the creek, stopping to kiss and whisper endearments. On the creek bank, they lay down together, fumbling and ignorant. He was twenty-seven to her eighteen, but neither of them had known another. And there was pain that first time for Rabbit but a happiness: this was the union her parents had known.

The night of Rabbit's bliss, Aggie awoke suddenly. Instantly, she knew her granddaughter had become a woman, though she didn't know Rabbit's beloved was a white man, and a slaveholder at that. And that Sunday at dinner, she took Rabbit aside, telling her she needed to know how a woman took care of herself, to keep from having a baby. Rabbit's eyes flew open—how did Aggie know?—and she tried to deny the accusation, but her grandmother put up a hand. Then she gave Rabbit a cloth-wrapped bundle of wild carrot seeds to drink for seven days, after she had lain with her beau. This was the safest way to keep a pregnancy from taking hold, for if that happened, then other solutions had to be sought to bring on her bleeding, and they were not as safe. And Aggie went further, embarrassing her granddaughter: Rabbit should learn to take her happiness before her man's, and to make sure he interrupted himself before his final pleasure arrived. For when a man took that final pleasure inside a woman, that increased the likelihood that he would leave a baby behind.

Aggie spoke to Rabbit not exactly as an equal, but there was a conviviality to her tone. And the tiny young girl—no, woman—felt pride. She had crossed over into a territory she had not known existed. And the next times that Rabbit met with her lover at the creek, she began to learn what pleasure was, and to feel the power in that joy. Yet forbidden love between two people who must keep their secret is full of strain.

And there came the night when Rabbit and Matthew were lying together at the creek, when finally, she revealed to him her deepest wish: she wanted to run away from Wood Place with Leena and Eliza Two and go north to seek her father. She didn't ask Matthew for help, as she'd assumed it was assured; thus, she was dismayed when he was silent. Her head was upon his pale chest, and she rose onto her elbow and looked at him. And Matthew told her such a thing was forbidden, for there was a law that had been passed eight years before to retrieve runaway slaves, who were called "fugitives." Not only were owners allowed to chase their slaves into the clutches of the north, but any white man who helped a slave escape was subject to losing his property—if he didn't possess one thousand dollars to pay the fines for assisting a runaway—and to suffer imprisonment besides.

He stumbled these words out quickly, for he'd had his own plan to reveal: he wanted to purchase Rabbit from Samuel and set her up in a small house in Milledgeville, and visit her several times a week. He'd started to save the money for her price as well as the house. And then he searched within the pocket of his jacket—discarded beside him in his lover's haste—and pulled out the present that he'd brought her for Christmas. A cameo brooch surrounded by pearls. He told Rabbit, he knew the brooch was not a ring, but he wanted to give her something as a promise. But Rabbit did not take the brooch. Instead, she asked him, what about her sisters—for she now considered Leena as kin, as much as Eliza Two. What would they do, while she was living in Milledgeville? And Matthew stammered on, explaining that they would have to be left on Wood Place, but he was sure that Samuel would treat them well, as he was certainly a very kind man.

And Rabbit narrowed her eyes, looking down at the white man to whom she'd given herself. She knew that he kept slaves but had put that in the back of her mind. Every lover lies to herself, in small or large ways. Yet she had thrown away every teaching of her childhood, that as a Negro girl she should avoid or hide from white men as best she could. She'd closed her eyes and ignored the truth of Matthew's heritage. And she was afraid again to tell him that Samuel, the man he thought was a benevolent gentleman, had caused her sister to be marked and shorn. The trust she had with Matthew flapped away, like a bird seeking shelter from the cold. Rabbit lay back on his chest and pulled him to her. She privately reasoned that she had a right to take her pleasure one last time.

The next day, when Matthew opened the door of the guesthouse, before him stood Pompey with the basket. He offered the obsequious words of a slave, but no excuse for Rabbit's absence. The next day and the next, Rabbit was absent again. Matthew could not inquire about her, for by then, Samuel had suggested to him that his courtship with Gloria had gone on long enough, and wasn't it time to start planning a wedding, and Matthew had agreed. He hadn't known how to extricate himself and keep his friendship with Samuel. And though he continued to visit the plantation every month, he could never catch a glimpse of Rabbit.

Worse than Matthew's romantic anguish was his ignorance: he'd thought that his offer of a soft life in a little house on a hidden street in Milledgeville had been a wonderful gift, like the brooch he had bought. Any other Negress would have been delighted. Where had he gone wrong?

The Day of the Daguerreotype

In 1839, a year before the birth of Rabbit and Eliza Two, a Frenchman with too many first names for us to list here had invented a process that permanently captured the images of humans. M. Daguerre showed the products of his fume-ridden invention, the wages of his camera obscura, in a building before learned men who thought highly of themselves, over the sea in Paris. It had been the sixth day of January. Earlier, M. Daguerre had transfixed a gentleman, M. Gaucheraud, with the capturing of a deceased spider underneath a microscope. So taken was the gentleman that he could not keep his secret and wrote about it in a local newspaper the day before the demonstration, stealing the surprise. His consternation and pleasure over this new toy mingled with his criticism of what the inventor had failed to do: "Nature in motion cannot be represented, or at least not without great difficulty, by the process in question." The criticism was obligatory. M. Gaucheraud did not want anyone to think him biased.

The invention crossed the sea shortly thereafter, and within years, a man traveling through Putnam County arrived in a covered wagon through the narrow, dangerously pitted portion of the main road, and used M. Daguerre's invention to capture the members of

Samuel's family: Lady, Victor, Grace, and Gloria, along with his future son-in-law, Matthew Thatcher. And because Samuel felt so
smug about finally securing a mate for his daughter, he even paid
the man who took that daguerreotype to take an image of Rabbit,
Eliza Two, and Leena. The three girls would pose with their arms
around each other's waists. Samuel had only wanted his Young
Friend captured, but she had begged him to let the other girls be
included. Usually Samuel was not so giving, but he relented. Daguerreotypes such as this were being taken throughout the south,
as plantation owners chronicled their lives, their falsely idyllic are-
nas, the white infant charges with dark nurses dressed in calico with
rings in their ears.

The Weeping Time

Samuel splurged in planning for his daughter's wedding. He had
sent away for the ivory silk, and in the months that it took to arrive, there was a tangled network of which he was only vaguely
aware that made his request come to fruition: the skeins of thread
manufactured by hungry worms in Asia, then sent to France, where
the cloth was woven and then shipped to Boston, then Savannah,
where Samuel had it transported to his store, and finally, to a particularly gifted slave's lap, a woman who was owned by a planter the
next town over, in Eatonton. She sewed the dress by hand, pains-
takingly, after Samuel drove Gloria in his carriage for three fittings.
The matching lace veil had not taken that long, as it only had been
made in some English housewife's cottage. Samuel decided that his
strange daughter would be married the following June.

When Samuel invited Matthew to travel with him to a slave auction in Savannah, Matthew did not want to leave the area; he hoped
that Rabbit would forgive him, and his plan would be fulfilled.
However, he wanted to please Samuel, who was his only friend—
once again—and Matthew agreed to travel to Savannah. Samuel was
merry: he meant to enjoy himself. They took the train to the city
and stayed at a fine hotel. The rooms were luxurious, with canopied

beds, and the further Samuel traveled away from his plantation, the higher his strength rose. He felt like a very young man again.

At the Savannah racetrack, the parcel for auction was huge, over four hundred pieces of slave merchandise—too much to hold the auction in the town square. Samuel paid for his four new slaves with a full bank draft. He did not want to accrue interest, and he advised Matthew to do the same. If he could not, Samuel assured his future son-in-law that with his own investments in the rail line, he could afford to loan Matthew the funds needed to purchase one lonely slave. Thinking of Rabbit, Matthew demurred. He was shocked at the roughhousing at the auction. There were much groping and intimate insults directed at the female slaves. Matthew and Samuel put several feet between themselves and the traders, who were partaking in the merry abuse, and hooting at an unusual sight: unlike the rest of the hundreds of slaves who created a high volume with their lamentations, one Negro man had grinned on the block without coaxing, even when the auctioneer had instructed a crying female to unbutton the Negro's trousers and expose his member for all. After striking the female several times, the auctioneer further forced her to stroke the naked flesh. It came to massive life.

The auction upset Matthew, provoking not only blushes when the buyers had shouted at the size of the Negro's member, but a later sickness in his stomach. Matthew had never been afflicted by slave trading. That some men ruled while others did not was an old story, one he hadn't written. Yet at the auction he had taken in the saddest scene. At the auction, a slave man, Number 319 in the catalog, had approached the white man who had purchased him and begged the man, begging him to buy Number 278, his ladylove. The slave thought he'd been successful, but the sale was bungled, and Matthew watched the man weep inconsolably as his lady was sold away separately. The rain had been unceasing.

On their return from Savannah, Samuel expressed his disappointment that there were no little mulatta girls for sale at the auction. He'd been expecting a greater selection, as he was past tired of his current Young Friend, Leena; she was far too old for his tastes. He talked openly and casually about the cost of such little girls, and how he had used them over the years. He remarked he was fortunate to be a well-off man. As Samuel spoke, Matthew stomach was turned, understanding for the first time the purpose of the adorable cottage that sat on the left side of the plantation house. But why hadn't Rabbit ever mentioned it? Suddenly he understood the insult—the outrage—that his offer to Rabbit had represented. When Matthew had asked Gloria who lived in the cottage, she'd told him, a princess in a tower. He had laughed as he always did at her odd phrasing. He did not love Gloria, but he had promised to marry her, the daughter of this disturbing man. And Matthew realized he was not outside this southern ugliness anymore. His sister Deborah had been right to scold him in her letters. He was firmly nestled inside the rotting carcass of the south.

When Samuel and Matthew arrived back at Wood Place, Lady delivered tragic news: while they'd been away, Gloria had fallen ill. The doctor had come and gone, but he could not alleviate her illness. She had passed away and already had been buried.

A Family Gathers

During the era that Rabbit lived, white women were considered to be frail and inferior to men. However, this perception of frailty never applied to Negro women, who were expected to thrive under any difficult circumstance, including ravishment, childbirth, and backbreaking labor in the fields. Rabbit had been reared on a plantation, and like every other plantation in the south, Wood Place did not treat Negro girls and women as precious. She had borne witness to the incredible requirements for strength that had been forced upon Negresses. As Aggie was fond of saying, "Root hog or die." And women of her kind had to dig in whatever dirt was beneath them. They had to dig and never cease. This was the reality of a Negress's life.

Though Rabbit grieved her separation from Matthew, she had never seen happiness allowed to flourish anyway. Not on Wood

Place. The Franklins were an abased, angry group living in their knot of shabby cabins on the south side of the plantation, and though the Pinchards were wealthy, they, too, were demoralized and miserable. The Quarters-folks lived in fear that Samuel would catch a whim and sell one of their children, or that his son Victor would do the same, once his father passed away.

Rabbit didn't allow Matthew's insult to distract her from her purpose: she wanted to leave Wood Place with Eliza Two and Leena, and search for their father. She didn't know what she expected after she left the plantation, but Nick was the sun and moon and every star in the sky for her. He would show her the way. And she was afraid that if she waited any longer that Samuel would die. True, he was a monster, but his crimes could be depended upon. Once Samuel was gone, however, a new master would have to be adapted to, and her opportunity for freedom could be lost. For now, Victor was an absence. He rarely spoke during the day, and at night, he roamed the countryside—no one knew in search of what.

One Sunday night in July, Rabbit gathered her family around her. She was afraid, for Aggie ever had expressed her fierce need to keep her family together. Yet when Rabbit told her family that she planned to leave—and wanted to take Leena and Eliza Two with her—Aggie told her that she already knew. She'd had a nighttime vision of a little girl she'd never seen before. In the dream, the child walked up to Rabbit and Leena, reaching out her hand. Then, from the corner, Tess roused from the chair, where she'd been sitting throughout dinner. Tess declared, sure enough, she'd seen that little girl in her dreams, as well. And Eliza Two shocked everyone by chiming in, the dream had come to her as well—and she didn't want Rabbit to be sad, but she wasn't going to leave. She wasn't afraid: Wood Place was her home, and not only the folks in this cabin, but those who lived in the Quarters.

Then, Pop George stood and called the name of each woman in the room. His face was at once young and ancient. Timelessness rested there. Love rested there. A knowledge that had been brought from across the water, as he spoke to his family. He told them he would send prayers to guide Rabbit's way, but before that, there needed to be fire.

The Night of the Fire

Samuel recovered quickly from the death of Gloria, if he even had mourned her at all. Yet his brief mourning was replaced by another such as he had never known before: in June, a plague struck his peaches, and dark spots covered the skins, changing the flavor to bitter.

It had been unusually wet that spring, and Samuel had forgotten to remind Pompey to prune back their branches, to keep the moisture from setting in. When Samuel confronted him, enraged over the loss of his most precious food, Pompey defended himself by reminding his owner that the last time he had pruned without permission, his master had slapped him and ordered Venie to take away his supper for two days.

Not only that, but even if Samuel wanted to lower his standards by eating peach preserves, there had been thefts and vandalism in the storehouse: some scallywag had broken the lock on the storehouse, taken the hams, and smashed the crocks of peaches. He'd ordered Pompey to rough up a few men to find the culprit, but bruises and loosened teeth had not encouraged confessions. Samuel was gloomy, recalling past encounters with his beloved peaches, and he gained more heft around his stomach because, though he ate second and third portions of his meals, nothing could fill the nostalgic hole.

Rabbit was his savior, distinguishing herself by making fresh blackberry cobbler for dessert, a dish with a subtle sprinkling of sugar and eastern spices. She had learned how to make Venie's French crust, too, which was good because that summer, the senior cook was pregnant and heavy on her feet. Other than the children, every resident on the farm knew that Holcomb Byrd James was the father of the child that Venie expected. Samuel did not approve, but he reasoned that a good overseer was hard to find.

The night that fire came to Wood Place, Rabbit outdid herself

with a particularly brilliant blackberry cobbler, which only Samuel
ate. When she'd served a bowl of cobbler to Grace, Samuel made
pejorative comments that she needed to watch her weight. Maybe if
she did, her husband would give her a child. Thus Grace pushed her
bowl away. Victor was at the table, but he did not defend his wife,
nor eat dessert. Lady was upstairs, lying down; she had not gotten
past the death of her daughter so easily.

When the shouts of fire began, Victor would be on one of his long
sojourns into the woods. He wouldn't hear the commotion, nor
would the Franklins on the far end of the plantation, though considering how the Pinchards had treated them, they probably wouldn't
have tried to put out the flames even if they had. Nor would Lady
or Grace be concerned; Grace would knock loudly on her mother-
in-law's door, shouting, come! Come and see! And she and Lady
would stand together at the window in their nightgowns, watching
the fire that was consuming the left cabin, grateful that the cursed
place was being destroyed. Some moments later, Lady would hear
Samuel screaming and encounter him crawling on the floor of the
hall outside his bedroom, vivid effluvia staining the white linen of
his pants. Before leaving him in the hallway to whatever fate God
decided, she spat upon his face. Though he survived, Lady's redress
would remain her secret, as a fever overtook Samuel for several days
and he would not remember her affront.

In the overseer's cabin, Holcomb awoke and heard screams, but
settled in deeper, his hand on the hill of Venie's stomach. He refused
to leave her in the night. Venie had not worked for more than two
or three hours a day in the kitchen as she waited for the birth of
their child. Thus, she had not seen Rabbit uncork a jug of pokeberry
wine and mix the contents into fresh, sugared blackberries before
placing the lattice of crust on top, though that wouldn't have bothered Venie. And Rabbit had stolen other jugs containing scuppernong brandy. Before starting the fire, she and Leena would kneel
and pray to God. Then they would douse the furniture, curtains,
and bedding in the left cabin, and a delicious smell would rise on the
wind when the flames took hold.

The Quarters-folks and the members of Rabbit's family would come out of their cabins and see the flames darting. Then all of them would turn and go back inside.

A Meeting at the Crossroads

The same evening of the fire in the left cabin, Matthew had decided to leave the south forever. He'd planned to drive his wagon to the train station, where he would travel by rail to the coast and then take a steamship north.

Not only was he heartbroken over the loss of Rabbit, Matthew had unsettling visions ever since the auction in Savannah. He would dream of disembodied breasts suckling infants who turned into skeletons, and songs that seemed instantly familiar, but which he'd never heard. He would awaken in time to see the apparition of a small Negro man running from his room. Things had worsened until Matthew began to hear the scuttling of shoes in daytime moments.

Yet he was filled with gratitude after receiving a letter from his sister. Deborah had invited him to visit her in Boston, and Matthew had written her to accept. When he arrived, he intended to send his deed to Jeremiah Franklin, his sometime overseer, whose nature was better suited to this land. Matthew knew he should have a care for his slaves, as Jeremiah was cruel, but it was past the time for salvation. Already, Matthew had aligned himself with the Devil, by partaking in the purchase of flesh. He had betrayed Rabbit and insulted her. He didn't deserve the blessing of such a woman.

He left late at night with a lantern, two medium-size valises, a basket of food, and a jug of strong, sugared coffee, not that he needed it, as sleeplessness tormented him. If Dori had packed him a jug of spirits along with the coffee, he would have drunk it, let inebriation take him over, climbed in the back of the wagon, and allowed the gray mares to lead him wherever they wanted: Hellfire. The bottom of a river. The town where the train station was. Back to his mother's womb, where something would recognize his malevolence and mercifully kill him. In his daze, Matthew could not be shocked by anything—and so, when he arrived at the crossroads, encountering the same small Negro man from his dreams did not trouble him. He signaled to the horses, and they stopped.

"Greetings, comrade," the small man said. "My name's Joe. Might I trouble you for transport?"

Matthew nodded his head, and in case the night had shielded his response, he spoke as well. "Yes, you can ride with me."

When the small man asked if they possibly could take a detour, Matthew handed him the reins. For some time, the horses trotted on, and then, they arrived at Wood Place, in time for them to witness the fire eating the left cabin, and ravenously at that.

Matthew saw several Negroes run into the woods, and then there was his beloved Rabbit holding the hand of a young woman. They were walking away in the other direction, away from the burning cabin. And Matthew didn't care about the consequences, that he'd face the weight of the law. That his money could be taken, and possibly his freedom. This was his chance to make the right choice, and Matthew allowed the small man to drive the wagon toward the woman he loved.

XI

And when we call for education we mean real education. We believe in work. We ourselves are workers, but work is not necessarily education. Education is the development of power and ideal. We want our children trained as intelligent human beings should be, and we will fight for all time against any proposal to educate black boys and girls simply as servants and underlings, or simply for the use of other people. They have a right to know, to think, to aspire.

—W. E. B. Du Bois, "The Niagara Movement Address"

"Ah wanted to preach a great sermon about colored women sittin' on high, but they wasn't no pulpit for me. . . . Ah said Ah'd save de text for you."

—Zora Neale Hurston, *Their Eyes Were Watching God*

WHO REMEMBERS THIS?

❖

The ticket agent squinted at my driver's license. I estimated him to be no more than twenty-five, but he was balding already. There were dashes of pink scalp under his red hair.

Though she knew I slept late on the weekends, my mother had rung me two weeks before in the morning, too close to dawn.

"I've been waiting for you to tell me your travel plans for Root's ceremony on Founder's Day."

"Mama, I don't think I can come. I was gone drive, but my transmission is tripping. I'll see you for the reunion."

"Is that all? I'll just order a ticket for you."

"No, Mama! I'm thirty-three years old. You can't keep spending money on me."

"Diane pays all the utilities in the house, so I'm all right."

"But, Mama—"

"Uncle Root is a very old man, and he hasn't seen you since last July. You have to come. You know you're his favorite."

"I call him every week."

"It's not the same. Now, I know you're writing that dissertation, but you have to show your face sometimes. You weren't even there when we buried Nana."

"You expected me to stop work for that?"

"Yes, I did. She was your father's mother. That's what people in families do. They come for the funerals of their grandmothers. You gone want somebody to be at your funeral one day."

"No, I won't, Mama. I'll be dead. You can cremate me and flush me down the toilet, for all I care."

"I wish you knew how stupid you sound. And stop trying to change the subject. I'm buying you that ticket, so I expect you to be there at the airport on Wednesday. David James is coming to get you. You know him and that girl got divorced, with his cheating self."

"Miss Rose told me they weren't together anymore, but how you know he stepped out?"

"'Cause I got some sense! All them James men cheat. It's in their blood."

"So after you low-rate him, you gone ask him to pick me up from the airport? Dang, Mama. That's cold."

"I didn't say David wasn't a nice guy. All I'm saying is look at the facts. Mr. J.W. was a cheater. His son Bo cheated on his first wife with David's mother. And David is Bo's son, so there you go."

"Fine. I'll see you on Wednesday."

"All right, baby. I love you very much. Travel safely."

The ticket agent straightened, his green eyes narrowing. "Miss Garfield, I'm sorry, but this doesn't look a thing like you. Do you have another form of identification?"

"Sure I do, but it's me, all right. And it's Ms., not Miss. You sure it doesn't look like me? I've lost a bit of weight."

"A bit? The woman in this picture is pretty heavy."

"And aren't you a gentleman for implying that I was fat?"

"It's not my intention to be rude. I'm just trying to make sure our country is safe."

"Every time I've come through this airport, someone asks me for another form of ID. I get patted down and have my bag randomly searched. But if it's random, why am I always the one searched? Why don't I get skipped sometimes?"

"Ms. Garfield, you wouldn't want us to be lazy about our jobs, and then have a terrorist sneak in, would you?"

"Do I look like a terrorist to you? Do terrorists wear horn-rimmed glasses and carry bags of potato chips and trashy gossip magazines?"

"I'm not sure, but if you gave me another form of identification, maybe I could verify that."

I gently placed my birth certificate on the counter. I wanted to slap it down, or even better, throw it at him. But I was Black, and he

wasn't, though he would deny that as motivation when he called a
rent-a-cop to flog me on some pretense of national security.

He looked as closely at the birth certificate as he had the license.

"So are you sure it's me now?"

"I suppose, Ms. Garfield."

He gave me back the license, and I didn't feel sorry for him anymore. Let him go bald immediately. He deserved it, the fascist abuser
of power. Let him go straight to Hell with gasoline drawers on.

In the baggage claim, David didn't see me beside the carousel. He
looked at the floor, his mouth covered with fingers splayed.

I came up behind him: "Boo!"

"Girl, stop playing! I almost knocked you out!"

"Please. I can kick your ass anytime. And why you so dressed up?"

"Some people have jobs, Ailey. We can't stay in the library all day
like the leisure class. Ooh, girl, look at you! You done got skinny!"

He wrapped an arm around me, lifting me from the ground, but
he couldn't be depended upon to tell the truth about the size of my
behind. He hadn't seen me naked since I was sixteen, in a faraway
time before stretch marks and orange-peel thighs.

He gently wrestled the bag from me, pushed down the handle,
and carried the suitcase. Grumbled that certain women needed to
let somebody be a gentleman. I walked in front of him, flipping my
hair as two brothers gave me the eye. It was dark in the garage, but
they seemed vaguely cute.

And there it was: the Eldorado. The same tank with the red velvet seats inside.

"Are you ever going to get a new car? And do you even have insurance?"

"Yes, I do. It's the law. And this is a registered classic." He opened
the door for me. "You better be glad I ain't asking for gas money."

"I got five on it." It was Boukie's saying from back in the day,
though he never put money in the tank.

"Yeah, I won't hold my breath on that!" On the journey, we
laughed and told stories about our beloved, cheap friend who had

become a teetotaling deacon at Mt. Calvary. Rhonda and Boukie were married now, with a passel of kids. The wedding had been a reluctant one, after his church minister had cautioned, he couldn't be having a single deacon spreading his seed throughout creation.

David slipped one hand off the steering wheel. He fingered a lock of my hair. Touched my cheekbone with his finger. "I like your hair longer. Remember when it was down your back? Man, that was pretty."

When we pulled off on the road to my granny's house, David and I stopped at the creek. He opened the car door and climbed out, and I saw him go to the base of a tree and pull out a plastic bag. A few moments later, he handed me a loose joint and a container of safety matches.

"Damn, Negro! You slick as grease."

"Nobody comes out here but me. I have it buried in a secret spot."

"Who you get this from, anyway?"

"Ma'am, that is covered by attorney-client privilege."

I took a hit, then opened the glove compartment, rummaging inside until I found an old *Jet* magazine folded to the "Beauty of the Week," a woman in a bikini with the roundest, most exquisite ass I'd ever seen. I waved the magazine, fanning the smoke in David's direction.

"Why'd you and Carla break up? I thought you were crazy about her."

"I was wondering when we'd get to that. You've gotten better, at least. It only took you a year to ask."

"David, answer the question."

"You need her to answer that. She's the one wanted the divorce."

"Did you cheat on her with some skank? Don't think I don't re-member Rhonda. Oh, I'm sorry, she's Mrs. Boukie Crawford now."

"Ailey, how you gone keep talking about that? That was almost twenty years ago. I was seventeen and stupid."

"I should have beat Rhonda down when I had the chance. Heifer."

"You still can. She and Boukie live right on Martin Luther King Jr. Drive. I can drop you off after supper."

He touched the knob of the radio, turned the volume up, and Luther Vandross's voice filled the car. The inside vibrated, the rear window beating out its own tune.

I turned the volume back down.

"David, did you cheat on Carla?"

"No, I did not. How could you even ask me that?"

"Then what happened with y'all?"

"None of your damned business. Carla and I might not be together anymore, but she is still the mother of my child. And I'm not going to talk about what happened between us. Some things are private, Ailey. So stop asking me." He looked out his window as Luther crooned about how he couldn't wait, now that he was in love.

At Miss Rose's, we sat in the kitchen while she moved around slowly, placing platters of fried chicken, macaroni and cheese, corn bread, sliced and salted tomatoes, and greens on the table.

"Baybay, you got time to carry Ailey back into town after supper?"

"Yes, ma'am."

He squirmed in his seat. He had the munchies, but neither one of us could start the meal until Miss Rose placed the last dish on the table and blessed the food.

She took a hand in each of hers. "Father God, we thank Thee for Thy gracious bounty and for this loving fellowship and we ask that You don't make it so long between our grandbaby's visits. But we so grateful to see this child here in the meantime. Thank you, Jesus. Thank you, Father God. Amen."

She sat down with a small groan, paused a moment, then lightly hit the table and looked at me.

"Ailey! Go on in that icebox and get them sweet potato pies. They covered in foil. Be careful, now. You know you clumsy."

"Aw, you didn't have to bake me any pies," David said. "I was glad to pick her up at the airport."

"Them pies not just for you, Baybay," she said. "One's for us, one's for Root and Belle, and one's for your mama. Tell Cloletha, I don't know if they as good as they should be. This batch of yams was kinda stringy. And I better not hear you ate up all them pies on the way back to town 'cause I know you been smoking them reefers."

He started coughing. I turned away from the refrigerator to hit him on the back.

"Ailey Pearl, don't you be trying to hide from me. You been smoking them reefers, too? Tell the truth and shame the Devil."

I stood by the refrigerator and put my hand up to my mouth, gnawing on my pinky nail. "No, ma'am, I was not! David was blowing smoke on me. That's why I smell like this."

He recovered his breath and laughed. I waited for him to betray me.

"She's right," David said. "You know she not like that."

"Lord, today, y'all chirren! Y'all ain't too big for me to strip a switch! Baybay, you ain't mines, but even if you was, you can't hold all the whippings you need."

He took her hand and kissed it. "I love you so much, Miss Rose."

"You pretty rascal!" She pulled her hand from his and speared a breast on the platter. "Ailey, eat this. You too skinny. You done fell way off."

"She supposed to have some meat on her, ain't she?" David asked. "She got that kind of frame."

"Shole do, and don't nobody want a bone but a dog."

I told them, they better stop teasing me, but give me that breast. I didn't mind getting the big piece of chicken.

———

The next morning, the bench dedication was long, with prayers and songs and stories. My mother and David James were on the first row of pews, in the old bourgie section. I sat on the chapel stage, beside Uncle Root. Dr. Oludara wore garb commensurate with her promotion to president of the college, a flowing purple-and-red dress. Around her head, brightly colored satin cloth, the regalia of her heritage.

Dr. Oludara spoke softly, but close to the microphone. Honoring Uncle Root, who'd never let his students forget the task before them. He'd remained at the college for over four decades, and for thirty of those years, he'd taught Freshman Orientation.

"Who remembers this?" She raised her index finger, and there were knowing chuckles from my mother and other, older people in the audience. She cleared her throat, deepening her voice into a high-toned drawl. "'My children, we are a distinguished race, although some would say otherwise. Our people depend on us. Our white brethren need the Negro, though they are unaware of it, for without the Negro, who would toil in his fields, or let the white man think himself divine? Every God needs an Adam to cast out of the Garden. And without the educated men of his race, the Negro would lose himself in the desert of the unlettered, the surest path to salvation. But without the sacrifices of the Negro woman'"—and here Dr. Oludara smiled broadly—"'without her struggles, who would my brother be? Unaided, unsupported, brutish—a heathen! My children, the Negro woman is the best our race has to offer. Cherish her. Love her. Never leave her behind.'" She bowed her head a few seconds, in reverence. Then: "Honored guests and alumni, I give you Dr. Jason Freeman Hargrace, class of 1926!"

There was a standing ovation, and the old man extended his hands to me, and I pulled him from his seat. At the podium, Dr. Oludara embraced the two of us, then swept her arm: the podium belonged to Uncle Root.

"I will not make a long speech, as I'm very old and I need to save what little time I have left." There was laughter. "I wish to thank you, President Oludara, and all the alumni. I am greatly humbled, and I accept this honor in the memories of my beloved mother, Maybelline Freeman, Dr. Terrence Carter Holmes, my professor, colleague, and friend, and my dear wife, Dr. Olivia Ellen Hargrace. And I pass my torch as the tender of the history of this college to my niece who stands beside me on this stage, Ailey Pearl Garfield, Routledge College, class of 1995."

He nodded his head in thanks as the crowd refused to be silent. For an entire minute, they kept clapping, and he pulled out his handkerchief. He wiped away tears.

At the reception in the faculty dining room, there were several of my old classmates. Though Abdul wasn't there, Tiffany stood in line with her husband, a Gamma who had graduated in my freshman year; she didn't wave or even acknowledge that she saw me. Keisha wasn't there, but Roz was, slender, her hair cut to the shoulders and colored auburn. Like me, she was single. She bragged that she was making too much money as a corporate lawyer to be tied down to somebody and pushing out his babies. She had dismissed Curt Waymon several years before.

After the buffet lunch was served and dishes cleared away, the Gamma brothers circled the old man and serenaded him with their fraternity song. When they broke apart, there was Patrick Lindsay. He was balding, his remaining curls cut low and surrounding a freckled scalp, but that same warmth beamed. He introduced himself to David, then embraced me, his arms hugging around my waist. We stood that way, facing each other, mere inches between us, until David had a coughing fit.

"Girl, you are fine as ever!" Pat said. "The glasses suit you."

"You're so sweet." I touched his face. "You're looking great yourself."

He'd wanted his wife to come, but she was breastfeeding, and it made her tired. They both taught at the University of Arkansas in the department of world languages. She was tenure-track, and he was visiting faculty but was hoping for a spousal hire. They'd met at Georgia, where they had been the only two Blacks in their program. He pulled out his billfold to show me her picture: a slender woman garbed in a sleeveless, loose linen dress. Her natural hair was shaved close to her skull. The fat baby in her arms had his mother's mahogany color and his father's brown-blond curls.

I leaned over the image, fighting emotion. Roz had told me that he was married, but somehow, I'd imagined him single, preserved in amber. Always available to me, if I ever got myself together.

"She's, like, a *Vogue* supermodel. She's so gorgeous. Look at those cheekbones. And your baby is so adorable! What's his name?"

"Léopold Aimé Lindsay."

"After your favorite Negritudes."

"Aw, girl, you remembered! Yeah, I guess he is kinda cute, even though he took all my hair. And my wife's a real good woman. The best woman a man could ask for." He put an arm around my shoulder, and then an arm around David's shoulder. He closed our circle. Pat directed his words to my escort but kept his eyes on me. "Let me tell you something. This girl, right here? I was in love with this girl! She had my nose so wide open I couldn't think about nobody else but Ailey Pearl Garfield. Then she stomped my heart in the dirt, and don't you know, I still don't know why? For years, I wondered if she'd take me back. Maybe I should call her and beg her, one more time. But then, finally, I had to move on."

"Oh, brother, I definitely know that feeling," David said. "It ain't hardly no fun."

They laughed at their common misery, and I didn't know whether to feel flattered or foolish.

ANY MORE WHITE FOLKS

◈

It had been five years since I'd found the daguerreotypes and the letters of Matthew Thatcher, Adeline Routledge, and Judith Hutchinson in the library of Routledge College, and had learned who these
women were, that they'd been enslaved on Wood Place Plantation.
When I'd dried my tears, I'd understood something else: only half
of the history had been told.

That Judith and Matthew probably had been more than friends
was obvious, but the college had concealed that fact, as had everyone going back to Adeline Routledge. When I asked Dr. Oludara,
and then Uncle Root, why this was the case, they both told me it had
been an open secret among the historians teaching at the school.
But no one in the college's administration had wanted to reveal
that Matthew and Judith were lovers: it was too explosive, in racial
terms. Too embarrassing and complicated. And so that part of the
college's founding had been buried.

Then I'd let myself be fooled: I became high with the ease of my
search. Even before I finished that final semester of my master's
program, I'd already outlined my doctoral dissertation on the two
formerly enslaved women who had escaped from Wood Place and
ended up in Boston. Dr. Whitcomb had been so proud of me: I'd
sailed through my coursework for the doctoral program with perfect grades, and I'd passed my comprehensive exams with distinction that next year. So I was disappointed to find that besides the
letters, there wasn't much else on Adeline and Judith to use for my
dissertation. There was so much more material on the Pinchards
and Matthew Thatcher—their lives, their land, the people that
they'd owned—but I didn't want to focus only on what I'd found
in the possessions of white men. The most interesting thing I'd discovered was of no use to my dissertation, though it was bound to
cause a stir in my family: it appeared that Samuel Pinchard's son

Victor had married a Grace Franklin, sibling to the same Franklins
from whom Chicasetta's most odious family was descended. Which
made us all distant cousins.

For a year, I was "all but dissertation" for my doctorate on Adeline
and Judith and Black women's education. I continued my research,
driving down to Georgia during my winter and fall breaks, and
spending time walking through my granny's farm. I sifted through
the overgrown ruins of the plantation house, where I found broken
shards of cooking pots, a corncob pipe, and twisted iron. The bricks
of the plantation had been made with stiff hog's hair. The cemetery
where my great-grandmother, father, and sister were buried contained the remains of generations of Wood Place enslaved folks. It
was segregated, with a grass-covered space separating the two sides
where the white Pinchards and the Black folks rested. In the latter
space, most of the graves didn't have stones.

But for months something bothered me, and when I woke one
morning, I was embarrassed I hadn't realized what it was before.
It was so simple: somehow the saga of Adeline and Judith was in-
terconnected with the lives of the other slaves at Wood Place. And
I had been ignoring the three people who could tell me at least a bit
about their stories.

———

In July, I drove down for the family reunion in Uncle Root's town
car. My own car finally had died, and he'd given me the long Lincoln
to take back to North Carolina, saying it was still a good automobile, and his driving days were over. I waited until after the reunion
to begin approaching this new aspect of my dissertation, about the
enslaved folks at Wood Place, until the days would settle back into
languor. I asked the old man, could I stay with him a few days more?

The morning that I interviewed him, he'd wanted our talk to
take place early in the day. He was sharpest before noon. When I
came down for the morning, he asked me, how formal did I want
him to be for our interview?

"You're not going to be on public television. I'll only be recording
you on this."

I showed him my new piece of equipment.

"Look at that tiny little thing! Isn't technology wonderful? Ailey, this is the first time I've ever been recorded. I want to be very professional."

"As opposed to what? I've never even seen you in jeans and a T-shirt."

"And you never will, as long as my head is hot!"

After I set the recorder on the coffee table, I looked at my legal pad. I'd written down basic questions. Dr. Whitcomb had told me, in his experience, even simple queries would yield great results, especially with elderly subjects. Just remember, don't try to control their answers. And keep my opinions to myself, if at all possible.

I clicked on the recorder.

"This is Ailey Pearl Garfield. I'm interviewing Dr. Jason Freeman Hargrace, a resident of Chicasetta, Georgia. Today's date is July 23, 2007. Dr. Hargrace, do you give me permission to record our conversation?"

"I do."

"Dr. Hargrace, can you tell me when and where you were born?"

"I was born Christmas Day in nineteen hundred and seven on Wood Place Plantation in Chicasetta, Georgia. My mother told me I was six weeks early, but her grandmother insisted the timing was off. I was a very fat baby."

"And who were your parents?"

"My mother's name was Maybelline Victorina Freeman. They called her Lil' May. My father's name was Thomas John Pinchard Sr. They called him Big Thom. His father was named Victor Pinchard. And Victor's father was Samuel Pinchard. My father was a white man, and my mother was a Negro. He was twenty-two years older. My mother's mother was named Sheba Freeman. We never knew the name of my mother's father, and we didn't know much about him, other than he was a scoundrel. My maternal great-grandmother was named Eliza Two Freeman, but we called her Meema. She was a slave and so were her parents. They were owned by the parents and grandparents of Big Thom Pinchard."

"Can you name any of your other ancestors of the Pinchard line?"

"You mean, can I name any more white folks in my bloodline?" He laughed. "I do know that Victor and Eliza Two's father were half brothers."

"Really?"

"Ah! The scholar picks up a pen! I see I've piqued your interest. Yes, they were half brothers. Samuel, their father, was the owner of Wood Place. The slaves called him 'Old Massa.' Whenever Meema talked about him, her mouth would shrink up like a prune."

He made a sour face.

The next question was sensitive. Though I'd talked through most of my findings with the old man, I hadn't told him about what might be shocking, at least to him. But how to proceed?

"Dr. Hargrace, may I ask you a question?"

"I thought you were doing that already."

"Um . . . well . . ."

"Go ahead, Ailey. I have no secrets from you."

"All right. Were you aware that . . . Big Thom's father, Victor . . . okay . . . um, were you aware that Victor . . . married a woman with the last name Franklin?"

He tilted his head. Reached for his cup of coffee. "You mean, as in the low-down, murderous Franklins of Chicasetta, Georgia?"

"Um . . . yes, sir. Those Franklins. Victor's wife was named Grace Bless Franklin. She was Big Thom's mother."

"Well, what do you know? I'll be goddamned! Excuse me, Ailey. I apologize for forgetting my manners. I was not reared to use profanity in front of ladies. Can we erase that part?"

"It's okay. I've heard worse in my life. Said worse, too."

"You mean, all this time, those Franklins actually owned that land?"

"Not exactly. Initially, they did own an adjoining parcel they'd won in the land lottery. But then they sold that parcel piecemeal through the years. Before the war, Jeremiah Franklin signed the last parcel over to Samuel Pinchard for a couple hundred dollars.

Jeremiah was Grace's brother. I guess that relationship meant Jeremiah felt like he somehow had a right to the land."

"This is so strange. Isn't this strange? Come now, Ailey, admit it. Or do I have to make a chicken face?"

"Uncle Root, stop! I'm trying to be serious here! Yes, I must say, I was very surprised to discover that information. So you didn't know about this?"

"No, I did not."

"But what about that stuff that Tommy Jr. kept? How come you didn't look at them . . ." I stopped. I had to remember this conversation was being recorded. We weren't just sitting up over coffee. "I mean, before your white half brother, Thomas Pinchard Jr., donated the family papers to the Old South Collections, did you have a chance to peruse those documents?"

"I did," Uncle Root said. "Actually, it was me who kept those three boxes of papers all that time. And a good thing. Otherwise, when the old plantation house burned down in 1934, those papers would have been destroyed."

"Really? There was another fire on Wood Place?"

"Oh yes. But nobody ever found out who burned it down or why."

"Is there a reason you chose not to look at the papers?"

"I tried once. But when I started looking through the documents from the very early years, I became enraged. Just because I'm an historian, doesn't mean I don't have feelings. And when I began to read, I got so angry, it seemed like I was vibrating! The casual way Samuel Pinchard talking about buying and selling and owning human beings. And some of those were my ancestors. I was afraid I'd do something stupid, like set those papers on fire. That's why I asked Tommy Jr. to donate them."

"May I ask, what is your response to learning that you're related to the Franklins?"

"Honestly, I'm a little confused, and I tend to be a clear thinker. You know, my father used to talk so badly about those Franklins. He did it constantly, sometimes right to their faces. He had abso-

lutely no respect for them. Called them white trash. Said they didn't
have the gumption to make their own way and that's why they
needed to lie about having a right to Wood Place. And here his own
mother was a Franklin! No wonder they were so angry. Not that it
excuses their behavior. There's never an excuse for membership in
the Klan or for murder."

"Do you think Meema—Eliza Two Freeman—knew about the
Franklins' relationship to your father's family?

"If she did, she never spoke about it in front of me. But Meema
never spoke about her relationship to Big Thom, either. She never
said a thing about his father and hers being half brothers. My mother
is the one who told me. It was a long time before I even knew that
Meema originally had been a Pinchard. My mother said the old lady
took the last name Freeman right after the Civil War. Meema didn't
say much, but when she did speak, she was a very direct person. A
straight shooter, as they say. My mother said Meema was furious
when Pearl was born looking just like Big Thom. Said my mother
had shamed the family. Pearl even had blond hair as a little girl,
before it darkened. There was a real social stigma placed on Negro
women engaging in those sorts of relationships; they were seen as
consorting with the enemy, but my father didn't seem to care about
stigmas on either side. He even bought her a wedding band, and
she wore it until she died. My mother wasn't demonstrative with
him, but he appeared to be very devoted to her."

"Dr. Hargrace, do you mind telling me one of your earliest memories?"

"I do remember my mother's funeral quite vividly, because my
father tried to throw himself into the coffin!"

"Really?"

"Oh yes! And it was shocking, even for me, and I was a little boy.
You know, white people don't usually carry on at funerals like we
Negroes do. Big Thom had been well behaved at the church service.
Nobody was going to tell him, it wasn't seemly for him to be there,
back in 1918, and holding the hands of his two Negro children. I
tried to pull away from him, but he wouldn't let me go. And then,

when we got to the cemetery out on the farm, he broke down, good-fashion. His face turned red and he started jumping around and flapping his arms. He kept screaming, 'Don't leave me, Lil' May! Don't leave me, honey!' I thought he was about to die, too, so I started crying, and then my father ran toward the coffin. It took six grown Negroes to hold him back, right before he fainted. Oh, they talked about that for a while! How a grown white man had acted more colored than anybody else at a Negro homegoing."

"Do you remember anything else?"

"Nothing special. We lived on the farm and there were animals and a big garden and there were cotton fields. Things like that. And when I was a little boy, they started planting soybeans so the soil wouldn't give out."

"And what about your . . . your unique interracial family situation?"

More of his laughter.

"Oh, we're calling it that! Well, my white father kept his promise to my Negro mother and took care of my sister and me. Pearl was eighteen when my mother died, and so she took over raising me. And my father provided the financial support. He bought all our clothes. He kept us in the house on his land that my mother had lived in. Miss Rose still lives in that same house. And he let us keep the beautiful furniture he gave my mother. I have some of it in my own house. Before my sister was born, there wasn't even a school for Negro children in town. Big Thom paid for the supplies for that school. I guess he called himself being a nice, white man doing that! And after he passed away, my brother, Tommy Jr., paid. My father sent me to Routledge College, and when he died, Tommy Jr. continued to pay for my education all through graduate school. Tommy bought me my first car. He put money in the bank for me. He even came north for my marriage to Olivia, and I lied to her family that he was Negro, though he didn't look it. At the reception, he took out his NAACP membership card and showed it around. I must say, that blew my mind!"

"What was your relationship to your brother? Was it close?"

"Not really, though he was crazy about Pearl. And he seemed to be fine with having Negro siblings. Maybe because he had grown up with my mother. She'd been his nanny for a few years. He didn't remember his own mother, of course. She had died when he was only a few days old."

"And, if you don't mind, what about your mother? What do you remember about her?"

"I loved her very much. Very much. She was very affectionate with my sister and me, which helped with our situation. Before my mother died, when she took Pearl and me out, white people stared at us like we were animals in a zoo. Negroes, they pretended there wasn't any difference, except my mother didn't have any friends outside of her brothers and their wives and children, and sometimes I had to fight in the schoolyard when the other Negro children would call me names. My mother and Pearl had warned me not to tattle on those children to the teacher, because their parents were sharecroppers on Big Thom's land. I didn't want to get their families in trouble. But whites? Every time they saw my mother with my sister and me, they acted like they'd heard the news for the first time. There was a lot of shame. I remember that. So much shame. I was very sad all the time. Until I met Olivia, I used to wish I'd never been born."

He cleared his throat several times. I didn't want to interject. I'd heard so many of the old man's stories, but I'd never heard this one. Nor had I ever witnessed this unabashed pain. Uncle Root needed to tell me everything. He was six months away from being a century old. If not now, when?

"Maybe my mother loved my father. I don't know, but it took me a while to consider that she might have taken up with Big Thom so her family would be taken care of. So they could stay on the land. What she went through, the humiliation in the community, so that her children and her family could be safe in this backwoods town. But as far as I know, she was never with another man. Big Thom and she doted on Pearl and me. She told us not to be embarrassed about the way we looked. My one regret is that my mother couldn't read or write, but she did love when I read to her. I was a really early reader. I'm not sure who taught me, but I could read very big books. *A Tale of Two Cities* was her favorite. She didn't care much for Shake-speare, but the way Dickens turned a phrase for her, she absolutely loved it! When I was little, I tried to teach her to read, many times. It never worked, but she could memorize long passages of Dickens or the Bible—anything—simply by hearing them out loud. She was a very brilliant woman. My sister was like that, too, and she never learned to read and write, either. I know now that Mama and Pearl probably suffered from what we call dyslexia, but back then, nobody knew what that was. The teachers at Red Mound didn't even know how to address the situation. Mostly, they thought Pearl was incor-rigibly stupid. Who knows how many other children never lived up to their potential because of something we hadn't even discovered? As a Negro man, I am very aware of my blessings. I'm lucky. So are you, Ailey. Do you know that?"

"Yes, sir, I do. Is there anything else you'd like to tell me?"

"Well, you can tell by looking at me that I could have passed. I could have gone to a school up north, a college with whites, and none of them would have known. I've found that only Negroes seem to recognize the little signs that give our race away. But I needed to be with my own and work among them. I've never regretted my decision to make my life here, among my people. I've been very happy. Very blessed. And I hope I may be allowed a bit of sentimen-tality when I say, Ailey Pearl, you make me so proud. You make our family proud. And my mother is smiling down at you from Heaven. I feel it."

"Dr. Hargrace, thank you so much for your time."

"Sugarfoot, it was my absolute pleasure."

MAMA'S BIBLE

❖

I'd planned to conduct my interview with Miss Rose on the same day I spoke with Uncle Root, but I found myself exhausted after talking to the old man. He told me that was to be expected. When we speak about history, we speak about somebody's life. This wasn't a television show or a play on a stage. So I called out to the farm and rescheduled my sit-down with Miss Rose for the next day.

When I drove up, she was sitting on the porch, peeling tomatoes. I leaned in for my kiss. She forgot her hands were wet with tomato juice and put a hand up to my face.

"I'm going to record you, if that's all right, Miss Rose. This will be a little formal. I'm going to ask you a bunch of questions. If you get uncomfortable, you just tell me."

"All right, baby."

There was a little table on the porch where Miss Rose had placed glasses of sweet tea. I moved one of the glasses aside and set up the tape recorder.

"This is Ailey Pearl Garfield. I'm interviewing Mrs. Miss Rose Collins Driskell, a resident of Chicasetta, Georgia. Today's date is July 24, 2007. Mrs. Driskell, do you give me permission to record our conversation?"

"Yes, I do."

"Mrs. Driskell, in what year were you born?"

"Oh, I ain't your granny no more?"

I laughed. So much for my acting in my official capacity as an historian. "You'll always be my granny!"

"I'm just teasing you, baby! Now, what you ask me again?"

"In what year were you born?"

"All right. Me and Huck was born on December third, nineteen and twenty. I done lived on this farm since that day. Never have lived no place else. Huck ain't never been no place at all. He don't like to leave home, but I done been to Atlanta, Milledgeville, and Macon."

"Huck would be Henry John Collins Jr. Is that correct?"

"Yes, that's my brother's name. We'se twins."

"And who are your parents?

"My daddy was named Henry John Collins Sr. My mama was named Pearl Thomasina Freeman. You want me to keep going back?"

"Yes, ma'am, if you would."

"My mama's mama was named Maybelline Victorina Freeman. They called her Lil' May. And my granddaddy was Thomas John Pinchard Sr. They called him Big Thom. He was a white man. He was fat, too. That's what they say. Grandma's mama was named Sheba Freeman. We ain't never know the name of Lil' May's daddy. He run off before somebody could make him do right. Sheba's mama was named Eliza Two Freeman. We called her Meema. Her husband was named Red. That was Sheba's daddy. They ain't have no more kids. Red used to live on the Benjamin Plantation. The Benjamins was Jewish folks. But then, after Red took up with Eliza, he moved to Wood Place. He used to be Red Benjamin, but he changed his name to Freeman, too. Red and Eliza, they was married official by a preacher after the war, but they had done took up before then. I do know that. But he died when he was young. Lockjaw. And Meema, she ain't never marry again. She didn't take up with no more mens, neither. Maybe it was 'cause of them scars on her face. She had these marks, real deep. Like that." Miss Rose ran her index finger over one cheek and then the other. "She was old when I was born, but she would have been a right pretty lady. Them marks kinda messed with her looks, though. You want to know about Grandma Maybelline's brothers and sisters and all that?"

"That's fine for now, if you don't mind, Mrs. Driskell. We'll probably come back to that at another time, though."

"All that's in Mama's Bible, if you want to see it."

"Dear Pearl kept a Bible?" I felt a rumble in my flesh: I'd found more documentation. "I mean, Mrs. Pearl Collins kept a Bible?"

"Shole did. She had me write down the names that she could re-member, before she died."

"Oh, excellent! Can I see that later?"

"You shole can, baby."

"Now, can you tell me your earliest memory of your time on Wood Place?"

"All right, let me see," she said. "When I was 'bout five years old, I ate too many peaches at preserve time and I got the worst ache in my stomach. Then my bowels got so loose, but my mama say, she ain't feel sorry for me. She say, it was my own fault 'cause she had done told me to stop eating them peaches, but when her back was turned, there I go. But Meema, she give me something, some kind of tea, and that stopped me going to the outhouse. When Meema died, she was past ninety, and she knowed all kind of things. Like that time you got stung by that wasp in the church outhouse, and I chewed up that tobacco and put it on there and it drawed out the pain. You remember that, baby?"

"Yes, ma'am, I certainly do remember. It was an efficacious treat-ment."

"What's that mean?"

"It means it worked!"

"I know that's right! Meema taught me 'bout that tobacco."

"How did she learn those things?"

"She say it was her own grandma. She was a Indian woman."

"Really? Do you know the name of Meema's grandmother?"

"They called her Aggie, and sometimes, Mama Gee. Ain't no-body know what her husband's name was, though. But they say the grandma had long hair, near-abouts to her knees."

Though I hadn't eaten anything that day—I'd been waiting until after this interview was over—my stomach lurched. Sweat broke out on my forehead.

"What's wrong, baby?" Miss Rose asked. "You want a drink of water?"

"Um . . . no. I'm all right. You were saying that Aggie had hair to her knees?"

"Real, real long. And she frown all the time. Don't never crack a smile. You sure you okay?"

"Um . . . no . . . I'm good . . . um . . ."

Miss Rose waved at a fruit fly. Asked me, did I mind going inside and getting a church fan out of the china cabinet? There was a whole stack of them. I clicked off the recording, grateful for a break. In the front room, I leaned against the china cabinet, breathed through my mouth. In my head, I heard Lydia's laughter. A familiar voice from my dreams joined her laughter, and I reached for a chair. I called through the screen door, give me another second. I was still looking for the fans.

When I returned, I turned the recorder back on, asking her, did she remember anything else from her childhood?

"Lots of things," Miss Rose said. "I remember a white man done came up here one day. He had some kind of contraption in the back of his car, say he want to sit it on the porch and let folks sing in it. My daddy knew them songs they used to sing in the fields and even before that. Oh, that man had a voice! Just like your uncle Huck. Meema, she ain't want Daddy to sing, but he say the man seemed all right as far as white people go. He sure was polite, I know that. When he tried to get Meema to sing, she say to that white man, say, 'I don't serve the Devil no more. I used to chop down that cotton in my time, yes, sir, but I don't chop nothing for the Devil, even if he do be a white man. Jesus and the Devil, they coming up the same road, just different sides. I guess they meet up at the crossing. I know that's blaspheme, but it's the truth. I knows it, 'cause I done seen it in a dream.' Everybody on that porch except that white man knew Meema ain't never chopped no cotton a day in her life, but nobody was gone contradict."

"How old were you then, Mrs. Driskell?"

"Me and Huck, we must have been about thirteen, and my baby sister, Annie Mae, she was little. About six or seven. She was Mama's surprise baby. Mama had lost some babies, and Uncle Tommy had took her to the doctor in town, and the doctor say, my mama couldn't have no more kids, but then here Annie Mae came. That was a long time after I ate all them peaches, but I still wouldn't eat them. I wouldn't eat peaches for years after that, until one time, Sister Johnson brought the best peach cobbler to church for fourth Sunday. I don't know what-all she put in that cobbler, but, child, I smelled it and just like that, peaches didn't make me sick no more. I wished my mama had asked Sister Johnson for that recipe, because I have tried and tried to make that cobbler, but I can't never get it right."

"So, the man came with his contraption that day . . ."

"Oh! I'm sorry, baby! Yes, the white man, he done came up to the house with his contraption, and when he said he'd heard tell Meema remembered things before Emancipation, I ain't even know what he was talking about."

"He knew she had been enslaved?"

"That's what he meant. But at the time, I was thinking, what that white man mean by Emancipation? Grown folks used to talk about slavery and freedom, but they ain't never use that word. He asked Meema what her last name was back in that time, and I could see she didn't want to say, but Negroes back then, we was afraid of the government. And this was a white man from the government. Uncle Tommy was alive back then, but still."

"This would be Thomas Pinchard Jr?"

"That was his government name. He was Mama's brother, but his daddy was related to Meema in some other kind of way, too. We was all related in betwixt and between. Kinda nasty if you ask me, but folks did that kind of thing back then, messing 'round with they cousins.

"And didn't nobody want to talk about how white men loved to chase them some Negro ladies. In this town, you can't go back but so far without finding out colored folks and white people is kin, but Uncle Tommy, he was good white folks. Not like the rest. He loved us, used to visit us on Sunday until the day he died. He give us what you call protection, but even Uncle Tommy couldn't beat the government. I could see that Meema was scared of that white man with the contraption, and she didn't scare easy. She told him what her name used to be, before she changed it. When I was a little girl, she was Eliza Two Freeman. All the folks on Wood Place besides us called her Miss Liza. But she was born Eliza Two Pinchard. The white man, he wrote that down and ask her some more questions. He want Meema to go back as far as she could remember."

I got a jolt of excitement again: it sounded like the white man had been part of the WPA project, recording the lives of formerly enslaved folks. If so, there would be a written narrative of Meema's recollections—and if I was really lucky maybe even the voice recordings the interviewer had made. But I still wanted to hear what Miss Rose had to say.

"What else did she remember?"

"Like what-all the slaves ate back then. Collards and turnip greens. Sweet potatoes. Pecans when they fell from the tree. Peanuts. Meema called them goobers, but same thing. Blackberries. Streak-o-lean and pig's feet. Stuff like that. Same food I eat that your mama be fussing at me about. I don't know what she saying, talking 'bout, don't eat no pork. What kind of colored folks don't eat no pork? That's just foolish talk."

"So, the white man and Meema talked . . ."

"They shole did. She wasn't giving him no big piece of information, not at first, but that white man's pen was moving across that paper like lightning, putting down things. He wrote down what-all her master planted: cotton in the big fields, a big vegetable garden for the big house, and that big peach orchard. That orchard burned down same time as the big house burned down. What's there now is what the fire ain't eat. You think that's a lot of peach trees now, but that orchard was big."

"Is that what the man asked Meema? About the fire?"

"No, that fire was after that white man. And that won't the first fire, neither. It was a bunch of them. Looked like somebody always was setting fires on Wood Place, but Meema wouldn't have told that man, no way. Not unless he asked her direct. She and that white man, they talked awhile about what work she had did in slavery time. She never would tell him she worked up there in the big house.

I don't know why. She told him how the cotton harvest went. What work the women did. What work the men did. He asked her about her family. She stayed quiet a long time. Then she said they was all dead. Her granny, her sister, her mama, her daddy. He tried to get her to tell him more about her family, but she wouldn't. Every time he would try to get to her talk about them, she'd raise her hand. He left, but that night, she wouldn't eat supper. She died 'bout a year after that."

"Did Meema ever talk about slavery to you, Mrs. Driskell?"

"She never did. But my mama, she knowed some things. It took a long time for me to find out. I was a grown lady when I found out. I thought it would make me feel better, to know, but that ain't happen. Mama told me Meema ain't want to talk about none of that to nobody. It cut her heart to bleeding even thinking about it, but Meema had told the white man the truth. Her daddy had ran off. Her mama lost her mind and died. Her grandma died. Her sister died. Meema and her was twins, like me and Huck. She used to get up in the middle of the night, screaming, 'Rabbit, Rabbit!'

"That's what Meema's sister was named. I don't know why somebody want to name her that, but they did. Meema be looking straight ahead, singing and crying. Used to be singing in words didn't nobody understand."

She sighed, moving the church fan. I waited for her to speak again.

"Them was hard times, baby. You understand me? Real hard times. White peoples, they was mean to coloreds. Y'all young folks don't know how mean they was. Ain't nobody gone kill a colored man for looking at a white woman now, but they would do them kind of things back then. They was killing colored men like it was Judgment Day. Hadn't been for Uncle Tommy, I don't know how hard it would have been for my family. My mama was a good-looking woman. Ain't no telling what some white man would have did to her if it hadn't been for Uncle Tommy. Ain't no telling what would have happened to my daddy trying to protect her. Uncle Tommy kept us safe. He was a good Christian. He was, but I ain't want to always be standing in no white man's shade. And all this time, I been asking myself, why couldn't them crackers just leave us colored folks alone? Let me tell you something. That white man with his contraption, he killed Meema. That's what he did, bringing all that up. He broke her heart. I loved Meema. She used to give me candy. Used to save it in her bureau drawer just for me. She was a good woman."

She took off her glasses. Covered her face. There was another long silence.

"I wish that white man never had came up here that day! I wish to God he never had!"

Her voice had lifted to an anguished shriek. I told her I hadn't meant to make her sad, but she didn't reply. The tape recorder kept rolling for the next fifteen minutes, as we didn't speak. Then my granny told me she was tired. She couldn't talk about this no more. She was gone lay down.

I stood first, holding out my hands. As she took them, I thanked her for her time.

"You welcome, baby. I'll see you on Sunday, at church."

LIKE AGATHA CHRISTIE

❖

After twenty years, Miss Sharon, Miss Cordelia's maid, had stopped pressing her hair: gray dreadlocks fell to her shoulders. There were glasses, too, but the smile with the glint of gold remained. She led me into the living room, where Miss Cordelia sat on the claw-foot sofa. There was a blanket over her legs. Her own hair was thinner, tinted a bluish color.

"My, you've grown, Ailey!"

"I'm thirty-four, Miss Cordelia."

Her arms shook a bit when she reached for me. I leaned and pecked on her cheek, hoping I wouldn't sneeze from her face powder. I didn't pull out my tape recorder yet. That shouldn't be the way, so I thanked Miss Sharon when she brought in the tea and the pound cake. I chatted about my family and graduate school. Waited until Miss Cordelia asked, did I still want to interview her?

"Yes, ma'am, I sure do! But only if that's all right."

"It sure is. I've been looking forward to this all week, ever since Root called me."

"Is it all right if I record you? I don't want to forget anything."

"Oh, this is so exciting!"

I pulled out the recorder. "This is Ailey Pearl Garfield. I am interviewing Mrs. Cordelia Pinchard Rice, a resident of Chicasetta, Georgia. Today's date is July 25, 2007. Mrs. Rice, do you give me permission to record our conversation?"

"I do, but you don't have to be so formal. You can call me Miss Cordelia."

We ran through the preliminary questions, beginning with her date and place of birth.

She laughed. "A true lady doesn't tell her age, Ailey. But all right, I was born July fifteenth, 1925."

"We have the same birthday, Miss Cordelia!"

"Well, I'll be!"

Then we turned to her parents' names and first memories.

"My mother's name was Lucille Sweet Pinchard. My father's name was Thomas John Pinchard Jr. I was born on Wood Place Plantation and lived there until it burned down. I was about nine then."

"Were you there when the fire started?"

"No, we were out of town. Mother and Daddy and I had driven to Atlanta to visit some people, and when we returned two days later, the plantation house was burned to the ground. Our furniture was in the house, our clothes, all our belongings. Mother took on something awful. 'My fur! My fur!' she screamed. Daddy had bought her a fur coat for Christmas, which was rather silly. How often can you wear a fur coat in Georgia? But Mother just loved that coat. Her daddy owned a few houses in town, and he gave this house to her. He was a rich man. After the fire, Daddy used to take me out to the farm to visit with the coloreds—I mean, Black people—and I would play with their children." She looked at me, blushing. "I'm an old lady, Ailey. Please forgive me."

I pretended to be clueless, furrowing my brow.

"Forgive you for what?"

"I have a hard time remembering what to call your people. There have been so many changes over the years. It's so hard to keep up."

"Miss Cordelia, don't you even worry about that." I was just grateful the lady didn't know any other names for Black people, because I needed this interview for my dissertation.

"You are so sweet."

"Thank you, Miss Cordelia. So are you." I picked up the recorder from the coffee table, moving a touch closer. "So . . . you used to play with the African American children on Wood Place?"

"Oh yes, but Mother didn't like it. She was very old-fashioned, but Daddy, he got along with everybody."

"Miss Cordelia, do you remember any of your other ancestors, before your mother and father?"

"Let's see. Big Thom's wife was Sarah Dawson Pinchard. They called her 'Sally.' She died having my father. Big Thom's father was Victor Thomas Pinchard, and his mother was named Grace. I don't know her maiden name. Big Thom had a twin sister, Petunia. Victor's father was Samuel, and his mother was named Eliza, but they called her 'Lady.' They said she was very beautiful, but we don't have any pictures of her. Samuel was the first person in these parts. There was nothing here when he came. Nothing but a bunch of trees and some savage Indians."

I needed to finish this dissertation. I really, really did, so I couldn't get insulted. And I repeated my need to myself when Miss Cordelia told me she never could have children, and since there weren't any other Pinchards besides her, she was the last of the line. I knew better than to bring up Dear Pearl's children. To mention that I was a direct Pinchard descendant.

"The doctors told me there was nothing wrong with me, but I just never did get pregnant, Ailey. It was the strangest thing. It took me a long time to stop being sad, but the year before he died, my husband, Horace, told me, we were enough for each other. It took him long enough to say it, but I'm glad he did. He gave me plenty trouble, but he was all right. He gave nice presents, especially when he'd been bad."

"Miss Cordelia, can you tell me your first memory?"

"Hmm. Well, I don't know if this is my first memory, but I hope this one will do. I was about four, so this was before everything burned down. Jinx Franklin came up to the house and knocked on the front door. He lived on our land and farmed for us, just like the coloreds—I mean, Black people. He was what we used to call 'white trash.' We only had three girls working in the house. There was Hettie. She was my nanny. I loved her as much as Mother, maybe even more. May Lois did the cooking, though she wasn't that good at it. I don't know why Mother tolerated her. Lacie was the maid. She cleaned the house. Lacie was younger and quite pretty. Probably younger than you. Mother didn't like her, but Daddy wouldn't let her fire her, because she was related to Root and Pearl somehow. I heard Mother say that she didn't trust a Pinchard man around a good-looking colored girl to save her soul. Because of Lil' May and Big Thom and all that. Am I being rude to bring that up?"

I kept my arm steady. "No, ma'am. Not at all. If I may say so, that's pretty common knowledge."

She giggled. "I guess it was! Anyway, we had some boys that used to work around the house, taking care of the cows and chickens and yard and such, but I don't remember their names. I do know that one of the boys was old, maybe my age now, but he got around well without a cane or anything. Do you notice that older people aren't as spry as they used to be? I wonder why that is. Root tells me, 'Cordelia, it's because of all the chemicals they put in the water and the food. They're poisoning us.' But I don't know."

"That's certainly something to think about."

"What was I talking about, Ailey?"

"You were mentioning that Mr. Franklin showed up that day at the house."

"That's right! That awful Jinx showed up to the front door, and Hettie answered, because Lacie was upstairs cleaning. We'd been playing a game. Hettie was fat, and she was out of breath. When she got to the door, she told Jinx to go around to the back, and he asked her why. She said, he knew why, and if he didn't, she didn't have time to tell him. Couldn't he see she was busy with Miss Cordelia? And, oh, he got so upset and took on! He started cussing up a blue streak right there on the front porch. And then, he called Hettie a bad word."

"What did Jinx call Hettie?"

"I can't say that word. All my life I haven't said that word, and I will not start now. Only the worst trash uses those words. And, my, those Franklins were just the rudest, most ill-mannered trash on God's green earth. The children used to stick their tongues out at me when Daddy drove us to town for church. I couldn't stand them!"

I shifted again. I wanted to ask about the Franklins. If the old man had been perplexed by the information that I'd given him, I suspected it would be worse with Miss Cordelia.

"Um . . . may I ask, did anyone in your family . . . um . . . ever tell you of a blood tie between the Pinchards and the Franklins?"

"A blood tie? What do you mean?"

"I mean . . . um . . . did anyone ever talk about you possibly being related to the Franklins?"

"Related? Of course not!"

"So . . . you never heard anything about that from your father, maybe? He never mentioned that?"

"No, he did not! I think I would remember something so ridiculous! What in the world are you talking about?"

Her voice rose, and soon, Miss Sharon had padded into the room. "Ma'am? Did you need something?"

"Bring me my fan!"

Miss Sharon widened her eyes at me: *What did you do?* When she returned with an Oriental-printed fan, I held out my hand, but the old lady grabbed it, saying she could fan herself. She wasn't that old.

"Miss Cordelia, I'm so sorry, ma'am," I said. "I didn't mean to insult you."

The fan fluttered. "There are just too many gossips in this town! And those Franklins always have been liars! I heard the one who's a policeman is halfway decent, but I don't believe it. I've never met a Franklin worth a nickel with a hole in it."

"Miss Cordelia, please forgive me. Will you accept my apology?"

She sighed and put the fan in her lap. "I suppose so, Ailey. As long as you promise not to repeat any more nasty gossip."

"I promise. You know, we historians have to track down every lead, even the false ones. We're like detectives."

"Like Agatha Christie?"

She laughed, and I joined her, relieved.

"Yes, ma'am! Exactly. Only, without all the trains and fancy clothes." I reached to the coffee table. I placed my hand on the recorder. "Would it be all right if we got back to your story, Miss Cordelia? Or are you too tired? Would you like to rest?"

"You are so sweet. No, I think I'm all right."

"Thank you so much. Gosh, I really appreciate you. Now, can you remember what happened after the fire at the big house?"

"Yes, I think so. After everything burned up, I was not sad at all to leave the country, but Mother never got past leaving. She said it was a shame not to try to rebuild the old house back up. She died when I was still a girl. I was heartbroken, but I was happy she passed on before Daddy did. She would have been so angry to find out the farm doesn't even belong to us anymore."

"It doesn't? Who does the farm belong to?"

"Why, Ailey, it belongs to your family."

"My family?"

"Yes, Ailey. Didn't you know that?"

"Um . . . no, ma'am."

"Well, I'll be. I thought Root or Miss Rose surely would have told you. You mean to tell me, after all these years, people think it's still mine? Daddy had sold about half the land and left that money to me. It was a lot. The other half, he willed to Root and Pearl."

"Did everyone know it was our land?"

"Oh my, no! It was a secret. Even my husband didn't know."

"Why do you think no one was told?"

"I guess because some people weren't very nice to coloreds— Black people—and such back then. And Root and Pearl and me, we didn't want any fuss or trouble. But I think things worked out just fine, don't you?"

"Yes, ma'am. I guess they did. All right, I think that's it, Miss Cordelia. Thank you so much for your time."

I turned off the recorder and slipped it into my bag.

"We're done already? I swan, I haven't had this much fun in years! The next time you come back, we'll have to talk more about Horace. He was a rascal, but so good-looking! I've lived an exciting life for an old lady. I don't have any complaints."

"Well, I just thank you so much again, Miss Cordelia. You are so wonderful to talk to me."

I rose, but she grabbed my hand. I couldn't hover over an old lady; that wouldn't be polite, so I sat down on the sofa.

"Ailey . . . I want to say I'm sorry. About . . . you know . . . all the things that happened . . . you know . . . slavery and that."

I suppressed a sigh. I was tired. I didn't feel like playing my role in this script.

"It's all right, Miss Cordelia. It's not your fault. Slavery happened before you were even born."

"No, Ailey, I really mean it. I'm just so sorry. But colored and white—Black and white, I mean—don't you think there's always been love between our families? Because I love Root so much. And I loved Pearl when she was alive. My daddy did, too. Pearl was . . . she was . . . she was my daddy's baby sister, and Root was his baby brother. Did you know that?"

"Yes, ma'am, I did know."

The times had changed so much, ever since Miss Cordelia had been born, but she was trying to give me something here. She wanted to ease a weight off her conscience. What she was offering me wasn't going to alter history or bring anyone back from the dead. But at least she finally had acknowledged that my family was her family. What could I gain from berating an old lady who couldn't even walk across the room without help?

"And yes, ma'am, Miss Cordelia. There sure has been love between us. All the love in the world."

But when I stood again, she still wouldn't let my hand go. She asked, I wasn't leaving just yet, was I? It was almost time for her afternoon soap operas. Miss Sharon always watched with her. We could all watch together, and there was plenty cake, if I wanted another piece.

I'd been looking forward to typing up my notes from the recording that afternoon. Then, too, when I arrived back at the old man's house, I was planning to fuss at him for keeping information from me, once again. Uncle Root thought he was slick: all these years, the family farm had belonged to him and no one else knew it. But I couldn't just grab my historical information and rush off. That wouldn't be kind.

I sat back down.

"More cake sounds lovely, Miss Cordelia."

NOT HASTY

❖

At the hospital, David unwrapped a peppermint and popped it into his mouth. He pulled out a small cologne sample from his pants pocket and dabbed a drop behind each ear with his index finger.

"How I look?" he asked.

"You look okay," I said.

"How I smell?" He lifted one arm and then the other, sniffing.

"Who are you trying to impress? Stop all that."

Another early morning phone call, only two weeks after I'd returned to North Carolina. This time, my mother had been weeping violently.

"What's wrong, Mama? Slow down, now."

"Ailey, he's in the hospital. They moved him to Atlanta."

"Who, Mama?"

"Root! The doctor at Crawford Long said it's only gone be a couple of days."

"You mean until he's dead? Are you serious? What happened?"

"They don't know, Ailey. His blood pressure kept spiking, and he was having trouble breathing. His regular doctor had him airlifted to Atlanta. Said they didn't have time for me to drive him. Ailey, please come. I don't know if I can go through this without you. Coco offered to fly down, but you know she's working."

"Of course I'll come, but can I borrow a few dollars? I'll pay you back when my fellowship check comes."

I put aside my panic and fear and moved into autopilot. I slid from under the sheets, dragging the phone cord to the closet. Something in case there was a funeral, dark this time. My navy crepe.

"You don't have to pay me back. It's all right. Thank you, baby. Mama loves you so much." I'd known it was critical when she'd referred to herself in the third person.

I grabbed David's hand, preparing myself to see Uncle Root lying against the hospital pillows, his fluffy, silver hair combed out. Wearing the silk pajamas that he favored, pressed by one of his many female relatives who were scheduled to drive over in shifts. Tears filled my eyes. David pulled me into a tight hug, kissing the top of my head.

"Aw, sweetheart. Everyone's got to pass."

"Your platitudes aren't consoling me, David."

"It might not be what you want to hear, but we've all got to go. Dr. Hargrace has had a long and good life, so don't cry, okay? Your mama and granny will be upset as it is. You've got to be strong now. That's your job."

"You're a little funky under your pits," I said. "Now that you mention it."

He pulled the tiny bottle of cologne back out.

In the hospital room, Uncle Root was perched on the edge of his hospital bed. He was telling a story, his head thrown back dramatically. Mama sat in the armchair by the door. She shook her head, grinning.

The old man held out his hands and David helped him down from the bed.

"Dr. Hargrace, you're looking well! This is a wonderful surprise. God is so good."

"He sure is! Don't count me out just yet." He turned to me and opened his arms. "There's my young scholar. What you know, sugarfoot? Coming to take me away from all this?"

The doctor decided not to keep Uncle Root for another day, saying he'd made a miraculous recovery for ninety-nine. Maybe it was the garlic he was eating, but it went without saying that he should take it easy.

––––––

Back at home Uncle Root shuffled into his study and stayed until I went in after him. I hovered, putting a palm on his shoulder, hoping he took the touch as love and not as a caution. If he fell, I could catch him before he hit the ground.

"What did I do with it?" A pile of books overturned and slid to the floor. He opened the drawers on his oak desk.

"Do with what? Uncle Root be careful, please. You know what the doctor said."

"Ah! Here it is!" He held up a bottle. "David's coming over this evening. You think he'll like this?"

"I'm sure, but you know he has to drive back to Atlanta."

"His mother lives not even a mile away. And if it gets too late, there's the other guest room. Unless you want to sneak him into your room."

He wiggled his eyebrows.

"Uncle Root, stop that! You ought to be ashamed of yourself."

"I know I should. However, I am not."

That evening Uncle Root, Mama, David, and I sat at the dining room table, eating pie. The old man had begged Mama to go in the kitchen and make some strong coffee; at his age, the caffeine couldn't hurt him anymore. When we moved into the living room, the old man produced the scotch, and Mama rose from her chair.

"I don't know about y'all, but I have to get up in the morning. Baybay, I'm sure Cloletha is wondering where you are."

"No, ma'am, she knows, and might I say, your coffee was downright heavenly. You should give me the recipe."

"It's ground coffee beans and water and a coffee maker. It's written on the back of the package."

"It was scrumptious all the same, Mrs. Garfield."

As she left, she giggled. "Lord have mercy, that boy."

"As I was saying, Du Bois had the right idea," Uncle Root said. "Yes, he ruled out some good men and women, but his principles continue to be effective."

"Dr. Hargrace, every time we get together, you know I'm going to take Booker T. Washington's side. He was for the Black community. All of it, not just one-tenth of one percent."

The old man lifted his index finger into the air; it shook slightly.

"And every time we have this same argument, you know I'm on the side of the great scholar."

"I know, but listen"—David picked up his glass from the marble-topped coffee table—"listen, now, if we let go of poor folks in this community, who's going to be left? A bunch of bourgie, light-skinned niggers—sorry, no offense—"

"—none taken—"

"—walking around with their behinds on their shoulders? Who was out there marching back in the civil rights movement? Working-class Black folks. Who was the majority getting lynched during Jim Crow days? Working-class Black folks. What about my mama and daddy? Neither one of them have been to college. What about Mrs. Garfield's brother? What about Miss Rose? Those are the folks Booker T. Washington was trying to protect. And I doubt when Dr. Du Bois was making up his Talented Tenth that he was even talking about all of us with degrees. I graduated from Morehouse and Emory, but dark as I am, would I even have counted to him? And don't get me started on how he left the States and ran to President Nkrumah in Ghana. What kind of devotion to the race is that?"

The old man nodded slowly, taking it all in. "All right. May I rebut?"

"You may."

"Though you resent his retreat to Ghana, Dr. Du Bois had a reason for that. He'd been accused of being a communist during the Red Scare. And even though he escaped imprisonment, what kind of peace could he have in this country after that? Further, there are plenty Negroes in Africa, and many of them are quite dark-skinned. But I'll give you the desertion charge. I'll give you that the great scholar wasn't looking out for all in our communities. I'll even give you that Booker T. Washington succeeded in doing just as much as Dr. Du Bois for the race, albeit in his own crude way, but David, you've got to admit that what Dr. Du Bois meant is everyone is not meant to be a leader of the race. Some folks bring us down, like that knucklehead Ailey brought to the picnic that time. What was his name?"

This had been a sore spot between us for a while. Even though I'd long stopped caring about Abdul, it still rubbed against my principles, the classist way Uncle Root low-rated him.

"You know his name," I said. "You might be old, but you ain't senile. At least, not yet."

"Ouch. I'll accept that insult because I love you so much. Oh yes, 'Abdul.' That was the knucklehead's name."

"You are so rude and snobby."

"Sugarfoot, I most certainly am not. What is it you young folks say?" He tapped his temple, then gestured widely with that hand. "Ah yes! I just keep it real."

"You were wrong. And Abdul was your fraternity brother, too?"

"Obviously, the standards for membership had been lowered since I'd joined the organization."

David broke in gently.

"Um, anyway, y'all, let me ask this. What did you think about the Million Man March? You know I attended—"

I gave a loud hoot: "Yeah, and that was some bullshit!"

Uncle Root giggled. "You are very loud. But I will not say you were wrong."

"Wait a minute," David said. "Don't you think the Million Man March was a good thing?"

I gave him the glass and told him, pour me some more scotch. When I took a drink, I expounded on my problems with that particular march. "Except for a bunch of crap rhetoric, what did them brothers, college educated or not, do at that march? And there was Farrakhan, trying to perpetuate like the second coming of Martin Luther King Jr."

"Ailey, we gave each other hope," David said. "Hope that brothers were going to work it out in this country. Like that Senator Obama, up in Chicago. He wants to help our people. And I think he could actually win, Ailey."

"There will never be a Black president in our lifetime," I said. "That is so ridiculous."

"I'd vote for him," David said. "And I know plenty other folks who would, too. And wouldn't that be something? A brother in the White House?"

"Oh, I've dreamed of such a day!" Uncle Root said. "To see a man my own color running this country."

"And what about a woman your own color?" I asked. "Why has that never occurred to you? I'll tell you why. Because you Black men need to get some feminist principles!"

A stream of raucous laughter from both men.

"What's so goddamned funny?" I asked.

"Negro men can't be feminists," the old man said. "That is a ridiculous notion."

"What about you, David?" I asked. "Would you call yourself a feminist?"

"I think I am," he said. "I mean, I've read my bell hooks, and she has some really great things to say."

"Is that so?" I asked. "Like what?"

"I've got to go back and read," he said. "I've had scotch. I can't quote right now. Dang."

"You are such a hypocrite," I said.

"Stop harassing him," the old man said.

"Uncle Root, you took Aunt Olivia's last name. If that's not a feminist act, I don't know what is."

"I liked the sound of it. And I liked the lady who had the name, too." Uncle Root winked broadly. "But honestly, Ailey, before we married, Olivia told me she wasn't about to take my name."

"Why not?" I asked.

"Olivia told me, it was one thing for her to carry her father's last name, because he was partly responsible for her being alive. But she wasn't about to carry some other man's load. She was a very independent woman. I was a young man with an ego, and that wrinkled me some, but when I thought on it, I stopped being bothered. You see, I was born with my mother's name, because I couldn't take my father's. Not as his legitimate child, because Georgia law didn't recognize our blood tie. My very presence was illegal. So I asked myself, what did it really matter if I took another woman's last name? Maybe if my mother had still been alive I wouldn't have, but she'd passed on by then."

"I guess I never thought about it like that," I said.

"And in this town, Ailey, if I hadn't changed my name, they wouldn't give a damn how many degrees I had or what I did for a living. All they were going to be thinking about was my white daddy. Like that peckerwood Jinx Franklin when I came back here."

David and I had heard the story many times, but we nestled into the cushions of the sofa.

"It was 1934, and Olivia had the summer off from her doctoral program at Mecca. I'd already finished with my program. I hadn't been home for a while, so we decided to drive down. It was a long journey in those days. When we finally arrived, I didn't want to wake Olivia. I stopped the car and left her napping and walked into Pinchard General Store, owned by my brother Tommy.

"I called myself 'passing,' though Tommy was in on the joke. I waited right in line with the whites, but when I emerged from the store, somebody recognized me. One of those Franklins.

"'Hey, you, boy! Jason Freeman!' That's what he said. And when he saw I hadn't learned a damned bit of sense, and thought I was better than God and six more men, he spat in the dust and called me a 'bastard.' Correction. He called me a 'half-nigger bastard.'"

David always had loved this story. "Aw, shit! Oops. Sorry."

"No need for apologies, my brother. By the time I was through, I showed him there wasn't any 'half' about it. But what made me go after him with the switchblade was that Jinx Franklin and his brothers had surrounded my car, and Olivia was awake."

I reached for my scotch glass again.

"Oh my God. Uncle Root, you never told me that."

"I thought I had," he said. "Yes, Ailey, those men were rocking the car back and forth. Poor Olivia was shrieking. Who knows what they were planning to do? I called out, 'You sumbitches! Get away from my woman!' I was scared to death that day, but I had to protect her. So now I hope I have sufficiently explained to you, David, why I am a follower of W. E. B. and not Booker T. If I had been a devotee of the second man, I wouldn't have had the courage to pull out my switchblade. And I hope I have explained to you, Ailey, why this Negro man is not a feminist. I wholeheartedly believe in equal rights for the sexes. If I didn't, I couldn't live among all you women. But there is one exception to my politics: I do not expect a lady to fight a man, white or otherwise, while I stand by and watch."

The man was old, and it was late. Or early, depending upon perspective. He extended both hands and David helped him rise from the wing chair. They walked slowly toward the stairs.

I propped open the front door and walked out to the glider, given to the old man when his sister had passed away and his niece had been so upset, she couldn't abide having her mother's things in sight.

The screen door creaked. David poked his head around the door.

"Hey, girl."

"Hey. Take a load off."

He slipped through the door and we sat together as the dark lightened. His arm around me, my head against his shoulder, until he said he needed to get back. He couldn't take another day off from work.

I knew he was going to kiss me. I'd sensed something alter between us as the birds forecast the day. And he did. It was even better than I recalled, not hasty or forbidden, but an exchange between two adults who weren't breaking any rules or betraying anyone. But I was taken aback when he asked for my number in North Carolina, when he said he didn't want to lose me again. It was a long-distance call, but he could afford it, if I could make the time. If I wanted to hear from him.

I told him he could have the number, but I'd decided to stay in Chicasetta for a while for my research. Dr. Whitcomb had told me I didn't have to be in town to work on my dissertation. I could email him the drafts of my chapters, and David told me he didn't know what-all that meant, but as long as I was in Chicasetta, that sounded real, real nice to him. And we sat there on the glider. And we kissed some more.

EVERY STRENGTH

❖

The spring after Uncle Root turned one hundred, Red Mound Church was designated an historical landmark. While they hadn't won the fight to keep the whole thing private, David and the old man had managed to work out certain provisions with the state. The farm would remain private. And the mound would be off-limits to visitors.

There had been changes at Red Mound. There was a plaque out front that identified the founding year of the church. And there was a new ramp for wheelchairs. Our church elder had retired, but his youngest son had taken over. This new Beasley was the first pastor who'd graduated college and who possessed a master's degree in theology. Frequently, his sermons focused on the beauty of nature: often on the mound in back of the church, where yellow sunflowers suddenly had joined the pink and blue wildflowers.

For the special dedication service, Elder Beasley the Younger asked Uncle Root to present the history of the church. It was only right: not only was he the oldest member, Uncle Root was the owner of the land on which the church resided. But Uncle Root asked me to do it. He was tired now, he told me.

Since I'd moved to Chicasetta, Uncle Root had been in and out of the hospital. He no longer hopped down from his bed. He could walk only a yard or two without leaning on someone's arm. My mother had a hospital bed installed in his dining room, after the table and chairs had been removed. He asked her to place them in storage. Under no circumstances was my mother to loan any of his furniture to Uncle Norman's wife. She might insist that she only wanted to borrow them, but once she got her hands on something, she'd never let it go.

That furniture was willed to me after he died, as well as the house itself. Every time Uncle Root talked about the items of my inheritance, I ordered him to change the subject. He'd make his silly face and tell me, since I'd commanded that he'd never die, God would certainly alter the cycle. He wasn't angry, though. He kept his patience with me and talked about God frequently. He didn't miss a Sunday service at church.

I didn't want to take Uncle Root's place at the dedication, but he'd scolded me. Other than him, who else knew more about the history leading up to the founding of the church? I'd read the papers of the Pinchard family. I knew the name of the first ancestor to arrive at Wood Place.

She was called Ahgayuh, also known as Aggie. Also known as Mama Gee. She married Midas and gave birth to Tess.

And Midas was sold, never to be heard from again.

And Tess married Nick and gave birth to the twins, Rabbit and Eliza Two.

And Nick ran away, but he lived and never forgot his family.

And Rabbit left Wood Place to seek freedom, left her twin behind, and changed her name to Judith Naomi Hutchinson.

And Eliza Two came to be known as Meema Freeman. And she married a man named Red Benjamin, and he took her last name. And Meema bore a daughter named Sheba.

And Red passed away, and his death made Meema a widowed woman. As gray strands began to wink in her hair, she found the Lord, who had been lost to her. She began to warn her daughter about religion, in hopes that the blood of Jesus would settle Sheba down.

After freedom came, the land where Meema and her family lived had no longer been called a "plantation." It had become a "farm," but there wasn't much of a difference in the lives of the Black families; after the Civil War, they were sharecroppers, which was very close to being slaves. The Black families of Wood Place barely broke even at the end of the yearly cotton harvest.

They lived in poverty. They wore ragged clothes. They didn't eat that well, either. Thirteen years after the so-called war to end slavery, whenever somebody Black in Chicasetta encountered white men in the town proper or out on country roads (even in the daylight), that somebody Black was shaking and obsequious. They looked at the ground and hunched their shoulders. They were frightened of being lynched, now that Black bodies no longer were worth valuable currency on the slave market. When white men demanded to know their allegiance to other white, powerful landowners in the county, when they pointed their shotguns at a dark chest, asking, "Nigger, who you for?" no one—man, woman, or child—was bold enough to say, "I'm not for nobody but myself. I'm free now." The Black somebody kept their eyes trained on the red dirt and whispered the names of their landlord. They hoped those syllables would provide a passport.

The church that Meema attended was constructed by Black men, those who had remained on Wood Place after the Civil War. Men who had not relied on their own fortune in their hands, who had not run through the forest away from the south, during the war. These men had stayed on Wood Place, and not because of any fairytale promise of good treatment, but because of their wives and children. These were the men who approached Pop George to ask their landlord (and former master) to sell them a parcel of land for the church.

Meema would tell her great-grandson Root that Pop George was the oldest living person on Wood Place. He was beloved to her. In the days before the war, he had been the caretaker of enslaved children, and she had been one of them. He had sat in his rocking chair with a pillow at his back and told stories. Two older children had run errands for him and brought food for the younger ones for meals. When she became an adult, Meema had been a caretaker as well, a "mammy," the tender of the children of Victor Pinchard. She and her husband and her child and Pop George had shared a two-room cabin that was spitting distance to the big, columned house where the rich, white folks lived.

After the war, Meema and Pop George continued to share the favor of their former master: they weren't charged rent for their spacious cabin, and no one who lived there had to chop cotton for a living, either. There was a large garden on the side of the cabin, and Meema freely picked peaches for preserves from the orchard on the farm. There were chickens in a coop out back of the cabin. In a pen, always a hog that was butchered every winter. As a very old man, Pop George didn't work anyway, and Meema's daughter and grandchildren didn't do much, either, except take care of the garden and animals. Meema's only paid labor was providing root remedies to women for their ailments, along with interpreting the dreams of the superstitious. Many of her clients were white ladies.

Thus, Meema and Pop George were "yard niggers." Pop George stayed in her cabin because he'd always lived with her family, even before she was born. He was very spry, so he didn't need Meema to help him bathe or walk around. She only cooked for him. In the evenings, they sat together in serenity. If the season meant that light reigned, Meema would pull their chairs outside of their cabin. She would quilt, piecing together discarded scraps from old clothes.

Pop George still would tell stories to children. Though slavery times were over, they were drawn to the cabin where he lived. Sometimes the children's parents came to visit as well, and maybe it was on one of those visits when one of the men approached the old man, telling him they needed land for a church. Since he had given Meema the only consistent peace she had known, when Pop George asked her to approach their former master instead, she told him she would do her best to acquire the land.

The day that Meema walked up to the big white house, she headed up to the kitchen house, and greeted Venie James, the cook. Meema asked her to send word to Victor Pinchard, the owner of the house and the farm. Please beg his pardon and ask him, could he spare some time for her?

Meema would not tell her descendants the exact exchange that took place in that kitchen between Victor and her, whether he called her "Auntie" in the way of paternalistic white southerners. There was no way he would have given a Black woman the honorific of "Miss" or "Mrs." That would put her on the level of a white woman, and that would never have done.

But by the end of the meeting, Meema had the promise that Victor would sell her a parcel of land. That parcel was not profitable for farming, though, so perhaps he was not so reluctant to part with it. Though the soil was very rich under the thick grass, the plot wasn't level. In centuries past, when the Creek had lived on the land, they had constructed a large mound in the center. If somebody wanted to plant anything there, they'd have to work around the mound.

The Black men of Wood Place began to collect dimes and nickels to purchase the land. That took a year. And then another year of saving change to purchase the lumber from Victor. Then another year to build the church. As sharecroppers, the men on the farm could hammer only on Sunday, after the open-air services on the grassy plot where their wives had envisioned a sanctuary. Pop George had been selected as the elder of the church. He sat in a cane-bottomed chair that was placed in the grass, holding the Bible open in his palms, though that was for show. He never had learned to read, but his memory was extraordinary. He possessed long passages of scripture in his head: Isaiah and Luke. Here and there a bit of Ruth and Esther.

During services, there were prayers and lined-out songs, not the tidy, blanched versions of the songs that would be paraded in front of white audiences in North America and in Europe, in years to come. These songs were messy and sweet. Deeply felt in the guts of folks who picked the white fluff from cotton plants. After services, the fellowship meal was laid out by the women. Then, with full stomachs, the men would begin their work of building the church. In the background, the mound that the Creeks had built rose over the folks.

But somebody else had wanted that land: a white man named Jeremiah Franklin.

He was mad about that land. It was in his blood, the need to finally own something for himself. Jeremiah was a sharecropper, too, on Wood Place. Victor had moved him from a cabin that stood by the mound to another plot near the southern property line of the thousand acres that Victor owned. A plot far away from the Black folks, because Jeremiah was, after all, a white man, too.

Meema told her great-grandson Root, Jeremiah was one of those types who always stayed mad. It was hard to know why, but commonsense dictated, he probably was angry to be poor in a white man's time. The war was over, and so was Reconstruction. Union soldiers had abandoned the south, and their protection of southern Black folks had left with them. Those few years of racial equality would forever appear as a fever dream. Once again, it was a white man's era in the south, but Jeremiah didn't have anything to show for being white. His labor in cotton fields corded his muscles. It was backbreaking work that took place when the sun was high and stained his neck a telltale red, the mark of poverty. Despite that labor, he was poor—poor as any Black man—and that probably hurt his feelings. No matter how low, everyone wants somebody to look down upon.

Jeremiah didn't own one acre to his name, and land was what white men throughout the history of this nation had killed and employed deceit to get. Land occupied a space in white pride, and a white man without land was no better than the Black man he had enslaved or the Indian he had stolen from, through murder and connivance and a lack of sympathy. White men had laughed at the anguish of the displaced Creeks: sooner or later, every conqueror laughs at his victim. That's what makes victory sweet, and more than that, justified.

Jeremiah approached Victor for the plot that had been promised to the Black sharecroppers for their church. Whether he knew the land was no longer available was not known. All that Venie James would report was that Jeremiah came for that same parcel that Meema had attained. He'd knocked on the door of the kitchen house. He told Venie to send word to Victor, but Jeremiah hadn't been polite: he hadn't even taken off his hat.

When Victor came to the kitchen, Jeremiah tried to order the cook to leave, but that didn't work. Venie sat in the corner of the kitchen house and listened to the entire conversation, then spread the news about how Jeremiah had asked to buy the parcel of land. How he had been summarily turned down, so that the land that Jeremiah had saved to buy would serve instead as the blessed earth for the church where Black sharecroppers would worship, which would be called Red Mound Church.

But that's not the end of the story, for Jeremiah bided his time.

That's what poor folks do, whether they are Black or white. Poor folks have patience. They're used to waiting a long time to receive what they view as justice. And in 1881, after the final plank of heart pine was set in the floor of the sanctuary, after Pop George had blessed their efforts, five white men rode up to the yard in front of Red Mound Church. Naturally, they were there to cause trouble, for all of them had the last name of Franklin. It was broad daylight, but they wore no hoods. In a few decades, they would officially be known as the Ku Klux Klan, but that year, they did not wear sheets or elaborate costumes. There was no official Klan in Chicasetta, a tiny town. That bureaucracy had spread nationally, but it took a while to arrive in the deep country. But let's say—for the sake of argument—that the Franklins were the Klan, Jeremiah was the chapter president, and his four sons were the members who regularly attended meetings.

They hopped off their horses and walked into the sanctuary. They kept their hats on and did not wipe their feet, tracking dirt across the heart-pine floor. Pop George was so busy preaching, so caught up in the Spirit that he didn't really hear the gasps of his congregation at first. When one of those Franklins pulled Pop George from his chair, his last strength sparked. He shouted to his flock to run, but several of the men ran toward the front of the church, including one named Holcomb Byrd James. Holcomb wanted to defy Pop George's orders and save the elder from sure death. His chest was barreled, and he was not afraid, but the old man screamed at Holcomb to run for his life. Pop George kept shouting for everybody to get out of there, and finally, Holcomb not only corralled

Venie and his own children, but Meema and her family, too. Everyone grabbed children and ran outside the church as the building caught fire.

Before she fainted, Meema would remember the smell of the bug juice, strong liquor made from corn. When she awoke, she was lying on the feather-stuffed bed in the front room of her cabin. Sheba, her daughter, was wiping her forehead with a water-soaked rag. She told her mother that Holcomb had carried her down the path from the church, and yes, Meema's grandchildren were alive.

The congregation waited two days to return, and Meema came with them. They all dug several hours through the rubble, but not even a splinter of Pop George's bones could be found.

On Sunday, the congregation held a homegoing for him next to the ruins of the church, though there wasn't a body. The women wailed, and the men shook their distraught shoulders. The following Sunday, the congregation met again, but they could not even lift a prayer. It seemed faith would be lost, but Meema had tied a clean white rag around her head. She was familiar with earlier fires, how they could break the spirit, so she gave the grandbaby she'd been rocking over to Venie, as Sheba was holding the other grandbaby and was pregnant again besides.

When Meema recalled this day to her descendants, her story would alter. She always would say that she stepped forward and began to line out a Spiritual, but through the years, the song would change. Sometimes it was "I want Jesus to walk with me." Other times, there were no words to Meema's tune, just a humming, as the others in the congregation played instruments of foot, hand, and tongue. Yet when they asked Meema to lead them in a word, she felt her strength wane. She reached her hand out, seeking aid, and Holcomb Byrd James stepped forward and began a long, passionate prayer.

Holcomb was only a sharecropper, but he had a high standing in the congregation. For starters, Venie, the cook at Wood Place, was his wife. And she kept her eyes and ears open and reported important news of the white folks living in the large house where the

Wood Place landlord resided, as the moods of their white employer greatly impacted Black folks living on his farm. Thus, the James family was greatly respected. And there was something else: before the Civil War, Holcomb had passed as a white man, when really he was the son of Cherokee Indians. He'd been the overseer on the Wood Place Plantation. But after the war, he'd become a share-cropper on the premises instead, relinquishing his position as over-seer. He did this because he didn't want to sneak around with Venie, who was the mother of his children. It was against the law for Blacks and whites to marry then, and it was against custom for a white man to live with a Black woman. A white man could rape a Black woman or pay her for sex and keep her a secret, but to live with her in an honorable way was not allowed, not in Georgia in the 1800s. But Holcomb wasn't going to use Venie like that. He wanted to marry her. So he gave up his past privileges and lived the life of a colored dirt farmer. And that made the folks respect him even more. And love him, too.

After Holcomb's long prayer, he told them to recall the difficult times that God's other children had gone through, many years be-fore: The Cherokee and the Creek, the original people who had lived on this land before it had been stolen. The slaves who had worked this earth with no hope of freedom. But some of these children had remained, and their children and so on. They were the mem-bers of the church's congregation, and surely God traveled among them. By the end of that service, Holcomb would be appointed the new elder of the church.

On the next Sunday, Meema climbed up onto the bench that had been dragged next to the rubble. Throughout the week folks had been expressing fear that the Franklins might return and enact more terror, and these murmurs had gotten back to Meema. She stood there, holding the shotgun she'd brought.

"Ain't nobody gone turn me from God," she said. "They might can kill me, but 'fore they do, I'm gone take somebody wit me."

Far from giving disapproval, Holcomb nodded enthusiastically. He advised that the congregation should elect her as a mother of the church, because Meema had surely been called by God, as those of the Old Testament had been called through blood and battle and burning bush. He urged the men to do the same, to bring their shotguns every Sunday. To get ready for what was coming in the days ahead, but to not be discouraged: though it was true that the Devil didn't sleep, neither did King Jesus.

And after the sanctuary was rebuilt, the Franklins didn't dare come back, for there had been hell to pay. When Victor Pinchard had learned of the devastation that Sunday, he'd ridden his horse out to Jeremiah's cabin. He'd talked down to the man, because he had not climbed off his animal. He told Jeremiah not to ever mess with Wood Place sharecroppers again, not unless he received permission. For it was one thing to lynch a few troublemaking niggers. That was all fine and dandy, but to show up on a Sunday when the well behaved were praying, and then to set fire to a church with an old darky inside? Only a redneck cracker would do a thing like that.

When he arrived back at his big, white house, Victor told this story to Venie James, who told the story to Meema. In this way, Meema understood that she should consider herself blessed to be a yard nigger for him. That Victor was supposed to be "good white folks." Like other lords of the manor, he would expect many displays of gratitude for his protection. And Meema obliged, smiling broadly whenever she encountered her landlord and former master. Repeatedly, she thanked him every year, when he gifted her that new hog that resided in the pen behind her cabin. She sent a few nice cuts of pig meat to his kitchen, too. On holidays she sent bottles of her homemade wine, so her landlord would know that her gratitude was certain.

But Meema Freeman didn't like Victor Pinchard, not at all. Nor had she liked his ill-mannered children, Thomas and Petunia, back when she had been their mammy. But she figured she'd use Victor, in order to protect her family and the Black sharecroppers of Wood Place. As Victor had used those same folks to make himself a rich white man, perched far above somebody like Jeremiah Franklin.

———

After the service, my mother and I lifted Uncle Root from his wheelchair, while David softly offered help. No, we had it, we told him. I was cranky, my tone brisk, but David wasn't bothered. He kissed my forehead and told me he'd been protective about Mr. J.W., too.

Usually Mama and I would push the wheelchair together across the field to the cemetery, where the old man liked to visit. But that afternoon, it was too much for Mama, it made her too sad: her husband and her child were buried in that place. So I told her I could push the old man by myself. Uncle Root kept both hands on the flowers piled high in his lap, bouquets for every woman in his family who was buried in that graveyard.

In the cemetery I put the brake on the chair and kneeled to begin the work of pulling weeds. I started with my father's grave, then moved to Lydia's. Before I'd moved to Chicasetta, I'd never done this work. As girls, Coco and I had reclined in the grass, her bossing me around in whatever game she thought up. The elders and Lydia had cleaned the graves in the cemetery, talking in cheerful voices. The only indication of the work's importance had been the short prayer after the cleaning was done, the squeeze from each hand holding mine.

After I shared my research with her, my mother had purchased a stone for Judith Hutchinson and placed it in a space beside that of Eliza Two and her only child, Sheba. She'd had the carver chisel both names—Judith Hutchinson and Rabbit Pinchard—along with BELOVED SISTER OF ELIZA TWO FREEMAN AND FORMER SLAVE. For a long time, we'd considered the last phrase. Did anyone want to be called "slave" on her tombstone? But what about the generations of our family to come? They needed to know the history, in case someone else was born as curious as I was.

There were markers for Ahgayuh—Mama Gee—and Tess, her daughter, but my mother hadn't bought those. Someone else had made sure that stones had been placed for them. Lil' May's was the most elaborate marker. A few family stories and some stones in a cemetery. These were the stingy remains of over two hundred years of family history. After I plucked the weeds, I placed the old man's flowers, unsure of whether to walk away to give him privacy. I'd made up my mind to leave when his voice stopped me.

"This was my mother," Uncle Root said. "This was my wife. This was my sister. That one was my great-great-niece." His voice caught, and I knew why. On grave-cleaning days, Mama and the others had not talked about the ones who had gone before, not until they'd left the cemetery behind. If you start to weep over the dead, you might never stop. "Why am I here when all my women are dead?"

I didn't know what to say to him. Though Uncle Root's mind was quick as ever, the once incredibly handsome, not-very-tall man now sat in a wheelchair. His body sank like the graves in the oldest part of the cemetery, the ones marked by bald rocks, or wooden crosses. Some had nothing except a slight depression in the ground. No words to tell onlookers who lay in which plot, only a hope that someone else would take up the charge of remembering to pluck the weeds. How foolish I'd been to think he wouldn't ever get to this point. Every strength must break apart. I should have known that, more than anyone.

"Uncle Root, how can you say that? Miss Rose is alive. Mama's alive. I'm here, and we all love you."

"Oh, child."

I kicked up the brake on his chair, but one of the wheels was caught in something. It had been so easy to push the chair over the field no more than a hundred yards. It never occurred to me that it would be a task to turn the chair around.

Then, from across the field, David called. Knowing what would happen in the cemetery, he had come to help us. He waved his arms wide, and the old man and I waited with our kin for him to join us.

THE VOICES OF CHILDREN

◈

In my dream, I'm settled down at the table in Dr. Oludara's office, reading articles for her. I open up a folder and see a moving picture. I lean closer and I expect to fall inside, but I don't. But then the picture is gone, the table is gone, and I'm standing underneath a peach tree in Miss Rose's orchard.

I walk through the peach trees and come out on the other side. I see my granny's house, but instead of Miss Rose, there is a white man sitting on the porch with a book in his hand. He looks up and doesn't see me, but I follow his gaze to the fields where my uncle works in the mornings, before he goes to his night shift at the factory. But there are plants with white puffs there, instead of the soybeans my uncle works. Cotton. And there's no tractor, only Black folks picking the puffs. Somehow, they are careful, even as their fingers are quick.

I hear the voices of children, and I see the long-haired lady and Lydia walking toward me. There are children on either side of them, their high voices chirping. Questions in the non sequiturs typical of the very young. The long-haired lady speaks to me in her rare, unknown vowels, and I think, after all this time, I still don't know who this woman is, even as something in the back of my mind urges me that I do.

"What's your name?" I ask.

She touches her chest and says something, but I don't understand. I shake my head, and she talks to Lydia, who seems to comprehend her perfectly.

"She says you know her name already."

"No. That's not true."

I know this is a dream. That I can't be killed or wounded, but I'm careful not to raise my voice. To not offend the woman who has been with me for so long.

"Yes, you do, baby sister," Lydia says. "You do. You just need to remember."

I open my mouth to answer, but it's as if I have glue in my mouth. My words are garbled, and I begin to choke, until Lydia pats my back. Breathe, she tells me, until I calm, and we begin to walk again.

We reach a cabin. It's propped up on a series of bricks. In the little dirt yard is a man in a rocking chair whose skin is the darkest I ever have seen, and his teeth are white and strong and beautiful. The children sit down in front of him. They wiggle and laugh. When the man snaps his fingers, they quiet. When he speaks, I know this language is English, but it sounds like complex music. I only understand every fourth or fifth word, so I put aside my need for comprehension, and pay attention to the sounds.

I listen to the children's response, their cries of appreciation. To the rise and fall of the man's voice, the music dipping into sage chords. I know the story will be over soon. That I will wake up with a question. And then another, but the question is what I have wanted. The question is the point. The question is my breath.

ACKNOWLEDGMENTS

❖

First, as always, I give unashamed glory and praise to my mighty good God, and to my Ancestors who continue to guide my path.

There is one Ancestor in particular who made my intellectual journey possible: the great W. E. B. Du Bois. My novel isn't based on his life, but rather on the lives of the inhabitants of one (fictitious) town in Georgia, a state he lived in for years. But I hope the spirit of the great scholar hovers over my book, and I hope that I have his blessing.

I was reared by a Georgian woman, who taught me southern home training, and how to listen to and revere old folks. I want to thank my mother, Dr. Trellie Lee James Jeffers (Spelman College, Class of 1955), for her sacrifices, her hard work, and her passing on her incredible intellect as well as her important cultural lessons to me. Thank you to Mama's parents, Florence Napier Paschal James and Charlie James, and Mama's siblings, Alvester James, Thedwron James, Edna James Hagan, Florence James Shields, Charles James, and Larry Paschal.

Thank you to my niece, wife-mother-caretaker extraordinaire Gabrielle Monique Morris, who holds it down for our family and keeps the Paschal-James matrilineal tradition thriving. Gabbie, I hope you know that you have made my work possible. I love you, baby girl.

My beloved "play brother," James William Richardson Jr., and my dear blood sister, Sidonie Colette Jeffers, have passed on to the Ancestors, but they are not forgotten.

I am so grateful to Native American colleagues who have accepted me as kin and encouraged my writing about Afro-Indigenous people(s) and history: Brother-Elder Geary Hobson, Kimberly Weiser, and Rachel Jackson. In particular, Brother Geary spent patient hours explaining to me Afro-Indigenous history and giving me the titles of books I should read. Neither Kimberly nor Brother Geary shamed me as I asked what I know (now) were very elementary questions about southeastern Indigenous history. Thank you to Faron Bear and Rain C. Goméz, too, for their encouragement of my Indigenous journey.

Gratitude to the organizations that provided me with financial support during the writing of this book: Aspen Summer Words Conference, Sewanee Writers Conference, and the University of Oklahoma.

As I always write on every acknowledgments page, I have been sustained by mentors through the years: Maggie Anderson, Lucille Clifton (rest in peace), Hank Lazer, David Lynn, Jerry Ward Jr., and Afaa M. Weaver. The elders guide me in a needful time.

Other various, wonderful human beings encouraged me while writing this book, in particular Barbara Soloski Albin, Huda Al-Murashi, Herman Beavers, Remica Bingham-Risher, Joan Brannon, Angela Brooks, Joanna Brooks, Kimberly Burns, Heidi Durrow, Julia Eagleton, Oscar Enriquez, Paul Erickson, Brigitte Fielder, John Freeman, Ernesto Fuentes, Helena de Groot, Logan Garrison, Shannon Gibney, Bailey Hoffner, Lynette Bloomberg, Wilhelmina Jenkins, Andrew Jeon, Tayari Jones, Randall Keenan, Keegan Long-Wheeler, Tanya Mears, Valerie Moore, Jim Moran, Fred Moten, Meredith Neuman, Emily Pawley, Laura Pegram, Michael Perry, Cherise Pollard, Riché Richardson, Bala Saho, Mungu Sanchez, Jonathan Senchyne, John Stewart, Jeanie Thompson, Natasha Trethewey, Jacqueline Allen Trimble, Margaret Porter Troupe, Quincy Troupe, Liz Van Hoose, Anthony Walton, Stephanie Powell Watts, and Crystal Wilkinson.

As always, gratitude to my African brothers—my "trois frères"—Chris Abani, Kwame Dawes, and Matthew Shenoda.

This is undoubtedly a woman's novel, and there are two women in particular who kept me going through the writing of this book. My literary agent, Sarah Burnes, and my Harper editor, Erin Wicks, two fiercely feminist, brilliant souls. They gave me courage when my confidence lagged and were honest but nurturing. Both Sarah

and Erin perform so much emotional labor and I want to acknowledge that, for the work of women is not always noticed or rewarded.

And finally, I am here on this earth to tend Ancestral altars. I am
here to speak of many tribes: the Cherokee, the Creek, the Wolof,
the Akan, the Yoruba. And the many gatherings that I cannot name.

I am here to give gratitude to those who came before. They live
within me: The people. The folks. Their songs.

ARCHIVAL CODA

❖

This is not an academic history book. This is a work of historical fiction, and so I'm not going to provide a ten-page bibliography of all the texts I read over a ten-year period. That would take too long.

Instead, I begin with the man whose name (hopefully) blesses me in this creative enterprise: William Edward Burghardt Du Bois. I read David Levering Lewis's hefty, utterly necessary biographies of the great scholar, *W.E.B. Du Bois: Biography of a Race, 1868–1919* and *W.E.B. Du Bois: The Fight for Equality and the American Century, 1919–1963* at least five times while writing this novel.

Du Bois wrote too many books for me to mention here, but the most beloved (for me) are *The Souls of Black Folk, Darkwater: Voices from Within the Veil,* and *Dusk of Dawn: An Essay Toward an Autobiography of a Race Concept.* In addition, I read the digitized correspondence of Du Bois on the Special Collections and University Archives website of the University of Massachusetts Amherst, paying close attention to his correspondence with Jessie Fauset. And webdubois.org is an excellent resource for the many out-of-print essays by Du Bois. Two excellent works on the woefully understudied Jessie Fauset are *Jessie Redmon Fauset, Black American Writer* by Carolyn Wedin Sylvander and *Women of the Harlem Renaissance* by Cheryl A. Wall.

This is a Black feminist novel. I'm unapologetic about that. Several works not only helped me with Ailey's intellectual progress as a young Black feminist/womanist, but also with character interactions. Kimberlé Crenshaw's "Mapping the Margins: Intersectionality, Identity Politics, and Violence Against Women of Color"; Jennifer L. Morgan's *Laboring Women: Reproduction and Gender in New World Slavery; All the Women Are White, All the Blacks Are Men, but Some of Us Are Brave,* edited by Akasha Gloria Hull, Patricia Bell-Scott, and Barbara Smith; bell hooks's *Ain't I a Woman: Black Women and Feminism*; and Alice Walker's *In Search of Our Mother's Gardens* are all like scripture to me. Zora Neale Hurston's *Their Eyes Were Watching God* was my first introduction (on the page) to a Black feminist heroine as well as to the African American southern vernacular that my mother's family spoke.

As painful as it was, reading about sexual violence toward Black women and girls helped me with necessary creative depictions. My book could not have been written without Harriet Jacobs's *Incidents in the Life of a Slave Girl*, Toni Morrison's *The Bluest Eye* as well as *Beloved*, and Alice Walker's *The Color Purple*—this last book is so special to me because Ms. Walker is a native of Eatonton, Georgia, the home of my maternal ancestors. (My mother was one of Ms. Walker's teachers.)

My mother—Trellie James Jeffers—published an early germinal essay about colorism in the Black community, "The Black Black Woman and the Black Middle Class," which allowed me to witness (vicariously) intra-racist sexism in African American communities. Another essay by her, "From the Old Slave Shack: Memoirs of a Teacher," offers historical background about Mama's experiences attending segregated schools in Eatonton, Georgia, in the 1930s and 1940s, before attending Spelman College in 1951.

The history of slavery provides the spine of this novel. Some texts that offered "deep background" were Boubacar Barry's *Senegambia and the Atlantic Slave Trade*, which excavates eighteenth-century slave trading history in Wolof-speaking areas of West Africa, and Walter Rucker's *Gold Coast Diasporas: Identity, Culture, and Power*, about Asante peoples of West Africa, those who would come to be called "Coromantee." Sylviane Diouf's *Servants of Allah: African Muslims Enslaved in the Americas* is a must-read for anyone interested in Muslim history on the American side of the Atlantic. And Marcus Rediker's *The Slave Ship: A Human History* gives background information about the brutal transatlantic slave trade. In addition, the digitized Georgia Archives provided information about eighteenth-century slave and Native American codes, as well as Land Lottery records. Henry Louis Gates's edited *The Classic Slave Narratives*, which include Jacobs's as well as Frederick Douglass's autobiographies, continue to be so important to me.

Ailey's family lives on land that was stolen from Native Americans; this is why this book begins with the original inhabitants of central Georgia. Four wonderful books on early Creek and Cherokee histories are Michael Green's *The Politics of Indian Removal: Creek Government and Society in Crisis*; Claudio Saunt's *A New Order of Things: Property, Power, and the Transformation of the Creek Indians, 1733–1816*; Theda Purdue's *Slavery and the Evolution of Cherokee Society, 1540–1866*; and Angela Pulley Hudson's *Creek Paths and Federal Roads: Indians, Settlers, and Slaves and the Making of the American South*.

And I must give a final shout-out to Tiya Miles, who does work in what is called Afro-Indigenous studies—or more colloquially Red-Black studies. When I read her two books, *The House on Diamond Hill: A Cherokee Plantation Story* and *Ties That Bind: The Story of an Afro-Cherokee Family in Slavery and Freedom*, I experienced something like a "happy" shout in church. Before I read these books, the Afro-Euro-Creek characters of Wood Place were still rolling around in my head. I was sure my novel was possible, but I didn't yet have the nerve to write it. Reading Tiya Miles's two books gave me that nerve. I remain so grateful for her important scholarship.